PENGUIN BOOKS

PHOENIX

David Herbert Lawrence was born at Eastwood, Nottinghamshire, in 1885, fourth of the five children of a miner and his middle-class wife. He attended Nottingham High School and Nottingham University College. His first novel, *The White Peacock,* was published in 1911, just a few weeks after the death of his mother, to whom he had been abnormally close. At this time he finally ended his relationship with Jessie Chambers (the Miriam of *Sons and Lovers*) and became engaged to Louie Burrows. His career as a schoolteacher was ended in 1911 by the illness which was ultimately diagnosed as tuberculosis.

In 1912 Lawrence eloped to Germany with Frieda Weekley, the German wife of his former modern languages tutor. They were married on their return to England in 1914. Lawrence was now living, precariously, by his writing. His greatest novels, *The Rainbow* and *Women in Love,* were completed in 1915 and 1916. The former was suppressed, and he could not find a publisher for the latter.

After the war Lawrence began his "savage pilgrimage" in search of a more fulfilling mode of life than industrial Western civilization could offer. This took him to Sicily, Ceylon, Australia and, finally, New Mexico. The Lawrences returned to Europe in 1925. Lawrence's last novel, *Lady Chatterley's Lover,* was banned in 1928, and his paintings were confiscated in 1929. He died in Vence in 1930 at the age of forty-four.

Lawrence spent most of his short life living. Nevertheless he produced an amazing quantity of work–novels, stories, poems, plays, essays, travel books, translations, and letters.... After his death Frieda wrote: "What he had seen and felt and known he gave in his writing to his fellow men, the splendour of living, the hope of more and more life... a heroic and immeasurable gift."

PHOENIX

The Posthumous Papers of

D. H. LAWRENCE

1936

Edited and with an Introduction by

EDWARD D. McDONALD

PENGUIN BOOKS

Penguin Books Ltd, Harmondsworth,
Middlesex, England
Penguin Books, 625 Madison Avenue,
New York, New York 10022, U.S.A.
Penguin Books Australia Ltd, Ringwood,
Victoria, Australia
Penguin Books Canada Limited, 2801 John Street,
Markham, Ontario, Canada L3R 1B4
Penguin Books (N.Z.) Ltd, 182–190 Wairau Road,
Auckland 10, New Zealand

First published in the United States of America by
The Viking Press 1936
First published in Great Britain by William Heinemann Ltd 1936
Viking Compass Edition published in the United States of America 1972
Reprinted 1974
Published in Penguin Books 1978
Reprinted 1980

LIBRARY OF CONGRESS CATALOGING IN PUBLICATION DATA
Lawrence, David Herbert, 1885–1930.
Phoenix.
A Penguin book.
Reprint of the 1972 ed. published by The Viking Press,
New York, in series: A Viking Compass book.
Includes index.
I. Title.
[PR6023.A93A116 1976] 828'.9'1208 76–28441
ISBN 0 14 00.4375 6

Printed in the United States of America by
The Murray Printing Company, Westford, Massachusetts
Set in Baskerville

CONTENTS

III. LOVE, SEX, MEN, AND WOMEN

IV. LITERATURE AND ART

VI. ETHICS, PSYCHOLOGY, PHILOSOPHY

VII. PERSONALIA AND FRAGMENTS

INTRODUCTION

At various times during his life D. H. Lawrence collected certain of his periodical non-fictional writings and shaped them into books. In this fashion he gave us first *Twilight in Italy*. Following at intervals came *Studies in Classical American Literature*, *Reflections on the Death of a Porcupine*, *Mornings in Mexico*, and finally *Assorted Articles*. Two of these are travel books; the others, to put the matter somewhat baldly, are ventures into criticism, metaphysics, and controversy. In spite of these five volumes—with which *Etruscan Places* might also properly be listed—a formidable number of sketches, essays, critical and other studies still remained uncollected, or even quite unpublished, at the time of Lawrence's death. Hence this posthumous collection.

Unique in design and scope, this volume may fairly be said to represent more broadly and more variously than any other book the non-fictional writings of D. H. Lawrence. In the present collection there is something of all the books mentioned above—and there is more besides. Here for the first time in a single volume are to be found sketches and essays written early in 1912 as well as some written in 1929, even in 1930. And practically all of the years that lie between make in turn their various contributions to *Phœnix*. Only one other book, namely the *Letters*, presents in its special way so comprehensive a picture of Lawrence's literary career from its beginning to its close.

At one time it was expected that Mr. Edward Garnett, distinguished critic, friend and adviser of Lawrence's youth, would collaborate in the editing of *Phœnix*, and he initiated much of the work of assembling and arranging the papers. He modestly withdrew, however, when it became apparent that the major part of the task would fall upon the present editor, who had readier access to the widely scattered material.

Phœnix was compiled from two sources: (a) from typescripts, in cases of unprinted matter; (b) from existing printed texts. Unfortunately original manuscripts were not available to the editor. Approximately one-third of the present volume has never before been printed. The larger portion, as has already been implied, was published in Lawrence's lifetime in various ways: chiefly in magazines, but also in newspapers, in anthologies, and as prefaces to books. To the previously unpublished matter belong the major part of a lengthy study of Thomas Hardy and all of an extensive treatise on popular education. Other entirely new material includes about twenty-five pieces which differ markedly as to length, subject, and importance. None of these is without great interest of one sort or another; some unquestionably deserve to be ranked among Lawrence's imperishable achievements.

The purpose of this introduction is to supply as unobtrusively as possible information and comment which seemed likely to contribute to a fuller understanding of some of the numerous selections which make up this volume. Since even a hint of pedantry would be out of place in a work by Lawrence, the body of this book has been kept largely free from editorial apparatus. The text is not broken up by extraneous matter. In the appendix are given all the available facts concerning the initial publication of the selections in this volume. If records of publication do not exist (or are unknown) this is also noted. In both instances these notations follow the order of the table of contents.

The arrangement of the contents under each of the seven headings is mainly chronological according to the dates of previous publication; and, in instances of unpublished matter, according to internal or other pertinent evidence as to the probable time of composition. But an effort was made to avoid scholarly fussiness in this business. Where Lawrence is concerned, too much significance can easily be placed upon dates of publication. This is true of his books; it is also true of his periodical and fugitive writings. Lawrence's troubles with publishers and the censorious are involved here. But this is not the whole story. Among Lawrence's rare natural gifts none was more evident than his faculty for carrying impressions and experiences, as it were, in solution in his mind. Here for a time they might remain fluid, awaiting the uses he was eventually to find for them. Again Lawrence would occasionally feel a special tenderness towards certain of his writings. These he would consciously withhold, usually to relinquish them, however unwillingly, in the end. Lawrence's habit of revising or, more accurately, of rewriting must also be remembered. For all these reasons dates of publication are in his case often very uncertain indications of the time of composition.

The most important problems connected with compiling and editing *Phœnix* were textual problems. The typescripts from which a considerable portion of this volume was made were on the whole just about what one acquainted with Lawrence's methods of work would expect them to be. As his letters show, Lawrence was for ever sending manuscripts here and there to be typed. He himself rarely composed on the typewriter. More rarely did he type final drafts, preferring to leave this task to others. Thus it must have been with the scripts here in question. Some were good, a few bad, the rest merely so-so. Evidence of revision by Lawrence was found on one typescript only, and in that instance the revisions were trivial. Needless to say every effort was made to provide for this posthumous volume an accurate and authentic text, one of which Lawrence himself would have approved and, so far as possible, did approve. In other words, whenever textual differences were found to exist between some of the typescripts and corresponding printed versions, proofs of which Lawrence might have seen, texts of the latter were preferred for reproduction here. Beyond this, editing as such was almost wholly restricted to technical details in order that a reasonable typographical consistency might be achieved. In some instances misspellings, more especially of proper names, were found and corrected. Certain other editorial problems are referred to below in discussing some of the separate selections. And now, these preliminaries disposed of, we come directly to the contents of the seven sections of *Phœnix*.

I. Nature and Poetical Pieces. "Whistling of Birds" was published April 11, 1919, in the *Athenæum,* of which Lawrence's friend, Mr. J. Middleton Murry, had recently become editor. The essay appeared under a pseudonym, *Grantorto*—a most unusual thing for Lawrence. Mr. Murry has shown that Lawrence consented to, even proposed, this arrangement. Still questions concerning it will probably always remain. Did Lawrence really believe that his proposal would be taken literally, and that an essay like "Whistling of Birds" would not be openly accredited to him? After all has been said, something unpleasant sticks to this episode. At the very least a certain sadness surrounds it. Just why *Grantorto?* What great wrong or insult? Did Lawrence's choice of pen-name reveal his resentment against a pseudonymity which he himself had suggested? All this as may be, Lawrence's situation in the spring of 1919 was very precarious. He was sick in body, low in spirit, alarmingly poor. England, he was convinced, would never find any use for him or his writing. Mr. Murry's assumption of the editorship of an important journal aroused hope in Lawrence's friends. Things would now be better. Lawrence himself was doubtful. His doubts were justified. No advantage accrued to him through Murry's connexion with the *Athenæum*. This is not the place to rehearse Catherine Carswell's charges against Murry for failing, as she says, to stand by Lawrence in a dark hour; nor to outline Murry's defence of his conduct at that time. The curious may consult Mrs. Carswell's *The Savage Pilgrimage* (1932) and Mr. Murry's *Reminiscences of D. H. Lawrence* (1933). Raking over the embers of old animosities is at best an unhappy prospect. Much pleasanter is it to call attention to the startling beauty of "Whistling of Birds." Here is a magnificent nature essay; here, too, in the form of a parable, is a glorious pæan acclaiming the passing of war and the coming of peace. In this essay Lawrence reveals his deepest, his most abiding love—the love of life. Little wonder that Mr. Murry should have found this essay "suitable" for the *Athenæum*. But why, after all explanations, pseudonymity? Why *Grantorto?*

"Adolf" and "Rex." A wild rabbit and a fox terrier. Two chapters out of Lawrence's childhood, with unforgettable portraits of his parents, portraits which restore a balance. For in these sketches Lawrence's father becomes a very appealing character; his mother something less than that. Of "Adolf" Lawrence frequently spoke with affection. At certain times he contemplated putting either one or both of these sketches in some collection of his writings, but never did. At long last it is done.

Now published for the first time, "Pan in America" was evidently written in New Mexico in 1924. In an undated letter to Mabel Dodge Luhan Lawrence writes from Lobo as follows: "My article—Pan in America—will, I think, have to have two parts. I'll see if I can finish first part this evening, and send it to Spoodle to type, if he comes." Spoodle was Lawrence's nick-name for Willard Johnson, in whose little magazine, the *Laughing Horse,* Lawrence first published some of the selections reprinted in this book.

Lawrence, who could kill no living thing, and least of all a bird, found it impossible to understand the appeal of hunting, especially as practised in Italy. In "Man Is a Hunter" he satirizes mildly, merely half-contemptuously, the idiotic doings of the Nimrods of Italy. At least two references from his letters are in point here. Writing to Mrs. Luhan from Ravello, March 18, 1926, he remarks: "We actually had two days of snow here, and the cacciatore are banging away at the tiny birds, it's like a festa with all the crackers going off. The robins and finches fly about in perfect bewilderment—and occasionally in bits. La caccia!" And in a letter, autumn, 1927, to Mr. and Mrs.

Aldous Huxley from the Villa Mirenda, near Florence, Lawrence writes: "Almost every day the morning starts a bit foggy, and Florence is always deeply buried. Then the sun comes out so *hot*.—Under the mist, the Cacciatore are banging away—it's a wonder they don't blow one another to bits—but I suppose sparrow-shot is small dust. And it's Sunday, *sacra festa*." Out of such experiences as these "Man Is a Hunter" was doubtless written, and probably at about the time of these letters, although there is no telling for certain.

No reference to "Mercury" is made in the *Letters*. Which is somehow strange, considering the importance of this essay. In that very splendid book on Lawrence by E. and A. Brewster the latter, in her reminiscences, describes going with her husband and Lawrence to Mercury Hill in October 1928. She writes: "Before leaving Baden-Baden we wanted to see the highest place in that region—Mercury Hill, because of the beautiful allegory Lawrence had written about it. One morning he led us through the dense shade of the Black Forest, dappled with the early light, to the entrance of the funicular, and seating himself on a nearby bench said he might wait if it did not turn too cold. . . . As we rattled and clattered back to the lower earth, Lawrence sat on the bench near the funicular entrance just as we had left him, still as a lizard in the sun out of the shadows of the deep woods. We walked silently home."

"The Nightingale" and the three essays which appear under the general title "Flowery Tuscany" reveal that exquisite sensitiveness which set Lawrence apart and gave him what Mr. Aldous Huxley has called "his superior otherness," a sensitiveness in which every nuance of feeling was in the highest degree true and individual. In *The Savage Pilgrimage* Catherine Carswell gives some pertinent information about "Flowery Tuscany." She writes: "Lawrence knew all about wild flowers and could name most of them. His friend Millicent Beveridge, whom he met later when in Sicily, has told me how she went walking with him once in the hills near Florence at the height of the Tuscan spring, and how as they went he named and discoursed upon at least thirty varieties. It was out of that walk that he wrote the three fragrant, categorical and joyous essays on 'Flowers in Tuscany' which appeared in the *Criterion*."

It has sometimes been asserted that Lawrence's opinion of Michelangelo's "David" is in dispute, or at any rate in doubt. If this be so, then the publication for the first time of Lawrence's essay on that famous statue ought to have special significance. It should perhaps be read with "Fireworks in Florence" in mind. In this essay, which will be found in the second section of the present volume, Lawrence refers to "David" as "the incarnation of the modern self-conscious young man, and very objectionable." That this represents his final judgment of the statue is at least questionable. No reference to "David" occurs in the *Letters*. Nor is anything said there about a related essay entitled "The Elephants of Dionysus," also heretofore unpublished.

In 1930 the Cresset Press, London, published Lawrence's *Birds, Beasts and Flowers,* with wood-engravings by Mr. Blair Hughes-Stanton. This edition of the poems was both limited and expensive. For each of the nine sections Lawrence wrote a mystical prefatory note. Because these notes have been virtually inaccessible to many readers, they were included in *Phœnix*.

II. Peoples, Countries, Races. Contemplating the essays in this section of *Phœnix*, one thinks inevitably of Mr. Aldous Huxley's sympathetic analysis of that strange and fateful compulsion in D. H. Lawrence, the compulsion to change and movement. In his introduction to the *Letters* Mr. Huxley writes: "It was, I think, the sense of being cut off that sent Lawrence on restless wanderings round the earth. His travels were at once a flight and a search: a search for some society with which he could establish contact, for a world where the times were not personal and conscious knowing had not yet perverted living; a search and at the same time a flight from the miseries and evils of a society into which he was born, and for which, in spite of his artist's detachment, he could not help feeling profoundly responsible." If, as Mr. Huxley concludes, Lawrence's "search was as fruitless as his flight was ineffective," we are still quite unjustified in believing that Lawrence from the outset could or should have known what he knew so pathetically in the end: the inevitability of disillusionment and failure.

What Lawrence sought was for him a profound personal need, not the satisfaction of a perverse and childish whim. This much is certain, countless intimations in the canons of Lawrence criticism to the contrary notwithstanding. To argue that Lawrence merely vaguely felt rather than understood the urgency of his need is to miss the point entirely. Those who would have had Lawrence's life cut to a pattern of their own designing have speculated again and again upon what his life might have been had he stuck to England—or perhaps to Europe. Their conjectures—and they are only that—are compounded largely of wishful thinking and disregard for realities. Without any of Lawrence's justification, all such commentators, big and little alike, have sought what doesn't exist and fled from what does. Had Lawrence made his fight solely in England, there probably would have been gains, but there certainly would have been losses. The latter we know and can appraise in wonder. The former, which are for ever unknowable, we can only surmise with regret.

The essays which appear under the general heading *Peoples, Countries, Races* are with a single exception directly related to Lawrence's travels. Three are joyful, rather youthful and topical sketches of experiences connected with Lawrence's first trip to the Continent. The remainder, except for "Nottingham and the Mining Countryside," record much later impressions of certain aspects of America, Mexico, Germany, France, and Italy. For the earliest essays the time is 1912; for the latest 1928 or 1929. "See Mexico After" and "Germans and Latins" are now published for the first time. The typescript of the latter bore, apparently by mistake, the title "Flowery Tuscany" and was attached, as the fourth essay, to the three nature pieces discussed above. The title "Germans and Latins" is, therefore, not Lawrence's but was chosen as being reasonably descriptive. "A Letter from Germany," republished here from the *New Statesman and Nation* for October 13, 1934, is of great interest. An editorial note which accompanied it reads as follows: "This letter written by D. H. Lawrence in 1928, shows a remarkable sensitiveness to the trend of events in Germany at a time when Hitlerism, as we know it, hardly existed." If this letter, as is certain, belongs to March 1924 rather than to 1928, then it becomes all the more remarkable that Lawrence should so early have sensed Germany's swing "away from the polarity of civilized Christian Europe" and have felt "the ancient spirit of prehistoric Germany coming back, at the end of history." Two other papers of the first importance represent very late work. "Nottingham and the Mining Countryside," especially valuable for its autobiographical matter, is a blistering indictment of the crass and blind materialism of English industrialism. "The real tragedy of England, as I see it, is the tragedy of ugliness. The country is so lovely: the man-made England is so vile." If the political and economic implications of this essay are not new, they are at any rate only too true. The mere bulk of Lawrence's writings about his life in Old and New Mexico is astonishingly large—and the quality in the main very high. Among these writings few deserve to rank above "New Mexico," the last essay in the section now under discussion. If one would know why Lawrence went to New Mexico, what he saw there, and what ultimate meaning he attached to his life there, one can scarcely do better than ponder this essay. For one thing, a good deal that others have said on these points then becomes largely superfluous.

The title "Christs in the Tirol" will be familiar to many readers of this book, though few of them will have read exactly what is here reprinted under that title. Now for the first time the original form of this sketch is reprinted from the *Westminster Gazette* for March 22, 1913. Considerably expanded with descriptive matter and otherwise altered, this essay was, in 1916, included in *Twilight in Italy* as "The Crucifix across the Mountains." Reduced to its original length, but with many textual changes, it reappeared under its first title in the *Atlantic Monthly* as recently as August 1933. Whence it was garnered into the American edition of *Love among the Haystacks*. In its different forms this beautiful essay is probably the most ubiquitous of Lawrence's writings.

III. Love, Sex, Men and Women. With the exception of "Love," first published in the *English Review* early in 1918, the essays in this section belong to the last few years of Lawrence's life. "All There," "Making Love to Music," and "Women Are So Cocksure" have apparently not heretofore been published. For both matter and manner they belong in that category of quasi-journalistic writings which came from Lawrence's pen with surprising frequency between 1927 and 1929. In her *Reminiscences* Mrs. Brewster refers to a sojourn of four months near the Lawrences at Gsteig, Switzerland, in 1928. Of this period she writes in part: "Lawrence was writing articles during those days for the newspapers, which have since been collected under the title *Assorted Articles*. Almost every day there would be a new one to read to us."

Existing evaluations of Lawrence as a writer are at best partial. One thinks of his great skill in controversy. Who has done justice to that? "Pornography and Obscenity" is an amazing diagnosis of "the grey disease of sex-hatred, coupled with the yellow disease of dirt-lust" with which, according to Lawrence, guardians of public morals are often afflicted. Soundly reasoned and vigorously written, this treatise makes the usual run of pronouncements on censorship seem dull and insipid—including those of Lord Brentford, one-time Home Secretary, at whom Lawrence's arguments were in part directed. In "The Real Thing" and "We Need One Another" are discussed what Lawrence, in the very maturity of his thinking, considered to be the fundamental needs of modern men and women. The final essay in this section is an amusing and characteristic example of how Lawrence frequently used his friends for "copy." Writing to Mrs. Aldous

Huxley from Gsteig in the summer of 1928, he describes a visit of some old friends, whose names are deleted from the published letter, as follows: "The ——'s came to tea and —— as near being in a real temper as ever I've seen her. She said: 'I don't know how it (the place) makes you feel, but I've lost *all* my *cosmic consciousness* and *all* my *universal love*. I don't care one bit about humanity.' " These phrases, italics and all, were the spring-board from which Lawrence plunged into a heady disquisition on how cosmic consciousness, universal love, and humanity affect, for better or worse, the individual. Hence "Nobody Loves Me."

IV. Literature and Art. The essays which appear under this heading present Lawrence in the role of critic of art and letters. Numerous, diverse, and heretofore uncollected, indeed largely inaccessible, these writings make a comprehensive view of Lawrence's critical work for the first time conveniently possible. A very appropriate introduction to these prefaces, reviews, and critical studies is to be found in the opening paragraphs of Lawrence's long paper on the novels of John Galsworthy, which appears as the last title but one in the section now under consideration. There Lawrence defines the function and limits of literary criticism. Denying the possibility of scientific criticism, and in other respects unduly restrictive, this definition nevertheless describes clearly and briefly Lawrence's own approach to literature —and perhaps, by inference, to art. His general thesis will be apparent from the following excerpt:

"Literary criticism can be no more than a reasoned account of the feeling produced upon the critic by the book he is criticizing. Criticism can never be a science: it is, in the first place, much too personal, and in the second, it is concerned with values that science ignores. The touchstone is emotion, not reason. We judge a work of art by its effect on our sincere and vital emotion, and nothing else. All the critical twiddle-twaddle about style and form, all this pseudo-scientific classification and analysing of books in an imitation-botanical fashion, is mere impertinence and mostly dull jargon."

In compiling the materials in this section every effort was made to represent adequately Lawrence's numerous and various ventures into literary and art criticism. Brought together here, along with essays on the novel and studies of Hardy and Galsworthy, are most of Lawrence's prefaces to books and all of his reviews. The prefaces fall principally into two classes: (a) introductions to books or translations by friends or acquaintances of Lawrence, such as S. S. Koteliansky, W. Siebenhaar, Harry Crosby, Frederick Carter, and others; (b) forewords to certain translations from the Italian by Lawrence himself and to a few more or less inaccessible books of his own, for example, the introductions to the American edition of *New Poems* and to the privately printed edition of *Pansies.* Two prefatory essays included in this section have never before been published. Both were apparently rejected in favour of shorter introductory notes. Hence their presence among Lawrence's unpublished papers. One of these, the typescript of which bore no title, had evidently been designed to serve as a preface to Lawrence's translation of Giovanni Verga's *Mastro-don Gesualdo.* Not quite so long as the later introduction to his translation to *Cavalleria Rusticana,* it is nevertheless Lawrence's most important general commentary on the work of Verga. The other, entitled "Foreword to Collected Poems," is of a much more personal nature than the preface published in *Collected Poems.* Lawrence's introduction to Harry Crosby's scarce *Chariot of the Sun* is also reprinted. This critical essay was first published in *Exchanges* under the title "Chaos in Poetry," and certain textual differences exist between the two versions, especially in the concluding paragraphs. Practically unknown except to bibliophiles, Lawrence's foreword to Edward D. McDonald's *Bibliography of the Writings of D. H. Lawrence* is made available in the present collection, as is also the preface to the limited and expensive edition of S. S. Koteliansky's translation of Dostoievsky's *The Grand Inquisitor.* The most puzzling of all the prefatory essays is one entitled simply "Introduction." But introduction to what? To a book which apparently never got beyond the manuscript stage. Fortunately "Introduction" is in part self-explanatory, but only in part. For a long time Lawrence was deeply interested in Mr. Frederick Carter's astrological designs and speculations. This interest, according to one account, began with the publication of Mr. Carter's *The Dragon of the Alchemists.* Some time thereafter Lawrence and Carter evidently agreed to collaborate in a study of the Apocalypse. Considerable progress to that end must have been made. At any rate, the Mandrake Press, shortly before it suspended, announced its intention to publish *The Revelation of St. John the Divine,* with notes and designs by Frederick Carter, and an introduction by D. H. Lawrence. The book never appeared. Four months after Lawrence's death "Introduction" was published, without any pertinent editorial comment, in the London *Mercury.* In the spring of 1931 Lawrence's *Apocalypse* appeared in Florence. In this book no reference was made to Frederick Carter or his work. One thing seems clear: "Introduction" resulted chiefly from Lawrence's interest in Mr. Carter's manuscript version of *The Dragon of the Apocalypse,* which Lawrence calls "the first *Dragon,*" and which he apparently preferred to a later version. "The *Dragon* as it exists now is no longer the *Dragon* which I read in Mexico. It has been made more—more argumentative, shall we say. Give me the old manuscript and let me write an introduction to that! I urge. But: No, says Carter. It isn't sound." When finally in 1932 Mr. Carter's *The Dragon of Revelation* was announced by Desmond Harmsworth, this publisher spoke of it as "the major document in an interesting and important collaboration," and inferentially of Lawrence's *Apocalypse* as the "first draft" of an introduction which, had Lawrence lived to see the project through, would have been his contribution to that collaboration.

The reviews reprinted in this section span almost twenty years of time—from early 1913 to within a few days of Lawrence's death. After a quarter of a century the reviews of 1913 are still alive and spirited, like those of later years. The authentic Lawrence stamp is upon all of them. From first to last Lawrence had one inexorable test for a book. For him a book was good only if it revealed some original vision of life, some living, venturesome faith, or some new awareness, to use his favorite word, of the mystery of consciousness. These things in some measure Lawrence insisted upon in all of his critical writings. Witness his first review, that of *Georgian Poetry: 1911–1912.* Rejoicing in English poetry's release from doubt and fear, he wrote: "God is there, faith, belief, love, everything. We are drunk with the joy of it, having got away from fear. In almost every poem in this book comes the note of exultation after fear, the exultation in the vast freedom, the illimitable wealth that we have suddenly got." At the same time, writing about Thomas Mann's *Death in Venice,* Lawrence flatly announced: "Already I find Thomas Mann . . . somewhat banal. His expression may be very fine. But by now what he expresses is stale." All this in 1913! Thomas Mann failed to meet Lawrence's highly subjective criteria. Hence his amusingly premature dismissal of the great German writer. In a burst of youthful self-assurance he closed the issue: "But Thomas Mann is old—and we are young."

As a reviewer Lawrence was occasionally very diverting and amusing. Witness his analysis of Stuart P. Sherman's *Americans.* At times he would claw a book savagely. His report on Mr. Carl Van Vechten's *Nigger Heaven* is a case in point. But after making necessary allowances for the completely personal character of Lawrence's critical standards, one usually finds that his reviews are serious efforts to arrive at the deeper implications of books. To this end he could be extremely patient with serious defects in a writer. This is convincingly shown by a review which he wrote during his last illness. The book was Mr. Eric Gill's *Art Nonsense and Other Essays.* The involved style and other faults of this book set Lawrence's nerves on edge. But once convinced that its author had looked into his soul and had spoken, however awkwardly, out of "his living experience" illuminating truths about men's relation to their work, then Lawrence, quickly dropping all fault-finding, proclaimed Mr. Gill "almost always good, simple and profound, truly a prophet." That Lawrence must have heard in *Art Nonsense* echoes of his own pronouncements on work is beside the point.

On July 15, 1914, Lawrence wrote to Mr. Edward Marsh in part as follows: "I am going to write a little book on Hardy's people. I think it will interest me." On September 5, 1914, he wrote to Mr. J. B. Pinker: "What a miserable world. What colossal idiocy, this war. Out of sheer rage I've begun my book about Thomas Hardy. It will be about anything but Thomas Hardy, I am afraid—queer stuff—but not bad." On October 13, 1914, to Mr. Edward Garnett: "I am writing my book more or less—very much less—about Thomas Hardy, I have done a third of it." And writing to Amy Lowell, November 18, 1914, Lawrence, among other things, had this to say: "I am finishing a book, supposed to be on Thomas Hardy, but in reality a sort of Confession of my Heart. I wonder if ever it will come out—& what you'd say to it."

The book referred to in these four letters, which is now published entire for the first time, bears the title, *Study of Thomas Hardy.* It is Lawrence's most pretentious critical work. Of the ten chapters which constitute this study only one has ever before been published. Chapter III, "Six Novels and the Real Tragedy," was published in the *Book Collector's Quarterly* for January–March 1932. This same chapter was reprinted in two issues of *John O'London's Weekly,* March 12 and 19, 1932. In both instances editorial notes accompanied publication. Because of its somewhat greater accuracy the note from the *Book Collector's Quarterly* is here reproduced. It is as follows: "This chapter, complete in itself, which gives a criticism of one distinguished novelist by another, forms part of a larger unfinished study, which was written shortly before the War, during the *Sons and Lovers* period. Lawrence gave it for safe keeping to Mr. J. Middleton Murry, in whose hands it lay, forgotten by both of them until today—this being the first time that any portion of it has been published. For its importance, as well as its intrinsic interest, we have therefore obtained the privilege of first printing it." In *The Savage Pilgrimage* Catherine Carswell asserts that the *Study of Thomas Hardy* was "everywhere rejected at the time," meaning presumably 1914–1915. Unfortunately she cites no proof for this statement. If the manuscript of this study was "everywhere rejected," then Lawrence must have offered it for publication. Hence he must have considered it whole and complete, not "unfinished." Whole and complete it certainly appears to be. Now that the *Study of Thomas Hardy* is at last generally available one may safely predict that it will arouse intense interest among the more serious readers of Lawrence. For, as the letters quoted above make clear, Hardy is merely the ostensible subject of this treatise; the real subject is Lawrence himself.

On February 28, 1927, Lawrence wrote to Miss Nancy Pearn in part as follows: "I am sending a 'Scrutiny' on John Galsworthy, for a book of 'scrutinies' by the younger writers on the elder. . . . I'm afraid it is not very nice to Galsworthy—but really, reading one novel after another just nauseated me up to the nose. Probably you like him, though— But I can't help it—either I must say what I say, or I put the whole thing in the fire."

The book here referred to was published in March 1928. Lawrence's contribution to it is reprinted in the collection of critical papers now being discussed. Compared with the *Study of Thomas Hardy* Lawrence's essay on Galsworthy is in manner distinctly pedestrian, and in tone unremittingly hostile. That Lawrence's criticism of the Forsyte novels is to some extent vitiated by personal animus towards Galsworthy can hardly be denied. The lives of these two writers seldom touched directly, but whenever they did friction points seem always to have been set up against a helpful relationship. Whose the blame? One likes to think that artists, different from the common run of men, are beyond prejudice. But, alas, the evidence does not support this pious thought. Neither Galsworthy nor Lawrence can be held wholly responsible for the instinctive and half-unconscious antagonism which existed between them. Galsworthy had praised parts ot *Sons and Lovers* highly and had strongly condemned other parts. *The Rainbow,* Galsworthy told Lawrence "calmly and ex cathedra, was a failure as a work of art." Then there is the much rehashed story of certain established writers (Galsworthy among them) refusing, in 1918, to join with Arnold Bennett in giving to Lawrence material or moral support, or both. And before this Galsworthy had seen the manuscript of *Women in Love*. What he thought of this novel is not of record. But possibly Lawrence knew.

In the recently published *The Life and Letters of John Galsworthy*, by H. V. Marrott, appears a notation by Galsworthy on a meeting with Lawrence, November 13, 1917. "Lunched with Pinker to meet D. H. Lawrence, that provincial genius. Interesting, but a type I could not get on with. Obsessed with self. Dead eyes, and a red beard, long narrow face. A strange bird." Desiring to find in this note something more than a series of deprecations, and putting the best possible construction upon it, one nevertheless sadly concludes that Galsworthy lacked the will to face the difficulties which, he must have felt, would attend any effort to get at the mystery of the "strange bird" who had come to lunch with him. Neither his naturally rich sympathies nor his artist's curiosity responded to the challenge in those "dead eyes" across the table.

Would the situation have been otherwise with *The Rainbow,* with *Women in Love,* between Lawrence and such writers as Bennett and Galsworthy had the War somehow not made normal human relations difficult, if not impossible? Who can say? In any event, behind Lawrence's destructive analysis of Galsworthy's novels may lie some of the personal history sketched in above.

In addition to the studies of Hardy and Galsworthy three general essays on the novel are included in the present collection of critical writings. "Surgery for the Novel–or a Bomb" and "Morality and the Novel" are reprinted from ephemeral literary journals, one American, the other English. These essays will be familiar only to avid readers of Lawrence. "Why the Novel Matters" has here its initial publication. In this illuminating paper Lawrence pays tribute to the novelist and to the novel as a literary form. "Being a novelist, I consider myself superior to the saint, the scientist, the philosopher and the poet. . . . The novel is the one bright book of life." The novel alone, Lawrence insists, is capable of presenting the whole of life. Compared with it, religion, science, philosophy, and poetry deal merely with parts abstracted from that whole. This theme, amplified and illustrated anew, appears again in "Morality and the Novel." That these two essays are also closely related in time of composition seems certain. With them, almost as surely, belongs "Art and Morality," wherein Lawrence, among other things, gustfully analyses the commonsense (or Kodak) approach to "the unsteady apples of Cézanne" and to the general problem of distortion in art.

"Introduction to These Paintings," the last essay in the present section, is reprinted from the expensive and largely inaccessible *The Paintings of D. H. Lawrence,* published by the Mandrake Press, London, 1929.

V. Education. Toward the end of 1918 Lawrence wrote to Katherine Mansfield in part as follows: "I've written three little essays, Education of the People. I told you Freeman, on the *Times,* asked me to do something for his Educational Supplement. Will you ask Jack please to send me, by return if possible, Freeman's initials, and the *Times* address, that will find him, so that I can send him the essays and see if he will print them. It will be nice if I can earn a little weekly money." Found to be unsuited to the requirements of the *Times,* the essays were returned to Lawrence with the suggestion that they were "rather a matter for a book than a supplement." Perhaps as a result of this suggestion the essays were shown to Mr. Stanley Unwin, who seems to have agreed provisionally to publish them. For in a letter dated January 23, 1919, and addressed to Catherine Carswell occurs the following reference: "Freeman sent me back my little essays. . . . Barbara saw the essays and showed them to Stanley Unwin, who wants me to write as much again, and he will publish in a little book, and give me £15 down. So it is not waste."

Nothing came of the plan to publish the expanded essays in book form. But even after this disappointment Lawrence might again have truly said: "So it is not waste." For his work on the educational essays must have led directly to the writing of that strangely wise and beautiful book, *Fantasia of the Unconscious.* It is difficult to offer proof for this assertion, but a comparison of *Fantasia* with "Education of the People," now published for the first time, makes formal proof quite unnecessary. Every important and vital issue propounded in the former is either tacitly or directly expressed in the latter. The present publication of "Education of the People" will, therefore, tend to remove some of the mystification which has surrounded the apparently unexpected appearance of *Fantasia of the Unconscious* in America in 1922, even though this book was, in fact, a continuation of Lawrence's *Psychoanalysis and the Unconscious* (1921). And now that "Education of the People" is made available, one fears that it may suffer the too obvious fate of its predecessors: neglect or wilful misinterpretation. Certainly it is easy to misread Lawrence's theories on popular education, far easier than to appraise them judicially. For these theories involve his fundamental beliefs concerning the relation of parents to children, parents to each other, teachers to pupils, citizens to the state; they embrace his disbeliefs in democracy, in socialism, in communism, and, above all, in the sort of fascism now currently in vogue. This in spite of the fact that much in Lawrence's rigid programme of elementary and secondary education suggests fascist regimentation and totalitarianism. But every such suggestion disappears with his insistence that "each individual is to be helped wisely, reverently, towards his natural fulfilment," and that it is the function of education "to recognize the true nature of each child, and to give each its natural chance." To this end Lawrence would entrust educational leadership–indeed all leadership–only to men richly endowed with a true religious faculty, which he defines as "the inward worship of the creative life-mystery: the implicit knowledge that life is unfathomable and unsearchable in its motives, not to be described, having no ascribable goal save the bringing forth of an ever-changing, ever-unfolding creation." All of which is a good long chalk from modern dogmas, whether educational or political. But as Lawrence once wrote of another of his mystical writings, "Education of the People" is of "no use for a five minutes' lunch."

VI. Ethics, Psychology, Philosophy. Of the fourteen essays in this section apparently ten have not heretofore been published. "The Reality of Peace" and "Life" appeared in the *English Review* in 1917 and 1918 respectively. At one time the former lay close to Lawrence's heart. On March 7, 1917, he wrote to Catherine Carswell in part as follows: "I have seven short articles–little essays–called *The Reality of Peace*. They are very beautiful, and, I think, very important. Something *must* be done with them. They are a new beginning." And on March 19, 1917, he addressed J. B. Pinker on the same subject: "I am sending you seven little articles called *The Reality of Peace*. . . . They are very beautiful and dear to me, and I feel very delicate and sensitive about them." Only four of these articles were published in the *English Review*. And only these four are here reprinted because the typescript of these essays unfortunately did not contain the other three. What has become of them? No reference to "Life" appears in the *Letters*. Like "The Reality of Peace," it is a venture into metaphysics.

The other two previously published essays, namely, "The Proper Study" and "On Being Religious," are in Lawrence's lighter and more popular vein. And so are some of the now initially published papers, to wit: "Books," "Thinking about Oneself," "Climbing down Pisgah," and "The Novel and the Feelings." With these may also be listed an unnamed article to which the somewhat stilted but apt title,

"The Individual Consciousness *v.* the Social Consciousness," has been assigned. This particular paper is undoubtedly related to the essay on Galsworthy which was discussed above. In any event, it and the selections listed immediately above reveal Lawrence busily and rather good-humoredly grinding away at some of his favourite axes. None belongs to his major canon.

A number of articles in the present section are from an editorial point of view very puzzling. This is especially true of an unfinished paper entitled "The Duc de Lauzun" and a closely related untitled essay here called "The Good Man." The former sticks pretty close to its subject, the Duc de Lauzun and eighteenth-century French manners as reflected by him. The latter, starting with the Duc, ranges far afield to modern Europe and America, to China and the Australian bush, only to find men everywhere fettered "in the bandages of old ideas and ideals." Both essays grew out of Lawrence's reading of the memoirs of the Duc de Lauzun—possibly in C. K. Scott-Moncrieff's translation (1928). But this is merely a surmise.

Those who know Lawrence's beautiful story, "The Escaped Cock," also called "The Man Who Died," will be interested in a short piece published here for the first time entitled "Resurrection," which is obviously closely related also to an essay published in *Assorted Articles* under the title, "The Risen Lord." Writing to Mrs. Luhan, May 28, 1927, Lawrence said something in point here: "I haven't been able to get my pictures snapped yet. But I've finished the Resurrection, also a story on the same theme." The references are clearly to a painting and to "The Escaped Cock." The two short pieces may safely be considered by-products of Lawrence's preoccupation with the story of the Resurrection.

"It is obvious that Whitman's Democracy is not merely a political system, or a system of government—or even a social system. It is an attempt to conceive a new way of life, to establish new values. It is a struggle to liberate human beings from the fixed, arbitrary control of ideals, into free spontaneity." Thus writes Lawrence in the last part of the long and important paper entitled "Democracy," which may have been written, one is justified in supposing, as early as, say, 1923. Now published for the first time, this treatise reveals anew Lawrence's admiration for Whitman's poetry and presents his most thorough-going exposition of the philosophy underlying that poetry.

"Introduction to Pictures," the last essay in the present section and never heretofore published, is indeed a puzzle. In it nothing is said directly, or even indirectly, about pictures. It is a long and organically complete dissertation on consciousness, elaborating once more its author's theories on that subject. It may safely be assigned to the later years of Lawrence's life. Beyond that one does not care to go. In all, a paper of more than ordinary interest and importance.

VII. Personalia and Fragments. One entry in this final section of *Phœnix* represents very early work. "The Miner at Home," an essentially autobiographical sketch, appeared in the London *Nation,* March 16, 1912. Reminiscent of *Sons and Lovers,* it is a beautifully direct piece of narrative writing. "Accumulated Mail" requires no comment. "The Late Mr. Maurice Magnus," which unhappily escaped inclusion in the *Letters,* is an interesting document in the controversy which arose over Lawrence's Introduction to Maurice Magnus's *Memoirs of the Foreign Legion* and Mr. Douglas's reply in *D. H. Lawrence and Maurice Magnus.* True, in "Accumulated Mail" Lawrence says he didn't know there was a controversy, but there was. Not so much between the principals, perhaps. Each had his say and then subsided. But numerous reviewers put in their oars, most of them pulling in Mr. Douglas's boat. The republication of Lawrence's letter apropos of his relations to Maurice Magnus will perhaps help to even things up a bit, when in the future the Lawrence-Douglas set-to helps to enliven the literary history of these times. Lawrence's Introduction is not reprinted in this volume, though it might well have been. For sheer writing power it still remains one of his most notable achievements.

Of the four unfinished pieces included in the present section "The Undying Man" and "Noah" are comparatively negligible. A long, untitled autobiographical fragment is of considerable interest. It is said that Lawrence, not long before his death, made several unsuccessful attempts to write a straightforward and extended account of his life. If this be true, then the paper now under consideration may very well be the result of one such attempt. It is obviously the first draft of an ambitious project, which Lawrence might ultimately have reshaped into a significant work of self-revelation.

And now, making an end, we come to the incomparably beautiful and moving fragment of a novel entitled "The Flying Fish." In her *Reminiscences* of Lawrence Mrs. Brewster gives some valuable information concerning this unfinished narrative. Describing an episode which occurred at Gsteig in the summer of 1928, she writes of Lawrence:

"One afternoon he sat holding a child's copybook saying he was going to read us an unfinished novel he had started on the way back from Mexico when he was very ill, and written down by Frieda from his dictation. It was called 'The Flying Fish' with the old haunting symbolism of *pisces*.

"As he read, it seemed to reach an ever higher and more serene beauty. Suddenly he stopped, saying: 'The last part will be regenerate man, a real life in this Garden of Eden.'

"We asked: 'What shall you make him do? What will he be like, the regenerate man, fulfilling life on earth?'

" 'I don't just know.' "

"The enduring beauty of 'The Flying Fish' made us ask at various times if he had not finished it, to which he would reply, that we must not urge him to finish it. 'I've an intuition I shall not finish that novel. It was written so near the borderline of death, that I never have been able to carry it through in the cold light of day.' "

And thus "The Flying Fish" remained to the very last a fragment. Perhaps it is better so: perfect in its incompleteness. One would not have it otherwise. For in this colourful fabric of rich and varied prose are beautifully fused the finest and highest qualities of D. H. Lawrence as writer and artist. It is scarcely necessary to say that Gethin Day, central character of "The Flying Fish," is Lawrence himself. Gethin Day's experiences were Lawrence's experiences: that desperate illness in Mexico, that sickening revulsion from the sinister and savage tropics, that nostalgic longing for his native land, that journey towards home by land and water, with its matchless descriptions of earth, sea, sky, and the living things which inhabit them. Here is no fictional account of a vagrant Englishman descended from an Elizabethan house, but the story of what Lawrence himself once saw, felt, suffered, and, almost miraculously, lived through.

—EDWARD D. McDONALD.

I

Nature and Poetical Pieces

WHISTLING OF BIRDS

The frost held for many weeks, until the birds were dying rapidly. Everywhere in the fields and under the hedges lay the ragged remains of lapwings, starlings, thrushes, redwings, innumerable ragged bloody cloaks of birds, whence the flesh was eaten by invisible beasts of prey.

Then, quite suddenly, one morning, the change came. The wind went to the south, came off the sea warm and soothing. In the afternoon there were little gleams of sunshine, and the doves began, without interval, slowly and awkwardly to coo. The doves were cooing, though with a laboured sound, as if they were still winter-stunned. Nevertheless, all the afternoon they continued their noise, in the mild air, before the frost had thawed off the road. At evening the wind blew gently, still gathering a bruising quality of frost from the hard earth. Then, in the yellow-gleamy sunset, wild birds began to whistle faintly in the blackthorn thickets of the stream-bottom.

It was startling and almost frightening after the heavy silence of frost. How could they sing at once, when the ground was thickly strewn with the torn carcasses of birds? Yet out of the evening came the uncertain, silvery sounds that made one's soul start alert, almost with fear. How could the little silver bugles sound the rally so swiftly, in the soft air, when the earth was yet bound? Yet the birds continued their whistling, rather dimly and brokenly, but throwing the threads of silver, germinating noise into the air.

It was almost a pain to realize, so swiftly, the new world. *Le monde est mort. Vive le monde!* But the birds omitted even the first part of the announcement, their cry was only a faint, blind, fecund *vive!*

There is another world. The winter is gone. There is a new world of spring. The voice of the turtle is heard in the land. But the flesh shrinks from so sudden a transition. Surely the call is premature while the clods are still frozen, and the ground is littered with the remains of wings! Yet we have no choice. In the bottoms of impenetrable blackthorn, each evening and morning now, out flickers a whistling of birds.

Where does it come from, the song? After so long a cruelty, how can they make it up so quickly? But it bubbles through them, they are like little well-heads, little fountain-heads whence the spring trickles and bubbles forth. It is not of their own doing. In their throats the new life distils itself into sound. It is the rising of silvery sap of a new summer, gurgling itself forth.

All the time, whilst the earth lay choked and killed and winter-mortified, the deep undersprings were quiet. They only wait for the ponderous encumbrance of the old order to give way, yield in the thaw, and there they are, a silver realm at once. Under the surge of ruin, unmitigated winter, lies the silver potentiality of all blossom. One day the black tide must spend itself and fade back. Then all-suddenly appears the crocus, hovering triumphant in the rear, and we know the order has changed, there is a new regime, sound of a new *vive! vive!*

It is no use any more to look at the torn remnants of birds that lie exposed. It is no longer any use remembering the sullen thunder of frost and the intolerable pressure of cold upon us. For whether we will or not, they are gone. The choice is not ours. We may remain wintry and destructive for a little longer, if we wish it, but the winter is gone out of us, and willy-nilly our hearts sing a little at sunset.

Even whilst we stare at the ragged horror of the birds scattered broadcast, part-eaten, the soft, uneven cooing of the pigeon ripples from the outhouses, and there is a faint silver whistling in the bushes come twilight. No matter, we stand and stare at the torn and unsightly ruins of life, we watch the weary, mutilated columns of winter retreating under our eyes. Yet in our ears are the silver vivid bugles of a new creation advancing on us from behind, we hear the rolling of the soft and happy drums of the doves.

We may not choose the world. We have hardly any choice for ourselves. We follow with our eyes the bloody and horrid line of march of extreme winter, as it passes away. But we cannot hold back the spring. We cannot make the birds silent, prevent the bubbling of the wood-pigeons. We cannot stay the fine world of silver-fecund creation from gathering itself and taking place upon us. Whether we will or no, the daphne tree will soon be giving off perfume, the lambs dancing on two feet, the celandines will twinkle all over the ground, there will be a new heaven and new earth.

For it is in us, as well as without us. Those who can may follow the columns of winter in their retreat from the earth. Some of us, we have no choice, the spring is within us, the silver fountain begins to bubble under our breast, there is gladness in spite of ourselves. And on the instant we accept the gladness! The first day of change, out whistles an unusual, interrupted pæan, a fragment that will augment itself imperceptibly. And this in spite of the extreme bitterness of the suffering, in spite of the myriads of torn dead.

Such a long, long winter, and the frost only broke yesterday. Yet it seems, already, we cannot remember it. It is strangely remote, like a far-off darkness. It is as unreal as a dream in the night. This is the morning of reality, when we are ourselves. This is natural and real, the glimmering of a new creation that stirs in us and about us. We know there was winter, long, fearful. We know the earth was strangled and mortified, we know the body of life was torn and scattered broadcast. But what is this retrospective knowledge? It is something extraneous to us, extraneous to this that we are now. And what we are, and what, it seems, we always have been, is this quickening lovely silver plasm of pure creativity. All the mortification and tearing, ah yes, it was upon us, encompassing us. It was like a storm or a mist or a falling from a height. It was estrangled upon us, like bats in our hair, driving us mad. But it was never really our innermost self. Within, we were always apart, we were this, this limpid fountain of silver, then quiescent, rising and breaking now into the flowering.

It is strange, the utter incompatibility of death with life. Whilst there is death, life is not to be found. It is all death, one overwhelming flood. And then a new tide rises, and it is all life, a fountain of silvery blissfulness. It is one or the other. We are for life, or we are for death, one or the other, but never in our essence both at once.

Death takes us, and all is torn redness, passing into darkness. Life rises, and we are faint fine jets of silver running out to blossom. All is incompatible with all. There is the silver-speckled, incandescent-lovely thrush, whistling pipingly his first song in the blackthorn thicket. How is he to be connected with the bloody, feathered unsightliness of the thrush-remnants just outside the bushes? There is no connexion. They are not to be referred the one to the other. Where one is, the other is not. In the kingdom of death the silvery song is not. But where there is life, there is no death. No death whatever, only silvery gladness, perfect, the other-world.

The blackbird cannot stop his song, neither can the pigeon. It takes place in him, even though all his race was yesterday destroyed.

He cannot mourn, or be silent, or adhere to the dead. Of the dead he is not, since life has kept him. The dead must bury their dead. Life has now taken hold on him and tossed him into the new ether of a new firmament, where he bursts into song as if he were combustible. What is the past, those others, now he is tossed clean into the new, across the untranslatable difference?

In his song is heard the first brokenness and uncertainty of the transition. The transit from the grip of death into new being is a death from death, in its sheer metempsychosis a dizzy agony. But only for a second, the moment of trajectory, the passage from one state to the other, from the grip of death to the liberty of newness. In a moment he is a kingdom of wonder, singing at the centre of a new creation.

The bird did not hang back. He did not cling to his death and his dead. There is no death, and the dead have buried their dead. Tossed into the chasm between two worlds, he lifted his wings in dread, and found himself carried on the impulse.

We are lifted to be cast away into the new beginning. Under our hearts the fountain surges, to toss us forth. Who can thwart the impulse that comes upon us? It comes from the unknown upon us, and it behoves us to pass delicately and exquisitely upon the subtle new wind from heaven, conveyed like birds in unreasoning migrations from death to life.

ADOLF

When we were children our father often worked on the night-shift. Once it was spring-time, and he used to arrive home, black and tired, just as we were downstairs in our nightdresses. Then night met morning face to face, and the contact was not always happy. Perhaps it was painful to my father to see us gaily entering upon the day into which he dragged himself soiled and weary. He didn't like going to bed in the spring morning sunshine.

But sometimes he was happy, because of his long walk through the dewy fields in the first daybreak. He loved the open morning, the crystal and the space, after a night down pit. He watched every bird, every stir in the trembling grass, answered the whinnying of the pewits and tweeted to the wrens. If he could, he also would have whinnied and tweeted and whistled in a native language that was not human. He liked non-human things best.

One sunny morning we were all sitting at table when we heard his heavy slurring walk up the entry. We became uneasy. His was always a disturbing presence, trammelling. He passed the window darkly, and we heard him go into the scullery and put down his tin bottle. But directly he came into the kitchen. We felt at once that he had something to communicate. No one spoke. We watched his black face for a second.

"Give me a drink," he said.

My mother hastily poured out his tea. He went to pour it out into his saucer. But instead of drinking he suddenly put something on the table among the teacups. A tiny brown rabbit! A small rabbit, a mere morsel, sitting against the bread as still as if it were a made thing.

"A rabbit! A young one! Who gave it you, father?"

But he laughed enigmatically, with a sliding motion of his yellow-grey eyes, and went to take off his coat. We pounced on the rabbit.

"Is it alive? Can you feel its heart beat?"

My father came back and sat down heavily in his armchair. He dragged his saucer to him, and blew his tea, pushing out his red lips under his black moustache.

"Where did you get it, father?"

"I picked it up," he said, wiping his naked forearm over his mouth and beard.

"Where?"

"It is a wild one!" came my mother's quick voice.

"Yes, it is."

"Then why did you bring it?" cried my mother.

"Oh, we wanted it," came our cry.

"Yes, I've no doubt you did——" retorted my mother. But she was drowned in our clamour of questions.

On the field path my father had found a dead mother rabbit and three dead little ones—this one alive, but unmoving.

"But what had killed them, daddy?"

"I couldn't say, my child. I s'd think she'd aten something."

"Why did you bring it!" again my mother's voice of condemnation. "You know what it will be."

My father made no answer, but we were loud in protest.

"He must bring it. It's not big enough to live by itself. It would die," we shouted.

"Yes, and it will die now. And then there'll be *another* outcry."

My mother set her face against the tragedy of dead pets. Our hearts sank.

"It won't die, father, will it? Why will it? It won't."

"I s'd think not," said my father.

"You know well enough it will. Haven't we had it all before!" said my mother.

"They dunna always pine," replied my father testily.

But my mother reminded him of other little wild animals he had brought, which had sulked and refused to live, and brought storms of tears and trouble in our house of lunatics.

Trouble fell on us. The little rabbit sat on our lap, unmoving, its eye wide and dark. We brought it milk, warm milk, and held it to its nose. It sat as still as if it was far away, retreated down some deep burrow, hidden, oblivious. We wetted its mouth and whiskers with drops of milk. It gave no sign, did not even shake off the wet white drops. Somebody began to shed a few secret tears.

"What did I say?" cried my mother. "Take it and put it down in the field."

Her command was in vain. We were driven to get dressed for school. There sat the rabbit. It was like a tiny obscure cloud. Watching it, the emotions died out of our breast. Useless to love it, to yearn over it. Its little feelings were all ambushed. They must be circumvented. Love and affection were a trespass upon it. A little wild thing, it became more mute and asphyxiated still in its own arrest, when we approached with love. We must not love it. We must circumvent it, for its own existence.

So I passed the order to my sister and my mother. The rabbit was not to be spoken to, nor even looked at. Wrapping it in a piece of flannel I put it in an obscure corner of the cold parlour, and put a saucer of milk before its nose. My mother was forbidden to enter the parlour whilst we were at school.

"As if I should take any notice of your nonsense," she cried affronted. Yet I doubt if she ventured into the parlour.

At midday, after school, creeping into the front room, there we saw the rabbit still and unmoving in the piece of flannel. Strange grey-brown neutralization of life, still living! It was a sore problem to us.

"Why won't it drink its milk, mother?" we whispered. Our father was asleep.

"It prefers to sulk its life away, silly little thing." A profound problem. Prefers to sulk its life away! We put young dandelion leaves to its nose. The sphinx was not more oblivious. Yet its eye was bright.

At tea-time, however, it had hopped a few inches, out of its flannel, and there it sat again, uncovered, a little solid cloud of muteness, brown, with unmoving whiskers. Only its side palpitated slightly with life.

Darkness came; my father set off to work. The rabbit was still unmoving. Dumb despair was coming over the sisters, a threat of tears before bedtime. Clouds of my mother's anger gathered as she muttered against my father's wantonness.

Once more the rabbit was wrapped in the old pit-singlet. But now it was carried into the scullery and put under the copper fireplace, that it might imagine itself inside a burrow. The saucers were placed about, four or five, here and there on the floor, so that if the little creature *should* chance to hop abroad, it could not fail to come upon some food. After this my mother was allowed to take from the scullery what she wanted and then she was forbidden to open the door.

When morning came and it was light, I went downstairs. Opening the scullery door, I heard a slight scuffle. Then I saw dabbles of milk all over the floor and tiny rabbit-droppings in the saucers. And there the miscreant, the tips of his ears showing behind a pair of boots. I peeped at him. He sat bright-eyed and askance, twitching his nose and looking at me while not looking at me.

He was alive—very much alive. But still we were afraid to trespass much on his confidence.

"Father!" My father was arrested at the door. "Father, the rabbit's alive."

"Back your life it is," said my father.

"Mind how you go in."

By evening, however, the little creature was tame, quite tame. He was christened Adolf. We were enchanted by him. We couldn't really love him, because he was wild and loveless to the end. But he was an unmixed delight.

We decided he was too small to live in a hutch—he must live at large in the house. My mother protested, but in vain. He was so tiny. So we had him upstairs, and he dropped his tiny pills on the bed and we were enchanted.

Adolf made himself instantly at home. He had the run of the house, and was perfectly happy, with his tunnels and his holes behind the furniture.

We loved him to take meals with us. He would sit on the table humping his back, sipping his milk, shaking his whiskers and his tender ears, hopping off and hobbling back to his saucer, with an air of supreme unconcern. Suddenly he was alert. He hobbled a few tiny paces, and reared himself up inquisitively at the sugar basin. He fluttered his tiny fore-paws, and then reached and laid them on the edge of the basin, whilst he craned his thin neck and peeped in. He trembled his whiskers at the sugar, then did his best to lift down a lump.

"*Do* you think I will have it! Animals in the sugar pot!" cried my mother, with a rap of her hand on the table.

Which so delighted the electric Adolf that he flung his hindquarters and knocked over a cup.

"It's your own fault, mother. If you left him alone——"

He continued to take tea with us. He rather liked warm tea. And he loved sugar. Having nibbled a lump, he would turn to the butter. There he was shooed off by our parent. He soon learned to treat her shooing with indifference. Still, she hated him to put his nose in the food. And he loved to do it. And one day between them they overturned the cream-jug. Adolf deluged his little chest, bounced back in terror, was seized by his little ears by my mother and bounced down on the hearth-rug. There he shivered in momentary discomfort, and suddenly set off in a wild flight to the parlour.

This last was his happy hunting ground. He had cultivated the bad habit of pensively nibbling certain bits of cloth in the hearth-rug. When chased from this pasture he would retreat under the sofa. There he would twinkle in Buddhist meditation until suddenly, no one knew why, he would go off like an alarm clock. With a sudden bumping scuffle he would whirl out of the room, going through the doorway with his little ears flying. Then we would hear his thunderbolt hurtling in the parlour, but before we could follow, the wild streak of Adolf would flash past us, on an electric wind that swept him round the scullery and carried him back, a little mad thing, flying possessed like a ball round the parlour. After which ebullition he would sit in a corner composed and distant, twitching his whiskers in abstract meditation. And it was in vain we questioned him about his outbursts. He just went off like a gun, and was as calm after it as a gun that smokes placidly.

Alas, he grew up rapidly. It was almost impossible to keep him from the outer door.

One day, as we were playing by the stile, I saw his brown shadow loiter across the road and pass into the field that faced the houses. Instantly a cry of "Adolf!"—a cry he knew full well. And instantly a wind swept him away down the sloping meadow, his tail twinkling and zigzagging through the grass. After him we pelted. It was a strange sight to see him, ears back, his little loins so powerful, flinging the world behind him. We ran ourselves out of breath, but could not catch him. Then somebody headed him off, and he sat with sudden unconcern, twitching his nose under a bunch of nettles.

His wanderings cost him a shock. One Sunday morning my father had just been quarrelling with a pedlar, and we were hearing the aftermath indoors, when there came a sudden unearthly scream from the yard. We flew out. There sat Adolf cowering under a bench, whilst a great black and white cat glowered intently at him, a few yards away. Sight not to be forgotten. Adolf rolling back his eyes and parting his strange muzzle in another scream, the cat stretching forward in a slow elongation.

Ha, how we hated that cat! How we pursued him over the chapel wall and across the neighbours' gardens.

Adolf was still only half grown.

"Cats!" said my mother. "Hideous detestable animals, why do people harbour them?"

But Adolf was becoming too much for her. He dropped too many pills. And suddenly to hear him clumping downstairs when she was alone in the house was startling. And to keep him from the door was impossible. Cats prowled outside. It was worse than having a child to look after.

Yet we would not have him shut up. He became more lusty, more callous than ever. He was a strong kicker, and many a scratch on face and arms did we owe to him. But he brought his own doom on himself. The lace curtains in the parlour–my mother was rather proud of them–fell on the floor very full. One of Adolf's joys was to scuffle wildly through them as though through some foamy undergrowth. He had already torn rents in them.

One day he entangled himself altogether. He kicked, he whirled round in a mad nebulous inferno. He screamed–and brought down the curtain-rod with a smash, right on the best beloved pelargonium, just as my mother rushed in. She extricated him, but she never forgave him. And he never forgave either. A heartless wildness had come over him.

Even we understood that he must go. It was decided, after a long deliberation, that my father should carry him back to the wildwoods. Once again he was stowed into the great pocket of the pit-jacket.

"Best pop him i' th' pot," said my father, who enjoyed raising the wind of indignation.

And so, next day, our father said that Adolf, set down on the edge of the coppice, had hopped away with utmost indifference, neither elated nor moved. We heard it and believed. But many, many were the heartsearchings. How would the other rabbits receive him? Would they smell his tameness, his humanized degradation, and rend him? My mother pooh-poohed the extravagant idea.

However, he was gone, and we were rather relieved. My father kept an eye open for him. He declared that several times passing the coppice in the early morning, he had seen Adolf peeping through the nettle-stalks. He had called him, in an odd, high-voiced, cajoling fashion. But Adolf had not responded. Wildness gains so soon upon its creatures. And they become so contemptuous then of our tame presence. So it seemed to me. I myself would go to the edge of the coppice, and call softly. I myself would imagine bright eyes between the nettle-stalks, flash of a white, scornful tail past the bracken. That insolent white tail, as Adolf turned his flank on us! It reminded me always of a certain rude gesture, and a certain unprintable phrase, which may not even be suggested.

But when naturalists discuss the meaning of the rabbit's white tail, that rude gesture and still ruder phrase always come to my mind. Naturalists say that the rabbit shows his white tail in order to guide his young safely after him, as a nursemaid's flying strings are the signal to her toddling charges to follow on. How nice and naïve! I only know that my Adolf wasn't naïve. He used to whisk his flank at me, push his white feather in my eye, and say *"Merde!"* It's a rude word—but one which Adolf was always semaphoring at me, flag-wagging it with all the derision of his narrow haunches.

That's a rabbit all over—insolence, and the white flag of spiteful derision. Yes, and he keeps his flag flying to the bitter end, sporting, insolent little devil that he is. See him running for his life. Oh, how his soul is fanned to an ecstasy of fright, a fugitive whirlwind of panic. Gone mad, he throws the world behind him, with astonishing hind legs. He puts back his head and lays his ears on his sides and rolls the white of his eyes in sheer ecstatic agony of speed. He knows the awful approach behind him; bullet or stoat. He knows! He knows, his eyes are turned back almost into his head. It is agony. But it is also ecstasy. Ecstasy! See the insolent white flag bobbing. He whirls on the magic wind of terror. All his pent-up soul rushes into agonized electric emotion of fear. He flings himself on, like a falling star swooping into extinction. White heat of the agony of fear. And at the same time, bob! bob! bob! goes the white tail, *merde! merde! merde!* it says to the pursuer. The rabbit can't help it. In his utmost extremity he still flings the insult at the pursuer. He is the inconquerable fugitive, the indomitable meek. No wonder the stoat becomes vindictive.

And if he escapes, this precious rabbit! Don't you see him sitting there, in his earthly nook, a little ball of silence and rabbit triumph? Don't you see the glint on his black eye? Don't you see, in his very immobility, how the whole world is *merde* to him? No conceit like the conceit of the meek. And if the avenging angel in the shape of the ghostly ferret steals down on him, there comes a shriek of terror out of that little hump of self-satisfaction sitting motionless in a corner. Falls the fugitive. But even fallen, his white feather floats. Even in death it seems to say: "I am the meek, I am the righteous, I am the rabbit. All you rest, you are evil doers, and you shall be *bien emmerdés!*"

REX

Since every family has its black sheep, it almost follows that every man must have a sooty uncle. Lucky if he hasn't two. However, it is only with my mother's brother that we are concerned. She had loved him dearly when he was a little blond boy. When he grew up black, she was always vowing she would never speak to him again. Yet when he put in an appearance, after years of absence, she invariably received him in a festive mood, and was even flirty with him.

He rolled up one day in a dog-cart, when I was a small boy. He was large and bullet-headed and blustering, and this time, sporty. Sometimes he was rather literary, sometimes coloured with business. But this time he was in checks, and was sporty. We viewed him from a distance.

The upshot was, would we rear a pup for him. Now my mother detested animals about the house. She could not bear the mix-up of human with animal life. Yet she consented to bring up the pup.

My uncle had taken a large, vulgar public-house in a large and vulgar town. It came to pass that I must fetch the pup. Strange for me, a member of the Band of Hope, to enter the big, noisy, smelly plate-glass and mahogany public-house. It was called The Good Omen. Strange to have my uncle towering over me in the passage, shouting "Hello, Johnny, what d'yer want?" He didn't know me. Strange to think he was my mother's brother, and that he had his bouts when he read Browning aloud with emotion and éclat.

I was given tea in a narrow, uncomfortable sort of living-room, half kitchen. Curious that such a palatial pub should show such miserable private accommodations, but so it was. There was I, unhappy, and glad to escape with the soft fat pup. It was winter-time, and I wore a big-flapped black overcoat, half cloak. Under the cloak-sleeves I hid the puppy, who trembled. It was Saturday, and the train was crowded, and he whimpered under my coat. I sat in mortal fear of being hauled out for travelling without a dog-ticket. However, we arrived, and my torments were for nothing.

The others were wildly excited over the puppy. He was small and fat and white, with a brown-and-black head: a fox terrier. My father said he had a lemon head—some such mysterious technical phraseology. It wasn't lemon at all, but coloured like a field bee. And he had a black spot at the root of his spine.

It was Saturday night—bath-night. He crawled on the hearth-rug like a fat white teacup, and licked the bare toes that had just been bathed.

"He ought to be called Spot," said one. But that was too ordinary. It was a great question, what to call him.

"Call him Rex—the King," said my mother, looking down on the fat, animated little teacup, who was chewing my sister's little toe and making her squeal with joy and tickles. We took the name in all seriousness.

"Rex—the King!" We thought it was just right. Not for years did I realize that it was a sarcasm on my mother's part. She must have wasted some twenty years or more of irony on our incurable naïveté.

It wasn't a successful name, really. Because my father and all the people in the street failed completely to pronounce the monosyllable Rex. They all said Rax. And it always distressed me. It always suggested to me seaweed, and rack-and-ruin. Poor Rex!

We loved him dearly. The first night we woke to hear him weeping and whinnying in loneliness at the foot of the stairs. When it could be borne no more, I slipped down for him, and he slept under the sheets.

"I won't have that little beast in the beds. Beds are not for dogs," declared my mother callously.

"He's as good as we are!" we cried, injured.

"Whether he is or not, he's not going in the beds."

I think now, my mother scorned us for our lack of pride. We were a little *infra dig.*, we children.

The second night, however, Rex wept the same and in the same way was comforted. The third night we heard our father plod downstairs, heard several slaps administered to the yelling, dismayed puppy, and heard the amiable, but to us heartless voice saying "Shut it then! Shut thy noise, 'st hear? Stop in thy basket, stop there!"

"It's a shame!" we shouted, in muffled rebellion, from the sheets.

"I'll give you shame, if you don't hold your noise and go to sleep," called our mother from her room. Whereupon we shed angry tears and went to sleep. But there was a tension.

"Such a houseful of idiots would make me detest the little beast, even if he was better than he is," said my mother.

But as a matter of fact, she did not detest Rexie at all. She only had to pretend to do so, to balance our adoration. And in truth, she did not care for close contact with animals. She was too fastidious. My father, however, would take on a real dog's voice, talking to the puppy: a funny, high, sing-song falsetto which he seemed to produce at the top of his head. " 'S a pretty little dog! 's a pretty little doggy!–ay!–yes!–he is, yes!–Wag thy strunt, then! Wag thy strunt, Rexie!–Ha-ha! Nay, tha munna——" This last as the puppy, wild with excitement at the strange falsetto voice, licked my father's nostrils and bit my father's nose with his sharp little teeth.

" 'E makes blood come," said my father.

"Serves you right for being so silly with him," said my mother. It was odd to see her as she watched the man, my father, crouching and talking to the little dog and laughing strangely when the little creature bit his nose and toused his beard. What does a woman think of her husband at such a moment?

My mother amused herself over the names we called him.

"He's an angel–he's a little butterfly–Rexie, my sweet!"

"Sweet! A dirty little object!" interpolated my mother. She and he had a feud from the first. Of course he chewed boots and worried our stockings and swallowed our garters. The moment we took off our stockings he would dart away with one, we after him. Then as he hung, growling, vociferously, at one end of the stocking, we at the other, we would cry:

"Look at him, mother! He'll make holes in it again." Whereupon my mother darted at him and spanked him sharply.

"Let go, sir, you destructive little fiend."

But he didn't let go. He began to growl with real rage, and hung on viciously. Mite as he was, he defied her with a manly fury. He did not hate her, nor she him. But they had one long battle with one another.

"I'll teach you, my Jockey! Do you think I'm going to spend my life darning after your destructive little teeth! I'll show you if I will!"

But Rexie only growled more viciously. They both became really angry, whilst we children expostulated earnestly with both. He would not let her take the stocking from him.

"You should tell him properly, mother. He won't be driven," we said.

"I'll drive him further than he bargains for. I'll drive him out of my sight for ever, that I will," declared my mother, truly angry.

He would put her into a real temper, with his tiny, growling defiance.

"He's sweet! A Rexie, a little Rexie!"

"A filthy little nuisance! Don't think I'll put up with him."

And to tell the truth, he was dirty at first. How could he be otherwise, so young! But my mother hated him for it. And perhaps this was the real start of their hostility. For he lived in the house with us. He would wrinkle his nose and show his tiny dagger-teeth in fury when he was thwarted, and his growls of real battle-rage against my mother rejoiced us as much as they angered her. But at last she caught him *in flagrante*. She pounced on him, rubbed his nose in the mess, and flung him out into the yard. He yelped with shame and disgust and indignation. I shall never forget the sight of him as he rolled over, then tried to turn his head away from the disgust of his own muzzle, shaking his little snout with a sort of horror, and trying to sneeze it off. My sister gave a yell of despair, and dashed out with a rag and a pan of water, weeping wildly. She sat in the middle of the yard with the befouled puppy, and shedding bitter tears she wiped him and washed him clean. Loudly she reproached my mother. "Look how much bigger you are than he is. It's a shame, it's a shame!"

"You ridiculous little lunatic, you've undone all the good it would do him, with your soft ways. Why is my life made a curse with animals! Haven't I enough as it is——"

There was a subdued tension afterwards. Rex was a little white chasm between us and our parent.

He became clean. But then another tragedy loomed. He must be docked. His floating puppy-tail must be docked short. This time my father was the enemy. My mother agreed with us that it was an unnecessary cruelty. But my father was adamant. "The dog'll look a fool all his life, if he's not docked." And there was no getting away from it. To add to the horror, poor Rex's tail must be *bitten* off. Why bitten? we asked aghast. We were assured that biting was the only way. A man would take the little tail and just nip it through with his teeth, at a certain joint. My father lifted his lips and bared his incisors, to suit the description. We shuddered. But we were in the hands of fate.

Rex was carried away, and a man called Rowbotham bit off the superfluity of his tail in the Nag's Head, for a quart of best and bitter. We lamented our poor diminished puppy, but agreed to find him more manly and *comme il faut*. We should always have been ashamed of his little whip of a tail, if it had not been shortened. My father said it had made a man of him.

Perhaps it had. For now his true nature came out. And his true nature, like so much else, was dual. First he was a fierce, canine little beast, a beast of rapine and blood. He longed to hunt, savagely. He lusted to set his teeth in his prey. It was no joke with him. The old canine Adam stood first in him, the dog with fangs and glaring eyes. He flew at us when we annoyed him. He flew at all intruders, particularly the postman. He was almost a peril to the neighbourhood. But not quite. Because close second in his nature stood that fatal need to love, the *besoin d'aimer* which at last makes an end of liberty. He had a terrible, terrible necessity to love, and this trammelled the native, savage hunting beast which he was. He was torn between two great impulses: the native impulse to hunt and kill, and the strange, secondary, supervening impulse to love and obey. If he had been left to my father and mother, he would have run wild and got himself shot. As it was, he loved us children with a fierce, joyous love. And we loved him.

When we came home from school we would see him standing at the end of the entry, cocking his head wistfully at the open country in front of him, and meditating whether to be off or not: a white, inquiring little figure, with green savage freedom in front of him. A cry from a far distance from one of us, and like a bullet he hurled himself down the road, in a mad game. Seeing him coming, my sister invariably turned and fled, shrieking with delighted terror. And he would leap straight up her back, and bite her and tear her clothes. But it was only an ecstasy of savage love, and she knew it. She didn't care if he tore her pinafores. But my mother did.

My mother was maddened by him. He was a little demon. At the least provocation, he flew. You had only to sweep the floor, and he bristled and sprang at the broom. Nor would he let go. With his scruff erect and his nostrils snorting rage, he would turn up the whites of his eyes at my mother, as she wrestled at the other end of the broom. "Leave go, sir, leave go!" She wrestled and stamped her foot, and he answered with horrid growls. In the end it was she who had to let go. Then she flew at him, and he flew at her. All the time we had him, he was within a hair's-breadth of savagely biting her. And she knew it. Yet he always kept sufficient self-control.

We children loved his temper. We would drag the bones from his mouth, and put him into such paroxysms of rage that he would twist his head right over and lay it on the ground upside-down, because he didn't know what to do with himself, the savage was so strong in him and he must fly at us. "He'll fly at your throat one of these days," said my father. Neither he nor my mother dared have touched Rex's bone. It was enough to see him bristle and roll the whites of his eyes when they came near. How near he must have been to driving his teeth right into us, cannot be told. He was a horrid sight snarling and crouching at us. But we only laughed and rebuked him. And he would whimper in the sheer torment of his need to attack us.

He never did hurt us. He never hurt anybody, though the neighbourhood was terrified of him. But he took to hunting. To my mother's disgust, he would bring large dead bleeding rats and lay them on the hearth-rug, and she had to take them up on a shovel. For he would not remove them. Occasionally he brought a mangled rabbit, and sometimes, alas, fragmentary poultry. We were in terror of prosecution. Once he came home bloody and feathery and rather sheepish-looking. We cleaned him and questioned him and abused him. Next day we heard of six dead ducks. Thank heaven no one had seen him.

But he was disobedient. If he saw a hen he was off, and calling would not bring him back. He was worst of all with my father, who would take him walks on Sunday morning. My mother would not walk a yard with him. Once, walking with my father, he rushed off at some sheep in a field. My father yelled in vain. The dog was at the sheep, and meant business. My father crawled through the hedge, and was upon him in time. And now the man was in a paroxysm of rage. He dragged the little beast into the road and thrashed him with a walking stick.

"Do you know you're thrashing that dog unmercifully?" said a passerby.

"Ay, an' mean to," shouted my father.

The curious thing was that Rex did not respect my father any the more, for the beatings he had from him. He took much more heed of us children, always.

But he let us down also. One fatal Saturday he disappeared. We hunted and called, but no Rex. We were bathed, and it was bedtime, but we would not go to bed. Instead we sat in a row in our nightdresses on the sofa, and wept without stopping. This drove our mother mad.

"Am I going to put up with it? Am I? And all for that hateful little beast of a dog! He shall go! If he's not gone now, he shall go."

Our father came in late, looking rather queer, with his hat over his eye. But in his staccato tippled fashion he tried to be consoling.

"Never mind, my duckie, I s'll look for him in the morning."

Sunday came—oh, such a Sunday. We cried, and didn't eat. We scoured the land, and for the first time realized how empty and wide the earth is, when you're looking for something. My father walked for many miles—all in vain. Sunday dinner, with rhubarb pudding, I remember, and an atmosphere of abject misery that was unbearable.

"Never," said my mother, "never shall an animal set foot in this house again, while I live. I knew what it would be! I knew."

The day wore on, and it was the black gloom of bed-time, when we heard a scratch and an impudent little whine at the door. In trotted Rex, mud-black, disreputable, and impudent. His air of off-hand "How d'ye do!" was indescribable. He trotted around with *suffisance,* wagging his tail as if to say, "Yes, I've come back. But I didn't need to. I can carry on remarkably well by myself." Then he walked to his water, and drank noisily and ostentatiously. It was rather a slap in the eye for us.

He disappeared once or twice in this fashion. We never knew where he went. And we began to feel that his heart was not so golden as we had imagined it.

But one fatal day reappeared my uncle and the dog-cart. He whistled to Rex, and Rex trotted up. But when he wanted to examine the lusty, sturdy dog, Rex became suddenly still, then sprang free. Quite jauntily he trotted round—but out of reach of my uncle. He leaped up, licking our faces, and trying to make us play.

"Why, what ha' you done wi' the dog—you've made a fool of him. He's softer than grease. You've ruined him. You've made a damned fool of him," shouted my uncle.

Rex was captured and hauled off to the dog-cart and tied to the seat. He was in a frenzy. He yelped and shrieked and struggled, and was hit on the head, hard, with the butt-end of my uncle's whip, which only made him struggle more frantically. So we saw him driven away, our beloved Rex, frantically, madly fighting to get to us from the high dog-cart, and being knocked down, whilst we stood in the street in mute despair.

After which, black tears, and a little wound which is still alive in our hearts.

I saw Rex only once again, when I had to call just once at The Good Omen. He must have heard my voice, for he was upon me in the passage before I knew where I was. And in the instant I knew how he loved us. He really loved us. And in the same instant there was my uncle with a whip, beating and kicking him back, and Rex cowering, bristling, snarling.

My uncle swore many oaths, how we had ruined the dog for ever, made him vicious, spoiled him for showing purposes, and been altogether a pack of mard-soft fools not fit to be trusted with any dog but a gutter-mongrel.

Poor Rex! We heard his temper was incurably vicious, and he had to be shot.

And it was our fault. We had loved him too much, and he had loved us too much. We never had another pet.

It is a strange thing, love. Nothing but love has made the dog lose his wild freedom, to become the servant of man. And this very servility or completeness of love makes him a term of deepest contempt—"You dog!"

We should not have loved Rex so much, and he should not have loved us. There should have been a measure. We tended, all of us, to overstep the limits of our own natures. He should have stayed outside human limits, we should have stayed outside canine limits. Nothing is more fatal than the disaster of too much love. My uncle was right, we had ruined the dog.

My uncle was a fool, for all that.

PAN IN AMERICA

At the beginning of the Christian era, voices were heard off the coasts of Greece, out to sea, on the Mediterranean, wailing: "Pan is dead! Great Pan is dead!"

The father of fauns and nymphs, satyrs and dryads and naiads was dead, with only the voices in the air to lament him. Humanity hardly noticed.

But who was he, really? Down the long lanes and overgrown ridings of history we catch odd glimpses of a lurking rustic god with a goat's white lightning in his eyes. A sort of fugitive, hidden among leaves, and laughing with the uncanny derision of one who feels himself defeated by something lesser than himself.

An outlaw, even in the early days of the gods. A sort of Ishmael among the bushes.

Yet always his lingering title: The Great God Pan. As if he was, or had been, the greatest.

Lurking among the leafy recesses, he was almost more demon than god. To be feared, not loved or approached. A man who should see Pan by daylight fell dead, as if blasted by lightning.

Yet you might dimly see him in the night, a dark body within the darkness. And then, it was a vision filling the limbs and the trunk of a man with power, as with new, strong-mounting sap. The Pan-power! You went on your way in the darkness secretly and subtly elated with blind energy, and you could cast a spell, by your mere presence, on women and on men. But particularly on women.

In the woods and the remote places ran the children of Pan, all the nymphs and fauns of the forest and the spring and the river and the rocks. These, too, it was dangerous to see by day. The man who looked up to see the white arms of a nymph flash as she darted behind the thick wild laurels away from him followed helplessly. He was a nympholept. Fascinated by the swift limbs and the wild, fresh sides of the nymph, he followed for ever, for ever, in the endless monotony of his desire. Unless came some wise being who could absolve him from the spell.

But the nymphs, running among the trees and curling to sleep under the bushes, made the myrtles blossom more gaily, and the spring bubble up with greater urge, and the birds splash with a strength of life. And the lithe flanks of the faun gave life to the oak-groves, the vast trees hummed with energy. And the wheat sprouted like green rain returning out of the ground, in the little fields, and the vine hung its black drops in abundance, urging a secret.

Gradually men moved into cities. And they loved the display of people better than the display of a tree. They liked the glory they got of overpowering one another in war. And, above all, they loved the vainglory of their own words, the pomp of argument and the vanity of ideas.

So Pan became old and grey-bearded and goat-legged, and his passion was degraded with the lust of senility. His power to blast and to brighten dwindled. His nymphs became coarse and vulgar.

Till at last the old Pan died, and was turned into the devil of the Christians. The old god Pan became the Christian devil, with the cloven hoofs and the horns, the tail, and the laugh of derision. Old Nick, the Old Gentleman who is responsible for all our wickednesses, but especially our sensual excesses—this is all that is left of the Great God Pan.

It is strange. It is a most strange ending for a god with such a name. Pan! All! That which is everything has goat's feet and a tail! With a black face!

This really is curious.

Yet this was all that remained of Pan, except that he acquired brimstone and hell-fire, for many, many centuries. The nymphs turned into the nasty-smelling witches of a Walpurgis night, and the fauns that danced became sorcerers riding the air, or fairies no bigger than your thumb.

But Pan keeps on being reborn, in all kinds of strange shapes. There he was, at the Renaissance. And in the eighteenth century he had quite a vogue. He gave rise to an "ism," and there were many pantheists, Wordsworth one of the first. They worshipped Nature in her sweet-and-pure aspect, her Lucy Gray aspect.

"Oft have I heard of Lucy Gray," the school-child began to recite, on examination-day.

"So have I," interrupted the bored inspector.

Lucy Gray, alas, was the form that William Wordsworth thought fit to give to the Great God Pan.

And then he crossed over to the young United States: I mean Pan did. Suddenly he gets a new name. He becomes the Oversoul, the Allness of everything. To this new Lucifer Gray of a Pan Whitman sings the famous *Song of Myself:* "I am All, and All is Me." That is: "I am Pan, and Pan is me."

The old goat-legged gentleman from Greece thoughtfully strokes his beard, and answers: "All A is B, but all B is not A." Aristotle did not live for nothing. All Walt is Pan, but all Pan is not Walt.

This, even to Whitman, is incontrovertible. So the new American pantheism collapses.

Then the poets dress up a few fauns and nymphs, to let them run riskily—oh, would there were any risk!—in their private "grounds." But, alas, these tame guinea-pigs soon became boring. Change the game.

We still *pretend* to believe that there is One mysterious Something-or-other back of Everything, ordaining all things for the ultimate good of humanity. It wasn't back of the Germans in 1914, of course, and whether it's back of the bolshevist is still a grave question. But still, it's back of *us,* so that's all right.

Alas, poor Pan! Is this what you've come to? Legless, hornless, faceless, even smileless, you are less than everything or anything, except a lie.

And yet here, in America, the oldest of all, old Pan is still alive. When Pan was greatest, he was not even Pan. He was nameless and unconceived, mentally. Just as a small baby new from the womb may say Mama! Dada! whereas in the womb it said nothing; so humanity, in the womb of Pan, said nought. But when humanity was born into a separate idea of itself, it said *Pan.*

In the days before man got too much separated off from the universe, he *was* Pan, along with all the rest.

As a tree still is. A strong-willed, powerful thing-in-itself, reaching up and reaching down. With a powerful will of its own it thrusts green hands and huge limbs at the light above, and sends huge legs and gripping toes down, down between the earth and rocks, to the earth's middle.

Here, on this little ranch under the Rocky Mountains, a big pine tree rises like a guardian spirit in front of the cabin where we live. Long, long ago the Indians blazed it. And the lightning, or the storm, has cut off its crest. Yet its column is always there, alive and changeless, alive and changing. The tree has its own aura of life. And in winter the snow slips off it, and in June it sprinkles down its little catkin-like pollen-tips, and it hisses in the wind, and it makes a silence within a silence. It is a great tree, under which the house is built. And the tree is still within the allness of Pan. At night, when the lamplight shines out of the window, the great trunk dimly shows, in the near darkness, like an Egyptian column, supporting some powerful mystery in the over-branching darkness. By day, it is just a tree.

It is just a tree. The chipmunks skelter a little way up it, the little black-and-white birds, tree-creepers, walk quick as mice on its rough perpendicular, tapping; the bluejays throng on its branches, high up, at dawn, and in the afternoon you hear the faintest rustle of many little wild doves alighting in its upper remoteness. It is a tree, which is still Pan.

And we live beneath it, without noticing. Yet sometimes, when one suddenly looks far up and sees those wild doves there, or when one glances quickly at the inhuman-human hammering of a woodpecker, one realizes that the tree is asserting itself as much as I am. It gives out life, as I give out life. Our two lives meet and cross one another, unknowingly: the tree's life penetrates my life, and my life the tree's. We cannot live near one another, as we do, without affecting one another.

The tree gathers up earth-power from the dark bowels of the earth, and a roaming sky-glitter from above. And all unto itself, which is a tree, woody, enormous, slow but unyielding with life, bristling with acquisitive energy, obscurely radiating some of its great strength.

It vibrates its presence into my soul, and I am with Pan. I think no man could live near a pine tree and remain quite suave and supple and compliant. Something fierce and bristling is communicated. The piny sweetness is rousing and defiant, like turpentine, the noise of the needles is keen with æons of sharpness. In the volleys of wind from the western desert, the tree hisses and resists. It does not lean eastward at all. It resists with a vast force of resistance, from within itself, and its column is a ribbed, magnificent assertion.

I have become conscious of the tree, and of its interpenetration into my life. Long ago, the Indians must have been even more acutely conscious of it, when they blazed it to leave their mark on it.

I am conscious that it helps to change me, vitally. I am even conscious that shivers of energy cross my living plasm, from the tree, and I become a degree more like unto the tree, more bristling and turpentiney, in Pan. And the tree gets a certain shade and alertness of my life, within itself.

Of course, if I like to cut myself off, and say it is all bunk, a tree is merely so much lumber not yet sawn, then in a great measure I shall *be* cut off. So much depends on one's attitude. One can shut many, many doors of receptivity in oneself; or one can open many doors that are shut.

I prefer to open my doors to the coming of the tree. Its raw earth-power and its raw sky-power, its resinous erectness and resistance, its sharpness of hissing needles and relentlessness of roots, all that goes to the primitive savageness of a pine tree, goes also to the strength of man.

Give me of your power, then, oh tree! And I will give you of mine.

And this is what men must have said, more naïvely, less sophisticatedly, in the days when all was Pan. It is what, in a way, the aboriginal Indians still say, and still *mean,* intensely: especially when they dance the sacred dance, with the tree; or with the spruce twigs tied above their elbows.

Give me your power, oh tree, to help me in my life. And I will give you my power: even symbolized in a rag torn from my clothing.

This is the oldest Pan.

Or again, I say: "Oh you, you big tree, standing so strong and swallowing juice from the earth's inner body, warmth from the sky, beware of me. Beware of me, because I am strongest. I am going to cut you down and take your life and make you into beams for my house, and into a fire. Prepare to deliver up your life to me."

Is this any less true than when the lumberman glances at a pine tree, sees if it will cut good lumber, dabs a mark or a number upon it, and goes his way absolutely without further thought or feeling? Is he truer to life? Is it truer to life to insulate oneself entirely from the influence of the tree's life, and to walk about in an inanimate forest of standing lumber, marketable in St. Louis, Mo.? Or is it truer to life to know, with a pantheistic sensuality, that the tree has its own life, its own assertive existence, its own living relatedness to me: that my life is added to, or militated against, by the tree's life?

Which is really truer?

Which is truer, to live among the living, or to run on wheels?

And who can sit with the Indians around a big camp-fire of logs, in the mountains at night, when a man rises and turns his breast and his curiously-smiling bronze face away from the blaze, and stands voluptuously warming his thighs and buttocks and loins, his back to the fire, faintly smiling the inscrutable Pan-smile into the dark trees surrounding, without hearing him say, in the Pan-voice: "Aha! Tree! Aha! Tree! Who has triumphed now? I drank the heat of your blood into my face and breast, and now I am drinking it into my loins and buttocks and legs, oh tree! I am drinking your heat right through me, oh tree! Fire is life, and I take your life for mine. I am drinking it up, oh tree, even into my buttocks. Aha! Tree! I am warm! I am strong! I am happy, tree, in this cold night in the mountains!"

And the old man, glancing up and seeing the flames flapping in flamy rags at the dark smoke, in the upper fire-hurry towards the stars and the dark spaces between the stars, sits stonily and inscrutably: yet one knows that he is saying: "Go back, oh fire! Go back like honey! Go back, honey of life, to where you came from, before you were hidden in the tree. The trees climb into the sky and steal the honey of the sun, like bears stealing from a hollow tree-trunk. But when the tree falls and is put on to the fire, the honey flames and goes straight back to where it came from. And the smell of burning pine is as the smell of honey."

So the old man says, with his lightless Indian eyes. But he is careful never to utter one word of the mystery. Speech is the death of Pan, who can but laugh and sound the reed-flute.

Is it better, I ask you, to cross the room and turn on the heat at the radiator, glancing at the thermometer and saying: "We're just a bit below the level, in here"? Then to go back to the newspaper!

What can a man do with his life but live it? And what does life consist in, save a vivid relatedness between the man and the living universe that surrounds him? Yet man insulates himself more and more into mechanism, and repudiates everything but the machine and the contrivance of which he himself is master, god in the machine.

Morning comes, and white ash lies in the fire-hollow, and the old man looks at it broodingly.

"The fire is gone," he says in the Pan silence, that is so full of unutterable things. "Look! there is no more tree. We drank his warmth, and he is gone. He is way, way off in the sky, his smoke is in the blueness, with the sweet smell of a pine-wood fire, and his yellow flame is in the sun. It is morning, with the ashes of night. There is no more tree. Tree is gone. But perhaps there is fire among the ashes. I shall blow it, and it will be alive. There is always fire, between the tree that goes and the tree that stays. One day I shall go——"

So they cook their meat, and rise, and go in silence.

There is a big rock towering up above the trees, a cliff. And silently a man glances at it. You hear him say, without speech:

"Oh, you big rock! If a man fall down from you, he dies. Don't let me fall down from you. Oh, you big pale rock, you are so still, you know lots of things. You know a lot. Help me, then, with your stillness. I go to find deer. Help me find deer."

And the man slips aside, and secretly lays a twig, or a pebble, some little object in a niche of the rock, as a pact between him and the rock. The rock will give him some of its radiant-cold stillness and enduring presence, and he makes a symbolic return, of gratitude.

Is it foolish? Would it have been better to invent a gun, to shoot his game from a great distance, so that he need not approach it with any of that living stealth and preparedness with which one live thing approaches another? Is it better to have a machine in one's hands, and so avoid the life-contact: the trouble! the pains! Is it better to see the rock as a mere nothing, not worth noticing because it has no value, and you can't eat it as you can a deer?

But the old hunter steals on, in the stillness of the eternal Pan, which is so full of soundless sounds. And in his soul he is saying: "Deer! Oh, you thin-legged deer! I am coming! Where are you, with your feet like little stones bounding down a hill? I know you. Yes, I know you. But you don't know me. You don't know where I am, and you don't know me, anyhow. But I know you. I am thinking of you. I shall get you. I've got to get you. I got to; so it will be.—I shall get you, and shoot an arrow right in you."

In this state of abstraction, and subtle, hunter's communion with the quarry—a weird psychic connexion between hunter and hunted —the man creeps into the mountains.

And even a white man who is a born hunter must fall into this state. Gun or no gun! He projects his deepest, most primitive hunter's consciousness abroad, and finds his game, not by accident, nor even chiefly by looking for signs, but primarily by a psychic attraction, a sort of telepathy: the hunter's telepathy. Then when he finds his quarry, he aims with a pure, spellbound volition. If there is no flaw in his abstracted huntsman's *will,* he cannot miss. Arrow or bullet, it flies like a movement of pure will, straight to the spot. And the deer, once she has let her quivering alertness be overmastered or stilled by the hunter's subtle, hypnotic, *following* spell, she cannot escape.

This is Pan, the Pan-mystery, the Pan-power. What can men who sit at home in their studies, and drink hot milk and have lamb's-wool slippers on their feet, and write anthropology, what *can* they possibly know about men, the men of Pan?

Among the creatures of Pan there is an eternal struggle for life, between lives. Man, defenceless, rapacious man, has needed the qualities of every living thing, at one time or other. The hard, silent abidingness of rock, the surging resistance of a tree, the still evasion of a puma, the dogged earth-knowledge of the bear, the light alertness of the deer, the sky-prowling vision of the eagle: turn by turn man has needed the power of every living thing. Tree, stone, or hill, river, or little stream, or waterfall, or salmon in the fall—man can be master and complete in himself, only by assuming the living powers of each of them, as the occasion requires.

He used to make himself master by a great effort of will, and sensitive, intuitive cunning, and immense labour of body.

Then he discovered the "idea." He found that all things were related by certain *laws.* The moment man learned to abstract, he began to make engines that would do the work of his body. So, instead of concentrating upon his quarry, or upon the living things which made his universe, he concentrated upon the engines or instruments which should intervene between him and the living universe, and give him mastery.

This was the death of the great Pan. The idea and the engine came between man and all things, like a death. The old connexion, the old Allness, was severed, and can never be ideally restored. Great Pan is dead.

Yet what do we live for, except to live? Man has lived to conquer the phenomenal universe. To a great extent he has succeeded. With all the mechanism of the human world, man is to a great extent master of all life, and of most phenomena.

And what then? Once you have conquered a thing, you have lost it. Its real relation to you collapses.

A conquered world is no good to man. He sits stupefied with boredom upon his conquest.

We need the universe to live again, so that we can live with it. A conquered universe, a dead Pan, leaves us nothing to live with.

You have to abandon the conquest, before Pan will live again. You have to live to live, not to conquer. What's the good of conquering even the North Pole, if after the conquest you've nothing left but an inert fact? Better leave it a mystery.

It was better to be a hunter in the woods of Pan, than it is to be a clerk in a city store. The hunter hungered, laboured, suffered tortures of fatigue. But at least he lived in a ceaseless living relation to his surrounding universe.

At evening, when the deer was killed, he went home to the tents, and threw down the deer-meat on the swept place before the tent of his women. And the women came out to greet him softly, with a sort of reverence, as he stood before the meat, the life-stuff. He came back spent, yet full of power, bringing the life-stuff. And the children looked with black eyes at the meat, and at that wonder-being, the man, the bringer of meat.

Perhaps the children of the store-clerk look at their father with a *tiny* bit of the same mystery. And perhaps the clerk feels a fragment of the old glorification, when he hands his wife the paper dollars.

But about the tents the women move silently. Then when the cooking-fire dies low, the man crouches in silence and toasts meat on a stick, while the dogs lurk round like shadows and the children watch avidly. The man eats as the sun goes down. And as the glitter departs, he says: "Lo, the sun is going, and I stay. All goes, but still I stay. Power of deer-meat is in my belly, power of sun is in my body. I am tired, but it is with power. There the small moon gives her first sharp sign. So! So! I watch her. I will give her something; she is very sharp and bright, and I do not know her power. Lo! I will give the woman something for this moon, which troubles me above the sunset, and has power. Lo! how very curved and sharp she is! Lo! how she troubles me!"

Thus, always aware, always watchful, subtly poising himself in the world of Pan, among the powers of the living universe, he sustains his life and is sustained. There is no boredom, because *everything* is alive and active, and danger is inherent in all movement. The contact between all things is keen and wary: for wariness is also a sort of reverence, or respect. And nothing, in the world of Pan, may be taken for granted.

So when the fire is extinguished, and the moon sinks, the man says to the woman: "Oh, woman, be very soft, be very soft and deep towards me, with the deep silence. Oh, woman, do not speak and stir and wound me with the sharp horns of yourself. Let me come into the deep, soft places, the dark, soft places deep as between the stars. Oh, let me lose there the weariness of the day: let me come in the power of the night. Oh, do not speak to me, nor break the deep night of my silence and my power. Be softer than dust, and darker than any flower. Oh, woman, wonderful is the craft of your softness, the distance of your dark depths. Oh, open silently the deep that has no end, and do not turn the horns of the moon against me."

This is the might of Pan, and the power of Pan.

And still, in America, among the Indians, the oldest Pan is alive. But here, also, dying fast.

It is useless to glorify the savage. For he will kill Pan with his own hands, for the sake of a motor-car. And a bored savage, for whom Pan is dead, is the stupefied image of all boredom.

And we cannot return to the primitive life, to live in tepees and hunt with bows and arrows.

Yet live we must. And once life has been conquered, it is pretty difficult to live. What are we going to do, with a conquered universe? The Pan relationship, which the world of man once had with all the world, was better than anything man has now. The savage, today, if you give him the chance, will become more mechanical and unliving than any civilized man. But civilized man, having conquered the universe, may as well leave off bossing it. Because, when all is said and done, life itself consists in a live relatedness between man and his universe: sun, moon, stars, earth, trees, flowers, birds, animals, men, everything—and not in a "conquest" of anything by anything. Even the conquest of the air makes the world smaller, tighter, and more airless.

And whether we are a store-clerk or a bus-conductor, we can still choose between the living universe of Pan, and the mechanical conquered universe of modern humanity. The machine has no windows. But even the most mechanized human being has only got his windows nailed up, or bricked in.

MAN IS A HUNTER

It is a very nice law which forbids shooting in England on Sundays. Here in Italy, on the contrary, you would think there was a law ordering every Italian to let off a gun as often as possible. Before the eyelids of dawn have come apart, long before the bells of the tiny church jangle to announce daybreak, there is a sputter and crackle as of irritating fireworks, scattering from the olive gardens and from the woods. You sigh in your bed. The Holy Day has started: the huntsmen are abroad; they will keep at it till heaven sends the night, and the little birds are no more.

The very word *cacciatore,* which means hunter, stirs one's bile. Oh, Nimrod, oh, Bahram, put by your arrows:

> And Bahram, the great hunter: the wild ass
> Stamps o'er his bed, and cannot wake his sleep.

Here, an infinite number of tame asses shoot over my head, if I happen to walk in the wood to look at the arbutus berries, and they never fail to rouse my ire, no matter how fast asleep it may have been.

Man is a hunter! *L'uomo è cacciatore:* the Italians are rather fond of saying it. It sounds so virile. One sees Nimrod surging through the underbrush, with his spear, in the wake of a bleeding lion. And if it is a question of a man who has got a girl into trouble: *"L'uomo è cacciatore"*—"man is a hunter"—what can you expect? It behoves the "game" to look out for itself. Man is a hunter!

There used to be a vulgar song: "If the Missis wants to go for a row, let 'er go." Here it should be: "If the master wants to run, with a gun, let him run." For the pine-wood is full of them, as a dog's back with fleas in summer. They crouch, they lurk, they stand erect, motionless as virile statues, with gun on the alert. Then *bang!* they have shot something, with an astonishing amount of noise. And then they run, with fierce and predatory strides, to the spot.

There is nothing there! Nothing! The game! *La caccia!*—where is it? If they had been shooting at the ghost of Hamlet's father, there could not be a blanker and more spooky emptiness. One expects to see a wounded elephant lying on its side, writhing its trunk; at the very least, a wild boar ploughing the earth in his death-agony. But no! There is nothing, just nothing at all. Man, being a hunter, is, fortunately for the rest of creation, a very bad shot.

Nimrod, in velveteen corduroys, bandolier, cartridges, game-bag over his shoulder and gun in his hand, stands with feet apart *virilissimo,* on the spot where the wild boar should be, and gazes downwards at some imaginary point in underworld space. So! Man is a hunter. He casts a furtive glance around, under the arbutus bush, and a tail of his eye in my direction, knowing I am looking on in raillery. Then he hitches his game-bag more determinedly over his shoulder, grips his gun, and strides off uphill, large strides, virile as Hector. Perhaps even he is a Hector, Italianized into Ettore. Anyhow, he's going to be the death of something or somebody, if only he can shoot straight.

A Tuscan pine-wood is by no means a jungle. The trees are umbrella-pines, with the umbrellas open, and bare handles. They are rather parsimoniously scattered. The undergrowth, moreover, is allowed to grow only for a couple of years or so; then it is most assiduously reaped, gleaned, gathered, cleaned up clean as a lawn, for cooking Nimrod's macaroni. So that, in a *pineta,* you have a piny roof over your head, and for the rest a pretty clear run for your money. So where can the game lurk? There is hardly cover for a bumble-bee. Where can the game be that is worth all this powder? The lions and wolves and boars that must prowl perilously round all these Nimrods?

You will never know. Or not until you are going home, between the olive-trees. The hunters have been burning powder in the open, as well as in the wood: a proper fusillade. Then, on the path between the olives, you may pick up a warm, dead bullfinch, with a bit of blood on it. The little grey bird lies on its side, with its frail feet closed, and its red breast ruffled. Nimrod, having hit for once, has failed to find his quarry.

So you will know better when the servant comes excitedly and asks: "Signore, do you want any game?" Game! Splendid idea! A couple of partridges? a hare? even a wild rabbit? Why, of course! So she arrives in triumph with a knotted red handkerchief, and the not very bulky game inside it. Untie the knots! Aha!–Alas! There, in a little heap on the table, three robins, two finches, four hedge-sparrows, and two starlings, in a fluffy, coloured, feathery little heap, all the small heads rolling limp. "Take them away," you say. "We don't eat little birds." "But these," she says, tipping up the starlings roughly, "these are big ones." "Not these, either, do we eat." "No?" she exclaims, in a tone which means: *"More fools you!"* And, digusted, disappointed at not having sold the goods, she departs with the game.

You will know best of all if you go to the market, and see whole yard-lengths of robins, like coral and onyx necklaces, and strings of bullfinches, goldfinches, larks, sparrows, nightingales, starlings, temptingly offered along with strings of sausages, these last looking like the strings of pearls in the show. If one bought the birds to wear as ornament, barbaric necklaces, it would be more conceivable. You can get quite a string of different-coloured ones for tenpence. But imagine the small mouthful of little bones each of these tiny carcasses must make!

But, after all, a partridge and a pheasant are only a bit bigger than a sparrow and a finch. And compared to a flea, a robin is big game. It is all a question of dimensions. Man is a hunter. "If the master wants to hunt, don't you grunt; let him hunt!"

MERCURY

It was Sunday, and very hot. The holiday-makers flocked to the hill of Mercury, to rise two thousand feet above the steamy haze of the valleys. For the summer had been very wet, and the sudden heat covered the land in hot steam.

Every time it made the ascent, the funicular was crowded. It hauled itself up the steep incline, that towards the top looked almost perpendicular, the steel thread of the rails in the gulf of pine-trees hanging like an iron rope against a wall. The women held their breath, and didn't look. Or they looked back towards the sinking levels of the river, steamed and dim, far-stretching over the frontier.

When you arrived at the top, there was nothing to do. The hill was a pine-covered cone; paths wound between the high tree-trunks, and you could walk round and see the glimpses of the world all round, all round: the dim, far river-plain, with a dull glint of the great stream, to westwards; southwards the black, forest-covered, agile-looking hills, with emerald-green clearings and a white house or two; east, the inner valley, with two villages, factory chimneys, pointed churches, and hills beyond; and north, the steep hills of forest, with reddish crags and reddish castle ruins. The hot sun burned overhead, and all was in steam.

Only on the very summit of the hill there was a tower, an outlook tower; a long restaurant with its beer-garden, all the little yellow tables standing their round disks under the horse-chestnut trees; then a bit of a rock-garden on the slope. But the great trees began again in wilderness a few yards off.

The Sunday crowd came up in waves from the funicular. In waves they ebbed through the beer-garden. But not many sat down to drink. Nobody was spending any money. Some paid to go up the outlook tower, to look down on a world of vapours and black, agile-crouching hills, and half-cooked towns. Then everybody dispersed along the paths, to sit among the trees in the cool air.

There was not a breath of wind. Lying and looking upwards at the shaggy, barbaric middle-world of the pine-trees, it was difficult to decide whether the pure high trunks supported the upper thicket of darkness, or whether they descended from it like great cords stretched downwards. Anyhow, in between the tree-top world and the earth-world went the wonderful clean cords of innumerable proud tree-trunks, clear as rain. And as you watched, you saw that the upper world was faintly moving, faintly, most faintly swaying, with a circular movement, though the lower trunks were utterly motionless and monolithic.

There was nothing to do. In all the world, there was nothing to do, and nothing to be done. Why have we all come to the top of the Merkur? There is nothing for us to do.

What matter? We have come a stride beyond the world. Let it steam and cook its half-baked reality below there. On the hill of Mercury we take no notice. Even we do not trouble to wander and pick the fat, blue, sourish bilberries. Just lie and see the rain-pure tree-trunks like chords of music between two worlds.

The hours pass by: people wander and disappear and reappear. All is hot and quiet. Humanity is rarely boisterous any more. You go for a drink: finches run among the few people at the tables: everybody glances at everybody, but with remoteness.

There is nothing to do but to return and lie down under the pine trees. Nothing to do. But why do anything, anyhow? The desire to do anything has gone. The tree-trunks, living like rain, they are quite active enough.

At the foot of the obsolete tower there is an old tablet-stone with a very much battered Mercury, in relief. There is also an altar, or votive stone, both from the Roman times. The Romans are supposed to have worshipped Mercury on the summit. The battered god, with his round sun-head, looks very hollow-eyed and unimpressive in the purplish-red sandstone of the district. And no one any more will throw grains of offering in the hollow of the votive stone: also common, purplish-red sandstone, very local and un-Roman.

The Sunday people do not even look. Why should they? They keep passing on into the pine-trees. And many sit on the benches; many lie upon the long chairs. It is very hot, in the afternoon, and very still.

Till there seems a faint whistling in the tops of the pine-trees, and out of the universal semi-consciousness of the afternoon arouses a bristling uneasiness. The crowd is astir, looking at the sky. And sure enough, there is a great flat blackness reared up in the western sky, curled with white wisps and loose breast-feathers. It looks very sinister, as only the elements still can look. Under the sudden weird whistling of the upper pine trees, there is a subdued babble and calling of frightened voices.

They want to get down; the crowd want to get down off the hill of Mercury, before the storm comes. At any price to get off the hill! They stream towards the funicular, while the sky blackens with incredible rapidity. And as the crowd presses down towards the little station, the first blaze of lightning opens out, followed immediately by a crash of thunder, and great darkness. In one strange movement, the crowd takes refuge in the deep veranda of the restaurant, pressing among the little tables in silence. There is no rain, and no definite wind, only a sudden coldness which makes the crowd press closer.

They press closer, in the darkness and the suspense. They have become curiously unified, the crowd, as if they had fused into one body. As the air sends a chill waft under the veranda the voices murmur plaintively, like birds under leaves, the bodies press closer together, seeking shelter in contact.

The gloom, dark as night, seems to continue a long time. Then suddenly the lightning dances white on the floor, dances and shakes upon the ground, up and down, and lights up the white striding of a man, lights him up only to the hips, white and naked and striding, with fire on his heels. He seems to be hurrying, this fiery man whose upper half is invisible, and at his naked heels white little flames seem to flutter. His flat, powerful thighs, his legs white as fire stride rapidly across the open, in front of the veranda, dragging little white flames at the ankles, with the movement. He is going somewhere, swiftly.

In the great bang of the thunder the apparition disappears. The earth moves, and the house jumps in complete darkness. A faint whimpering of terror comes from the crowd, as the cold air swirls in. But still, upon the darkness, there is no rain. There is no relief: a long wait.

Brilliant and blinding, the lightning falls again; a strange bruising thud comes from the forest, as all the little tables and the secret tree-trunks stand for one unnatural second exposed. Then the blow of the thunder, under which the house and the crowd reel as under an explosion. The storm is playing directly upon the Merkur. A belated sound of tearing branches comes out of the forest.

And again the white splash of the lightning on the ground: but nothing moves. And again the long, rattling, instantaneous volleying of the thunder, in the darkness. The crowd is panting with fear, as the lightning again strikes white, and something again seems to burst, in the forest, as the thunder crashes.

At last, into the motionlessness of the storm, in rushes the wind, with the fiery flying of bits of ice, and the sudden sea-like roaring of the pine trees. The crowd winces and draws back, as the bits of ice hit in the face like fire. The roar of the trees is so great, it becomes like another silence. And through it is heard the crashing and splintering of timber, as the hurricane concentrates upon the hill.

Down comes the hail, in a roar that covers every other sound, threshing ponderously upon the ground and the roofs and the trees. And as the crowd surges irresistibly into the interior of the building, from the crushing of this ice-fall, still amid the sombre hoarseness sounds the tinkle and crackle of things breaking.

After an eternity of dread, it ends suddenly. Outside is a faint gleam of yellow light, over the snow and the endless debris of twigs and things broken. It is very cold, with the atmosphere of ice and deep winter. The forest looks wan, above the white earth, where the ice-balls lie in their myriads, six inches deep, littered with all the twigs and things they have broken.

"Yes! Yes!" say the men, taking sudden courage as the yellow light comes into the air. "Now we can go!"

The first brave ones emerge, picking up the big hailstones, pointing to the overthrown tables. Some, however, do not linger. They hurry to the funicular station, to see if the apparatus is still working.

The funicular station is on the north side of the hill. The men come back, saying there is no one there. The crowd begins to emerge upon the wet, crunching whiteness of the hail, spreading around in curiosity, waiting for the men who operate the funicular.

On the south side of the outlook tower two bodies lay in the cold but thawing hail. The dark-blue of the uniforms showed blackish. Both men were dead. But the lightning had completely removed the clothing from the legs of one man, so that he was naked from the hips down. There he lay, his face sideways on the snow, and two drops of blood running from his nose into his big, blond, military moustache. He lay there near the votive stone of the Mercury. His companion, a young man, lay face downwards, a few yards behind him.

The sun began to emerge. The crowd gazed in dread, afraid to touch the bodies of the men. Why had they, the dead funicular men, come round to this side of the hill, anyhow?

The funicular would not work. Something had happened to it in the storm. The crowd began to wind down the bare hill, on the sloppy ice. Everywhere the earth bristled with broken pine boughs and twigs. But the bushes and the leafy trees were stripped absolutely bare, to a miracle. The lower earth was leafless and naked as in winter.

"Absolute winter!" murmured the crowd, as they hurried, frightened, down the steep, winding descent, extricating themselves from the fallen pine-branches.

Meanwhile the sun began to steam in great heat.

THE NIGHTINGALE

Tuscany is full of nightingales, and in spring and summer they sing all the time, save in the middle of the night and the middle of the day. In the little, leafy woods that hang on the steep of the hill towards the streamlet, as maidenhair hangs on a rock, you hear them piping up again in the wanness of dawn, about four o'clock in the morning: "Hello! Hello! Hello!" It is the brightest sound in the world, a nightingale piping up. Every time you hear it, you feel wonder and, it must be said, a thrill, because the sound is so bright, so glittering, it has so much power behind it.

"There goes the nightingale," you say to yourself. It sounds in the half-dawn as if the stars were darting up from the little thicket and leaping away into the vast vagueness of the sky, to be hidden and gone. But the song rings on after sunrise, and each time you listen again, startled, you wonder: "Now *why* do they say he is a sad bird?"

He is the noisiest, most inconsiderate, most obstreperous and jaunty bird in the whole kingdom of birds. How John Keats managed to begin his "Ode to a Nightingale" with: "My heart aches, and a drowsy numbness pains my senses," is a mystery to anybody acquainted with the actual song. You hear the nightingale silverily shouting: "What? What? What, John? Heart aches and a drowsy numbness pains? Tra-la-la! Tri-li-lilylilylilylily!"

And why the Greeks said he, or she, was sobbing in a bush for a lost lover, again I don't know. "Jug-jug-jug!" say the medieval writers, to represent the rolling of the little balls of lightning in the nightingale's throat. A wild, rich sound, richer than the eyes in a peacock's tail:

> And the bright brown nightingale, amorous,
> Is half assuaged for Itylus.

They say, with that "Jug! jug! jug!," that she is sobbing. How they hear it is a mystery. How anyone who didn't have his ears on upside down ever heard the nightingale "sobbing," I don't know.

Anyhow it's a male sound, a most intensely and undilutedly male sound. A pure assertion. There is not a hint nor a shadow of echo and hollow recall. Nothing at all like a hollow low bell! Nothing in the world so unforlorn.

Perhaps that is what made Keats straightway feel forlorn.

> Forlorn! the very word is like a bell
> To toll me back from thee to my sole self!

Perhaps that is the reason of it; why they all hear sobs in the bush, when the nightingale sings, while any honest-to-God listening person hears the ringing shouts of small cherubim. Perhaps because of the discrepancy.

Because, in sober fact, the nightingale sings with a ringing, pinching vividness and a pristine assertiveness that makes a mere man stand still. A kind of brilliant calling and interweaving of glittering exclamation such as must have been heard on the first day of creation, when the angels suddenly found themselves created, and shouting aloud before they knew it. Then there must have been a to-do of angels in the thickets of heaven: "Hello! Hello! Behold! Behold! Behold! It is I! It is I! What a mar-mar-marvellous occurrence! What!"

For the pure splendidness of vocal assertion: "Lo! It is I!" you have to listen to the nightingale. Perhaps for the visual perfection of the same assertion, you have a look at a peacock shaking all his eyes. Among all the creatures created in final splendor, these two are perhaps the most finally perfect; the one is invisible, triumphing sound, the other is voiceless visibility. The nightingale is a quite undistinguished grey-brown bird, if you do see him, although he's got that tender, hopping mystery about him, of a thing that is rich alive inside. Just as the peacock, when he does make himself heard, is awful, but still impressive: such a fearful shout from out of the menacing jungle. You can actually see him, in Ceylon, yell from a high bough, then stream away past the monkeys, into the impenetrable jungle that seethes and is dark.

And perhaps for this reason—the reason, that is, of pure, angel-keen or demon-keen assertion of true self—the nightingale makes a man feel sad, and the peacock often makes him angry. It is a sadness that is half envy. The birds are so triumphantly positive in their created selves, eternally new from the hand of the rich, bright God, and perfect. The nightingale ripples with his own perfection. And the peacock arches all his bronze and purple eyes with assuredness.

This—this rippling assertion of a perfect bit of creation—this green shimmer of a perfect beauty in a bird—makes men angry or melancholy, according as it assails the eye or the ear.

The ear is much less cunning than the eye. You can say to somebody: "I like you awfully, you look so beautiful this morning," and she will believe it utterly, though your voice may really be vibrating with mortal hatred. The ear is so stupid, it will accept any amount of false money in words. But let one tiny gleam of the mortal hatred come into your eye, or across your face, and it is detected immediately. The eye is so shrewd and rapid.

For this reason we get the peacock at once, in all his showy, male self-assertion; and we say, rather sneeringly: "Fine feathers make fine birds!" But when we hear the nightingale, we don't know what we hear, we only know we feel sad, forlorn. And so we say it is the nightingale that is sad.

The nightingale, let us repeat, is the most unsad thing in the world; even more unsad than the peacock full of gleam. He has nothing to be sad about. He feels perfect with life. It isn't conceit. He just feels life-perfect, and he trills it out—shouts, jugs, gurgles, trills, gives long, mock-plaintiff calls, makes declarations, assertions, and triumphs; but he never reflects. It is pure music, in so far as you could never put words to it. But there are words for the feelings aroused in us by the song. No, even that is not true. There are no words to tell what one really feels, hearing the nightingale. It is something so much purer than words, which are all tainted. Yet we can say, it is some sort of feeling of triumph in one's own life-perfection.

> 'Tis not through envy of thy happy lot,
> But being too happy in thine happiness,—
> That thou, light-wingèd Dryad of the trees,
> In some melodious plot
> Of beechen green, and shadows numberless,
> Singest of summer in full-throated ease.

Poor Keats, he has to be "too happy" in the nightingale's happiness, not being very happy in himself at all. So he wants to drink the blushful Hippocrene, and fade away with the nightingale into the forest dim.

> Fade far away, dissolve, and quite forget
> What thou among the leaves hast never known,
> The weariness, the fever, and the fret. . . .

It is such sad, beautiful poetry of the human male. Yet the next line strikes me as a bit ridiculous.

> Here, where men sit and hear each other groan;
> Where palsy shakes a few, sad, last gray hairs. . . .

This is Keats, not at all the nightingale. But the sad human male still tries to break away, and get over into the nightingale world. Wine will not take him across. Yet he will go.

Away! away! for I will fly to thee,
  Not charioted by Bacchus and his pards,
But on the viewless wings of Poesy. . . .

He doesn't succeed, however. The viewless wings of Poesy carry him only into the bushes, not into the nightingale world. He is still outside.

Darkling I listen; and for many a time
  I have been half in love with easeful Death. . . .

The nightingale never made any man in love with easeful death, except by contrast. The contrast between the bright flame of positive pure self-aliveness, in the bird, and the uneasy flickering of yearning selflessness, for ever yearning for something outside himself, which is Keats:

To cease upon the midnight with no pain,
  While thou art pouring forth thy soul abroad
    In such an ecstasy!
Still wouldst thou sing, and I have ears in vain,–
  To thy high requiem become a sod.

How astonished the nightingale would be if he could be made to realize what sort of answer the poet was answering to his song. He would fall off the bough with amazement.

Because a nightingale, when you answer him back, only shouts and sings louder. Suppose a few other nightingales pipe up in neighbouring bushes—as they always do. Then the blue-white sparks of sound go dazzling up to heaven. And suppose you, mere mortal, happen to be sitting on the shady bank having an altercation with the mistress of your heart, hammer and tongs, then the chief nightingale swells and goes at it like Caruso in the Third Act—simply a brilliant, bursting frenzy of music, singing you down, till you simply can't hear yourself speak to quarrel.

There was, in fact, something very like a nightingale in Caruso—that bird-like, bursting, miraculous energy of song, and fullness of himself, and self-luxuriance.

Thou wast not born for death, immortal Bird!
  No hungry generations tread thee down.

Not yet in Tuscany, anyhow. They are twenty to the dozen. Whereas the cuckoo seems remote and low-voiced, calling his low, half secretive call as he flies past. Perhaps it really is different in England.

The voice I hear this passing night was heard
  In ancient days by emperor and clown:
Perhaps the self-same song that found a path
Through the sad heart of Ruth, when, sick for home,
  She stood in tears amid the alien corn.

And why in tears? Always tears. Did Diocletian, I wonder, among the emperors, burst into tears when he heard the nightingale, and Æsop among the clowns? And Ruth, really? Myself, I strongly suspect that young lady of setting the nightingale singing, like the nice damsel in Boccaccio's story, who went to sleep with the lively bird in her hand, *"—tua figliuola è stata sì vaga dell'usignuolo, ch'ella l'ha preso e tienlosi in mano!"*

And what does the hen nightingale think of it all, as she mildly sits upon the eggs and hears milord giving himself forth? Probably she likes it, for she goes on breeding him as jaunty as ever. Probably she prefers his high cockalorum to the poet's humble moan:

> Now more than ever seems it rich to die,
> To cease upon the midnight with no pain. . . .

That wouldn't be much use to the hen nightingale. And one sympathizes with Keats's Fanny, and understands why she wasn't having any. Much good such a midnight would have been to *her!*

Perhaps, when all's said and done, the female of the species gets more out of life when the male isn't wanting to cease upon the midnight, with or without pain. There are better uses for midnights. And a bird that sings because he's full of his own bright life, and leaves her to keep the eggs cozy, is perhaps preferable to one who moans, even with love of her.

Of course, the nightingale is utterly unconscious of the little dim hen, while he sings. And he never mentions her name. But she knows well enough that the song is half her; just as she knows the eggs are half him. And just as she doesn't want him coming in and putting a heavy foot down on her little bunch of eggs, he doesn't want her poking into his song, and fussing over it, and mussing it up. Every man to his trade, and every woman to hers:

> Adieu! adieu! thy plaintive anthem fades. . . .

It never was a plaintive anthem—it was Caruso at his jauntiest. But don't try to argue with a poet.

FLOWERY TUSCANY

I

Each country has its own flowers, that shine out specially there. In England it is daisies and buttercups, hawthorn and cowslips. In America, it is goldenrod, stargrass, June daisies, Mayapple and asters, that we call Michaelmas daisies. In India, hibiscus and dattura and champa flowers, and in Australia mimosa, that they call wattle, and sharp-tongued strange heath-flowers. In Mexico it is cactus flowers, that they call roses of the desert, lovely and crystalline among many thorns; and also the dangling yard-long clusters of the cream bells of the yucca, like dropping froth.

But by the Mediterranean, now as in the days of the Argosy, and, we hope, for ever, it is narcissus and anemone, asphodel and myrtle. Narcissus and anemone, asphodel, crocus, myrtle, and parsley, they leave their sheer significance only by the Mediterranean. There are daisies in Italy too: at Pæstum there are white little carpets of daisies, in March, and Tuscany is spangled with celandine. But for all that, the daisy and the celandine are English flowers, their best significance is for us and for the North.

The Mediterranean has narcissus and anemone, myrtle and asphodel and grape hyacinth. These are the flowers that speak and are understood in the sun round the Middle Sea.

Tuscany is especially flowery, being wetter than Sicily and more homely than the Roman hills. Tuscany manages to remain so remote, and secretly smiling to itself in its many sleeves. There are so many hills popping up, and they take no notice of one another. There are so many little deep valleys with streams that seem to go their own little way entirely, regardless of river or sea. There are thousands, millions of utterly secluded little nooks, though the land has been under cultivation these thousands of years. But the intensive culture of vine and olive and wheat, by the ceaseless industry of naked human hands and winter-shod feet, and slow-stepping, soft-eyed oxen does not devastate a country, does not denude it, does not lay it bare, does not uncover its nakedness, does not drive away either Pan or his children. The streams run and rattle over wild rocks of secret places, and murmur through blackthorn thickets where the nightingales sing all together, unruffled and undaunted.

It is queer that a country so perfectly cultivated as Tuscany, where half the produce of five acres of land will have to support ten human mouths, still has so much room for the wild flowers and the nightingale. When little hills heave themselves suddenly up, and shake themselves free of neighbours, man has to build his garden and his vineyard, and sculp his landscape. Talk of hanging gardens of Babylon, all Italy, apart from the plains, is a hanging garden. For centuries upon centuries man has been patiently modelling the surface of the Mediterranean countries, gently rounding the hills, and graduating the big slopes and the little slopes into the almost invisible levels of terraces. Thousands of square miles of Italy have been lifted in human hands, piled and laid back in tiny little flats, held up by the drystone walls, whose stones came from the lifted earth. It is a work of many, many centuries. It is the gentle sensitive sculpture of all the landscape. And it is the achieving of the peculiar Italian beauty which is so exquisitely natural, because man, feeling his way sensitively to the fruitfulness of the earth, has moulded the earth to his necessity without violating it.

Which shows that it *can* be done. Man *can* live on the earth and by the earth without disfiguring the earth. It has been done here, on all these sculptured hills and softly, sensitively terraced slopes.

But, of course, you can't drive a steam plough on terraces four yards wide, terraces that dwindle and broaden and sink and rise a little, all according to the pitch and the breaking outline of the mother hill. Corn has got to grow on these little shelves of earth, where already the grey olive stands semi-invisible, and the grapevine twists upon its own scars. If oxen can step with that lovely pause at every little stride, they can plough the narrow field. But they will have to leave a tiny fringe, a grassy lip over the drystone wall below. And if the terraces are too narrow to plough, the peasant digging them will still leave the grassy lip, because it helps to hold the surface in the rains.

And here the flowers take refuge. Over and over and over and over has this soil been turned, twice a year, sometimes three times a year, for several thousands of years. Yet the flowers have never been driven out. There is a very rigorous digging and sifting, the little bulbs and tubers are flung away into perdition, not a weed shall remain.

Yet spring returns, and on the terrace lips, and in the stony nooks between terraces, up rise the aconites, the crocuses, the narcissus and the asphodel, the inextinguishable wild tulips. There they are, for ever hanging on the precarious brink of an existence, but for ever triumphant, never quite losing their footing. In England, in America, the flowers get rooted out, driven back. They become fugitive. But in the intensive cultivation of ancient Italian terraces, they dance round and hold their own.

Spring begins with the first narcissus, rather cold and shy and wintry. They are the little bunchy, creamy narcissus with the yellow cup like the yolk of the flower. The natives call these flowers *tazzette,* little cups. They grow on the grassy banks rather sparse, or push up among thorns.

To me they are winter flowers, and their scent is winter. Spring starts in February, with the winter aconite. Some icy day, when the wind is down from the snow of the mountains, early in February, you will notice on a bit of fallow land, under the olive trees, tight, pale-gold little balls, clenched tight as nuts, and resting on round ruffs of green near the ground. It is the winter aconite suddenly come.

The winter aconite is one of the most charming flowers. Like all the early blossoms, once her little flower emerges it is quite naked. No shutting a little green sheath over herself, like the daisy or the dandelion. Her bubble of frail, pale, pure gold rests on the round frill of her green collar, with the snowy wind trying to blow it away.

But without success. The *tramontana* ceases, comes a day of wild February sunshine. The clenched little nuggets of the aconite puff out, they become light bubbles, like small balloons, on a green base. The sun blazes on, with February splendour. And by noon, all under the olives are wide-open little suns, the aconites spreading all their rays; and there is an exquisitely sweet scent, honey-sweet, not narcissus-frosty; and there is a February humming of little brown bees.

Till afternoon, when the sun slopes, and the touch of snow comes back into the air.

But at evening, under the lamp on the table, the aconites are wide and excited, and there is a perfume of sweet spring that makes one almost start humming and trying to be a bee.

Aconites don't last very long. But they turn up in all odd places—on clods of dug earth, and in land where the broad-beans are thrusting up, and along the lips of terraces. But they like best land left fallow for one winter. There they throng, showing how quick they are to seize on an opportunity to live and shine forth.

In a fortnight, before February is over, the yellow bubbles of the aconite are crumpling to nothingness. But already in a cosy-nook the violets are dark purple, and there is a new little perfume in the air.

Like the debris of winter stand the hellebores, in all the wild places, and the butcher's broom is flaunting its last bright red berry. Hellebore is Christmas roses, but in Tuscany the flowers never come white. They emerge out of the grass towards the end of December, flowers wintry of winter, and they are delicately pale green, and of a lovely shape, with yellowish stamens. They have a peculiar wintry quality of invisibility, so lonely rising from the sere grass, and pallid green, held up like a little hand-mirror that reflects nothing. At first they are single upon a stem, short and lovely, and very wintry-beautiful, with a will not to be touched, not to be noticed. One instinctively leaves them alone. But as January draws towards February, these hellebores, these greenish Christmas roses become more assertive. Their pallid water-green becomes yellower, pale sulphur-yellow-green, and they rise up, they are in tufts, in throngs, in veritable bushes of greenish open flowers, assertive, bowing their faces with a hellebore assertiveness. In some places they throng among the bushes and above the water of the stream, giving the peculiar pale glimmer almost of primroses, as you walk among them. Almost of primroses, yet with a coarse hellebore leaf and an up-rearing hellebore assertiveness, like snakes in winter.

And as one walks among them, one brushes the last scarlet off the butcher's broom. This low little shrub is the Christmas holly of Tuscany, only a foot or so high, with a vivid red berry stuck on in the middle of its sharp hard leaf. In February the last red ball rolls off the prickly plume, and winter rolls with it. The violets already are emerging from the moisture.

But before the violets make any show, there are the crocuses. If you walk up through the pine-wood, that lifts its umbrellas of pine so high, up till you come to the brow of the hill at the top, you can look south, due south, and see snow on the Apennines, and on a blue afternoon, seven layers of blue-hilled distance.

Then you sit down on that southern slope, out of the wind, and there it is warm, whether it be January or February, *tramontana* or not. There the earth has been baked by innumerable suns, baked and baked again; moistened by many rains, but never wetted for long. Because it is rocky, and full to the south, and sheering steep in the slope.

And there, in February, in the sunny baked desert of that crumbly slope, you will find the first crocuses. On the sheer aridity of crumbled stone you see a queer, alert little star, very sharp and quite small. It has opened out rather flat, and looks like a tiny freesia flower, creamy, with a smear of yellow yolk. It has no stem, seems to have been just lightly dropped on the crumbled, baked rock. It is the first hill-crocus.

II

North of the Alps, the everlasting winter is interrupted by summers that struggle and soon yield; south of the Alps, the everlasting summer is interrupted by spasmodic and spiteful winters that never get a real hold, but that are mean and dogged. North of the Alps, you may have a pure winter's day in June. South of the Alps, you may have a midsummer day in December or January or even February. The in-between, in either case, is just as it may be. But the lands of the sun are south of the Alps, for ever.

Yet things, the flowers especially, that belong to both sides of the Alps, are not much earlier south than north of the mountains. Through all the winter there are roses in the garden, lovely creamy roses, more pure and mysterious than those of summer, leaning perfect from the stem. And the narcissus in the garden are out by the end of January, and the little simple hyacinths early in February.

But out in the fields, the flowers are hardly any sooner than English flowers. It is mid-February before the first violets, the first crocus, the first primrose. And in mid-February one may find a violet, a primrose, a crocus in England, in the hedgerows and the garden corner.

And still there is a difference. There are several kinds of wild crocus in this region of Tuscany: being little spiky mauve ones, and spiky little creamy ones, that grow among the pine-trees of the bare slopes. But the beautiful ones are those of a meadow in the corner of the woods, the low hollow meadow below the steep, shadowy pine-slopes, the secretive grassy dip where the water seeps through the turf all winter, where the stream runs between thick bushes, where the nightingale sings his mightiest in May, and where the wild thyme is rosy and full of bees, in summer.

Here the lavender crocuses are most at home—here sticking out of the deep grass, in a hollow like a cup, a bowl of grass, come the lilac-coloured crocuses, like an innumerable encampment. You may see them at twilight, with all the buds shut, in the mysterious stillness of the grassy underworld, palely glimmering like myriad folded tents. So the apaches still camp, and close their tepees, in the hollows of the great hills of the West, at night.

But in the morning it is quite different. Then the sun shines strong on the horizontal green cloud-puffs of the pines, the sky is clear and full of life, the water runs hastily, still browned by the last juice of crushed olives. And there the earth's bowl of crocuses is amazing. You cannot believe that the flowers are really still. They are open with such delight, and their pistil-thrust is so red-orange, and they are so many, all reaching out wide and marvellous, that it suggests a perfect ecstasy of radiant, thronging movement, lit-up violet and orange, and surging in some invisible rhythm of concerted, delightful movement. You cannot believe they do not move, and make some sort of crystalline sound of delight. If you sit still and watch, you begin to move with them, like moving with the stars, and you feel the sound of their radiance. All the little cells of the flowers must be leaping with flowery life and utterance.

And the small brown honey-bees hop from flower to flower, dive down, try, and off again. The flowers have been already rifled, most of them. Only sometimes a bee stands on his head, kicking slowly inside the flower, for some time. He has found something. And all the bees have little loaves of pollen, bee-bread, in their elbow-joints.

The crocuses last in their beauty for a week or so, and as they begin to lower their tents and abandon camp, the violets begin to thicken. It is already March. The violets have been showing like tiny dark hounds for some weeks. But now the whole pack comes forth, among the grass and the tangle of wild thyme, till the air all sways subtly scented with violets, and the banks above where the crocuses had their tents are now swarming brilliant purple with violets. They are the sweet violets of early spring, but numbers have made them bold, for they flaunt and ruffle till the slopes are a bright blue-purple blaze of them, full in the sun, with an odd late crocus still standing wondering and erect amongst them.

And now that it is March, there is a rush of flowers. Down by the other stream, which turns sideways to the sun, and has tangles of brier and bramble, down where the hellebore has stood so wan and dignified all winter, there are now white tufts of primroses, suddenly come. Among the tangle and near the water-lip, tufts and bunches of primroses, in abundance. Yet they look more wan, more pallid, more flimsy than English primroses. They lack some of the full wonder of the northern flowers. One tends to overlook them, to turn to the great, solemn-faced purple violets that rear up from the bank, and above all, to the wonderful little towers of the grape-hyacinth.

I know no flower that is more fascinating, when it first appears, than the blue grape-hyacinth. And yet, because it lasts so long, and keeps on coming so repeatedly, for at least two months, one tends later on to ignore it, even to despise it a little. Yet that is very unjust.

The first grape-hyacinths are flowers of blue, thick and rich and meaningful, above the unrenewed grass. The upper buds are pure blue, shut tight; round balls of pure, perfect warm blue, blue, blue; while the lower bells are darkish blue-purple, with the spark of white at the mouth. As yet, none of the lower bells has withered, to leave the greenish, separate sparseness of fruiting that spoils the grape-hyacinth later on, and makes it seem naked and functional. All hyacinths are like that in the seeding.

But, at first, you have only a compact tower of night-blue clearing to dawn, and extremely beautiful. If we were tiny as fairies, and lived only a summer, how lovely these great trees of bells would be to us, towers of night and dawn-blue globes. They would rise above us thick and succulent, and the purple globes would push the blue ones up, with white sparks of ripples, and we should see a god in them.

As a matter of fact, someone once told me they were the flowers of the many-breasted Artemis; and it is true, the Cybele of Ephesus, with her clustered breasts was like a grape-hyacinth at the bosom.

This is the time, in March, when the sloe is white and misty in the hedge-tangle by the stream, and on the slope of land the peach tree stands pink and alone. The almond blossom, silvery pink, is passing, but the peach, deep-toned, bluey, not at all ethereal, this reveals itself like flesh, and the trees are like isolated individuals, the peach and the apricot.

A man said this spring: "Oh, I *don't* care for peach blossom! It is such a vulgar pink!" One wonders what anybody means by a "vulgar" pink. I think pink flannelette is rather vulgar. But probably it's the flannelette's fault, not the pink. And peach blossom has a beautiful sensual pink, far from vulgar, most rare and private. And pink is so beautiful in a landscape, pink houses, pink almond, pink peach and purply apricot, pink asphodels.

It is so conspicuous and so individual, that pink among the coming green of spring, because the first flowers that emerge from winter seem always white or yellow or purple. Now the celandines are out, and along the edges of the *podere,* the big, sturdy, black-purple anemones, with black hearts.

They are curious, these great, dark-violet anemones. You may pass them on a grey day, or at evening or early morning, and never see them. But as you come along in the full sunshine, they seem to be baying at you with all their throats, baying deep purple into the air. It is because they are hot and wide open now, gulping the sun. Whereas when they are shut, they have a silkiness and a curved head, like the curve of an umbrella handle, and a peculiar outward colourlessness, that makes them quite invisible. They may be under your feet, and you will not see them.

Altogether anemones are odd flowers. On these last hills above the plain, we have only the big black-purple ones, in tufts here and there, not many. But two hills away, the young green corn is blue with the lilac-blue kind, still the broad-petalled sort with the darker heart. But these flowers are smaller than our dark-purple, and frailer, more silky. Ours are substantial, thickly vegetable flowers, and not abundant. The others are lovely and silky-delicate, and the whole corn is blue with them. And they have a sweet, sweet scent, when they are warm.

Then on the priest's *podere* there are the scarlet, Adonis-blood anemones: only in one place, in one long fringe under a terrace, and there by a path below. These flowers above all you will never find unless you look for them in the sun. Their silver silk outside makes them quite invisible, when they are shut up.

Yet, if you are passing in the sun, a sudden scarlet faces on to the air, one of the loveliest scarlet apparitions in the world. The inner surface of the Adonis-blood anemone is as fine as velvet, and yet there is no suggestion of pile, not as much as on a velvet rose. And from this inner smoothness issues the red colour, perfectly pure and unknown of earth, no earthiness, and yet solid, not transparent. How a colour manages to be perfectly strong and impervious, yet of a purity that suggests condensed light, yet not luminous, at least, not transparent, is a problem. The poppy in her radiance is translucent, and the tulip in her utter redness has a touch of opaque earth. But the Adonis-blood anemone is neither translucent nor opaque. It is just pure condensed red, of a velvetiness without velvet, and a scarlet without glow.

This red seems to me the perfect premonition of summer—like the red on the outside of apple blossom—and later, the red of the apple. It is the premonition in redness of summer and of autumn.

The red flowers are coming now. The wild tulips are in bud, hanging their grey leaves like flags. They come up in myriads, wherever they get a chance. But they are holding back their redness till the last days of March, the early days of April.

Still, the year is warming up. By the high ditch the common magenta anemone is hanging its silky tassels, or opening its great magenta daisy-shape to the hot sun. It is much nearer to red than the big-petalled anemones are; except the Adonis-blood. They say these anemones sprang from the tears of Venus, which fell as she went looking for Adonis. At that rate, how the poor lady must have wept, for the anemones by the Mediterranean are common as daisies in England.

The daisies are out here too, in sheets, and they too are red-mouthed. The first ones are big and handsome. But as March goes on, they dwindle to bright little things, like tiny buttons, clouds of them together. That means summer is nearly here.

The red tulips open in the corn like poppies, only with a heavier red. And they pass quickly, without repeating themselves. There is little lingering in a tulip.

In some places there are odd yellow tulips, slender, spiky, and Chinese-looking. They are very lovely, pricking out their dulled yellow in slim spikes. But they too soon lean, expand beyond themselves, and are gone like an illusion.

And when the tulips are gone, there is a moment's pause, before summer. Summer is the next move.

III

In the pause towards the end of April, when the flowers seem to hesitate, the leaves make up their minds to come out. For some time, at the very ends of the bare boughs of fig trees, spurts of pure green have been burning like little cloven tongues of green fire vivid on the tips of the candelabrum. Now these spurts of green spread out, and begin to take the shape of hands, feeling for the air of summer. And tiny green figs are below them, like glands on the throat of a goat.

For some time, the long stiff whips of the vine have had knobby pink buds, like flower buds. Now these pink buds begin to unfold into greenish, half-shut fans of leaves with red in the veins, and tiny spikes of flower, like seed-pearls. Then, in all its down and pinky dawn, the vine-rosette has a frail, delicious scent of a new year.

Now the aspens on the hill are all remarkable with the translucent membranes of blood-veined leaves. They are gold-brown, but not like autumn, rather like the thin wings of bats when like birds—call them birds—they wheel in clouds against the setting sun, and the sun glows through the stretched membrane of their wings, as through thin, brown-red stained glass. This is the red sap of summer, not the red dust of autumn. And in the distance the aspens have the tender panting glow of living membrane just come awake. This is the beauty of the frailty of spring.

The cherry tree is something the same, but more sturdy. Now, in the last week of April, the cherry blossom is still white, but waning and passing away: it is late this year; and the leaves are clustering thick and softly copper in their dark, blood-filled glow. It is queer about fruit trees in this district. The pear and the peach were out together. But now the pear tree is a lovely thick softness of new and glossy green, vivid with a tender fullness of apple-green leaves, gleaming among all the other green of the landscape, the half-high wheat, emerald, and the grey olive, half-invisible, the browning green of the dark cypress, the black of the evergreen oak, the rolling, heavy green puffs of the stone-pines, the flimsy green of small peach and almond trees, the sturdy young green of horse-chestnut. So many greens, all in flakes and shelves and tilted tables and round shoulders and plumes and shaggles and uprisen bushes, of greens and greens, sometimes blindingly brilliant at evening, when the landscape looks as if it were on fire from inside, with greenness and with gold.

The pear is perhaps the greenest thing in the landscape. The wheat may shine lit-up yellow, or glow bluish, but the pear tree is green in itself. The cherry has white, half-absorbed flowers, so has the apple. But the plum is rough with her new foliage, and inconspicuous, inconspicuous as the almond, the peach, the apricot, which one can no longer find in the landscape, though twenty days ago they were the distinguished pink individuals of the whole countryside. Now they are gone. It is the time of green, pre-eminent green, in ruffles and flakes and slabs.

In the wood, the scrub-oak is only just coming uncrumpled, and the pines keep their hold on winter. They are wintry things, stone-pines. At Christmas, their heavy green clouds are richly beautiful. When the cypresses raise their tall and naked bodies of dark green, and the osiers are vivid red-orange, on the still blue air, and the land is lavender, then, in mid-winter, the landscape is most beautiful in colour, surging with colour.

But now, when the nightingale is still drawing out his long, wistful, yearning, teasing plaint-note, and following it up with a rich and joyful burble, the pines and the cypresses seem hard and rusty, and the wood has lost its subtlety and its mysteriousness. It still seems wintry in spite of the yellowing young oaks, and the heath in flower. But hard, dull pines above, and hard, dull, tall heath below, all stiff and resistant, this is out of the mood of spring.

In spite of the fact that the stone-white heath is in full flower, and very lovely when you look at it, it does not, casually, give the impression of blossom. More the impression of having its tips and crests all dipped in hoarfrost; or in a whitish dust. It has a peculiar ghostly colourlessness amid the darkish colourlessness of the wood altogether, which completely takes away the sense of spring.

Yet the tall white heath is very lovely, in its invisibility. It grows sometimes as tall as a man, lifting up its spires and its shadowy-white fingers with a ghostly fullness, amid the dark, rusty green of its lower bushiness; and it gives off a sweet honeyed scent in the sun, and a cloud of fine white stone-dust, if you touch it. Looked at closely, its little bells are most beautiful, delicate and white, with the brown-purple inner eye and the dainty pin-head of the pistil. And out in the sun at the edge of the wood, where the heath grows tall and thrusts up its spires of dim white next a brilliant, yellow-flowering vetch-bush, under a blue sky, the effect has a real magic.

And yet, in spite of all, the dim whiteness of all the flowering heath-fingers only adds to the hoariness and out-of-date quality of the pine-woods, now in the pause between spring and summer. It is the ghost of the interval.

Not that this week is flowerless. But the flowers are little lonely things, here and there: the early purple orchid, ruddy and very much alive, you come across occasionally, then the little groups of bee-orchid, with their ragged concerted indifference to their appearance. Also there are the huge bud-spikes of the stout, thick-flowering pink orchid, huge buds like fat ears of wheat, hard-purple and splendid. But already odd grains of the wheat-ear are open, and out of the purple hangs the delicate pink rag of a floweret. Also there are very lovely and choice cream-coloured orchids with brown spots on the long and delicate lip. These grow in the more moist places, and have exotic tender spikes, very rare-seeming. Another orchid is a little, pretty yellow one.

But orchids, somehow, do not make a summer. They are too aloof and individual. The little slate-blue scabious is out, but not enough to raise an appearance. Later on, under the real hot sun, he will bob into notice. And by the edges of the paths there are odd rosy cushions of wild thyme. Yet these, too, are rather samples than the genuine thing. Wait another month, for wild thyme.

The same with the irises. Here and there, in fringes along the upper edge of terraces, and in odd bunches among the stones, the dark-purple iris sticks up. It is beautiful, but it hardly counts. There is not enough of it, and it is torn and buffeted by too many winds. First the wind blows with all its might from the Mediterranean, not cold, but infinitely wearying, with its rude and insistent pushing. Then, after a moment of calm, back comes a hard wind from the Adriatic, cold and disheartening. Between the two of them, the dark-purple iris flutters and tatters and curls as if it were burnt: while the little yellow rock-rose streams at the end of its thin stalk, and wishes it had not been in such a hurry to come out.

There is really no hurry. By May, the great winds will drop, and the great sun will shake off his harassments. Then the nightingale will sing an unbroken song, and the discreet, barely audible Tuscan cuckoo will be a little more audible. Then the lovely pale-lilac irises will come out in all their showering abundance of tender, proud, spiky bloom, till the air will gleam with mauve, and a new crystalline lightness will be everywhere.

The iris is half-wild, half-cultivated. The peasants sometimes dig up the roots, iris root, orris root (orris powder, the perfume that is still used). So, in May, you will find ledges and terraces, fields just lit up with the mauve light of irises, and so much scent in the air, you do not notice it, you do not even know it. It is all the flowers of iris, before the olive invisibly blooms.

There will be tufts of iris everywhere, rising up proud and tender. When the rose-coloured wild gladiolus is mingled in the corn, and the love-in-the-mist opens blue: in May and June, before the corn is cut.

But as yet it is neither May nor June, but end of April, the pause between spring and summer, the nightingale singing interruptedly, the bean-flowers dying in the bean-fields, the bean-perfume passing with spring, the little birds hatching in the nests, the olives pruned, and the vines, the last bit of late ploughing finished, and not much work to hand, now, not until the peas are ready to pick, in another two weeks or so. Then all the peasants will be crouching between the pea-rows, endlessly, endlessly gathering peas, in the long pea-harvest which lasts two months.

So the change, the endless and rapid change. In the sunny countries, the change seems more vivid, and more complete than in the grey countries. In the grey countries, there is a grey or dark permanency, over whose surface passes change ephemeral, leaving no real mark. In England, winters and summers shadowily give place to one another. But underneath lies the grey substratum, the permanency of cold, dark reality where bulbs live, and reality is bulbous, a thing of endurance and stored-up, starchy energy.

But in the sunny countries, change is the reality and permanence is artificial and a condition of imprisonment. In the North, man tends instinctively to imagine, to conceive that the sun is lighted like a candle, in an everlasting darkness, and that one day the candle will go out, the sun will be exhausted, and the everlasting dark will resume uninterrupted sway. Hence, to the northerner, the phenomenal world is essentially tragical, because it is temporal and must cease to exist. Its very existence implies ceasing to exist, and this is the root of the feeling of tragedy.

But to the southerner, the sun is so dominant that, if every phenomenal body disappeared out of the universe, nothing would remain but bright luminousness, sunniness. The absolute is sunniness; and shadow, or dark, is only merely relative: merely the result of something getting between one and the sun.

This is the instinctive feeling of the ordinary southerner. Of course, if you start to *reason,* you may argue that the sun is a phenomenal body. Therefore it came into existence, therefore it will pass out of existence, therefore the very sun is tragic in its nature.

But this is just argument. We think, because we have to light a candle in the dark, therefore some First Cause had to kindle the sun in the infinite darkness of the beginning.

The argument is entirely shortsighted and specious. We do not know in the least whether the sun ever came into existence, and we have not the slightest possible ground for conjecturing that the sun will ever pass out of existence. All that we do know, by actual experience, is that shadow comes into being when some material object intervenes between us and the sun, and that shadow ceases to exist when the intervening object is removed. So that, of all temporal or transitory or bound-to-cease things that haunt our existence, shadow or darkness, is the one which is purely and simply temporal. We can think of death, if we like, as of something permanently intervening between us and the sun: and this is at the root of the southern, under-world idea of death. But this doesn't alter the sun at all. As far as experience goes, in the human race, the one thing that is always there is the shining sun, and dark shadow is an accident of intervention.

Hence, strictly, there is no tragedy. The universe contains no tragedy, and man is only tragical because he is afraid of death. For my part, if the sun always shines, and always will shine, in spite of millions of clouds of words, then death, somehow, does not have many terrors. In the sunshine, even death is sunny. And there is no end to the sunshine.

That is why the rapid change of the Tuscan spring is utterly free, for me, of any sense of tragedy. "Where are the snows of yesteryear?" Why, precisely where they ought to be. Where are the little yellow aconites of eight weeks ago? I neither know nor care. They were sunny and the sun shines, and sunniness means change, and petals passing and coming. The winter aconites sunnily came, and sunnily went. What more? The sun always shines. It is our fault if we don't think so.

THE ELEPHANTS OF DIONYSUS

Dionysus, returning from India a victor with his hosts, met the Amazons once more towards the Ephesian coasts. O small-breasted, brilliant Amazons, will you never leave off attacking the Bull-foot, for whom the Charites weave ivy-garlands? Garlands and flutes. Oh, listen to the flutes! Oh, draw near, there is going to be sacrifice to the god of delight!

But the Amazons swept out of cover with bare limbs flashing and bronze spears lifted. O Dionysus! Iacchus! Iacchus! how fierce they are against you, fiercer than your own panthers. Ah, the shock of the enraged Amazons! Ah, elephants of the East, trumpeting round Dionysus!

They have fled again, lo! the Amazons have fled like a sudden ceasing of a hail-storm. They are gone, they are vanished. Ah no! here are some, suppliant in the temple. Pardon, Lord Dionysus! Oh, pardon!

But inveterate are the Amazons: over the sea, over the sea to Samos. In Samos shall be no cry of Iacchus! None shall cry: Come! Come in the spring-time! For Amazons range along the coast, inveterate; defy thee, Dionysus.

The god takes ship, and his dark-faced following, elephants stand in the boats. And the Amazons wail when they see again the long-nosed beasts bulk up. Ah, how will they devour us! Bitter, bitter the fight! Spare them not this time, Lord Dionysus! Bitter, bitter the fight! And bright-red Amazon blood spreads over the rocks and the earth, yet the last ones pierce the elephants. The rocks are torn with the piercing death-cries of elephants, the great and piercing cry of elephants, dying at the hands of the last of the Amazons, rips the island rocks.

Dionysus has conquered the Amazons. The elephants are dead. And the rocks of Samos, called Phloion, remain torn.

DAVID

Perpetual sound of water. The Arno, having risen with rain, is swirling brown: *café-au-lait*. It was a green river, suggesting olive trees and the hills. It is a rushing mass of *café-au-lait,* and it has already eaten one great slice from the flight of black steps. *Café-au-lait* is not respectful. But a world of women has brought us to it.

Morning in Florence. Dark, grey, and raining, with a perpetual sound of water. Over the bridge, carriages trotting under great ragged umbrellas. Two white bullocks urged from beneath a bright green umbrella, shambling into a trot as the whip-thong flickers between their soft shanks. Two men arm-in-arm under one umbrella, going nimbly. Mid-day from San Ministo—and cannon-shots. Why cannon-shots? Innumerable umbrellas over the bridge, "like flowers of infernal moly."

David in the Piazza livid with rain. Unforgettable, now I am safe in my upper room again. Livid—unnatural. He is made so natural that he is against nature, there in his corpse-whiteness in the rain. The Florentines say that a hot excitement, an anticipatory orgasm, possesses him at midnight of the New Year. Once told, impossible to forget. A year's waiting. It will happen to him, this orgasm, this further exposure of his nakedness. Uncomfortable. The Neptune, the Bandinelli statues, great stone creatures, do not matter. Water trickles over their flanks and down between their thighs, without effect. But David—always so sensitive. Corpse-white and sensitive. The water sinks into him, cold, diluting his stagnant springs. And yet he waits with that tense anticipation. As if to clutch the moment. Livid! The Florentine.

Perpetual sound of water. When the sun shines, it shines with grand brilliance, and then the Arno creeps underneath like a cat, like a green-eyed cat in a strange garden. We scarcely observe. We seem to hear the sun clapping in the air, noiseless and brilliant. The aerial and inaudible music of all the sun-shaken ether, inaudible, yet surely like chimes of glass. What is a river, then, but a green thread fluttering? And now! And particularly last night. Last night the river churned and challenged with strange noises. Not a Florentine walked by the parapet. Last night enormous cat-swirls breathed hoarse beyond the bank, the weir was a fighting flurry of waters. Like enormous cats interlocked in fight, uttering strange noises. Weight of dark, recoiling water. How is this Italy?

Florence—she puts up no fight. Who hears the river in Turin? Turin camps flat in defiance. Great snowy Alps, like inquisitive gods from the North, encircle her. She sticks a brandished statue at the end of the street, full in the vista of glistening, peering snow. She pokes her finger in the eye of the gods. But Florence, the Lily-town among her hills! Her hills, her hovering waters. She can be hot, brilliant, burnt dry. But look at David! What's the matter with him? Not sun but cold rain. Children of the South, exposing themselves to the rain. Savonarola, like a hot coal quenched. The South, the North: the fire, the wet downfall. Once there was a pure equilibrium, and the Lily blossomed. But the Lily now—livid! David, livid, almost quenched, yet still strained and waiting, tense for that orgasm. Crowds will gather at New Year's midnight.

The Lily, the flower of adolescence. Water-born. You cannot dry a lily-bulb. Take away its watery preponderance, surcharge an excess of water, and it is finished. Its flesh is dead. Ask a gardener. A water-blossom dripped from the North. How it blossomed here in the flowery town. Obviously northerners must love Florence. Here is their last point, their most southerly. The extreme south of the Lily's flowering. It is said the fruits are best at their extremity of climate. The southern apple is sweetest at his most northerly limit. The Lily, the Water-born, most dazzling nearest the sun. Florence, the flower-town. David!

Michelangelo's David is the presiding genius of Florence. Not a shadow of a doubt about it. Once and for all, Florence. So young: sixteen, they say. So big: and stark-naked. Revealed. Too big, too naked, too exposed. Livid, under today's sky. The Florentine! The Tuscan pose—half self-conscious all the time. Adolescent. Waiting. The tense look. No escape. The Lily. Lily or iris, what does it matter? Whitman's Calamus, too.

Does he listen? Does he, with his young troubled brow, listen? What does he hear? Weep of waters? Even on bluest, hottest day, the same tension. Listen! The weep of waters. The wintry North. The naked exposure. Stripped so bare, the very kernel of youth. Stripped even to the adolescent orgasm of New Year's night—at midwinter. Unbearable.

Dionysus and Christ of Florence. A clouded Dionysus, a refractory Christ. Dionysus, brightness of sky and moistness of earth: so they tell us is the meaning. Giver of riches. Riches of transport, the vine. Nymphs and Hamadryads, Silenus, Pan and the Fauns and

Satyrs: clue to all these, Dionysus, Iacchus, Dithyrambus. David?—Dionysus, source of reed-music, water-born melody. "The Crocus and the Hyacinth in deep grass"—lily-flowers. Then wine. Dew and fire, as Pater says. Eleutherios, the Deliverer. What did he deliver? Michelangelo asked himself that; and left us the answer. Dreams, transports. Dreams, brilliant consciousness, vivid self-revelation. Michelangelo's Dionysus, and Michelangelo's David—what is the difference? The cloud on David. The four months of winter were sacred to Dionysus: months of wine and dreams and transport of self-realization. Months of the inner fire. The vine. Fire which even now, at New Year's night, comes up in David. To have no issue. A cloud is on him.

Semele, scarred with lightning, gave birth prematurely to her child. The Cinque-Cento. Too fierce a mating, too fiery and potent a sire. The child was sewn again into the thigh of Zeus, re-entered into the loins of the lightning. So the brief fire-brand. It was fire overwhelming, over-weening, briefly married to the dew, that begot this child. The South to the North. Married! The child, the fire-dew, Iacchus, David.

Fire-dew, yet still too fiery. Plunge him further into the dew. Dithyrambus, the twice-born, born first of fire, then of dew. Dionysus leaping into the mists of the North, to escape his foes. David, by the Arno.

So Florence, this Lily. Here David trembled to his first perfection, on the brink of the dews. Here his soul found its perfect embodiment, in the trembling union of southern flame and northern waters. David, Dithyrambus; the adolescent. The shimmer, the instant of unstable combination, the soul for one moment perfectly embodied. Fire and dew, they call it. David, the Lily-flame, the Florentine.

The soul that held the fire and the dew clipped together in one lily-flame, where is it? David. Where is he? Cinque-Cento, a fleeting moment of adolescence. In that one moment the two eternal elements were held in consummation, forming the perfect embodiment of the human soul. And then gone. David, the Lily, the Florentine—Venus of the Scallop-Shell—Leonardo's John the Baptist. The moment of adolescence—gone. The subtle, evanescent lily-soul. They are wistful, all of them: Botticelli's women; Leonardo's, Michelangelo's men: wistful, knowing the loss even in the very moment of perfection. A day-lily, the Florentine. David frowning, Mona Lisa sadly, subtly smiling, beyond bitterness, Botticelli getting rapture out of sadness, his Venus wistfully Victrix. Fire and dew for one moment proportionate, immediately falling into disproportion.

They all knew. They knew the quenching of the flame, the breaking of the lily-balance, the passing of perfection and the pure pride of life, the inestimable loss. It had to be. They knew the mists of the North damping down. Born of the fire, they had still to be born of the mist. Christ, with his submission, universal humility, finding one level, like mist settling, like water. A new flood. Savonarola smokily quenched. The fire put out, or at least overwhelmed. Then Luther and the North.

Michelangelo, Leonardo, Botticelli, how well they knew, artistically, what was coming. The magnificent pride of life and perfection granted only to bud. The transient lily. Adam, David, Venus on her shell, the Madonna of the Rocks: they listen, all of them. What do they hear? Perpetual sound of waters. The level sweep of waters, waters overwhelming. Morality, chastity–another world drowned: equality, democracy, the masses, like drops of water in one sea, overwhelming all outstanding loveliness of the individual soul. Quenching of all flame in the great watery passivity which bears down at last so ponderous. Christ-like submissiveness which, once it bursts its bounds, floods the face of the earth with such devastation.

Pride of life! The perfect soul erect, holding the eternal elements consummate in itself. Thus for one moment the young lily David. For one moment Dionysus touched the hand of the Crucified: for one moment, and then was dragged down. Meekness flooded the soul of Dithyrambus, mist overwhelmed him. The elements supervene in the human soul, men become nature-worshippers; light, landscape and mists–these take the place of human individuality. Dionysus pale and corpse-like, there in the Piazza della Signoria. David, Venus, Saint John, all overcome with mist and surrender of the soul.

Yet no final surrender. Leonardo laughs last, even at the Crucified. David, with his knitted brow and full limbs, is unvanquished. Livid, maybe, corpse-coloured, quenched with innumerable rains of morality and democracy. Yet deep fountains of fire lurk within him. Must do. Witness the Florentines gathered at New Year's night to watch that fiery fruitless orgasm. They laugh, but it is Leonardo's laugh. The fire is not ridiculous. It surges recurrent. Never to be quenched. Stubborn. The Florentine.

One day David finishes his adolescence. One day he reaps his mates. It is a throbbing through the centuries of unquenchable fire, that will still leap out to consummation. The pride of life. The pride of the fulfilled self. The bud is not nipped; it awaits its maturity. Not the frail lily. Not even the clinging purple vine. But the full tree of life in blossom.

NOTES FOR *BIRDS, BEASTS AND FLOWERS*

FRUITS

"For fruits are all of them female, in them lies the seed. And so when they break and show the seed, then we look into the womb and see its secrets. So it is that the pomegranate is the apple of love to the Arab, and the fig has been a catch-word for the female fissure for ages. I don't care a fig for it! men say. But why a fig? The apple of Eden, even, was Eve's fruit. To her it belonged, and she offered it to the man. Even the apples of knowledge are Eve's fruit, the woman's. But the apples of life the dragon guards, and no woman gives them. . . ."

"No sin is it to drink as much as a man can take and get home without a servant's help, so he be not stricken in years."

TREES

"It is said, a disease has attacked the cypress trees of Italy, and they are all dying. Now even the shadow of the lost secret is vanishing from earth."

"Empedokles says trees were the first living creatures to grow up out of the earth, before the sun was spread out and before day and night were distinguished; from the symmetry of their mixture of fire and water, they contain the proportion of male and female; they grow, rising up owing to the heat which is in the earth, so that they are parts of the earth just as embryos are parts of the uterus. Fruits are excretions of the water and fire in plants."

FLOWERS

"And long ago, the almond was the symbol of resurrection.–But tell me, tell me, why should the almond be the symbol of resurrection?–

Have you not seen, in the mild winter sun of the southern Mediterranean, in January and in February, the re-birth of the almond tree, all standing in clouds of glory?–

Ah yes! ah yes! would I might see it again!

Yet even this is not the secret of the secret. Do you know what was called the almond bone, the last bone of the spine? This was the seed of the body, and from the grave it could grow into a new body again, like almond blossom in January.–No, no, I know nothing of that.–"

"Oh Persephone, Persephone, bring back to me from Hades the life of a dead man.–"

"Wretches, utter wretches, keep your hands from beans! saith Empedokles. For according to some, the beans were the beans of votes, and votes were politics. But others say it was a food-taboo. Others also say the bean was one of the oldest symbols of the male organ, for the peas-cod is later than the beans-cod."

"But blood is red, and blood is life. Red was the colour of kings. Kings, far-off kings, painted their faces vermilion, and were almost gods."

THE EVANGELISTIC BEASTS

"Oh, put them back, put them back in the four corners of the heavens, where they belong, the Apocalyptic beasts. For with their wings full of stars they rule the night, and man that watches through the night lives four lives, and man that sleeps through the night sleeps four sleeps, the sleep of the lion, the sleep of the bull, the sleep of the man, and the eagle's sleep. After which the lion wakes, and it is day. Then from the four quarters the four winds blow, and life has its changes. But when the heavens are empty, empty of the four great Beasts, the four Natures, the four Winds, the four Quarters, then sleep is empty too, man sleeps no more like the lion and the bull, nor wakes from the light-eyed eagle sleep."

CREATURES

"But fishes are very fiery, and take to the water to cool themselves."

"To those things that love darkness, the light of day is cruel and a pain. Yet the light of lamps and candles has no fears for them; rather they draw near to taste it, as if saying: Now what is this?

So we see that the sun is more than burning, more than the burning of fires or the shining of lamps. Because with his rays he hurts the creatures that live by night, and lamplight and firelight do them no hurt. Therefore the sun lives in his shining, and is not like fires, that die."

REPTILES

"Homer was wrong in saying, 'Would that strife might pass away from among gods and men!' He did not see that he was praying for the destruction of the universe; for, if his prayer were heard, all things would pass away–for in the tension of opposites all things have their being–"

"For when Fire in its downward path chanced to mingle with the dark breath of the earth, the serpent slid forth, lay revealed. But he was moist and cold, the sun in him darted uneasy, held down by moist earth, never could he rise on his feet. And this is what put poison in his mouth. For the sun in him would fain rise halfway, and move on feet. But moist earth weighs him down, though he dart and twist, still he must go with his belly on the ground.– The wise tortoise laid his earthy part around him, he cast it round him and found his feet. So he is the first of creatures to stand upon his toes, and the dome of his house is his heaven. Therefore it is charted out, and is the foundation of the world."

BIRDS

"Birds are the life of the skies, and when they fly, they reveal the thoughts of the skies. The eagle flies nearest to the sun, no other bird flies so near.

So he brings down the life of the sun, and the power of the sun, in his wings, and men who see him wheeling are filled with the elation of the sun. But all creatures of the sun must dip their mouths in blood, the sun is for ever thirsty, thirsting for the brightest exhalation of blood.

You shall know a bird by his cry, and great birds cry loud, but sing not. The eagle screams when the sun is high, the peacock screams at the dawn, rooks call at evening, when the nightingale sings. And all birds have their voices, each means a different thing."

ANIMALS

"Yes, and if oxen or lions had hands, and could paint with their hands, and produce works of art as men do, horses would paint the forms of the gods like horses, and oxen like oxen, and make their bodies in the image of their several kinds."

"Once, they say, he was passing by when a dog was being beaten, and he spoke this word: 'Stop! don't beat it! For it is the soul of a friend I recognized when I heard its voice.' "

"Swine wash in mire, and barnyard fowls in dust."

GHOSTS

"And as the dog with its nostrils tracking out the fragments of the beasts' limbs, and the breath from their feet that they leave in the soft grass, runs upon a path that is pathless to men, so does the soul follow the trail of the dead, across great spaces. For the journey is a far one, to sleep and a forgetting, and often the dead look back, and linger, for now they realize all that is lost. Then the living soul comes up with them, and great is the pain of greeting, and deadly the parting again. For oh, the dead are disconsolate, since even death can never make up for some mistakes."

II

Peoples, Countries, Races

GERMAN IMPRESSIONS:

I. French Sons of Germany

In Metz I prefer the Frenchmen to the Germans. I am more at my ease with them. It is a question of temperament.

From the Cathedral down to the river is all French. The Cathedral seems very German. It is nothing but nave: a tremendous lofty nave, and nothing else: a great jump at heaven, in the conception; a rather pathetic fall to earth in execution. Still, the splendid conception is there.

So I go down from the Cathedral to the French quarter. It is full of smells, perhaps, but it is purely itself. A Frenchman has the same soul, whether he is eating his dinner or kissing his baby. A German has no soul when he is eating his dinner, and is beautiful when he kisses his baby. So I prefer the Frenchman who hasn't the tiresome split between his animal nature and his spiritual, in whom the two are fused.

The barber drinks. He has wild hair and bloodshot eyes. Still, I dare trust my throat and chin to him. I address him in German. He dances before me, answering in mad French, that he speaks no German. Instantly I love him in spite of all.

"You are a foreigner here?" I remark.

He cannot lather me, he is so wildly excited. "No he was born in Metz, his father was born in Metz, his grandfather was born in Metz. For all he knows, Adam was born in Metz. But no Leroy has ever spoken German; no, not a syllable. It would split his tongue—he could not, you see, Sir, he could not; his construction would not allow of it."

With all of which I agree heartily; whereupon he looks lovingly upon me and continues to lather.

"His wife was a Frenchwoman, born in Paris. I must see his wife." He calls her by some name I do not know, and she appears—fat and tidy.

"You are a subject of France?" my barber demands furiously.

"Certainly," she begins. "I was born in Paris——" As they both talk at once, I can't make out what they say. But they are happy, they continue. At last, with a final flourish of the razor, I am shaved. The barber is very tipsy.

"Monsieur is from Brittany?" he asks me tenderly.

Alas! I am from England.

"But, why?" cries Madame; "you have not an English face; no, never. And a German face—pah! impossible."

In spite of all I look incurably English. Nevertheless, I start a story about a great-grandfather who was refugee in England after the revolution. They embrace me, they love me. And I love them.

"Sir," I say, "will you give me a morsel of soap? No, not shaving soap."

"This is French soap, this is German," he says. The French is in a beautiful flowery wrapper, alas! much faded.

"And what is the difference?" I ask.

"The French, of course, is *better*. The German is five pfennigs—one sou, Monsieur—the cheaper."

Of course, I take the French soap. The barber grandly gives my twenty-pfennig tip to the lathering boy, who has just entered, and he bows me to the door. I am in the street, breathless.

A German officer, in a flowing cloak of bluey-grey—like ink and milk—looks at me coldly and inquisitively. I look at him with a "Go to the devil" sort of look, and pass along. I wonder to myself if my dislike of these German officers is racial, or owing to present national feeling, or if it is a temperamental aversion. I decide on the last. A German soldier spills something out of a parcel on to the road and looks round like a frightened boy. I want to shelter him.

I pass along, look at the ridiculous imitation-medieval church that is built on the islet—or peninsula—in the middle of the river, on the spot that has been called for ages "The Place of Love." I wonder how the Protestant conscience of this ugly church remains easy upon such foundation. I think of the famous "three K's" that are allotted to German women, *"Kinder, Küche, Kirche,"* and pity the poor wretches.

Over the river, all is barracks—barracks, and soldiers on foot, and soldiers on horseback. Everywhere these short, baggy German soldiers, with their fair skins and rather stupid blue eyes! I hurry to get away from them. To the right is a steep hill, once, I suppose, the scarp of the river.

At last I found a path, and turned for a little peace to the hillside and the vineyards. The vines are all new young slips, climbing up their sticks. The whole hillside bristles with sticks, like an angry hedgehog. Across lies Montigny; to the right, Metz itself, with its cathedral like a brown rat humped up. I prefer my hillside. In this Mosel valley there is such luxuriance of vegetation. Lilac bushes are only heaps of purple flowers. Some roses are out. Here on the wild hillside there are lively vetches of all sorts, and white poppies and red; and then the vine shoots, with their tips of most living, sensitive pink and red, just like blood under the skin.

I am happy on the hillside. It is a warm, grey day. The Mosel winds below. The vine sticks bristle against the sky. The little church of the village is in front. I climb the hill, past a Madonna shrine that stands out by the naked path. The faded blue "Lady" is stuck with dying white lilac. She looks rather ugly, but I do not mind. Odd men, and women, are working in the vineyards. They are very swarthy, and they have very small-bladed spades, which glisten in the sun.

At last I come to the cemetery under the church. As I marvel at the bead-work wreaths, with ridiculous little naked china figures of infants floating in the middle, I hear voices, and looking up, see two German soldiers on the natural platform, or terrace, beside the church. Along the vineyard path are squares of yellow and black and white, like notice boards. The two soldiers, in their peculiar caps, almost similar to our round sailors' hats, or blue cooks' caps, are laughing. They watch the squares, then me.

When I go up to the church and round to the terrace, they are gone. The terrace is a natural platform, a fine playground, very dark with great horse-chestnuts in flower, and walled up many feet from the hillside, overlooking the far valley of the Mosel. As I sit on a bench, the hens come pecking round me. It is perfectly still and lovely, the only sound being from the boys' school.

Somewhere towards eleven o'clock two more soldiers came. One led his horse, the other was evidently not mounted. They came to the wall, or parapet, to look down the valley at the fort. Meanwhile, to my great joy, the mare belonging to the mounted soldier cocked up her tail and cantered away under the horse-chestnuts, down the village. Her owner went racing, shouting after her, making the peculiar *hu-hu!* these Germans use to their horses. She would have been lost had not two men rushed out of the houses, and, shouting in French, stopped her. The soldier jerked her head angrily, and led her back. He was a short, bear-like little German, she was a wicked and delicate mare. He kept her bridle as he returned. Meanwhile, his companion, his hands clasped on his knees, shouted with laughter.

Presently, another, rather taller, rather more manly soldier appeared. He had a sprig of lilac between his teeth. The foot-soldier recounted the escapade with the mare, whereupon the newcomer roared with laughter and suddenly knocked the horse under the jaw. She reared in terror. He got hold of her by the bridle, teasing her. At last her owner pacified her. Then the newcomer would insist on sticking a piece of lilac in her harness, against her ear. It frightened her, she reared, and she panted, but he would not desist. He teased her, bullied her, coaxed her, took her unawares; she was in torment as he pawed at her head to stick in the flower, she would not allow him. At last, however, he succeeded. She, much discomfited, wore lilac against her ear.

Then the children came out of school—boys, in their quaint pinafores. It is strange how pleasant, how quaint, and manly these little children are; the tiny boys of six seemed more really manly than the soldiers of twenty-one, more alert to the real things. They cried to each other in their keen, naïve way, discussing the action at the fortress, of which I could make out nothing.

And one of the soldiers asked them, "How old are you, Johnny?" Human nature is very much alike. The boys used French in their play, but they answered the soldiers in German.

As I was going up the hill there came on a heavy shower. I sheltered as much as I could under an apple-tree thick with pink blossom; then I hurried down to the village. "Café—Restauration" was written on one house. I wandered into the living-room beyond the courtyard.

"Where does one drink?" I asked the busy, hard-worked-looking woman. She answered me in French, as she took me in. At once, though she was a drudge, her fine spirit of politeness made me comfortable.

"This is not France?" I asked of her.

"Oh, no—but always the people have been French," and she looked at me quickly from her black eyes. I made my voice tender as I answered her.

Presently I said: "Give me some cigarettes, please."

"French or German?" she asked.

"What's the difference?" I inquired.

"The French, of course, are better."

"Then French," I said, laughing, though I do not really love the black, strong French cigarettes.

"Sit and talk to me a minute," I said to her. "It is so nice not to speak German."

"Ah, Monsieur!" she cried, and she loved me. She could not sit, no. She could only stay a minute. Then she sent her man.

I heard her in the other room bid him come. He was shy—he would not. "Ssh!" I heard her go as she pushed him through the door.

He was very swarthy, burned dark with the sun. His eyes were black and very bright. He was a man of about forty-five. I could not persuade him to sit down or to drink with me; he would accept only a cigarette. Then, laughing, he lighted me my cigarette. He was a gentleman, and he had white teeth.

The village, he told me, was Sey: a French name, but a German village.

"And you are a German subject?" I asked.

He bowed to me. He said he had just come in from the vines, and must go back immediately. Last year they had had a bad disease, so that all the plants I had seen were new. I hoped he would get rich with them. He smiled with a peculiar sad grace.

"Not rich, Monsieur, but not a failure this time."

He had a daughter, Angèle: "In Paris—in *France*."

He bowed and looked at me meaningly. I said I was glad. I said:

"I do not like Metz: too many soldiers. I do not like German soldiers."

"They are scarcely polite," he said quietly.

"You find it?" I asked.

He bowed his acquiescence.

It is a strange thing that these two Frenchmen were the only two men—not acquaintances—whom I felt friendly towards me in the whole of Metz.

II. Hail in the Rhineland

We were determined to take a long walk this afternoon, in spite of the barometer, which persisted in retreating towards "storm." The morning was warm and mildly sunny. The blossom was still falling from the fruit-trees down the village street, and drifting in pink and white all along the road. The barber was sure it would be fine. But then he'd have sworn to anything I wanted, he liked me so much since I admired, in very bad German, his moustache.

"I may trim your moustache?" he asked.

"You can do what you like with it," I said.

As he was clipping it quite level with my lip he asked:

"You like a short moustache?"

"Ah," I answered, "I could never have anything so beautiful and upstanding as yours."

Whereupon immediately he got excited, and vowed my moustache should stand on end even as Kaiserly as did his own.

"Never," I vowed.

Then he brought me a bottle of mixture, and a gauze bandage, which I was to bind under my nose, and there I should be, in a few weeks, with an upstanding moustache sufficient as a guarantee for any man. But I was modest; I refused even to try.

"No," I said, "I will remember yours." He pitied me, and vowed it would be fine for the afternoon.

I told Johanna so, and she took her parasol. It was really sunny, very hot and pretty, the afternoon. Besides, Johanna's is the only parasol I have seen in Waldbröl, and I am the only Englishman any woman for miles around could boast. So we set off.

We were walking to Nümbrecht, some five or six miles away. Johanna moved with great dignity, and I held the parasol. Every man, even the workmen on the fields, bowed low to us, and every woman looked at us yearningly. And to every women, and to every man, Johanna gave a bright "Good day."

"They like it so much," she said. And I believed her.

There was a scent of apple-blossom quite strong on the air. The cottages, set at random and painted white, with their many numbers painted black, have a make-believe, joyful, childish look.

Everywhere the broom was out, great dishevelled blossoms of ruddy gold sticking over the besom strands. The fields were full of dandelion pappus, floating misty bubbles crowded thick, hiding the green grass with their globes. I showed Johanna how to tell the time. "One!" I puffed; "two-three-four-five-six! Six o'clock, my dear."

"Six o'clock what?" she asked.

"Anything you like," I said.

"At six o'clock there will be a storm. The barometer is never wrong," she persisted.

I was disgusted with her. The beech wood through which we were walking was a vivid flame of green. The sun was warm.

"Johanna," I said. "Seven ladies in England would walk out with me, although they *knew* that at six o'clock a thunder-shower would ruin their blue dresses. Besides, there are two holes in your mittens, and black mittens show so badly."

She quickly hid her arms in the folds of her skirts. "Your English girls have queer taste, to walk out seven at a time with you."

We were arguing the point with some ferocity when, descending a hill in the wood, we came suddenly upon a bullock-wagon. The cows stood like blocks in the harness, though their faces were black with flies. Johanna was very indignant. An old man was on the long, railed wagon, which was piled with last year's brown oak-leaves. A boy was straightening the load, and waiting at the end of the wagon ready to help, a young, strong man, evidently his father, who was struggling uphill with an enormous sack-cloth bundle—enormous, full of dead leaves. The new leaves of the oaks overhead were golden brown, and crinkled with young vigour. The cows stood stolid and patient, shutting their eyes, weary of the plague of flies. Johanna flew to their rescue, fanning them with a beech-twig.

"Ah, poor little ones!" she cried. Then, to the old man, in tones of indignation: "These flies will eat up your oxen."

"Yes—their wicked little mouths," he agreed.

"Cannot you prevent them?" she asked.

"They are everywhere," he answered, and he smacked a fly on his hand.

"But you can do something," she persisted.

"You could write a card and stick it between their horns, 'Settling of flies strictly forbidden here,'" I said.

"'*Streng verboten,*'" he repeated as he laughed.

Johanna looked daggers at me.

"Thank you, young fellow," she said sarcastically. I stuck leafy branches in the head-harness of the cattle. The old man thanked me with much gratitude.

"It is hot weather!" I remarked.

"It will be a thunderstorm, I believe," he answered.

"At six o'clock?" cried Johanna.

But I was along the path.

We went gaily through the woods and open places, and had nearly come to Nümbrecht, when we met a very old man, coming very slowly up the hill with a splendid young bull, of buff-colour and white, which, in its majestic and leisurely way, was dragging a harrow that rode on sledges.

"Fine weather," I remarked, forgetting.

"Jawohl!" he answered. "But there will be a thunderstorm."

"And I knew it," said Johanna.

But we were at Nümbrecht. Johanna drank her mineral water and raspberry juice. It was ten minutes to six.

"It is getting dark," remarked Johanna.

"There is no railway here?" I asked.

"Not for six miles," she replied pointedly.

The landlord was a very handsome man.

"It is getting dark," said Johanna to him.

"There will be a thunderstorm, Madame," he replied with beautiful grace. "Madame is walking?"

"From Waldbröl," she replied. By this time she was statuesque. The landlord went to the door. Girls were leading home the cows.

"It is coming," he said, and immediately there was a rumbling of thunder.

Johanna went to the door.

"An enormous black cloud. The sky is black," she announced. I followed to her side. It was so.

"The barber——" I said.

"Must you live by the word of the barber?" said Johanna.

The landlord retired indoors. He was a very handsome man, all the hair was positively shaved from his head. And I knew Johanna liked the style.

I fled to Stollwerck's chocolate machine, and spent a few anxious moments extracting burnt almonds. The landlord reappeared.

"There is an omnibus goes to Waldbröl for the station and the east. It passes the door in ten minutes," he said gracefully. No English landlord could have equalled him. I thanked him with all my heart.

The omnibus was an old brown cab—a growler. Its only occupant was a brown-paper parcel for Frau ——.

"You don't mind riding?" I said tenderly to Johanna.

"I had rather we were at home. I am terribly afraid of thunderstorms," she answered.

We drove on. A young man in black stopped the omnibus. He bowed to us, then mounted the box with the driver.

"It is Thienes, the Bretzel baker," she said. *Bretzel* is a very twisty little cake like *Kringel.*

I do not know why, but after this Johanna and I sat side by side in tense silence. I felt very queerly.

"There, the rain!" she suddenly cried.

"Never mind," I pleaded.

"Oh, I like riding in here," she said.

My heart beat, and I put my hand over hers. She pretended not to notice, which made my heart beat more. I don't know how it would have ended. Suddenly there was such a rattle outside, and something pounding on me. Johanna cried out. It was a great hailstorm–the air was a moving white storm–enormous balls of ice, big as marbles, then bigger, like balls of white carbon that housewives use against moths, came striking in. I put up the window. It was immediately cracked, so I put it down again. A hailstone as big as a pigeon-egg struck me on the knee, hurt me, and bounced against Johanna's arm. She cried out with pain. The horses stood still and would not move. There was a roar of hail. All round, on the road balls of ice were bouncing viciously up again. We could not see six yards out of the carriage.

Suddenly the door opened, and Thienes, excusing himself, appeared. I dragged him in. He was a fresh young man, with naïve, wide eyes. And his best suit of lustrous black was shining now with wet.

"Had you no cover?" we said.

He showed his split umbrella, and burst into a torrent of speech. The hail drummed bruisingly outside.

It had come like horse-chestnuts of ice, he said.

The fury of the storm lasted for five minutes, all of which time the horses stood stock still. The hailstones shot like great white bullets into the carriage. Johanna clung to me in fear. There was a solid sheet of falling ice outside.

At last the horses moved on. I sat eating large balls of ice and realizing myself. When at last the fall ceased Thienes *would* get out on to the box again. I liked him; I wanted him to stay. But he would not.

The country was a sight. All over the road, and fallen thick in the ruts, were balls of ice, pure white, as big as very large marbles, and some as big as bantam-eggs. The ditches looked as if stones and stones weight of loaf sugar had been emptied into them–white balls and cubes of ice everywhere. Then the sun came out, and under the brilliant green birches a thick white mist, only a foot high, sucked at the fall of ice. It was very cold. I shuddered.

"I was only flirting with Johanna," I said to myself. "But, by Jove, I was nearly dished."

The carriage crunched over the hail. All the road was thick with twigs, as green as spring. It made me think of the roads strewed for the Entry to Jerusalem. Here it was cherry boughs and twigs and tiny fruits, a thick carpet; next, brilliant green beech; next, pine-brushes, very beautiful, with their creamy pollen cones, making the road into a green bed; then fir twigs, with pretty emerald new shoots like stars, and dark sprigs over the hailstones. Then we passed two small dead birds, fearfully beaten. Johanna began to cry. But we were near a tiny, lonely inn, where the carriage stopped. I said I *must* give Thienes a *Schnapps,* and I jumped out. The old lady was sweeping away a thick fall of ice-stones from the doorway.

When I next got into the carriage, I suppose I smelled of *Schnapps,* and was not lovable. Johanna stared out of the window, away from me. The lovely dandelion bubbles were gone, there was a thicket of stripped stalks, all broken. The corn was broken down, the road was matted with fruit twigs. Over the Rhineland was a grey, desolate mist, very cold.

At the next stopping place, where the driver had to deliver a parcel, a young man passed with a very gaudily apparelled horse, great red trappings. He was a striking young fellow. Johanna watched him. She was not *really* in earnest with me. We might have both made ourselves unhappy for life, but for this storm. A middle-aged man, very brown and sinewy with work, came to the door. He was rugged, and I liked him. He showed me his hand. The back was bruised, and swollen, and already going discoloured. It made me wince. But he laughed rather winsomely, even as if he were glad.

"A hailstone!" he said, proudly.

We watched the acres of ice-balls slowly pass by, in silence. Neither of us spoke. At last we came to the tiny station, at home. There was the station-master, and, of all people, the barber.

"I can remember fifty-five years," said the station-master, "but nothing like this."

"Not round, but squares, two inches across, of ice," added the barber, with gusto.

"At the shop they have sold out of tiles, so many smashed," said the station-master.

"And in the green-house roofs, at the Asylum, not a shred of glass," sang the barber.

"The windows at the station smashed——"

"And a man"–I missed the name–"hurt quite badly by——" rattled the barber.

"But," I interrupted, "you said it would be fine."

"And," added Johanna, "we went on the strength of it." It is queer, how sarcastic she can be, without *saying* anything really meaningful.

We were four dumb people. But I had a narrow escape, and Johanna had a narrow escape, and we both know it, and thank the terrific hail-storm, though at present *she* is angry–vanity, I suppose.

CHRISTS IN THE TIROL

The real Tirol does not seem to extend far south of the Brenner, and northward it goes right to the Starnberger See. Even at Sterzing the rather gloomy atmosphere of the Tirolese Alps is being dispersed by the approach of the South. And, strangely enough, the roadside crucifixes become less and less interesting after Sterzing. Walking down from Munich to Italy, I have stood in front of hundreds of *Martertafeln;* and now I miss them; these painted shrines by the Garda See are not the same.

I, who see a tragedy in every cow, began by suffering from the Secession pictures in Munich. All these new paintings seemed so shrill and restless. Those that were meant for joy shrieked and pranced for joy, and sorrow was a sensation to be relished, curiously; as if we were epicures in suffering, keen on a new flavour. I thought with kindliness of England, whose artists so often suck their sadness like a lollipop, mournfully, and comfortably.

Then one must walk, as it seems, for miles and endless miles past crucifixes, avenues of them. At first they were mostly factory made, so that I did not notice them, any more than I noticed the boards with warnings, except just to observe they were there. But coming among the Christs carved in wood by the peasant artists, I began to feel them. Now, it seems to me, they create almost an atmosphere over the northern Tirol, an atmosphere of pain.

I was going along a marshy place at the foot of the mountains, at evening, when the sky was a pale, dead colour and the hills were nearly black. At a meeting of the paths was a crucifix, and between the feet of the Christ a little red patch of dead poppies. So I looked at him. It was an old shrine, and the Christus was nearly like a man. He seemed to me to be real. In front of me hung a Bavarian peasant, a Christus, staring across at the evening and the black hills. He had broad cheek-bones and sturdy limbs, and he hung doggedly on the cross, hating it. He reminded me of a peasant farmer, fighting slowly and meanly, but not giving in. His plain, rudimentary face stared stubbornly at the hills, and his neck was stiffened, as if even yet he were struggling away from the cross he resented. He would not yield to it. I stood in front of him, and realized him. He might have said, "Yes, here I am, and it's bad enough, and it's suffering, and it doesn't come to an end. *Perhaps* something will happen, will help. If it doesn't, I s'll have to go on with it." He seemed stubborn and struggling from the root of his soul, his human soul. No Godship had been thrust upon him. He was human clay, a peasant Prometheus-Christ, his poor soul bound in him, blind, but struggling stubbornly against the fact of the nails. And I looked across at the tiny square of orange light, the window of a farmhouse on the marsh. And, thinking of the other little farms, of how the man and his wife and his children worked on till dark, intent and silent, carrying the hay in their arms out of the streaming thunder-rain which soaked them through, I understood how the Christus was made.

And after him, when I saw the Christs posing on the Cross, à la Guido Reni, I recognized them as the mere conventional symbol, meaning no more Christ than St. George and the Dragon on a five-shilling-piece means England.

There are so many Christs carved by men who have carved to get at the meaning of their own soul's anguish. Often, I can distinguish one man's work in a district. In the Zemm valley, right in the middle of the Tirol, there are some half-dozen crucifixes by the same worker, who has whittled away in torment to see himself emerge out of the piece of timber, so that he can understand his own suffering, and see it take on itself the distinctness of an eternal thing, so that he can go on further, leaving it. The chief of these crucifixes is a very large one, deep in the Klamm, where it is always gloomy and damp. The river roars below, the rock wall opposite reaches high overhead, pushing back the sky. And by the track where the pack-horses go, in the cold gloom, hangs the large, pale Christ. He has fallen forward, just dead, and the weight of his full-grown, mature body is on the nails of the hands. So he drops, as if his hands would tear away, and he would fall to earth. The face is strangely brutal, and is set with an ache of weariness and pain and bitterness, and his rather ugly, passionate mouth is shut with bitter despair. After all, he had wanted to live and to enjoy his manhood. But fools had ruined his body, and thrown his life away, when he wanted it. No one had helped. His youth and health and vigour, all his life, and himself, were just thrown away as waste. He had died in bitterness. It is sombre and damp, silent save for the roar of water. There hangs the falling body of the man who had died in bitterness of spirit, and the driver of the pack-horses takes off his hat, cringing in his sturdy cheerfulness as he goes beneath.

He is afraid. I think of the carver of the crucifix. He also was more or less afraid. They all, when they carved or erected these crucifixes, had fear at the bottom of their hearts. And so the monuments to physical pain are found everywhere in the mountain gloom. By the same hand that carved the big, pale Christ I found another crucifix, a little one, at the end of a bridge. This Christ had a fair beard instead of a black one, and his body was hanging differently. But there was about him the same bitterness, the same despair, even a touch of cynicism. Evidently the artist could not get beyond the tragedy that tormented him. No wonder the peasants are afraid, as they take off their hats in passing up the valley.

They are afraid of physical pain. It terrifies them. Then they raise, in their startled helplessness of suffering, these Christs, these human attempts at deciphering the riddle of pain. In the same way they paint the humorous little pictures of some calamity—a man drowned in a stream or killed by a falling tree—and nail it up near the scene of the accident. *"Memento mori,"* they say everywhere. And so they try to get used to the idea of death and suffering, to rid themselves of some of the fear thereof. And all tragic art is part of the same attempt.

But some of the Christs are quaint. One I know is very elegant, brushed and combed. "I'm glad I am no lady," I say to him. For he is a pure lady-killer. But he ignores me utterly, the exquisite. The man who made him must have been dying to become a gentleman.

And a fair number are miserable fellows. They put up their eyebrows plaintively, and pull down the corners of their mouths. Sometimes they gaze heavenwards. They are quite sorry for themselves.

"Never mind," I say to them. "It'll be worse yet, before you've done."

Some of them look pale and done-for. They didn't make much fight; they hadn't much pluck in them. They make me sorry.

"It's a pity you hadn't got a bit more kick in you," I say to them. And I wonder why in England one sees always this pale, pitiful Christ with no "go" in him. Is it because our national brutality is so strong and deep that we must create for ourselves an anæmic Christus, for ever on the whine; either that, or one of those strange neutrals with long hair, that are supposed to represent to our children the Jesus of the New Testament.

In a tiny glass case beside the high-road where the Isar is a very small stream, sits another Christ that makes me want to laugh, and makes me want to weep also. His little head rests on his hand, his elbow on his knee, and he meditates, half-wearily. I am strongly reminded of Walther von der Vogelweide and the German medieval spirit. Detached, he sits, and dreams, and broods, in his little golden crown of thorns, and his little cloak of red flannel, that some peasant woman has stitched for him.

"Couvre-toi de gloire, Tartarin—couvre-toi de flanelle," I think to myself.

But he sits, a queer little man, fretted, plunged in anxiety of thought, and yet dreaming rather pleasantly at the same time. I think he is the forefather of the warm-hearted German philosopher and professor.

He is the last of the remarkable Christs of the peasants that I have seen. Beyond the Brenner an element of unreality seems to creep in. The Christs are given great gashes in the breast and knees, and from the brow and breast and hands and knees streams of blood trickle down, so that one sees a weird striped thing in red and white that is not at all a Christus. And the same red that is used for the blood serves also to mark the path, so that one comes to associate the *Martertafeln* and their mess of red stripes with the stones smeared with scarlet paint for guidance. The wayside chapels, going south, become fearfully florid and ornate, though still one finds in them the little wooden limbs, arms and legs and feet, and little wooden cows or horses, hung up by the altar, to signify a cure in these parts. But there is a tendency for the Christs themselves to become either neuter or else sensational. In a chapel near St. Jakob, a long way from the railway, sat the most ghastly Christus I can imagine. He is seated, after the crucifixion. His eyes, which are turned slightly to look at you, are bloodshot till they glisten scarlet, and even the iris seems purpled. And the misery, the almost criminal look of hate and misery on the bloody, disfigured face is shocking. I was amazed at the ghastly thing: moreover, it was fairly new.

South of the Brenner again, in the Austrian Tirol, I have not seen anyone salute the Christus: not even the guides. As one goes higher the crucifixes get smaller and smaller. The wind blows the snow under the tiny shed of a tiny Christ: the guides tramp stolidly by, ignoring the holy thing. That surprised me. But perhaps these were particularly unholy men. One does not expect a great deal of an Austrian, except real pleasantness.

So, in Austria, I have seen a fallen Christus. It was on the Jaufen, not very far from Meran. I was looking at all the snowpeaks all around, and hurrying downhill, trying to get out of a piercing wind, when I almost ran into a very old *Martertafel.* The wooden shed was silver-grey with age, and covered on the top with a thicket of lichen, weird, grey-green, sticking up its tufts. But on the rocks at the foot of the cross was the armless Christ, who had tumbled down and lay on his back in a weird attitude. It was one of the old, peasant Christs, carved out of wood, and having the long, wedge-shaped shins and thin legs that are almost characteristic. Considering the great sturdiness of a mountaineer's calves, these thin, flat legs are interesting. The arms of the fallen Christ had broken off at the shoulders, and they hung on their nails, as *ex voto* limbs hang in the shrines. But these arms dangled from their palms, one at each end of the cross, the muscles, carved in wood, looking startling, upside down. And the icy wind blew them backwards and forwards. There, in that bleak place among the stones, they looked horrible. Yet I dared not touch either them or the fallen image. I wish some priest would go along and take the broken thing away.

So many Christs there seem to be: one in rebellion against his cross, to which he was nailed; one bitter with the agony of knowing he must die, his heart-beatings all futile; one who felt sentimental; one who gave in to his misery; one who was a sensationalist; one who dreamed and fretted with thought. Perhaps the peasant carvers of crucifixes are right, and all these were found on the same cross. And perhaps there were others too: one who waited for the end, his soul still with a sense of right and hope; one ashamed to see the crowd make beasts of themselves, ashamed that he should provide for their sport; one who looked at them and thought: "And I am of you. I might be among you, yelling at myself in that way. But I am not, I am here. And so—"

All those Christs, like a populace, hang in the mountains under their little sheds. And perhaps they are falling, one by one. And I suppose we have carved no Christs, afraid lest they should be too like men, too like ourselves. What we worship must have exotic form.

AMERICA, LISTEN TO YOUR OWN

"America has no *tradition*. She has no culture-history."

Therefore, she is damned.

Europe invariably arrives at this self-congratulatory conclusion, usually from the same stock starting-point, the same phrase about tradition and culture. Moreover it usually gets Americans in the eye, for they really haven't anything more venerable than the White House, or more primitive than Whistler. Which they ought to be thankful for, boldly proclaiming this thankfulness.

Americans in Italy, however, are very humble and deprecating. They know their nakedness, and beg to be forgiven. They prostrate themselves with admiration, they knock their foreheads in front of our elegant fetishes. Poor, void America, crude, barbaric America, the Cinquescents knew her not. How thankful she ought to be! She doesn't know when she is well off.

Italy consists of just one big arrangement of things to be admired. Every step you take, you get a church or a coliseum between your eyes, and down you have to go, on your knees in admiration. Down go the Americans, till Italy fairly trembles with the shock of their dropping knees.

It is a pity. It is a pity that Americans are always so wonderstruck by our—note the possessive adjective—cultural monuments. Why they are any more mine than yours, I don't know—except that I have a British passport to validify my existence, and you have an American. However . . .

After all, a heap of stone is only a heap of stone—even if it is Milan Cathedral. And who knows that it isn't a horrid bristly burden on the face of the earth? So why should the *Corriere della Sera* remark with such sniffy amusement: "Of course they were duly impressed, and showed themselves overcome with admiration"—*they* being the Knights of Columbus, *i Cavaliere di Colombo*.

The Knights of Columbus were confessedly funny in Milan. But once more, why not? The dear, delicate-nosed, supercilious Anna Comnena found Bohemund and Tancred and Godfrey of Bouillon funny enough, in Constantinople long ago. And well-nurtured Romans never ceased to be amused by the gaping admiration of Goths and Scythians inside some forum or outside some temple, until the hairy barbarians stopped gaping and started to pull the wonder to pieces.

Of course, Goths and Scythians and Tancred and Bohemund had no tradition behind them. Luckily for them, for they would never have got so far with such impedimenta. As a matter of fact, once they *had* a tradition they were fairly harnessed. And if Rome could only have harnessed them in time, she might have made them pull her ponderous uncouth Empire across a few more centuries. However, men with such good names as Alaric and Attila were not going to open their mouths so easily to take the bit of Roman tradition.

You might as well sneer at a lad for not having a grey beard as jibe at a young people for not having a tradition. A tradition, like a bald head, comes with years, fast enough. And culture, more often than not, is a weary saddle for a jaded race.

A thing of beauty is a joy for ever. Let us live in hopes. But it isn't the end of all joys. There are as good fish in the sea as ever came out of it: quite as good as that prickly sea-urchin of Milan Cathedral, O Knights of Columbus! As for the sea–*la mer, c'est moi. La mer, c'est aussi vous, o Chevaliers de Colombe*. Which is to say, there are quite as many wonders enfathomed in the human spirit as ever have come out of it: be they Milan Cathedral or the Coliseum or the Bridge of Sighs. And in the strange and undrawn waters of the Knights of Columbus, what wonders of beauty, etc., do not swim unrevealed? A fig for the spiny cathedral of Milan. Whence all this prostration before it?

A thing of beauty is a joy for ever. But there's more than one old joy. It isn't the limit. Do you expect me to gasp in front of Ghirlandajo, that life has reached its limit, and there's no more to be done? You can't fix a high-water mark to human activity: not till you start to die. Here is Europe swimming in the stagnation of the ebb, and congratulating itself on the long line of Cathedrals, Coliseums, Ghirlandajos which mark the horizon of the old high water: people swarming like the little crabs in the lagoons of Venice, in seas gone dead, and scuttling and gaping and pluming themselves conceitedly on the vision of St. Mark's and San Giorgio, looming up magic on the sky-and-water line beyond.

Alas for a people when its tradition is established, and its limit of beauty defined. Alas for a race which has an exhibition of modern paintings such as the one in the Gardens at Venice, in this year of grace 1920. What else is left but to look back to Tintoret? Let it look back then.

Let the beauty of Venice be a sort of zenith to us, beyond which there is no seeing. Let Lincoln Cathedral fan her wings in our highest heaven, like an eagle at our pitch of flight. We can do no more. We have reached our limits of beauty. But these are not the limits of all beauty. They are not the limit of all things: only of *us*.

Therefore St. Mark's need be no reproach to an American. It isn't *his* St. Mark's. It is ours. And we like crabs ramble in the slack waters and gape at the excess of our own glory. Behold our golden Venice, our Lincoln Cathedral like a dark bird in the sky at twilight. And think of our yesterdays! What would you not give, O America, for our yesterdays? Far more than they are worth, I assure you. What would not *I* give for your tomorrows!

One begins to understand the barbarian rage against the great monuments of civilization. "Go beyond *that,* if you can." We say to the Americans, pointing to Venice among the waters. And the American humbly admits that it can't be done. Rome said the same thing to Attila, years gone by. "Get beyond Aquileia, get beyond Padua, you barbarian!" Attila promptly kicked Aquileia and Padua to smithereens, and walked past. Hence Venice. If Attila or some other barbaric villain hadn't squashed the cities of the Adriatic head, we should have had no Venice. Shall be bewail Aquileia or praise our Venice? Is Attila a reprehensible savage, or a creator in wrath?

Of course, it is simple for America. Venice isn't really in her way, as Aquileia was in the way of Attila, or Rome in the way of the Goths. Attila and the Goths *had* to do some kicking. The Americans can merely leave us to our monuments.

There are limits. But there are no limits to the human race. The human race has no limits. The Milanese fished that prickly sea-bear of a cathedral out of the deeps of their own soul, and have never been able to get away from it. But the Knights of Columbus depart by the next train.

Happy is the nation which hasn't got a tradition and which lacks cultural monuments. How gay Greece must have been, while Egypt was sneering at her for an uneducated young nobody, and what a good time Rome was having, whilst Hellas was looking down a cultured and supercilious nose at her. There's as fine fish in the sea as ever came out of it.

America, therefore, should leave off being *quite* so prostrate with admiration. Beauty is beauty, and must have its wistful time-hallowed dues. But the human soul is father and mother of all man-created beauty. An old race, like an old parent, sits watching the golden past. But the golden glories of the old are only fallen leaves about the feet of the young. It is an insult to life itself to be *too* abject, too prostrate before Milan Cathedral or a Ghirlandajo. What is Milan Cathedral but a prickly, empty burr dropped off the tree of life! The nut was eaten even in Sforza days.

What a young race wants is not a tradition nor a bunch of culture monuments. It wants an inspiration. And you can't acquire an inspiration as you can a culture or a tradition, by going to school and by growing old.

You must first have faith. Not rowdy and tub-thumping, but steady and deathless, faith in your own unrevealed, unknown destiny. The future is not a finished product, like the past. The future is a strange, urgent, poignant responsibility, something which urges inside a young race like sap, or like pregnancy, urging towards fulfilment. This urge you must never betray and never deny. It is more than all tradition, more than all law, more than all standards or monuments. Let the old world and the old way have been what they may, this is something other. Abide by that which is coming, not by that which has come.

And turn for the support and the confirmation not to the perfected past, that which is set in perfection as monuments of human passage. But turn to the unresolved, the rejected.

Let Americans turn to America, and to that very America which has been rejected and almost annihilated. Do they want to draw sustenance for the future? They will never draw it from the lovely monuments of our European past. These have an almost fatal narcotic, dream-luxurious effect upon the soul. America must turn again to catch the spirit of her own dark, aboriginal continent.

That which was abhorrent to the Pilgrim Fathers and to the Spaniards, that which was called the Devil, the black Demon of savage America, this great aboriginal spirit the Americans must recognize again, recognize and embrace. The devil and anathema of our forefathers hides the Godhead which we seek.

Americans must take up life where the Red Indian, the Aztec, the Maya, the Incas left it off. They must pick up the life-thread where the mysterious Red race let it fall. They must catch the pulse of the life which Cortés and Columbus murdered. There lies the real continuity: not between Europe and the new States, but between the murdered Red America and the seething White America. The President should not look back towards Gladstone or Cromwell or Hildebrand, but towards Montezuma. A great and lovely life-form, unperfected, fell with Montezuma. The responsibility for the producing and the perfecting of this life-form devolves upon the new American. It is time he accepted the full responsibility. It means a surpassing of the old European life-form. It means a departure from the old European morality, ethic. It means even a departure from the old range of emotions and sensibilities. The old emotions are crystallized for ever among the European monuments of beauty. There we can leave them, along with the old creeds and the old ethical laws outside of life. Montezuma had other emotions, such as we have not known or admitted. We must start from Montezuma, not from St. Francis or St. Bernard.

As Venice wedded the Adriatic, let America embrace the great dusky continent of the Red Man. It is a mysterious, delicate process, no theme for tub-thumping and shouts of Expositions. And yet it is a theme upon which American writers have touched and touched again, uncannily, unconsciously, blindfold as it were. Whitman was almost conscious; only the political democracy issue confused him. Now is the day when Americans must become fully self-reliantly conscious of their own inner responsibility. They must be ready for a new act, a new extension of life. They must pass the bounds.

To your tents, O America. Listen to your own, don't listen to Europe.

INDIANS AND AN ENGLISHMAN

Supposing one fell onto the moon, and found them talking English, it would be something the same as falling out of the open world plump down here in the middle of America. "Here" means New Mexico, the Southwest, wild and woolly and artistic and sage-brush desert.

It is all rather like comic opera played with solemn intensity. All the wildness and woolliness and westernity and motor-cars and art and sage and savage are so mixed up, so incongruous, that it is a farce, and everybody knows it. But they refuse to play it as farce. The wild and woolly section insists on being heavily dramatic, bold and bad on purpose; the art insists on being real American and artistic; motor-cars insist on being thrilled, moved to the marrow; highbrows insist on being ecstatic; Mexicans insist on being Mexicans, squeezing the last black drop of macabre joy out of life; and Indians wind themselves in white cotton sheets like Hamlet's father's ghost, with a lurking smile.

And here am I, a lone lorn Englishman, tumbled out of the known world of the British Empire onto this stage: for it persists in seeming like a stage to me, and not like the proper world.

Whatever makes a proper world, I don't know. But surely two elements are necessary: a common purpose and a common sympathy. I can't see any common purpose. The Indians and Mexicans don't even seem very keen on dollars. That full moon of a silver dollar doesn't strike me as overwhelmingly hypnotic out here. As for a common sympathy or understanding, that's beyond imagining. West is wild and woolly and bad-on-purpose; commerce is a little self-conscious about its own pioneering importance—Pioneers! O Pioneers!—highbrow is bent on getting to the bottom of everything and saving the lost soul down there in the depths; Mexican is bent on being Mexican and not gringo; and the Indian is all the things that all the others aren't. And so everybody smirks at everybody else, and says tacitly: "Go on; you do your little stunt, and I'll do mine," and they're like the various troupes in a circus, all performing at once, with nobody for Master of Ceremonies.

It seems to me, in this country, everything is taken so damn seriously that nothing remains serious. Nothing is so farcical as insistent drama. Everybody is lurkingly conscious of this. Each section or troupe is quite willing to admit that all the other sections are buffoon stunts. But it itself is the real thing, solemnly bad in its badness, good in its goodness, wild in its wildness, woolly in its woolliness, arty in its artiness, deep in its depths–in a word, earnest.

In such a masquerade of earnestness, a bewildered straggler out of the far-flung British Empire, myself! Don't let me for a moment pretend to *know* anything. I know less than nothing. I simply gasp like a bumpkin in a circus ring, with the horse-lady leaping over my head, the Apache war-whooping in my ear, the Mexican staggering under crosses and bumping me as he goes by, the artist whirling colours across my dazzled vision, the highbrows solemnly declaiming at me from all the cross-roads. If, dear reader, you, being the audience who has paid to come in, feel that you must take up an attitude to me, let it be one of amused pity.

One has to take sides. First, one must be either pro-Mexican or pro-Indian; then, either art or intellect; then, Republican or Democrat; and so on. But as for me, poor lamb, if I bleat at all in the circus ring, it will be my own shorn lonely bleat of a lamb who's lost his mother.

The first Indians I really saw were the Apaches in the Apache Reservation of this state. We drove in a motor-car, across desert and mesa, down cañons and up divides and along arroyos and so forth, two days, till at afternoon our two Indian men ran the car aside from the trail and sat under the pine tree to comb their long black hair and roll it into the two roll-plaits that hang in front of their shoulders, and put on all their silver-and-turquoise jewellery and their best blankets: because we were nearly there. On the trail were horsemen passing, and wagons with Ute Indians and Navajos.

"De donde viene Usted?" . . .

We came at dusk from the high shallows and saw on a low crest the points of Indian tents, the tepees, and smoke, and silhouettes of tethered horses and blanketed figures moving. In the shadow a rider was following a flock of white goats that flowed like water. The car ran to the top of the crest, and there was a hollow basin with a lake in the distance, pale in the dying light. And this shallow upland basin, dotted with Indian tents, and the fires flickering in front, and crouching blanketed figures, and horsemen crossing the dusk from tent to tent, horsemen in big steeple hats sitting glued on their ponies, and bells tinkling, and dogs yapping, and tilted wagons trailing in on the trail below, and a smell of wood-smoke and of cooking, and wagons coming in from far off, and tents pricking on the ridge of the round *vallum,* and horsemen dipping down and emerging again, and more red sparks of fires glittering, and crouching bundles of women's figures squatting at a fire before a little tent made of boughs, and little girls in full petticoats hovering, and wild barefoot boys throwing bones at thin-tailed dogs, and tents away in the distance, in the growing dark, on the slopes, and the trail crossing the floor of the hollows in the low dusk.

There you had it all, as in the hollow of your hand. And to my heart, born in England and kindled with Fenimore Cooper, it wasn't the wild and woolly West, it was the nomad nations gathering still in the continent of hemlock trees and prairies. The Apaches came and talked to us, in their steeple black hats and plaits wrapped with beaver fur, and their silver and beads and turquoise. Some talked strong American, and some talked only Spanish. And they had strange lines in their faces.

The two kivas, the rings of cut aspen trees stuck in the ground like the walls of a big hut of living trees, were on the plain, at either end of the race-track. And as the sun went down, the drums began to beat, the drums with their strong-weak, strong-weak pulse that beat on the plasm of one's tissue. The car slid down to the south kiva. Two elderly men held the drum, and danced the pàt-pat, pàt-pat quick beat on flat feet, like birds that move from the feet only, and sang with wide mouths: Hie! Hie! Hie! Hy-a! Hy-a! Hy-a! Hie! Hie! Hie! Ay-away-away-a! Strange dark faces with wide, shouting mouths and rows of small, close-set teeth, and strange lines on the faces, part ecstasy, part mockery, part humorous, part devilish, and the strange, calling, summoning sound in a wild song-shout, to the thud-thud of the drum. Answer of the same from the other kiva, as of a challenge accepted. And from the gathering darkness around, men drifting slowly in, each carrying an aspen twig, each joining to cluster close in two rows upon the drum, holding each his aspen twig inwards, their faces all together, mouths all open in the song-shout, and all of them all the time going on the two feet, pat-pat, pàt-pat, to the thud-thud of the drum and the strange, plangent yell of the chant, edging inch by inch, pàt-pat, pàt-pat, pàt-pat, sideways in a cluster along the track, towards the distant cluster of the challengers from the other kiva, who were sing-shouting and edging onwards, sideways, in the dusk, their faces all together, their leaves all inwards, towards the drum, and their feet going pàt-pat, pàt-pat on the dust, with their buttocks stuck out a little, faces all inwards, shouting open-mouthed to the drum, and half laughing, half mocking, half devilment, half fun. *Hie! Hie! Hie! Hie-away-awaya!* The strange yell, song, shout rising so lonely in the dusk, as if pine trees could suddenly, shaggily sing. Almost a pre-animal sound, full of triumph in life, and devilment against other life, and mockery, and humorousness, and the pàt-pat, pàt-pat of the rhythm. Sometimes more youths coming up, and as they draw near laughing, they give the war-whoop, like a turkey giving a startled shriek and then gobble-gobbling with laughter—Ugh!—the shriek half laughter, then the gobble-gobble-gobble like a great demoniac chuckle. The chuckle in the war-whoop.—They produce the gobble from the deeps of the stomach, and say it makes them feel good.

Listening, an acute sadness, and a nostalgia, unbearably yearning for something, and a sickness of the soul came over me. The gobble-gobble chuckle in the whoop surprised me in my very tissues. Then I got used to it, and could hear in it the humanness, the playfulness, and then, beyond that, the mockery and the diabolical, pre-human, pine-tree fun of cutting dusky throats and letting the blood spurt out unconfined. Gobble-agobble-agobble, the unconfined loose blood, gobble-agobble, the dead, mutilated lump, gobble-agobble-agobble, the fun, the greatest man-fun. The war-whoop!

So I felt. I may have been all wrong, and other folk may feel much more natural and reasonable things. But so I felt. And the sadness and the nostalgia of the song-calling, and the resinous continent of pine trees and turkeys, the feet of birds treading a dance, far off, when man was dusky and not individualized.

I am no ethnologist. The point is, what is the feeling that passes from an Indian to me, when we meet? We are both men, but how do we feel together? I shall never forget that first evening when I first came into contact with Red Men, away in the Apache country. It was not what I had thought it would be. It was something of a shock. Again something in my soul broke down, letting in a bitterer dark, a pungent awakening to the lost past, old darkness, new terror, new root-griefs, old root-richnesses.

The Apaches have a cult of water-hatred; they never wash flesh or rag. So never in my life have I smelt such an unbearable sulphur-human smell as comes from them when they cluster: a smell that takes the breath from the nostrils.

We drove the car away half a mile or more, back from the Apache hollow, to a lonely ridge, where we pitched camp under pine trees.

Our two Indians made the fire, dragged in wood, then wrapped themselves in their best blankets and went off to the tepees of their friends. The night was cold and starry.

After supper I wrapped myself in a red serape up to the nose, and went down alone to the Apache encampment. It is good, on a chilly night in a strange country, to be wrapped almost to the eyes in a good Navajo blanket. Then you feel warm inside yourself, and as good as invisible, and the dark air thick with enemies. So I stumbled on, startling the hobbled horses that jerked aside from me. Reaching the rim-crest one saw many fires burning in red spots round the slopes of the hollow, and against the fires many crouching figures. Dogs barked, a baby cried from a bough shelter, there was a queer low crackle of voices. So I stumbled alone over the ditches and past the tents, down to the kiva. Just near was a shelter with a big fire in front, and a man, an Indian, selling drinks, no doubt Budweiser beer and grape-juice, non-intoxicants. Cowboys in chaps and big hats were drinking too, and one screechy, ungentle cowgirl in khaki. So I went on in the dark up the opposite slope. The dark Indians passing in the night peered at me. The air was full of a sort of sportiveness, playfulness, that had a jeering, malevolent vibration in it, to my fancy. As if this play were another kind of harmless-harmful warfare, overbearing. Just the antithesis of what I understand by jolliness: ridicule. Comic sort of bullying. No jolly, free laughter. Yet a great deal of laughter. But with a sort of gibe in it.

This, of course, may just be the limitation of my European fancy. But that was my feeling. One felt a stress of will, of human wills, in the dark air, gibing even in the comic laughter. And a sort of unconscious animosity.

Again a sound of a drum down below, so again I stumbled down to the kiva. A bunch of young men were clustered–seven or eight round a drum, and standing with their faces together, loudly and mockingly singing the song-yells, some of them treading the pàt-pat, some not bothering. Just behind was the blazing fire and the open shelter of the drink-tent, with Indians in tall black hats and long plaits in front of their shoulders, and bead-braided waistcoats, and hands in their pockets; some swathed in sheets, some in brilliant blankets, and all grinning, laughing. The cowboys with big spurs still there, horses' bridles trailing, and cowgirl screeching her laugh. One felt an inevitable silent gibing, animosity in each group, one for the other. At the same time, an absolute avoidance of any evidence of this.

The young men round the drum died out and started again. As they died out, the strange uplifted voice in the kiva was heard. It seemed to me the outside drumming and singing served to cover the voice within the kiva.

The kiva of young green trees was just near, two paces only. On the ground outside, boughs and twigs were strewn round to prevent anyone's coming close to the enclosure. Within was the firelight. And one could see through the green of the leaf-screen, men round a fire inside there, and one old man, the same old man always facing the open entrance, the fire between him and it. Other Indians sat in a circle, of which he was the key. The old man had his dark face lifted, his head bare, his two plaits falling on his shoulders. His close-shutting Indian lips were drawn open, his eyes were as if half-veiled, as he went on and on, on and on, in a distinct, plangent, recitative voice, male and yet strangely far-off and plaintive, reciting, reciting, reciting like a somnambulist, telling, no doubt, the history of the tribe interwoven with the gods. Other Apaches sat round the fire. Those nearest the old teller were stationary, though one chewed gum all the time and one ate bread-cake and others lit cigarettes. Those nearer the entrance rose after a time, restless. At first some strolled in, stood a minute, then strolled out, desultory. But as the night went on, the ring round the fire inside the wall of green young trees was complete, all squatting on the ground, the old man with the lifted face and parted lips and half-unseeing eyes going on and on, across the fire. Some men stood lounging with the half self-conscious ease of the Indian behind the seated men. They lit cigarettes. Some drifted out. Another filtered in. I stood wrapped in my blanket in the cold night, at some little distance from the entrance, looking on.

A big young Indian came and pushed his face under my hat to see who or what I was.

"Buenos!"

"Buenos!"

"Qué quiere?"

"No hablo español."

"Oh, only English, eh? You can't come in here."

"I don't want to."

"This Indian church."

"Is it?"

"I don't let people come, only Apache, only Indian."

"You keep watch?"

"I keep watch, yes; Indian church, eh?"

"And the old man preaches?"

"Yes, he preaches."

After which I stood quite still and uncommunicative. He waited for a further development. There was none. So, after giving me another look, he went to talk to other Indians, *sotto voce,* by the door. The circle was complete; groups stood behind the squatting ring, some men were huddled in blankets, some sitting just in trousers and shirt, in the warmth near the fire, some wrapped close in white cotton sheets. The firelight shone on the dark, unconcerned faces of the listeners, as they chewed gum, or ate bread, or smoked a cigarette. Some had big silver ear-rings swinging, and necklaces of turquoise. Some had waistcoats all bead braids. Some wore store shirts and store trousers, like Americans. From time to time one man pushed another piece of wood on the fire.

They seemed to be paying no attention; it all had a very perfunctory appearance. But they kept silent, and the voice of the old reciter went on blindly, from his lifted, bronze mask of a face with its wide-opened lips. They furl back their teeth as they speak, and they use a sort of resonant tenor voice that has a plangent, half-sad, twanging sound, vibrating deep from the chest. The old man went on and on, for hours, in that urgent, far-off voice. His hair was grey, and parted, and his two round plaits hung in front of his shoulders on his shirt. From his ears dangled pieces of blue turquoise, tied with string. An old green blanket was wrapped round above his waist, and his feet in old moccasins were crossed before the fire. There was a deep pathos, for me, in the old, mask-like, virile figure, with its metallic courage of persistence, old memory, and its twanging male voice. So far, so great a memory. So dauntless a persistence in the piece of living red earth seated on the naked earth, before the fire; this old, bronze-resonant man with his eyes as if glazed in old memory, and his voice issuing in endless plangent monotony from the wide, unfurled mouth.

And the young men, who chewed chewing-gum and listened without listening. The voice no doubt registered on their underconsciousness, as they looked around, and lit a cigarette, and spat sometimes aside. With their day-consciousness they hardly attended.

As for me, standing outside, beyond the open entrance, I was no enemy of theirs; far from it. The voice out of the far-off time was not for my ears. Its language was unknown to me. And I did not wish to know. It was enough to hear the sound issuing plangent from the bristling darkness of the far past, to see the bronze mask of the face lifted, the white, small, close-packed teeth showing all the time. It was not for me, and I knew it. Nor had I any curiosity to understand. The soul is as old as the oldest day, and has its own hushed echoes, its own far-off tribal understandings sunk and incorporated. We do not need to live the past over again. Our darkest tissues are twisted in this old tribal experience, our warmest blood came out of the old tribal fire. And they vibrate still in answer, our blood, our tissue. But me, the conscious me, I have gone a long road since then. And as I look back, like memory terrible as bloodshed, the dark faces round the fire in the night, and one blood beating in me and them. But I don't want to go back to them, ah, never. I never want to deny them or break with them. But there is no going back. Always onward, still further. The great devious onward-flowing stream of conscious human blood. From them to me, and from me on.

I don't want to live again the tribal mysteries my blood has lived long since. I don't want to know as I have known, in the tribal exclusiveness. But every drop of me trembles still alive to the old sound, every thread in my body quivers to the frenzy of the old mystery. I know my derivation. I was born of no virgin, of no Holy Ghost. Ah, no, these old men telling the tribal tale were my fathers. I have a dark-faced, bronze-voiced father far back in the resinous ages. My mother was no virgin. She lay in her hour with this dusky-lipped tribe-father. And I have not forgotten him. But he, like many an old father with a changeling son, he would like to deny me. But I stand on the far edge of their firelight, and am neither denied nor accepted. My way is my own, old red father; I can't cluster at the drum any more.

TAOS

The Indians say Taos is the heart of the world. Their world, maybe. Some places seem temporary on the face of the earth: San Francisco, for example. Some places seem final. They have a true nodality. I never felt that so powerfully as, years ago, in London. The intense powerful nodality of that great heart of the world. And during the war that heart, for me, broke. So it is. Places can lose their living nodality. Rome, to me, has lost hers. In Venice one feels the magic of the glamorous old node that once united East and West, but it is the beauty of an after-life.

Taos pueblo still retains its old nodality. Not like a great city. But, in its way, like one of the monasteries of Europe. You cannot come upon the ruins of the old great monasteries of England, beside their waters, in some lovely valley, now remote, without feeling that here is one of the choice spots of the earth, where the spirit dwelt. To me it is so important to remember that when Rome collapsed, when the great Roman Empire fell into smoking ruins, and bears roamed in the streets of Lyon and wolves howled in the deserted streets of Rome, and Europe really was a dark ruin, then, it was not in castles or manors or cottages that life remained vivid. Then those whose souls were still alive withdrew together and gradually built monasteries, and these monasteries and convents, little communities of quiet labour and courage, isolated, helpless, and yet never overcome in a world flooded with devastation, these alone kept the human spirit from disintegration, from going quite dark, in the Dark Ages. These men made the Church, which again made Europe, inspiring the martial faith of the Middle Ages.

Taos pueblo affects me rather like one of the old monasteries. When you get there you feel something final. There is an arrival. The nodality still holds good.

But this is the pueblo. And from the north side to the south side, from the south side to the north side, the perpetual silent wandering intentness of a full-skirted, black-shawled, long-fringed woman in her wide white deerskin boots, the running of children, the silent sauntering of dark-faced men, bare-headed, the two plaits in front of their thin shoulders, and a white sheet like a sash swathed round their loins. They must have something to swathe themselves in.

And if it were sunset, the men swathing themselves in their sheets like shrouds, leaving only the black place of the eyes visible. And women, darker than ever, with shawls over their heads, busy at the ovens. And cattle being driven to sheds. And men and boys trotting in from the fields, on ponies. And as the night is dark, on one of the roofs, or more often on the bridge, the inevitable drum-drum-drum of the tomtom, and young men in the dark lifting their voices to the song, like wolves or coyotes crying in music.

There it is, then, the pueblo, as it has been since heaven knows when. And the slow dark weaving of the Indian life going on still, though perhaps more waveringly. And oneself, sitting there on a pony, a far-off stranger with gulfs of time between me and this. And yet, the old nodality of the pueblo still holding, like a dark ganglion spinning invisible threads of consciousness. A sense of dryness, almost of weariness, about the pueblo. And a sense of the inalterable. It brings a sick sort of feeling over me, always, to get into the Indian vibration. Like breathing chlorine.

The next day, in the morning, we went to help erect the great stripped maypole. It was the straight, smoothed yellow trunk of a big tree. Of course one of the white boys took the bossing of the show. But the Indians were none too ready to obey, and their own fat dark-faced boss gave counter-orders. It was the old, amusing contradiction between the white and the dark races. As for me, I just gave a hand steadying the pole as it went up, outsider at both ends of the game.

An American girl came with a camera, and got a snap of us all struggling in the morning light with the great yellow trunk. One of the Indians went to her abruptly, in his quiet, insidious way.

"You give me that Kodak. You ain't allowed take no snaps here. You pay fine—one dollar."

She was frightened, but she clung to her camera.

"You're not going to take my Kodak from me," she said.

"I'm going to take that film out. And you pay one dollar fine, see?"

The girl relinquished the camera; the Indian took out the film.

"Now you pay me one dollar, or I don't give you back the Kodak."

Rather sullenly, she took out her purse and gave the two silver half-dollars. The Indian returned the camera, pocketed the money, and turned aside with a sort of triumph. Done it over one specimen of the white race.

There were not very many Indians helping to put up the pole.

"I never see so few boys helping put up the pole," said Tony Romero to me.

"Where are they all?" I asked. He shrugged his shoulders.

Dr. West, a woman doctor from New York who has settled in one of the villages, was with us. Mass was being said inside the church, and she would have liked to go in. She is well enough known, too. But two Indians were at the church door, and one put his elbow in front of her.

"You Catholic?"

"No, I'm not."

"Then you can't come in."

The same almost jeering triumph in giving the white man—or the white woman—a kick. It is the same the whole world over, between dark-skin and white. Dr. West, of course, thinks everything Indian wonderful. But she wasn't used to being rebuffed, and she didn't like it. But she found excuses.

"Of course," she said, "they're quite right to exclude the white people, if the white people can't behave themselves. It seems there were some Americans, boys and girls, in the church yesterday, insulting the images of the saints, shrieking, laughing, and saying they looked like monkeys. So now *no* white people are allowed inside the church."

I listened, and said nothing. I had heard the same story at Buddhist temples in Ceylon. For my own part, I have long since passed the stage when I want to crowd up and stare at anybody's spectacle, white man's or dark man's.

I stood on one of the first roofs of the north pueblo. The iron bell of the church began to bang-bang-bang. The sun was down beyond the far-off, thin clear line of the western mesa, the light had ceased glowing on the piñon-dotted foot-hills beyond the south pueblo. The square beneath was thick with people. And the Indians began to come out of church.

Two Indian women brought a little dressed-up Madonna to her platform in the green starting-bower. Then the men slowly gathered round the drum. The bell clanged. The tomtom beat. The men slowly uplifted their voices. The wild music resounded strangely against the banging of that iron bell, the silence of the many faces, as the group of Indians in their sheets and their best blankets, and in their ear-rings and brilliant scarlet trousers, or emerald trousers, or purple trousers, trimmed with beads, trod the slow bird-dance sideways, in feet of beaded moccasins, or yellow doeskin moccasins, singing all the time like drumming coyotes, slowly down and across the bridge to the south side, and up the incline to the south kiva. One or two Apaches in their beaded waistcoats and big black hats were among the singers, distinguishable by their thick build also. An old Navajo chief was among the encouragers.

As dusk fell, the singers came back under a certain house by the south kiva, and as they passed under the platform they broke and dispersed; it was over. They seemed as if they were grinning subtly as they went: grinning at being there in all that white crowd of inquisitives. It must have been a sort of ordeal to sing and tread the slow dance between that solid wall of silent, impassive white faces. But the Indians seemed to take no notice. And the crowd only silently, impassively watched. Watched with that strange, static American quality of *laissez-faire* and of indomitable curiosity.

AU REVOIR, U. S. A.

Say au revoir
But not good-bye
This parting brings
A bitter sigh. . . .

It really does, when you find yourself in an unkempt Pullman trailing through endless deserts, south of El Paso, fed on doubtful scraps at enormous charge and at the will of a rather shoddy smallpox-marked Mexican Pullman-boy who knows there's been a revolution and that his end is up. Then you remember the neat and nice nigger who looked after you as far as El Paso, before you crossed the Rio Grande into desert and chaos, and you sigh, if you have time before a curse chokes you.

Yet, U. S. A., you do put a strain on the nerves. Mexico puts a strain on the temper. Choose which you prefer. Mine's the latter. I'd rather be in a temper than be pulled taut. Which is what the U. S. A. did to me. Tight as a fiddle string, tense over the bridge of the solar plexus. Anyhow the solar plexus goes a bit loose and has a bit of play down here.

I still don't know why the U. S. A. pulls one so tight and makes one feel like a chicken that is being drawn. The people on the whole are quite as amenable as people anywhere else. They don't pick your pocket, or even your personality. They're not unfriendly. It's not the people. Something in the air tightens one's nerves like fiddle strings, screws them up, squeak-squeak! . . . till one's nerves will give out nothing but a shrill fine shriek of overwroughtness. Why, in the name of heaven? Nobody knows. It's just the spirit of place.

You cross the Rio Grande and change from tension into exasperation. You feel like hitting the impudent Pullman waiter with a beer-bottle. In the U. S. A. you don't even think of such a thing.

Of course, one might get used to a state of tension. And then one would pine for the United States. Meanwhile one merely snarls back at the dragons of San Juan Teotihuacan.

It's a queer continent—as much as I've seen of it. It's a fanged continent. It's got a rattlesnake coiled in its heart, has this democracy of the New World. It's a dangerous animal, once it lifts its head again. Meanwhile, the dove still nests in the coils of the rattlesnake, the stone coiled rattlesnake of Aztec eternity. The dove lays her eggs on his flat head.

The old people had a marvellous feeling for snakes and fangs, down here in Mexico. And after all, Mexico is only the sort of solar plexus of North America. The great paleface overlay hasn't gone into the soil half an inch. The Spanish churches and palaces stagger, the most rickety things imaginable, always just on the point of falling down. And the peon still grins his Indian grin behind the Cross. And there's quite a lively light in his eyes, much more so than in the eyes of the northern Indian. He knows his gods.

These old civilizations down here, they never got any higher than Quetzalcoatl. And he's just a sort of feathered snake. Who needed the smoke of a little heart's-blood now and then, even he.

"Only the ugly is æsthetic now," said the young Mexican artist. Personally, he seems as gentle and self-effacing as the nicest of lambs. Yet his caricatures are hideous, hideous without mirth or whimsicality. Blood-hideous. Grim, earnest hideousness.

Like the Aztec things, the Aztec carvings. They all twist and bite. That's all they do. Twist and writhe and bite, or crouch in lumps. And coiled rattlesnakes, many, like dark heaps of excrement. And out at San Juan Teotihuacan where are the great pyramids of a vanished, pre-Aztec people, as we are told—and the so-called Temple of Quetzalcoatl—there, behold you, huge gnashing heads jut out jagged from the wall-face of the low pyramid, and a huge snake stretches along the base, and one grasps at a carved fish, that swims in old stone and for once seems harmless. Actually a harmless fish!

But look out! The great stone heads snarl at you from the wall, trying to bite you: and one great dark, green blob of an obsidian eye, you never saw anything so blindly malevolent: and then white fangs. Great white fangs, smooth today, the white fangs, with tiny cracks in them. Enamelled. These bygone pyramid-building Americans, who were a dead-and-gone mystery even to the Aztecs, when the Spaniards arrived, they applied their highest art to the enamelling of the great fangs of these venomous stone heads, and there is the enamel today, white and smooth. You can stroke the great fang with your finger and see. And the blob of an obsidian eye looks down at you.

It's a queer continent. The anthropologists may make what prettiness they like out of myths. But come here, and you'll see that the gods bit. There is none of the phallic preoccupation of the old Mediterranean. Here they hadn't got even as far as hot-blooded sex.

Fangs, and cold serpent folds, and bird-snakes with fierce cold blood and claws.

I admit that I feel bewildered. There is always something a bit amiably comic about Chinese dragons and contortions. There's nothing amiably comic in these ancient monsters. They're dead in earnest about biting and writhing, snake-blooded birds.

And the Spanish white superimposition, with rococo church-towers among pepper-trees and column cactuses, seems so rickety and temporary, the pyramids seem so indigenous, rising like hills out of the earth itself. The one goes down with a clatter, the other remains.

And this is what seems to me the difference between Mexico and the United States. And this is why, it seems to me, Mexico exasperates, whereas the U. S. A. puts an unbearable tension on one. Because here in Mexico the fangs are still obvious. Everybody knows the gods are going to bite within the next five minutes. While in the United States, the gods have had their teeth pulled, and their claws cut, and their tails docked, till they seem real mild lambs. Yet all the time, inside, it's the same old dragon's blood. The same old American dragon's blood.

And that discrepancy of course is a strain on the human psyche.

A LETTER FROM GERMANY

We are going back to Paris tomorrow, so this is the last moment to write a letter from Germany. Only from the fringe of Germany, too.

It is a miserable journey from Paris to Nancy, through that Marne country, where the country still seems to have had the soul blasted out of it, though the dreary fields are ploughed and level, and the pale wire trees stand up. But it is all void and null. And in the villages, the smashed houses in the street rows, like rotten teeth between good teeth.

You come to Strasburg, and the people still talk Alsatian German, as ever, in spite of French shop-signs. The place feels dead. And full of cotton goods, white goods, from Mülhausen, from the factories that once were German. Such cheap white cotton goods, in a glut.

The cathedral front rearing up high and flat and fanciful, a sort of darkness in the dark, with round rose windows and long, long prisons of stone. Queer, that men should have ever wanted to put stone upon fanciful stone to such a height, without having it fall down. The Gothic! I was always glad when my card-castle fell. But these Goths and Alemans seemed to have a craze for peaky heights.

The Rhine is still the Rhine, the great divider. You feel it as you cross. The flat, frozen, watery places. Then the cold and curving river. Then the other side, seeming so cold, so empty, so frozen, so forsaken. The train stands and steams fiercely. Then it draws through the flat Rhine plain, past frozen pools of flood-water, and frozen fields, in the emptiness of this bit of occupied territory.

Immediately you are over the Rhine, the spirit of place has changed. There is no more attempt at the bluff of geniality. The marshy places are frozen. The fields are vacant. There seems nobody in the world.

It is as if the life had retreated eastwards. As if the Germanic life were slowly ebbing away from contact with western Europe, ebbing to the deserts of the east. And there stand the heavy, ponderous, round hills of the Black Forest, black with an inky blackness of Germanic trees, and patched with a whiteness of snow. They are like a series of huge, involved black mounds, obstructing the vision eastwards. You look at them from the Rhine plain, and know that you stand on an actual border, up against something.

The moment you are in Germany, you know. It feels empty, and, somehow, menacing. So must the Roman soldiers have watched those black, massive round hills: with a certain fear, and with the knowledge that they were at their own limit. A fear of the invisible natives. A fear of the invisible life lurking among the woods. A fear of their own opposite.

So it is with the French: this almost mystic fear. But one should not insult even one's fears.

Germany, this bit of Germany, is very different from what it was two-and-a-half years ago, when I was here. Then it was still open to Europe. Then it still looked to western Europe for a reunion, for a sort of reconciliation. Now that is over. The inevitable, mysterious barrier has fallen again, and the great leaning of the Germanic spirit is once more eastwards, towards Russia, towards Tartary. The strange vortex of Tartary has become the positive centre again, the positivity of western Europe is broken. The positivity of our civilization has broken. The influences that come, come invisibly out of Tartary. So that all Germany reads *Beasts, Men and Gods* with a kind of fascination. Returning again to the fascination of the destructive East, that produced Attila.

So it is at night. Baden-Baden is a little quiet place, all its guests gone. No more Turgenievs or Dostoievskys or Grand Dukes or King Edwards coming to drink the waters. All the outward effect of a world-famous watering-place. But empty now, a mere Black Forest village with the wagon-loads of timber going through, to the French.

The Rentenmark, the new gold mark of Germany, is abominably dear. Prices are high in England, but English money buys less in Baden than it buys in London, by a long chalk. And there is no work–consequently no money. Nobody buys anything, except absolute necessities. The shop-keepers are in despair. And there is less and less work.

Everybody gives up the telephone–can't afford it. The tram-cars don't run, except about three times a day to the station. Up to the Annaberg, the suburb, the lines are rusty, no trams ever go. The people can't afford the ten pfennigs for the fare. Ten pfennigs is an important sum now: one penny. It is really a hundred milliards of marks.

Money becomes insane, and people with it.

At night the place is almost dark, economizing light. Economy,

economy, economy—that too becomes an insanity. Luckily the government keeps bread fairly cheap.

But at night you feel strange things stirring in the darkness, strange feelings stirring out of this still-unconquered Black Forest. You stiffen your backbone and you listen to the night. There is a sense of danger. It is not the people. They don't seem dangerous. Out of the very air comes a sense of danger, a queer, *bristling* feeling of uncanny danger.

Something has happened. Something has happened which has not yet eventuated. The old spell of the old world has broken, and the old, bristling, savage spirit has set in. The war did not break the old peace-and-production hope of the world, though it gave it a severe wrench. Yet the old peace-and-production hope still governs, at least the consciousness. Even in Germany it has not quite gone.

But it feels as if, virtually, it were gone. The last two years have done it. The hope in peace-and-production is broken. The old flow, the old adherence is ruptured. And a still older flow has set in. Back, back to the savage polarity of Tartary, and away from the polarity of civilized Christian Europe. This, it seems to me, has already happened. And it is a happening of far more profound import than any actual *event*. It is the father of the next phase of events.

And the feeling never relaxes. As you travel up the Rhine valley, still the same latent sense of danger, of silence, of suspension. Not that the people are actually planning or plotting or preparing. I don't believe it for a minute. But something has happened to the human soul, beyond all help. The human soul recoiling now from unison, and making itself strong elsewhere. The ancient spirit of pre-historic Germany coming back, at the end of history.

The same in Heidelberg. Heidelberg full, full, full of people. Students the same, youths with rucksacks the same, boys and maidens in gangs come down from the hills. The same, and not the same. These queer gangs of *Young Socialists,* youths and girls, with their non-materialistic professions, their half-mystic assertions, they strike one as strange. Something primitive, like loose, roving gangs of broken, scattered tribes, so they affect one. And the swarms of people somehow produce an impression of silence, of secrecy, of stealth. It is as if everything and everybody recoiled away from the old unison, as barbarians lurking in a wood recoil out of sight. The old habits remain. But the bulk of the people have no money. And the whole stream of feeling is reversed.

So you stand in the woods above the town and see the Neckar flowing green and swift and slippery out of the gulf of Germany, to the Rhine. And the sun sets slow and scarlet into the haze of the Rhine valley. And the old, pinkish stone of the ruined castle across looks sultry, the marshalry is in shadow below, the peaked roofs of old, tight Heidelberg compressed in its river gateway glimmer and glimmer out. There is a blue haze.

And it all looks as if the years were wheeling swiftly backwards, no more onwards. Like a spring that is broken, and whirls swiftly back, so time seems to be whirling with mysterious swiftness to a sort of death. Whirling to the ghost of the old Middle Ages of Germany, then to the Roman days, then to the days of the silent forest and the dangerous, lurking barbarians.

Something about the Germanic races is unalterable. White-skinned, elemental, and dangerous. Our civilization has come from the fusion of the dark-eyes with the blue. The meeting and mixing and mingling of the two races has been the joy of our ages. And the Celt has been there, alien, but necessary as some chemical re-agent to the fusion. So the civilization of Europe rose up. So these cathedrals and these thoughts.

But now the Celt is the disintegrating agent. And the Latin and southern races are falling out of association with the northern races, the northern Germanic impulse is recoiling towards Tartary, the destructive vortex of Tartary.

It is a fate; nobody now can alter it. It is a fate. The very blood changes. Within the last three years, the very constituency of the blood has changed, in European veins. But particularly in Germanic veins.

At the same time, we have brought it about ourselves–by a Ruhr occupation, by an English nullity, and by a German false will. We have done it ourselves. But apparently it was not to be helped.

Quos vult perdere Deus, dementat prius.

SEE MEXICO AFTER, BY LUIS Q.

My home's in Mexico,
That's where you want to go.
Life's one long cine *show. . . .*

As a matter of fact, I am a hard-worked, lean individual poked in the corner of a would-be important building in Mexico D. F.

That's that.

I am–married, so this is not a matrimonial ad. But I am, as I said, lean, pale, hard-worked, with indiscriminate fair hair and, I hope, nice blue eyes. Anyhow they aren't black. And I am young. And I am Mexican: oh, don't doubt it for a second. *Mejicano soy.* La-la-la-la! I'll jabber your head off in Spanish. But where is my gun and red sash?

Ay de mi! That's how one sighs in Spanish. I am sighing because I am Mexican, for who would be a Mexican? Where would he be if he was one? I am an official–without doubt important, since every four-farthing sparrow, etc. And being an important official, I am always having to receive people. Receive. Deceive. Believe. Rather, they're not usually people. They're almost always commissions.

"Please to meet you, Mister," they say. "Not American, are you?"

I seize my chin in trepidation. "Good God! Am I?" There is a Monroe doctrine, and there is a continent, or two continents. Am I American? by any chance?

"Pardon me one moment!" I say, with true Mexican courtesy.

And I dash upstairs to the top floor–the fourth–no elevators–to my little corner office that looks out over the flat roofs and bubbly church-domes and streaks of wire of Mexico D. F. I rush to the window, I look out, and ah!–Yes! *Qué tal? Amigo!* How lucky you're there! Say, boy, will you tell me whether you're American or not? Because if you are, I am.

This interesting announcement is addressed to my old friend Popo, who is lounging his heavy shoulders under the sky, smoking a cigarette end, *à la Mexicaine.* Further, since I'm paid to give information, Popo is the imperturbable volcano, known at length as Popocatepetl, with the accent on the tay, so I beg you not to put it on the cat, who is usually loitering in the vicinity of Mexico D. F.

No, I shan't tell you what the D. F. is: or *who* it is. Take it for yourself if you like. I never come pulling the tail of your D. C.–Washington.

Popo gives another puff to his eternal cigarette, and replies, as every Mexican should:

"Quien sabe?"

"Who knows?–Ask me another, boy!"

Ca!–as a matter of fact, we don't say *Caramba!* very much. But I'll say it to please. I say it. I tear my hair. I dash downstairs to the Committee, or rather Commission, which is waiting with bated breath (mint) to know whether I'm American or not. I smile ingratiatingly.

"Do pardon me for the interruption, gentlemen. (One of them is usually a lady, but she's best interpreted by *gentlemen*.) You ask me, am I American?–*Quien sabe?"*

"Then you're *not*."

"Am I not, gentlemen? *Ay de mi!"*

"Ever been in America?"

Good God! Again? Ah, my chin, let me seize thee!

Once more I flee upstairs and poke myself out of that window and say *Oiga! Viejo! Oiga* is a very important word. And I am in the Bureau of Information.

"Oiga! Viejo! Are you in America?"

"Quien sabe?" He bumps the other white shoulder at me. Snow!

"Oh, gentlemen!" I pant. *"Quien sabe?"*

"Then you haven't."

"But I've been to New York."

"Why didn't you say so?"

"Have I been to America?"

"Hey! Who's running this Information Bureau?"

"I am. Let me run it."

So I dart upstairs again, and address myself to Popo.

"Popo! I have been to America, *via* New York, and you haven't."

Down I dart, to my Commission. On the way I remember how everything–I mean the loud walls–in New York, said SEE AMERICA FIRST. Thank God! I say to myself, wiping my wet face before entering to the Commission: On American evidence, I've seen him, her, or it. But whether *en todo* or *en parte, quien sabe?*

I open the door, and I give a supercilious sniff. Such are my American manners.

I am just smelling my Commission.–As usual! I say to myself, snobbishly: *Oil!*

There are all sorts and sizes of commissions, every sort and size and condition of commission. But oil predominates. Usually, I can smell oil down the telephone.

There are others—Railway Commissions, Mines Commissions, American Women's Christian Missions, American Bankers' Missions, American Bootleggers' Missions, American Episcopalian, Presbyterian, Mormon, and Jewish Missions, American Tramps' Missions . . .

I, however, in my little office, am Mohammed. If you would like to see Mexico summed up into one unique figure, see me, *à la* Mohammed, in my little office, saying: Let these mountains come to *me*.

And they come. They come in whole ranges, in sierras, in cordilleras. I smell oil, and I see the backbone of America walking up the stair-case (no elevator). I hear the chink of silver, and behold the entire Sierra Madre marching me-wards. Ask me if [*sic*] leave Mohammed with cold feet! Oh, I am *muy Mejicano,* I am!

I feel I am SEEING AMERICA FIRST, and they are seeing Mexico after. I feel myself getting starrier and stripyer every day, I see such a lot of America first.

But what happens to them, when they see Mexico after?

Quien sabe!

I am always murmuring: You see, Mexico and America are not in the same boat.

I want to add: They're not even floating on the same ocean. I doubt if they're gyrating in the same cosmos.

But superlatives are not well-mannered.

Still, it is hard on a young man like me to be merely Mexican, when my father, merely by moving up the map a little while he was still strong and lusty, might have left me hundred-per-cent American. I'm sure I should have been plus.

It is hard on me, I say. As it is hard on Popo. He might have been Mount Brown or Mount Abraham. How can any mountain, when you come to think of it, be Popocatepetl?—and *tay*-petl at that!

There, there! let me soothe myself.

In fact, I am always a little sorry for the Americans who come seeing Mexico after. "I am left such a long way behind!" as the burro said when he fell down an abandoned mine.

Still, the commissioners and missioners often stay quite brisk. They really do wonders. They put up chimneys and they make all sorts of wheels go round. The Mexicans are simply enraptured. But after a while, being nothing but naughty boys and greasers, they are pining to put their spokes in those wheels. Mischief, I tell you. *Brummmm!* go the spokes! And the wheels pause to wonder, while the bits fly. That's fun!

Other gentlemen who are very sharp-eyed, seeing Mexico after, are the political see-ers. America is too hot for them, as a rule, so they move into cool, cool Mexico. They are some boys, they are! At least, so they tell me. And they belong to weird things that only exist as initials, such I.W.W.'s and A.F.L.'s and P.J.P.'s. Give me a job, say these gentlemen, and I'll take the rest.

Why certainly, what could be more accommodating! Whereupon instantly, these gentlemen acquire the gift of Spanish, with an almost Pentecostal suddenness; they pat you on the shoulder and tell you sulphureous Mexican stories which certainly you would never have heard but for them. Oh, hot stuff! Hot dog! They even cry aloud *Perro caliente!*—and the walls of the city quake.

Moreover they proceed to organize our labour, after having so firmly insisted that we haven't any. But we produce some, for their sakes. And they proceed to organize it: without music. And in throes of self-esteem they cry: Ah, Mexico's the place. America can't touch it! God bless Mexico!

Whereupon all the Mexicans present burst into tears.

You want no darn gringoes and gringo capital down here! they say.

We cross ourselves rapidly! Absit omen.

But alas, these thrilling gentlemen always leave us. They return with luggage, having come without, to AMERICA.

Well, *adiós!* eh, boy? Come up there one day. Show you something.

Tears; the train moves out.

No, I am Mexican. I might as well be Jonah in the whale's belly, so perfectly, so mysteriously am I nowhere.

But they come. They come as tourists, for example, looking round the whale's interior.

"My wife's a college graduate," says the he-man.

She looks it. And she may thank her lucky stars—Rudolph Valentino is the first-magnitude—she will go on looking it all her days.

Ah, the first time she felt Rudolfino's Italianino-Argentino-swoon-between-o kisses! On the screen, of course— Ah, that first time!

On the back porch, afterwards: Bill, I'm so tired of clean, hygienic kisses.

Poor Bill spits away his still-good, five-cent, mint-covered Wrigley's chewing-gum gag, and with it, the last straw he had to cling to.

Now, aged thirty-four, and never quite a Valentino, he's brought her to see Mexico after–she'd seen Ramon Novarro's face, with the skin-you-love-to-touch. On the screen, of course.

Bill has brought her south. She has crossed the border with Bill. Ah, her eyes at the Pullman window! Where is the skin I would love to touch? they cry. And a dirty Indian pushes his black face and glaring eyes towards her, offering to sell her enchiladas.

It is no use *my* being sorry for her. Bill is better-looking than I am. So she re-falls in love with Bill; the dark-eyed flour-faced creatures make such eyes at him, down here. Call them women! Downtrodden things!

The escaped husband is another one. He drinks, swears, looks at all the women meaningly over a red nose, and lives with a prostitute. Hot *dog!*

Then the young lady collecting information! Golly! Quite nice-looking too. And the things she does! One would think the invisible unicorn that protects virgins was ramping round her every moment. But it's not that. Not even the toughest bandit, not even Pancho Villa, could carry off all that information, though she as good as typed out her temptation to him.

Then the home-town aristocrats, of Little Bull, Arizona, or of Old Hat, Illinois. They are just looking round for something: seeing Mexico after: and very rarely finding it. It really is extraordinary the things there are in Little Bull and in Old Hat, that there aren't in Mexico. Cold slaw, for example! Why, in Little Bull—–!

San Juan Teotihuacan! Hey, boy, why don't you get the parson to sprinkle him with a new tag? Never stand a name like that for half a day, in Little Bull, Illinois. Or was it Arizona?

Such a pity, to have to see Mexico after you've seen America first: or at least, Little Bull, which is probably more so.

The ends won't meet. America isn't just *a* civilization, it is CIVILIZATION. So what is Mexico? Beside Little Bull, what is Mexico?

Of course Mexico went in for civilization long, long, long ago. But it got left. The snake crawled on, leaving the tail behind him.

The snake crawled, lap by lap, all round the globe, till it got back to America. And by that time he was some snake, was civilization. But where was his tail? He'd forgotten it?

Hey, boy! What's that?

Mexico!

Mexico!–the snake didn't know his own tail. *Mexico!* Garn!

That's nothing. It's mere nothing, but the darn silly emptiness where I'm not. Not yet.

So he opens his mouth, and Mexico, his old tail, shivers.

But before civilization swallows its own tail, that tail will buzz. For civilization's a rattler: anyhow Mexico is.

EUROPE *V.* AMERICA

A young American said to me: "I am not very keen on Europe, but should like to see it, and have done with it." He is an ass. How can one "see" Europe and have done with it? One might as well say: I want to see the moon next week and have done with it. If one doesn't want to see the moon, he doesn't look. And if he doesn't want to see Europe, he doesn't look either. But neither of 'em will go away because he's not looking.

There's no "having done with it." Europe is here, and will be here, long after he has added a bit of dust to America. To me, I simply don't see the point of that American trick of saying one is "through with a thing," when the thing is a good deal better than oneself.

I can hear that young man saying: "Oh, I'm through with the moon, she's played out. She's a dead old planet anyhow, and was never more than a side issue." So was Eve only a side issue. But when a man is through with her, he's through with most of his life.

It's the same with Europe. One may be sick of certain aspects of European civilization. But they're in ourselves, rather than in Europe. As a matter of fact, coming back to Europe, I realize how much more *tense* the European civilization is, in the Americans, than in the Europeans. The Europeans still have a vague idea that the universe is greater than they are, and isn't going to change very radically, not for all the telling of all men put together. But the Americans are tense, somewhere inside themselves, as if they felt that once they slackened, the world would really collapse. It wouldn't. If the American tension snapped tomorrow, only that bit of the world which is tense and American would come to an end. Nothing more.

How could I say: I am through with America? America is a great continent; it won't suddenly cease to be. Some part of me will always be conscious of America. But probably some part greater still in me will always be conscious of Europe, since I am a European.

As for Europe's being old, I find it much younger than America. Even these countries of the Mediterranean, which have known quite a bit of history, seem to me much, much younger even than Taos, not to mention Long Island, or Coney Island.

In the people here there is still, at the bottom, the old, young insouciance. It isn't that the young *don't care:* it is merely that, at the bottom of them there *isn't* care. Instead there is a sort of bubbling-in of life. It isn't till we grow old that we grip the very sources of our life with care, and strangle them.

And that seems to me the rough distinction between an American and a European. They are both of the same civilization, and all that. But the American grips himself, at the very sources of his consciousness, in a grip of care: and then, to so much of the rest of life, is indifferent. Whereas, the European hasn't got so much care in him, so he cares much more for life and living.

That phrase again of wanting to see Europe and have done with it shows that strangle-hold so many Americans have got on themselves. Why don't they say: I'd like to see Europe, and then, if it means something to me, good! and if it doesn't mean much to me, so much the worse for both of us. *Vogue la galère!*

I've been a fool myself, saying: Europe is finished for me. It wasn't Europe at all, it was myself, keeping a strangle-hold on myself. And that strangle-hold I carried over to America; as many a man–and woman, worse still–has done before me.

Now, back in Europe, I feel a real relief. The past is too big, and too intimate, for one generation of men to get a strangle-hold on it. Europe is squeezing the life out of herself, with her mental education and fixed ideas. But she hasn't got her hands round her own throat not half so far as America has hers; here the grip is already falling slack; and if the system collapses, it'll only be another system collapsed, of which there have been plenty. But in America, where men grip themselves so much more intensely and suicidally–the women worse–the system has its hold on the very sources of consciousness, so God knows what would happen, if the system broke.

No, it's a relief to be by the Mediterranean, and gradually let the tight coils inside oneself come slack. There is much more life in a deep insouciance, which really is the clue to faith, than in this frenzied, keyed-up care, which is characteristic of our civilization, but which is at its worst, or at least its intensest, in America.

PARIS LETTER

I promised to write a letter to you from Paris. Probably I should have forgotten, but I saw a little picture–or sculpture–in the Tuileries, of Hercules slaying the Centaur, and that reminded me. I had so much rather the Centaur had slain Hercules, and men had never developed souls. Seems to me they're the greatest ailment humanity ever had. However, they've got it.

Paris is still monumental and handsome. Along the river where its splendours are, there's no denying its man-made beauty. The poor, pale little Seine runs rapidly north to the sea, the sky is pale, pale jade overhead, greenish and Parisian, the trees of black wire stand in rows, and flourish their black wire brushes against a low sky of jade-pale cobwebs, and the huge dark-grey palaces rear up their masses of stone and slope off towards the sky still with a massive, satisfying suggestion of pyramids. There is something noble and man-made about it all.

My wife says she wishes that grandeur still squared its shoulders on the earth. She wishes she could sit sumptuously in the river windows of the Tuileries, and see a royal spouse–who wouldn't be me–cross the bridge at the head of a tossing, silk and silver cavalcade. She wishes she had a bevy of ladies-in-waiting around her, as a peacock has its tail, as she crossed the weary expanses of pavement in the Champs Elysées.

Well, she can have it. At least, she can't. The world has lost its faculty for splendour, and Paris is like an old, weary peacock that sports a bunch of dirty twigs at its rump, where it used to have a tail. Democracy has collapsed into more and more democracy, and men, particularly Frenchmen, have collapsed into little, rather insignificant, rather wistful, rather nice and helplessly commonplace little fellows who rouse one's mother-instinct and make one feel they should be tucked away in bed and left to sleep, like Rip Van Winkle, till the rest of the storms rolled by.

It's a queer thing to sit in the Tuileries on a Sunday afternoon and watch the crowd drag through the galleries. Instead of a gay and wicked court, the weary, weary crowd, that looks as if it had nothing at heart to keep it going. As if the human creature had been dwindling and dwindling through the processes of democracy, amid the ponderous ridicule of the aristocratic setting, till soon he will dwindle right away.

Oh, those galleries. Oh, those pictures and those statues of nude, nude women: nude, nude, insistently and hopelessly nude. At last the eyes fall in absolute weariness, the moment they catch sight of a bit of pink-and-white painting, or a pair of white marble *fesses*. It becomes an inquisition; like being forced to go on eating pink marzipan icing. And yet there is a fat and very undistinguished bourgeois with a little beard and a fat and hopelessly petit-bourgeoise wife and awful little girl, standing in front of a huge heap of twisting marble, while he, with a goose-grease unctuous simper, strokes the marble hip of the huge marble female, and points out its niceness *to his wife*. She is not in the least jealous. She knows, no doubt, that her own hip and the marble hip are the only ones he will stroke without paying prices, one of which, and the last he could pay, would be the price of spunk.

It seems to me the French are just worn out. And not nearly so much with the late great war as with the pink nudities of women. The men are just worn out, making offerings on the shrine of Aphrodite in elastic garters. And the women are worn out, keeping the men up to it. The rest is all nervous exasperation.

And the table. One shouldn't forget that other, four-legged mistress of man, more unwitherable than Cleopatra. The table. The good kindly tables of Paris, with Coquilles Saint Martin, and escargots and oysters and Chateaubriands and the good red wine. If they can afford it, the men sit and eat themselves pink. And no wonder. But the Aphrodite in a hard black hat opposite, when she has eaten herself also pink, is going to insist on further delights, to which somebody has got to play up. Weariness isn't the word for it.

May the Lord deliver us from our own enjoyments, we gasp at last. And he won't. We actually have to deliver ourselves.

One goes out again from the restaurant comfortably fed and soothed with a food and drink, to find the pale-jade sky of Paris crumbling in a wet dust of rain; motor-cars skidding till they turn clean around, and are facing south when they were going north: a boy on a bicycle coming smack, and picking himself up with his bicycle pump between his legs: and the men still fishing, as if it were a Sisyphus penalty, with long sticks fishing for invisible fishes in the Seine: and the huge buildings of the Louvre and the Tuileries standing ponderously, with their Parisian suggestion of pyramids.

And no, in the old style of grandeur I never want to be grand.

That sort of regality, that builds itself up in piles of stone and masonry, and prides itself on living inside the monstrous heaps, once they're built, is not for me. My wife asks why she can't live in the Petit Palais, while she's in Paris. Well, even if she might, she'd live alone.

I don't believe any more in democracy. But I can't believe in the old sort of aristocracy, either, nor can I wish it back, splendid as it was. What I believe in is the old Homeric aristocracy, when the grandeur was inside the man, and he lived in a simple wooden house. Then, the men that were grand inside themselves, like Ulysses, were the chieftains and the aristocrats by instinct and by choice. At least we'll hope so. And the Red Indians only knew the aristocrat by instinct. The leader was leader in his own being, not because he was somebody's son or had so much money.

It's got to be so again. They say it won't work. I say, why not? If men could once recognize the natural aristocrat when they set eyes on him, they can still. They can still choose him if they would.

But this business of dynasties is weariness. House of Valois, House of Tudor! Who would want to be a House, or a bit of a House! Let a man be a man, and damn the House business. I'm absolutely a democrat as far as that goes.

But that men are all brothers and all equal is a greater lie than the other. Some men are always aristocrats. But it doesn't go by birth. A always contains B, but B is not contained in C.

Democracy, however, says that there is no such thing as an aristocrat. All men have two legs and one nose, ergo, they are all alike. Nosily and leggily, maybe. But otherwise, very different.

Democracy says that B is not contained in C, and neither is it contained in A. B, that is, the aristocrat, does not exist.

Now this is palpably a greater lie than the old dynastic life. Aristocracy truly does not go by birth. But it still goes. And the tradition of aristocracy will help it a lot.

The aristocrats tried to fortify themselves inside these palaces and these splendours. Regal Paris built up the external evidences of her regality. But the two-limbed man inside these vast shells died, poor worm, of over-encumbrance.

The natural aristocrat has got to fortify himself inside his own will, according to his own strength. The moment he builds himself external evidences, like palaces, he builds himself in, and commits his own doom. The moment he depends on his jewels, he has lost his virtue.

It always seems to me that the next civilization won't want to raise these ponderous, massive, deadly buildings that refuse to crumble away with their epoch and weigh men helplessly down. Neither palaces nor cathedrals nor any other hugenesses. Material simplicity is after all the highest sign of civilization. Here in Paris one knows it finally. The ponderous and depressing museum that is regal Paris. And living humanity like poor worms struggling inside the shell of history, all of them inside the museum. The dead life and the living life, all one museum.

Monuments, museums, permanencies, and ponderosities are all anathema. But brave men are for ever born, and nothing else is worth having.

FIREWORKS IN FLORENCE

Yesterday being St. John's Day, the 24th June, and St. John being the patron saint of Florence, his day being also the day of midsummer festival, when, in the north, you jump through the flames: for all these reasons Florence was lit up, and there was a show of fireworks from the Piazzale. There must be fire of some sort on Midsummer Day: so let it be fireworks.

The illuminations were rather scanty. The Palazzo Vecchio had frames of little electric bulbs round the windows. But above that, all along the battlements of the square roof, and in the arches of the thin-necked tower, and between the battlements at the top of the tower, the flames were orange-ruddy, and they danced about in one midsummer witch-night dance, a hundred or two little ruddy dancements among the black, hard battlements, and round the lofty, unrelenting square crown of the old building. It was at once medieval and fascinating, in the soft, hot, moonlit night. The Palazzo Vecchio has come down to our day, but it hasn't yet quite come down to us. It lifts its long slim neck like a hawk rearing up to look around, and in the darkness its battlements in silhouette look like black feathers. Like an alert fierce bird from the Middle Ages it lifts its head over the level town, eagle with serrated plumes. And one feels it is a wonder that the modern spirit hasn't given it a knock over the head, it is so silently fierce and haughty and severe with splendour.

On Midsummer Night the modern spirit had only fixed itself, like so many obstinate insects, in the squares of paltry electric bulb lights on the hard façade. Stupid, staring, unwinking, unalive, unchanging beads of electric lights! As if there could be anything festive or midsummerish about them, in their idiotic fixity like bright colourless brass nail-heads nailed on the night.

Thus far had the modern spirit nailed itself on the old Palazzo. But above, where the battlements ruffled like pinion-tips upon the blond sky, and the dark-necked tower suddenly shot up, the modern spirit unexplainedly ceased, and the Middle Ages flourished. There the illuminations must have been oil flare-lamps, old oil torch lamps, because the flames were like living bodies, so warm and alive, and they danced about perpetually in the warm bland air of night, like Shiva dancing her myriad-movement dance. And all this alive dancement the severe old building carried calmly, with pride and dignity, its neck in the sky. As for the rows of electric bulbs below, like buttons on the breast of a page-boy, they didn't exist.

If anything is detestable, it is hard, stupid fixity, that doesn't know how to flicker and waver and be alive, but must keep on going on being the same, like the buttons on a coat; the coat wears out, but the idiotic buttons are the same as ever.

The people were streaming out of the piazza, all in one direction, and all quiet, and all seeming small and alive under the tall buildings. Of course the Palazzo Vecchio and the Uffizi aren't really tall: in terms of the Woolworth Tower, that is, or the Flatiron Building. But underneath their walls people move diminished, in small, alert, lively throngs, just as in the street-scenes of the old pictures: throngs and groups of striding and standing and streaming people who are quick and alive, and still have a certain alert human dignity, in spite of their being so diminished. And that again is different from the effect of looking down from the top of the Flatiron Building, let us say. There you see people little and scurrying and insect-like, rather repulsive, like the thick mechanical hurrying of ants.

Out of the Piazza Signoria the people were all flowing in one direction, towards the dark mouth of the Uffizi, towards the river. The fountain was shooting up a long, leaning stem of water, and the rather stupid thick Bandinelli statue below glistened all over, in his thick nakedness, but not unpleasant, really. Michelangelo's *David,* in the dry dimness, continued to smirk and trail his foot self-consciously, the incarnation of the modern self-conscious young man, and very objectionable.

But the crowd streamed on, towards the Lungarno, under the big-headed David, unheeding. It is a curious thing, that in spite of that extremely obtrusive male statue of David which stands and has stood for so long a time there in the Piazza, where every Friday the farmers from the country throng to discuss prices, still the name *David* is practically unknown among the ordinary people. They have never heard it. It is meaningless sound to them. It might as well be Popocatepetl. Tell them your name is David, and they remain utterly impervious and blank. You cannot bring them to utter it.

On the Lungarno the crowd is solid. There is no traffic. The whole length of the riverside has become one long theatre pit, where the whole populace of Florence waits to see the fireworks. In countless numbers they stand and wait, the whole city, yet quiet almost as mice.

The fireworks will go off from the Piazzale Michelangelo, which is like a platform, a little platform away above the left bank of the river. So the crowd solidly lines the right bank, the whole city.

In the sky a little to the south, the fair, warm moon, almost full, lingers in a fleece of iridescent cloud, as if also wanting to look on, but from an immeasurable distance. There is no drawing near, on the moon's part.

The crowd is quiet, and perfectly well-behaved. No excitement, and absolutely no exuberance. In a sense, there is no holiday spirit at all. A man hawks half-a-dozen balloons, but nobody buys them. There is a little flare-lit stall, where they cook those little aniseed waffles. And nobody seems to buy them. Only the men who silently walk through the throng with little tubs of ice-cream do a trade. But almost without a sound.

It seems long to wait. Down on the grass by the still full river, under the embankment, are throngs of people. Even those boats in which during the day one sees men getting gravel are full of spectators. But you wouldn't know, unless you looked over the rampart. They are so still. In the river's underworld.

It is weary to wait. The young men, all wearing no hats, stroll, winding among the throng of immovable citizens and wives. There is nothing to see. Best sit in the motor-car by the kerb.

By the car stand two women with a police-dog on a chain. The dog, alert, nervous, uneasy, crouches and then rises restlessly. *Bang!* Up goes the first rocket, like a golden tadpole wiggling up in the sky, then a burst of red and green sparks. The dog winces, and crouches under the running-board of the car. *Bang! Bang! Crackle!* More rockets, more showers of stars and fizzes of aster-petal light in the sky. The dog whimpers, the mistresses divide their attention between the heavens and him. In the sky, the moon draws further and further off, while still watching palely. At an immense distance, the moon, pallid far. Nearer, in the high sky, a rolling and fuming of smoke, a whistling of rockets, a spangling and splashing of fragments of coloured lights, and, most impressive of all, the continuous explosions, crepitation within the air itself, the high air bursting outwards from within itself, in continual shocks. It is more like an air-raid than anything. And perhaps the deepest impression made on the psyche is that of a raid in the air.

The dog suffers and suffers more. He tries to hide away, not to look at all. But there is an extra bang and a fusillade! He has to look! *bish!* the sky-asters burst one beyond the other! He cannot bear it. He shivers like a glass cup that is going to shatter. His mistresses try to comfort him. They want to look at the fireworks but their interest in the dog is more real. And he, he wants to cover his ears, and bury his head, but at every new bang! he starts afresh and rises, and turns round. Sometimes he sits like a statue of pure distress, still as bronze. Then he curls away upon himself again, curling to get away. While the high sky bursts and reverberates, wiggles with tadpoles of golden fire, and plunges with splashes of light, spangles of colour, as if someone had thrown a stone into the ether from above, and then pelted the ether with stones.

The crowd watches in silence. Young men wander by, and in the subdued tone of mocking irony common to the Italians, they say *bello! bello! bellezza!* But it is pure irony. As the light goes up, you see the dark trees and cypresses standing tall and black, like Dantesque spectators, on the sky-line. And down below, you see the townspeople standing motionless, with uplifted faces. Also, rather frequently, a young man with his arm round his white-dressed sweetheart, caressing her and making public love to her. Love-making, it seems, like everything else, must be public nowadays. The stag goes into the depths of the forest. But the young city buck likes the light to flare up and reveal his arm round the shoulders of his girl, his hand stroking her neck.

Up on the Piazzale, they are letting off the figure-pieces: wheels that turn round showerily in red and green and white fire, fuming dense smoke, that moves in curious slow volumes, all penetrated with colour. Now there is a red piece: and on top of the old water-tower a column of red fire and reddish smoke. It looks as if a city in the distance were being burnt by the enemy. And again the fusillade of a raid, while the smoke rolls ponderously, the colour dies out, only the iridescence of the far, unreachable naked moon tinges the low fume.

In heaven are more rockets. There are lovely ones that lean down in the sky like great spider lilies, with long outcurving petals of soft light, and at the end of each petal, a sudden drop of pure green, ready to fall like dew. But some strange hand of evanescence brushes it away, and it is gone, and the next rocket bursting shows all the smoke-threads still stretching, like the spectre of the great fire lily, up in the sky: like the greyness of wild clematis fronds in autumn, crumbling together, as the succeeding rocket bursts in brilliance.

Meanwhile, in another world, and a world more real, the explosion and percussions and fusillades keep up, and penetrate into the soul with a sense of fear. The dog, reduced and shattered, tries to get used to it, but can't succeed.

There is a great spangling and sparkling and trailing of long lights in the sky and long sprays of whitish, successively-bursting fire-blossoms, and other big many-petalled flowers curving their petals downwards like a grasping hand. Ah, at last, it is all happening at once!

And as the eye is thrilled and dazzled, the ear almost ceases to hear. Yet the moment the sky empties, it is the percussion of explosions on the heart that one feels.

It is quickly all over. The chauffeur is gabbling *sotto voce* that it is shorter than last year. The crowd is dispersing so quickly and silently, as if they were running away. And you feel they are all mocking quietly at the spectacle. *Panem et circenses* is all very well, but when the great crowd quietly jeers at your circus, it leaves you at a loss.

The cathedral dome, the top of Giotti's tower, like a lily-stem, and the straight lines of the top of the Baptistery are outlined with rather sparse electric bulbs. It looks very unfinished. Yet, with that light above illuminating the pale and coloured marbles ghostly, and the red tiles of the dome in the night-sky, and the abrupt end of the lily-stem without a flower, and the old hard lines of the Baptistery's top, there is a lovely ethereal quality to the great cathedral group; and you think again of the Lily of Florence–"The Lily of Florence shall become the cauliflower of Rovenzano," somebody said.

But not yet, anyhow.

[GERMANS AND LATINS]

It is already summer in Tuscany, the sun is hot, the earth is baked hard, and the soul has changed her rhythm. The nightingales sing all day and all night—not at all sadly, but brightly, vividly, impudently, with a trilling power of assertion quite disproportionate to the size of the shy bird. Why the Greeks should have heard the nightingale weeping or sobbing is more than I can understand. Anyhow, perhaps the Greeks were looking for the tragic, rather than the rhapsodic consummation to life. They were predisposed.

Tomorrow, however, is the first of May, and already summer is here. Yesterday, in the flood of sunshine on the Arno at evening, I saw two German boys steering out of the Por Santa Maria onto the Ponte Vecchio in Florence. They were dark-haired, not blonds, but otherwise the true *Wandervögel* type, in shirts and short trousers and thick boots, hatless, coat slung in the rucksack, shirt-sleeves rolled back above the brown muscular arms, shirt-breast open from the brown, scorched breast, and the face and neck glowing sun-darkened as they strode into the flood of evening sunshine, out of the narrow street. They were talking loudly to one another in German, as if oblivious of their surroundings, in that thronged crossing of the Ponte Vecchio. And they strode with strong strides, heedless, marching past the Italians as if the Italians were but shadows. Strong, heedless, travelling intently, bent a little forward from the rucksacks in the plunge of determination to travel onwards, looking neither to right nor left, conversing in strong voices only with one another, where were they going, in the last golden light of the sun-flooded evening, over the Arno? Were they leaving town, at this hour? Were they pressing on, to get out of the Porta Romana before nightfall, going southwards?

In spite of the fact that one is used to these German youths, in Florence especially, in summer, still the mind calls a halt each time they appear and pass by. If swans or wild geese flew honking, low over the Arno in the evening light, moving with that wedge-shaped, intent, unswerving progress that is so impressive, they would create the same impression on one. They would bring that sense of remote, far-off lands which these Germans bring, and that sense of mysterious, unfathomable purpose.

Now no one knows better than myself that Munich or Frankfortam-Main are not far-off, remote, lonely lands: on the contrary: and that these boys are not mysteriously migrating from one unknown to another. They are just wandering for wandering's sake, and moving instinctively, perhaps, towards the sun, and towards Rome, the old centre-point. There is really nothing more remarkable in it than in the English and Americans sauntering diffidently and, as it were, obscurely along the Lungarno. The English in particular seem to move under a sort of Tarnhelm, having a certain power of invisibility. They manage most of the time to efface themselves, deliberately, from the atmosphere. And the Americans, who don't try to efface themselves, give the impression of not being really there. They have left their real selves way off in the United States, in Europe they are like rather void *Doppelgänger*. I am speaking, of course, of the impression of the streets. Inside the hotels, the trains, the tea-rooms and the restaurants, it is another affair. There you may have a little England, very insular, or a little America, very money-rich democratic, or a little Germany, assertive, or a little Scandinavia, domestic. But I am not speaking of indoor impressions. Merely of the streets.

And in the streets of Florence or Rome, the *Wandervögel* make a startling impression, whereas the rest of the foreigners impress one rather negatively. When I am in Germany, then Germany seems to me very much like anywhere else, especially England or America.

And when I see the *Wandervögel* pushing at evening out of the Por Santa Maria, across the blaze of sun and into the Ponte Vecchio, then Germany becomes again to me what it was to the Romans: the mysterious, half-dark land of the north, bristling with gloomy forests, resounding to the cry of wild geese and of swans, the land of the stork and the bear and the *Drachen* and the *Greifen*.

I know it is not so. Yet the impression comes back over me, as I see the youths pressing heedlessly past. And I know it is the same with the Italians. They see, as their ancestors saw in the Goths and the Vandals, *i barbari,* the barbarians. That is what the little policeman with his staff and his peaked cap thinks, as the boys from the north go by: *i barbari!* Not with dislike or contempt: not at all: but with the old, weird wonder. So he might look up at wild swans flying over the Ponte Vecchio: wild strangers from the north.

So strong is the impression the *Wandervögel* make on the imagination! It is not that I am particularly impressionable. I know the Italians feel very much as I do.

And when one sees English people with rucksacks and shirt-sleeves rolled back and hob-nailed boots, as one does sometimes, even in Tuscany, one notices them, but they make very little impression. They are rather odd than extraordinary. They are just *gli escursionisti,* quite comprehensible: part of the fresh-air movement. The Italians will laugh at them, but they know just what to think about them.

Whereas about the *Wandervögel* they do not quite know what to think, nor even what to feel: since we even only feel the things we know how to feel. And we do not know what to feel about these *Wandervögel* boys. They bring with them such a strong feeling of *somewhere else,* of an unknown country, an unknown race, a powerful, still unknown northland.

How wonderful it must have been, at the end of the old Roman Empire, for the Roman citizens to see the big, bare-limbed Goths, with their insolent-indifferent blue eyes, stand looking on at the market-places! They were there like a vision. *Non angli sed angeli,* as we were told the first great Pope said of the British slaves. Creatures from the beyond, presaging another world of men.

So it was then. So it is, to a certain extent, even now. Strange wanderers towards the sun, forerunners of another world of men. That is how one still feels, as one sees the *Wandervögel* cross the Ponte Vecchio. They carry with them another world, another air, another meaning of life. The meaning is not explicit, not as much as it is even in storks or wild geese. But there it lies, implicit.

Curious how different it is with the well-dressed Germans. They are very often quite domesticated, and in the sense that Ibsen's people are ridiculous, just a little ridiculous. They are *so* bourgeois, so much more a product of civilization than the producers of civilization. They are *so* much buttoned up inside their waistcoats, and stuck inside their trousers, and encircled in their starched collars. They are not so grotesquely self-conscious and physically withered or non-existent as the equivalent English bourgeois tourist. And they are never quite so utterly domesticated as the equivalent Scandinavian. But they have so often the unsure look of children who have been turned out in their best clothes by their mama, and told to go and enjoy themselves: Now enjoy yourselves! That is a little absurd.

The Italians, whatever they are, are what they are. So you know them, you feel that they have developed themselves into an expression of themselves, as far as they go. With the English, weird fish as they are very often, you feel the same: whatever they are, they are what they are, they can't be much different, poor dears. But with the Germans abroad, you feel: These people ought really to be something else. They are not themselves, in their Sunday clothes. They are being something they are not.

And one has the feeling even stronger, with many Russians. One feels: These people are not themselves at all. They are the roaring echoes of other people, older races, other languages. Even the things they say aren't really Russian things: they're all sorts of half-translations from Latin or French or English or God-knows-what.

Some of this feeling one has about the Germans one meets abroad: as if they were talking in translation: as if the ideas, however original, always had a faint sound of translations. As if they were never *quite* themselves.

Then, when one sees the *Wandervögel,* comes the shock of realization, and one thinks: There they go, the real Germans, seeking the sun! They have really nothing to say. They are roving, roving, roving, seeking themselves. That is it, with these "barbarians." They are still seeking themselves. And they have not yet found themselves. They are turning to the sun again, in the great adventure of seeking themselves.

Man does not start ready-made. He is a weird creature that slowly evolves himself through the ages. He need never stop evolving himself, for a human being who was completely himself has never even been conceived. The great Goethe was half-born, Shakespeare the same, Napoleon only a third-born. And most people are hardly born at all, into individual consciousness.

But with the Italians and the French, the mass-consciousness which governs the individual is really derived from the individual. Whereas with the German and the Russian, it seems to me not so. The mass-consciousness has been *taken over,* by great minds like Goethe or Frederick, from other people, and does not spring inherent from the Teutonic race itself. In short, the Teutonic mind, young, powerful, active, is always thinking in terms of somebody else's experience, and almost never in terms of its own experience.

Then comes a great unrest. It seems to show so plainly in the *Wandervögel.* Thinking in terms of somebody else's experience at last becomes utterly unsatisfactory. Then thought altogether falls into chaos—and then into discredit. The young don't choose to think any more. Blindly, they turn to the sun.

Because the sun is anti-thought. Thought is of the shade. In bright sunshine no man thinks. So the *Wandervögel* turn instinctively to the sun, which melts thoughts away, and sets the blood running with another, non-mental consciousness.

And this is why, at times of great change, the northern nations turn to the sun. And this is why, when revolutions come, they often come in May. It is the sun making the blood revolt against old conceptions. And this is why the nations of the sun do not live the life of thought, therefore they are more "themselves." In the grey shadow the northern nations mould themselves according to a few ideas, until their whole life is buttoned and choked up. Then comes a revulsion. They cast off the clothes and turn to the sun, as the *Wandervögel* do, strange harbingers.

NOTTINGHAM AND THE MINING COUNTRYSIDE

I was born nearly forty-four years ago, in Eastwood, a mining village of some three thousand souls, about eight miles from Nottingham, and one mile from the small stream, the Erewash, which divides Nottinghamshire from Derbyshire. It is hilly country, looking west to Crich and towards Matlock, sixteen miles away, and east and north-east towards Mansfield and the Sherwood Forest district. To me it seemed, and still seems, an extremely beautiful countryside, just between the red sandstone and the oak-trees of Nottingham, and the cold limestone, the ash-trees, the stone fences of Derbyshire. To me, as a child and a young man, it was still the old England of the forest and agricultural past; there were no motor-cars, the mines were, in a sense, an accident in the landscape, and Robin Hood and his merry men were not very far away.

The string of coal-mines of B.W. & Co. had been opened some sixty years before I was born, and Eastwood had come into being as a consequence. It must have been a tiny village at the beginning of the nineteenth century, a small place of cottages and fragmentary rows of little four-roomed miners' dwellings, the homes of the old colliers of the eighteenth century, who worked in the bits of mines, foot-rill mines with an opening in the hillside into which the miners walked, or windlass mines, where the men were wound up one at a time, in a bucket, by a donkey. The windlass mines were still working when my father was a boy—and the shafts of some were still there, when I was a boy.

But somewhere about 1820 the company must have sunk the first big shaft—not very deep—and installed the first machinery of the real industrial colliery. Then came my grandfather, a young man trained to be a tailor, drifting from the south of England, and got the job of company tailor for the Brinsley mine. In those days the company supplied the men with the thick flannel vests, or singlets, and the moleskin trousers lined at the top with flannel, in which the colliers worked. I remember the great rolls of coarse flannel and pit-cloth which stood in the corner of my grandfather's shop when I was a small boy, and the big, strange old sewing-machine, like nothing else on earth, which sewed the massive pit-trousers. But when I was only a child the company discontinued supplying the men with pit-clothes.

My grandfather settled in an old cottage down in a quarry-bed, by the brook at Old Brinsley, near the pit. A mile away, up at Eastwood, the company built the first miners' dwellings—it must be nearly a hundred years ago. Now Eastwood occupies a lovely position on a hilltop, with the steep slope towards Derbyshire and the long slope towards Nottingham. They put up a new church, which stands fine and commanding, even if it has no real form, looking across the awful Erewash Valley at the church of Heanor, similarly commanding, away on a hill beyond. What opportunities, what opportunities! These mining villages *might* have been like the lovely hill-towns of Italy, shapely and fascinating. And what happened?

Most of the little rows of dwellings of the old-style miners were pulled down, and dull little shops began to rise along the Nottingham Road, while on the down-slope of the north side the company erected what is still known as the New Buildings, or the Square. These New Buildings consist of two great hollow squares of dwellings planked down on the rough slope of the hill, little four-room houses with the "front" looking outward into the grim, blank street, and the "back," with a tiny square brick yard, a low wall, and a w.c. and ash-pit, looking into the desert of the square, hard, uneven, jolting black earth tilting rather steeply down, with these little back yards all round, and openings at the corners. The squares were quite big, and absolutely desert, save for the posts for clothes lines, and people passing, children playing on the hard earth. And they were shut in like a barracks enclosure, very strange.

Even fifty years ago the squares were unpopular. It was "common" to live in the Square. It was a little less common to live in the Breach, which consisted of six blocks of rather more pretentious dwellings erected by the company in the valley below, two rows of three blocks, with an alley between. And it was most "common," most degraded of all to live in Dakins Row, two rows of the old dwellings, very old, black, four-roomed little places, that stood on the hill again, not far from the Square.

So the place started. Down the steep street between the squares, Scargill Street, the Wesleyans' chapel was put up, and I was born in the little corner shop just above. Across the other side the Square the miners themselves built the big, barn-like Primitive Methodist chapel. Along the hill-top ran the Nottingham Road, with its scrappy, ugly mid-Victorian shops. The little market-place, with a superb outlook, ended the village on the Derbyshire side, and was just left bare, with the Sun Inn on one side, the chemist across, with the gilt pestle-and-mortar, and a shop at the other corner, the corner of Alfreton Road and Nottingham Road.

In this queer jumble of the old England and the new, I came into consciousness. As I remember, little local speculators already began to straggle dwellings in rows, always in rows, across the fields: nasty red-brick, flat-faced dwellings with dark slate roofs. The bay-window period only began when I was a child. But most of the country was untouched.

There must be three or four hundred company houses in the squares and the streets that surround the squares, like a great barracks wall. There must be sixty or eighty company houses in the Breach. The old Dakins Row will have thirty to forty little holes. Then counting the old cottages and rows left with their old gardens down the lanes and along the twitchells, and even in the midst of Nottingham Road itself, there were houses enough for the population, there was no need for much building. And not much building went on when I was small.

We lived in the Breach, in a corner house. A field-path came down under a great hawthorn hedge. On the other side was the brook, with the old sheep-bridge going over into the meadows. The hawthorn hedge by the brook had grown tall as tall trees, and we used to bathe from there in the dipping-hole, where the sheep were dipped, just near the fall from the old mill-dam, where the water rushed. The mill only ceased grinding the local corn when I was a child. And my father, who always worked in Brinsley pit, and who always got up at five o'clock, if not at four, would set off in the dawn across the fields at Coney Grey, and hunt for mushrooms in the long grass, or perhaps pick up a skulking rabbit, which he would bring home at evening inside the lining of his pit-coat.

So that the life was a curious cross between industrialism and the old agricultural England of Shakespeare and Milton and Fielding and George Eliot. The dialect was broad Derbyshire, and always "thee" and "thou." The people lived almost entirely by instinct, men of my father's age could not really read. And the pit did not mechanize men. On the contrary. Under the butty system, the miners worked underground as a sort of intimate community, they knew each other practically naked, and with curious close intimacy, and the darkness and the underground remoteness of the pit "stall," and the continual presence of danger, made the physical, instinctive, and intuitional contact between men very highly developed, a contact almost as close as touch, very real and very powerful. This physical awareness and intimate *togetherness* was at its strongest down pit. When the men came up into the light, they blinked. They had, in a measure, to change their flow. Nevertheless, they brought with them above ground the curious dark intimacy of the mine, the naked sort of contact, and if I think of my childhood, it is always as if there was a lustrous sort of inner darkness, like the gloss of coal, in which we moved and had our real being. My father loved the pit. He was hurt badly, more than once, but he would never stay away. He loved the contact, the intimacy, as men in the war loved the intense male comradeship of the dark days. They did not know what they had lost till they lost it. And I think it is the same with the young colliers of today.

Now the colliers had also an instinct of beauty. The colliers' wives had not. The colliers were deeply alive, instinctively. But they had no daytime ambition, and no daytime intellect. They avoided, really, the rational aspect of life. They preferred to take life instinctively and intuitively. They didn't even care very profoundly about wages. It was the women, naturally, who nagged on this score. There was a big discrepancy, when I was a boy, between the collier who saw, at the best, only a brief few hours of daylight–often no daylight at all during the winter weeks–and the collier's wife, who had all the day to herself when the man was down pit.

The great fallacy is, to pity the man. He didn't dream of pitying himself, till agitators and sentimentalists taught him to. He was happy: or more than happy, he was fulfilled. Or he was fulfilled on the receptive side, not on the expressive. The collier went to the pub and drank in order to continue his intimacy with his mates. They talked endlessly, but it was rather of wonders and marvels, even in politics, than of facts. It was hard facts, in the shape of wife, money, and nagging home necessities, which they fled away from, out of the house to the pub, and out of the house to the pit.

The collier fled out of the house as soon as he could, away from the nagging materialism of the woman. With the women it was always: This is broken, now you've got to mend it! or else: We want this, that and the other, and where is the money coming from? The collier didn't know and didn't care very deeply–his life was otherwise. So he escaped. He roved the countryside with his dog, prowling for a rabbit, for nests, for mushrooms, anything. He loved the countryside, just the indiscriminating feel of it. Or he loved just to sit on his heels and watch—anything or nothing. He was not intellectually interested. Life for him did not consist in facts, but in a flow. Very often, he loved his garden. And very often he had a genuine love of the beauty of flowers. I have known it often and often, in colliers.

Now the love of flowers is a very misleading thing. Most women love flowers as possessions, and as trimmings. They can't look at a flower, and wonder a moment, and pass on. If they see a flower that arrests their attention, they must at once pick it, pluck it. Possession! A possession! Something added on to *me!* And most of the so-called love of flowers today is merely this reaching out of possession and egoism: something I've *got:* something that embellishes *me*. Yet I've seen many a collier stand in his back garden looking down at a flower with that odd, remote sort of contemplation which shows a *real* awareness of the presence of beauty. It would not even be admiration, or joy, or delight, or any of those things which so often have a root in the possessive instinct. It would be a sort of contemplation: which shows the incipient artist.

The real tragedy of England, as I see it, is the tragedy of ugliness. The country is so lovely: the man-made England is so vile. I know that the ordinary collier, when I was a boy, had a peculiar sense of beauty, coming from his intuitive and instinctive consciousness, which was awakened down pit. And the fact that he met with just cold ugliness and raw materialism when he came up into daylight, and particularly when he came to the Square or the Breach, and to his own table, killed something in him, and in a sense spoiled him as a man. The woman almost invariably nagged about material things. She was taught to do it; she was encouraged to do it. It was a mother's business to see that her sons "got on," and it was the man's business to provide the money. In my father's generation, with the old wild England behind them, and the lack of education, the man was not beaten down. But in my generation, the boys I went to school with, colliers now, have all been beaten down, what with the din-din-dinning of Board Schools, books, cinemas, clergymen, the whole national and human consciousness hammering on the fact of material prosperity above all things.

The men are beaten down, there is prosperity for a time, in their defeat—and then disaster looms ahead. The root of all disaster is disheartenment. And men are disheartened. The men of England, the colliers in particular, are disheartened. They have been betrayed and beaten.

Now though perhaps nobody knew it, it was ugliness which really betrayed the spirit of man, in the nineteenth century. The great crime which the moneyed classes and promoters of industry committed in the palmy Victorian days was the condemning of the workers to ugliness, ugliness, ugliness: meanness and formless and ugly surroundings, ugly ideals, ugly religion, ugly hope, ugly love, ugly clothes, ugly furniture, ugly houses, ugly relationship between workers and employers. The human soul needs actual beauty even more than bread. The middle classes jeer at the colliers for buying pianos—but what is the piano, often as not, but a blind reaching out for beauty. To the woman it is a possession and a piece of furniture and something to feel superior about. But see the elderly colliers trying to learn to play, see them listening with queer alert faces to their daughter's execution of *The Maiden's Prayer,* and you will see a blind, unsatisfied craving for beauty. It is far more deep in the men than the women. The women want show. The men want beauty, and still want it.

If the company, instead of building those sordid and hideous Squares, then, when they had that lovely site to play with, there on the hill top: if they had put a tall column in the middle of the small market-place, and run three parts of a circle of arcade round the pleasant space, where people could stroll or sit, and with handsome houses behind! If they had made big, substantial houses, in apartments of five or six rooms, and with handsome entrances. If above all, they had encouraged song and dancing—for the miners still sang and danced—and provided handsome space for these. If only they had encouraged some form of beauty in dress, some form of beauty in interior life—furniture, decoration. If they had given prizes for the handsomest chair or table, the loveliest scarf, the most charming room that the men or women could make! If only they had done this, there would never have been an industrial problem. The industrial problem arises from the base forcing of all human energy into a competition of mere acquisition.

You may say the working man would not have accepted such a form of life: the Englishman's home is his castle, etc., etc.—"my own little home." But if you can hear every word the next-door people say, there's not much castle. And if you can see everybody in the square if they go to the w.c.! And if your one desire is to get out of your "castle" and your "own little home"!—well, there's not much to be said for it. Anyhow, it's only the woman who idolizes "her own little home"—and it's always the woman at her worst, her most greedy, most possessive, most mean. There's nothing to be said for the "little home" any more: a great scrabble of ugly pettiness over the face of the land.

As a matter of fact, till 1800 the English people were strictly a rural people—very rural. England has had towns for centuries, but they have never been real towns, only clusters of village streets. Never the real *urbs*. The English character has failed to develop the real *urban* side of a man, the civic side. Siena is a bit of a place, but it is a real city, with citizens intimately connected with the city. Nottingham is a vast place sprawling towards a million, and it is nothing more than an amorphous agglomeration. There *is* no Nottingham, in the sense that there is Siena. The Englishman is stupidly undeveloped, as a citizen. And it is partly due to his "little home" stunt, and partly to his acceptance of hopeless paltriness in his surrounding. The new cities of America are much more genuine cities, in the Roman sense, than is London or Manchester. Even Edinburgh used to be more of a true city than any town England ever produced.

That silly little individualism of "the Englishman's home is his castle" and "my own little home" is out of date. It would work almost up to 1800, when every Englishman was still a villager, and a cottager. But the industrial system has brought a great change. The Englishman still likes to think of himself as a "cottager"—"my home, my garden." But it is puerile. Even the farm-labourer today is psychologically a town-bird. The English are town-birds through and through, today, as the inevitable result of their complete industrialization. Yet they don't know how to build a city, how to think of one, or how to live in one. They are all suburban, pseudo-cottagy, and not one of them knows how to be truly urban—the citizen as the Romans were citizens—or the Athenians—or even the Parisians, till the war came.

And this is because we have frustrated that instinct of community which would make us unite in pride and dignity in the bigger gesture of the citizen, not the cottager. The great city means beauty, dignity, and a certain splendour. This is the side of the Englishman that has been thwarted and shockingly betrayed. England is a mean and petty scrabble of paltry dwellings called "homes." I believe in their heart of hearts all Englishmen loathe their little homes—but not the women. What we want is a bigger gesture, a greater scope, a certain splendour, a certain grandeur, and beauty, big beauty. The American does far better than we, in this.

And the promoter of industry, a hundred years ago, dared to perpetrate the ugliness of my native village. And still more monstrous, promoters of industry today are scrabbling over the face of England with miles and square miles of red-brick "homes," like horrible scabs. And the men inside these little red rat-traps get more and more helpless, being more and more humiliated, more and more dissatisfied, liked trapped rats. Only the meaner sort of women go on loving the little home which is no more than a rat-trap to her man.

Do away with it all, then. At no matter what cost, start in to alter it. Never mind about wages and industrial squabbling. Turn the attention elsewhere. Pull down my native village to the last brick. Plan a nucleus. Fix the focus. Make a handsome gesture of radiation from the focus. And then put up big buildings, handsome, that sweep to a civic centre. And furnish them with beauty. And make an absolute clean start. Do it place by place. Make a new England. Away with little homes! Away with scrabbling pettiness and paltriness. Look at the contours of the land, and build up from these, with a sufficient nobility. The English may be mentally or spiritually developed. But as citizens of splendid cities they are more ignominious than rabbits. And they nag, nag, nag all the time about politics and wages and all that, like mean narrow housewives.

NEW MEXICO

Superficially, the world has become small and known. Poor little globe of earth, the tourists trot round you as easily as they trot round the Bois or round Central Park. There is no mystery left, we've been there, we've seen it, we know all about it. We've done the globe, and the globe is done.

This is quite true, superficially. On the superficies, horizontally, we've been everywhere and done everything, we know all about it. Yet the more we know, superficially, the less we penetrate, vertically. It's all very well skimming across the surface of the ocean, and saying you know all about the sea. There still remain the terrifying under-deeps, of which we have utterly no experience.

The same is true of land travel. We skim along, we get there, we see it all, we've done it all. And as a rule, we never once go through the curious film which railroads, ships, motor-cars, and hotels stretch over the surface of the whole earth. Peking is just the same as New York, with a few different things to look at; rather more Chinese about, etc. Poor creatures that we are, we crave for experience, yet we are like flies that crawl on the pure and transparent mucous-paper in which the world like a bon-bon is wrapped so carefully that we can never get at it, though we see it there all the time as we move about it, apparently in contact, yet actually as far removed as if it were the moon.

As a matter of fact, our great-grandfathers, who never went anywhere, in actuality had more experience of the world than we have, who have seen everything. When they listened to a lecture with lantern-slides, they really held their breath before the unknown, as they sat in the village school-room. We, bowling along in a rickshaw in Ceylon, say to ourselves: "It's very much what you'd expect." We really know it all.

We are mistaken. The know-it-all state of mind is just the result of being outside the mucous-paper wrapping of civilization. Underneath is everything we don't know and are afraid of knowing.

I realized this with shattering force when I went to New Mexico.

New Mexico, one of the United States, part of the U. S. A. New Mexico, the picturesque reservation and playground of the eastern states, very romantic, old Spanish, Red Indian, desert mesas, pueblos, cowboys, penitentes, all that film-stuff. Very nice, the great South-

West, put on a sombrero and knot a red kerchief round your neck, to go out in the great free spaces!

That is New Mexico wrapped in the absolutely hygienic and shiny mucous-paper of our trite civilization. That is the New Mexico known to most of the Americans who know it at all. But break through the shiny sterilized wrapping, and actually *touch* the country, and you will never be the same again.

I think New Mexico was the greatest experience from the outside world that I have ever had. It certainly changed me for ever. Curious as it may sound, it was New Mexico that liberated me from the present era of civilization, the great era of material and mechanical development. Months spent in holy Kandy, in Ceylon, the holy of holies of southern Buddhism, had not touched the great psyche of materialism and idealism which dominated me. And years, even in the exquisite beauty of Sicily, right among the old Greek paganism that still lives there, had not shattered the essential Christianity on which my character was established. Australia was a sort of dream or trance, like being under a spell, the self remaining unchanged, so long as the trance did not last too long. Tahiti, in a mere glimpse, repelled me: and so did California, after a stay of a few weeks. There seemed a strange brutality in the spirit of the western coast, and I felt: O, let me get away!

But the moment I saw the brilliant, proud morning shine high up over the deserts of Santa Fé, something stood still in my soul, and I started to attend. There was a certain magnificence in the high-up day, a certain eagle-like royalty, so different from the equally pure, equally pristine and lovely morning of Australia, which is so soft, so utterly pure in its softness, and betrayed by green parrot flying. But in the lovely morning of Australia one went into a dream. In the magnificent fierce morning of New Mexico one sprang awake, a new part of the soul woke up suddenly, and the old world gave way to a new.

There are all kinds of beauty in the world, thank God, though ugliness is homogeneous. How lovely is Sicily, with Calabria across the sea like an opal, and Etna with her snow in a world above and beyond! How lovely is Tuscany, with little red tulips wild among the corn: or bluebells at dusk in England, or mimosa in clouds of pure yellow among the grey-green dun foliage of Australia, under a soft, blue, unbreathed sky! But for a *greatness* of beauty I have never experienced anything like New Mexico. All those mornings when I went with a hoe along the ditch to the Cañon, at the ranch, and stood, in the fierce, proud silence of the Rockies, on their foot-hills, to look far over the desert to the blue mountains away in Arizona, blue as chalcedony, with the sage-brush desert sweeping grey-blue in between, dotted with tiny cube-crystals of houses, the vast amphitheatre of lofty, indomitable desert, sweeping round to the ponderous Sangre de Cristo, mountains on the east, and coming up flush at the pine-dotted foot-hills of the Rockies! What splendour! Only the tawny eagle could really sail out into the splendour of it all. Leo Stein once wrote to me: It is the most æsthetically-satisfying landscape I know. To me it was much more than that. It had a splendid silent terror, and a vast far-and-wide magnificence which made it way beyond mere æsthetic appreciation. Never is the light more pure and overweening than there, arching with a royalty almost cruel over the hollow, uptilted world. For it is curious that the land which has produced modern political democracy at its highest pitch should give one the greatest sense of overweening, terrible proudness and mercilessness: but so beautiful, God! so beautiful! Those that have spent morning after morning alone there pitched among the pines above the great proud world of desert will know, almost unbearably how beautiful it is, how clear and unquestioned is the might of the day. Just day itself is tremendous there. It is so easy to understand that the Aztecs gave hearts of men to the sun. For the sun is not merely hot or scorching, not at all. It is of a brilliant and unchallengeable purity and haughty serenity which would make one sacrifice the heart to it. Ah, yes, in New Mexico the heart is sacrificed to the sun and the human being is left stark, heartless, but undauntedly religious.

And that was the second revelation out there. I had looked over all the world for something that would strike *me* as religious. The simple piety of some English people, the semi-pagan mystery of some Catholics in southern Italy, the intensity of some Bavarian peasants, the semi-ecstasy of Buddhists or Brahmins: all this had seemed religious all right, as far as the parties concerned were involved, but it didn't involve me. I looked on at their religiousness from the outside. For it is still harder to feel religion at will than to love at will.

I had seen what I felt was a hint of wild religion in the so-called devil dances of a group of naked villagers from the far-remote jungle in Ceylon, dancing at midnight under the torches, glittering wet with sweat on their dark bodies as if they had been gilded, at the celebration of the Pera-hera, in Kandy, given to the Prince of Wales. And the utter dark absorption of these naked men, as they danced with their knees wide apart, suddenly affected me with a *sense* of religion, I *felt* religion for a moment. For religion is an experience, an uncontrollable sensual experience, even more so than love: I use sensual to mean an experience deep down in the senses, inexplicable and inscrutable.

But this experience was fleeting, gone in the curious turmoil of the Pera-hera, and I had no permanent feeling of religion till I came to New Mexico and penetrated into the old human race-experience there. It is curious that it should be in America, of all places, that a European should really experience religion, after touching the old Mediterranean and the East. It is curious that one should get a sense of living religion from the Red Indians, having failed to get it from Hindus or Sicilian Catholics or Cingalese.

Let me make a reservation. I don't stand up to praise the Red Indian as he reveals himself in contact with white civilization. From that angle, I am forced to admit he *may* be thoroughly objectionable. Even my small experience knows it. But also I know he *may* be thoroughly nice, even in his dealings with white men. It's a question of individuals, a good deal, on both sides.

But in this article, I don't want to deal with the everyday or superficial aspect of New Mexico, outside the mucous-paper wrapping, I *want* to go beneath the surface. But therefore the American Indian in his behaviour as an American citizen doesn't really concern me. What concerns me is what he is–or what he seems to me to be, in his ancient, ancient race-self and religious-self.

For the Red Indian seems to me much older than Greeks, or Hindus or any Europeans or even Egyptians. The Red Indian, as a civilized and truly religious man, civilized beyond taboo and totem, as he is in the south, is religious in perhaps the oldest sense, and deepest, of the word. That is to say, he is a remnant of the most deeply religious race still living. So it seems to me.

But again let me protect myself. The Indian who sells you baskets on Albuquerque station or who slinks around Taos plaza may be an utter waster and an indescribably low dog. Personally he may be even less religious than a New York sneak-thief. He may have broken with his tribe, or his tribe itself may have collapsed finally from its old religious integrity, and ceased, really to exist. Then he is only fit for rapid absorption into white civilization, which must make the best of him.

But while a tribe retains its religion and keeps up its religious practices, and while any member of the tribe shares in those practices, then there is a tribal integrity and a living tradition going back far beyond the birth of Christ, beyond the pyramids, beyond Moses. A vast old religion which once swayed the earth lingers in unbroken practice there in New Mexico, older, perhaps, than anything in the world save Australian aboriginal taboo and totem, and that is not yet religion.

You can feel it, the atmosphere of it, around the pueblos. Not, of course, when the place is crowded with sight-seers and motor-cars. But go to Taos pueblo on some brilliant snowy morning and see the white figure on the roof: or come riding through at dusk on some windy evening, when the black skirts of the silent women blow around the white wide boots, and you will feel the old, old root of human consciousness still reaching down to depths we know nothing of: and of which, only too often, we are jealous. It seems it will not be long before the pueblos are uprooted.

But never shall I forget watching the dancers, the men with the fox-skin swaying down from their buttocks, file out at San Geronimo, and the women with seed rattles following. The long, streaming, glistening black hair of the men. Even in ancient Crete long hair was sacred in a man, as it is still in the Indians. Never shall I forget the utter absorption of the dance, so quiet, so steadily, timelessly rhythmic, and silent, with the ceaseless down-tread, always to the earth's centre, the very reverse of the upflow of Dionysiac or Christian ecstasy. Never shall I forget the deep singing of the men at the drum, swelling and sinking, the deepest sound I have heard in all my life, deeper than thunder, deeper than the sound of the Pacific Ocean, deeper than the roar of a deep waterfall: the wonderful deep sound of men calling to the unspeakable depths.

Never shall I forget coming into the little pueblo of San Filipi one sunny morning in spring, unexpectedly, when bloom was on the trees in the perfect little pueblo more old, more utterly peaceful and idyllic than anything in Theocritus, and seeing a little casual dance. Not impressive as a spectacle, only, to me, profoundly moving because of the truly terrifying religious absorption of it.

Never shall I forget the Christmas dances at Taos, twilight, snow, the darkness coming over the great wintry mountains and the lonely pueblo, then suddenly, again, like dark calling to dark, the deep Indian cluster-singing around the drum, wild and awful, suddenly rousing on the last dusk as the procession starts. And then the bonfires leaping suddenly in pure spurts of high flame, columns of sudden flame forming an alley for the procession.

Never shall I forget the khiva of birch-trees, away in the Apaché country, in Arizona this time, the tepees and flickering fires, the neighing of horses unseen under the huge dark night, and the Apaches all abroad, in their silent moccasined feet: and in the khiva, beyond a little fire, the old man reciting, reciting in the unknown Apache speech, in the strange wild Indian voice that re-echoes away back to before the Flood, reciting apparently the traditions and legends of the tribe, going on and on, while the young men, the *braves* of today, wandered in, listened, and wandered away again, overcome with the power and majesty of that utterly old tribal voice, yet uneasy with their half-adherence to the modern civilization, the two things in contact. And one of these *braves* shoved his face under my hat, in the night, and stared with his glittering eyes close to mine. He'd have killed me then and there, had he dared. He didn't dare: and I knew it: and he knew it.

Never shall I forget the Indian races, when the young men, even the boys, run naked, smeared with white earth and stuck with bits of eagle fluff for the swiftness of the heavens, and the old men brush them with eagle feathers, to give them power. And they run in the strange hurling fashion of the primitive world, hurled forward, not making speed deliberately. And the race is not for victory. It is not a contest. There is no competition. It is a great cumulative effort. The tribe this day is adding up its male energy and exerting it to the utmost–for what? To get power, to get strength: to come, by sheer cumulative, hurling effort of the bodies of men, into contact with the great cosmic source of vitality which gives strength, power, energy to the men who can grasp it, energy for the zeal of attainment.

It was a vast old religion, greater than anything we know: more starkly and nakedly religious. There is no God, no conception of a god. All is god. But it is not the pantheism we are accustomed to, which expresses itself as "God is everywhere, God is in everything." In the oldest religion, everything was alive, not supernaturally but naturally alive. There were only deeper and deeper streams of life, vibrations of life more and more vast. So rocks were alive, but a mountain had a deeper, vaster life than a rock, and it was much harder for a man to bring his spirit, or his energy, into contact with the life of the mountain, and so draw strength from the mountain, as from a great standing well of life, than it was to come into contact with the rock. And he had to put forth a great religious effort. For the whole life-effort of man was to get his life into direct contact with the elemental life of the cosmos, mountain-life, cloud-life, thunder-life, air-life, earth-life, sun-life. To come into immediate *felt* contact, and so derive energy, power, and a dark sort of joy. This effort into sheer naked contact, *without an intermediary or mediator,* is the root meaning of religion, and at the sacred races the runners hurled themselves in a terrible cumulative effort, through the air, to come at last into naked contact with the very life of the air, which is the life of the clouds, and so of the rain.

It was a vast and pure religion, without idols or images, even mental ones. It is the oldest religion, a cosmic religion the same for all peoples, not broken up into specific gods or saviours or systems. It is the religion which precedes the god-concept, and is therefore greater and deeper than any god-religion.

And it lingers still, for a little while, in New Mexico: but long enough to have been a revelation to me. And the Indian, however objectionable he may be on occasion, has still some of the strange beauty and pathos of the religion that brought him forth and is now shedding him away into oblivion. When Trinidad, the Indian boy, and I planted corn at the ranch, my soul paused to see his brown hands softly moving the earth over the maize in pure ritual. He was back in his old religious self, and the ages stood still. Ten minutes later he was making a fool of himself with the horses. Horses were never part of the Indian's religious life, never would be. He hasn't a tithe of the feeling for them that he has for a bear, for example. So horses don't like Indians.

But there it is: the newest democracy ousting the oldest religion! And once the oldest religion is ousted, one feels the democracy and all its paraphernalia will collapse, and the oldest religion, which comes down to us from man's pre-war days, will start again. The sky-scraper will scatter on the winds like thistledown, and the genuine America, the America of New Mexico, will start on its course again. This is an interregnum.

III

Love, Sex, Men, and Women

LOVE

ALL THERE

MAKING LOVE TO MUSIC

WOMEN ARE SO COCKSURE

PORNOGRAPHY AND OBSCENITY

WE NEED ONE ANOTHER

THE REAL THING

NOBODY LOVES ME

LOVE

Love is the happiness of the world. But happiness is not the whole of fulfilment. Love is a coming together. But there can be no coming together without an equivalent going asunder. In love, all things unite in a oneness of joy and praise. But they could not unite unless they were previously apart. And, having united in a whole circle of unity, they can go no further in love. The motion of love, like a tide, is fulfilled in this instance; there must be an ebb.

So that the coming together depends on the going apart; the systole depends on the diastole; the flow depends upon the ebb. These can never be love universal and unbroken. The sea can never rise to high tide over all the globe at once. The undisputed reign of love can never be.

Because love is strictly a travelling. "It is better to travel than to arrive," somebody has said. This is the essence of unbelief. It is a belief in absolute love, when love is by nature relative. It is a belief in the means, but not in the end. It is strictly a belief in force, for love is a unifying force.

How shall we believe in force? Force is instrumental and functional; it is neither a beginning nor an end. We travel in order to arrive; we do not travel in order to travel. At least, such travelling is mere futility. We travel in order to arrive.

And love is a travelling, a motion, a speed of coming together. Love is the force of creation. But all force, spiritual or physical, has its polarity, its positive and its negative. All things that fall, fall by gravitation to the earth. But has not the earth, in the opposite of gravitation, cast off the moon and held her at bay in our heavens during all the æons of time?

So with love. Love is the hastening gravitation of spirit towards spirit, and body towards body, in the joy of creation. But if all be united in one bond of love, then there is no more love. And therefore, for those who are in love with love, to travel is better than to arrive. For in arriving one passes beyond love, or, rather, one encompasses love in a new transcendence. To arrive is the supreme joy after all our travelling.

The bond of love! What worse bondage can we conceive than the bond of love? It is an attempt to wall in the high tide; it is a will to arrest the spring, never to let May dissolve into June, never to let the hawthorn petal fall for the berrying.

This has been our idea of immortality, this infinite of love, love universal and triumphant. And what is this but a prison and a bondage? What is eternity but the endless passage of time? What is infinity but an endless progressing through space? Eternity, infinity, our great ideas of rest and arrival, what are they but ideas of endless travelling? Eternity is the endless travelling through time, infinity is the endless travelling through space; no more, however we try to argue it. And immortality, what is it, in our idea, but an endless continuing in the same sort? A continuing, a living for ever, a lasting and enduring for ever—what is this but travelling? An assumption into heaven, a becoming one with God—what is this, likewise, but a projection into the infinite? And how is the infinite an arrival? The infinite is no arrival. When we come to find exactly what we mean by God, by the infinite, by our immortality, it is a meaning of endless continuing in the same line and in the same sort, endless travelling in one direction. This is infinity, endless travelling in one direction. And the God of Love is our idea of the progression *ad infinitum* of the force of love. Infinity is no arrival. It is as much a cul-de-sac as is the bottomless pit. And what is the infinity of love but a cul-de-sac or a bottomless pit?

Love is a progression towards the goal. Therefore it is a progression away from the opposite goal. Love travels heavenwards. What then does love depart from? Hellwards, what is there? Love is at last a positive infinite. What then is the negative infinite? Positive and negative infinite are the same, since there is only one infinite. How then will it matter whether we travel heavenwards, *ad infinitum,* or in the opposite direction, to infinity. Since the infinity obtained is the same in either case, the infinite of pure homogeneity, which is nothingness, or everythingness, it does not matter which.

Infinity, the infinite, is no goal. It is a cul-de-sac, or, in another sense, it is the bottomless pit. To fall down the bottomless pit is to travel for ever. And a pleasant-walled cul-de-sac may be a perfect heaven. But to arrive in a sheltered, paradisiacal cul-de-sac of peace and unblemished happiness, this will not satisfy us. And to fall for ever down the bottomless pit of progression, this will not do either.

Love is not a goal; it is only a travelling. Likewise death is not a goal; it is a travelling asunder into elemental chaos. And from the elemental chaos all is cast forth again into creation. Therefore death also is but a cul-de-sac, a melting-pot.

There is a goal, but the goal is neither love nor death. It is a goal neither infinite nor eternal. It is the realm of calm delight, it is the other-kingdom of bliss. We are like a rose, which is a miracle of pure centrality, pure absolved equilibrium. Balanced in perfection in the midst of time and space, the rose is perfect in the realm of perfection, neither temporal nor spatial, but absolved by the quality of perfection, pure immanence of absolution.

We are creatures of time and space. But we are like a rose; we accomplish perfection, we arrive in the absolute. We are creatures of time and space. And we are at once creatures of pure transcendence, absolved from time and space, perfected in the realm of the absolute, the other-world of bliss.

And love, love is encompassed and surpassed. Love always has been encompassed and surpassed by the fine lovers. We are like a rose, a perfect arrival.

Love is manifold, it is not of one sort only. There is the love between man and woman, sacred and profane. There is Christian love, "thou shalt love thy neighbour as thyself." And there is the love of God. But always love is a joining together.

Only in the conjunction of man and woman has love kept a duality of meaning. Sacred love and profane love, they are opposed, and yet they are both love. The love between man and woman is the greatest and most complete passion the world will ever see, because it is dual, because it is of two opposing kinds. The love between man and woman is the perfect heart-beat of life, systole, diastole.

Sacred love is selfless, seeking not its own. The lover serves his beloved and seeks perfect communion of oneness with her. But whole love between man and woman is sacred and profane together. Profane love seeks its own. I seek my own in the beloved, I wrestle with her to wrest it from her. We are not clear, we are mixed and mingled. I am in the beloved also, and she is in me. Which should not be, for this is confusion and chaos. Therefore I will gather myself complete and free from the beloved, she shall single herself out in utter contradistinction to me. There is twilight in our souls, neither light nor dark. The light must draw itself together in purity, the dark must stand on the other hand; they must be two complete in opposition, neither one partaking of the other, but each single in its own stead.

We are like a rose. In the pure passion for oneness, in the pure passion for distinctness and separateness, a dual passion of unutterable separation and lovely conjunction of the two, the new configuration takes place, the transcendence, the two in their perfect singleness, transported into one surpassing heaven of a rose-blossom.

But the love between a man and a woman, when it is whole, is dual. It is the melting into pure communion, and it is the friction of sheer sensuality, both. In pure communion I become whole in love. And in pure, fierce passion of sensuality I am burned into essentiality. I am driven from the matrix into sheer separate distinction. I become my single self, inviolable and unique, as the gems were perhaps once driven into themselves out of the confusion of earths. The woman and I, we are the confusion of earths. Then in the fire of their extreme sensual love, in the friction of intense, destructive flames, I am destroyed and reduced to her essential otherness. It is a destructive fire, the profane love. But it is the only fire that will purify us into singleness, fuse us from the chaos into our own unique gem-like separateness of being.

All whole love between man and woman is thus dual, a love which is the motion of melting, fusing together into oneness, and a love which is the intense, frictional, and sensual gratification of being burnt down, burnt apart into separate clarity of being, unthinkable otherness and separateness. But not all love between man and woman is whole. It may be all gentle, the merging into oneness, like St. Francis and St. Clare, or Mary of Bethany and Jesus. There may be no separateness discovered, no singleness won, no unique otherness admitted. This is a half love, what is called sacred love. And this is the love which knows the purest happiness. On the other hand, the love may be all a lovely battle of sensual gratification, the beautiful but deadly counterposing of male against female, as Tristan and Isolde. These are the lovers that top the summit of pride, they go with the grandest banners, they are the gem-like beings, he pure male singled and separated out in superb jewel-like isolation of arrogant manhood, she purely woman, a lily balanced in rocking pride of beauty and perfume of womanhood. This is the profane love, that ends in flamboyant and lacerating tragedy when the two which are so singled out are torn finally apart by death. But if profane love ends in piercing tragedy, none the less the sacred love ends in a poignant yearning and exquisite submissive grief. St. Francis dies and leaves St. Clare to her pure sorrow.

There must be two in one, always two in one—the sweet love

of communion and the fierce, proud love of sensual fulfilment, both together in one love. And then we are like a rose. We surpass even love, love is encompassed and surpassed. We are two who have a pure connexion. We are two, isolated like gems in our unthinkable otherness. But the rose contains and transcends us, we are one rose, beyond.

The Christian love, the brotherly love, this is always sacred. I love my neighbour as myself. What then? I am enlarged, I surpass myself, I become whole in mankind. In the whole of perfect humanity I am whole. I am the microcosm, the epitome of the great microcosm. I speak of the perfectibility of man. Man can be made perfect in love, he can become a creature of love alone. Then humanity shall be one whole of love. This is the perfect future for those who love their neighbours as themselves.

But, alas! however much I may be the microcosm, the exemplar of brotherly love, there is in me this necessity to separate and distinguish myself into gem-like singleness, distinct and apart from all the rest, proud as a lion, isolated as a star. This is a necessity within me. And as this necessity is unfulfilled, it becomes stronger and stronger and it becomes dominant.

Then I shall hate the self that I am, powerfully and profoundly shall I hate this microcosm that I have become, this epitome of mankind. I shall hate myself with madness the more I persist in adhering to my achieved self of brotherly love. Still I shall persist in representing a whole loving humanity, until the unfulfilled passion for singleness drives me into action. Then I shall hate my neighbour as I hate myself. And then, woe betide my neighbour and me! Whom the gods wish to destroy they first make mad. And this is how we become mad, by being impelled into activity by the subconscious reaction against the self we maintain, without ever ceasing to maintain this detested self. We are bewildered, dazed. In the name of brotherly love we rush into stupendous blind activities of brotherly hate. We are made mad by the split, the duality in ourselves. The gods wish to destroy us because we serve them too well. Which is the end of brotherly love, *liberté, fraternité, égalité*. How can there be liberty when I am not free to be other than fraternal and equal? I must be free to be separate and unequal in the finest sense, if I am to be free. *Fraternité* and *égalité,* these are tyranny of tyrannies.

There must be brotherly love, a wholeness of humanity. But there must also be pure, separate individuality, separate and proud as a lion or a hawk. There must be both. In the duality lies fulfilment. Man must act in concert with man, creatively and happily. This is greatest happiness. But man must also act separately and distinctly, apart from every other man, single and self-responsible and proud with unquenchable pride, moving for himself without reference to his neighbour. These two movements are opposite, yet they do not negate each other. We have understanding. And if we understand, then we balance perfectly between the two motions, we are single, isolated individuals, we are a great concordant humanity, both, and then the rose of perfection transcends us, the rose of the world which has never yet blossomed, but which will blossom from us when we begin to understand both sides and to live in both directions, freely and without fear, following the inmost desires of our body and spirit, which arrive to us out of the unknown.

Lastly, there is the love of God; we become whole with God. But God as we know Him is either infinite love or infinite pride and power, always one or the other, Christ or Jehovah, always one half excluding the other. Therefore, God is for ever jealous. If we love one God, we must hate this one sooner or later, and choose the other. This is the tragedy of religious experience. But the Holy Spirit, the unknowable, is single and perfect for us.

There is that which we cannot love, because it surpasses either love or hate. There is the unknown and the unknowable which propounds all creation. This we cannot love, we can only accept it as a term of our own limitation and ratification. We can only know that from the unknown, profound desires enter in upon us, and that the fulfilling of these desires is the fulfilling of creation. We know that the rose comes to blossom. We know that we are incipient with blossom. It is our business to go as we are impelled, with faith and pure spontaneous morality, knowing that the rose blossoms, and taking that knowledge for sufficient.

ALL THERE

What you want to do, said Jimmy to Ciss, is to forget yourself.–So I can think of you all the time, I suppose, said Cecilia.–Well, not necessarily all the time. Now and then would do. But it'd do you a lot of good to forget yourself, persisted Jim.–I agree, snapped Cecilia. But why don't you make me? Why don't you give a girl a bit of a lift? You don't exactly sweep me off my feet, or lift me clean out of myself, I must say!–Dash it all, a fellow might as well try to sweep the Albert Memorial off its feet. Seems to me you're cemented in! cried the exasperated Jim.–In what?–Eh?–What am I cemented in? demanded Cecilia.–Oh, how should I know? In your own idea of yourself! cried he, desperately.

Silence! One of those fatal and Egyptian silences that can intervene between the fair sex and the unfair.

I should love to forget myself, if I were allowed, resumed Cecilia.–Who prevents you?–You do!–I wish I knew how.–You throw me back on myself every time.–Throw you back on yourself! cried the mortified Jim. Why, I've never seen you come an inch forward, away from yourself, yet.–I'm always coming forward to you, and you throw me back on myself, she declared.–Coming forward to me! he cried, in enraged astonishment. I wish you'd tell me when the move begins.–You wouldn't see it, if I hooted like a bus.–I believe you, he groaned, giving up.

The gulf yawned between them. I, miserable ostrich, hid my head in the sands of the *Times*. The clock had the impertinence to tick extra cheerfully.

Don't you think it's a boy's duty to make a girl forget herself? she asked of me, mercilessly.–If there's a good band, said I.–Precisely! cried Jim. The minute the saxophone lets on, she's as right as rain.–Of course! she said. Because then I don't have to forget myself, I'm all there.–We looked at her in some astonishment, and Jim, being a cub, did the obvious.–Do you mean to say that the rest of the time you're not all there? he asked, with flat-footed humour.–Witty boy! she said witheringly. No, naturally I leave my wits at home, when I go out with you.–Sounds like it! said Jim.

Now look here! said I. Do you mean to say you only feel quite yourself when you're dancing?–Not always then, she retorted.–And never any other time?–Never! The word fell on top of us with a smack, and left us flat. Oh, go on! cried Jimmy. What about the other day at Cromer?–What about it? said she.–Ah! What were the wild waves saying! cried he knowingly.–You may ask me, she replied. They hummed and hawed, but they never got a word out, as far as I'm concerned.–Do you mean to say you weren't happy! cried he, mortified.–I certainly never forgot myself, not for a moment, she replied. He made a gesture of despair.

But what do you mean? said I. Do you mean you were never all there, or that you were too much there? Which? She became suddenly attentive, and Jimmy looked at her mockingly, with a sort of got-her-on-toast look.–Why? she drawled languidly. I suppose when you can't forget yourself, it's because some of you's left out, and you feel it.–So you are only painfully aware of yourself when you're not altogether yourself–like a one-legged man trying to rub his missing toes, because they ache? said I. She pondered a moment. –I suppose that's about the size of it, she admitted.–And nothing of you is left out in jazz? Jimmy demanded.–Not in good jazz, if the boy can dance, she replied.–Well, I think you'll grant me that, said Jim. To which she did not reply.

So it takes a jazz band to get you all there? I asked.–Apparently, she replied.–Then why aren't you content to be only half there, till the band toots up?–Oh, I am. It's only friend James gets the wind up about the missing sections.–Hang it all! cried James—— But I held up my hand like a high-church clergyman, and hushed him off.–Then why don't you marry a boy who will prefer you only half there? I demanded of her.–What! marry one of those coat-hangers? You see me! she said, with cool contempt.

Then the point, said I, is that Jimmy leaves some of you out, and so he never sweeps you off your feet. And so you can't forget yourself, because part of you isn't embraced by Jimmy, and that part stands aside and gibbers.–Gibbers is the right word, like a lucky monkey! said Jim spitefully.–Better a whole monkey than half a man! said she.–So what's to be done about it? said I. Why not think about it? Which bit of the woman does Jimmy leave out of his manly embrace?–Oh, about nine-tenths of her! said she.–Nine-tenths of her being too conceited for nuts! said Jimmy.

Look here! said I. This is vulgar altercation.–What do you expect, with a whipper-snapper like Jimmy? said she.–My stars! if that two-stepping Trissie says another word——! cried Jim.

Peace! said I. And give the last word to me, for I am the latter-day Aristotle, who has more to say even than a woman. Next time,

O James, when you have your arms, both of them, around Cecilia—— Which will be never! said Cecilia——then, I continued, you must say to yourself, I have here but one-tenth of my dear Ciss, the remaining nine-tenths being mysteriously elsewhere. Yet this one-tenth is a pretty good armful, not to say handful, and will do me very nicely; so forward the light brigade! And you, Cecilia, under the same circumstance, will say to yourself: Alas so little of me is concerned, that why should I concern myself? Jimmy gets his tenth. Let's see him make the most of it.

MAKING LOVE TO MUSIC

"To me, dancing," said Romeo, "is just making love to music."

"That's why you never will dance with me, I suppose," replied Juliet.

"Well, you know, you are a bit too much of an individual."

It is a curious thing, but the ideas of one generation become the instincts of the next. We are all of us, largely, the embodied ideas of our grandmothers, and, without knowing it, we behave as such. It is odd that the grafting works so quickly, but it seems to. Let the ideas change rapidly, and there follows a correspondingly rapid change in humanity. We become what we think. Worse still, we have become what our grandmothers thought. And our children's children will become the lamentable things that we are thinking. Which is the psychological visiting of the sins of the fathers upon the children. For we do not become just the lofty or beautiful thoughts of our grandmothers. Alas no! We are the embodiment of the most potent ideas of our progenitors, and these ideas are mostly private ones, not to be admitted in public, but to be transmitted as instincts and as the dynamics of behaviour to the third and fourth generation. Alas for the thing that our grandmothers brooded over in secret, and willed in private. That thing are we.

What did they wish and will? One thing is certain: they wished to be made love to, to music. They wished man were not a coarse creature, jumping to his goal, and finished. They wanted heavenly strains to resound, while he held their hand, and a new musical movement to burst forth, as he put his arm round their waist. With infinite variations the music was to soar on, from level to level of love-making, in a delicious dance, the two things inextricable, the two persons likewise.

To end, of course, before the so-called consummation of love-making, which, to our grandmothers in their dream, and therefore to us in actuality, is the grand anti-climax. Not a consummation, but a humiliating anti-climax.

This is the so-called act of love itself, the actual knuckle of the whole bone of contention: a humiliating anti-climax. The bone of contention, of course, is sex. Sex is very charming and very delightful, so long as you make love to music, and you tread the clouds with Shelley, in a two-step. But to come at last to the grotesque bathos of capitulation: no, sir! Nay-nay!

Even a man like Maupassant, an apparent devotee of sex, says the same thing: and Maupassant is grandfather, or great-grandfather, to very many of us. Surely, he says, the act of copulation is the Creator's cynical joke against us. To have created in us all these beautiful and noble sentiments of love, to set the nightingale and all the heavenly spheres singing, merely to throw us into this grotesque posture, to perform this humiliating act, is a piece of cynicism worthy, not of a benevolent Creator, but of a mocking demon.

Poor Maupassant, there is the clue to his own catastrophe! He wanted to make love to music. And he realized, with rage, that copulate to music you cannot. So he divided himself against himself, and damned his eyes in disgust, then copulated all the more.

We, however, his grandchildren, are shrewder. Man *must* make love to music, and woman *must* be made love to, to a string and saxophone accompaniment. It is our inner necessity. Because our grandfathers, and especially our great-grandfathers, left the music most severely out of their copulations. So now we leave the copulation most severely out of our musical love-making. We *must* make love to music: it is our grandmothers' dream, become an inward necessity in us, an unconscious motive force. Copulate you cannot, to music. So cut out that part, and solve the problem.

The popular modern dances, far from being "sexual," are distinctly anti-sexual. But there, again, we must make a distinction. We should say, the modern jazz and tango and Charleston, far from being an incitement to copulation, are in direct antagonism to copulation. Therefore it is all nonsense for the churches to raise their voice against dancing, against "making love to music." Because the Church, and society at large, has no particular antagonism to sex. It would be ridiculous, for sex is so large and all-embracing that the religious passion itself is largely sexual. But, as they say, "sublimated." This is the great recipe for sex: only sublimate it! Imagine the quicksilver heated and passing off in weird, slightly poisonous vapour, instead of heavily rolling together and fusing: and there you have the process: sublimation: making love to music! Morality has really no quarrel at all with "sublimated" sex. Most "nice" things are "sublimated sex." What morality hates, what the Church hates, what modern *mankind* hates—for what, after all, is "morality" except the instinctive revulsion of the majority?—is just copulation. The modern youth especially just have an instinctive aversion from copulation. They love sex. But they inwardly loathe copulation, even when they play at it. As for playing at it, what else are they to do, given the toys? But they don't like it. They do it in a sort of self-spite. And they turn away, with disgust and relief, from this bed-ridden act, to make love once more to music.

And really, surely this is all to the good. If the young don't really *like* copulation, then they are safe. As for marriage, they will marry, according to their grandmothers' dream, for quite other reasons. Our grandfathers, or great-grandfathers, married crudely and unmusically, for copulation. That was the actuality. So the dream was all of music. The dream was the mating of two souls, to the faint chiming of the Seraphim. We, the third and fourth generation, we are the dream made flesh. They dreamed of a marriage with all things gross—meaning especially copulation—left out, and only the pure harmony of equality and intimate companionship remaining. And the young live out the dream. They marry: they copulate in a perfunctory and half-disgusted fashion, merely to show they can do it. And so they have children. But the marriage is made to music, the gramophone and the wireless orchestrate each small domestic act, and keep up the jazzing jig of connubial felicity, a felicity of companionship, equality, forbearance, and mutual sharing of everything the married couple have in common. Marriage set to music! The worn-out old serpent in this musical Eden of domesticity is the last, feeble instinct for copulation, which drives the married couple to clash upon the boring organic differences in one another, and prevents them from being twin souls in almost identical bodies. But we are wise, and soon learn to leave the humiliating act out altogether. It is the only wisdom.

We are such stuff as our grandmothers' dreams were made on, and our little life is rounded by a band.

The thing you wonder, as you watch the modern dancers making love to music, in a dance-hall, is what kind of dances will our children's children dance? Our mothers' mothers danced quadrilles and sets of Lancers, and the waltz was almost an indecent thing to them. Our mothers' mothers' mothers danced minuets and Roger de Coverleys, and smart and bouncing country-dances which worked up the blood and danced a man nearer and nearer to copulation.

But lo! even while she was being whirled round in the dance, our great-grandmother was dreaming of soft and throbbing music, and the arms of "one person," and the throbbing and sliding unison of this one more elevated person, who would never coarsely bounce her towards bed and copulation, but would slide on with her for ever, down the dim and sonorous vistas, making love without end to music without end, and leaving out entirely that disastrous, music-less full-stop of copulation, the end of ends.

So she dreamed, our great-grandmother, as she crossed hands and was flung around, and buffeted and busked towards bed, and the bouncing of the *bête à deux dos*. She dreamed of men that were only embodied souls, not tiresome and gross males, lords and masters. She dreamed of "one person" who was all men in one, universal, and beyond narrow individualism.

So that now, the great-granddaughter is made love to by all men —to music—as if it were one man. To music, all men, as if it were one man, make love to her, and she sways in the arms, not of an individual, but of the modern species. It is wonderful. And the modern man makes love, to music, to all women, as if she were one woman. All woman, as if she were one woman! It is almost like Baudelaire making love to the vast thighs of Dame Nature herself, except that that dream of our great-grandfather is still too copulative, though all-embracing.

But what is the dream that is simmering at the bottom of the soul of the modern young woman as she slides to music across the floor, in the arms of the species, or as she waggles opposite the species, in the Charleston? If she is content, there is no dream. But woman is never content. If she were content, the Charleston and the Black Bottom would not oust the tango.

She is not content. She is even less content, in the morning after the night before, than was her great-grandmother, who had been bounced by copulatory attentions. She is even less content; therefore her dream, though not risen yet to consciousness, is even more devouring and more rapidly subversive.

What is her dream, this slender, tender lady just out of her teens, who is varying the two-step with the Black Bottom? What can her dream be? Because what her dream is, that her children, and my children, or children's children, will become. It is the very ovum of the future soul, as my dream is the sperm.

There is not much left for her to dream of, because whatever she wants she can have. All men, or no men, this man or that, she has the choice, for she has no lord and master. Sliding down the endless avenues of music, having an endless love endlessly made to her, she has this too. If she wants to be bounced into copulation, at a dead end, she can have that too: just to prove how monkeyish it is, and what a fumbling in the cul-de-sac.

Nothing is denied her, so there is nothing to want. And without desire, even dreams are lame. Lame dreams! Perhaps she has lame dreams, and wishes, last wish of all, she had no dreams at all.

But while life lasts, and is an affair of sleeping and waking, this is the one wish that will never be granted. From dreams no man escapeth, no woman either. Even the little blonde who is preferred by gentlemen has a dream somewhere, if she, and we, and he, did but know it. Even a dream beyond emeralds and dollars.

What is it? What is the lame and smothered dream of the lady? Whatever it is, she will never know: not till somebody has told it her, and then gradually, and after a great deal of spiteful repudiation, she will recognize it, and it will pass into her womb.

Myself, I do not know what the frail lady's dream may be. But depend upon one thing, it will be something very different from the present business. The dream and the business!—an eternal antipathy. So the dream, whatever it may be, will *not* be "making love to music." It will be something else.

Perhaps it will be the re-capturing of a dream that started in mankind, and never finished, was never fully unfolded. The thought occurred to me suddenly when I was looking at the remains of paintings on the walls of Etruscan tombs at Tarquinia. There the painted women dance, in their transparent linen with heavier, coloured borders, opposite the naked-limbed men, in a splendour and an abandon which is not at all abandoned. There is a great beauty in them, as of life which has not finished. The dance is Greek, if you like, but not finished off like the Greek dancing. The beauty is not so pure, if you will, as the Greek beauty; but also it is more ample, not so narrowed. And there is not the slight element of abstraction, of inhumanity, which underlies all Greek expression, the tragic will.

The Etruscans, at least before the Romans smashed them, do not seem to have been tangled up with tragedy, as the Greeks were from the first. There seems to have been a peculiar large carelessness about them, very human and non-moral. As far as one can judge, they never said: certain acts are immoral, just because we say so! They seem to have had a strong feeling for taking life sincerely as a pleasant thing. Even death was a gay and lively affair.

Moralists will say: Divine law wiped them out. The answer to that is, divine law wipes everything out in time, even itself. And if the smashing power of the all-trampling Roman is to be identified with divine law, then all I can do is to look up another divinity.

No, I do believe that the unborn dream at the bottom of the soul of the shingled, modern young lady is this Etruscan young woman of mine, dancing with such abandon opposite her naked-limbed, strongly dancing young man, to the sound of the double flute. They are wild with a dance that is heavy and light at the same time, and not a bit anti-copulative, yet not bouncingly copulative either.

That was another nice thing about the Etruscans: there was a phallic symbol everywhere, so everybody was used to it, and they no doubt all offered it small offerings, as the source of inspiration. Being part of the everyday life, there was no need to get it on the brain, as we tend to do.

And apparently the men, the men slaves at least, went gaily and jauntily round with no clothes on at all, and being therefore of a good brown colour, wore their skin for livery. And the Etruscan ladies thought nothing of it. Why should they? We think nothing of a naked cow, and we still refrain from putting our pet-dogs into pants or petticoats: marvellous to relate: but then, our ideal is Liberty, after all! So if the slave was stark-naked, who gaily piped to the lady as she danced, and if her partner was three-parts naked, and herself nothing but a transparency, well, nobody thought anything about it; there was nothing to shy off from, and all the fun was in the dance.

There it is, the delightful quality of the Etruscan dance. They are neither making love to music, to avoid copulation, nor are they bouncing towards copulation with a brass band accompaniment. They are just dancing a dance with the elixir of life. And if they have made a little offering to the stone phallus at the door, it is because when one is full of life one is full of possibilities, and the phallus gives life. And if they have made an offering also to the queer ark of the female symbol, at the door of a woman's tomb, it is because the womb too is the source of life, and a great fountain of dance-movements.

It is we who have narrowed the dance down to two movements: either bouncing towards copulation, or sliding and shaking and waggling, to elude it. Surely it is ridiculous to make love to music, and to music to be made love to! Surely the music is to dance to! And surely the modern young woman feels this, somewhere deep inside.

To the music one should dance, and dancing, dance. The Etruscan young woman is going gaily at it, after two-thousand-five-hundred years. She is not making love to music, nor is the dark-limbed youth, her partner. She is just dancing her very soul into existence, having made an offering on one hand to the lively phallus of man, on the other hand, to the shut womb-symbol of woman, and put herself on real good terms with both of them. So she is quite serene, and dancing herself as a very fountain of motion and of life, the young man opposite her dancing himself the same, in contrast and balance, with just the double flute to whistle round their naked heels.

And I believe this is, or will be, the dream of our pathetic, music-shunned young girl of today, and the substance of her children's children, unto the third and fourth generation.

WOMEN ARE SO COCKSURE

My destiny has been cast among cocksure women. Perhaps when man begins to doubt himself, woman, who should be nice and peacefully hen-sure, becomes instead insistently cocksure. She develops convictions, or she catches them. And then woe betide everybody.

I began with my mother. She was convinced about some things: one of them being that a man ought not to drink beer. This conviction developed from the fact, naturally, that my father drank beer. He sometimes drank too much. He sometimes boozed away the money necessary for the young family. Therefore the drinking of beer became to my mother the cardinal sin. No other sin was so red, so red-hot. She was like a bull before this red sin. When my father came in tipsy, she saw scarlet.

We dear children were trained never, *never* to fall into this sin. We were sent to the Band of Hope, and told harrowing stories of drunkenness; we wept bitterly over the heroic youth who had taken the pledge and sworn never never to touch nor to taste, and who clenched his teeth when his cruel comrades tried to force beer down his throat: but alas, he had lost one of his front teeth, and through this narrow gap beer trickled even down his gullet. So he died of a broken heart.

My mother, though a woman with a real sense of humour, kept her face straight and stern while we recounted this fearsome episode. And we were rigidly sent to the Band of Hope.

Years passed. Children became young men. It was evident my mother's sons were not going to hell down the beer-mug: they didn't care enough about it. My mother relaxed. She would even watch with pleasure while I drank a glass of ale, the fearful enemy, at supper. There was no longer a serpent in the glass, dash it down, dash it down.

"But, mother, if you don't mind if I drink a little beer, why did you mind so much about my father?"

"You don't realize what I had to put up with."

"Yes, I do. But you made it seem a sin, a horror. You terrified our lives with the bogy of strong drink. You were absolutely sure it was utter evil. Why isn't it utter evil any more?"

"You're different from your father——"

But she was just a little shame-faced. Life changes our feelings.

We may get mellower, or we may get harder, as time goes on. But we change. What outrages our feelings in the twenties will probably not outrage them in the fifties, not at all. And the change is much more striking in women than in men. Particularly in those women who are the moral force in the household, as my mother was.

My mother spoilt her life with her moral frenzy against John Barleycorn. To be sure she had occasion to detest the alcoholic stuff. But why the moral frenzy? It made a tragedy out of what was only a nuisance. And at fifty, when the best part of life was gone, she realized it. And then what would she not have given to have her life again, her young children, her tipsy husband, and a proper natural insouciance, to get the best out of it all. When woman tries to be too much mistress of fate, particularly of other people's fates, what a tragedy!

As sure as a woman has the whip-hand over her destiny and the destinies of those near her, so sure will she make a mess of her own destiny, and a muddle of the others'. And just as inevitably as the age of fifty will come upon her, so inevitably will come the realization that she has got herself into a hole. *She ought not to have been so cocksure.*

Beware, oh modern women, the age of fifty. It is then that the play is over, the theatre shuts, and you are turned out into the night. If you have been making a grand show of your life, all off your own bat, and being grand mistress of your destiny, all triumphant, the clock of years tolls fifty, and the play is over. You've had your turn on the stage. Now you must go, out into the common night, where you may or may not have a true place of shelter.

It is dangerous for anybody to be cocksure. But it is peculiarly dangerous for a woman. Being basically a creature of emotion, she will direct all her emotion force full on to what seems to her the grand aim of existence. For twenty, thirty years she may rush ahead to the grand goal of existence. And then the age of fifty approaches—the speed slackens—the driving force begins to fail—the grand goal is not only no nearer, it is all too near. It is all round about. It is a waste of unspeakable dreariness.

There were three sisters. One started out to be learned and to give herself to social reform. She was absolutely cocksure about being able to bring the world nearer salvation. The second obstinately decided to live her own life and to be herself. "The aim of my life is to be myself." She was cocksure about what her self was and how to be it. The aim of the third was to gather roses, whilst she might.

She had real good times with her lovers, with her dress-makers, with her husband and her children. All three had everything life could offer.

The age of fifty draws near. All three are in the state of vital bankruptcy of the modern woman of that age. The one is quite cynical about reform, the other begins to realize that the "self" she was so cocksure about doesn't exist, and she wonders what does exist. To the third the world is a dangerous and dirty place, and she doesn't know where to put herself.

Of all things, the most fatal to a woman is to have an aim, and be cocksure about it.

What they are depends, as usual, entirely on the individual. What is pornography to one man is the laughter of genius to another.

The word itself, we are told, means "pertaining to harlots"—the graph of the harlot. But nowadays, what is a harlot? If she was a woman who took money from a man in return for going to bed with him—really, most wives sold themselves, in the past, and plenty of harlots gave themselves, when they felt like it, for nothing. If a woman hasn't got a tiny streak of a harlot in her, she's a dry stick as a rule. And probably most harlots had somewhere a streak of womanly generosity. Why be so cut and dried? The law is a dreary thing, and its judgments have nothing to do with life.

The same with the word *obscene:* nobody knows what it means. Suppose it were derived from *obscena:* that which might not be represented on the stage; how much further are you? None! What is obscene to Tom is not obscene to Lucy or Joe, and really, the meaning of a word has to wait for majorities to decide it. If a play shocks ten people in an audience, and doesn't shock the remaining five hundred, then it is obscene to ten and innocuous to five hundred; hence, the play is not obscene, by majority. But *Hamlet* shocked all the Cromwellian Puritans, and shocks nobody today, and some of Aristophanes shocks everybody today, and didn't galvanize the later Greeks at all, apparently. Man is a changeable beast, and words change their meanings with him, and things are not what they seemed, and what's what becomes what isn't, and if we think we know where we are it's only because we are so rapidly being translated to somewhere else. We have to leave everything to the majority, everything to the majority, everything to the mob, the mob, the mob. They know what is obscene and what isn't, they do. If the lower ten million doesn't know better than the upper ten men, then there's something wrong with mathematics. Take a vote on it! Show hands, and prove it by count! *Vox populi, vox Dei. Odi profanum vulgum! Profanum vulgum.*

So it comes down to this: if you are talking to the mob, the meaning of your words is the mob-meaning, decided by majority. As somebody wrote to me: the American law on obscenity is very plain, and America is going to enforce the law. Quite, my dear, quite, quite, quite! The mob knows all about obscenity. Mild little words that rhyme with spit or farce are the height of obscenity. Supposing a printer put "h" in the place of "p," by mistake, in that mere word spit? Then the great American public knows that this man has committed an obscenity, an indecency, that his act was lewd, and as a compositor he was pornographical. You can't tamper with the great public, British or American. *Vox populi, vox Dei,* don't you know. If you don't we'll let you know it. At the same time, this *vox Dei* shouts with praise over moving-pictures and books and newspaper accounts that seem, to a sinful nature like mine, completely disgusting and obscene. Like a real prude and Puritan, I have to look the other way. When obscenity becomes mawkish, which is its palatable form for the public, and when the *Vox populi, vox Dei* is hoarse with sentimental indecency, then I have to steer away, like a Pharisee, afraid of being contaminated. There is a certain kind of sticky universal pitch that I refuse to touch.

So again, it comes down to this: you accept the majority, the mob, and its decisions, or you don't. You bow down before the *Vox populi, vox Dei,* or you plug your ears not to hear its obscene howl. You perform your antics to please the vast public, *Deus ex machina,* or you refuse to perform for the public at all, unless now and then to pull its elephantine and ignominious leg.

When it comes to the meaning of anything, even the simplest word, then you must pause. Because there are two great categories of meaning, for ever separate. There is mob-meaning, and there is individual meaning. Take even the word *bread.* The mob-meaning is merely: stuff made with white flour into loaves that you eat. But take the individual meaning of the word bread: the white, the brown, the corn-pone, the home-made, the smell of bread just out of the oven, the crust, the crumb, the unleavened bread, the shew-bread, the staff of life, sour-dough bread, cottage loaves, French bread, Viennese bread, black bread, a yesterday's loaf, rye, graham, barley, rolls, *Bretzeln, Kringeln,* scones, damper, matsen—there is no end to it all, and the word bread will take you to the ends of time and space, and far-off down avenues of memory. But this is individual. The word bread will take the individual off on his own journey, and its meaning will be his own meaning, based on his own genuine imagination reactions. And when a word comes to us in its individual character, and starts in us the individual responses, it is great pleasure to us. The American advertisers have discovered this, and some of the cunningest American literature is to be found in advertisements of soap-suds, for example. These advertisements are *almost* prose-poems. They give the word soap-suds a bubbly, shiny individual meaning, which is very skilfully poetic, would, perhaps, be quite poetic to the mind which could forget that the poetry was bait on a hook.

Business is discovering the individual, dynamic meaning of words, and poetry is losing it. Poetry more and more tends to far-fetch its word-meanings, and this results once again in mob-meanings, which arouse only a mob-reaction in the individual. For every man has a mob-self and an individual self, in varying proportions. Some men are almost all mob-self, incapable of imaginative individual responses. The worst specimens of mob-self are usually to be found in the professions, lawyers, professors, clergymen and so on. The business man, much maligned, has a tough outside mob-self, and a scared, floundering yet still alive individual self. The public, which is feeble-minded like an idiot, will never be able to preserve its individual reactions from the tricks of the exploiter. The public is always exploited and always will be exploited. The methods of exploitation merely vary. Today the public is tickled into laying the golden egg. With imaginative words and individual meanings it is tricked into giving the great goose-cackle of mob-acquiescence. *Vox populi, vox Dei.* It has always been so, and will always be so. Why? Because the public has not enough wit to distinguish between mob-meanings and individual meanings. The mass is for ever vulgar, because it can't distinguish between its own original feelings and feelings which are diddled into existence by the exploiter. The public is always profane, because it is controlled from the outside, by the trickster, and never from the inside, by its own sincerity. The mob is always obscene, because it is always second-hand.

Which brings us back to our subject of pornography and obscenity. The reaction to any word may be, in any individual, either a mob-reaction or an individual reaction. It is up to the individual to ask himself: Is my reaction individual, or am I merely reacting from my mob-self?

When it comes to the so-called obscene words, I should say that hardly one person in a million escapes mob-reaction. The first reaction is almost sure to be mob-reaction, mob-indignation, mob-condemnation. And the mob gets no further. But the real individual has second thoughts and says: Am I really shocked? Do I *really* feel outraged and indignant? And the answer of any individual is bound to be: No, I am not shocked, not outraged, nor indignant. I know the word, and take it for what it is, and I am not going to be jockeyed into making a mountain out of a mole-hill, not for all the law in the world.

Now if the use of a few so-called obscene words will startle man or woman out of a mob-habit into an individual state, well and good. And word prudery is so universal a mob-habit that it is time we were startled out of it.

But still we have only tackled obscenity, and the problem of pornography goes even deeper. When a man is startled into his individual self, he still may not be able to know, inside himself, whether Rabelais is or is not pornographic: and over Aretino or even Boccaccio he may perhaps puzzle in vain, torn between different emotions.

One essay on pornography, I remember, comes to the conclusion that pornography in art is that which is calculated to arouse sexual desire, or sexual excitement. And stress is laid on the fact, whether the author or artist *intended* to arouse sexual feelings. It is the old vexed question of intention, become so dull today, when we know how strong and influential our unconscious intentions are. And why a man should be held guilty of his conscious intentions, and innocent of his unconscious intentions, I don't know, since every man is more made up of unconscious intentions than of conscious ones. I am what I am, not merely what I think I am.

However! We take it, I assume, that *pornography* is something base, something unpleasant. In short, we don't like it. And why don't we like it? Because it arouses sexual feelings?

I think not. No matter how hard we may pretend otherwise, most of us rather like a moderate rousing of our sex. It warms us, stimulates us like sunshine on a grey day. After a century or two of Puritanism, this is still true of most people. Only the mob-habit of condemning any form of sex is too strong to let us admit it naturally. And there are, of course, many people who are genuinely repelled by the simplest and most natural stirrings of sexual feeling. But these people are perverts who have fallen into hatred of their fellow men: thwarted, disappointed, unfulfilled people, of whom, alas, our civilization contains so many. And they nearly always enjoy some unsimple and unnatural form of sex excitement, secretly.

Even quite advanced art critics would try to make us believe that any picture or book which had "sex appeal" was *ipso facto* a bad book or picture. This is just canting hypocrisy. Half the great poems, pictures, music, stories of the whole world are great by virtue of the beauty of their sex appeal. Titian or Renoir, the Song of

Solomon or *Jane Eyre,* Mozart or "Annie Laurie," the loveliness is all interwoven with sex appeal, sex stimulus, call it what you will. Even Michelangelo, who rather hated sex, can't help filling the Cornucopia with phallic acorns. Sex is a very powerful, beneficial and necessary stimulus in human life, and we are all grateful when we feel its warm, natural flow through us, like a form of sunshine.

So we can dismiss the idea that sex appeal in art is pornography. It may be so to the grey Puritan, but the grey Puritan is a sick man, soul and body sick, so why should we bother about his hallucinations? Sex appeal, of course, varies enormously. There are endless different kinds, and endless degrees of each kind. Perhaps it may be argued that a mild degree of sex appeal is not pornographical, whereas a high degree is. But this is a fallacy. Boccaccio at his hottest seems to me less pornographical than *Pamela* or *Clarissa Harlowe* or even *Jane Eyre,* or a host of modern books or films which pass uncensored. At the same time Wagner's *Tristan and Isolde* seems to me very near to pornography, and so, even, do some quite popular Christian hymns.

What is it, then? It isn't a question of sex appeal, merely: nor even a question of deliberate intention on the part of the author or artist to arouse sexual excitement. Rabelais sometimes had a deliberate intention, so in a different way, did Boccaccio. And I'm sure poor Charlotte Brontë, or the authoress of *The Sheik,* did not have any deliberate intention to stimulate sex feelings in the reader. Yet I find *Jane Eyre* verging towards pornography and Boccaccio seems to me always fresh and wholesome.

The late British Home Secretary, who prides himself on being a very sincere Puritan, grey, grey in every fibre, said with indignant sorrow in one of his outbursts on improper books: "—and these two young people, who had been perfectly pure up till that time, after reading this book went and had sexual intercourse together!!!" *One up to them!* is all we can answer. But the grey Guardian of British Morals seemed to think that if they had murdered one another, or worn each other to rags of nervous prostration, it would have been much better. The grey disease!

Then what is pornography, after all this? It isn't sex appeal or sex stimulus in art. It isn't even a deliberate intention on the part of the artist to arouse or excite sexual feelings. There's nothing wrong with sexual feelings in themselves, so long as they are straightforward and not sneaking or sly. The right sort of sex stimulus is invaluable to human daily life. Without it the world grows grey.

I would give everybody the gay Renaissance stories to read, they would help to shake off a lot of grey self-importance, which is our modern civilized disease.

But even I would censor genuine pornography, rigorously. It would not be very difficult. In the first place, genuine pornography is almost always underworld, it doesn't come into the open. In the second, you can recognize it by the insult it offers, invariably, to sex, and to the human spirit.

Pornography is the attempt to insult sex, to do dirt on it. This is unpardonable. Take the very lowest instance, the picture post-card sold under hand, by the underworld, in most cities. What I have seen of them have been of an ugliness to make you cry. The insult to the human body, the insult to a vital human relationship! Ugly and cheap they make the human nudity, ugly and degraded they make the sexual act, trivial and cheap and nasty.

It is the same with the books they sell in the underworld. They are either so ugly they make you ill, or so fatuous you can't imagine anybody but a cretin or a moron reading them, or writing them.

It is the same with the dirty limericks that people tell after dinner, or the dirty stories one hears commercial travellers telling each other in a smoke-room. Occasionally there is a really funny one, that redeems a great deal. But usually they are just ugly and repellent, and the so-called "humour" is just a trick of doing dirt on sex.

Now the human nudity of a great many modern people is just ugly and degraded, and the sexual act between modern people is just the same, merely ugly and degrading. But this is nothing to be proud of. It is the catastrophe of our civilization. I am sure no other civilization, not even the Roman, has showed such a vast proportion of ignominious and degraded nudity, and ugly, squalid dirty sex. Because no other civilization has driven sex into the underworld, and nudity to the w.c.

The intelligent young, thank heaven, seem determined to alter in these two respects. They are rescuing their young nudity from the stuffy, pornographical hole-and-corner underworld of their elders, and they refuse to sneak about the sexual relation. This is a change the elderly grey ones of course deplore, but it is in fact a very great change for the better, and a real revolution.

But it is amazing how strong is the will in ordinary, vulgar people, to do dirt on sex. It was one of my fond illusions, when I was young, that the ordinary healthy-seeming sort of men, in railway carriages, or the smoke-room of an hotel or a pullman, were healthy in their feelings and had a wholesome rough devil-may-care attitude towards sex. All wrong! All wrong! Experience teaches that common individuals of this sort have a disgusting attitude towards sex, a disgusting contempt of it, a disgusting desire to insult it. If such fellows have intercourse with a woman, they triumphantly feel that they have done her dirt, and now she is lower, cheaper, more contemptible than she was before.

It is individuals of this sort that tell dirty stories, carry indecent picture post-cards, and know the indecent books. This is the great pornographical class—the really common men-in-the-street and women-in-the-street. They have as great a hate and contempt of sex as the greyest Puritan, and when an appeal is made to them, they are always on the side of the angels. They insist that a film-heroine shall be a neuter, a sexless thing of washed-out purity. They insist that real sex-feeling shall only be shown by the villain or villainess, low lust. They find a Titian or a Renoir really indecent, and they don't want their wives and daughters to see it.

Why? Because they have the grey disease of sex-hatred, coupled with the yellow disease of dirt-lust. The sex functions and the excrementory functions in the human body work so close together, yet they are, so to speak, utterly different in direction. Sex is a creative flow, the excrementory flow is towards dissolution, de-creation, if we may use such a word. In the really healthy human being the distinction between the two is instant, our profoundest instincts are perhaps our instincts of opposition between the two flows.

But in the degraded human being the deep instincts have gone dead, and then the two flows become identical. *This* is the secret of really vulgar and of pornographical people: the sex flow and the excrement flow is the same to them. It happens when the psyche deteriorates, and the profound controlling instincts collapse. Then sex is dirt and dirt is sex, and sexual excitement becomes a playing with dirt, and any sign of sex in a woman becomes a show of her dirt. This is the condition of the common, vulgar human being whose name is legion, and who lifts his voice and it is the *Vox populi, vox Dei*. And this is the source of all pornography.

And for this reason we must admit that *Jane Eyre* or Wagner's *Tristan* are much nearer to pornography than is Boccaccio. Wagner and Charlotte Brontë were both in the state where the strongest instincts have collapsed, and sex has become something slightly obscene, to be wallowed in, but despised. Mr. Rochester's sex passion is not "respectable" till Mr. Rochester is burned, blinded, disfigured, and reduced to helpless dependence. Then, thoroughly humbled and humiliated, it may be merely admitted. All the previous titillations are slightly indecent, as in *Pamela* or *The Mill on the Floss* or *Anna Karenina*. As soon as there is sex excitement with a desire to spite the sexual feeling, to humiliate it and degrade it, the element of pornography enters.

For this reason, there is an element of pornography in nearly all nineteenth century literature and very many so-called pure people have a nasty pornographical side to them, and never was the pornographical appetite stronger than it is today. It is a sign of a diseased condition of the body politic. But the way to treat the disease is to come out into the open with sex and sex stimulus. The real pornographer truly dislikes Boccaccio, because the fresh healthy naturalness of the Italian story-teller makes the modern pornographical shrimp feel the dirty worm he is. Today Boccaccio should be given to everybody young or old, to read if they like. Only a natural fresh openness about sex will do any good, now we are being swamped by secret or semi-secret pornography. And perhaps the Renaissance story-tellers, Boccaccio, Lasca, and the rest, are the best antidote we can find now, just as more plasters of Puritanism are the most harmful remedy we can resort to.

The whole question of pornography seems to me a question of secrecy. Without secrecy there would be no pornography. But secrecy and modesty are two utterly different things. Secrecy has always an element of fear in it, amounting very often to hate. Modesty is gentle and reserved. Today, modesty is thrown to the winds, even in the presence of the grey guardians. But secrecy is hugged, being a vice in itself. And the attitude of the grey ones is: Dear young ladies, you may abandon all modesty, so long as you hug your dirty little secret.

This "dirty little secret" has become infinitely precious to the mob of people today. It is a kind of hidden sore or inflammation which, when rubbed or scratched, gives off sharp thrills that seem delicious. So the dirty little secret is rubbed and scratched more and more, till it becomes more and more secretly inflamed, and the nervous and psychic health of the individual is more and more impaired. One might easily say that half the love novels and half the love films today depend entirely for their success on the secret rubbing of the dirty little secret. You can call this sex excitement if you like, but it is sex excitement of a secretive, furtive sort, quite special. The plain and simple excitement, quite open and wholesome, which you find in some Boccaccio stories is not for a minute to be confused with the furtive excitement aroused by rubbing the dirty little secret in all secrecy in modern best-sellers. This furtive, sneaking, cunning rubbing of an inflamed spot in the imagination is the very quick of modern pornography, and it is a beastly and very dangerous thing. You can't so easily expose it, because of its very furtiveness and its sneaking cunning. So the cheap and popular modern love novel and love film flourishes and is even praised by moral guardians, because you get the sneaking thrill fumbling under all the purity of dainty underclothes, without one single gross word to let you know what is happening.

Without secrecy there would be no pornography. But if pornography is the result of sneaking secrecy, what is the result of pornography? What is the effect on the individual?

The effect on the individual is manifold, and always pernicious. But one effect is perhaps inevitable. The pornography of today, whether it be the pornography of the rubber-goods shop or the pornography of the popular novel, film, and play, is an invariable stimulant to the vice of self-abuse, onanism, masturbation, call it what you will. In young or old, man or woman, boy or girl, modern pornography is a direct provocative of masturbation. It cannot be otherwise. When the grey ones wail that the young man and the young woman went and had sexual intercourse, they are bewailing the fact that the young man and the young woman didn't go separately and masturbate. Sex must go somewhere, especially in young people. So, in our glorious civilization, it goes in masturbation. And the mass of our popular literature, the bulk of our popular amusements just exists to provoke masturbation. Masturbation is the one thoroughly secret act of the human being, more secret even than excrementation. It is the one functional result of sex-secrecy, and it is stimulated and provoked by our glorious popular literature of pretty pornography, which rubs on the dirty secret without letting you know what is happening.

Now I have heard men, teachers and clergymen, commend masturbation as the solution of an otherwise insoluble sex problem. This at least is honest. The sex problem is there, and you can't just will it away. There it is, and under the ban of secrecy and taboo in mother and father, teacher, friend, and foe, it has found its own solution, the solution of masturbation.

But what about the solution? Do we accept it? Do all the grey ones of this world accept it? If so, they must now accept it openly.

We can none of us pretend any longer to be blind to the fact of masturbation, in young and old, man and woman. The moral guardians who are prepared to censor all open and plain portrayal of sex must now be made to give their only justification: We prefer that the people shall masturbate. If this preference is open and declared, then the existing forms of censorship are justified. If the moral guardians prefer that the people shall masturbate, then their present behaviour is correct, and popular amusements are as they should be. If sexual intercourse is deadly sin, and masturbation is comparatively pure and harmless, then all is well. Let things continue as they now are.

Is masturbation so harmless, though? Is it even comparatively pure and harmless? Not to my thinking. In the young, a certain amount of masturbation is inevitable, but not therefore natural. I think, there is no boy or girl who masturbates without feeling a sense of shame, anger, and futility. Following the excitement comes the shame, anger, humiliation, and the sense of futility. This sense of futility and humiliation deepens as the years go on, into a suppressed rage, because of the impossibility of escape. The one thing that it seems impossible to escape from, once the habit is formed, is masturbation. It goes on and on, on into old age, in spite of marriage or love affairs or anything else. And it always carries this secret feeling of futility and humiliation, futility and humiliation. And this is, perhaps, the deepest and most dangerous cancer of our civilization. Instead of being a comparatively pure and harmless vice, masturbation is certainly the most dangerous sexual vice that a society can be afflicted with, in the long run. Comparatively pure it may be—purity being what it is. But harmless! ! !

The great danger of masturbation lies in its merely exhaustive nature. In sexual intercourse, there is a give and take. A new stimulus enters as the native stimulus departs. Something quite new is added as the old surcharge is removed. And this is so in all sexual intercourse where two creatures are concerned, even in the homosexual intercourse. But in masturbation there is nothing but loss. There is no reciprocity. There is merely the spending away of a certain force, and no return. The body remains, in a sense, a corpse, after the act of self-abuse. There is no change, only deadening. There is what we call dead loss. And this is not the case in any act of sexual intercourse between two people. Two people may destroy one another in sex. But they cannot just produce the null effect of masturbation.

The only positive effect of masturbation is that it seems to release a certain mental energy, in some people. But it is mental energy which manifests itself always in the same way, in a vicious circle of analysis and impotent criticism, or else a vicious circle of false and easy sympathy, sentimentalities. The sentimentalism and the niggling analysis, often self-analysis, of most of our modern literature, is a sign of self-abuse. It is the manifestation of masturbation, the sort of conscious activity stimulated by masturbation, whether male or female. The outstanding feature of such consciousness is that there is no real object, there is only subject. This is just the same whether it be a novel or a work of science. The author never escapes from himself, he pads along within the vicious circle of himself. There is hardly a writer living who gets out of the vicious circle of himself—or a painter either. Hence the lack of creation, and the stupendous amount of production. It is a masturbation result, within the vicious circle of the self. It is self-absorption made public.

And of course the process is exhaustive. The real masturbation of Englishmen began only in the nineteenth century. It has continued with an increasing emptying of the real vitality and the real *being* of men, till now people are little more than shells of people. Most of the responses are dead, most of the awareness is dead, nearly all the constructive activity is dead, and all that remains is a sort of shell, a half-empty creature fatally self-preoccupied and incapable of either giving or taking. Incapable either of giving or taking, in the vital self. And this is masturbation result. Enclosed within the vicious circle of the self, with no vital contacts outside, the self becomes emptier and emptier, till it is almost a nullus, a nothingness.

But null or nothing as it may be, it still hangs on to the dirty little secret, which it must still secretly rub and inflame. For ever the vicious circle. And it has a weird, blind will of its own.

One of my most sympathetic critics wrote: "If Mr. Lawrence's attitude to sex were adopted, then two things would disappear, the love lyric and the smoking-room story." And this, I think, is true. But it depends on which love lyric he means. If it is the: *Who is Sylvia, what is she?*—then it may just as well disappear. All that pure and noble and heaven-blessed stuff is only the counterpart to the smoking-room story. *Du bist wie eine Blume!* Jawohl! One can see the elderly gentleman laying his hands on the head of the pure maiden and praying God to keep her for ever so pure, so clean and beautiful. Very nice for him! Just pornography! Tickling the dirty little secret and rolling his eyes to heaven! He knows perfectly well that if God keeps the maiden so clean and pure and beautiful—in his vulgar sense of clean and pure—for a few more years, then she'll be an unhappy old maid, and not pure nor beautiful at all, only stale and pathetic. Sentimentality is a sure sign of pornography. Why should "sadness strike through the heart" of the old gentleman, because the maid was pure and beautiful? Anybody but a masturbator would have been glad and would have thought: What a lovely bride for some lucky man! —But no, not the self-enclosed, pornographic masturbator. Sadness has to strike into his beastly heart!—Away with such love lyrics, we've had too much of their pornographic poison, tickling the dirty little secret and rolling the eyes to heaven.

But if it is a question of the sound love lyric, *My love is like a red, red rose——!* then we are on other ground. My love is like a red, red rose only when she's *not* like a pure, pure lily. And nowadays the pure, pure lilies are mostly festering, anyhow. Away with them and their lyrics. Away with the pure, pure lily lyric, along with the smoking-room story. They are counterparts, and the one is as pornographic as the other. *Du bist wie eine Blume* is really as pornographic as a dirty story: tickling the dirty little secret and rolling the eyes to heaven. But oh, if only Robert Burns had been accepted for what he is, then love might still have been like a red, red rose.

The vicious circle, the vicious circle! The vicious circle of masturbation! The vicious circle of self-consciousness that is never *fully* self-conscious, never fully and openly conscious, but always harping on the dirty little secret. The vicious circle of secrecy, in parents, teachers, friends—everybody. The specially vicious circle of family. The vast conspiracy of secrecy in the press, and at the same time, the endless tickling of the dirty little secret. The needless masturbation! and the endless purity! The vicious circle!

How to get out of it? There is only one way: Away with the secret! No more secrecy! The only way to stop the terrible mental itch about sex is to come out quite simply and naturally into the open with it. It is terribly difficult, for the secret is cunning as a crab. Yet the thing to do is to make a beginning. The man who said to his exasperating daughter: "My child, the only pleasure I ever had out of you was the pleasure I had in begetting you" has already done a great deal to release both himself and her from the dirty little secret.

How to get out of the dirty little secret! It is, as a matter of fact, extremely difficult for us secretive moderns. You can't do it by being wise and scientific about it, like Dr. Marie Stopes: though to be wise and scientific like Dr. Marie Stopes is better than to be utterly hypocritical, like the grey ones. But by being wise and scientific in the serious and earnest manner you only tend to disinfect the dirty little secret, and either kill sex altogether with too much seriousness and intellect, or else leave it a miserable disinfected secret. The unhappy "free and pure" love of so many people who have taken out the dirty little secret and thoroughly disinfected it with scientific words is apt to be more pathetic even than the common run of dirty-little-secret love. The danger is, that in killing the dirty little secret, you kill dynamic sex altogether, and leave only the scientific and deliberate mechanism.

This is what happens to many of those who become seriously "free" in their sex, free and pure. They have mentalized sex till it is nothing at all, nothing at all but a mental quantity. And the final result is disaster, every time.

The same is true, in an even greater proportion, of the emancipated bohemians: and very many of the young are bohemian today, whether they ever set foot in Bohemia or not. But the bohemian is "sex free." The dirty little secret is no secret either to him or her. It is, indeed, a most blatantly open question. There is nothing they don't say: everything that can be revealed is revealed. And they do as they wish.

And then what? They have apparently killed the dirty little secret, but somehow, they have killed everything else too. Some of the dirt still sticks, perhaps; sex remains still dirty. But the thrill of secrecy is gone. Hence the terrible dreariness and depression of modern Bohemia, and the inward dreariness and emptiness of so many young people of today. They have killed, they imagine, the dirty little secret. The thrill of secrecy is gone. Some of the dirt remains. And for the rest, depression, inertia, lack of life. For sex is the fountain-head of our energetic life, and now the fountain ceases to flow.

Why? For two reasons. The idealists along the Marie Stopes line, and the young bohemians of today have killed the dirty little secret as far as their personal self goes. But they are still under its dominion socially. In the social world, in the press, in literature, film, theatre, wireless, everywhere purity and the dirty little secret reign supreme. At home, at the dinner table, it is just the same. It is the same wherever you go. The young girl, and the young woman is by tacit assumption pure, virgin, sexless. *Du bist wie eine Blume.* She, poor thing, knows quite well that flowers, even lilies, have tippling yellow anthers and a sticky stigma, sex, rolling sex. But to the popular mind flowers are sexless things, and when a girl is told she is like a flower, it means she is sexless and ought to be sexless. She herself knows quite well she isn't sexless and she isn't merely like a flower. But how bear up against the great social life forced on her? She can't! She succumbs, and the dirty little secret triumphs. She loses her interest in sex, as far as men are concerned, but the vicious circle of masturbation and self-consciousness encloses her even still faster.

This is one of the disasters of young life today. Personally, and among themselves, a great many, perhaps a majority of the young people of today have come out into the open with sex and laid salt on the tail of the dirty little secret. And this is a very good thing. But in public, in the social world, the young are still entirely under the shadow of the grey elderly ones. The grey elderly ones belong to the last century, the eunuch century, the century of the mealy-mouthed lie, the century that has tried to destroy humanity, the nineteenth century. All our grey ones are left over from this century. And they rule us. They rule us with the grey, mealy-mouthed, canting lie of that great century of lies which, thank God, we are drifting away from. But they rule us still with the lie, for the lie, in the name of the lie. And they are too heavy and too numerous, the grey ones. It doesn't matter what government it is. They are all grey ones, left over from the last century, the century of mealy-mouthed liars, the century of purity and the dirty little secret.

So there is one cause for the depression of the young: the public reign of the mealy-mouthed lie, purity and the dirty little secret, which they themselves have privately overthrown. Having killed a good deal of the lie in their own private lives, the young are still enclosed and imprisoned within the great public lie of the grey ones. Hence the excess, the extravagance, the hysteria, and then the weakness, the feebleness, the pathetic silliness of the modern youth. They are all in a sort of prison, the prison of a great lie and a society of elderly liars. And this is one of the reasons, perhaps the main reason why the sex-flow is dying out of the young, the real energy is dying away. They are enclosed within a lie, and the sex won't flow. For the length of a complete lie is never more than three generations, and the young are the fourth generation of the nineteenth century lie.

The second reason why the sex-flow is dying is of course, that the young, in spite of their emancipation, are still enclosed within the vicious circle of self-conscious masturbation. They are thrown back into it, when they try to escape, by the enclosure of the vast public lie of purity and the dirty little secret. The most emancipated bohemians, who swank most about sex, are still utterly self-conscious and enclosed within the narcissus-masturbation circle. They have perhaps less sex even than the grey ones. The whole thing has been driven up into their heads. There isn't even the lurking hole of a dirty little secret. Their sex is more mental than their arithmetic; and as vital physical creatures they are more non-existent than ghosts. The modern bohemian is indeed a kind of ghost, not even narcissus, only the image of narcissus reflected on the face of the audience. The dirty little secret is most difficult to kill. You may put it to death publicly a thousand times, and still it reappears, like a crab, stealthily from under the submerged rocks of the personality. The French, who are supposed to be so open about sex, will perhaps be the last to kill the dirty little secret. Perhaps they don't want to. Anyhow, mere publicity won't do it.

You may parade sex abroad, but you will not kill the dirty little secret. You may read all the novels of Marcel Proust, with everything there in all detail. Yet you will not kill the dirty little secret. You will perhaps only make it more cunning. You may even bring about a state of utter indifference and sex-inertia, still without killing the dirty little secret. Or you may be the most wispy and enamoured little Don Juan of modern days, and still the core of your spirit merely be the dirty little secret. That is to say, you will still be in the narcissus-masturbation circle, the vicious circle of self-enclosure. For whenever the dirty little secret exists, it exists as the centre of the vicious circle of masturbation self-enclosure. And whenever you have the vicious circle of masturbation self-enclosure, you have at the core the dirty little secret. And the most high-flown sex-emancipated young people today are perhaps the most fatally and nervously enclosed within the masturbation self-enclosure. Nor do they want to get out of it, for there would be nothing left to come out.

But some people surely do want to come out of the awful self-enclosure. Today, practically everybody is self-conscious and imprisoned in self-consciousness. It is the joyful result of the dirty little secret. Vast numbers of people don't want to come out of the prison of their self-consciousness: they have so little left to come out with. But some people, surely, want to escape this doom of self-enclosure which is the doom of our civilization. There is surely a proud minority that wants once and for all to be free of the dirty little secret.

And the way to do it is, first, to fight the sentimental lie of purity and the dirty little secret wherever you meet it, inside yourself or in the world outside. Fight the great lie of the nineteenth century, which has soaked through our sex and our bones. It means fighting with almost every breath, for the lie is ubiquitous.

Then secondly, in his adventure of self-consciousness a man must come to the limits of himself and become aware of something beyond him. A man must be self-conscious enough to know his own limits, and to be aware of that which surpasses him. What surpasses me is the very urge of life that is within me, and this life urges me to forget myself and to yield to the stirring half-born impulse to smash up the vast lie of the world, and make a new world. If my life is merely to go on in a vicious circle of self-enclosure, masturbating self-consciousness, it is worth nothing to me. If my individual life is to be enclosed within the huge corrupt lie of society today, purity and the dirty little secret, then it is worth not much to me. Freedom is a very great reality. But it means, above all things, freedom from lies. It is first, freedom from myself, from the lie of myself, from the lie of my all-importance, even to myself; it is freedom from the self-conscious masturbating thing I am, self-enclosed. And second, freedom from the vast lie of the social world, the lie of purity and the dirty little secret. All the other monstrous lies lurk under the cloak of this one primary lie. The monstrous lie of money lurks under the cloak of purity. Kill the purity-lie, and the money-lie will be defenceless.

We have to be sufficiently conscious, and self-conscious, to know our own limits and to be aware of the greater urge within us and beyond us. Then we cease to be primarily interested in ourselves. Then we learn to leave ourselves alone, in all the affective centres: not to force our feelings in any way, and never to force our sex. Then we make the great onslaught on to the outside lie, the inside lie being settled. And that is freedom and the fight for freedom.

The greatest of all lies in the modern world is the lie of purity and the dirty little secret. The grey ones left over from the nineteenth century are the embodiment of this lie. They dominate in society, in the press, in literature, everywhere. And, naturally, they lead the vast mob of the general public along with them.

Which means, of course, perpetual censorship of anything that would militate against the lie of purity and the dirty little secret, and perpetual encouragement of what may be called permissible pornography, pure, but tickling the dirty little secret under the delicate underclothing. The grey ones will pass and will commend floods of evasive pornography, and will suppress every outspoken word.

The law is a mere figment. In his article on the "Censorship of Books," in the *Nineteenth Century,* Viscount Brentford, the late Home Secretary, says: "Let it be remembered that the publishing of an obscene book, the issue of an obscene post-card or pornographic photograph—are all offences against the law of the land, and the Secretary of State who is the general authority for the maintenance of law and order most clearly and definitely cannot discriminate between one offence and another in discharge of his duty."

So he winds up, *ex cathedra* and infallible. But only ten lines above he has written: "I agree, that if the law were pushed to its logical conclusion, the printing and publication of such books as *The Decameron,* Benvenuto Cellini's *Life,* and Burton's *Arabian Nights* might form the subject of proceedings. But the ultimate sanction of all law is public opinion, and I do not believe for one moment that prosecution in respect of books that have been in circulation for many centuries would command public support."

Ooray then for public opinion! It only needs that a few more years shall roll. But now we see that the Secretary of State most clearly and definitely *does* discriminate between one offence and another in discharge of his duty. Simple and admitted discrimination on his part! Yet what is this public opinion? Just more lies on the part of the grey ones. They would suppress Benvenuto tomorrow, if they dared. But they would make laughing-stocks of themselves, because *tradition* backs up Benvenuto. It isn't public opinion at all. It is the grey ones afraid of making still bigger fools of themselves. But the case is simple. If the grey ones are going to be backed by a general public, then every new book that would smash the mealy-mouthed lie of the nineteenth century will be suppressed as it appears. Yet let the grey ones beware. The general public is nowadays a very unstable affair, and no longer loves its grey ones so dearly, with their old lie. And there is another public, the small public of the minority, which hates the lie and the grey ones that perpetuate the lie, and which has its own dynamic ideas about pornography and obscenity. You can't fool all the people all the time, even with purity and a dirty little secret.

And this minority public knows well that the books of many contemporary writers, both big and lesser fry, are far more pornographical than the liveliest story in *The Decameron:* because they tickle the dirty little secret and excite to private masturbation, which the wholesome Boccaccio never does. And the minority public knows full well that the most obscene painting on a Greek vase—*Thou still unravished bride of quietness*—is not as pornographical as the close-up kisses on the film, which excite men and women to secret and separate masturbation.

And perhaps one day even the general public will desire to look the thing in the face, and see for itself the difference between the sneaking masturbation pornography of the press, the film, and present-day popular literature, and then the creative portrayals of the sexual impulse that we have in Boccaccio or the Greek vase-paintings or some Pompeian art, and which are necessary for the fulfilment of our consciousness.

As it is, the public mind is today bewildered on this point, bewildered almost to idiocy. When the police raided my picture show, they did not in the least know what to take. So they took every picture where the smallest bit of the sex organ of either man or woman showed. Quite regardless of subject or meaning or anything else: they would allow anything, these dainty policemen in a picture show, except the actual sight of a fragment of the human *pudenda*. This was the police test. The dabbing on of a postage stamp—especially a green one that could be called a leaf—would in most cases have been quite sufficient to satisfy this "public opinion."

It is, we can only repeat, a condition of idiocy. And if the purity-with-a-dirty-little-secret lie is kept up much longer, the mass of society will really be an idiot, and a dangerous idiot at that. For the public is made up of individuals. And each individual has sex, and is pivoted on sex. And if, with purity and dirty little secrets, you drive every individual into the masturbation self-enclosure, and keep him there, then you will produce a state of general idiocy. For the masturbation self-enclosure produces idiots. Perhaps if we are all idiots, we shan't know it. But God preserve us.

WE NEED ONE ANOTHER

We may as well admit it: men and women need one another. We may as well, after all our kicking against the pricks, our revolting and our sulking, give in and be graceful about it. We are all individualists: we are all egoists: we all believe intensely in freedom, our own at all events. We all want to be absolute, and sufficient unto ourselves. And it is a great blow to our self-esteem that we simply *need* another human being. We don't mind airily picking and choosing among women—or among men, if we are a woman. But to have to come down to the nasty, sharp-pointed brass tacks of admitting: My God, I can't live without that obstreperous woman of mine!—this is terribly humiliating to our isolated conceit.

And when I say: "without that woman of mine" I do not mean a mistress, the sexual relation in the French sense. I mean the woman, my relationship to the woman herself. There is hardly a man living who can exist at all cheerfully without a relationship to some particular woman: unless, of course, he makes another man play the role of woman. And the same of woman. There is hardly a woman on earth who can live cheerfully without some intimate relationship to a man; unless she substitutes some other woman for the man.

So there it is. Now for three thousand years men, and women, have been struggling against this fact. In Buddhism, particularly, a man could never possibly attain the supreme Nirvana if he so much as saw a woman out of the corner of his eye. "Alone I did it!" is the proud assertion of the gentleman who attains Nirvana. And "Alone I did it!" says the Christian whose soul is saved. They are the religions of overweening individualism, resulting, of course, in our disastrous modern egoism of the individual. Marriage, which on earth is a sacrament, is dissolved by the decree absolute of death. In heaven there is no giving and taking in marriage. The soul in heaven is supremely individual, absolved from every relationship except that with the Most High. In heaven there is neither marriage nor love, nor friendship nor fatherhood nor motherhood, nor sister nor brother nor cousin: there is just me, in my perfected isolation, placed in perfect relation to the Supreme, the Most High.

When we talk of heaven we talk, really, of that which we would most like to attain, and most like to be here on earth. The condition of heaven is the condition to be longed for, striven for, now.

Now, if I say to a woman, or to a man: "Would you like to be purely free of all human relationships, free from father and mother, brother and sister, husband, lover, friend, or child? free from all these human entanglements, and reduced purely to your own pure self, connected only with the Supreme Power, the Most High?" Then what would the answer be? What is the answer, I ask you? What is your own sincere answer?

I expect, in almost all cases, it is an emphatic "yes." In the past, most men would have said "yes," and most women "no." But today, I think, many men might hesitate, and nearly all women would unhesitatingly say "yes."

Modern men, however, have so nearly achieved this Nirvana-like condition of having no real human relationships at all, that they are beginning to wonder what and where they are. What are you, when you've asserted your grand independence, broken all the ties, or "bonds," and reduced yourself to a "pure" individuality? What are you?

You may imagine you are something very grand, since few individuals even approximate to this independence without falling into deadly egoism and conceit: and emptiness. The real danger is, reduced to your own single merits and cut off from the most vital human contacts, the danger is that you are left just simply next to nothing. Reduce any individual, man or woman, to his elements, or her elements, and what is he? what is she? Extremely little! Take Napoleon, and stick him alone on a miserable island, and what is he?—a peevish, puerile little fellow. Put Mary Stuart in a nasty stone castle of a prison, and she becomes merely a catty little person. Now Napoleon was not a peevish, puerile little fellow, even if he became such when isolated on St. Helena. And Mary Queen of Scots was only a catty little person when she was isolated in Fotheringay or some such hole. This grand isolation, this reducing of ourselves to our very elemental selves, is the greatest fraud of all. It is like plucking the peacock naked of all his feathers to try to get at the real bird. When you've plucked the peacock bare, what have you got? Not the peacock, but the naked corpse of a bird.

And so it is with us and our grand individualism. Reduce any of us to the *mere* individual that we are, and what do we become? Napoleon becomes a peevish, puerile little fellow, Mary Queen of Scots becomes a catty little person, St. Simeon Stylites, stuck up on his pillar, becomes a conceited lunatic, and we, wonderful creatures as we are, become trashy, conceited little modern egoists. The world today is full of silly, impertinent egoists who have broken all the finer human ties, and base their claims to superiority on their own emptiness and nullity. But the empty ones are being found out. Emptiness, which makes a fair noise, deceives for a short time only.

The fact remains that when you cut off a man and isolate him in his own pure and wonderful individuality, you haven't got the man at all, you've only got the dreary fag-end of him. Isolate Napoleon, and he is nothing. Isolate Immanuel Kant, and his grand ideas will still go on tick-tick-ticking inside his head, but unless he could write them down and communicate them, they might as well be the ticking of the death-watch beetle. Take even Buddha himself, if he'd been whisked off to some lonely place and planted cross-legged under a bhô-tree and nobody had ever seen him or heard any of his Nirvana talk, then I doubt he would have got much fun out of Nirvana, and he'd have been just a crank. In absolute isolation, I doubt if any individual amounts to much; or if any soul is worth saving, or even having. "And I, if I be lifted up, will draw all men unto me." But if there were no other men to be lifted, the whole show would be a fiasco.

So that everything, even individuality itself, depends on relationship. "God cannot do without me," said an eighteenth-century Frenchman. What he meant was, that if there were no human beings, if Man did not exist, then God, the God of Man, would have no meaning. And it is true. If there were no men and women, Jesus would be meaningless. In the same way, Napoleon on St. Helena became meaningless, and the French nation lost a great part of its meaning without him in connexion with his army and the nation; a great power streamed out of Napoleon, and from the French people there streamed back to him a great responsive power, and therein lay his greatness and theirs. That is, in the relationship. The light shines only when the circuit is completed. The light does not shine with one half of the current. Every light is some sort of completed circuit. And so is every life, if it is going to be a life.

We have our very individuality in relationship. Let us swallow this important and prickly fact. Apart from our connexions with other people, we are barely individuals, we amount, all of us, to next to nothing. It is in the living touch between us and other people, other lives, other phenomena that we move and have our being. Strip us of our human contacts and of our contact with the living earth and the sun, and we are almost bladders of emptiness.

Our individuality means nothing. A skylark that was alone on an island would be songless and meaningless, his individuality gone, running about like a mouse in the grass. But if there were one female with him, it would lift him singing into the air, and restore him his real individuality.

And so with men and women. It is in relationship to one another that they have their true individuality and their distinct being: in contact, not out of contact. This is sex, if you like. But it is no more sex than sunshine on the grass is sex. It is a living contact, give and take: the great and subtle relationship of men and women, man and woman. In this and through this we become real individuals, without it, without the real contact, we remain more or less nonentities.

But, of course, it is necessary to have the contact alive and unfixed. It is not a question of: Marry the woman and have done with it–that is only one of the stupid recipes for avoiding contact and killing contact. There are many popular dodges for killing every possibility of true contact: like sticking a woman on a pedestal, or the reverse, sticking her beneath notice; or making a "model" housewife of her, or a "model" mother, or a "model" help-meet. All mere devices for avoiding any contact with her. A woman is not a "model" anything. She is not even a distinct and definite personality. It is time we got rid of these fixed notions. A woman is a living fountain whose spray falls delicately around her, on all that come near. A woman is a strange soft vibration on the air, going forth unknown and unconscious, and seeking a vibration of response. Or else she is a discordant, jarring, painful vibration, going forth and hurting everyone within range. And a man the same. A man, as he lives and moves and has being, is a fountain of life-vibration, quivering and flowing towards someone, something that will receive his outflow and send back an inflow, so that a circuit is completed, and there is a sort of peace. Or else he is a source of irritation, discord, and pain, harming everyone near him.

But while we remain healthy and positive, we seek all the time to come into true human relationship with other human beings. Yet it has to happen, the relationship, almost unconsciously. We can't *deliberately* do much with a human connexion, except smash it: and that is usually not difficult. On the positive side we can only most carefully let it take place, without interfering or forcing.

We are labouring under a false conception of ourselves. For centuries, man has been the conquering hero, and woman has been merely the string to his bow, part of his accoutrement. Then woman was allowed to have a soul of her own, a separate soul. So the separating business started, with all the clamour of freedom and independence. Now the freedom and independence have been rather overdone, they lead to an empty nowhere, the rubbish-heap of all our dead feelings and waste illusions.

The conquering hero business is as obsolete as Marshal Hindenburg, and about as effective. The world sees attempts at revival of this stunt, but they are usually silly, in the end. Man is no longer a conquering hero. Neither is he a supreme soul isolated and alone in the universe, facing the unknown in the eternity of death. That stunt is also played out, though the pathetic boys of today keep on insisting on it, especially the pathetic boys who wrap themselves in the egoistic pathos of their sufferings during the late war.

But both stunts are played out, both the conquering hero and the pathetic hero clothed in suffering and facing Eternity in the soul's last isolation. The second stunt is, of course, more popular today, and still dangerous to the self-pitying, played-out specimens of the younger generation. But for all that, it is a dead stunt, finished.

What a man has to do today is to admit, at last, that all these fixed ideas are no good. As a fixed object, even as an individuality or a personality, no human being, man or woman, amounts to much. The great I AM does not apply to human beings, so they may as well leave it alone. As soon as anybody, man or woman, becomes a great I AM, he becomes nothing. Man or woman, each is a flow, a flowing life. And without one another, we can't flow, just as a river cannot flow without banks. A woman is one bank of the river of my life, and the world is the other. Without the two shores, my life would be a marsh. It is the relationship to woman, and to my fellowmen, which makes me myself a river of life.

And it is this, even, that gives me my soul. A man who has never had a vital relationship to any other human being doesn't really have a soul. We cannot feel that Immanuel Kant ever had a soul. A soul is something that forms and fulfils itself in my contacts, my living touch with people I have loved or hated or truly known. I am born with the clue to my soul. The wholeness of my soul I must achieve. And by my soul I mean my wholeness. What we suffer from today is the lack of a sense of our own wholeness, or completeness, which is peace. What we lack, what the young lack, is a sense of being whole in themselves. They feel so scrappy, they have no peace.

And by peace I don't mean inertia, but the full flowing of life, like a river.

We lack peace because we are not whole. And we are not whole because we have known only a tithe of the vital relationships we might have had. We live in an age which believes in stripping away the relationships. Strip them away, like an onion, till you come to pure, or blank nothingness. Emptiness. That is where most men have come now: to a knowledge of their own complete emptiness. They wanted so badly to be "themselves" that they became nothing at all: or next to nothing.

It is not much fun, being next to nothing. And life ought to be fun, the greatest fun. Not merely "having a good time," in order to "get away from yourself." But real fun in being yourself. Now there are two great relationships possible to human beings: the relationship of man to woman, and the relationship of man to man. As regards both, we are in a hopeless mess.

But the relationship of man to woman is the central fact in actual human life. Next comes the relationship of man to man. And, a long way after, all the other relationships, fatherhood, motherhood, sister, brother, friend.

A young man said to me the other day, rather sneeringly, "I'm afraid I can't believe in the regeneration of England by sex." I said to him: "I'm sure you can't." He was trying to inform me that he was above such trash as sex, and such commonplace as women. He was the usual vitally below par, hollow, and egoistic young man, infinitely wrapped up in himself, like a sort of mummy that will crumble if unwrapped.

And what is sex, after all, but the symbol of the relation of man to woman, woman to man? And the relation of man to woman is wide as all life. It consists in infinite different flows between the two beings, different, even apparently contrary. Chastity is part of the flow between man and woman, as to physical passion. And beyond these, an infinite range of subtle communication which we know nothing about. I should say that the relation between any two decently married people changes profoundly every few years, often without their knowing anything about it; though every change causes pain, even if it brings a certain joy. The long course of marriage is a long event of perpetual change, in which a man and a woman mutually build up their souls and make themselves whole. It is like rivers flowing on, through new country, always unknown.

But we are so foolish, and fixed by our limited ideas. A man says: "I don't love my wife any more, I no longer want to sleep with her." But why should he always want to sleep with her? How does he know what other subtle and vital interchange is going on between him and her, making them both whole, in this period when he doesn't want to sleep with her? And she, instead of jibbing and saying that all is over and she must find another man and get a divorce—why doesn't she pause, and listen for a new rhythm in her soul, and look for the new movement in the man? With every change, a new being emerges, a new rhythm establishes itself; we renew our life as we grow older, and there is real peace. Why, oh, why do we want one another to be always the same, fixed, like a menu-card that is never changed?

If only we had more sense. But we are held by a few fixed ideas, like sex, money, what a person "ought" to be, and so forth, and we miss the whole of life. Sex is a changing thing, now alive, now quiescent, now fiery, now apparently quite gone, quite gone. But the ordinary man and woman haven't the gumption to take it in all its changes. They demand crass, crude sex-desire, they demand it always, and when it isn't forthcoming, then—smash-bash! smash up the whole show. Divorce! Divorce!

I am so tired of being told that I want mankind to go back to the condition of savages. As if modern city people weren't about the crudest, rawest, most crassly savage monkeys that ever existed, when it comes to the relation of man and woman. All I see in our vaunted civilization is men and women smashing each other emotionally and psychically to bits, and all I ask is that they should pause and consider.

For sex, to me, means the whole of the relationship between man and woman. Now this relationship is far greater than we know. We only know a few crude forms—mistress, wife, mother, sweetheart. The woman is like an idol, or a marionette, always forced to play one role or another: sweetheart, mistress, wife, mother. If only we could break up this fixity, and realize the unseizable quality of real woman: that a woman is a flow, a river of life, quite different from a man's river of life: and that each river must flow in its own way, though without breaking its bounds: and that the relation of man to woman is the flowing of two rivers side by side, sometimes even mingling, then separating again, and travelling on. The relationship is a life-long change and a life-long travelling. And that is sex. At periods, sex-desire itself departs completely. Yet the great flow of the relationship goes on all the same, undying, and this is the flow of living sex, the relation between man and woman, that lasts a lifetime, and of which sex-desire is only one vivid, most vivid, manifestation.

THE REAL THING

Most revolutions are explosions: and most explosions blow up a great deal more than was intended. It is obvious, from later history, that the French didn't really want to blow up the whole monarchic and aristocratic system, in the 1790's. Yet they did it, and try as they might, they could never really put anything together again. The same with the Russians: they want to blow a gateway in a wall, and they blow the whole house down.

All fights for freedom, that succeed, go too far, and become in turn the infliction of a tyranny. Like Napoleon or a soviet. And like the freedom of women. Perhaps the greatest revolution of modern times is the emancipation of women; and perhaps the deepest fight for two thousand years and more has been the fight for woman's independence, or freedom, call it what you will. The fight was deeply bitter, and, it seems to me, it is won. It is even going beyond, and becoming a tyranny of woman, of the individual woman in the house, and of the feminine ideas and ideals in the world. Say what we will, the world is swayed by feminine emotion today, and the triumph of the productive and domestic activities of man over all his previous military or adventurous or flaunting activities is a triumph of the woman in the home.

The male is subservient to the female need, and outwardly, man is submissive to the demands of woman.

But inwardly, what has happened? It cannot be denied that there has been a fight. Woman has not won her freedom without fighting for it; and she still fights, fights hard, even when there is no longer any need. For man has fallen. It would be difficult to point to a man in the world today who is not subservient to the great woman-spirit that sways modern mankind. But still not peacefully. Still the sway of a struggle, the sway of conflict.

Woman in the mass has fought her fight politically. But woman the individual has fought her fight with individual man, with father, brother, and particularly with husband. All through the past, except for brief periods of revolt, woman has played a part of submission to man. Perhaps the inevitable nature of man and woman demands such submission. But it must be an instinctive, unconscious submission, made in unconscious faith. At certain periods this blind faith of woman in man seems to weaken, then break. It always happens at the end of some great phase, before another phase sets in. It always seems to start, in man, an overwhelming worship of woman, and a glorification of queens. It always seems to bring a brief spell of glory, and a long spell of misery after. Man yields in glorifying the woman, the glory dies, the fight goes on.

It is not necessarily a sex struggle. The sexes are not by nature pitted against one another in hostility. It only happens so, in certain periods: when man loses his unconscious faith in himself, and woman loses her faith in him, unconsciously and then consciously. It is not biological sex struggle. Not at all. Sex is the great uniter, the great unifier. Only in periods of the collapse of instinctive life-assurance in men does sex become a great weapon and divider.

Man loses his faith in himself, and woman begins to fight him. Cleopatra really fought Antony—that's why he killed himself. But he had first lost faith in himself, and leaned on love, which is a sure sign of weakness and failure. And when woman once begins to fight her man, she fights and fights, as if for freedom. But it is not even freedom she wants. Freedom is a man's word: its meaning, to a woman, is really rather trivial. She fights to escape from a man who doesn't really believe in himself; she fights and fights, and there is no freedom from the fight. Woman is truly less free today than ever she has been since time began, in the womanly sense of freedom. Which means, she has less peace, less of that lovely womanly peace that flows like a river, less of the lovely, flower-like repose of a happy woman, less of the nameless joy in life, purely unconscious, which is the very breath of a woman's being, than ever she has had since she and man first set eyes on one another.

Today, woman is always tense and strung-up, alert, and bare-armed, not for love but for battle. In her shred of a dress and her little helmet of a hat, her cropped hair and her stark bearing she is a sort of soldier, and look at her as one may, one can see nothing else. It is not her fault. It is her doom. It happens when man loses his primary faith in himself and in his very life.

Now through the ages thousands of ties have been formed between men and women. In the ages of discredit, these ties are felt as bonds, and must be fought loose. It is a great tearing and snapping of sympathies, and of unconscious sympathetic connexions. It is a great rupture of unconscious tenderness and unconscious flow of strength between man and woman. Man and woman are not two separate and complete entities. In spite of all protestation, we must continue to assert it. Man and woman are not even two separate persons: not even two separate consciousnesses, or minds. In spite of vehement cries to the contrary, it is so. Man is connected with woman for ever, in connexions visible and invisible, in a complicated life-flow that can never be analysed. It is not only man and wife: the woman facing me in the train, the girl I buy cigarettes from, all send forth to me a stream, a spray, a vapour of female life that enters my bloood and my soul, and makes me me. And back again, I send the stream of male life which soothes and satisfies and builds up the woman. So it still is, very often, in public contacts. The more general stream of life-flow between men and women is not so much broken and reversed as the private flow. Hence we all tend more and more to live in public. In public men and women are still kind to another, very often.

But in private, the fight goes on. It had started in our great-grandmothers; it was going strong in our grandmothers; and in our mothers it was the dominant factor in life. The women *thought* it was a fight for righteousness. They *thought* they were fighting the man to make him "better," and to make life "better" for the children.

We know now this ethical excuse was only an excuse. We know now that our fathers were fought and beaten by our mothers, not because our mothers really knew what was "better," but because our fathers had lost their instinctive hold on the life-flow and the life-reality, that therefore the female had to fight them at any cost, blind, and doomed. We saw it going on as tiny children, the battle. We believed the moral excuse. But we lived to be men, and to be fought in turn. And now we know there is no excuse, moral or immoral. It is just phenomenal. And our mothers, who asserted such a belief in "goodness," were tired of that self-same goodness even before their death.

No, the fight was, and is, for itself, and it is pitiless—except in spasms and pauses. A woman does not fight a man for his love—though she may say so a thousand times over. She fights him because she knows, instinctively, he *cannot* love. He has lost his peculiar belief in himself, his instinctive faith in his own life-flow, and so he cannot love. He *cannot*. The more he protests, the more he asserts, the more he kneels, the more he worships, the less he loves. A woman who is worshipped, or even adored, knows perfectly well, in her instinctive depths, that she is not loved, that she is being swindled. She encourages the swindle, oh enormously, it flatters her vanity. But in the end comes Nemesis and the Furies, pursuing the unfortunate pair. Love between man and woman is neither worship nor adoration, but something much deeper, much less showy and gaudy, part of the very breath, and as ordinary, if we may say so, as breathing. Almost as necessary. In fact, love between man and woman is really just a kind of breathing.

No woman ever got a man's love by fighting for it: at least, by fighting *him*. No man ever loved a woman until she left off fighting him. And when will she leave off fighting him? When he has, apparently, submitted to her (for the submission is always, at least partly, false and a fraud)? No, then least of all. When a man has submitted to a woman, she usually fights him worse than ever, more ruthlessly. Why doesn't she leave him? Often she does. But what then? She merely takes up with another man in order to resume the fight. The need to fight with man is upon her, inexorable.

Why can't she live alone? She can't. Sometimes she can join with other women, and keep up the fight in a group. Sometimes she *must* live alone, for no man will come forward to fight with her. Yet, sooner or later, the need for contact with a man comes over a woman again. It is imperative. If she is rich, she hires a dancing partner, a gigolo, and humiliates him to the last dregs. The fight is not ended. When the great Hector is dead, it is not enough. He must be trailed naked and defiled; tied by the heels to the tail of a contemptuous chariot.

When is the fight over? Ah when! Modern life seems to give no answer. Perhaps when a man finds his strength and his rooted belief in himself again. Perhaps when the man has died, and been painfully born again with a different breath, a different courage, and a different kind of care, or carelessness. But most men can't and daren't die in their old, fearful selves. They cling to their women in desperation, and come to hate them with cold and merciless hate, the hate of a child that is persistently ill-treated. Then when the hate dies, the man escapes into the final state of egoism, when he has no true feelings any more, and cannot be made to suffer.

That is where the young are now. The fight is more or less fizzling out, because both parties have become hollow. There is a perfect cynicism. The young men know that most of the "benevolence" and "motherly love" of their adoring mothers was simply egoism again, and an extension of self, and a love of having absolute power over another creature. Oh, these women who secretly lust to have absolute power over their own children—for their own good! Do they think the children are deceived? Not for a moment! You can read in the eyes of the small modern child: "My mother is trying to bully me with every breath she draws, but though I am only six, I can really resist her." It is the fight, the fight. It has degenerated into the mere fight to impose the will over some other creature, mostly now, mother over her children. She fails again, abjectly. But she goes on.

For the great fight with the man has come almost to an end. Why? Is it because man has found a new strength, has died the death in his old body and been born with a new strength and a new sureness? Alas, apparently not so at all. Man has dodged, sidetracked. Tortured and cynical and unbelieving, he has let all his feelings go out of him, and remains a shell of a man, very nice, very pleasant, in fact the best of modern men. Because nothing really moves him except one thing, a threat against his own safety. He is terrified of not feeling "safe." So he keeps his woman there between him and the world of dangerous feelings and demands.

But he feels nothing. It is the great *counterfeit* liberation, this counterfeit of Nirvana and the peace that passeth all understanding. It is a sort of Nirvana, and a sort of peace: in sheer nullity. At first, the woman cannot realize it. She rages, she goes mad. Woman after woman you can see smashing herself against the figure of a man who has achieved the state of false peace, false strength, false power: the egoist. The egoist, he who has no more spontaneous feelings, and can be made to suffer humanly no more. He who derives all his life henceforth at second-hand, and is animated by self-will and some sort of secret ambition to *impose* himself, either on the world or another individual. See a man or a woman trying to impose herself, himself, and you have an egoist in natural action. But the true *pose* of the modern egoist is that of perfect suaveness and kindness and humility: oh, always delicately humble!

When a man achieves this triumph of egoism: and many men have achieved it today, practically all the successful ones, certainly all the charming ones, and all the "artistic" ones: then the woman concerned is apt to go really a little mad. She gets no more responses. The fight has suddenly given out. She throws herself against a man, and he is not there, only the sort of glassy image of him receives her shocks and feels nothing. She becomes wild, outrageous. The explanation of the impossible behaviour of some women in their thirties lies here. Suddenly nothing comes back at them in the fight, and they go crazy, demented, as if they were on the brink of a fearful abyss. Which they are.

And then they either go to pieces, or else, with one of those sudden turns typical of women, they suddenly realize. And then, almost instantly, their whole behaviour changes. It is over. The fight is finished. The man has side-tracked. He becomes, in a sense, negligible, though the basic animosity is only rarefied, made more subtle. And so you have the smart young woman in her twenties. She no longer fights her man—or men. She leaves him to his devices, and as far as possible invents her own. She may have a child to bully. But as a rule she pushes the child away as far as she can. No, she is now quite alone. If the man has no real feelings, she has none either. No matter how she feels about her husband, unless she is in a state of nervous rage she calls him angel of light, and winged messenger, and loveliest man, and my beautiful pet boy. She flips it all over him, like eau de cologne. And he takes it quite for granted, and suggests the next amusement. And their life is "one round of pleasure," to use the old banality: until the nerves collapse. Everything is counterfeit: counterfeit complexion, counterfeit jewels, counterfeit elegance, counterfeit charm, counterfeit endearment, counterfeit passion, counterfeit culture, counterfeit love of Blake, or of *The Bridge of San Luis Rey,* or Picasso, or the latest film-star. Counterfeit sorrows and counterfeit delights, counterfeit woes and moans, counterfeit ecstasies, and, under all, a hard, hard realization that we live by money, and money alone: and a terrible lurking fear of nervous collapse, collapse.

These are, of course, the extreme cases of the modern young. They are those who have got way beyond tragedy or real seriousness, that old-fashioned stuff. They are—they don't know where they are. And they don't care. But they are at the far end of the great fight between men and women.

Judging them as a result, the fight hardly seems to have been worth it. But we are looking on them still as fighters. Perhaps there is something else, positive, as a result.

In their own way, many of these young ones who have gone through everything and reached a stage of emptiness and disillusion unparalleled since the decadent Romans of Ravenna, in the fifth century, they are now, in very fear and forlornness, beginning to put out feelers towards some other way of trust. They begin to realize that if they are not careful, they will have missed life altogether. Missed the bus! They, the smart young who are so swift at hopping onto a thing, to have missed life itself, not to have hopped onto it! Missed the bus! to use London slang. Let the great chance slip by, while they were fooling round! The young are just beginning uneasily to realize that this may be the case. They are just beginning uneasily to realize that all that "life" which they lead, rushing around and being so smart, perhaps isn't life after all, and they are missing the real thing.

What then? What *is* the real thing? Ah, there's the rub. There are millions of ways of living, and it's all life. But what is the real thing in life? What is it that makes you *feel* right, makes life really feel good?

It is the great question. And the answers are old answers. But every generation must frame the answer in its own way. What makes life good to me is the sense that, even if I am sick and ill, I am alive, alive to the depths of my soul, and in touch somewhere in touch with the vivid life of the cosmos. Somehow my life draws strength from the depths of the universe, from the depths among the stars, from the great "world." Out of the great world comes my strength and my reassurance. One could say "God," but the word "God" is somehow tainted. But there *is* a flame or a Life Everlasting wreathing through the cosmos for ever and giving us our renewal, once we can get in touch with it.

It is when men lose their contact with this eternal life-flame, and become merely personal, things in themselves, instead of things kindled in the flame, that the fight between man and woman begins. It cannot be avoided; any more than nightfall or rain. The more conventional and correct a woman may be, the more outwardly devastating she is. Once she feels the loss of the greater control and the greater sustenance, she becomes emotionally destructive, she can no more help it than she can help being a woman, when the great connexion is lost.

And then there is nothing for men to do but to turn back to life itself. Turn back to the life that flows invisibly in the cosmos, and will flow for ever, sustaining and renewing all living things. It is not a question of sins or morality, of being good or being bad. It is a question of renewal, of being renewed, vivified, made new and vividly alive and aware, instead of being exhausted and stale, as men are today. How to be renewed, reborn, revivified? That is the question men must ask themselves, and women too.

And the answer will be difficult. Some trick with glands or secretions, or raw food, or drugs won't do it. Neither will some wonderful revelation or message. It is not a question of knowing something, but of doing something. It is a question of getting into contact again with the *living* centre of the cosmos. And how are we to do it?

NOBODY LOVES ME

Last year, we had a little house up in the Swiss mountains, for the summer. A friend came to tea: a woman of fifty or so, with her daughter: old friends. "And how are you all?" I asked, as she sat, flushed and rather exasperated after the climb up to the chalet on a hot afternoon, wiping her face with a too-small handkerchief. "Well!" she replied, glancing almost viciously out of the window at the immutable slopes and peaks opposite, "I don't know how *you* feel about it—but—these mountains!—well!—I've lost *all* my *cosmic consciousness,* and *all* my *love for humanity.*"

She is, of course, New England of the old school—and usually transcendentalist calm. So that her exasperated frenzy of the moment—it was really a frenzy—coupled with the New England language and slight accent, seemed to me really funny. I laughed in her face, poor dear, and said: "Never mind! Perhaps you can do with a rest from your cosmic consciousness and your love of humanity."

I have often thought of it since: of what she really meant. And every time, I have had a little pang, realizing that I was a bit spiteful to her. I admit, her New England transcendental habit of loving the cosmos *en bloc* and humanity *en masse* did rather get on my nerves, always. But then she had been brought up that way. And the fact of loving the cosmos didn't prevent her from being fond of her own garden—though it did, a bit; and her love of humanity didn't prevent her from having a real affection for her friends, except that she felt that she *ought* to love them in a selfless and general way, which was rather annoying. Nevertheless, that, to me, rather silly language about cosmic consciousness and love of humanity did stand for something that was not merely cerebral. It stood, and I realized it afterwards, for her peace, her inward peace with the universe and with man. And this she could *not* do without. One may be at war with society, and still keep one's deep peace with mankind. It is not pleasant to be at war with society, but sometimes it is the only way of preserving one's peace of soul, which is peace with the living, struggling, *real* mankind. And this latter one cannot afford to lose. So I had no right to tell my friend she could do with a rest from her love of humanity. She couldn't, and none of us can: if we interpret *love of humanity* as that feeling of being at one with the struggling soul, or spirit, or whatever it is, of our fellow-men.

Now the wonder to me is that the young do seem to manage to get on without any "cosmic consciousness" or "love of humanity." They have, on the whole, shed the cerebral husk of generalizations from their emotional state: the cosmic and humanity touch. But it seems to me they have also shed the flower that was inside the husk. Of course, you can hear a girl exclaim: *"Really,* you know, the colliers are darlings, and it's a shame the way they're treated." She will even rush off and register a vote for her darlings. But she doesn't really care—and one can sympathize with her. This caring about the wrongs of unseen people has been rather overdone. Nevertheless, though the colliers or cotton-workers or whatever they be are a long way off and we can't do anything about it, still, away in some depth of us, we know that we are connected vitally, if remotely, with these colliers or cotton-workers, we dimly realize that mankind is one, almost one flesh. It is an abstraction, but it is also a physical fact. In some way or other, the cotton-workers of Carolina, or the rice growers of China, are connected with me and, to a faint yet real degree, part of me. The vibration of life which they give off reaches me, touches me, and affects me all unknown to me. For we are more or less connected, all more or less in touch: all humanity. That is, until we have killed the sensitive responses in ourselves, which happens today only too often.

Dimly, this is what my transcendentalist meant by her "love of humanity," though she tended to kill the real thing by labelling it so philanthropically and bossily. Dimly, she meant her sense of participating in the life of all humanity, which is a sense we all have, delicately and deeply, when we are at peace in ourselves. But let us lose our inward peace, and at once we are likely to substitute for this delicate inward sense of participating in the life of all mankind another thing, a nasty pronounced benevolence, which wants to do good to all mankind, and is only a form of self-assertion and of bullying. From this sort of love of humanity, good Lord deliver us! and deliver poor humanity. My friend was a tiny bit tainted with this form of self-importance, as all transcendentalists were. So if the mountains, in their brutality, took away the tainted love, good for them. But my dear Ruth—I shall call her Ruth—had more than this. She had, woman of fifty as she was, an almost girlish naïve sense of living at peace, real peace, with her fellow-men. And this she could not afford to lose. And save for that taint of generalization and *will,* she would never have lost it, even for that half-hour in the Swiss mountains. But she meant the "cosmos" and "humanity" to fit her will and her feelings, and the mountains made her realize that the cosmos *wouldn't.* When you come up against the cosmos, your consciousness is likely to suffer a jolt. And humanity, when you come down to it, is likely to give your "love" a nasty jar. But there you are.

When we come to the younger generation, however, we realize that "cosmos consciousness" and "love of humanity" have really been left out of their composition. They are like a lot of brightly coloured bits of glass, and they only feel just what they bump against, when they're shaken. They make an accidental pattern with other people, and for the rest they know nothing and care nothing.

So that cosmic consciousness and love of humanity, to use the absurd New England terms, are really dead. They were tainted. Both the cosmos and humanity were too much manufactured in New England. They weren't the real thing. They were, very often, just noble phrases to cover up self-assertion, self-importance, and malevolent bullying. They were just activities of the ugly, self-willed ego, determined that humanity and the cosmos should exist as New England allowed them to exist, or not at all. They were tainted with bullying egoism, and the young, having fine noses for this sort of smell, would have none of them.

The way to kill any feeling is to insist on it, harp on it, exaggerate it. Insist on loving humanity, and sure as fate you'll come to hate everybody. Because, of course, if you insist on loving humanity, then you insist that it shall be lovable: which half the time it isn't. In the same way, insist on loving your husband, and you won't be able to help hating him secretly. Because of course nobody is *always* lovable. If you insist they shall be, this imposes a tyranny over them, and they become less lovable. And if you force yourself to love them—or pretend to—when they are not lovable, you falsify everything, and fall into hate. The result of forcing any feeling is the death of that feeling, and the substitution of some sort of opposite. Whitman insisted on sympathizing with everything and everybody: so much so, that he came to believe in death only, not just his own death, but the death of all people. In the same way the slogan "Keep Smiling!" produces at last a sort of savage rage in the breast of the smilers, and the famous "cheery morning greeting" makes the gall accumulate in all the cheery ones.

It is no good. Every time you force your feelings, you damage yourself and produce the opposite effect to the one you want. Try to force yourself to love somebody, and you are bound to end by detesting that same somebody. The only thing to do is to have the feelings you've really got, and not make up any of them. And that is the only way to leave the other person free. If you feel like murdering your husband, then don't say, "Oh, but I love him dearly. I'm devoted to him." That is not only bullying yourself, but bullying him. He doesn't want to be *forced,* even by love. Just say to yourself: "I could murder him, and that's a fact. But I suppose I'd better not." And then your feelings will get their own balance.

The same is true of love of humanity. The last generation, and the one before that *insisted* on loving humanity. They cared terribly for the poor suffering Irish and Armenians and Congo rubber Negroes and all that. And it was a great deal of it fake, self-conceit, self-importance. The bottom of it was the egoistic thought: "I'm so good, I'm so superior, I'm so benevolent, I care intensely about the poor suffering Irish and the martyred Armenians and the oppressed Negroes, and I'm going to save them, even if I have to upset the English and the Turks and the Belgians severely." This love of mankind was half self-importance and half a desire to interfere and put a spoke in other people's wheels. The younger generation, smelling the rat under the lamb's-wool of Christian Charity, said to themselves: No love of humanity for me!

They have, if the truth be told, a secret detestation of all oppressed or unhappy people who need "relief." They rather hate "the poor colliers," "the poor cotton-workers," "the poor starving Russians," and all that. If there came another war, how they would loathe "the stricken Belgians"! And so it is: the father eats the pear, and the son's teeth are set on edge.

Having overdone the sympathy touch, especially the love of humanity, we have now got the recoil away from sympathy. The young don't sympathize, and they don't want to. They are egoists, and frankly so. They say quite honestly: "I don't give a hoot in hell for the poor oppressed this-that-and-the-other." And who can blame them? Their loving forebears brought on the Great War. If love of humanity brought on the Great War, let us see what frank and honest egoism will do. Nothing so horrible, we can bet.

The trouble about frank and accepted egoism is its unpleasant effect on the egoist himself. Honesty is very good, and it is good to cast off all the spurious sympathies and false emotions of the prewar world. But casting off spurious sympathy and false emotion need not entail the death of all sympathy and all deep emotion, as it seems to do in the young. The young quite deliberately *play* at sympathy and emotion. "Darling child, how lovely you look to-night! I *adore* to look at you!"—and in the next breath, a little arrow of spite. Or the young wife to her husband: "My beautiful love, I feel so precious when you hold me like that, my perfect dear! But shake me a cocktail, angel, would you? I need a good kick—you *angel* of light!"

The young, at the moment, have a perfectly good time strumming on the keyboard of emotion and sympathy, tinkling away at all the exaggerated phrases of rapture and tenderness, adoration and delight, while they feel—nothing, except a certain amusement at the childish game. It is so *chic* and charming to use all the most precious phrases of love and endearment amusingly, just amusingly, like the tinkling in a music-box.

And they would be very indignant if told they had no love of humanity. The English ones profess the most amusing and histrionic love of England, for example. "There is only one thing I care about, except my beloved Philip, and that is England, our precious England. Philip and I are both prepared to die for England, at any moment." At the moment, England does not seem to be in any danger of asking them, so they are quite safe. And if you gently inquire: "But what, in your imagination, is England?" they reply fervently: "The great tradition of the English, the great idea of England"—which seems comfortably elastic and non-committal.

And they cry: "I would give anything for the cause of freedom. Hope and I have wept tears, and saddened our precious marriage-bed, thinking of the trespass on English liberty. But we are calmer now, and determined to fight calmly to the utmost." Which calm fight consists in taking another cocktail and sending out a wildly emotional letter to somebody perfectly irresponsible. Then all is over, and freedom is forgotten, and perhaps religion gets a turn, or a wild outburst over some phrase in the burial service.

This is the advanced young of today. I confess it is amusing, while the coruscation lasts. The trying part is when the fireworks have finished—and they don't last very long, even with cocktails—and the grey stretches intervene. For with the advanced young, there is no warm daytime and silent night. It is all fireworks of excitement and stretches of grey emptiness; then more fireworks. And, let the grisly truth be owned, it is rather exhausting.

Now in the grey intervals in the life of the modern young one fact emerges in all its dreariness, and makes itself plain to the young themselves, as well as the onlooker. The fact that they are empty: that they care about nothing and nobody: not even the Amusement they seek so strenuously. Of course this skeleton is not to be taken out of the cupboard. "Darling angel man, don't start being a nasty white ant. Play the game, angel-face, play the game; don't start saying unpleasant things and rattling a lot of dead men's bones! Tell us something nice, something amusing. Or let's be *really* serious, you know, and talk about bolshevism or *la haute finance*. Do be an angel of light, and cheer us up, you nicest precious pet!"

As a matter of fact, the young are becoming afraid of their own emptiness. It's awful fun throwing things out of the window. But when you've thrown everything out, and you've spent two or three days sitting on the bare floor, your bones begin to ache, and you begin to wish for some of the old furniture, even if it was the ugliest Victorian horsehair.

At least, that's how it seems to me the young women begin to feel. They are frightened at the emptiness of their house of life, now they've thrown everything out of the window. Their young Philips and Peters and so on don't seem to make the slightest move to put any new furniture in the house of the young generation. The only new piece they introduce is a cocktail-shaker and perhaps a wireless set. For the rest, it can stay blank.

And the young women begin to feel a little uneasy. Women don't like to feel empty. A woman hates to feel that she believes in nothing and stands for nothing. Let her be the silliest woman on earth, she will take something seriously: her appearance, her clothes, her house, something. And let her be not so very silly, and she wants more than that. She wants to feel, instinctively, that she amounts to something and that her life stands for something. Women, who so often are angry with men because men cannot "just live," but must always be wanting some purpose in life, are themselves, perhaps, the very root of the male necessity for a purpose in life. It seems to me that in a woman the need to feel that her life *means* something, stands for something, and amounts to something is much more imperative than in a man. The woman herself may deny it emphatically; because, of course, it is the man's business to supply her life with this "purpose." But a man can be a tramp, purposeless, and be happy. Not so a woman. It is a very, very rare woman who can be happy if she feels herself "outside" the great purpose of life. Whereas, I verily believe, vast numbers of men would gladly drift away as wasters, if there were anywhere to drift to.

A woman cannot bear to feel empty and purposeless. But a man may take a real pleasure in that feeling. A man can take real pride and satisfaction in pure negation: "I am quite empty of feeling, I don't care the slightest bit in the world for anybody or anything except myself. But I do care for myself, and I'm going to survive in spite of them all, and I'm going to have my own success without caring the least in the world how I get it. Because I'm cleverer than they are, I'm cunninger than they are, even if I'm weak. I must build myself proper protections, and entrench myself, and then I'm safe. I can sit inside my glass tower and feel nothing and be touched by nothing, and yet exert my power, my will, through the glass walls of my ego."

That, roughly, is the condition of a man who accepts the condition of true egoism, and emptiness, in himself. He has a certain pride in the condition, since in pure emptiness of real feeling he can still carry out his ambition, his will to egoistic success.

Now I doubt if any woman can feel like this. The most egoistic woman is always in a tangle of hate, if not of love. But the true male egoist neither hates nor loves. He is quite empty, at the middle of him. Only on the surface he has feelings: and these he is always trying to get away from. Inwardly, he feels nothing. And when he feels nothing, he exults in his ego and knows he is safe. Safe, within his fortifications, inside his glass tower.

But I doubt if women can even understand this condition in a man. They mistake the emptiness for depth. They think the false calm of the egoist who really feels nothing, is strength. And they imagine that all the defences which the confirmed egoist throws up, the glass tower of imperviousness, are screens to a real man, a positive being. And they throw themselves madly on the defences, to tear them down and come at the real man, little knowing that there *is* no real man, the defences are only there to protect a hollow emptiness, an egoism, not a human man.

But the young are beginning to suspect. The young women are beginning to respect the defences, for they are more afraid of coming upon the ultimate nothingness of the egoist, than of leaving him undiscovered. Hollowness, nothingness–it frightens the woman. They cannot be *real* nihilists. But men can. Men can have a savage satisfaction in the annihilation of all feeling and all connexion, in a resultant state of sheer negative emptiness, when there is nothing left to throw out of the window, and the window is sealed.

Women wanted freedom. The result is a hollowness, an emptiness which frightens the stoutest heart. Women then turn to women for love. But that doesn't last. It can't. Whereas the emptiness persists and persists.

The love of humanity is gone, leaving a great gap. The cosmic consciousness has collapsed upon a great void. The egoist sits grinning furtively in the triumph of his own emptiness. And now what is woman going to do? Now that the house of life is empty, now that she's thrown all the emotional furnishing out of the window, and the house of life, which is her eternal home, is empty as a tomb, now what is dear forlorn woman going to do?

IV

Literature and Art

PREFACES AND INTRODUCTIONS TO BOOKS

REVIEWS OF BOOKS

STUDY OF THOMAS HARDY

SURGERY FOR THE NOVEL—OR A BOMB

ART AND MORALITY

MORALITY AND THE NOVEL

WHY THE NOVEL MATTERS

JOHN GALSWORTHY

INTRODUCTION TO THESE PAINTINGS

PREFACES AND INTRODUCTIONS TO BOOKS

All Things Are Possible, by Leo Shestov

In his paragraph on The Russian Spirit, Shestov gives us the real clue to Russian literature. European culture is a rootless thing in the Russians. With us, it is our very blood and bones, the very nerve and root of our psyche. We think in a certain fashion, we feel in a certain fashion, because our whole substance is of this fashion. Our speech and feeling are organically inevitable to us.

With the Russians it is different. They have only been inoculated with the virus of European culture and ethic. The virus works in them like a disease. And the inflammation and irritation comes forth as literature. The bubbling and fizzing is almost chemical, not organic. It is an organism seething as it accepts and masters the strange virus. What the Russian is struggling with, crying out against, is not life itself: it is only European culture which has been introduced into his psyche, and which hurts him. The tragedy is not so much a real soul tragedy, as a surgical one. Russian art, Russian literature after all does not stand on the same footing as European or Greek or Egyptian art. It is not spontaneous utterance. It is not the flowering of a race. It is a surgical outcry, horrifying, or marvellous, lacerating at first; but when we get used to it, not really so profound, not really ultimate, a little extraneous.

What is valuable is the evidence against European culture, implied in the novelists, here at last expressed. Since Peter the Great Russia has been accepting Europe, and seething Europe down in a curious process of catabolism. Russia has been expressing nothing inherently Russian. Russia's modern Christianity even was not Russian. Her genuine Christianity, Byzantine and Asiatic, is incomprehensible to us. So with her true philosophy. What she has actually uttered is her own unwilling, fantastic reproduction of European truths. What she has really to utter the coming centuries will hear. For Russia will certainly inherit the future. What we already call the greatness of Russia is only her pre-natal struggling.

It seems as if she had at last absorbed and overcome the virus of old Europe. Soon her new, healthy body will begin to act in its own reality, imitative no more, protesting no more, crying no more, but full and sound and lusty in itself. Real Russia is born. She will laugh at us before long. Meanwhile she goes through the last stages of reaction against us, kicking away from the old womb of Europe.

In Shestov one of the last kicks is given. True, he seems to be only reactionary and destructive. But he can find a little amusement at last in tweaking the European nose, so he is fairly free. European idealism is anathema. But more than this, it is a little comical. We feel the new independence in his new, half-amused indifference.

He is only tweaking the nose of European idealism. He is preaching nothing: so he protests time and again. He absolutely refutes any imputation of a central idea. He is so afraid lest it should turn out to be another hateful hedge-stake of an ideal.

"Everything is possible"—this is his really central cry. It is not nihilism. It is only a shaking free of the human psyche from old bonds. The positive central idea is that the human psyche, or soul, really believes in itself, and in nothing else.

Dress this up in a little comely language, and we have a real ideal, that will last us for a new, long epoch. The human soul itself is the source and well-head of creative activity. In the unconscious human soul the creative prompting issues first into the universe. Open the consciousness to this prompting, away with all your old sluice-gates, locks, dams, channels. No ideal on earth is anything more than an obstruction, in the end, to the creative issue of the spontaneous soul. Away with all ideals. Let each individual act spontaneously from the for ever incalculable prompting of the creative well-head within him. There is no universal law. Each being is, at his purest, a law unto himself, single, unique, a Godhead, a fountain from the unknown.

This is the ideal which Shestov refuses positively to state, because he is afraid it may prove in the end a trap to catch his own spirit. So it may. But it is none the less a real, living ideal for the moment, the very salvation. When it becomes ancient, and like the old lion who lay in his cave and whined, devours all its servants, then it can be dispatched. Meanwhile it is a really liberating word.

Shestov's style is puzzling at first. Having found the "ands" and "buts" and "becauses" and "therefores" hampered him, he clips them all off deliberately and even spitefully, so that his thought is like a man with no buttons on his clothes, ludicrously hitching along all undone. One must be amused, not irritated. Where the arm-holes were a bit tight, Shestov cuts a slit. It is baffling, but really rather piquant. The real conjunction, the real unification lies in the reader's own amusement, not in the author's unbroken logic.

The American Edition of *New Poems*, by D. H. Lawrence

It seems when we hear a skylark singing as if sound were running into the future, running so fast and utterly without consideration, straight on into futurity. And when we hear a nightingale, we hear the pause and the rich, piercing rhythm of recollection, the perfected past. The lark may sound sad, but with the lovely lapsing sadness that is almost a swoon of hope. The nightingale's triumph is a pæan, but a death-pæan.

So it is with poetry. Poetry is, as a rule, either the voice of the far future, exquisite and ethereal, or it is the voice of the past, rich, magnificent. When the Greeks heard the *Iliad* and the *Odyssey,* they heard their own past calling in their hearts, as men far inland sometimes hear the sea and fall weak with powerful, wonderful regret, nostalgia; or else their own future rippled its time-beats through their blood, as they followed the painful, glamorous progress of the Ithacan. This was Homer to the Greeks: their Past, splendid with battles won and death achieved, and their Future, the magic wandering of Ulysses through the unknown.

With us it is the same. Our birds sing on the horizons. They sing out of the blue, beyond us, or out of the quenched night. They sing at dawn and sunset. Only the poor, shrill, tame canaries whistle while we talk. The wild birds begin before we are awake, or as we drop into dimness, out of waking. Our poets sit by the gateways, some by the east, some by the west. As we arrive and as we go out our hearts surge with response. But whilst we are in the midst of life, we do not hear them.

The poetry of the beginning and the poetry of the end must have that exquisite finality, perfection which belongs to all that is far off. It is in the realm of all that is perfect. It is of the nature of all that is complete and consummate. This completeness, this consummateness, the finality and the perfection are conveyed in exquisite form: the perfect symmetry, the rhythm which returns upon itself like a dance where the hands link and loosen and link for the supreme moment of the end. Perfected bygone moments, perfected moments in the glimmering futurity, these are the treasured gemlike lyrics of Shelley and Keats.

But there is another kind of poetry: the poetry of that which is at hand: the immediate present. In the immediate present there is no perfection, no consummation, nothing finished. The strands are all flying, quivering, intermingling into the web, the waters are shaking the moon. There is no round, consummate moon on the face of running water, nor on the face of the unfinished tide. There are no gems of the living plasm. The living plasm vibrates unspeakably, it inhales the future, it exhales the past, it is the quick of both, and yet it is neither. There is no plasmic finality, nothing crystal, permanent. If we try to fix the living tissue, as the biologists fix it with formation, we have only a hardened bit of the past, the bygone life under our observation.

Life, the ever-present, knows no finality, no finished crystallization. The perfect rose is only a running flame, emerging and flowing off, and never in any sense at rest, static, finished. Herein lies its transcendent loveliness. The whole tide of all life and all time suddenly heaves, and appears before us as an apparition, a revelation. We look at the very white quick of nascent creation. A water-lily heaves herself from the flood, looks around, gleams, and is gone. We have seen the incarnation, the quick of the ever-swirling flood. We have seen the invisible. We have seen, we have touched, we have partaken of the very substance of creative change, creative mutation. If you tell me about the lotus, tell me of nothing changeless or eternal. Tell me of the mystery of the inexhaustible, forever-unfolding creative spark. Tell me of the incarnate disclosure of the flux, mutation in blossom, laughter and decay perfectly open in their transit, nude in their movement before us.

Let me feel the mud and the heavens in my lotus. Let me feel the heavy, silting, sucking mud, the spinning of sky winds. Let me feel them both in purest contact, the nakedness of sucking weight, nakedly passing radiance. Give me nothing fixed, set, static. Don't give me the infinite or the eternal: nothing of infinity, nothing of eternity. Give me the still, white seething, the incandescence and the coldness of the incarnate moment: the moment, the quick of all change and haste and opposition: the moment, the immediate present, the Now. The immediate moment is not a drop of water running downstream. It is the source and issue, the bubbling up of the stream. Here, in this very instant moment, up bubbles the stream of time, out of the wells of futurity, flowing on to the oceans of the past. The source, the issue, the creative quick.

There is poetry of this immediate present, instant poetry, as well as poetry of the infinite past and the infinite future. The seething poetry of the incarnate Now is supreme, beyond even the everlasting gems of the before and after. In its quivering momentaneity it surpasses the crystalline, pearl-hard jewels, the poems of the eternities. Do not ask for the qualities of the unfading timeless gems. Ask for the whiteness which is the seethe of mud, ask for that incipient putrescence which is the skies falling, ask for the never-pausing, never-ceasing life itself. There must be mutation, swifter than iridescence, haste, not rest, come-and-go, not fixity, inconclusiveness, immediacy, the quality of life itself, without denouement or close. There must be the rapid momentaneous association of things which meet and pass on the for ever incalculable journey of creation: everything left in its own rapid, fluid relationship with the rest of things.

This is the unrestful, ungraspable poetry of the sheer present, poetry whose very permanency lies in its wind-like transit. Whitman's is the best poetry of this kind. Without beginning and without end, without any base and pediment, it sweeps past for ever, like a wind that is for ever in passage, and unchainable. Whitman truly looked before and after. But he did not sigh for what is not. The clue to all his utterance lies in the sheer appreciation of the instant moment, life surging itself into utterance at its very well-head. Eternity is only an abstraction from the actual present. Infinity is only a great reservoir of recollection, or a reservoir of aspiration: man-made. The quivering nimble hour of the present, this is the quick of Time. This is the immanence. The quick of the universe is the *pulsating, carnal self,* mysterious and palpable. So it is always.

Because Whitman put this into his poetry, we fear him and respect him so profoundly. We should not fear him if he sang only of the "old unhappy far-off things," or of the "wings of the morning." It is because his heart beats with the urgent, insurgent Now, which is even upon us all, that we dread him. He is so near the quick.

From the foregoing it is obvious that the poetry of the instant present cannot have the same body or the same motion as the poetry of the before and after. It can never submit to the same conditions. It is never finished. There is no rhythm which returns upon itself, no serpent of eternity with its tail in its own mouth. There is no static perfection, none of that finality which we find so satisfying because we are so frightened.

Much has been written about free verse. But all that can be said, first and last, is that free verse is, or should be direct utterance from the instant, whole man. It is the soul and the mind and body surging at once, nothing left out. They speak all together. There is some confusion, some discord. But the confusion and the discord only belong to the reality, as noise belongs to the plunge of water. It is no use inventing fancy laws for free verse, no use drawing a melodic line which all the feet must toe. Free verse toes no melodic line, no matter what drill-sergeant. Whitman pruned away his clichés—perhaps his clichés of rhythm as well as of phrase. And this is about all we can do, deliberately, with free verse. We can get rid of the stereotyped movements and the old hackneyed associations of sound or sense. We can break down those artificial conduits and canals through which we do so love to force our utterance. We can break the stiff neck of habit. We can be in ourselves spontaneous and flexible as flame, we can see that utterance rushes out without artificial form or artificial smoothness. But we cannot positively prescribe any motion, any rhythm. All the laws we invent or discover—it amounts to pretty much the same—will fail to apply to free verse. They will only apply to some form of restricted, limited unfree verse.

All we can say is that free verse does *not* have the same nature as restricted verse. It is not of the nature of reminiscence. It is not the past which we treasure in its perfection between our hands. Neither is it the crystal of the perfect future, into which we gaze. Its tide is neither the full, yearning flow of aspiration, nor the sweet, poignant ebb of remembrance and regret. The past and the future are the two great bournes of human emotion, the two great homes of the human days, the two eternities. They are both conclusive, final. Their beauty is the beauty of the goal, finished, perfected. Finished beauty and measured symmetry belong to the stable, unchanging eternities.

But in free verse we look for the insurgent naked throb of the instant moment. To break the lovely form of metrical verse, and to dish up the fragments as a new substance, called *vers libre,* this is what most of the free-versifiers accomplish. They do not know that free verse has its own *nature,* that it is neither star nor pearl, but instantaneous like plasm. It has no goal in either eternity. It has no finish. It has no satisfying stability, satisfying to those who like the immutable. None of this. It is the instant; the quick; the very jetting source of all will-be and has-been. The utterance is like a spasm, naked contact with all influences at once. It does not want to get anywhere. It just takes place.

For such utterance any externally applied law would be mere

shackles and death. The law must come new each time from within. The bird is on the wing in the winds, flexible to every breath, a living spark in the storm, its very flickering depending upon its supreme mutability and power of change. Whence such a bird came: whither it goes: from what solid earth it rose up, and upon what solid earth it will close its wings and settle, this is not the question. This is a question of before and after. Now, *now,* the bird is on the wing in the winds.

Such is the rare new poetry. One realm we have never conquered: the pure present. One great mystery of time is terra incognita to us: the instant. The most superb mystery we have hardly recognized: the immediate, instant self. The quick of all time is the instant. The quick of all the universe, of all creation, is the incarnate, carnal self. Poetry gave us the clue: free verse: Whitman. Now we know.

The ideal—what is the ideal? A figment. An abstraction. A static abstraction, abstracted from life. It is a fragment of the before or the after. It is a crystallized aspiration, or a crystallized remembrance: crystallized, set, finished. It is a thing set apart, in the great storehouse of eternity, the storehouse of finished things.

We do not speak of things crystallized and set apart. We speak of the instant, the immediate self, the very plasm of the self. We speak also of free verse.

All this should have come as a preface to *Look! We Have Come Through!* But is it not better to publish a preface long after the book it belongs to has appeared? For then the reader will have had his fair chance with the book, alone.

[*Mastro-don Gesualdo*, by Giovanni Verga]

It seems curious that modern Italian literature has made so little impression on the European consciousness. A hundred years ago, when Manzoni's *I Promessi Sposi* came out, it met with European applause. Along with Sir Walter Scott and Byron, Manzoni stood for "Romance" to all Europe. Yet where is Manzoni now, even compared to Scott and Byron? Actually, I mean. Nominally, *I Promessi Sposi* is a classic; in fact, it is usually considered *the* classic Italian novel. It is set in all "literature courses." But who reads it? Even in Italy, who reads it? And yet, to my thinking, it is one of the best and most interesting novels ever written: surely a greater book than *Ivanhoe* or *Paul et Virginie* or *Werther*. Why then does nobody read it? Why is it found boring? When I gave a good English translation to the late Katharine Mansfield, she said, to my astonishment: I couldn't read it. Too long and boring.

It is the same with Giovanni Verga. After Manzoni, he is Italy's accepted greatest novelist. Yet nobody takes any notice of him. He is, as far as anybody knows his name, just the man who wrote the libretto to *Cavalleria Rusticana*. Whereas, as a matter of fact, Verga's story *Cavalleria Rusticana* is as much superior to Mascagni's rather cheap music as wine is superior to sugar-water. Verga is one of the greatest masters of the short story. In the volume *Novelle Rusticane* and in the volume entitled *Cavalleria Rusticana* are some of the best short stories ever written. They are sometimes as short and as poignant as Chekhov. I prefer them to Chekhov. Yet nobody reads them. They are "too depressing." They don't depress me half as much as Chekhov does. I don't understand the popular taste.

Verga wrote a number of novels, of different sorts: very different. He was born about 1850, and died, I believe, at the beginning of 1921. So he is a modern. At the same time, he is a classic. And at the same time, again, he is old-fashioned.

The earlier novels are rather of the French type of the seventies —Octave Feuillet, with a touch of Gyp. There is the depressing story of the Sicilian young man who made a Neapolitan marriage, and on the last page gives his wife a much-belated slap across the face. There is the gruesome book, *Tigre Reale*, of the Russian countess—or princess, whatever it is—who comes to Florence and gets fallen in love with by the young Sicilian, with all the subsequent horrid affair: the weird woman dying of consumption, the man weirdly infatuated, in the suicidal South-Italian fashion. It is a bit in the manner of Matilda Serao. And though unpleasant, it is impressive.

Verga himself was a Sicilian, from one of the lonely agricultural villages in the south of the island. He was a gentleman—but not a rich one, presumably: with some means. As a young man, he went to Naples, then he worked at journalism in Milan and Florence. And finally he retired to Catania, to an exclusive, aristocratic old age. He was a shortish, broad man with a big red moustache. He never married.

His fame rests on his two long Sicilian novels, *I Malavoglia* and *Mastro-don Gesualdo,* also on the books of short pieces, *Cavalleria Rusticana, Novelle Rusticane,* and *Vagabondaggio*. These are all placed in Sicily, as is the short novel, *Storia di Una Capinera.* Of this last little book, one of the leading literary young Italians in Rome said to me the other day: Ah, yes, Verga! *Some* of his things! But a thing like *Storia di Una Capinera,* now, is ridiculous.

But why? It is rather sentimental, maybe. But it is no more sentimental than *Tess.* And the sentimentality seems to me to belong to the Sicilian characters in the book, it is true to type, quite as much so as the sentimentality of a book like Dickens's *Christmas Carol,* or George Eliot's *Silas Marner,* both of which works are "ridiculous," if you like, without thereby being wiped out of existence.

The trouble with Verga, as with all Italians, is that he never seems quite to know where he is. When one reads Manzoni, one wonders if he is not more "Gothic" or Germanic, than Italian. And Verga, in the same way, seems to have a borrowed outlook on life: but this time, borrowed from the French. With d'Annunzio the same, it is hard to believe he is really being himself. He gives one the impression of "acting up." Pirandello goes on with the game today. The Italians are always that way: always acting up to somebody else's vision of life. Men like Hardy, Meredith, Dickens, they are just as sentimental and false as the Italians, in their own way. It only happens to be our own brand of falseness and sentimentality.

And yet, perhaps, one can't help feeling that Hardy, Meredith, Dickens, and Maupassant and even people like the Goncourts and Paul Bourget, false in part though they be, are still looking on life with their own eyes. Whereas the Italians give one the impression that they are always borrowing somebody else's eyes to see with, and then letting loose a lot of emotion into a borrowed vision.

This is the trouble with Verga. But on the other hand, everything he does has a weird quality of Verga in it, quite distinct and like nothing else. And yet, perhaps the gross vision of the man is not quite his own. All his movements are his own. But his main motive is borrowed.

This is the unsatisfactory part about all Italian literature, as far as I know it.

The main motive, the gross vision of all the nineteenth-century literature, is what we may call the emotional-democratic vision or motive. It seems to me that since 1860, or even 1830, the Italians have always borrowed their ideals of democracy from the northern nations, and poured great emotion into them, without ever being really grafted by them. Some of the most wonderful martyrs for democracy have been Neapolitan men of birth and breeding. But none the less, it seems a mistake: an attempt to live by somebody else's lights.

Verga's first Sicilian novel, *I Malavoglia,* is of this sort. It was considered his greatest work. It is a great book. But it is *parti pris.* It is one-sided. And therefore it dates. There is too much, too much of the tragic fate of the poor, in it. There is a sort of wallowing in tragedy: the tragedy of the humble. It belongs to a date when the "humble" were almost the most fashionable thing. And the Malavoglia family are most humbly humble. Sicilians of the sea-coast, fishers, small traders–their humble tragedy is so piled on, it becomes almost disastrous. The book was published in America under the title of *The House by the Medlar Tree,* and can still be obtained. It is a great book, a great picture of poor life in Sicily, on the coast just north of Catania. But it is rather overdone on the pitiful side. Like the woebegone pictures by Bastien Lepage. Nevertheless, it is essentially a true picture, and different from anything else in literature. In most books of the period–even in *Madame Bovary,* to say nothing of Balzac's earlier *Lys dans la Vallée*–one has to take off about twenty per cent of the tragedy. One does it in Dickens, one does it in Hawthorne, one does it all the time, with all the great writers. Then why not with Verga? Just knock off about twenty per cent of the tragedy in *I Malavoglia,* and see what a great book remains. Most books that live, live in spite of the author's laying it on thick. Think of *Wuthering Heights.* It is quite as impossible to an Italian as even *I Malavoglia* is to us. But it is a great book.

The trouble with realism—and Verga was a realist—is that the writer, when he is a truly exceptional man like Flaubert or like Verga, tries to read his own sense of tragedy into people much smaller than himself. I think it is a final criticism against *Madame Bovary* that people such as Emma Bovary and her husband Charles simply are too insignificant to carry the full weight of Gustave Flaubert's sense of tragedy. Emma and Charles Bovary are a couple of little people. Gustave Flaubert is not a little person. But, because he is a realist and does not believe in "heroes," Flaubert insists on pouring his own deep and bitter tragic consciousness into the little skins of the country doctor and his uneasy wife. The result is a discrepancy. *Madame Bovary* is a great book and a very wonderful picture of life. But we cannot help resenting the fact that the great tragic soul of Gustave Flaubert is, so to speak, given only the rather commonplace bodies of Emma and Charles Bovary. There's a misfit. And to get over the misfit, you have to let in all sorts of seams of pity. Seams of pity, which won't be hidden.

The great tragic soul of Shakespeare borrows the bodies of kings and princes—not out of snobbism, but out of natural affinity. You can't put a great soul into a commonplace person. Commonplace persons have commonplace souls. Not all the noble sympathy of Flaubert or Verga for Bovarys and Malavoglias can prevent the said Bovarys and Malavoglias from being commonplace persons. They were deliberately chosen because they *were* commonplace, and not heroic. The authors insisted on the treasure of the humble. But they had to lend the humble by far the best part of their own treasure, before the said humble could show any treasure at all.

So, if *I Malavoglia* dates, so does *Madame Bovary*. They belong to the emotional-democratic, treasure-of-the-humble period of the nineteenth century. The period is just rather out of fashion. We still feel the impact of the treasure-of-the-humble too much. When the emotion will have quite gone out of us, we can accept *Madame Bovary* and *I Malavoglia* in the same free spirit with the same detachment as that in which we accept Dickens or Richardson.

Mastro-don Gesualdo, however, is not nearly so much treasure-of-the-humble as *I Malavoglia.* Here, Verga is not dealing with the disaster of poverty, and calling it tragedy. On the contrary, he is a little bored by poverty. He must have a hero who wins out, and makes his pile, and then succumbs under the pile.

Mastro-don Gesualdo started life as a barefoot peasant brat, not a don at all. He becomes very rich. But all he gets of it is a great tumour of bitterness inside, which kills him.

Verga must have known, in actual life, the prototype of Gesualdo. We see him in the marvellous realistic story in *Cavalleria Rusticana,* of a fat little peasant who has become enormously rich, grinding his labourers, and now is diseased and must die. This little fellow is quite unheroic. He has the indomitable greedy will, but nothing else of Gesualdo's rather attractive character.

Gesualdo is attractive, and, in a sense, heroic. But still he is not allowed to emerge in the old heroic sense, with swagger and nobility and head-and-shoulders taller than anything else. He is allowed to have exceptional qualities, and above all, exceptional force. But these things do not make a hero of a man. A hero must be a hero by grace of God, and must have an inkling of the same. Even the old Paladin heroes had a great idea of themselves as exemplars. And Hamlet had the same. "O cursed spite that ever I was born to set it right." Hamlet didn't succeed in setting anything right, but he felt that way. And so all heroes must feel.

But Gesualdo, and Jude, and Emma Bovary are not allowed to feel any of these feelings. As far as *destiny* goes, they felt no more than anybody else. And this is because they belong to the realistic world.

Gesualdo is just an ordinary man with extraordinary energy. That, of course, is the intention. But he is a Sicilian. And here lies the difficulty. Because the realistic-democratic age has dodged the dilemma of having no heroes by having every man his own hero. This is reached by what we call subjective intensity, and in this subjectively-intense every-man-his-own-hero business the Russians have carried us to the greatest lengths. The merest scrub of a pick-pocket is so phenomenally aware of his own soul, that we are made to bow down before the imaginary coruscations that go on inside him. That is almost the whole of Russian literature: the phenomenal coruscations of the souls of quite commonplace people.

Of course your soul will coruscate, if you think it does. That's why the Russians are so popular. No matter how much of a shabby animal you may be, you can learn from Dostoievsky and Chekhov, etc., how to have the most tender, unique, coruscating soul on earth. And so you may be most vastly important to yourself. Which is the private aim of all men. The hero had it openly. The com-monplace person has it inside himself, though outwardly he says: Of course I'm no better than anybody else! His very asserting it shows he doesn't think it for a second. Every character in Dostoievsky or Chekhov thinks himself *inwardly* a nonesuch, absolutely unique.

And here you get the blank opposite, in the Sicilians. The Sicilians simply don't have any subjective idea of themselves, or any souls. Except, of course, that funny little *alter ego* of a soul which can be prayed out of purgatory into paradise, and is just as objective as possible.

The Sicilian, in our sense of the word, doesn't have any soul. He just hasn't got our sort of subjective consciousness, the soulful idea of himself. Souls, to him, are little naked people uncomfortably hopping on hot bricks, and being allowed at last to go up to a garden where there is music and flowers and sanctimonious society, Paradise. Jesus is a man who was crucified by a lot of foreigners and villains, and who can help you against the villainous lot nowadays: as well as against witches and the rest.

The self-tortured Jesus, the self-tortured Hamlet, simply does not exist. Why should a man torture himself? Gesualdo would ask in amazement. Aren't there scoundrels enough in the world to torture him?

Of course, I am speaking of the Sicilians of Verga's day, fifty and sixty years ago, before the great emigration to America, and the great return, with dollars and bits of self-aware souls: at least politically self-aware.

So that in *Mastro-don Gesualdo* you have the very antithesis of what you get in *The Brothers Karamazov*. Anything more un-Russian than Verga it would be hard to imagine: save Homer. Yet Verga has the same sort of pity as the Russians. And, with the Russians, he is a realist. He won't have heroes, nor appeals to gods above nor below.

The Sicilians of today are supposed to be the nearest thing to the classic Greeks that is left to us: that is, they are the nearest descendants on earth. In Greece today there are no Greeks. The nearest thing is the Sicilian, the eastern and south-eastern Sicilian.

And if you come to think of it, Gesualdo Motta might really be a Greek in modern setting, except that he is not intellectual. But this many Greeks were not. And he has the energy, the quickness, the vividness of the Greek, the same vivid passion for wealth, the same ambition, the same lack of scruples, the same queer openness, without ever really openly committing himself. He is not a bit furtive, like an Italian. He is astute instead, far too astute and Greek to let himself be led by the nose. Yet he has a certain frankness, far more than an Italian. And far less fear than an Italian. His boldness and his queer sort of daring are Sicilian rather than Italian, so is his independent manliness.

He is Greek above all in not having any soul or any lofty ideals. The Greeks were far more bent on making an audacious, splendid impression than on fulfilling some noble purpose. They loved the splendid look of a thing, the splendid ring of words. Even tragedy was to them a grand gesture, rather than something to mope over. Peak and pine they would not, and unless some Fury pursued them to punish them for their sins, they cared not a straw for sins: their own or anyone else's.

As for being burdened with souls, they were not such fools.

But alas, ours is the day of souls, when soul pays, and when having a soul is as important to the young as solitaire to a valetudinarian. If you don't have feelings about your soul, what sort of person can you be?

And Gesualdo didn't have feelings about his soul. He was remorselessly and relentlessly objective, like all people that belong to the sun. In the sun, men are objective, in the mist and snow, subjective. Subjectivity is largely a question of the thickness of your overcoat.

When you get to Ceylon, you realize that, to the swarthy Cingalese, even Buddhism is a purely objective affair. And we have managed to spiritualize it to such a subjective pitch.

Then you have the setting to the hero. The south-Sicilian setting to *Mastro-don Gesualdo* is perhaps nearer to the true medieval than anything else in modern literature, even barring the Sardinian medievalism of Grazia Deledda. You have the Sicily of the Bourbons, the Sicily of the kingdom of Naples. The island is incredibly poor and incredibly backward. There are practically no roads for wheeled vehicles, and consequently no wheeled vehicles, neither carts nor carriages, outside the towns. Everything is packed on asses or mules, man travels on horseback or on foot, or, if sick, in a mule-litter. The land is held by the great landowners, the peasants are almost serfs. It is as wild, as poor, and in the ducal houses of Palermo even as splendid and ostentatious as Russia.

Yet how different from Russia! Instead of the wild openness of the north, you have the shut-in, guarded watchfulness of the old Mediterranean. For centuries, the people of the Mediterranean have lived on their guard, intensely on their guard, on the watch, wary, always wary, and holding aloof. So it is even today, in the villages: aloof, holding aloof, each individual inwardly holding aloof from the others; and this in spite of the returned "Americans."

How utterly different it is from Russia, where the people are always—in the books—expanding to one another, and pouring out tea and their souls to one another all night long. In Sicily, by nightfall, nearly every man is barricaded inside his own house. Save in the hot summer, when the night is more or less turned into day.

It all seems, to some people, dark and squalid and brutal and boring. There is no soul, no enlightenment at all. There is not one single enlightened person. If there had been, he would have departed long ago. He could not have stayed.

And for people who seek enlightenment, oh, how boring! But if you have any physical feeling for life, apart from nervous feelings such as the Russians have, nerves, nerves—if you have any appreciation for the southern way of life, then what a strange, deep fascination there is in *Mastro-don Gesualdo!* Perhaps the deepest nostalgia I have ever felt has been for Sicily, reading Verga. Not for England or anywhere else—for Sicily, the beautiful, that which goes deepest into the blood. It is so clear, so beautiful, so like the physical beauty of the Greek.

Yet the lives of the people all seem so squalid, so pottering, so despicable: like a crawling of beetles. And then, the moment you get outside the grey and squalid walls of the village, how wonderful in the sun, with the land lying apart. And isolated, the people too have some of the old Greek singleness, carelessness, dauntlessness. It is only when they bunch together as citizens that they are squalid. In the countryside, they are portentous and subtle, like the wanderers in the Odyssey. And their relations are all curious and immediate, objective. They are so little aware of themselves, and so much aware of their own effects.

It all depends what you are looking for. Gesualdo's lifelong love-affair with Diodata is, according to our ideas, quite impossible. He puts no value on sentiment at all: or almost none: again a real Greek. Yet there is a strange forlorn beauty in it, impersonal, a bit like Rachel or Rebecca. It is of the old, old world, when man is aware of his own belongings, acutely, but only very dimly aware of his own feelings. And feelings you are not aware of, you don't have.

Gesualdo seems so potent, so full of potency. Yet nothing emerges, and he never says anything. It is the very reverse of the Russian, who talks and talks, out of impotence.

And you have a wretched, realistic kind of tragedy for the end. And you feel, perhaps the book was all about nothing, and Gesualdo wasn't worth the labour of Verga.

But that is because we are spiritual snobs, and think, because a man can fume with "To be or not to be," therefore he is a person to be taken account of. Poor Gesualdo had never heard of: To be or not to be, and he wouldn't have taken any notice if he had. He lived blindly, with the impetuosity of blood and muscles, sagacity and will, and he never woke up to himself. Whether he would have been any the better for waking up to himself, who knows!

A Bibliography of D. H. Lawrence, by Edward D. McDonald

There doesn't seem much excuse for me, sitting under a little cedar tree at the foot of the Rockies, looking at the pale desert disappearing westward, with hummocks of shadow rising in the stillness of incipient autumn, this morning, the near pine trees perfectly still, the sunflowers and the purple Michaelmas daisies moving for the first time, this morning, in an invisible breath of breeze, to be writing an introduction to a bibliography.

Books to me are incorporate things, voices in the air, that do not disturb the haze of autumn, and visions that don't blot the sunflowers. What do I care for first or last editions? I have never read one of my own published works. To me, no book has a date, no book has a binding.

What do I care if "e" is somewhere upside down, or "g" comes from the wrong font? I really don't.

And when I force myself to remember, what pleasure is there in that? The very first copy of *The White Peacock* that was ever sent out, I put into my mother's hands when she was dying. She looked at the outside, and then at the title-page, and then at me, with darkening eyes. And though she loved me so much, I think she doubted whether it could be much of a book, since no one more important than I had written it. Somewhere, in the helpless privacies of her being, she had wistful respect for me. But for me in the face of the world, not much. This David would never get a stone across at Goliath. And why try? Let Goliath alone! Anyway, she was beyond reading my first immortal work. It was put aside, and I never wanted to see it again. She never saw it again.

After the funeral, my father struggled through half a page, and it might as well have been Hottentot.

"And what dun they gi'e thee for that, lad?"

"Fifty pounds, father."

"Fifty pounds!" He was dumbfounded, and looked at me with shrewd eyes, as if I were a swindler. "Fifty pounds! An' tha's niver done a day's hard work in thy life."

I think to this day, he looks upon me as a sort of cleverish swindler, who gets money for nothing: a sort of Ernest Hooley. And my sister says, to my utter amazement: "You always were lucky!"

Somehow, it is the actual corpus and substance, the actual paper and rag volume of any of my works, that calls up these personal feelings and memories. It is the miserable tome itself which somehow delivers me to the vulgar mercies of the world. The voice inside is mine for ever. But the beastly marketable chunk of published volume is a bone which every dog presumes to pick with me.

William Heinemann published *The White Peacock*. I saw him once; and then I realized what an immense favour he was doing me. As a matter of fact, he treated me quite well.

I remember at the last minute, when the book was all printed and ready to bind: some even bound: they sent me in great haste a certain page with a marked paragraph. Would I remove this paragraph, as it might be considered "objectionable," and substitute an exactly identical number of obviously harmless words. Hastily I did so. And later, I noticed that the two pages, on one of which was the altered paragraph, were rather loose, not properly bound into the book. Only my mother's copy had the paragraph unchanged.

I have wondered often if Heinemann's just altered the "objectionable" bit in the first little batch of books they sent out, then left the others as first printed. Or whether they changed all but the one copy they sent me ahead.

It was my first experience of the objectionable. Later, William Heinemann said he thought *Sons and Lovers* one of the dirtiest books he had ever read. He refused to publish it. I should not have thought the deceased gentleman's reading had been so circumspectly narrow.

I forget the first appearance of *The Trespasser* and *Sons and Lovers*. I always hide the fact of publication from myself as far as possible. One writes, even at this moment, to some mysterious presence in the air. If that presence were not there, and one thought of even a single solitary actual reader, the paper would remain for ever white.

But I always remember how, in a cottage by the sea, in Italy, I rewrote almost entirely that play, *The Widowing of Mrs. Holroyd,* right on the proofs which Mitchell Kennerley had sent me. And he nobly forbore with me.

But then he gave me a nasty slap. He published *Sons and Lovers* in America, and one day, joyful, arrived a cheque for twenty pounds. Twenty pounds in those days was a little fortune: and as it was a windfall, it was handed over to Madame; the first pin-money she had seen. Alas and alack, there was an alteration in the date of the cheque, and the bank would not cash it. It was returned to Mitchell

Kennerley, but that was the end of it. He never made good, and never to this day made any further payment for *Sons and Lovers*. Till this year of grace 1924, America has had that, my most popular book, for nothing—as far as I am concerned.*

Then came the first edition of *The Rainbow*. I'm afraid I set my rainbow in the sky too soon, before, instead of after, the deluge. Methuen published that book, and he almost wept before the magistrate, when he was summoned for bringing out a piece of indecent literature. He said he did not know the dirty thing he had been handling, he had not read the work, his reader had misadvised him—and Peccavi! Peccavi! wept the now be-knighted gentleman. Then around me arose such a fussy sort of interest, as when a really scandalous bit of scandal is being whispered about one. In print my fellow-authors kept scrupulously silent, lest a bit of the tar might stick to them. Later Arnold Bennett and May Sinclair raised a kindly protest. But John Galsworthy told me, very calmly and *ex cathedra,* he thought the book a failure as a work of art. They think as they please. But why not wait till I ask them, before they deliver an opinion to me? Especially as impromptu opinions by elderly authors are apt to damage him who gives as much as him who takes.

There is no more indecency or impropriety in *The Rainbow* than there is in this autumn morning—I, who say so, ought to know. And when I open my mouth, let no dog bark.

So much for the first edition of *The Rainbow*. The only copy of any of my books I ever keep is my copy of Methuen's *Rainbow*. Because the American editions have all been mutilated. And this is almost my favourite among my novels: this, and *Women in Love*. And I should really be best pleased if it were never reprinted at all, and only those blue, condemned volumes remained extant.

Since *The Rainbow,* one submits to the process of publication as to a necessary evil: as souls are said to submit to the necessary evil of being born into the flesh. The wind bloweth where it listeth. And one must submit to the processes of one's day. Personally, I have no belief in the vast public. I believe that only the winnowed few can care. But publishers, like thistle, must set innumerable seeds on the wind, knowing most will miscarry.

To the vast public, the autumn morning is only a sort of stage background against which they can display their own mechanical

* In a letter to Mr. Edward Garnett, dated April 22, 1914, Lawrence acknowledges the receipt of £35 from Mr. Mitchell Kennerley. *Letters of D. H. Lawrence,* p. 192 (American edition).

importance. But to some men still the trees stand up and look around at the daylight, having woven the two ends of darkness together into visible being and presence. And soon, they will let go the two ends of darkness again, and disappear. A flower laughs once, and having had his laugh, chuckles off into seed, and is gone. Whence? Whither? Who knows, who cares? That little laugh of achieved being is all.

So it is with books. To every man who struggles with his own soul in mystery, a book that is a book flowers once, and seeds, and is gone. First editions or forty-first are only the husks of it.

Yet if it amuses a man to save the husks of the flower that opened once for the first time, one can understand that too. It is like the costumes that men and women used to wear, in their youth, years ago, and which now stand up rather faded in museums. With a jolt they reassemble for us the day-to-day actuality of the bygone people, and we see the trophies once more of man's eternal fight with inertia.

Max Havelaar, by E. D. Dekker (Multatuli, pseud.)

Max Havelaar was first published in Holland, nearly seventy years ago, and it created a *furore*. In Germany it was the book of the moment, even in England it had a liberal vogue. And to this day it remains vaguely in the minds of foreigners as the one Dutch classic.

I say vaguely, because many well-read people know nothing about it. Mr. Bernard Shaw, for example, confessed that he had never heard of it. Which is curious, considering the esteem in which it was held by men whom we might call the pre-Fabians, both in England and in America, sixty years ago.

But then *Max Havelaar*, when it appeared, was hailed as a book with a purpose. And the Anglo-Saxon mind loves to hail such books. They are so obviously in the right. The Anglo-Saxon mind also loves to forget completely, in a very short time, any book with a purpose. It is a bore, with its insistency.

So we have forgotten, with our usual completeness, all about *Max Havelaar* and about Multatuli, its author. Even the pseudonym, Multatuli (Latin for: I suffered much, or: I endured much), is to us irritating as it was exciting to our grandfathers. We don't care for poor but noble characters who are aware that they have suffered much. There is too much self-awareness.

On the surface, *Max Havelaar* is a tract or a pamphlet very much in the same line as *Uncle Tom's Cabin*. Instead of "pity the poor Negro slave" we have "pity the poor oppressed Javanese"; with the same urgent appeal for legislation, for the government to do something about it. Well, the government did something about Negro slaves, and *Uncle Tom's Cabin* fell out of date. The Netherlands government is also said to have done something in Java for the poor Javanese, on the strength of Multatuli's book. So that *Max Havelaar* became a back number.

So far so good. If by writing tract-novels you can move governments to improve matters, then write tract-novels by all means. If the government, however, plays up, and does its bit, then the tract-novel has served its purpose, and descends from the stage like a political orator who has made his point.

This is all in the course of nature. And because this is the course of nature, many educated Hollanders today become impatient when they hear educated Germans or English or Americans referring to *Max Havelaar* as "the one Dutch classic." So Americans would feel if they heard *Uncle Tom's Cabin* referred to as "the one American classic." *Uncle Tom* is a back number in the English-speaking world, and *Max Havelaar* is, to the Dutch-speaking world, another.

If you ask a Hollander for a really good Dutch novelist he refers you to the man who wrote: *Old People and the Things that Pass,* (Louis Couperus)—or else to somebody you know nothing about.

As regards the Dutch somebody I know nothing about, I am speechless. But as regards *Old People and the Things that Pass* I still think *Max Havelaar* a far more real book. And since *Old People* etc. is quite a good contemporary novel, one needs to find out why *Max Havelaar* is better.

I have not tried to read *Uncle Tom's Cabin* since I was a boy, and wept. I will try again, when I come across a copy. But I am afraid it will pall. I know I shan't weep.

Then why doesn't *Max Havelaar* pall? Why can one still read every word of it? As far as composition goes, it is the greatest mess possible. How the reviewers of today would tear it across and throw it in the w.p.b! But the reviewers of today, like the clergy, feel that they must justify God to man, and when they find they can't do it, when the book or the Almighty seems really unjustifiable, in the sight of common men, they apply the w.p.b.

It is surely the mistake of modern criticism, to conceive the public, the man-in-the-street, as the real god, who must be served and flattered by every book that appears, even if it were the Bible. To my thinking, the critic, like a good beadle, should rap the public on the knuckles and make it attend during divine service. And any good book is divine service.

The critic, having dated *Max Havelaar* a back number, hits him on the head if he dares look up, and says: Down! Revere the awesome modernity of the holy public!

I say: Not at all! The thing in *Max* that the public once loved, the tract, is really a back number. But there is so very little of the tract, actually, and what there is, the author has retracted so comically, as he went, that the reader can grin as he goes.

It was a stroke of cunning journalism on Multatuli's part (Dostoievsky also made such strokes of cunning journalism) to put his book through on its face value as a tract. What Multatuli really wanted was to get his book over. He wanted to be heard. He wanted to be read. *I want to be heard. I will be heard!* he vociferates on the last pages. He himself must have laughed in his sleeve as he vociferated. But the public gaped and fell for it.

He was the passionate missionary for the poor Javanese! Because he knew missionaries were, and are, listened to! And the Javanese were a good stick with which to beat the dog. The successful public being the dog. Which dog he longed to beat. To give it the trouncing of its life!

He did it, in missionary guise, in *Max Havelaar*. The book isn't really a tract, it is a satire. Multatuli isn't really a preacher, he's a satirical humourist. Straight on in the life of Jean Paul Richter the same bitter, almost mad-dog aversion from humanity that appeared in Jean Paul, appears again in Multatuli, as it appears in the later Mark Twain. Dostoievsky was somewhat the same, but in him the missionary had swallowed the mad dog of revulsion, so that the howls of derision are all ventriloquistic undertone.

Max Havelaar isn't a tract or a pamphlet, it is a satire. The satire on the Dutch bourgeois, in Drystubble, is final. The coffee-broker is reduced to his ultimate nothingness, in pure humour. It is the reduction of the prosperous business man in America and England today, just the same, essentially the same: and it is a death-stroke.

Similarly, the Java part of the book is a satire on colonial administration, and on government altogether. It is quite direct and straightforward satire, so it is wholesome. Multatuli never quite falls down the fathomless well of his own revulsion, as Dostoievsky did, to become a lily-mouthed missionary rumbling with ventral howls of derision and dementia. At his worst, Multatuli is irritatingly sentimental, harping on pity when he is inspired by hate. Maybe he deceives himself. But never for long.

His sympathy with the Javanese is also genuine enough; there was a man in him whose bowels of compassion were moved. Whereas a great nervous genius like Dostoievsky never felt a moment of real physical sympathy in his life. But with Multatuli, the sympathy for the Javanese is rather an excuse for hating the Dutch authorities still further. It is the sympathy of a man preoccupied with other feelings.

We see this in the famous idyll of Saïdyah and Adinda, once the most beloved and most quoted part of the book. We see how it bored the author to write it, after the first few pages. He *tells* us it bored him. It bored him to write sympathetically. He was by nature a satirical humorist, and it was far more exciting for him to be attacking the Dutch officials than sympathizing with the Javanese.

This is again obvious in his partiality for the old Native Prince, the Regent. It is obvious that all the *actual* oppression of the poor Javanese came from the Javanese themselves, the native princes. It isn't the Dutch officials who steal Saïdyah's buffalo: it is the princely Javanese. The oppression has been going on, Havelaar himself says it, *since the beginning of time*. Not since the coming of the Dutch. Indeed, it is the Oriental idea that the prince shall oppress his humble subjects. So why blame the Dutch officials so absolutely? Why not take the old native Regent by the beard?

But no! Multatuli, Max Havelaar, swims with pity for the poor and oppressed, but only because he hates the powers-that-be so intensely. He doesn't hate the powers because he loves the oppressed. The boot is on the other leg. The chick of pity comes out of the egg of hate. It is perhaps always so, with pity. But here we have to distinguish compassion from pity.

Surely, when Saïdyah sets off into the world, or is defended by the buffalo, it is compassion Multatuli feels for him, not pity. But the end is pity only.

The bird of hate hatches the chick of pity. The great dynamic force in Multatuli is as it was, really, in Jean Paul and in Swift and Gogol and in Mark Twain, hate, a passionate, honourable hate. It is honourable to hate Drystubble, and Multatuli hated him. It is honourable to hate cowardly officialdom, and Maltatuli hated that. Sometimes, it is even honourable, and necessary, to hate society, as Swift did, or to hate mankind altogether, as often Voltaire did.

For man tends to deteriorate into that which Drystubble was, and the Governor-General and Slimering, something hateful, which must be destroyed. Then in comes Maltatuli, like Jack and the Beanstalk, to fight the giant.

And when Jack fights the giant, he *must* have recourse to a trick. David thought of a sling and stone. Multatuli took a sort of missionary disguise. The gross public accepted the disguise, and David's stone went home. *À la guerre comme à la guerre*.

When there are no more Drystubbles, no more Governor-Generals or Slimerings, then *Max Havelaar* will be out of date. The book is a pill rather than a comfit. The jam of pity was put on to get the pill down. Our fathers and grandfathers licked the jam off. We can still go on taking the pill, for the social constipation is as bad as ever.

Cavalleria Rusticana, by Giovanni Verga

Cavalleria Rusticana is in many ways the most interesting of the Verga books. The volume of short stories under this title appeared in 1880, when the author was forty years old, and when he had just "retired" from the world.

The Verga family owned land around Vizzini, a biggish village in southern Sicily; and here, in and around Vizzini, the tragedies of Turiddu and La Lupa and Jeli take place. But it was only in middle life that the drama of peasant passion really made an impression on Giovanni Verga. His earlier imagination, naturally, went out into the great world.

The family of the future author lived chiefly at Catania, the seaport of east Sicily, under Etna. And Catania was really Verga's home town, just as Vizzini was his home village.

But as a young man of twenty he already wanted to depart into the bigger world of "the Continent," as the Sicilians called the mainland of Italy. It was the Italy of 1860, the Italy of Garibaldi, and the new era. Verga seems to have taken little interest in politics. He had no doubt the southern idea of himself as a gentleman and an aristocrat, beyond politics. And he had the ancient southern thirst for show, for lustre, for glory, a desire to figure grandly among the first society of the world. His nature was proud and unmixable. At the same time, he had the southern passionate yearning for tenderness and generosity. And so he ventured into the world, without much money; and, in true southern fashion, he was dazzled. To the end of his days he was dazzled by elegant ladies in elegant equipages: one sees it, amusingly, in all his books.

He was a handsome man, by instinct haughty and reserved: because, partly, he was passionate and emotional, and did not choose to give himself away. A true provincial, he had to try to enter the *beau monde*. He lived by journalism, more or less: certainly the Vizzini lands would not keep him in affluence. But still, in his comparative poverty, he must enter the *beau monde*.

He did so: and apparently with a certain success. And for nearly twenty years he lived in Milan, in Florence, in Naples, writing, and imagining he was fulfilling his thirst for glory by having love-affairs with elegant ladies: most elegant ladies, as he assures us.

To this period belong the curiously unequal novels of the city world: *Eva, Tigre Reale, Eros.* They are interesting, alive, bitter, somewhat unhealthy, smelling of the seventies and of the Paris of the Goncourts, and, in some curious way, abortive. The man had not found himself. He was in his wrong element, fooling himself and being fooled by show, in a true Italian fashion.

Then, towards the age of forty, came the recoil, and the *Cavalleria Rusticana* volume is the first book of the recoil. It was a recoil away from the *beau monde* and the "Continent," back to Sicily, to Catania, to the peasants. Verga never married: but he was deeply attached to his own family. He lived in Catania, with his sister. His brother, or brother-in-law, who had looked after the Vizzini property, was ill. So for the first time in his life Giovanni Verga had to undertake the responsibility for the family estate and fortune. He had to go to Vizzini and more or less manage the farm work–at least keep an eye on it. He said he hated the job, that he had no capacity for business, and so on. But we may be sure he managed very well. And certainly from this experience he gained his real fortune, his genuine sympathy with peasant life, instead of his spurious sympathy with elegant ladies. His great books all followed *Cavalleria Rusticana:* and *Mastro-don Gesualdo* and the *Novelle Rusticane* ("Little Novels of Sicily") and most of the sketches have their scenes laid in or around Vizzini.

So that *Cavalleria Rusticana* marks a turning-point in the man's life. Verga still looks back to the city elegance, and makes such a sour face over it, it is really funny. The sketch he calls "Fantasticheria" ("Caprice") and the last story in the book, "Il Come, il Quando, et il Perché" ("The How, When, and Wherefore") both deal with the elegant little lady herself. The sketch "Caprice" we may take as autobiographical–the story not entirely so. But we have enough data to go on.

The elegant little lady is the same, pretty, spoilt, impulsive emotional, but without passion. The lover, Polidori, is only half-sketched. But evidently he is a passionate man who *thinks* he can play at love and then is mortified to his very soul because he finds it is only a game. The tone of mortification is amusingly evident both in the sketch and in the story. Verga is profoundly and everlastingly offended with the little lady, with all little ladies, for not taking him absolutely seriously as an amorous male, when all the time he doesn't quite take himself seriously, and doesn't take the little lady seriously at all.

Nevertheless, the moment of sheer roused passion is serious in the man: and apparently not so in the woman. Each time the moment comes, it involves the whole nature of the man and does not involve the whole nature of the woman: she still clings to her social safeguards. It is the difference between a passionate nature and an emotional nature. But then the man goes out deliberately to make love to the emotional elegant woman who is truly social and not passionate. So he has only himself to blame if his passionate nose is out of joint.

It is most obviously out of joint. His little picture of the elegant little lady jingling her scent-bottle and gazing in nervous anxiety for the train from Catania which will carry her away from Aci-Trezza and her too-intense lover, back to her light, gay, secure world on the mainland is one of the most amusingly biting things in the literature of love. How glad she must have been to get away from him! And how bored she must have been by his preaching the virtues of the humble poor, holding them up before her to make her feel small. We may be sure she doesn't feel small, only nervous and irritable. For apparently she had no deep warmth or generosity of nature.

So Verga recoiled to the humble poor, as we see in his "Caprice" sketch. Like a southerner, what he did he did wholesale. Floods of savage and tragic pity he poured upon the humble fisher-folk of Aci-Trezza, whether they asked for it or not—partly to spite the elegant little lady. And this particular flood spreads over the whole of his long novel concerning the fisher-folk of Aci-Trezza: *I Malavoglia*. It is a great novel, in spite of the pity: but always in spite of it.

In *Cavalleria Rusticana,* however, Verga had not yet come to the point of letting loose his pity. He is still too much and too profoundly offended, as a passionate male. He recoils savagely away from the sophistications of the city life of elegant little ladies, to the peasants in their most crude and simple, almost brute-like aspect.

When one reads, one after the other, the stories of Turiddu, La Lupa, Jeli, Brothpot, Rosso Malpelo, one after the other, stories of crude killing, it seems almost too much, too crude, too violent, too much a question of mere brutes.

As a matter of fact, the judgment is unjust. Turiddu is not a brute: neither is Alfio. Both are men of sensitive and even honourable nature. Turiddu knows he is wrong, and would even let himself be killed, he says, but for the thought of his old mother. The elegant Maria and her Erminia are never so sensitive and direct in expressing themselves; not so frankly warm-hearted.

As for Jeli, who could call him a brute? or Nanni? or Brothpot? They are perhaps not brutal enough. They are too gentle and forbearing, too delicately naïve. And so grosser natures trespass on them unpardonably; and the revenge flashes out.

His contemporaries abused Verga for being a realist of the Zola school. The charge is unjust. The base of the charge against Zola is that he made his people too often merely physical-functional arrangements, physically and materially functioning without any "higher" nature. The charge against Zola is often justifiable. It is completely justifiable against the earlier d'Annunzio. In fact, the Italian tends on the one hand to be this creature of physical-functional activity and nothing else, spasmodically sensual and materialist; hence the violent Italian outcry against the portrayal of such creatures, and d'Annunzio's speedy transition to neurotic Virgins of the Rocks and ultra-refinements.

But Verga's people are always people in the purest sense of the word. They are not intellectual, but then neither was Hector nor Ulysses intellectual. Verga, in his recoil, mistrusted everything that smelled of sophistication. He had a passion for the most naïve, the most unsophisticated manifestation of human nature. He was not seeking the brute, the animal man, the so-called cave-man. Far from it. He knew already too well that the brute and the cave-man lie quite near under the skin of the ordinary successful man of the world. There you have the predatory cave-man of vulgar imagination, thinly hidden under expensive cloth.

What Verga's soul yearned for was the purely naïve human being, in contrast to the sophisticated. It seems as if Sicily, in some way, under all her amazing forms of sophistication and corruption, still preserves some flower of pure human candour: the same thing that fascinated Theocritus. Theocritus was an Alexandrine courtier, singing from all his "musk and insolence" of the pure idyllic Sicilian shepherds. Verga is the Theocritus of the nineteenth century, born among the Sicilian shepherds, and speaking of them in prose more sadly than Theocritus, yet with some of the same eternal Sicilian dawn-freshness in his vision. It is almost bitter to think that Rosso Malpelo must often have looked along the coast and seen the rocks that the Cyclops flung at Ulysses; and that Jeli must some time or other have looked to the yellow temple-ruins of Girgenti.

Verga was fascinated, after his mortification in the *beau monde,* by pure naïveté and by the spontaneous passion of life, that spurts beyond all convention or even law. Yet as we read, one after the other, of these betrayed husbands killing the co-respondents, it seems a little mechanical. Alfio, Jeli, Brothpot, Gramigna ending their life in prison: it seems a bit futile and hopeless, mechanical again.

The fault is partly Verga's own, the fault of his own obsession. He felt himself in some way deeply mortified, insulted in his ultimate sexual or male self, and he enacted over and over again the drama of revenge. We think to ourselves, ah, how stupid of Alfio, of Jeli, of Brothpot, to have to go killing a man and getting themselves shut up in prison for life, merely because the man had committed adultery with their wives. Was it worth it? Was the wife worth one year of prison, to a man, let alone a lifetime?

We ask the question with our reason, and with our reason we answer No! Not for a moment was any of these women worth it. Nowadays we have learnt more sense, and we let her go her way. So the stories are too old-fashioned.

And again, it was not for love of their wives that Jeli and Alfio and Brothpot killed the other man. It was because people talked. It was because of the fiction of "honour." We have got beyond all that.

We are so much more reasonable. All our life is so much more reasoned and reasonable. *Nous avons changé tout cela.*

And yet, as the years go by, one wonders if mankind is so radically changed. One wonders whether reason, sweet reason, has really changed us, or merely delayed or diverted our reactions. Are Alfio and Jeli and Gramigna utterly out of date, a thing superseded for ever? Or are they eternal?

Is man a sweet and reasonable creature? Or is he, basically, a passional phenomenon? Is man a phenomenon on the face of the earth, or a rational consciousness? Is human behaviour to be reasonable, throughout the future, reasoned and rational?—or will it always display itself in strange and violent phenomena?

Judging from all experience, past and present, one can only decide that human behaviour is ultimately one of the natural phenomena, beyond all reason. Part of the phenomenon, for the time being, is human reason, the control of reason, and the power of the Word. But the Word and the reason are themselves only part of the coruscating phenomenon of human existence; they are, so to speak, one rosy shower from the rocket, which gives way almost instantly to the red shower of ruin or the green shower of despair.

Man is a phenomenon on the face of the earth. But the phenomena have their laws. One of the laws of the phenomenon called a human being is that, hurt this being mortally at its sexual root, and it will recoil ultimately into some form of killing. The recoil may be prompt, or delay by years or even by generations. But it will come. We may take it as a law.

We may take it as another law that the very deepest quick of a man's nature is his own pride and self-respect. The human being, weird phenomenon, may be patient for years and years under insult, insult to his very quick, his pride in his own natural being. But at last, O phenomenon, killing will come of it. All bloody revolutions are the result of the long, slow, accumulated insult to the quick of pride in the mass of men.

A third law is that the naïve or innocent core in a man is always his vital core, and infinitely more important than his intellect or his reason. It is only from his core of unconscious naïveté that the human being is ultimately a responsible and dependable being. Break this human core of naïveté–and the evil of the world all the time tries to break it, in Jeli, in Rosso Malpelo, in Brothpot, in all these Verga characters–and you get either a violent reaction, or, as is usual nowadays, a merely rational creature whose core of spontaneous life is dead. Now the rational creature, who is merely rational, by some cruel trick of fate remains rational only for one or two generations at best. Then he is quite mad. It is one of the terrible qualities of the reason that it has no life of its own, and unless continually kept nourished or modified by the naïve life in man and woman, it becomes a purely parasitic and destructive thing. Make any human being a really rational being, and you have made him a parasitic and destructive force. Make any people mainly rational in their life, and their inner activity will be the activity of destruction. The more the populations of the world become only rational in their consciousness, the swifter they bring about their destruction pure and simple.

Verga, like every great artist, had sensed this. What he bewails really, as the tragedy of tragedies, in this book, is the ugly trespass of the sophisticated greedy ones upon the naïve life of the true human being: the death of the naïve, pure being–or his lifelong imprisonment–and the triumph or the killing of the sophisticated greedy ones.

This is the tragedy of tragedies in all time, but particularly in our epoch: the killing off of the naïve innocent life in all of us, by which alone we can continue to live, and the ugly triumph of the sophisticated greedy.

It may be urged that Verga commits the Tolstoian fallacy, of repudiating the educated world and exalting the peasant. But this is not the case. Verga is very much the gentleman, exclusively so, to the end of his days. He did not dream of putting on a peasant's smock, or following the plough. What Tolstoi somewhat perversely worshipped in the peasants was poverty itself, and humility, and what Tolstoi perversely hated was instinctive pride or spontaneous passion. Tolstoi has a perverse pleasure in making the later Vronsky abject and pitiable: because Tolstoi so meanly envied the healthy passionate male in the young Vronsky. Tolstoi cut off his own nose to spite his face. He envied the reckless passionate male with a carking envy, because he must have felt himself in some way wanting in comparison. So he exalts the peasant: not because the peasant may be a more natural and spontaneous creature than the city man or the guardsman, but just because the peasant is poverty-stricken and humble. This is malice, the envy of weakness and deformity.

We know now that the peasant is no better than anybody else; no better than a prince or a selfish young army officer or a governor or a merchant. In fact, in the mass, the peasant is worse than any of these. The peasant mass is the ugliest of all human masses, most greedily selfish and brutal of all. Which Tolstoi, leaning down from the gold bar of heaven, will have had opportunity to observe. If we have to trust to a *mass,* then better trust the upper or middle-class mass, all masses being odious.

But Verga by no means exalts the peasants as a class: nor does he believe in their poverty and humility. Verga's peasants are certainly not Christ-like, whatever else they are. They are most normally ugly and low, the bulk of them. And individuals are sensitive and simple.

Verga turns to the peasants only to seek for a certain something which, as a healthy artist, he worshipped. Even Tolstoi, as a healthy artist, worshipped it the same. It was only as a moralist and a personal being that Tolstoi was perverse. As a true artist, he worshipped, as Verga did, every manifestation of pure, spontaneous, passionate life, life kindled to vividness. As a perverse moralist with a sense of some subtle deficiency in himself, Tolstoi tries to insult and to damp out the vividness of life. Imagine any great artist making the vulgar social condemnation of Anna and Vronsky figure as divine punishment! Where now is the society that turned its back on Vronsky and Anna? Where is it? And what is its condemnation worth, today?

Verga turned to the peasants to find, *in individuals,* the vivid spontaneity of sensitive passionate life, non-moral and non-didactic. He found it always *defeated.* He found the vulgar and the greedy always destroying the sensitive and the passionate. The vulgar and the greedy are themselves usually peasants: Verga was far too sane to put an aureole round the whole class. Still more are the women greedy and egoistic. But even so, Turiddu and Jeli and Rosso Malpelo and Nanni and Gramigna and Brothpot are not humble. They have no saint-like, self-sacrificial qualities. They are only naïve, passionate, and natural. They are "defeated" not because there is any glory or sanctification in defeat; there is no martyrdom about it. They are defeated because they are too unsuspicious, not sufficiently armed and ready to do battle with the greedy and the sophisticated. When they do strike, they destroy themselves too. So the real tragedy is that they are not sufficiently conscious and developed to defend their own naïve sensitiveness against the inroads of the greedy and the vulgar. The greedy and the vulgar win all the time: which, alas, is only too true, in Sicily as everywhere else. But Giovanni Verga certainly doesn't help them, by preaching humility. He does show them the knife of revenge at their throat.

And these stories, instead of being out of date, just because the manners depicted are more or less obsolete, even in Sicily, which is a good deal Americanized and "cleaned up," as the reformers would say; instead of being out of date, they are dynamically perhaps the most up to date of stories. The Chekhovian after-influenza effect of inertia and will-lessness is wearing off, all over Europe. We realize we've had about enough of being null. And if Chekhov represents the human being driven into an extremity of self-consciousness and faintly-wriggling inertia, Verga represents him as waking suddenly from inaction into the stroke of revenge. We shall see which of the two visions is more deeply true to life.

"Cavalleria Rusticana" and "La Lupa" have always been hailed as masterpieces of brevity and gems of literary form. Masterpieces they are, but one is now a little sceptical of their form. After the enormous diffusiveness of Victor Hugo, it was perhaps necessary to make the artist more self-critical and self-effacing. But any wholesale creed in art is dangerous. Hugo's romanticism, which consisted in letting himself go, in an orgy of effusive self-conceit, was not much worse than the next creed the French invented for the artist, of self-effacement. Self-effacement is quite as self-conscious, and perhaps even more conceited than letting oneself go. Maupassant's self-effacement becomes more blatant than Hugo's self-effusion. As for the perfection of form achieved—Mérimée achieved the highest, in his dull stories like "Mateo Falcone" and "L'Enlèvement de la Redoute." But they are hopelessly literary, fabricated. So is most of Maupassant. And if *Madame Bovary* has form, it is a pretty flat form.

But Verga was caught up by the grand idea of self-effacement in art. Anything more confused, more silly, really, than the pages prefacing the excellent story "Gramigna's Lover" would be hard to find, from the pen of a great writer. The moment Verga starts talking theories, our interest wilts immediately. The theories were none of his own: just borrowed from the literary smarties of Paris. And poor Verga looks a sad sight in Paris ready-mades. And when he starts putting his theories into practice, and effacing himself, one is far more aware of his interference than when he just goes ahead. Naturally! Because self-effacement is, of course, self-conscious, and any form of emotional self-consciousness hinders a first-rate artist: though it may help the second-rate.

Therefore in "Cavalleria Rusticana" and in "La Lupa" we are just a bit too much aware of the author and his scissors. He has clipped too many away. The transitions are too abrupt. All is over in a gasp: whereas a story like "La Lupa" covers at least several years of time.

As a matter of fact, we need more looseness. We need an apparent formlessness, definite form is mechanical. We need more easy transition from mood to mood and from deed to deed. A great deal of the meaning of life and of art lies in the apparently dull spaces, the pauses, the unimportant passages. They are truly passages, the places of passing over.

So that Verga's deliberate missing-out of transition passages is, it seems to me, often a defect. And for this reason a story like "La Lupa" loses a great deal of its life. It may be a masterpiece of concision, but it is hardly a masterpiece of narration. It is so short, our acquaintance with Nanni and Maricchia is so fleeting, we forget them almost at once. "Jeli" makes a far more profound impression, so does "Rosso Malpelo." These seem to me the finest stories in the book, and among the finest stories ever written. Rosso Malpelo is an extreme of the human consciousness, subtle and appalling as anything done by the Russians, and at the same time substantial, not introspective vapours. You will never forget him.

And it needed a deeper genius to write "Rosso Malpelo" than to write "Cavalleria Rusticana" or "La Lupa." But the literary smarties, being so smart, have always praised the latter two above the others.

This business of missing out transition passages is quite deliberate on Verga's part. It is perhaps most evident in this volume, because it is here that Verga practises it for the first time. It was a new dodge, and he handled it badly. The sliding-over of the change from Jeli's boyhood to his young manhood is surely too deliberately confusing!

But Verga had a double motive. First was the Frenchy idea of self-effacement, which, however, didn't go very deep, as Verga was too much of a true southerner to know quite what it meant. But the second motive was more dynamic. It was connected with Verga's whole recoil from the sophisticated world, and it effected a revolution in his style. Instinctively he had come to hate the tyranny of a persistently logical sequence, or even a persistently chronological sequence. Time and the syllogism both seemed to represent the sophisticated falsehood and a sort of bullying, to him.

He tells us himself how he came across his new style:

"I had published several of my first novels. They went well: I was preparing others. One day, I don't know how, there came into my hands a sort of broadside, a halfpenny sheet, sufficiently ungrammatical and disconnected, in which a sea-captain succinctly relates all the vicissitudes through which his sailing-ship has passed. Seaman's language, short, without an unnecessary phrase. It struck me, and I read it again; it was what I was looking for, without definitely knowing it. Sometimes, you know, just a sign, an indication is enough. It is a revelation. . . ."

This passage explains all we need to know about Verga's style, which is perhaps at its most extreme in this volume. He was trying to follow the workings of the unsophisticated mind, and trying to reproduce the pattern.

Now the emotional mind, if we may be allowed to say so, is not logical. It is a psychological fact, that when we are thinking emotionally or passionately, thinking and feeling at the same time, we do not think rationally: and therefore, and therefore, and therefore. Instead, the mind makes curious swoops and circles. It touches the point of pain or interest, then sweeps away again in a cycle, coils round and approaches again the point of pain or interest. There is a curious spiral rhythm, and the mind approaches again and again the point of concern, repeats itself, goes back, destroys the time-sequence entirely, so that time ceases to exist, as the mind stoops to the quarry, then leaves it without striking, soars, hovers, turns, swoops, stoops again, still does not strike, yet is nearer, nearer, reels away again, wheels off into the air, even forgets, quite forgets, yet again turns, bends, circles slowly, swoops and stoops again, until at last there is the closing-in, and the clutch of a decision or a resolve.

This activity of the mind is strictly timeless, and illogical. Afterwards you can deduce the logical sequence and the time sequence, as historians do from the past. But in the happening, the logical and the time sequence do not exist.

Verga tried to convey this in his style. It gives at first the sense of jumble and incoherence. The beginning of the story "Brothpot" is a good example of this breathless muddle of the peasant mind. When one is used to it, it is amusing, and a new movement in deliberate consciousness: though the humorists have used the form before. But at first it may be annoying. Once he starts definitely narrating, however, Verga drops the "muddled" method, and seeks only to be concise, often too concise, too abrupt in the transition. And in the matter of punctuation he is, perhaps deliberately, a puzzle, aiming at the same muddled swift effect of the emotional mind in its movements. He is doing, as a great artist, what men like James Joyce do only out of contrariness and desire for a sensation. The emotional mind, however apparently muddled, has its own rhythm, its own commas and colons and full-stops. They are not always as we should expect them, but they are there, indicating that other rhythm.

Everybody knows, of course, that Verga made a dramatized version of "Cavalleria Rusticana," and that this dramatized version is the libretto of the ever-popular little opera of the same name. So that Mascagni's rather feeble music has gone to immortalize a man like Verga, whose only *popular* claim to fame is that he wrote the aforesaid libretto. But that is fame's fault, not Verga's.

Instead of bewailing a lost youth, a man nowadays begins to wonder, when he reaches my ripe age of forty-two, if ever his past will subside and be comfortably bygone. Doing over these poems makes me realize that my teens and my twenties are just as much me, here and now and present, as ever they were, and that pastness is only an abstraction. The actuality, the body of feeling, is essentially alive and here.

And I remember the slightly self-conscious Sunday afternoon, when I was nineteen, and I "composed" my first two "poems." One was to "Guelder-roses," and one to "Campions," and most young ladies would have done better: at least I hope so. But I thought the effusions very nice, and so did Miriam.

Then much more vaguely I remember subsequent half-furtive moments when I would absorbedly scribble at verse for an hour or so, and then run away from the act and the production as if it were secret sin. It seems to me that "knowing oneself" was a sin and a vice for innumerable centuries, before it became a virtue. It seems to me, it is still a sin and vice, when it comes to new knowledge. In those early days—for I was very green and unsophisticated at twenty —I used to feel myself at times haunted by something, and a little guilty about it, as if it were an abnormality. Then the haunting would get the better of me, and the ghost would suddenly appear, in the shape of a usually rather incoherent poem. Nearly always I shunned the apparition once it had appeared. From the first, I was a little afraid of my real poems—not my "compositions," but the poems that had the ghost in them. They seemed to me to come from somewhere, I didn't quite know where, out of a me whom I didn't know and didn't want to know, and to say things I would much rather not have said: for choice. But there they were. I never read them again. Only I gave them to Miriam, and she loved them, or she seemed to. So when I was twenty-one, and went to Nottingham University as a day-student, I began putting them down in a little college note-book, which was the foundation of the poetic me. *Sapientiae Urbs Conditur,* it said on the cover. Never was anything less true. The city is founded on a passionate unreason.

To this day, I still have the uneasy haunted feeling, and would rather not write most of the things I do write—including this Note.

Only now I know my demon better, and, after bitter years, respect him more than my other, milder and nicer self. Now I no longer like my "compositions." I once thought the poem "Flapper" a little masterpiece: when I was twenty: because the demon isn't in it. And I must have burnt many poems that had the demon fuming in them. The fragment "Discord in Childhood" was a long poem, probably was good, but I destroyed it. Save for Miriam, I perhaps should have destroyed them all. She encouraged my demon. But alas, it was me, not he, whom she loved. So for her too it was a catastrophe. My demon is not easily loved: whereas the ordinary me is. So poor Miriam was let down. Yet in a sense, she let down my demon, till he howled. And there it is. And no more *past* in me than my blood in my toes or my nose.

I have tried to arrange the poems in chronological order: that is, in the order in which they were written. The first are either subjective, or Miriam poems. "The Wild Common" was very early and very confused. I have rewritten some of it, and added some, till it seems complete. It has taken me twenty years to say what I started to say, incoherently, when I was nineteen, in this poem. The same with "Virgin Youth," and others of the subjective poems with the demon fuming in them smokily. To the demon, the past is not past. The wild common, the gorse, the virgin youth are here and now. The same: the same me, the same one experience. Only now perhaps I can give it more complete expression.

The poems to Miriam, at least the early ones like "Dog-Tired" and "Cherry-Robbers" and "Renascence," are not much changed. But some of the later ones had to be altered, where sometimes the hand of commonplace youth had been laid on the mouth of the demon. It is not for technique these poems are altered: it is to say the real say.

Other verses, those I call the imaginative, or fictional, like "Love on the Farm" and "Wedding Morn," I have sometimes changed to get them into better form, and take out the dead bits. It took me many years to learn to play with the form of a poem: even if I can do it now. But it is only in the less immediate, the more fictional poems that the form has to be played with. The demon, when he's really there, makes his own form willy-nilly, and is unchangeable.

The poems to Miriam run into the first poems to my mother. Then when I was twenty-three, I went away from home for the first time, to the south of London. From the big new red school where I taught, we could look north and see the Crystal Palace: to me, who saw it for the first time, in lovely autumn weather, beautiful and softly blue on its hill to the north. And past the school, on an embankment, the trains rushed south to Brighton or to Kent. And round the school the country was still only just being built over, and the elms of Surrey stood tall and noble. It was different from the Midlands.

Then began the poems to Helen, and all that trouble of "Lilies in the Fire": and London, and school, a whole new world. Then starts the rupture with home, with Miriam, away there in Nottinghamshire. And gradually the long illness, and then the death of my mother; and in the sick year after, the collapse of Miriam, of Helen, and of the other woman, the woman of "Kisses in the Train" and "The Hands of the Betrothed."

Then, in that year, for me everything collapsed, save the mystery of death, and the haunting of death in life. I was twenty-five, and from the death of my mother, the world began to dissolve around me, beautiful, iridescent, but passing away substanceless. Till I almost dissolved away myself, and was very ill: when I was twenty-six.

Then slowly the world came back: or I myself returned: but to another world. And in 1912, when I was still twenty-six, the other phase commenced, the phase of *Look! We Have Come Through!*—when I left teaching, and left England, and left many other things, and the demon had a new run for his money.

But back in England during the war, there are the War poems from the little volume: *Bay*. These, beginning with "Tommies in the Train," make up the end of the volume of *Rhyming Poems*. They are the end of the cycle of purely English experience, and death experience.

The first poems I had published were "Dreams Old" and "Dreams Nascent," which Miriam herself sent to Ford Madox Hueffer, in 1910, I believe, just when the *English Review* had started so brilliantly. Myself, I had offered the little poem "Study" to the Nottingham University *Magazine,* but they returned it. But Hueffer accepted the "Dreams" poems for the *English Review,* and was very kind to me, and was the first man I ever met who had a real and a true feeling for literature. He introduced me to Edward Garnett, who, somehow, introduced me to the world. How well I remember the evenings at Garnett's house in Kent, by the log fire. And there I wrote the best of the dialect poems. I remember Garnett disliked the old ending to "Whether or Not." Now I see he was right, it was the voice of the commonplace me, not the demon. So I have altered it. And there again, those days of Hueffer and Garnett are not past at all, once I recall them. They were good to the demon, and the demon is timeless. But the ordinary meal-time me has yesterdays.

And that is why I have altered "Dreams Nascent," that exceedingly funny and optimistic piece of rhymeless poetry which Ford Hueffer printed in the *English Review,* and which introduced me to the public. The public seemed to like it. The M.P. for school-teachers said I was an ornament to the educational system, whereupon I knew it must be the ordinary me which had made itself heard, and not the demon. Anyhow, I was always uneasy about it.

There is a poem added to the second volume, which had to be left out of *Look! We Have Come Through!* when that book was first printed, because the publishers objected to mixing love and religion, so they said, in the lines:

> But I hope I shall find eternity
> With my face down buried between her breasts. . . .

But surely there are many eternities, and one of them Adam spends with his face buried and at peace between the breasts of Eve: just as Eve spends one of her eternities with her face hidden in the breast of Adam. But the publishers coughed out that gnat, and I was left wondering, as usual.

Some of the poems in *Look!* are rewritten, but not many, not as in the first volume. And *Birds, Beasts and Flowers* are practically untouched. They are what they are. They are the same me as wrote "The Wild Common," or "Renascence."

Perhaps it may seem bad taste to write this so personal foreword. But since the poems are so often personal themselves, and hang together in a life, it is perhaps only fair to give the demon his body of mere man, as far as possible.

Chariot of the Sun, by Harry Crosby *

Poetry, they say, is a matter of words. And this is just as much true as that pictures are a matter of paint, and frescoes a matter of water and colour-wash. It is such a long way from being the whole truth that it is slightly silly if uttered sententiously.

Poetry is a matter of words. Poetry is a stringing together of words into a ripple and jingle and a run of colours. Poetry is an interplay of images. Poetry is the iridescent suggestion of an idea. Poetry is all these things, and still it is something else. Given all these ingredients, you have something very like poetry, something for which we might borrow the old romantic name of poesy. And poesy, like bric-à-brac, will for ever be in fashion. But poetry is still another thing.

The essential quality of poetry is that it makes a new effort of attention, and "discovers" a new world within the known world. Man, and the animals, and the flowers, all live within a strange and for ever surging chaos. The chaos which we have got used to we call a cosmos. The unspeakable inner chaos of which we are composed we call consciousness, and mind, and even civilization. But it is, ultimately, chaos, lit up by visions, or not lit up by visions. Just as the rainbow may or may not light up the storm. And, like the rainbow, the vision perisheth.

But man cannot live in chaos. The animals can. To the animal all is chaos, only there are a few recurring motions and aspects within the surge. And the animal is content. But man is not. Man must wrap himself in a vision, make a house of apparent form and stability, fixity. In his terror of chaos he begins by putting up an umbrella between himself and the everlasting whirl. Then he paints the under-side of his umbrella like a firmament. Then he parades around, lives and dies under his umbrella. Bequeathed to his descendants, the umbrella becomes a dome, a vault, and men at last begin to feel that something is wrong.

Man fixes some wonderful erection of his own between himself and the wild chaos, and gradually goes bleached and stifled under his parasol. Then comes a poet, enemy of convention, and makes a slit in the umbrella; and lo! the glimpse of chaos is a vision, a window to the sun. But after a while, getting used to the vision, and not

* The text of this preface is taken from Lawrence's typescript, not from *Chariot of the Sun*.

liking the genuine draught from chaos, commonplace man daubs a simulacrum of the window that opens on to chaos, and patches the umbrella with the painted patch of the simulacrum. That is, he has got used to the vision; it is part of his house-decoration. So that the umbrella at last looks like a glowing open firmament, of many aspects. But alas! it is all simulacrum, in innumerable patches. Homer and Keats, annotated and with glossary.

This is the history of poetry in our era. Someone sees Titans in the wild air of chaos, and the Titan becomes a wall between succeeding generations and the chaos they should have inherited. The wild sky moved and sang. Even that became a great umbrella between mankind and the sky of fresh air; then it became a painted vault, a fresco on a vaulted roof, under which men bleach and go dissatisfied. Till another poet makes a slit on to the open and windy chaos.

But at last our roof deceives us no more. It is painted plaster, and all the skill of all the human ages won't take us in. Dante or Leonardo, Beethoven or Whitman: lo! it is painted on the plaster of our vault. Like St. Francis preaching to the birds in Assisi. Wonderfully like air and birdy space and chaos of many things—partly because the fresco is faded. But even so, we are glad to get out of that church, and into the natural chaos.

This is the momentous crisis for mankind, when we have to get back to chaos. So long as the umbrella serves, and poets make slits in it, and the mass of people can be gradually educated up to the vision in the slit: which means they patch it over with a patch that looks just like the vision in the slit: so long as this process can continue, and mankind can be educated up, and thus built in, so long will a civilization continue more or less happily, completing its own painted prison. It is called completing the consciousness.

The joy men had when Wordsworth, for example, made a slit and saw a primrose! Till then, men had only seen a primrose dimly, in the shadow of the umbrella. They saw it through Wordsworth in the full gleam of chaos. Since then, gradually, we have come to see primavera nothing but primrose. Which means, we have patched over the slit.

And the greater joy when Shakespeare made a big rent and saw emotional, wistful man outside in the chaos, beyond the conventional idea and painted umbrella of moral images and iron-bound paladins, which had been put up in the Middle Ages. But now, alas, the roof of our vault is simply painted dense with Hamlets and

Macbeths, the side walls too, and the order is fixed and complete. Man can't be any different from his image. Chaos is all shut out.

The umbrella has got so big, the patches and plaster are so tight and hard, it can be slit no more. If it were slit, the rent would no more be a vision, it would only be an outrage. We should dab it over at once, to match the rest.

So the umbrella is absolute. And so the yearning for chaos becomes a nostalgia. And this will go on till some terrific wind blows the umbrella to ribbons, and much of mankind to oblivion. The rest will shiver in the midst of chaos. For chaos is always there, and always will be, no matter how we put up umbrellas of visions.

What about the poets, then, at this juncture? They reveal the inward desire of mankind. What do they reveal? They show the desire for chaos, and the fear of chaos. The desire for chaos is the breath of their poetry. The fear of chaos is in their parade of forms and technique. Poetry is made of words, they say. So they blow bubbles of sound and image, which soon burst with the breath of longing for chaos, which fills them. But the poetasters can make pretty shiny bubbles for the Christmas-tree, which never burst, because there is no breath of poetry in them, but they remain till we drop them.

What, then, of *Chariot of the Sun?* It is a warlike and bronzy title for a sheaf of flimsies, almost too flimsy for real bubbles. But incongruity is man's recognition of chaos.

If one had to judge these little poems for their magic of words, as one judges Paul Valéry, for example, they would look shabby. There is no obvious incantation of sweet noise; only too often the music of one line deliberately kills the next, breathlessly staccato. There is no particular jewellery of epithet. And no handsome handling of images. Where deliberate imagery is used, it is perhaps a little clumsy. There is no coloured thread of an idea; and no subtle ebbing of a theme into consciousness, no recognizable vision, new gleam of chaos let in to a world of order. There is only a repetition of sun, sun, sun, not really as a glowing symbol, more as a bewilderment and a narcotic. The images in "Sun Rhapsody" shatter one another, line by line. For the sun,

> it is a forest without trees
> it is a lion in a cage of breeze
> it is the roundness of her knees
> great Hercules
> and all the seas
> and our soliloquies

The rhyme is responsible for a great deal. The lesser symbols are as confusing: sunmaids who are naiads of the water world, hiding in a cave. Only the forest becomes suddenly logical.

> I am a tree whose roots are tangled in the sun
> All men and women are trees whose roots are tangled in the sun
> Therefore humanity is the forest of the sun.

What is there, then, in this poetry, where there seems to be nothing? For if there is nothing, it is merely nonsense.

And, almost, it is nonsense. Sometimes, as in the "verse" beginning: "sthhe fous on ssu eod," since I at least can make no head or tail of it, and the mere sound is impossible, and the mere look of it is not inspiring, to me it is just nonsense. But in a world overloaded with shallow "sense," I can bear a page of nonsense, just for a pause.

For the rest, what is there? Take, at random, the poem called "Néant:"

> Red sunbeams from an autumn sun
> Shall be the strongest wall
> To shield the sunmaids of my soul
> From worlds inimical.
>
> Yet sunflakes falling in the sea
> Beyond the outer shore
> Reduplicate their epitaph
> To kill the conqueror.

It is a tissue of incongruity, in sound and sense. It means nothing, and it says nothing. And yet it has something to say. It even carries a dim suggestion of that which refuses to be said.

And therein lies the charm. It is a glimpse of chaos not reduced to order. But the chaos *alive,* not the chaos of matter. A glimpse of the living, untamed chaos. For the grand chaos is all alive, and everlasting. From it we draw our breath of life. If we shut ourselves off from it, we stifle. The animals live with it, as they live in grace. But when man became conscious, and aware of *himself,* his own littleness and puniness in the whirl of the vast chaos of God, he took fright, and began inventing God in his own image.

Now comes the moment when the terrified but inordinately conceited human consciousness must at last submit, and own itself part of the vast and potent living chaos. We must keep true to ourselves. But we must breathe in life from the living and unending chaos. We shall put up more umbrellas. They are a necessity of our consciousness. But never again shall we be able to put up The Absolute Umbrella, either religious or moral or rational or scientific or practical. The vast parasol of our conception of the universe, the cosmos, the firmament of suns and stars and space, this we can roll up like any other green sunshade, and bring it forth again when we want it. But we mustn't imagine it always spread above us. It is no more absolutely there than a green sunshade is absolutely there. It is casually there, only; because it is as much a contrivance and invention of our mind as a green sunshade is. Likewise the grand conception of God: this already shuts up like a Japanese parasol, rather clumsily, and is put by for Sundays, or bad weather, or a "serious" mood.

Now we see the charm of *Chariot of the Sun.* It shuts up all the little and big umbrellas of poesy and importance, has no outstanding melody or rhythm or image or epithet or even sense. And we feel a certain relief. The sun is very much in evidence, certainly, but it is a bubble reality that always explodes before you can really look at it. And it upsets all the rest of things with its disappearing.

Hence the touch of true poetry in this sun. It bursts all the bubbles and umbrellas of reality, and gives us a breath of the live chaos. We struggle out into the fathomless chaos of things passing and coming, and many suns and different darknesses. There is a bursting of bubbles of reality, and the pang of extinction that is also liberation into the roving, uncaring chaos which is all we shall ever know of God.

To me there is a breath of poetry, like an uneasy waft of fresh air at dawn, before it is light. There is an acceptance of the limitations of consciousness, and a leaning-up against the sun-imbued world of chaos. It is poetry at the moment of inception in the soul, before the germs of the known and the unknown have fused to begin a new body of concepts. And therefore it is useless to quote fragments. They are too nebulous and *not there.* Yet in the whole there is a breath of real poetry, the essential quality of poetry. It makes a new act of attention, and wakes us to a nascent world of inner and outer suns. And it has the poetic faith in the chaotic splendour of suns.

It is poetry of suns which are the core of chaos, suns which are fountains of shadow and pools of light and centres of thought and lions of passion. Since chaos has a core which is itself quintessentially chaotic and fierce with incongruities. That such a sun should have a chariot makes it only more chaotic.

And in the chaotic re-echoing of the soul, wisps of sound curl round with curious soothing—

> Likewise invisible winds
> Drink fire, and all my heart is sun-consoled.

And a poem such as "Water-Lilies" has a lovely suffusion in which the visual image passes at once into sense of touch, and back again, so that there is an iridescent confusion of sense-impression, sound and touch and sight all running into one another, blending into a vagueness which is a new world, a vagueness and a suffusion which liberates the soul, and lets a new flame of desire flicker delicately up from the numbed body.

The suffused fragments are the best, those that are only comprehensible with the senses, with visions passing into touch and to sound, then again touch, and the bursting of the bubble of an image. There is always sun, but there is also water, most palpably water. Even some of the suns are wetly so, wet pools that wet us with their touch. Then loose suns like lions, soft gold lions and white lions half-visible. Then again the elusive gleam of the sun of livingness, soft as gold and strange as the lion's eyes, the livingness that never ceases and never will cease. In this there is faith, soft, intangible, suffused faith that is the breath of all poetry, part of the breathing of the myriad sun in chaos. Such sun breathes its way into words, and the words become poetry, by suffusion. On the part of the poet it is an act of faith, pure attention and purified receptiveness. And without such faith there is no poetry. There is even no life. The poetry of conceit is a dead-sea fruit. The poetry of sunless chaos is already a bore. The poetry of a regulated cosmos is nothing but a wire bird-cage. Because in all living poetry the living chaos stirs, sun-suffused and sun-impulsive, and most subtly chaotic. All true poetry is most subtly and sensitively chaotic, outlawed. But it is the impulse of the sun in chaos, not conceit.

> The Sun in unconcealèd rage
> Glares down across the magic of the world.

The sun within us, that sways us incalculably.

> At night
> Swift to the Sun
> Deep imaged in my soul
> But during the long day black lands
> To cross

And it is faith in the incalculable sun, inner and outer, which keeps us alive.

Sunmaid
Left by the tide
I bring you a conch-shell
That listening to the Sun you may
Revive

And there is always the battle of the sun, against the corrosive acid vapour of vanity and poisonous conceit, which is the breath of the world.

Dark clouds
Are not so dark
As our embittered thoughts
Which carve strange silences within
The Sun

That the next "cinquain" may not be poetry at all is perhaps just as well, to keep us in mind of the world of conceit outside. It is the expired breath, with its necessary carbonic acid. It is the cold shadow across the sun, and saves us from the strain of the monos, from homogeneity and exaltation and forcedness and all-of-a-pieceness, which is the curse of the human consciousness. What does it matter if half the time a poet fails in his effort at expression! The failures make it real. The act of attention is not so easy. It is much easier to write poesy. Failure is part of the living chaos. And the groping reveals the act of attention, which suddenly passes into pure expression.

But I shall not be frightened by a sound
Of Something moving cautiously around.

Whims, and fumblings, and effort, and nonsense, and echoes from other poets, these all go to make up the living chaos of a little book of real poetry, as well as pure little poems like "Sun-Ghost," "To Those Who Return," "Torse de Jeune Femme au Soleil," "Poem for the Feet of Polia." Through it all runs the intrinsic naïveté without which no poetry can exist, not even the most sophisticated. This naïveté is the opening of the soul to the sun of chaos, and the soul may open like a lily or a tiger-lily or a dandelion or a deadly nightshade or a rather paltry chickweed flower, and it will be poetry of its own sort. But open it must. This opening, and this alone, is the essential act of attention, the essential poetic and vital act. We may fumble in the act, and a hailstone may hit us. But it is in the course of things. In this act, and this alone, we truly *live:* in that innermost naïve opening of the soul, like a flower, like an animal, like a coloured snake, it does not matter, to the sun of chaotic livingness.

Now, after a long bout of conceit and self-assurance and flippancy, the young are waking up to the fact that they are starved of life and of essential sun, and at last they are being driven, out of sheer starvedness, to make the act of submission, the act of attention, to open into inner naïveté, deliberately and dauntlessly, admit the chaos and the sun of chaos. This is the new naïveté, chosen, recovered, regained. Round it range the white and golden soft lions of courage and the sun of dauntlessness, and the whorled ivory horn of the unicorn is erect and ruthless, as a weapon of defence. The naïve, open spirit of man will no longer be a victim, to be put on a cross, nor a beggar, to be scorned and given a pittance. This time it will be erect and a bright lord, with a heart open to the wild sun of chaos, but with the yellow lions of the sun's danger on guard in the eyes.

The new naïveté, erect, and ready, sufficiently sophisticated to wring the neck of sophistication, will be the new spirit of poetry and the new spirit of life. Tender, but purring like a leopard that may snarl, it may be clumsy at first, and make gestures of self-conscious crudity. But it is a real thing, the real creature of the inside of the soul. And to the young it is the essential reality, the liberation into the real self. The liberation into the wild air of chaos, the being part of the sun. A long course of merely negative "freedom" reduces the soul and body both to numbness. They can feel no more and respond no more. Only the mind remains awake, and suffers keenly from the sense of nullity; to be young, and to feel you have every "opportunity," every "freedom" to live, and yet not to be able to live, because the responses have gone numb in the body and soul, this is the nemesis that is overtaking the young. It drives them silly.

But there is the other way, back to the sun, to faith in the speckled leopard of the mixed self. What is more chaotic than a dappled leopard trotting through dappled shade? And that is our life, really. Why try to whitewash ourselves?—or to camouflage ourselves into an artificially chaotic pattern? All we have to do is to accept the true chaos that we are, like the jaguar dappled with black suns in gold.

An island of rigid conventions, the rigid conventions of barbarism, and at the same time the fierce violence of the instinctive passions. A savage tradition of chastity, with a savage lust of the flesh. A barbaric overlordship of the gentry, with a fierce indomitableness of the servile classes. A lack of public opinion, a lack of belonging to any other part of the world, a lack of mental awakening, which makes inland Sardinia almost as savage as Benin, and makes Sardinian singing as wonderful and almost as wild as any on earth. It is the human instinct still uncontaminated. The money-sway still did not govern central Sardinia, in the days of Grazia Deledda's books, twenty, a dozen years ago, before the war. Instead, there was a savage kind of aristocracy and feudalism, and a rule of ancient instinct, instinct with the definite but indescribable tang of the aboriginal people of the island, not absorbed into the world: instinct often at war with the Italian government; a determined, savage individualism often breaking with the law, or driven into brigandage: but human, of the great human mystery.

It is this old Sardinia, at last being brought to heel, which is the real theme of Grazia Deledda's books. She is fascinated by her island and its folks, more than by the problems of the human psyche. And therefore this book, *The Mother,* is perhaps one of the least typical of her novels, one of the most "Continental." Because here, she has a definite universal theme: the consecrated priest and the woman. But she keeps on forgetting her theme. She becomes more interested in the death of the old hunter, in the doings of the boy Antiochus, in the exorcising of the spirit from the little girl possessed. She is herself somewhat bored by the priest's hesitations; she shows herself suddenly impatient, a pagan sceptical of the virtues of chastity, even in consecrated priests; she is touched, yet annoyed, by the pathetic, tiresome old mother who made her son a priest out of ambition, and who simply expires in the terror of a public exposure: and, in short, she makes a bit of a mess of the book, because she started a problem she didn't quite dare to solve. She shirks the issue atrociously. But neither will the modern spirit solve the problem by killing off the fierce instincts that made the problem. As for Grazia Deledda, first she started by sympathizing with the mother, and then must sympathize savagely with the young woman, and then can't make up her mind. She kills off the old mother in disgust at the old woman's triumph, so leaving the priest and the young woman hanging in space. As a sort of problem-story, it is disappointing. No doubt, if the priest had gone off with the woman, as he first intended, then all the authoress's sympathy would have fallen to the old abandoned mother. As it is, the sympathy falls between two stools, and the title *La Madre* is not really justified. The mother turns out not to be the heroine.

But the interest of the book lies, not in plot or characterization, but in the presentation of sheer instinctive life. The love of the priest for the woman is sheer instinctive passion, pure and undefiled by sentiment. As such it is worthy of respect, for in other books on this theme the instinct is swamped and extinguished in sentiment. Here, however, the instinct of direct sex is so strong and so vivid, that only the other blind instinct of mother-obedience, the child-instinct, can overcome it. All the priest's education and Christianity are really mere snuff of the candle. The old, wild instinct of a mother's ambition for her son defeats the other wild instinct of sexual mating. An old woman who has never had any sex-life–and it is astonishing, in barbaric half-civilization, how many people are denied a sex-life–she succeeds, by her old barbaric maternal power over her son, in finally killing his sex-life too. It is the suicide of semi-barbaric natures under the sway of a dimly comprehended Christianity, and falsely conceived ambition.

The old, blind life of instinct, and chiefly frustrated instinct and the rage thereof, as it is seen in the Sardinian hinterland, this is Grazia Deledda's absorption. The desire of the boy Antiochus to be a priest is an instinct: perhaps an instinctive recoil from his mother's grim priapism. The dying man escapes from the village, back to the rocks, instinctively needing to die in the wilds. The feeling of Agnes, the woman who loves the priest, is sheer female instinctive passion, something as in Emily Brontë. It too has the ferocity of frustrated instinct, and is bare and stark, lacking any of the graces of sentiment. This saves it from "dating" as d'Annunzio's passions date. Sardinia is by no means a land for Romeos and Juliets, nor even Virgins of the Rocks. It is rather the land of *Wuthering Heights*.

The book, of course, loses a good deal in translation, as is inevitable. In the mouths of the simple people, Italian is a purely instinctive language, with the rhythm of instinctive rather than mental processes. There are also many instinct-words with meanings never clearly mentally defined. In fact, nothing is brought to real mental clearness, everything goes by in a stream of more or less vague, more or less realized, feeling, with a natural mist or glow of sensation over everything, that counts more than the actual words said; and which, alas, it is almost impossible to reproduce in the more cut-and-dried northern languages, where every word has its fixed value and meaning, like so much coinage. A language can be killed by over-precision, killed especially as an effective medium for the conveyance of instinctive passion and instinctive emotion. One feels this, reading a translation from the Italian. And though Grazia Deledda is not masterly as Giovanni Verga is, yet, in Italian at least, she can put us into the mood and rhythm of Sardinia, like a true artist, an artist whose work is sound and enduring.

Bottom Dogs, by Edward Dahlberg

When we think of America, and of her huge success, we never realize how many failures have gone, and still go, to build up that success. It is not till you live in America, and go a little under the surface, that you begin to see how terrible and brutal is the mass of failure that nourishes the roots of the gigantic tree of dollars. And this is especially so in the country, and in the newer parts of the land, particularly out west. There you see how many small ranches have gone broke in despair, before the big ranches scoop them up and profit by all the back-breaking, profitless, grim labour of the pioneer. In the west you can still see the pioneer work of tough, hard first-comers, individuals, and it is astounding to see how often these individuals, pioneer first-comers who fought like devils against their difficulties, have been defeated, broken, their efforts and their amazing hard work lost, as it were, on the face of the wilderness. But it is these hard-necked failures who really broke the resistance of the stubborn, obstinate country, and made it easier for the second wave of exploiters to come in with money and reap the harvest. The real pioneer in America fought like hell and suffered till the soul was ground out of him: and then, nine times out of ten, failed, was beaten. That is why pioneer literature, which, even from the glimpses one has of it, contains the amazing Odyssey of the brute fight with savage conditions of the western continent, hardly exists, and is absolutely unpopular. Americans will not stand for the pioneer stuff, except in small, sentimentalized doses. They know too well the grimness of it, the savage fight and the savage failure which broke the back of the country but also broke something in the human soul. The spirit and the will survived: but something in the soul perished: the softness, the floweriness, the natural tenderness. How could it survive the sheer brutality of the fight with that American wilderness, which is so big, vast, and obdurate!

The savage America was conquered and subdued at the expense of the instinctive and intuitive sympathy of the human soul. The fight was too brutal. It is a great pity some publisher does not undertake a series of pioneer records and novels, the genuine, unsweetened stuff. The books exist. But they are shoved down into oblivion by the common will-to-forget. They show the strange brutality of the struggle, what would have been called in the old language the breaking of the heart. America was not colonized and "civilized" until the heart was broken in the American pioneer. It was a price that was paid. The heart was broken. But the will, the determination to conquer the land and make it submit to productivity, this was not broken. The will-to-success and the will-to-produce became clean and indomitable once the sympathetic heart was broken.

By the sympathetic heart, we mean that instinctive belief which lies at the core of the human heart, that people and the universe itself are *ultimately* kind. This belief is fundamental and, in the old language, is embodied in the doctrine: God is good. Now given an opposition too ruthless, a fight too brutal, a betrayal too bitter, this belief breaks in the heart, and is no more. Then you have either despair, bitterness, and cynicism, or you have the much braver reaction which says: God is not good, but the human will is indomitable, it cannot be broken, it will succeed against all odds. It is not God's business to be good and kind, that is man's business. God's business is to be indomitable. And man's business is essentially the same.

This is, roughly, the American position today, as it was the position of the Red Indian, when the white man came, and of the Aztec and of the Peruvian. So far as we can make out, neither Redskin nor Aztec nor Inca had any conception of a "good" God. They conceived of implacable, indomitable Powers, which is very different. And that seems to me the essential American position today. Of course the white American believes that man should behave in a kind and benevolent manner. But this is a social belief and a social gesture, rather than an individual flow. The flow from the heart, the warmth of fellow-feeling which has animated Europe and been the best of her humanity, individual, spontaneous, flowing in thousands of little passionate currents often conflicting, this seems unable to persist on the American soil. Instead you get the social creed of benevolence and uniformity, a mass *will,* and an inward individual retraction, an isolation, an amorphous separateness like grains of sand, each grain isolated upon its own will, its own indomitableness, its own implacability, its own unyielding, yet heaped together with all the other grains. This makes the American mass the easiest mass in the world to rouse, to move. And probably, under a long stress, it would make it the most difficult mass in the world to hold together.

The deep psychic change which we call the breaking of the heart, the collapse of the flow of spontaneous warmth between a man and his fellows, happens of course now all over the world. It seems to have happened to Russia in one great blow. It brings a people into a much more complete social unison, for good or evil. But it throws them apart in their private, individual emotions. Before, they were like cells in a complex tissue, alive and functioning diversely in a vast organism composed of family, clan, village, nation. Now, they are like grains of sand, friable, heaped together in a vast inorganic democracy.

While the old sympathetic flow continues, there are violent hostilities between people, but they are not secretly repugnant to one another. Once the heart is broken, people become repulsive to one another, secretly, and they develop social benevolence. They smell in each other's nostrils. It has been said often enough of more primitive or old-world peoples, who live together in a state of blind mistrust but also of close physical connexion with one another, that they have no noses. They are so close, the flow from body to body is so powerful, that they hardly smell one another, and hardly are aware at all of offensive human odours that madden the new civilizations. As it says in this novel: The American senses other people by their sweat and their kitchens. By which he means, their repulsive effluvia. And this is basically true. Once the blood-sympathy breaks, and only the nerve-sympathy is left, human beings become secretly intensely repulsive to one another, physically, and sympathetic only mentally and spiritually. The secret physical repulsion between people is responsible for the perfection of American "plumbing," American sanitation, and American kitchens, utterly white-enamelled and antiseptic. It is revealed in the awful advertisements such as those about "halitosis," or bad breath. It is responsible for the American nausea at coughing, spitting, or any of those things. The American townships don't mind hideous litter of tin cans and paper and broken rubbish. But they go crazy at the sight of human excrement.

And it is this repulsion from the physical neighbour that is now coming up in the consciousness of the great democracies, in England, America, Germany. The old flow broken, men could enlarge themselves for a while in transcendentalism, Whitmanish "adhesiveness" of the social creature, noble supermen, lifted above the baser functions. For the last hundred years man has been elevating himself above his "baser functions" and posing around as a transcendentalist, a superman, a perfect social being, a spiritual entity. And now, since the war, the collapse has come.

Man has no ultimate control of his own consciousness. If his nose doesn't notice stinks, it just doesn't, and there's the end of it. If his nose is so sensitive that a stink overpowers him, then again he's helpless. He can't prevent his senses from transmitting and his mind from registering what it does register.

And now, man has begun to be overwhelmingly conscious of the repulsiveness of his neighbour, particularly of the physical repulsiveness. There it is, in James Joyce, in Aldous Huxley, in André Gide, in modern Italian novels like *Parigi*—in all the very modern novels, the dominant note is the repulsiveness, intimate physical repulsiveness of human flesh. It is the expression of absolutely genuine experience. What the young feel intensely, and no longer so secretly, is the extreme repulsiveness of other people.

It is, perhaps, the inevitable result of the transcendental bodiless brotherliness and social "adhesiveness" of the last hundred years. People rose superior to their bodies, and soared along, till they had exhausted their energy in this performance. The energy once exhausted, they fell with a struggling plunge, not down into their bodies again, but into the cesspools of the body.

The modern novel, the very modern novel, has passed quite away from tragedy. An American novel like *Manhattan Transfer* has in it still the last notes of tragedy, the sheer spirit of suicide. An English novel like *Point Counter Point* has gone beyond tragedy into exacerbation, and continuous nervous repulsion. Man is so nervously repulsive to man, so screamingly, nerve-rackingly repulsive! This novel goes one further. Man just *smells,* offensively and unbearably, not to be borne. The human stink!

The inward revulsion of man away from man, which follows on the collapse of the physical sympathetic flow, has a slowly increasing momentum, a wider and wider swing. For a long time, the *social* belief and benevolence of man towards man keeps pace with the secret physical repulsion of man away from man. But ultimately, inevitably, the one outstrips the other. The benevolence exhausts itself, the repulsion only deepens. The benevolence is external and extra-individual. But the revulsion is inward and personal. The one gains over the other. Then you get a gruesome condition, such as is displayed in this book.

The only motive power left is the sense of revulsion away from people, the sense of the repulsiveness of the neighbour. It is a condition we are rapidly coming to—a condition displayed by the intellectuals much more than by the common people. Wyndham Lewis gives a display of the utterly repulsive effect people have on him, but he retreats into the intellect to make his display. It is a question of manner and manners. The effect is the same. It is the same exclamation: They stink! My God, they stink!

And in this process of recoil and revulsion, the affective consciousness withers with amazing rapidity. Nothing I have ever read has astonished me more than the "orphanage" chapters of this book. There I realized with amazement how rapidly the human psyche can strip itself of its awarenesses and its emotional contacts, and reduce itself to a sub-brutal condition of simple gross persistence. It is not animality—far from it. Those boys are much less than animals. They are cold wills functioning with a minimum of consciousness. The amount that they are *not* aware of is perhaps the most amazing aspect of their character. They are brutally and deliberately *unaware*. They have no hopes, no desires even. They have even no will-to-exist, for existence even is too high a term. They have a strange, stony will-to-persist, that is all. And they persist by reaction, because they still feel the repulsiveness of each other, of everything, even of themselves.

Of course the author exaggerates. The boy Lorry "always had his nose in a book"—and he must have got things out of the books. If he had taken the intellectual line, like Mr. Huxley or Mr. Wyndham Lewis, he would have harped on the intellectual themes, the essential feeling being the same. But he takes the non-intellectual line, is in revulsion against the intellect too, so we have the stark reduction to a persistent minimum of the human consciousness. It is a minimum lower than the savage, lower than the African Bushman. Because it is a *willed* minimum, sustained from inside by resistance, brute resistance against any flow of consciousness except that of the barest, most brutal egoistic self-interest. It is a phenomenon, and pre-eminently an American phenomenon. But the flow of repulsion, inward physical revulsion of man away from man, is passing over all the world. It is only perhaps in America, and in a book such as this, that we see it most starkly revealed.

After the orphanage, the essential theme is repeated over a wider field. The state of revulsion continues. The young Lorry is indomitable. You can't destroy him. And at the same time, you can't catch him. He will recoil from everything, and nothing on earth will make him have a positive feeling, of affection or sympathy or connexion. His mother?–we see her in her decaying repulsiveness. He has a certain loyalty, because she is his sort: it is part of his will-to-persist. But he must turn his back on her with a certain disgust.

The tragedian, like Theodore Dreiser and Sherwood Anderson, still dramatizes his defeat and is in love with himself in his defeated role. But the Lorry Lewis is in too deep a state of revulsion to dramatize himself. He almost deliberately finds himself repulsive too. And he goes on, just to see if he can hit the world without destroying himself. Hit the world not to destroy it, but to experience in himself how repulsive it is.

Kansas City; Beatrice, Nebraska; Omaha; Salt Lake City; Portland, Oregon; Los Angeles, he finds them all alike, nothing if not repulsive. He covers the great tracts of prairie, mountain, forest, coast-range, without seeing anything but a certain desert scaliness. His consciousness is resistant, shuts things out, and reduces itself to a minimum.

In the Y.M.C.A. it is the same. He has his gang. But the last word about them is that they stink, their effluvia is offensive. He goes with women, but the thought of women is inseparable from the thought of sexual disease and infection. He thrills to the repulsiveness of it, in a terrified, perverted way. His associates–which means himself also–read Zarathustra and Spinoza, Darwin and Hegel. But it is with a strange external, superficial mind that has no connexion with the affective and effective self. One last desire he has–to write, to put down his condition in words. His will-to-persist is intellectual also. Beyond this, nothing.

It is a genuine book, as far as it goes, even if it is an objectionable one. It is, in psychic disintegration, a good many stages ahead of *Point Counter Point*. It reveals a condition that not many of us have reached, but towards which the trend of consciousness is taking us, all of us, especially the young. It is, let us hope, a *ne plus ultra*. The next step is legal insanity, or just crime. The book is perfectly sane: yet two more strides, and it is criminal insanity. The style seems to me excellent, fitting the matter. It is sheer bottom-dog style, the bottom-dog mind expressing itself direct, almost as if it barked. That directness, that unsentimental and non-dramatized thoroughness of setting down the under-dog mind surpasses anything I know. I don't want to read any more books like this. But I am glad to have read this one, just to know what is the last word in repulsive consciousness, consciousness in a state of repulsion. It helps one to understand the world, and saves one the necessity of having to follow out the phenomenon of physical repulsion any further, for the time being.

The Story of Doctor Manente, by A. F. Grazzini

It is rather by accident than design that *The Story of Doctor Manente* should be the first book to appear in this Lungarno Series. Yet the accident is also fortunate, since it would be difficult to find a work more typical of the times. It is true, Lasca was not a sensitive genius like Boccaccio: but then the Renaissance was by no means a sensitive period. Boccaccio was far lovelier than the ordinary, or even than most extraordinary men of his day. Whereas Lasca is of the day and of the city, and as such, as a local and temporal writer, he is a typical Florentine.

Again, this famous story is a magnificent account of what is perhaps the best Florentine *beffa,* or *burla* (practical joke) on record. The work is a *novella,* a short novel, composed of various parts which fit together with the greatest skill. In this respect the story is far superior to most of Boccaccio's long *novelle,* which are full of unnecessary stuff, often tedious. Here we are kept sharp to essentials, and yet we are given a complete and living atmosphere. Anyone who knows Florence today can picture the whole thing perfectly, the big complicated *palazzi* with far-off attics and hidden chambers, the inns of the country where men sit on benches outside, and drink and talk on into the night, the houses with the little courtyards at the back, where everybody looks out of the window and knows all about everybody's affairs. The presentation of the story is masterly, and could hardly be bettered, setting a pattern for later works. In character, each man is himself. One can see the sly, frail Lorenzo playing this rather monstrous joke. One can see Doctor Manente through and through. The Grand Vicar, so authoritative and easily cowed, what a fine picture of an Italian inquisitor, how different from the Spanish type! The people are people, they are Italians and Florentines, absolutely. There they are, in their own ordinary daylight, not lifted into the special gleam of poetry, as Boccaccio's people so often are. And we have to admit, if Boccaccio is more universal, Lasca is more Tuscan. The Italians are, when you come down to it, peculiarly *terre à terre,* right down on the earth. It is part of their wholesome charm. But the rather fantastic side of their nature sometimes makes them want to be angels or winged lions or soaring eagles, and then they are often ridiculous, though occasionally sublime. But the people itself is of the earth, wholesomely and soundly so, and unless perverted, will remain so. The great artists were wild coruscations which shone and expired. The people remains the people, and wine and spaghetti are their forms of poetry: good forms too. The peasants who bargain every Friday, year in, year out, in the Piazza della Signoria, where the great white statue of Michelangelo's *David* stands livid, have *never even heard* of the name *David.* If you say to them: My name is *David,* they say: What? To them it is no name. Their outward-roaming consciousness has never even roamed so far as to read the name of the statue they almost touch each Friday. Inquiry is not their affair. They are centripetal.

And that is Italian. This soaring people sticks absolutely to the earth, and keeps the strength of the earth. The cities may go mad; they do. But the real Italian people is on the earth, and the cities will never lift them up. The bulk of the Italian people will never be "interested." They are centripetal, and only the little currents near to them matter.

So Doctor Manente! His courage and his force of life under all his trial are wonderful. Think of the howls, laments, prayers, sighs, and recriminations the northerner would have raised, under the circumstances. Not so the Doctor! He refuses to take an objective view of his mishaps, he refuses to *think,* but eats and drinks handsomely, sleeps, builds castles in the air, and sings songs, even improvising. We feel, when he comes back into the world, he is still good and fat. Mental torture has not undermined him. He has refused to *think,* and so saved himself the worst suffering. And how can we fail to admire the superb earthly life-courage which this reveals! It is the strength and courage of trees, deep rooted in substance, in substantial earth, and centripetal. So the Italian is, really, *rooted in substance,* not in dreams, ideas, or ideals, but *physically* self-centred, like a tree.

But the Italian also gets stuck sometimes, in this self-centred physicality of his nature, and occasionally has wild revolts from it. Then you get the sombre curses of Dante, the torments of Michelangelo and Leonardo, the sexless flights of Fra Angelico and Botticelli, the anguish of the idealists. The Italian at his best doesn't quarrel with substance on behalf of his soul or his spirit. When he does, you see strange results.

Among which are the famous *burle,* or *beffe* of the Renaissance period: the famous and infamous practical jokes. Apparently the Florentines actually did play these cruel jokes on one another, all the time: it was a common sport. It is so even in Boccaccio, though we feel that he was too true a poet really to appreciate the game. Lasca, who was a real Florentine of the town and taverns, was in heaven when there was a good, cruel joke being perpetrated. Lorenzo de' Medici, who writes so touchingly of the violet, did actually play these pranks on his acquaintances–and if this is not a true story, historically it might just as well be so. The portrait of Lorenzo given here is true to life: that even the most gentle modern Italian critics admit. But they deny the story any historical truth; on very insufficient grounds, really. The modern mind, however, dislikes the *beffa,* and would like to think it never really existed. "Of course Lorenzo never really played this trick." But the chances are that he did. And denying the historical truth of every recorded *beffa* does not wipe the *beffa* out of existence. On the contrary, it only leaves us blind to the real Renaissance spirit in Italy.

If every exalted soul who stares at Fra Angelico and Filippo Lippi, Botticelli and Michelangelo and Piero della Francesca, were compelled at the same time to study the practical-joke stories which play around the figures of these men and which fill the background of the great artists, then we should have a considerable change in feeling when we visited the Uffizi Gallery. We might be a little less exalted: we should certainly be more amused and more *on the spot,* instead of floating in the vapour of ecstasized admiration.

The *beffa* is real, the *beffa* is earnest, and what in heaven was its goal? We can only understand it, I think, if we remember the true substantial, *terre à terre* nature of the Italian. This self-centred physical nature can become crude, gross, even bestial and monstrous. We see it in d'Annunzio's peasant stories. We see it in the act of that Gonzaga of Mantua (if I remember right) who met his only son walking near the palace, and because the child did not salute with sufficient obsequiousness, kicked the boy ferociously in the groin, so that he died. The two centuries preceding the Renaissance had been full of such ferocity, beastliness. The spirit of Tuscany recoiled against it, and used every weapon of wit and intelligence against the egoistic brute of the preceding ages. And Italy is always having these periods of self-shame and recoil, not always into wit and fine intelligence, often into squeamish silliness. Indeed the Renaissance itself fizzled out into silly squeamishness, even in Lasca's day.

There seems to be a cycle: a period of brutishness, a conquering of the brutish energy by intelligence, a flowering of the intelligence, then a fizzling down into nervous fuss. The *beffa* belongs to the period when the brute force is conquered by wit and intelligence, but is not extinguished. It is a form of revenge taken by wit on the self-centred physical fellow. The *beffe* are sometimes simply repulsive. But on the whole it is a sport for spurring up the sluggish intelligence, or taming the forward brute. If a man was a bit fat and simple, but especially if he overflowed in physical self-assertion, was importunate, pedantic, hypocritical, ignorant, all infallible signs of self-centred physical egoism, then the wits marked him down as a prey. He was made the victim of some *beffa*. This put the fear of God into him and into his like. He and his lot did not dare to assert themselves, their pedantry or self-importance or ignorance or brutality or hypocrisy, so flagrantly. Chastened, they learned better manners. And so civilization moves on, wit and intelligence taking their revenge on insolent animal spirits, till the animal spirits are cowed, and wit and intelligence become themselves insolent, then feeble, then silly, then null, as we see during the latter half of the sixteenth century, and the first half of the seventeenth, even in Florence and Rome.

Like all other human corrective measures the *beffa* was often cruelly unjust and degenerated into a mere lust for sporting with a victim. Nimble wits, which had been in suppression during the preceding centuries, now rose up to take a cruel revenge on the somewhat fat and slower-witted citizen.

It is said that the Brunelleschi, who built the Cathedral dome in Florence, played the cruel and unjustified *beffa* on the *Fat Carpenter,* in the well-known story of that name. Here, the Magnificent Lorenzo plays a joke almost as unjustifiable and cruel, on Doctor Manente. All Florence rings with joy over the success of these terrific pieces of horse-play. The gentle Boccaccio tries to record such jokes with gusto. Nobody seems to have pitied the victim. Doctor Manente certainly never pitied himself; there is that to his credit, vastly: when we think how a modern would howl to the world at large. No, they weren't sorry for themselves—they were tough without being hard-boiled. The courage of life is splendid in them. We badly need some of it today, in this self-pitying age when we are so sorry for ourselves that we have to be soothed by art as by candy. Renaissance art has some of its roots in the cruel *beffa*—you can see it even in Botticelli's *Spring:* it is glaring in Michelangelo. Michelangelo struck his languishing Adam high on the Sistine ceiling for safety, for in Florence they'd have played a rare *beffa* on that chap.

So we have the story of Doctor Manente, history alive and kick-

The Privately Printed Edition of *Pansies*, by D. H. Lawrence

This little bunch of fragments is offered as a bunch of *pensées*, *anglicé* pansies; a handful of thoughts. Or, if you will have the other derivation of pansy, from *panser*, to dress or soothe a wound, these are my tender administrations to the mental and emotional wounds we suffer from. Or you can have heartsease if you like, since the modern heart could certainly do with it.

Each little piece is a thought; not a bare idea or an opinion or a didactic statement, but a true thought, which comes as much from the heart and the genitals as from the head. A thought, with its own blood of emotion and instinct running in it like the fire in a fire-opal, if I may be so bold. Perhaps if you hold up my pansies properly to the light, they may show a running vein of fire. At least, they do not pretend to be half-baked lyrics or melodies in American measure. They are thoughts which run through the modern mind and body, each having its own separate existence, yet each of them combining with all the others to make up a complete state of mind.

It suits the modern temper better to have its state of mind made up of apparently irrelevant thoughts that scurry in different directions, yet belong to the same nest; each thought trotting down the page like an independent creature, each with its own small head and tail, trotting its own little way, then curling up to sleep. We prefer it, at least the young seem to prefer it to those solid blocks of mental pabulum packed like bales in the pages of a proper heavy book. Even we prefer it to those slightly didactic opinions and slices of wisdom which are laid horizontally across the pages of Pascal's *Pensées* or La Bruyère's *Caractères*, separated only by *pattes de mouches*, like faint sprigs of parsley. Let every *pensée* trot on its own little paws, not be laid like a cutlet trimmed with a *patte de mouche*.

Live and let live, and each pansy will tip you its separate wink. The fairest thing in nature, a flower, still has its roots in earth and manure; and in the perfume there hovers still the faint strange scent of earth, the under-earth in all its heavy humidity and darkness. Certainly it is so in pansy-scent, and in violet-scent; mingled with the blue of the morning the black of the corrosive humus. Else the scent would be just sickly sweet.

So it is: we all have our roots in earth. And it is our roots that now need a little attention, need the hard soil eased away from them, and softened so that a little fresh air can come to them, and they can breathe. For by pretending to have no roots, we have trodden the earth so hard over them that they are starving and stifling below the soil. We have roots, and our roots are in the sensual, instinctive and intuitive body, and it is here we need fresh air of open consciousness.

I am abused most of all for using the so-called "obscene" words. Nobody quite knows what the word "obscene" itself means, or what it is intended to mean: but gradually all the *old* words that belong to the body below the navel, have come to be judged obscene. Obscene means today that the policeman thinks he has a right to arrest you, nothing else.

Myself, I am mystified at this horror over a mere word, a plain simple word that stands for a plain simple thing. "In the beginning was the Word, and the Word was God and the Word was with God." If that is true, then we are very far from the beginning. When did the Word "fall"? When did the Word become unclean "below the navel"? Because today, if you suggest that the word arse was in the beginning and was God and was with God, you will just be put in prison at once. Though a doctor might say the same of the word *ischial tuberosity,* and all the old ladies would piously murmur "Quite!" Now that sort of thing is idiotic and humiliating. Whoever the God was that made us, He made us complete. He didn't stop at the navel and leave the rest to the devil. It is too childish. And the same with the Word which is God. If the Word is God–which in the sense of the human it is–then you can't suddenly say that all the words which belong below the navel are obscene. The word arse is as much god as the word face. It must be so, otherwise you cut off your god at the waist.

What is obvious is that the words in these cases have been dirtied by the mind, by unclean mental associations. The words themselves are clean, so are the things to which they apply. But the mind drags in a filthy association, calls up some repulsive emotion. Well, then, cleanse the mind, that is the real job. It is the mind which is the Augean stables, not language. The word arse is clean enough. Even the part of the body it refers to is just as much me as my hand and my brain are me. It is not for *me* to quarrel with my own natural make-up. If I am, I am all that I am. But the impudent and dirty mind won't have it. It hates certain parts of the body, and makes the words representing these parts scapegoats. It pelts them out of the consciousness with filth, and there they hover, never dying, never dead, slipping into the consciousness again unawares, and pelted out again with filth, haunting the margins of the consciousness like jackals or hyenas. And they refer to parts of our own living bodies, and to our most essential acts. So that man turns himself into a thing of shame and horror. And his consciousness shudders with horrors that he has made for himself.

That sort of thing has got to stop. We can't have the consciousness haunted any longer by repulsive spectres which are no more than poor simple scapegoat words representing parts of man himself; words that the cowardly and unclean mind has driven out into the limbo of the unconscious, whence they return upon us looming and magnified out of all proportion, frightening us beyond all reasons. We must put an end to that. It is the self divided against itself most dangerously. The simple and natural "obscene" words must be cleaned up of all their depraved fear-associations, and re-admitted into the consciousness to take their natural place. Now they are magnified out of all proportion, so is the mental fear they represent. We must accept the word arse as we accept the word face, since arses we have and always shall have. We can't start cutting off the buttocks of unfortunate mankind, like the ladies in the Voltaire story, just to fit the mental expulsion of the word.

This scapegoat business does the mind itself so much damage. There is a poem of Swift's which should make us pause. It is written to Celia, his Celia–and every verse ends with the mad, maddened refrain: "But–Celia, Celia, Celia shits!" Now that, stated baldly, is so ridiculous it is almost funny. But when one remembers the gnashing insanity to which the great mind of Swift was reduced by that and similar thoughts, the joke dies away. Such thoughts poisoned him, like some terrible constipation. They poisoned his mind. And why, in heaven's name? The *fact* cannot have troubled him, since it applied to himself and to all of us. It was not the fact that Celia shits which so deranged him, it was the *thought*. His mind couldn't bear the thought. Great wit as he was, he could not see how ridiculous his revulsions were. His arrogant mind overbore him. He couldn't even see how much worse it would be if Celia didn't shit. His physical sympathies were too weak, his guts were too cold to sympathize with poor Celia in her natural functions. His insolent and sicklily squeamish mind just turned her into a thing of horror, because she was merely natural and went to the w.c. It is monstrous! One feels like going back across all the years to poor Celia, to say to her: It's all right, don't you take any notice of that mental lunatic.

And Swift's form of madness is very common today. Men with cold guts and over-squeamish minds are always thinking those things and squirming. Wretched man is the victim of his own little revulsions, which he magnifies into great horrors and terrifying taboos. We are all savages, we all have taboos. The Australian black may have the kangaroo for his taboo. And then he will probably die of shock and terror if a kangaroo happens to touch him. Which is what I would call a purely unnecessary death. But modern men have even more dangerous taboos. To us, certain words, certain ideas are taboo, and if they come upon us and we can't drive them away, we die or go mad with a degraded sort of terror. Which is what happened to Swift. He was such a great wit. And the modern mind altogether is falling into this form of degraded taboo-insanity. I call it a waste of sane human consciousness. But it is very dangerous, dangerous to the individual and utterly dangerous to society as a whole. Nothing is so fearful in a mass-civilization like ours as a mass-insanity.

The remedy is, of course, the same in both cases: lift off the taboo. The kangaroo is a harmless animal, the word shit is a harmless word. Make either into a taboo, and it becomes more dangerous. The result of taboo is insanity. And insanity, especially mob-insanity, mass-insanity, is the fearful danger that threatens our civilization. There are certain persons with a sort of rabies, who live only to infect the mass. If the young do not watch out, they will find themselves, before so very many years are past, engulfed in a howling manifestation of mob-insanity, truly terrifying to think of. It will be better to be dead than to live to see it. Sanity, wholeness, is everything. In the name of piety and purity, what a mass of disgusting insanity is spoken and written. We shall have to fight the mob, in order to keep sane, and to keep society sane.

The Grand Inquisitor, by F. M. Dostoievsky

It is a strange experience, to examine one's reaction to a book over a period of years. I remember when I first read *The Brothers Karamazov*, in 1913, how fascinated yet unconvinced it left me. And I remember Middleton Murry * saying to me: "Of course the whole clue to Dostoievsky is in that Grand Inquisitor story." And I remember saying: "Why? It seems to me just rubbish."

And it was true. The story seemed to me just a piece of showing off: a display of cynical-satanical pose which was simply irritating. The cynical-satanical pose always irritated me, and I could see nothing else in that black-a-vised Grand Inquisitor talking at Jesus at such length. I just felt it was all pose; he didn't really mean what he said; he was just showing off in blasphemy.

Since then I have read *The Brothers Karamazov* twice, and each time found it more depressing because, alas, more drearily true to life. At first it had been lurid romance. Now I read *The Grand Inquisitor* once more, and my heart sinks right through my shoes. I still see a trifle of cynical-satanical showing-off. But under that I hear the final and unanswerable criticism of Christ. And it is a deadly, devastating summing-up, unanswerable because borne out by the long experience of humanity. It is reality versus illusion, and the illusion was Jesus', while time itself retorts with the reality.

If there is any question: Who is the grand Inquisitor?—then surely we must say it is Ivan himself. And Ivan is the thinking mind of the human being in rebellion, thinking the whole thing out to the bitter end. As such he is, of course, identical with the Russian revolutionary of the thinking type. He is also, of course, Dostoievsky himself, in his thoughtful, as apart from his passional and inspirational self. Dostoievsky half hated Ivan. Yet, after all, Ivan is the greatest of the three brothers, pivotal. The passionate Dmitri and the inspired Alyosha are, at last, only offsets to Ivan.

And we cannot doubt that the Inquisitor speaks Dostoievsky's own final opinion about Jesus. The opinion is, baldly, this: Jesus, you are inadequate. Men must correct you. And Jesus in the end gives the kiss of acquiescence to the Inquisitor, as Alyosha does to Ivan. The two inspired ones recognize the inadequacy of their in-

* Before this preface was published in *The Grand Inquisitor* the name of Katherine Mansfield was substituted for that of Middleton Murry.

spiration: the thoughtful one has to accept the responsibility of a complete adjustment.

We may agree with Dostoievsky or not, but we have to admit that his criticism of Jesus is the final criticism, based on the experience of two thousand years (he says fifteen hundred) and on a profound insight into the nature of mankind. Man can but be true to his own nature. No inspiration whatsoever will ever get him permanently beyond his limits.

And what are the limits? It is Dostoievsky's first profound question. What are the limits to the nature, not of Man in the abstract, but of men, mere men, everyday men?

The limits are, says the Grand Inquisitor, three. Mankind in the bulk can never be "free," because man on the whole makes three grand demands on life, and cannot endure unless these demands are satisfied.

1. He demands bread, and not merely as foodstuff, but as a miracle, given from the hand of God.
2. He demands mystery, the sense of the miraculous in life.
3. He demands somebody to bow down to, and somebody before whom all men shall bow down.

These three demands, for miracle, mystery and authority, prevent men from being "free." They are man's "weakness." Only a few men, the elect, are capable of abstaining from the absolute demand for bread, for miracle, mystery, and authority. These are the strong, and they must be as gods, to be able to be Christians fulfilling all the Christ-demand. The rest, the millions and millions of men throughout time, they are as babes or children or geese, they are too weak, "impotent, vicious, worthless and rebellious" even to be able to share out the earthly bread, if it is left to them.

This, then, is the Grand Inquisitor's summing-up of the nature of mankind. The inadequacy of Jesus lies in the fact that Christianity is too difficult for men, the vast mass of men. It could only be realized by the few "saints" or heroes. For the rest, man is like a horse harnessed to a load he cannot possibly pull. "Hadst Thou respected him less, Thou wouldst have demanded less of him, and that would be nearer to love, for his burden would be lighter."

Christianity, then, is the ideal, but it is impossible. It is impossible because it makes demands greater than the nature of man can bear. And therefore, to get a livable, working scheme, some of the elect, such as the Grand Inquisitor himself, have turned round to "him," that other great Spirit, Satan, and have established

Church and State on "him." For the Grand Inquisitor finds that to be able to live at all, mankind must be loved more tolerantly and more contemptuously than Jesus loved it, loved, for all that, more truly, since it is loved for itself, for what it is, and not for what it ought to be. Jesus loved mankind for what it ought to be, free and limitless. The Grand Inquisitor loves it for what it is, with all its limitations. And he contends his is the kinder love. And yet he says it is Satan. And Satan, he says at the beginning, means annihilation, and not-being.

As always in Dostoievsky, the amazing perspicacity is mixed with ugly perversity. Nothing is pure. His wild love for Jesus is mixed with perverse and poisonous hate of Jesus: his moral hostility to the devil is mixed with secret worship of the devil. Dostoievsky is always perverse, always impure, always an evil thinker and a marvellous seer.

Is it true that mankind demands, and will always demand, miracle, mystery, and authority? Surely it is true. Today, man gets his sense of the miraculous from science and machinery, radio, aeroplane, vast ships, zeppelins, poison gas, artificial silk: these things nourish man's sense of the miraculous as magic did in the past. But now, man is master of the mystery, there are no occult powers. The same with mystery: medicine, biological experiment, strange feats of the psychic people, spiritualists, Christian scientists—it is all mystery. And as for authority, Russia destroyed the Tsar to have Lenin and the present mechanical despotism, Italy has the rationalized despotism of Mussolini, and England is longing for a despot.

Dostoievsky's diagnosis of human nature is simple and unanswerable. We have to submit, and agree that men are like that. Even over the question of sharing the bread, we have to agree that man is too weak, or vicious, or something, to be able to do it. He has to hand the common bread over to some absolute authority, Tsar or Lenin, to be shared out. And yet the mass of men are *incapable* of looking on bread as a mere means of sustenance, by which man sustains himself for the purpose of true living, true life being the "heavenly bread." It seems a strange thing that men, the mass of men, cannot understand that *life* is the great reality, that true living fills us with vivid life, "the heavenly bread," and earthly bread merely supports this. No, men cannot understand, never have understood that simple fact. They cannot see the distinction between bread, or property, money, and vivid life. They think that property and money are the same thing as vivid life. Only the few, the potential heroes or the "elect," can see the simple distinction. The mass *cannot* see it, and will never see it.

Dostoievsky was perhaps the first to realize this devastating truth, which Christ had not seen. A truth it is, none the less, and once recognized it will change the course of history. All that remains is for the elect to take charge of the bread—the property, the money—and then give it back to the masses as if it were really the gift of life. In this way, mankind might live happily, as the Inquisitor suggests. Otherwise, with the masses making the terrible mad mistake that money is life, and that therefore no one shall control the money, men shall be "free" to get what they can, we are brought to a condition of competitive insanity and ultimate suicide.

So far, well and good, Dostoievsky's diagnosis stands. But is it then to betray Christ and turn over to Satan if the elect should at last realize that instead of refusing Satan's three offers, the heroic Christian must now accept them. Jesus refused the three offers out of pride and fear: he wanted to be greater than these, and "above" them. But we now realize, no man, not even Jesus, is really "above" miracle, mystery, and authority. The one thing that Jesus is truly above, is the confusion between money and life. Money is not life, says Jesus, therefore you can ignore it and leave it to the devil.

Money is not life, it is true. But ignoring money and leaving it to the devil means handing over the great mass of men to the devil, for the mass of men *cannot* distinguish between money and life. It is hard to believe: certainly Jesus didn't believe it: and yet, as Dostoievsky and the Inquisitor point out, it is so.

Well, and what then? Must we therefore go over to the devil? After all, the whole of Christianity is not contained in the rejection of the three temptations. The essence of Christianity is a love of mankind. If a love of mankind entails accepting the bitter limitation of the mass of men, their inability to distinguish between money and life, then accept the limitation, and have done with it. Then take over from the devil the money (or bread), the miracle, and the sword of Cæsar, and, for the love of mankind, give back to men the bread, with its wonder, and give them the miracle, the marvellous, and give them, in a hierarchy, someone, some men, in higher and higher degrees, to bow down to. Let them bow down, let them bow down *en masse,* for the mass, who do not understand the difference between money and life, should always bow down to the elect, who do.

And is that serving the devil? It is certainly not serving the spirit of annihilation and not-being. It is serving the great wholeness of mankind, and in that respect, it is Christianity. Anyhow, it is the service of Almighty God, who made men what they are, limited and unlimited.

Where Dostoievsky is perverse is in his making the old, old, wise governor of men a Grand Inquisitor. The recognition of the weakness of man has been a common trait in all great, wise rulers of people, from the Pharaohs and Darius through the great patient Popes of the early Church right down to the present day. They have known the weakness of men, and felt a certain tenderness. This is the spirit of all great government. But it was not the spirit of the Spanish Inquisition. The Spanish Inquisition in 1500 was a newfangled thing, peculiar to Spain, with her curious death-lust and her bullying, and, strictly, a Spanish-political instrument, not Catholic at all, but rabidly national. The Spanish Inquisition actually was diabolic. It could not have produced a Grand Inquisitor who put Dostoievsky's sad questions to Jesus. And the man who put those sad questions to Jesus could not possibly have been a Spanish Inquisitor. He could not possibly have burnt a hundred people in an *auto-da-fé*. He would have been too wise and far-seeing.

So that, in this respect, Dostoievsky showed his epileptic and slightly criminal perversity. The man who feels a certain tenderness for mankind in its weakness or limitation is not therefore diabolic. The man who realizes that Jesus asked too much of the mass of men, in asking them to choose between earthly and heavenly bread, and to judge between good and evil, is not therefore satanic. Think how difficult it is to know the difference between good and evil! Why, sometimes it is evil to be good. And how is the ordinary man to understand that? He can't. The extraordinary men have to understand it for him. And is that going over to the devil? Or think of the difficulty in choosing between the earthly and heavenly bread. Lenin, surely a pure soul, rose to great power simply to give men—what? The earthly bread. And what was the result? Not only did they lose the heavenly bread, but even the earthly bread disappeared out of wheat-producing Russia. It is most strange. And all the socialists and the generous thinkers of today, what are they striving for? The same: to share out more evenly the earthly bread. Even *they*, who are practising Christianity *par excellence,* cannot properly choose between the heavenly and earthly bread. For the poor, they choose the earthly bread, and once more the heavenly bread is lost: and once more, as soon as it is really chosen, the earthly bread begins to disappear. It is a great mystery. But today, the most passionate believers in Christ believe that all you have to do is to struggle to give earthly bread (good houses, good sanitation, etc.) to the poor, and that is in itself the heavenly bread. But it isn't. Especially for the poor, it isn't. It is for them the loss of heavenly bread. And the poor are the vast majority. Poor things, how everybody hates them today! For benevolence is a form of hate.

What then is the heavenly bread? Every generation must answer for itself. But the heavenly bread is life, is living. Whatever makes life vivid and delightful is the heavenly bread. And the earthly bread must come as a by-product of the heavenly bread. The vast mass will never understand this. Yet it is the essential truth of Christianity, and of life itself. The few will understand. Let them take the responsibility.

Again, the Inquisitor says that it is a weakness in men, that they must have miracle, mystery and authority. But is it? Are they not bound up in our emotions, always and for ever, these three demands of miracle, mystery, and authority? If Jesus cast aside miracle in the Temptation, still there is miracle again in the Gospels. And if Jesus refused the earthly bread, still he said: "In my Father's house are many mansions." And for authority: "Why call ye me Lord, Lord, and do not the things which I say?"

The thing Jesus was trying to do was to supplant physical emotion by moral emotion. So that earthly bread becomes, in a sense, immoral, as it is to many refined people today. The Inquisitor sees that this is the mistake. The earthly bread must in itself be the miracle, and be bound up with the miracle.

And here, surely, he is right. Since man began to think and to feel vividly, seed-time and harvest have been the two great sacred periods of miracle, rebirth, and rejoicing. Easter and harvest-home are festivals of the earthly bread, and they are festivals which go to the roots of the soul. For it is the earthly bread as a miracle, a yearly miracle. All the old religions saw it: the Catholic still sees it, by the Mediterranean. And this is not weakness. This is *truth*. The rapture of the Easter kiss, in old Russia, is intimately bound up with the springing of the seed and the first footstep of the new earthly bread. It is the rapture of the Easter kiss which makes the bread worth eating. It is the absence of the Easter kiss which makes the Bolshevist bread barren, dead. They eat dead bread, now.

The earthly bread is leavened with the heavenly bread. The heavenly bread is life, is contact, and is consciousness. In sowing the seed man has his contact with earth, with sun and rain: and he *must not* break the contact. In the awareness of the springing of the corn he has his ever-renewed consciousness of miracle, wonder, and mystery: the wonder of creation, procreation, and re-creation, following the mystery of death and the cold grave. It is the grief of Holy Week and the delight of Easter Sunday. And man must not, must not lose this supreme state of consciousness out of himself, or he has lost the best part of him. Again, the reaping and the harvest are another contact, with earth and sun, a rich touch of the cosmos, a living stream of activity, and then the contact with harvesters, and the joy of harvest-home. All this is life, life, it is the heavenly bread which we eat in the course of getting the earthly bread. Work is, or should be, our heavenly bread of activity, contact and consciousness. All work that is not this, is anathema. True, the work is hard; there is the sweat of the brow. But what of it? In decent proportion, this is life. The sweat of the brow is the heavenly butter.

I think the older Egyptians understood this, in the course of their long and marvellous history. I think that probably, for thousands of years, the masses of the Egyptians were happy, in the hierarchy of the State.

Miracle and mystery run together, they merge. Then there is the third thing, authority. The word is bad: a policeman has authority, and no one bows down to him. The Inquisitor means: "that which men bow down to." Well, they bowed down to Cæsar, and they bowed down to Jesus. They will bow down, first, as the Inquisitor saw, to the one who has the power to control the bread.

The bread, the earthly bread, while it is being reaped and grown, it is life. But once it is harvested and stored, it becomes a commodity, it becomes riches. And then it becomes a danger. For men think, if they only possessed the hoard, they need not work; which means, really, they need not live. And that is the real blasphemy. For while we live we must live, we must not wither or rot inert.

So that ultimately men bow down to the man, or group of men, who can and dare take over the hoard, the store of bread, the riches, to distribute it among the people again. The lords, the givers of bread. How profound Dostoievsky is when he says that the people will forget that it is their own bread which is being given back to them. While they keep their own bread, it is not much better than stone to them—inert possessions. But given back to them from the great Giver, it is divine once more, it has the quality of miracle to make it taste well in the mouth and in the belly.

Men bow down to the lord of bread, first and foremost. For, by knowing the difference between earthly and heavenly bread, he is able calmly to distribute the earthly bread, and to give it, for the commonalty, the heavenly taste which they can never give it. That is why, in a democracy, the earthly bread loses its taste, the salt loses its savour, and there is no one to bow down to.

It is not man's weakness that he needs someone to bow down to. It is his nature, and his strength, for it puts him into touch with far, far greater life than if he stood alone. All life bows to the sun. But the sun is very far away to the common man. It needs someone to bring it to him. It needs a lord: what the Christians call one of the elect, to bring the sun to the common man, and put the sun in his heart. The sight of a true lord, a noble, a nature-hero puts the sun into the heart of the ordinary man, who is no hero, and therefore cannot know the sun direct.

This is one of the real mysteries. As the Inquisitor says, the mystery of the elect is one of the inexplicable mysteries of Christianity, just as the lord, the natural lord among men, is one of the inexplicable mysteries of humanity throughout time. We must accept the mystery, that's all.

But to do so is not diabolic.

And Ivan need not have been so tragic and satanic. He had made a discovery about men, which was due to be made. It was the rediscovery of a fact which was known universally almost till the end of the eighteenth century, when the illusion of the perfectibility of men, of all men, took hold of the imagination of the civilized nations. It was an illusion. And Ivan has to make a restatement of the old truth, that most men *cannot* choose between good and evil, because it is so extremely difficult to know which is which, especially in crucial cases: and that most men *cannot* see the difference between life-values and money-values: they can only see money-values; even nice simple people who *live* by the life-values, kind and natural, yet can only estimate value in terms of money. So let the specially gifted few make the decision between good and evil, and establish the life-values against the money-values. And let the many accept the decision, with gratitude, and bow down to the few, in the hierarchy. What is there diabolical or satanic in that? Jesus kisses the Inquisitor: Thank you, you are right, wise old man! Alyosha kisses Ivan: Thank you, brother, you are right, you take a burden off me! So why should Dostoievsky drag in Inquisitors and *autos-da-fé,* and Ivan wind up so morbidly suicidal? Let them be glad they've found the truth again.

[*The Dragon of the Apocalypse,* by Frederick Carter] *

It is some years now since Frederick Carter first sent me the manuscript of his *Dragon of the Apocalypse.* I remember it arrived when I was staying in Mexico, in Chapala. The village post-master sent for me to the post-office: Will the honourable Señor please come to the post-office. I went, on a blazing April morning, there in the northern tropics. The post-master, a dark, fat Mexican with moustaches, was most polite: but also rather mysterious. There was a packet—did I know there was a packet? No, I didn't. Well, after a great deal of suspicious courtesy, the packet was produced; the rather battered typescript of the *Dragon,* together with some of Carter's line-engravings, mainly astrological, which went with it. The post-master handled them cautiously. What was it? What was it? It was a book, I said, the manuscript of a book, in English. Ah, but what sort of a book? What was the book about? I tried to explain, in my hesitating Spanish, what the *Dragon* was about, with its line-drawings. I didn't get far. The post-master looked darker and darker, more uneasy. At last he suggested, was it *magic?* I held my breath. It seemed like the Inquisition again. Then I tried to accommodate him. No, I said, it was not magic, but the *history* of magic. It was the history of what magicians had thought, in the past, and these were the designs they had used. Ah! The postman was relieved. The history of magic! A scholastic work! And these were the designs they had used! He fingered them gingerly, but fascinated.

And I walked home at last, under the blazing sun, with the bulky package under my arm. And then, in the cool of the patio, I read the beginning of the first *Dragon.*

The book was not then what it is now. Then, it was nearly all astrology, and very little argument. It was confused: it was, in a sense, a chaos. And it hadn't very much to do with St. John's *Revelation.* But that didn't matter to me. I was very often smothered in words. And then would come a page, or a chapter, that would release my imagination and give me a whole great sky to move in. For the first time I strode forth into the grand fields of the sky. And it was a real experience, for which I have been always grateful. And always the sensation comes back to me, of the dark shade on

* See Introduction to present volume, pp. xviii–xix.

the veranda in Mexico, and the sudden release into the great sky of the old world, the sky of the zodiac.

I have read books of astronomy which made me dizzy with the sense of illimitable space. But the heart melts and dies—it is the disembodied mind alone which follows on through this horrible hollow void of space, where lonely stars hang in awful isolation. And this is not a release. It is a strange thing, but when science extends space *ad infinitum,* and we get the terrible sense of limitlessness, we have at the same time a secret sense of imprisonment. Three-dimensional space is homogeneous, and no matter *how* big it is, it is a kind of prison. No matter how vast the range of space, there is no release.

Why then, this sense of release, of marvellous release, in reading the *Dragon?* I don't know. But anyhow, the *whole* imagination is released, not a part only. In astronomical space, one can only *move,* one cannot be. In the astrological heavens, that is to say, the ancient zodiacal heavens, the whole man is set free, once the imagination crosses the border. The whole man, bodily and spiritual, walks in the magnificent fields of the stars, and the stars have names, and the feet tread splendidly upon—we know not what, but the heavens, instead of untreadable space.

It is an experience. To enter the astronomical sky of space is a great sensational experience. To enter the astrological sky of the zodiac and the living, roving planets is another experience, another *kind* of experience; it is truly imaginative, and to me, more valuable. It is not a mere extension of what we know: an extension that becomes awful, then appalling. It is the entry into another world, another kind of world, measured by another dimension. And we find some prisoned self in us coming forth to live in this world.

Now it is ridiculous for us to deny any experience. I well remember my first real experience of space, reading a book of modern astronomy. It was rather awful, and since then I rather hate the mere suggestion of illimitable space.

But I also remember very vividly my first experience of the astrological heavens, reading Frederick Carter's *Dragon:* the sense of being the Macrocosm, the great sky with its meaningful stars and its profoundly meaningful motions, its wonderful bodily vastness, not empty, but all alive and doing. And I value this experience more. For the sense of astronomical space merely paralyses me. But the sense of the living astrological heavens gives me an extension of my being, I become big and glittering and vast with a sumptuous vastness. I am the Macrocosm, and it is wonderful. And since I am not afraid to feel my own nothingness in front of the vast void of astronomical space, neither am I afraid to feel my own splendidness in the zodiacal heavens.

The *Dragon* as it exists now is no longer the *Dragon* which I read in Mexico. It has been made more—more argumentative, shall we say. Give me the old manuscript and let me write an introduction to that! I urge. But: No, says Carter. It isn't *sound.*

Sound what? He means his old astrological theory of the Apocalypse was not sound, as it was exposed in the old manuscript. But who cares? We do not care, vitally, about theories of the Apocalypse: what the Apocalypse means. What we care about is the release of the imagination. A real release of the imagination renews our strength and our vitality, makes us feel stronger and happier. Scholastic works don't release the imagination: at the best, they satisfy the intellect, and leave the body an unleavened lump. But when I get the release into the zodiacal cosmos my very feet feel lighter and stronger, my very knees are glad.

What does the Apocalypse matter, unless in so far as it gives us imaginative release into another vital world? After all, what meaning *has* the Apocalypse? For the ordinary reader, not much. For the ordinary student and biblical student, it means a prophetic vision of the martyrdom of the Christian Church, the Second Advent, the destruction of worldly power, particularly the power of the great Roman Empire, and then the institution of the Millennium, the rule of the risen Martyrs of Christendom for the space of one thousand years: after which, the end of everything, the Last Judgment, and souls in heaven; all earth, moon and sun being wiped out, all stars and all space. The New Jerusalem, and Finis!

This is all very fine, but we know it pretty well by now, so it offers no imaginative release to most people. It is the orthodox interpretation of the Apocalypse, and probably it is the true superficial meaning, or the final intentional meaning of the work. But what of it? It is a bore. Of all the stale buns, the New Jerusalem is one of the stalest. At the best, it was only invented for the Aunties of this world.

Yet when we read Revelation, we feel at once there are meanings behind meanings. The visions that we have known since childhood are not so easily exhausted by the orthodox commentators. And the phrases that have haunted us all our life, like: And I saw heaven opened, and behold! A white horse!—these are not explained quite away by orthodox explanations. When all is explained and expounded and commented upon, still there remains a curious fitful, half-spurious and half-splendid wonder in the work. Sometimes the great figures loom up marvellous. Sometimes there is a strange sense of incomprehensible drama. Sometimes the figures have a life of their own, inexplicable, which cannot be explained away or exhausted.

And gradually we realize that we are in the world of symbol as well as of allegory. Gradually we realize the book has no one meaning. It has meanings. Not meaning *within* meaning: but rather, meaning against meaning. No doubt the last writer left the Apocalypse as a sort of complete Christian allegory, a Pilgrim's Progress to the Judgment Day and the New Jerusalem: and the orthodox critics can explain the allegory fairly satisfactorily. But the Apocalypse is a compound work. It is no doubt the work of different men, of different generations and even different centuries.

So that we don't have to look for a *meaning,* as we can look for a meaning in an allegory like *Pilgrim's Progress,* or even like Dante. John of Patmos didn't *compose* the Apocalypse. The Apocalypse is the work of no one man. The Apocalypse began probably two centuries before Christ, as some small book, perhaps, of Pagan ritual, or some small pagan-Jewish Apocalypse written in symbols. It was written over by other Jewish apocalyptists, and finally came down to John of Patmos. He turned it more or less, rather less than more, into a Christian allegory. And later scribes trimmed up his work.

So the ultimate intentional, Christian meaning of the book is, in a sense, only plastered over. The great images incorporated are like the magnificent Greek pillars plastered into the Christian Church in Sicily: they are not merely allegorical figures: they are symbols, they belong to a bigger age than that of John of Patmos. And as symbols they defy John's superficial allegorical meaning. You can't give a great symbol a "meaning," any more than you can give a cat a "meaning." Symbols are organic units of consciousness with a life of their own, and you can never explain them away, because their value is dynamic, emotional, belonging to the sense–consciousness of the body and soul, and not simply mental. An allegorical image has a *meaning*. Mr. Facing-both-ways has a meaning. But I defy you to lay your finger on the full meaning of Janus, who is a symbol.

It is necessary for us to realize very definitely the difference between allegory and symbol. Allegory is narrative description using, as a rule, images to express certain definite qualities. Each image means something, and is a term in the argument and nearly always for a moral or didactic purpose, for under the narrative of an allegory lies a didactic argument, usually moral. Myth likewise is descriptive narrative using images. But myth is never an argument, it never has a didactic nor a moral purpose, you can draw no conclusion from it. Myth is an attempt to narrate a whole human experience, of which the purpose is too deep, going too deep in the blood and soul, for mental explanation or description. We *can* expound the myth of Chronos very easily. We can explain it, we can even draw the moral conclusion. But we only look a little silly. The myth of Chronos lives on beyond explanation, for it describes a profound experience of the human body and soul, an experience which is never exhausted and never will be exhausted, for it is being felt and suffered now, and it will be felt and suffered while man remains man. You may explain the myths away: but it only means you go on suffering blindly, stupidly, "in the unconscious," instead of healthily and with the imaginative comprehension playing upon the suffering.

And the images of myth are symbols. They don't "mean something." They stand for units of human *feeling*, human experience. A complex of emotional experience is a symbol. And the power of the symbol is to arouse the deep emotional self, and the dynamic self, beyond comprehension. Many ages of accumulated experience still throb within a symbol. And we throb in response. It takes centuries to create a really significant symbol: even the symbol of the Cross, or of the horse-shoe, or the horns. No man can invent symbols. He can invent an emblem, made up of images: or metaphors: or images: but not symbols. Some images, in the course of many generations of men, become symbols, embedded in the soul and ready to start alive when touched, carried on in the human consciousness for centuries. And again, when men become unresponsive and half dead, symbols die.

Now the Apocalypse has many splendid old symbols, to make us throb. And symbols suggest schemes of symbols. So the Apocalypse, with its symbols, suggests schemes of symbols, deep underneath its Christian, allegorical surface meaning of the Church of Christ.

And one of the chief schemes of symbols which the Apocalypse will suggest to any man who has a feeling for symbols, as contrasted with the orthodox feeling for allegory, is the astrological scheme. Again and again the symbols of the Apocalypse are astrological, the movement is star-movement, and these suggest an astrological scheme. Whether it is worth while to work out the astrological scheme from the impure text of the Apocalypse depends on the man who finds it worth while. Whether the scheme *can* be worked out remains for us to judge. In all probability there was once an astrological scheme there.

But what is certain is that the astrological symbols and suggestions are still there, they give us the lead. And the lead leads us sometimes out into a great imaginative world where we feel free and delighted. At least, that is my experience. So what does it matter whether the astrological scheme can be restored intact or not? Who cares about explaining the Apocalypse, either allegorically or astrologically or historically or any other way. All ones cares about is the lead, the lead that the symbolic figures give us, and their dramatic movement: the lead, and where it will lead us to. If it leads to a release of the imagination into some new sort of world, then let us be thankful, for that is what we want. It matters so little to us who care more about life than about scholarship, what is correct or what is not correct. What does "correct" mean, anyhow? *Sanahorias* is the Spanish for carrots: I hope I am correct. But what are carrots correct for?

What the ass wants is carrots; not the idea of carrots, nor thought-forms of carrots, but carrots. The Spanish ass doesn't even know that he is eating *sanahorias*. He just eats and feels blissfully full of carrot. Now does *he* have more of the carrot, who eats it, or do I, who know that in Spanish it is called a *sanahoria* (I hope I am correct) and in botany it belongs to the *umbelliferæ*?

We are full of the wind of thought-forms, and starved for a good carrot. I don't care *what* a man sets out to prove, so long as he will interest me and carry me away. I don't in the least care whether he proves his point or not, so long as he has given me a real imaginative experience by the way, and not another set of bloated thought-forms. We are starved to death, fed on the eternal sodom-apples of thought-forms. What we want is *complete* imaginative experience, which goes through the whole soul and body. Even at the expense of reason we want imaginative experience. For reason is certainly not the final judge of life.

Though, if we pause to think about it, we shall realize that it is not Reason herself whom we have to defy, it is her myrmidons, our accepted ideas and thought-forms. Reason can adjust herself to almost anything, if we will only free her from her crinoline and powdered wig, with which she was invested in the eighteenth and nineteenth centuries. Reason is a supple nymph, and slippery as a fish by nature. She had as leave give her kiss to an absurdity any day, as to syllogistic truth. The absurdity may turn out truer.

So we need not feel ashamed of flirting with the zodiac. The zodiac is well worth flirting with. But not in the rather silly modern way of horoscopy and telling your fortune by the stars. Telling your fortune by the stars, or trying to get a tip from the stables, before a horse-race. You want to know what horse to put your money on. Horoscopy is just the same. They want their "fortune" told, never their misfortune.

Surely one of the greatest imaginative experiences the human race has ever had was the Chaldean experience of the stars, including the sun and moon. Sometimes it seems it must have been greater experience than any God-experience. For God is only a great imaginative experience. And sometimes it seems as if the experience of the living heavens, with a living yet not human sun, and brilliant living stars in *live* space must have been the most magnificent of all experiences, greater than any Jehovah or Baal, Buddha or Jesus. It may seem an absurdity to talk of *live* space. But is it? While we are warm and well and "unconscious" of our bodies, are we not all the time ultimately conscious of our bodies in the same way, as live or living space? And is not this the reason why void space so terrifies us?

I would like to know the stars again as the Chaldeans knew them, two thousand years before Christ. I would like to be able to put my ego into the sun, and my personality into the moon, and my character into the planets, and live the life of the heavens, as the early Chaldeans did. The human consciousness is really homogeneous. There is no complete forgetting, even in death. So that somewhere within us the old experience of the Euphrates, Mesopotamia between the rivers, lives still. And in my Mesopotamian self I long for the sun again, and the moon and stars, for the Chaldean sun and the Chaldean stars. I long for them terribly. Because *our* sun and *our* moon are only thought-forms to us, balls of gas, dead globes of extinct volcanoes, things we *know* but never feel by experience. By *experience,* we should feel the sun as the savages feel him, we should "know" him as the Chaldeans knew him, in a terrific embrace. But our experience of the sun is dead, we are cut off. All we have now is the thought-form of the sun. He is a blazing ball of gas, he has spots occasionally, from some sort of indigestion, and he makes you brown and healthy if you let him. The first two "facts" we should never have known if men with telescopes, called astronomers, hadn't told us. It is obvious, they are mere thought-forms. The third "fact," about being brown and healthy, we believe because the doctors have told us it is so. As a matter of fact, many neurotic people become more and more neurotic, the browner and "healthier" they become by sun-baking. The sun can rot as well as ripen. So the third fact is also a thought-form.

And that is all we have, poor things, of the sun. Two or three cheap and inadequate thought-forms. Where, for us, is the great and royal sun of the Chaldeans? Where even, for us, is the sun of the Old Testament, coming forth like a strong man to run a race? We have lost the sun. We have lost the sun, and we have found a few miserable thought-forms. A ball of blazing gas! With spots! He browns you!

To be sure, we are not the first to lose the sun. The Babylonians themselves began the losing of him. The great and living heavens of the Chaldeans deteriorated already in Belshazzar's day to the fortune-telling disc of the night skies. But that was man's fault, not the heavens'. Man always deteriorates. And when he deteriorates he always becomes inordinately concerned about his "fortune" and his fate. While life itself is fascinating, fortune is completely uninteresting, and the idea of fate does not enter. When men become poor in life then they become anxious about their fortune and frightened about their fate. By the time of Jesus, men had become so anxious about their fortunes and so frightened about their fates, that they put up the grand declaration that life was one long misery and you couldn't expect your fortune till you got to heaven; that is, till after you were dead. This was accepted by all men, and has been the creed till our day, Buddha and Jesus alike. It has provided us with a vast amount of thought-forms, and landed us in a sort of living death.

So now we want the sun again. Not the spotted ball of gas that browns you like a joint of meat, but the living sun, and the living moon of the old Chaldean days. Think of the moon, think of Artemis and Cybele, think of the white wonder of the skies, so rounded, so velvety, moving so serene; and then think of the pock-marked horror of the scientific photographs of the moon!

But when we have seen the pock-marked face of the moon in scientific photographs, need that be the end of the moon for us? Even rationally? I think not. It is a great blow: but the imagination can recover from it. Even if we have to believe the pock-marked photograph, even if we believe in the cold and snow and utter deadness of the moon—which we *don't* quite believe—the moon is not therefore a dead nothing. The moon is a white strange world, great, white, soft-seeming globe in the night sky, and what she actually communicates to me across space I shall never fully know. But the moon that pulls the tides, and the moon that controls the menstrual periods of women, and the moon that touches the lunatics, she is not the mere dead lump of the astronomist. The moon is the great moon still, she gives forth her soft and feline influences, she sways us still, and asks for sympathy back again. In her so-called deadness there is enormous potency still, and power even over our lives. The Moon! Artemis! the great goddess of the splendid past of men! Are you going to tell me she is a dead lump?

She is not dead. But maybe we are dead, half-dead little modern worms stuffing our damp carcasses with thought-forms that have no sensual reality. When we describe the moon as dead, we are describing the deadness in ourselves. When we find space so hideously void, we are describing our own unbearable emptiness. Do we imagine that we, poor worms with spectacles and telescopes and thought-forms, are really more conscious, more vitally aware of the universe than the men in the past were, who called the moon Artemis, or Cybele, or Astarte? Do we imagine that we really, livingly know the moon better than they knew her? That our knowledge of the moon is more real, more "sound"? Let us disabuse ourselves. We know the moon in terms of our own telescopes and our own deadness. We know everything in terms of our own deadness.

But the moon is Artemis still, and a dangerous goddess she is, as she always was. She throws her cold contempt on you as she passes over the sky, poor, mean little worm of a man who thinks she is nothing but a dead lump. She throws back the cold white vitriol of her angry contempt on to your mean, tense nerves, nervous man, and she is corroding you away. Don't think you can escape the moon, any more than you can escape breathing. She is on the air you breathe. She is active within the atom. Her sting is part of the activity of the electron.

Do you think you can put the universe apart, a dead lump here, a ball of gas there, a bit of fume somewhere else? How puerile it is, as if the universe were the back yard of some human chemical works! How gibbering man becomes, when he is really clever, and thinks he is giving the ultimate and final description of the universe! Can't he see that he is merely describing himself, and that the self he is describing is merely one of the more dead and dreary states that man can exist in? When man changes his state of being, he needs an entirely different description of the universe, and so the universe changes its nature to him entirely. Just as the nature of our universe is entirely different from the nature of the Chaldean Cosmos. The Chaldeans described the Cosmos as they found it: Magnificent. We describe the universe as we find it: mostly void, littered with a certain number of dead moons and unborn stars, like the back yard of a chemical works.

Is our description true? Not for a single moment, once you change your state of mind: or your state of soul. It is true for our present deadened state of mind. Our state of mind is becoming unbearable. We shall have to change it. And when we have changed it, we shall change our description of the universe entirely. We shall not call the moon Artemis, but the new name will be nearer to Artemis than to a dead lump or an extinct globe. We shall not get back the Chaldean vision of the living heavens. But the heavens will come to life again for us, and the vision will express also the new men that we are.

And so the value of these studies in the Apocalypse. They wake the imagination and give us at moments a new universe to live in. We may think it is the old cosmos of the Babylonians, but it isn't. We can never recover an old vision, once it has been supplanted. But what we can do is to discover a new vision in harmony with the memories of old, far-off, far, far-off experience that lie within us. So long as we are not deadened or drossy, memories of Chaldean experience still live within us, at great depths, and can vivify our impulses in a new direction, once we awaken them.

Therefore we ought to be grateful for a book like this of the *Dragon*. What does it matter if it is confused? What does it matter if it repeats itself? What does it matter if in parts it is not very interesting, when in other parts it is intensely so, when it suddenly opens doors and lets out the spirit into a new world, even if it is a very old world! I admit that I cannot see eye to eye with Mr. Carter about the Apocalypse itself. I cannot, myself, feel that old John of Patmos spent his time on his island lying on his back and gazing at the resplendent heavens; then afterwards writing a book in which all the magnificent cosmic and starry drama is deliberately wrapped up in Jewish-Christian moral threats and vengeances, sometimes rather vulgar.

But that, no doubt, is due to our different approach to the book. I was brought up on the Bible, and seem to have it in my bones.

From early childhood I have been familiar with Apocalyptic language and Apocalyptic image: not because I spent my time reading Revelation, but because I was sent to Sunday School and to Chapel, to Band of Hope and to Christian Endeavour, and was always having the Bible read at me or to me. I did not even listen attentively. But language has a power of echoing and re-echoing in my unconscious mind. I can wake up in the night and "hear" things being said–or hear a piece of music–to which I had paid no attention during the day. The very sound itself registers. And so the sound of Revelation had registered in me very early, and I was as used to: "I was in the Spirit on the Lord's day, and heard behind me a great voice, as of a trumpet, saying: I am Alpha and the Omega"–as I was to a nursery rhyme like "Little Bo-Peep"! I didn't know the meaning, but then children so often prefer sound to sense. "Alleluia: for the Lord God omnipotent reigneth." The Apocalypse is full of sounding phrases, beloved by the uneducated in the chapels for their true liturgical powers. "And he treadeth the winepress of the fierceness and wrath of Almighty God."

No, for me the Apocalypse is altogether too full of fierce feeling, fierce and moral, to be a grand disguised star-myth. And yet it has intimate connexion with star-myths and the movement of the astrological heavens: a sort of submerged star-meaning. And nothing delights me more than to escape from the all-too-moral chapel meaning of the book, to another wider, older, more magnificent meaning. In fact, one of the real joys of middle age is in coming back to the Bible, reading a new translation, such as Moffatt's, reading the modern research and modern criticism of some Old Testament books, and of the Gospels, and getting a whole new conception of the Scriptures altogether. Modern research has been able to put the Bible back into its living connexions, and it is splendid: no longer the Jewish-moral book and a stick to beat an immoral dog, but a fascinating account of the adventure of the Jewish–or Hebrew or Israelite nation, among the great old civilized nations of the past, Egypt, Assyria, Babylon, and Persia: then on into the Hellenic world, the Seleucids, and the Romans, Pompey and Anthony. Reading the Bible in a new translation, with modern notes and comments, is more fascinating than reading Homer, for the adventure goes even deeper into time and into the soul, and continues through the centuries, and moves from Egypt to Ur and to Nineveh, from Sheba to Tarshish and Athens and Rome. It is the very quick of ancient history.

And the Apocalypse, the last and presumably the latest of the books of the Bible, also comes to life with a great new life, once we look at its symbols and take the lead that they offer us. The text leads most easily into the great chaotic Hellenic world of the first century: Hellenic, not Roman. But the symbols lead much further back.

They lead Frederick Carter back to Chaldea and to Persia, chiefly, for his skies are the late Chaldean, and his mystery is chiefly Mithraic. Hints, we have only hints from the outside. But the rest is within us, and if we can take a hint, it is extraordinary how far and into what fascinating worlds the hints can lead us. The orthodox critics will say: Fantasy! Nothing but fantasy! But then, thank God for fantasy, if it enhances our life.

And even so, the "reproach" is not quite just. The Apocalypse has an old, submerged astrological meaning, and probably even an old astrological scheme. The hints are too obvious and too splendid: like the ruins of an old temple incorporated in a Christian chapel. Is it any more fantastic to try to reconstruct the embedded temple, than to insist that the embedded images and columns are mere rubble in the Christian building, and have no meaning? It is as fantastic to deny meaning when meaning is there, as it is to invent meaning when there is none. And it is much duller. For the invented meaning may still have a life of its own.

REVIEWS OF BOOKS

Georgian Poetry: 1911–1912

Georgian Poetry is an anthology of verse which has been published during the reign of our present king, George V. It contains one poem of my own, but this fact will not, I hope, preclude my reviewing the book.

This collection is like a big breath taken when we are waking up after a night of oppressive dreams. The nihilists, the intellectual, hopeless people–Ibsen, Flaubert, Thomas Hardy–represent the dream we are waking from. It was a dream of demolition. Nothing was, but was nothing. Everything was taken from us. And now our lungs are full of new air, and our eyes see it is morning, but we have not forgotten the terror of the night. We dreamed we were falling through space into nothingness, and the anguish of it leaves us rather eager.

But we are awake again, our lungs are full of new air, our eyes of morning. The first song is nearly a cry, fear and the pain of remembrance sharpening away the pure music. And that is this book.

The last years have been years of demolition. Because faith and belief were getting pot-bound, and the Temple was made a place to barter sacrifices, therefore faith and belief and the Temple must be broken. This time art fought the battle, rather than science or any new religious faction. And art has been demolishing for us: Nietzsche, the Christian religion as it stood; Hardy, our faith in our own endeavour; Flaubert, our belief in love. Now, for us, it is all smashed, we can see the whole again. We were in prison, peeping at the sky through loop-holes. The great prisoners smashed at the loop-holes, for lying to us. And behold, out of the ruins leaps the whole sky.

It is we who see it and breathe in it for joy. God is there, faith, belief, love, everything. We are drunk with the joy of it, having got away from the fear. In almost every poem in the book comes this note of exultation after fear, the exultation in the vast freedom, the illimitable wealth that we have suddenly got.

> But send desire often forth to scan
> The immense night that is thy greater soul,

says Mr. Abercrombie. His deadly sin is Prudence, that will not risk to avail itself of the new freedom. Mr. Bottomley exults to find men for ever building religions which yet can never compass all.

> Yet the yielding sky
> Invincible vacancy was there discovered.

Mr. Rupert Brooke sees

> every glint
> Posture and jest and thought and tint
> Freed from the mask of transiency
> Triumphant in eternity,
> Immote, immortal

and this at Afternoon Tea. Mr. John Drinkwater sings:

> We cherish every hour that strays
> Adown the cataract of days:
> We see the clear, untroubled skies,
> We see the glory of the rose——

Mr. Wilfrid Wilson Gibson hears the "terror turned to tenderness," then

> I watched the mother sing to rest
> The baby snuggling on her breast.

And to Mr. Masefield:

> When men count
> Those hours of life that were a bursting fount
> Sparkling the dusty heart with living springs,
> There seems a world, beyond our earthly things,
> Gated by golden moments.

It is all the same—hope, and religious joy. Nothing is really wrong. Every new religion is a waste-product from the last, and every religion stands for us for ever. We love Christianity for what it has brought us, now that we are no longer upon the cross.

The great liberation gives us an overwhelming sense of joy, *joie d'être, joie de vivre*. This sense of exceeding keen relish and appreciation of life makes romance. I think I could say every poem in the book is romantic, tinged with a love of the marvellous, a joy of natural things, as if the poet were a child for the first time on the seashore, finding treasures. "Best trust the happy moments," says Mr. Masefield, who seems nearest to the black dream behind us. There is Mr. W. H. Davies's lovely joy, Mr. De La Mare's perfect appreciation of life at still moments, Mr. Rupert Brooke's brightness, when he "lived from laugh to laugh," Mr. Edmund Beale Sargant's pure, excited happiness in the woodland–it is all the same, keen zest in life found wonderful. In Mr. Gordon Bottomley it is the zest of activity, of hurrying, labouring men, or the zest of the utter stillness of long snows. It is a bookful of Romance that has not quite got clear of the terror of realism.

There is no *carpe diem* touch. The joy is sure and fast. It is not the falling rose, but the rose for ever rising to bud and falling to fruit that gives us joy. We have faith in the vastness of life's wealth. We are always rich: rich in buds and in shed blossoms. There is no winter that we fear. Life is like an orange tree, always in leaf and bud, in blossom and fruit.

And we ourselves, in each of us, have everything. Somebody said: "The Georgian poets are not love poets. The influence of Swinburne has gone." But I should say the Georgian poets are just ripening to be love poets. Swinburne was no love poet. What are the Georgian poets, nearly all, but just bursting into a thick blaze of being? They are not poets of passion, perhaps, but they are essentially passionate poets. The time to be impersonal has gone. We start from the joy we have in being ourselves, and everything must take colour from that joy. It is the return of the blood, that has been held back, as when the heart's action is arrested by fear. Now the warmth of blood is in everything, quick, healthy, passionate blood. I look at my hands as I write and know they are mine, with red blood running its way, sleuthing out Truth and pursuing it to eternity, and I am full of awe for this flesh and blood that holds this pen. Everything that ever was thought and ever will be thought, lies in this body of mine. This flesh and blood sitting here writing, the great impersonal flesh and blood, greater than me, which I am proud to belong to, contains all the future. What is it but the quick of all growth, the seed of all harvest, this body of mine? And grapes and corn and birds and rocks and visions, all are in my fingers. I am so full of wonder at my own miracle of flesh and blood that I could not contain myself, if I did not remember we are all alive, have all of us living bodies. And that is a joy greater than any dream of immortality in the spirit, to me. It reminds me of Rupert Brooke's moment triumphant in its eternality; and of Michelangelo, who is also the moment triumphant in its eternality; just the opposite from Corot, who is the eternal triumphing over the moment, at the moment, at the very point of sweeping it into the flow.

Of all love poets, we are the love poets. For our religion is loving. To love passionately, but completely, is our one desire.

What is "The Hare" but a complete love poem, with none of the hackneyed "But a bitter blossom was born" about it, nor yet the Yeats, "Never give all the heart." Love is the greatest of all things, no "bitter blossom" nor such-like. It is sex-passion, so separated, in which we do not believe. The *Carmen* and *Tosca* sort of passion is not interesting any longer, because it can't progress. Its goal and aim is possession, whereas possession in love is only a means to love. And because passion cannot go beyond possession, the passionate heroes and heroines–Tristans and what-not–must die. We believe in the love that is happy ever after, progressive as life itself.

I worship Christ, I worship Jehovah, I worship Pan, I worship Aphrodite. But I do not worship hands nailed and running with blood upon a cross, nor licentiousness, nor lust. I want them all, all the gods. They are all God. But I must serve in real love. If I take my whole, passionate, spiritual and physical love to the woman who in return loves me, that is how I serve God. And my hymn and my game of joy is my work. All of which I read in the anthology of *Georgian Poetry*.

German Books: Thomas Mann

Thomas Mann is perhaps the most famous of German novelists now writing. He, and his elder brother, Heinrich Mann, with Jakob Wassermann, are acclaimed the three artists in fiction of present-day Germany.

But Germany is now undergoing that craving for form in fiction, that passionate desire for the mastery of the medium of narrative, that will of the writer to be greater than and undisputed lord over the stuff he writes, which is figured to the world in Gustave Flaubert.

Thomas Mann is over middle age, and has written three or four books: *Buddenbrooks,* a novel of the patrician life of Lübeck; *Tristan,* a collection of six *Novellen; Königliche Hoheit,* an unreal Court romance; various stories, and lastly, *Der Tod in Venedig.* The author himself is the son of a Lübeck *Patrizier.*

It is as an artist rather than as a story-teller that Germany worships Thomas Mann. And yet it seems to me, this craving for form is the outcome, not of artistic conscience, but of a certain attitude to life. For form is not a personal thing like style. It is impersonal like logic. And just as the school of Alexander Pope was logical in its expressions, so it seems the school of Flaubert is, as it were, logical in its æsthetic form. "Nothing outside the definite line of the book," is a maxim. But can the human mind fix absolutely the definite line of a book, any more than it can fix absolutely any definite line of action for a living being?

Thomas Mann, however, is personal, almost painfully so, in his subject-matter. In "Tonio Kröger," the long *Novelle* at the end of the *Tristan* volume, he paints a detailed portrait of himself as a youth and younger man, a careful analysis. And he expresses at some length the misery of being an artist. "Literature is not a calling, it is a curse." Then he says to the Russian painter girl: "There is no artist anywhere but longs again, my love, for the common life." But any young artist might say that. It is because the stress of life in a young man, but particularly in an artist, is very strong, and has as yet found no outlet, so that it rages inside him in *Sturm und Drang.* But the condition is the same, only more tragic, in the Thomas Mann of fifty-three. He has never found any outlet for himself, save his art. He has never given himself to anything but his art. This is all well and good, if his art absorbs and satisfies him, as it has done some great men, like Corot. But then there are the other artists, the more human, like Shakespeare and Goethe, who must give themselves to life as well as to art. And if these were afraid, or despised life, then with their surplus they would ferment and become rotten. Which is what ails Thomas Mann. He is physically ailing, no doubt. But his complaint is deeper: it is of the soul.

And out of this soul-ailment, this unbelief, he makes his particular art, which he describes, in "Tonio Kröger," as *"Wählerisch, erlesen, kostbar, fein, reizbar gegen das Banale, und aufs höchste empfindlich in Fragen des Taktes und Geschmacks."* He is a disciple, in method, of the Flaubert who wrote: "I worked sixteen hours yesterday, today the whole day, and have at last finished one page." In writing of the *Leitmotiv* and its influence, he says: "Now this method alone is sufficient to explain my slowness. It is the result neither of anxiety nor indigence, but of an overpowering sense of responsibility for the choice of every word, the coining of every phrase . . . a responsibility that longs for perfect freshness, and which, after two hours' work, prefers not to undertake an important sentence. For which sentence is important, and which not? Can one know before hand whether a sentence, or part of a sentence may not be called upon to appear again as *Motiv,* peg, symbol, citation or connexion? And a sentence which must be heard twice must be fashioned accordingly. It must—I do not speak of beauty—possess a certain high level, and symbolic suggestion, which will make it worthy to sound again in any epic future. So every point becomes a standing ground, every adjective a decision, and it is clear that such work is not to be produced off-hand."

This, then, is the method. The man himself was always delicate in constitution. "The doctors said he was too weak to go to school, and must work at home." I quote from Aschenbach, in *Der Tod in Venedig.* "When he fell, at the age of fifty-three, one of his closest observers said of him: 'Aschenbach has always lived like this'—and he gripped his fist hard clenched; 'never like this'—and he let his open hand lie easily on the arm of the chair."

He forced himself to write, and kept himself to the work. Speaking of one of his works, he says: "It was pardonable, yea, it showed plainly the victory of his morality, that the uninitiated reader supposed the book to have come of a solid strength and one long breath; whereas it was the result of small daily efforts and hundreds of single inspirations."

And he gives the sum of his experience in the belief: *"dass beinahe alles Grosse, was dastehe, als ein Trotzdem dastehe, trotz Kummer und Qual, Armut, Verlassenheit, Körperschwäche, Laster, Leidenschaft und tausend hemmnischen Zustände gekommen sei."* And then comes the final revelation, difficult to translate. He is speaking of life as it is written into his books:

"For endurance of one's fate, grace in suffering, does not only mean passivity, but is an active work, a positive triumph, and the Sebastian figure is the most beautiful symbol, if not of all art, yet of the art in question. If one looked into this portrayed world and saw the elegant self-control that hides from the eyes of the world to the last moment the inner undermining, the biological decay; saw the yellow ugliness which, sensuously at a disadvantage, could blow its choking heat of desire to a pure flame, and even rise to sovereignty in the kingdom of beauty; saw the pale impotence which draws out of the glowing depths of its intellect sufficient strength to subdue a whole vigorous people, bring them to the foot of the Cross, to the feet of impotence; saw the amiable bearing in the empty and severe service of Form; saw the quickly enervating longing and art of the born swindler: if one saw such a fate as this, and all the rest it implied, then one would be forced to doubt whether there were in reality any other heroism than that of weakness. Which heroism, in any case, is more of our time than this?"

Perhaps it is better to give the story of *Der Tod in Venedig,* from which the above is taken, and to whose hero it applies.

Gustav von Aschenbach, a fine, famous author, over fifty years of age, coming to the end of a long walk one afternoon, sees as he is approaching a burying place, near Munich, a man standing between the chimeric figures of the gateway. This man in the gate of the cemetery is almost the *Motiv* of the story. By him, Aschenbach is infected with a desire to travel. He examines himself minutely, in a way almost painful in its frankness, and one sees the whole soul of this author of fifty-three. And it seems, the artist has absorbed the man, and yet the man is there, like an exhausted organism on which a parasite has fed itself strong. Then begins a kind of Holbein *Totentanz.* The story is quite natural in appearance, and yet there is the gruesome sense of symbolism throughout. The man near the burying ground has suggested travel—but whither? Aschenbach sets off to a watering place on the Austrian coast of the Adriatic, seeking some adventure, some passionate adventure, to which his sick soul and unhealthy body have been kindled. But finding himself on the Adriatic, he knows it is not thither that his desire draws him, and he takes ship for Venice. It is all real, and yet with a curious sinister unreality, like decay, the "biological decay." On board there is a man who reminds one of the man in the gateway, though there is no connexion. And then, among a crowd of young Poles who are crossing, is a ghastly fellow, whom Aschenbach sees is an old man dressed up as young, who capers unsuspected among the youths, drinks hilariously with them, and falls hideously drunk at last on the deck, reaching to the author, and slobbering about *"dem allerliebsten, dem schönsten Liebchen."* Suddenly the upper plate of his false teeth falls on his underlip.

Aschenbach takes a gondola to the Lido, and again the gondolier reminds one of the man in the cemetery gateway. He is, moreover, one who will make no concession, and, in spite of Aschenbach's demand to be taken back to St. Mark's, rows him in his black craft to the Lido, talking to himself softly all the while. Then he goes without payment.

The author stays in a fashionable hotel on the Lido. The adventure is coming, there by the pallid sea. As Aschenbach comes down into the hall of the hotel, he sees a beautiful Polish boy of about fourteen, with honey-coloured curls clustering round his pale face, standing with his sisters and their governess.

Aschenbach loves the boy—but almost as a symbol. In him he loves life and youth and beauty, as Hyacinth in the Greek myth. This, I suppose, is blowing the choking heat to pure flame, and raising it to the kingdom of beauty. He follows the boy, watches him all day long on the beach, fascinated by beauty concrete before him. It is still the *Künstler* and his abstraction: but there is also the "yellow ugliness, sensually at a disadvantage," of the elderly man below it all. But the picture of the writer watching the folk on the beach gleams and lives with a curious, gold-phosphorescent light, touched with the brightness of Greek myth, and yet a modern seashore with folks on the sands, and a half-threatening, diseased sky.

Aschenbach, watching the boy in the hotel lift, finds him delicate, almost ill, and the thought that he may not live long fills the elderly writer with a sense of peace. It eases him to think the boy should die.

Then the writer suffers from the effect of the *sirocco,* and intends to depart immediately from Venice. But at the station he finds with joy that his luggage has gone wrong, and he goes straight back to the hotel. There, when he sees Tadzin again, he knows why he could not leave Venice.

There is a month of hot weather, when Aschenbach follows Tadzin about, and begins to receive a look, loving, from over the lad's shoulder. It is wonderful, the heat, the unwholesomeness, the passion in Venice. One evening comes a street singer, smelling of carbolic acid, and sings beneath the veranda of the hotel. And this time, in gruesome symbolism, it is the man from the burying ground distinctly.

The rumour is, that the black cholera is in Venice. An atmosphere of secret plague hangs over the city of canals and palaces. Aschenbach verifies the report at the English bureau, but cannot bring himself to go away from Tadzin, nor yet to warn the Polish family. The secretly pest-smitten days go by. Aschenbach follows the boy through the stinking streets of the town and loses him. And on the day of the departure of the Polish family, the famous author dies of the plague.

It is absolutely, almost intentionally, unwholesome. The man is sick, body and soul. He portrays himself as he is, with wonderful skill and art, portrays his sickness. And since any genuine portrait is valuable, this book has its place. It portrays one man, one atmosphere, one sick vision. It claims to do no more. And we have to allow it. But we know it is unwholesome–it does not strike me as being morbid for all that, it is too well done–and we give it its place as such.

Thomas Mann seems to me the last sick sufferer from the complaint of Flaubert. The latter stood away from life as from a leprosy. And Thomas Mann, like Flaubert, feels vaguely that he has in him something finer than ever physical life revealed. Physical life is a disordered corruption, against which he can fight with only one weapon, his fine æsthetic sense, his feeling for beauty, for perfection, for a certain fitness which soothes him, and gives him an inner pleasure, however corrupt the stuff of life may be. There he is, after all these years, full of disgusts and loathing of himself as Flaubert was, and Germany is being voiced, or partly so, by him. And so, with real suicidal intention, like Flaubert's, he sits, a last too-sick disciple, reducing himself grain by grain to the statement of his own disgust, patiently, self-destructively, so that his statement at least may be perfect in a world of corruption. But he is so late.

Already I find Thomas Mann, who, as he says, fights so hard against the banal in his work, somewhat banal. His expression may be very fine. But by now what he expresses is stale. I think we have learned our lesson, to be sufficiently aware of the fulsomeness of life. And even while he has a rhythm in style, yet his work has none of the rhythm of a living thing, the rise of a poppy, then the after uplift of the bud, the shedding of the calyx and the spreading wide of the petals, the falling of the flower and the pride of the seed-head. There is an unexpectedness in this such as does not come from their carefully plotted and arranged developments. Even *Madame Bovary* seems to me dead in respect to the living rhythm of the whole work. While it is there in *Macbeth* like life itself.

But Thomas Mann is old–and we are young. Germany does not feel very young to me.

Americans, by Stuart P. Sherman

Professor Sherman once more coaxing American criticism the way it should go.

Like Benjamin Franklin, one of his heroes, he attempts the invention of a creed that shall "satisfy the professors of all religions, and offend none."

He smites the marauding Mr. Mencken with a velvet glove, and pierces the obstinate Mr. More with a reproachful look. Both gentlemen, of course, will purr and feel flattered.

That's how Professor Sherman treats his enemies: buns to his grizzlies.

Well, Professor Sherman, being a professor, has got to be nice to everybody about everybody. What else does a professor sit in a chair of English for, except to dole out sweets?

Awfully nice, rather cloying. But there, men *are* but children of a later growth.

So much for the professor's attitude. As for his "message." He steers his little ship of Criticism most obviously between the Scylla of Mr. Mencken and the Charybdis of Mr. P. E. More. I'm sorry I never heard before of either gentleman: except that I dimly remember having read, in the lounge of a Naples hotel, a bit of an article by a Mr. Mencken, in German, in some German periodical: all amounting to nothing.

But Mr. Mencken is the Scylla of American Criticism, and hence, of American democracy. There is a verb "to menckenize," and a noun "menckenism." Apparently to *menckenize* is to manufacture jeering little gas-bomb phrases against everything deep and earnest, or high and noble, and to paint the face of corruption with phosphorus, so it shall glow. And a *menckenism* is one of the little stink-gas phrases.

Now the *nouveau riche jeune fille* of the *bourgeoisie,* as Professor Sherman puts it; in other words, the profiteers' flappers all read Mr. Mencken and swear by him: swear that they don't give a nickel for any Great Man that ever was or will be. Great Men are all a bombastical swindle. So asserts the *nouveau riche jeune fille,* on whom, apparently, American democracy rests. And Mr. Mencken "learnt it her." And Mr. Mencken got it in Germany, where all stink-gas comes from, according to Professor Sherman. And Mr.

Mencken does it to poison the noble and great old spirit of American democracy, which is grandly Anglo-Saxon in origin, but absolutely American in fact.

So much for the Scylla of Mr. Mencken. It is the first essay in the book. The Charybdis of Mr. P. E. More is the last essay: to this monster the professor warbles another tune. Mr. More, author of the *Shelburne Essays,* is learned, and steeped in tradition, the very antithesis of the nihilistic stink-gassing Mr. Mencken. But alas, Mr. More is remote: somewhat haughty and supercilious at his study table. And even, alasser! with all his learning and remoteness, he hunts out the risky Restoration wits to hob-nob with on high Parnassus; Wycherley, for example; he likes his wits smutty. He even goes and fetches out Aphra Behn from her disreputable oblivion, to entertain her in public.

And there you have the Charybdis of Mr. More: snobbish, distant, exclusive, disdaining even the hero from the Marne who mends the gas bracket: and at the same time absolutely *preferring* the doubtful odour of Wycherley because it is–well, malodorous, says the professor.

Mr. Mencken: Great Men and the Great Past are an addled egg full of stink-gas.

Mr. P. E. More: Great Men of the Great Past are utterly beyond the *mobile vulgus.* Let the *mobile vulgus* (in other words, the democratic millions of America) be cynically scoffed at by the gentlemen of the Great Past, especially the naughty ones.

To the Menckenites, Professor Sherman says: Jeer not at the Great Past and at the Great Dead. Heroes are heroes still, they do not go addled, as you would try to make out, nor turn into stink-bombs. Tradition is honourable still, and will be honourable for ever, though it may be splashed like a futurist's picture with the rotten eggs of menckenism.

To the smaller and more select company of Moreites: Scorn not the horny hand of noble toil: "–the average man is, like (Mr. More) himself, at heart a mystic, vaguely hungering for a peace that diplomats cannot give, obscurely seeking the permanent amid the transitory: a poor swimmer struggling for a rock amid the flux of waters, a lonely pilgrim longing for the shadow of a mighty rock in a weary land. And if 'P. E. M.' had a bit more of that natural sympathy of which he is so distrustful, he would have perceived that what more than anything else today keeps the average man from lapsing into Yahooism is the religion of democracy, consisting of a little bundle of general principles which make him respect himself and his neighbour; a bundle of principles kindled in crucial times by an intense emotion, in which his self-interest, his petty vices, and his envy are consumed as with fire; and he sees the common weal as the mighty rock in the shadow of which his little life and personality are to be surrendered, if need be, as things negligible and transitory."

All right, Professor Sherman. All the profiteers, and shovers, and place-grabbers, and bullies, especially bullies, male and female, all that sort of gentry of the late war were, of course, outside the average. The supermen of the occasion.

The Babbitts, while they were on the make.

And as for the mighty rocks in weary lands, as far as my experience goes, they have served the pilgrims chiefly as sanitary offices and places in whose shadows men shall leave their offal and tin cans.

But there you have a specimen of Professor Sherman's "style." And the thin ends of his parabola.

The great arch is of course the Religion of Democracy, which the professor italicizes. If you want to trace the curve you must follow the course of the essays.

After Mr. Mencken and Tradition comes Franklin. Now Benjamin Franklin is one of the founders of the Religion of Democracy. It was he who invented the creed that should satisfy the professors of all religions, not of universities only, and offend none. With a deity called Providence. Who turns out to be a sort of superlative Mr. Wanamaker, running the globe as a revolving dry-goods store, according to a profit-and-loss system; the profit counted in plump citizens whose every want is satisfied: like chickens in an absolutely coyote-proof chicken-run.

In spite of this new attempt to make us like Dr. Franklin, the flesh wearies on our bones at the thought of him. The professor hints that the good old gentleman on Quaker Oats was really an old sinner. If it had been proved to us, we *might* have liked him. As it is, he just wearies the flesh on our bones. *Religion civile,* indeed.

Emerson. The next essay is called "The Emersonian Liberation." Well, Emerson is a great man still: or a great individual. And heroes are heroes still, though their banners may decay, and stink.

It is true that lilies may fester. And virtues likewise. The great Virtue of one age has a trick of smelling far worse than weeds in the next.

It is a sad but undeniable fact.

Yet why so sad, fond lover, prithee why so sad? Why should Virtue remain incorruptible, any more than anything else? If stars wax and wane, why should Goodness shine for ever unchanged? That too makes one tired. Goodness sweals and gutters, the light of the Good goes out with a stink, and lo, somewhere else a new light, a new Good. Afterwards, it may be shown that it is eternally the same Good. But to us poor mortals at the moment, it emphatically isn't.

And that is the point about Emerson and the Emersonian Liberation—save the word! Heroes are heroes still: safely dead. Heroism is always heroism. But the hero who was heroic one century, uplifting the banner of a creed, is followed the next century by a hero heroically ripping that banner to rags. *Sic transit veritas mundi.*

Emerson was an idealist: a believer in "continuous revelation," continuous inrushes of inspirational energy from the Over-Soul. Professor Sherman says: "His message when he leaves us is not, 'Henceforth be masterless,' but, 'Bear thou henceforth the sceptre of thine own control through life and the passion of life.' "

When Emerson says: "I am surrounded by messengers of God who send me credentials day by day," then all right for him. But he cozily forgot that there are many messengers. He knew only a sort of smooth-shaven Gabriel. But as far as we remember, there is Michael too: and a terrible discrepancy between the credentials of the pair of 'em. Then there are other cherubim with outlandish names, bringing very different messages than those Ralph Waldo got: Israfel, and even Mormon. And a whole bunch of others. But Emerson had a stone-deaf ear for all except a nicely aureoled Gabriel *qui n'avait pas de quoi.*

Emerson listened to one sort of message and only one. To all the rest he was blank. Ashtaroth and Ammon are gods as well, and hand out their own credentials. But Ralph Waldo wasn't having any. They could never ring *him* up. He was only connected on the Ideal phone. "We are all aiming to be idealists," says Emerson, "and covet the society of those who make us so, as the sweet singer, the orator, the ideal painter."

Well, we're pretty sick of the ideal painters and the uplifting singers. As a matter of fact we have worked the ideal bit of our nature to death, and we shall go crazy if we can't start working from some other bit. Idealism now is a sick nerve, and the more you rub on it the worse you feel afterwards. Your later reactions aren't pretty at all. Like Dostoievsky's Idiot, and President Wilson sometimes.

Emerson believes in having the courage to treat all men as equals. It takes some courage *not* to treat them so now.

"Shall I not treat all men as gods?" he cries.

If you like, Waldo, but we've got to pay for it, when you've made them *feel* that they're gods. A hundred million American godlets is rather much for the world to deal with.

The fact of the matter is, all those gorgeous inrushes of exaltation and spiritual energy which made Emerson a great man, now make us sick. They are with us a drug habit. So when Professor Sherman urges us in Ralph Waldo's footsteps, he is really driving us nauseously astray. Which perhaps is hard lines on the professor, and us, and Emerson. But it wasn't I who started the mills of God a-grinding.

I like the essay on Emerson. I like Emerson's real courage. I like his wild and genuine belief in the Over-Soul and the inrushes he got from it. But it is a museum-interest. Or else it is a taste of the old drug to the old spiritual drug-fiend in me.

We've got to have a different sort of sardonic courage. And the sort of credentials we are due to receive from the god in the shadow would have been real bones out of hell-broth to Ralph Waldo. *Sic transeunt Dei hominorum.*

So no wonder Professor Sherman sounds a little wistful, and somewhat pathetic, as he begs us to follow Ralph Waldo's trail.

Hawthorne: A Puritan Critic of Puritanism. This essay is concerned chiefly with an analysis and praise of *The Scarlet Letter.* Well, it is a wonderful book. But why does nobody give little Nathaniel a kick for his duplicity? Professor Sherman says there is nothing erotic about *The Scarlet Letter.* Only neurotic. It wasn't the sensual act itself had any meaning for Hawthorne. Only the Sin. He knew there's nothing deadly in the act itself. But if it is Forbidden, immediately it looms lurid with interest. He is not concerned for a moment with what Hester and Dimmesdale really felt. Only with their situations as Sinners. And Sin looms lurid and thrilling, when after all it is only just a normal sexual passion. This luridness about the book makes one feel like spitting. It is somewhat worked up: invented in the head and grafted on to the lower body, like some serpent of supposition under the fig-leaf. It depends so much on *coverings.* Suppose you took off the fig-leaf, the serpent isn't there. And so the relish is all two-faced and tiresome. *The Scar-*

let Letter is a masterpiece, but in duplicity and half-false excitement.

And when one remembers *The Marble Faun,* all the parochial priggishness and poor-bloodedness of Hawthorne in Italy, one of the most bloodless books ever written, one feels like giving Nathaniel a kick in the seat of his poor little pants and landing him back in New England again. For the rolling, many-godded medieval and pagan world was too big a prey for such a ferret.

Walt Whitman. Walt is the high priest of the Religion of Democracy. Yet "at the first bewildering contact one wonders whether his urgent touch is of lewdness or divinity," says Professor Sherman.

"All I have said concerns you." But it doesn't. One ceases to care about so many things. One ceases to respond or to react. And at length other things come up, which Walt and Professor Sherman never knew.

"Whatever else it involves, democracy involves at least one grand salutary elementary admission, namely, that the world exists for the benefit and for the improvement of all the decent individuals in it." O Lord, how long will you submit to this Insurance Policy interpretation of the Universe! How "decent"? Decent in what way? Benefit! Think of the world's existing for people's "benefit and improvement."

So wonderful says Professor Sherman, the way Whitman identifies himself with everything and everybody: Runaway slaves and all the rest. But we no longer want to take the whole hullabaloo to our bosom. We no longer want to "identify ourselves" with a lot of other things and other people. It *is* a sort of lewdness. *Noli me tangere,* "you." I don't want "you."

Whitman's "you" doesn't get me.

We don't want to be embracing everything any more. Or to be embraced in one of Waldo's vast promiscuous armfuls. *Merci, monsieur!*

We've had enough democracy.

Professor Sherman says that if Whitman had lived "at the right place in these years of Proletarian Millennium, he would have been hanged as a reactionary member of the *bourgeoise.*" ('Tisn't my spelling.)

And he gives Whitman's own words in proof: "The true gravitation hold of liberalism in the United States will be a more universal ownership of property, general homesteads, general comforts—a vast intertwining reticulation of wealth. . . . She (Democracy) asks for men and women with occupations, well-off, owners of houses and acres, and with cash in the bank and with some craving for literature too"—so that they can buy certain books. Oh, Walt!

Allons! The road is before us.

Joaquin Miller: Poetical Conquistador of the West. A long essay with not much spirit in it, showing that Miller was a true son of the Wild and Woolly West, in so far as he was a very good imitation of other people's poetry (note the Swinburnian bit) and a rather poor assumer of other people's played-out poses. A self-conscious little "wild" man, like the rest of the "wild" men. The Wild West is a pose that pays Zane Grey today, as it once paid Miller and Bret Harte and Buffalo Bill.

A note on Carl Sandburg. That Carl is a super-self-conscious literary gent stampeding around with red-ochre blood on his hands and smeared-on soot darkening his craggy would-be-criminal brow: but that his heart is as tender as an old tomato.

Andrew Carnegie. That Andy was the most perfect American citizen Scotland ever produced, and the sweetest example of how beautifully the *Religion Civile* pays, in cold cash.

Roosevelt and the National Psychology. Theodore didn't have a spark of magnanimity in his great personality, says Professor Sherman, what a pity! And you see where it lands you, when you play at being pro-German. You go quite out of fashion.

Evolution of the Adams Family. Perfect Pedigree of the most aristocratic Democratic family. Your aristocracy is played out, my dear fellows, but don't cry about it, you've always got your Democracy to fall back on. If you don't like falling back on it of your own free will, you'll be shoved back on it by the Will of the People.

"Man is the animal that destiny cannot break."

But the Will of the People can break Man and the animal man, and the destined man, all the lot, and grind 'em to democratic powder, Professor Sherman warns us.

Allons! en-masse is before us.

But when Germany is thoroughly broken, Democracy finally collapses. (My own prophecy.)

An Imaginary Conversation with Mr. P. E. More: You've had the gist of that already.

Well there is Professor Sherman's dish of cookies which he bids you eat and have. An awfully sweet book, all about having your cookies and eating 'em. The cookies are Tradition, and Heroes, and Great Men, and $350,000,000 in your pocket. And eating 'em is Democracy, Serving Mankind, piously giving most of the $350,-000,000 back again. "Oh, nobly and heroically get $350,000,000 together," chants Professor Sherman in this litany of having your cookies and eating 'em, "and then piously and munificently give away $349,000,000 again."

P.S. You can't get past Arithmetic.

A Second Contemporary Verse Anthology

"It is not merely an assembly of verse, but the spiritual record of an entire people."—This from the wrapper of *A Second Contemporary Verse Anthology*. The spiritual record of an entire people sounds rather impressive. The book as a matter of fact is a collection of pleasant verse, neat and nice and easy as eating candy.

Naturally, any collection of contemporary verse in any country at any time is bound to be more or less a box of candy. Days of Horace, days of Milton, days of Whitman, it would be pretty much the same, more or less a box of candy. Would it be at the same time the spiritual record of an entire people? Why not? If we had a good representative anthology of the poetry of Whitman's day, and if it contained two poems by Whitman, then it would be a fairly true spiritual record of the American people of that day. As if the whole nation had whispered or chanted its inner experience into the horn of a gramophone.

And the bulk of the whisperings and murmurings would be candy: sweet nothings, tender trifles, and amusing things. For of such is the bulk of the spiritual experience of any entire people.

The Americans have always been good at "occasional" verse. Sixty years ago they were very good indeed: making their little joke against themselves and their century. Today there are fewer jokes. There are also fewer footprints on the sands of time. Life is still earnest, but a little less real. And the soul has left off asserting that dust it isn't nor to dust returneth. The spirit of verse prefers now a "composition salad" of fruits of sensation, in a cooked mayonnaise of sympathy. Odds and ends of feelings smoothed into unison by some prevailing sentiment:

> My face is wet with the rain
> But my heart is warm to the core. . . .

Or you can call it a box of chocolate candies. Let me offer you a sweet! Candy! Isn't everything candy?

> There be none of beauty's daughters
> With a magic like thee—
> And like music on the waters
> Is thy sweet voice to me.

Is that candy? Then what about this?

But you are a girl and run
  Fresh bathed and warm and sweet,
After the flying ball
  On little, sandalled feet.

One of those two fragments is a classic. And one is a scrap from the contemporary spiritual record.

The river boat had loitered down its way,
The ropes were coiled, and business for the day
Was done——

Now fades the glimmering landscape on the sight,
And all the air a solemn stillness holds;
Save where——

Two more bits. Do you see any intrinsic difference between them? After all, the one *means* as much as the other. And what is there in the mere stringing together of words?

For some mysterious reason, there is everything.

When lilacs last in the dooryard bloomed——

It is a string of words, but it makes me prick my innermost ear. So do I prick my ear to: "Fly low, vermilion dragon." But the next line: "With the moon horns," makes me lower that same inward ear once more, in indifference.

There is an element of danger in all new utterance. We prick our ears like an animal in a wood at a strange sound.

Alas! though there is a modicum of "strange sound" in this contemporary spiritual record, we are not the animal to prick our ears at it. Sounds sweetly familiar, linked in a new crochet pattern. "Christ, what are patterns for?" But why invoke Deity? Ask the *Ladies' Home Journal*. You may know a new utterance by the element of danger in it. "My heart aches," says Keats, and you bet it's no joke.

Why do I think of stairways
With a rush of hurt surprise?

Heaven knows, my dear, unless you once fell down.

The element of danger. Man is always, all the time and for ever on the brink of the unknown. The minute you realize this, you prick your ears in alarm. And the minute any man steps alone, with his whole naked self, emotional and mental, into the everlasting hinterland of consciousness, you hate him and you wonder over him. Why can't he stay cozily playing word-games around the camp fire?

Now it is time to invoke the Deity, who made man an adventurer into the everlasting unknown of consciousness.

The spiritual record of any people is 99 per cent a record of games around a camp fire: word-games and picture-games. But the one per cent is a step into the grisly dark, which is for ever dangerous and wonderful. Nothing is wonderful unless it is dangerous. Dangerous to the *status quo* of the soul. And therefore to some degree detestable.

When the contemporary spiritual record warbles away about the wonder of the blue sky and the changing seas, etc., etc., etc., it is all candy. The sky is a blue hand-mirror to the modern poet and he goes on smirking before it. The blue sky of our particular heavens is painfully well known to us all. In fact, it is like the glass bowl to the goldfish, a *ne plus ultra* in which he sees himself as he goes round and round.

The actual heavens can suddenly roll up like the heavens of Ezekiel. That's what happened at the Renaissance. The old heavens shrivelled and men found a new empyrean above them. But they didn't get at it by playing word-games around the camp fire. Somebody has to jump like a desperate clown through the vast blue hoop of the upper air. Or hack a slow way through the dome of crystal.

Play! Play! Play! All the little playboys and playgirls of the western world, playing at goodness, playing at badness, playing at sadness, and playing deafeningly at gladness. Playboys and playgirls of the western world, harmlessly fulfilling their higher destinies and registering the spiritual record of an entire people. Even playing at death, and playing with death. Oh, poetry, you child in a bathing-dress, playing at ball!

You say nature is always nature, the sky is always the sky. But sit still and consider for one moment what sort of nature it was the Romans saw on the face of the earth, and what sort of heavens the medievals knew above them, and your sky will begin to crack like glass. The world is what it is, and the chimerical universe of the ancients was always child's play. The camera cannot lie. And the eye of man is nothing but a camera photographing the outer world in colour-process.

This sounds very well. But the eye of man photographs the chimera of nature, as well as the so-called scientific vision. The eye of man photographs gorgons and chimeras, as the eye of the spider photographs images unrecognizable to us and the eye of the horse photographs flat ghosts and looming motions. We are at the phase of scientific vision. This phase will pass and this vision will seem as chimerical to our descendants as the medieval vision seems to us.

The upshot of it all is that we are pot-bound in our consciousness. We are like a fish in a glass bowl, swimming round and round and gaping at our own image reflected on the walls of the infinite: the infinite being the glass bowl of our conception of life and the universe. We are prisoners inside our own conception of life and being. We have exhausted the possibilities of the universe, as we know it. All that remains is to telephone to Mars for a new word of advice.

Our consciousness is pot-bound. Our ideas, our emotions, our experiences are all pot-bound. For us there is nothing new under the sun. What there is to know, we know it already, and experience adds little. The girl who is going to fall in love knows all about it beforehand from books and the movies. She knows what she wants and she wants what she knows. Like candy. It is still nice to eat candy, though one has eaten it every day for years. It is still nice to eat candy. But the spiritual record of eating candy is a rather thin noise.

There is nothing new under the sun, once the consciousness becomes pot-bound. And this is what ails all art today. But particularly American art. The American consciousness is peculiarly pot-bound. It doesn't even have that little hole in the bottom of the pot through which desperate roots straggle. No, the American consciousness is not only potted in a solid and everlasting pot, it is placed moreover in an immovable ornamental vase. A double hide to bind it and a double bond to hide it.

European consciousness still has cracks in its vessel and a hole in the bottom of its absoluteness. It still has strange roots of memory groping down to the heart of the world.

But American consciousness is absolutely free of such danglers. It is free from all loop-holes and crevices of escape. It is absolutely safe inside a solid and ornamental concept of life. There it is Free! Life is good, and all men are meant to have a good time. Life is good! that is the flower-pot. The ornamental vase is: Having a good time.

So they proceed to have it, even with their woes. The young maiden knows exactly when she falls in love: she knows exactly how she feels when her lover or husband betrays her or when she betrays him: she knows precisely what it is to be a forsaken wife, an adoring mother, an erratic grandmother. All at the age of eighteen.

Vive la vie!

There is nothing new under the sun, but you can have a jolly good old time all the same with the old things. A nut sundae or a new beau, a baby or an automobile, a divorce or a troublesome appendix: my dear, that's Life! You've got to get a good time out of it, anyhow, so here goes!

In which attitude there is a certain piquant stoicism. The stoicism of having a good time. The heroism of enjoying yourself. But, as I say, it makes rather thin hearing in a spiritual record. *Rechauffés* of *rechauffés*. Old soup of old bones of life, heated up again for a new consommé. Nearly always called *printanière*.

I know a forest, stilly-deep . . .

Mark the poetic novelty of stilly-deep, and then say there is nothing new under the sun.

My soul-harp never thrills to peaceful tunes;

I should say so.

For after all, the thing to do
Is just to put your heart in song—

Or in pickle.

I sometimes wish that God were back
  In this dark world and wide;
For though some virtues he might lack,
  He had his pleasant side.

"Getting on the pleasant side of God, and how to stay there."—Hints by a Student of Life.

Oh, ho! Now I am masterful!
Now I am filled with power.
Now I am brutally myself again
And my own man.

For I have been among my hills today,
On the scarred dumb rocks standing;

And it made a man of him . . .

Open confession is good for the soul.

The spiritual record of an entire . . . what?

Hadrian the Seventh, by Baron Corvo

In *Hadrian the Seventh,* Frederick Baron Corvo falls in, head over heels, in deadly earnest. A man must keep his earnestness nimble, to escape ridicule. The so-called Baron Corvo by no means escapes. He reaches heights, or depths, of sublime ridiculousness.

It doesn't kill the book, however. Neither ridicule nor dead earnest kills it. It is extraordinarily alive, even though it has been buried for twenty years. Up it rises to confront us. And, great test, it does not "date" as do Huysmans's books, or Wilde's or the rest of them. Only a first-rate book escapes its date.

Frederick Rolfe was a fantastic figure of the nineties, the nineties of the *Yellow Book,* Oscar Wilde, Aubrey Beardsley, Simeon Solomon, and all the host of the godly. The whole decade is now a little ridiculous, ridiculous decadence as well as ridiculous pietism. They said of Rolfe that he was certainly possessed of a devil. At least his devil is still alive, it hasn't turned into a sort of gollywog, like the bulk of the nineties' devils.

Rolfe was one of the Catholic converts of the period, very intense. But if ever a man was a Protestant in all his being, this one was. The acuteness of his protest drove him, like a crazy serpent, into the bosom of the Roman Catholic Church.

He seems to have been a serpent of serpents in the bosom of all the nineties. That in itself endears him to one. The way everyone dropped him with a shudder is almost fascinating.

He died about 1912, when he was already forgotten: an outcast and in a sense a wastrel.

We can well afford to remember him again: he was not nothing, as so many of the estimables were. He was a gentleman of education and culture, pining, for the show's sake, to be a priest. The Church shook him out of her bosom before he could take orders. So he wrote himself Fr. Rolfe. It would do for Frederick, and if you thought it meant Father Rolfe, good old you!

But then his other passion, for medieval royalism, overcame him, and he was Baron Corvo when he signed his name. Lord Rook, Lord Raven, the bird was the same as Fr. Rolfe.

Hadrian the Seventh is, as far as his connexion with the Church was concerned, largely an autobiography of Frederick Rolfe. It is the story of a young English convert, George Arthur Rose (Rose for

Rolfe), who has had bitter experience with the priests and clergy, and years of frustration and disappointment, till he arrives at about the age of forty, a highly-bred, highly-sensitive, super-æsthetic man, ascetic out of æstheticism, athletic the same, religious the same. He is to himself beautiful, with a slim, clean-muscled grace, much given to cold baths, white-faced with a healthy pallor, and pure, that is sexually chaste, because of his almost morbid repugnance for women. He had no desires to conquer or to purify. Women were physically repulsive to him, and therefore chastity cost him nothing, the Church would be a kind of asylum.

The priests and clergy, however, turned him down, or dropped him like the proverbial snake in the bosom, and inflamed him against them, so that he was burned through and through with white, ceaseless anger. His anger had become so complete as to be pure: it really was demonish. But it was all nervous and imaginative, an imaginative, sublimated hate, of a creature born crippled in its affective organism.

The first part of the book, describing the lonely man in a London lodging, alone save for his little cat, whose feline qualities of aloofness and self-sufficiency he so much admires, fixes the tone at once. And in the whole of literature I know nothing that resembles those amazing chapters, when the bishop and the archbishop come to him, and when he is ordained and makes his confession. Then the description of the election of the new pope, the cardinals shut up in the Vatican, the failure of the Way of Scrutiny and the Way of Access, the fantastic choice, by the Way of Compromise, of George Arthur Rose, is too extraordinary and daring ever to be forgotten.

From being a rejected aspirant to the priesthood, George Arthur Rose, the man in the London lodging, finds himself suddenly not only consecrated, but elected head of all the Catholic Church. He becomes Pope Hadrian the Seventh.

Then the real fantasy and failure begins. George Arthur Rose, triple-crowned and in the chair of Peter, is still very much Frederick Rolfe, and perfectly consistent. He is the same man, but now he has it all his own way: a White Pope, pure, scrupulous, chaste, living on two dollars a day, an æsthetic idealist, and really, a super-Protestant. He has the British instinct of authority, which is now gloriously gratified. But he has no inward *power,* power to make true change in the world. Once he is on the throne of high power, we realize his futility.

He is, like most modern men, especially reformers and idealists, through and through a Protestant. Which means, his life is a changeless fervour of protest. He can't help it. Everything he comes into contact with he must criticize, with all his nerves, and react from. Fine, subtle, sensitive, and almost egomaniac, he can accept nothing but the momentary thrill of æsthetic appreciation. His life-flow is like a stream washing against a false world, and ebbing itself out in a marsh and a hopeless bog.

So it is with George Arthur Rose, become Pope Hadrian the Seventh, while he is still in a state of pure protest, he is vivid and extraordinary. But once he is given full opportunity to do as he wishes, and his *raison d'être* as a Protestant is thereby taken away, he becomes futile, and lapses into the ridiculous.

He can criticize men, exceedingly well: hence his knack of authority. But the moment he has to build men into a new form, construct something out of men by making a new unity among them, swarming them upon himself as bees upon a queen, he is ridiculous and powerless, a fraud.

It is extraordinary how *blind* he is, with all his keen insight. He no more "gets" his cardinals than we get the men on Mars. He can criticize them, and analyse them, and reject or condone them. But the real old Adam that is in them, the old male instinct for *power,* this, to him, does not exist.

In actual life, of course, the cardinals would drop a Hadrian down the oubliette, in ten minutes, and without any difficulty at all, once he was inside the Vatican. And Hadrian would be utterly flabbergasted, and call it villainy.

And what's the good of being Pope, if you've nothing but protest and æsthetics up your sleeve? Just like the reformers who are excellent, while fighting authority. But once authority disappears, they fall into nothingness. So with Hadrian the Seventh. As Pope, he is a fraud. His critical insight makes him a politician of the League of Nations sort, on a vast and curious scale. His medievalism makes him a truly comical royalist. But as a *man,* a real power in the world, he does not exist.

Hadrian unwinding the antimacassar is a sentimental farce. Hadrian persecuted to the point of suicide by a blowsy lodging-house keeper is a bathetic farce. Hadrian and the Socialist "with gorgonzola teeth" is puerile beyond words. It is all amazing, that a man with so much insight and fineness, on the one hand, should be so helpless and just purely ridiculous, when it comes to actualities.

He simply has no conception of what it is to be a natural or honestly animal man, with the repose and the power that goes with the honest animal in man. His attempt to appreciate his Cardinal Ragna—probably meant for Rampolla—is funny. It is as funny as would be an attempt on the part of the late President Wilson to appreciate Hernán Cortés, or even Theodore Roosevelt, supposing they were put face to face.

The time has come for stripping: cries Hadrian. Strip then, if there are falsities to throw away. But if you go on and on and on peeling the onion down, you'll be left with blank nothing between your hands, at last. And this is Hadrian's plight. He is assassinated in the streets of Rome by a Socialist, and dies supported by three Majesties, sublimely absurd. And there is nothing to it. Hadrian has stripped himself and everything else till nothing is left but absurd conceit, expiring in the arms of the Majesties.

Lord! be to me a Saviour, not a judge! is Hadrian's prayer: when he is not affectedly praying in Greek. But why should such a white streak of blamelessness as Hadrian need saving so badly? Saved from what? If he has done his best, why mind being judged—at least by Jesus, who in this sense is any man's peer?

The brave man asks for justice: the rabble cries for favours! says some old writer. Why does Hadrian, in spite of all his protest, go in with the rabble?

It is a problem. The book remains a clear and definite book of our epoch, not to be swept aside. If it is the book of a demon, as the contemporaries said, it is the book of a man-demon, not of a mere poseur. And if some of it is caviare, at least it came out of the belly of a live fish.

The Origins of Prohibition, by J. A. Krout

This is a book which one may honestly call "an excellent piece of work." Myself, I feel I have done a more or less excellent piece of work, in having read it. Because it wearied me a little.

But then, I am not an American, and have never, to my knowledge, had a single relative in the United States. And I am a novelist, not a scientific historian. All the American names mean nothing to me, and to this day I don't know where Rhode Island is. So there are limits to my sympathy.

Yet I have read the book, and realize it is a sound piece of work: an attempt to convey, dispassionately, the attitude of the American people to alcoholic drinks, since the early days of the colonies. This is not, strictly, an inquiry into the *origins* of prohibition. For that, one would have to go deeper. It is a record of the development of the prohibitionist feeling: almost, a statistical record. There are copious notes, and an extraordinary bibliography: good scholarship, but, on the whole, flat reading.

One wonders if anything should try to be so angelically dispassionate: anything except an adding-up machine. Reading the chapters about excise laws, and political campaigns, a deep depression comes over one. There are gleams of warmth and vividness elsewhere. The very words malmsey, and sack, and pale sherry, cheer one up a bit. And the famous cycle molasses–rum–slaves–molasses–rum–slaves–makes one pause: as does the glimpse of Washington's army getting its whisky rations. As soon as we catch sight of an actual individual, like Dr. Rush, we prick up our ears–but Dr. Rush turns out rather boring. The Washingtonians, with the Cold Water Army, and Hawkins and Gough, might really have been lively; while to step into the sobbing literature of teetotalism is a relaxation. But the author is inexorable. He won't laugh, and he won't let us laugh. He won't get angry, and he prevents our getting angry. He refuses to take an attitude, except that of impartiality, which is the worst of all attitudes. So he leaves us depressed, not wanting to hear another word about temperance, teetotalism, prohibition. We want to relegate the whole business into the class of "matters indifferent," where John Knox put it.

We can't, quite, since prohibition has us by the leg. So perhaps it is as well to read the book, which helps us to come to a decision. For myself–dropping all pretence at impartiality–it makes me regret that ardent spirits were ever discovered. Why, oh, why, as soon as the New World waved the sugar-cane, did it start turning molasses into rum? And as soon as the wheat rose in the colonies, why did it disappear into whisky? Apparently, until the time of the Renaissance and the discovery of America, men actually drank no liquors–or very little. Beer, cider, wine, these had kept the world going, more or less, till the days of Columbus. Why did all Europe and America suddenly, after the Renaissance, demand powerful liquor? get drunk quick? It is a mystery, and a tragedy, and part of our evolution.

That distilled liquor has been more of a curse than a blessing to mankind, few, surely, will deny. It is only the curse of whisky which has driven wine and beer into disrepute. Until a few decades ago, even the temperance societies had nothing to say against beer. But now it is the whole hog.

In the conclusion, which is cautiously called "A Summary View," the author finds that prohibition in America was inevitable: firstly, because a self-governing people must be self-responsible. "Intemperance might be tolerated in a divine-right monarchy, but in a republic it endangered the very existence of the state. No popular government could long endure, unless the electorate was persuaded or forced to follow the straight and narrow path of sobriety."–"It was ridiculous to talk of the *will of the sovereign people,* when intoxicated citizens were taken to the polls."

This is confused thinking. How can the electorate of a popular government be *forced* to follow the straight and narrow path? Persuaded, an electorate may be. But how, and by whom can it be *forced?*

The answer is, by itself: an electorate forcing itself to do a thing it doesn't want to do, and doesn't intend to do, is indeed making a display of the sovereign will of the people.

But this is the anomaly of popular government. Obviously America failed to *persuade* herself, or to be persuaded, into the straight and narrow path of sobriety. So she went one worse, and forced herself.

And this is the dreary, depressing reality. A republic with a "popular government" can only exist honourably when the bulk of the individuals choose, of their own free will, to follow the straight and narrow path necessary to the common good. That is, when every man governs himself, responsibly, from within. Which, say what we may, was the very germ of the "American idea."

The dreary and depressing fact is that this germ is dying, if not dead. Temperance reformers decided, after long experience, that America was not to be persuaded. Her citizens could not, or would not control themselves, with regard to liquor.

Therefore they must be coerced. By whom? By the electorate itself. Every man voting prohibition for his neighbour voted it for himself, of course. But somewhere he made a mental reservation. He intended, himself, to have his little drink still, if he wanted it. Since he, good citizen, knew better than to abuse himself.

The cold misery of every man seeking to coerce his neighbour, in the name of righteousness, creeps out of these pages and makes depressing reading.

The second reason why prohibition was inevitable—because it is advantageous to industry—is sound as far as economics go. But how far do national economics go, even in America, in the ordinary individual? And even then, it is temperance, not prohibition, which is truly advantageous to industry.

One is chilled and depressed. The saloon was bad, and is best abolished. Myself, I believe that. But in prohibition one sees an even worse thing: a nation, knowing it cannot control itself from the inside, self-responsibly, each man vindictively votes to coerce his neighbour.

Because surely, seeing the state of things, a great number of the voters voting for prohibition must have reserved for themselves the private right to a drink, all the same.

A man may vote from his honourable national self: or he may vote from his vindictive herd self. Which self voted, you will only know by the smell, afterwards.

In the American Grain, by William Carlos Williams

Mr. Williams quotes Poe's distinction between "nationality in letters" and the *local* in literature. Nationality in letters is deplorable, whereas the *local* is essential. All creative art must rise out of a specific soil and flicker with a spirit of place.

The local, of course, in Mr. Williams's sense, is the very opposite of the parochial, the parish-pump stuff. The local in America is America itself. Not Salem, or Boston, or Philadelphia, or New York, but that of the American subsoil which spouts up in any of those places into the lives of men.

In these studies of "American" heroes, from Red Eric of Greenland, and Columbus and Cortés and Montezuma, on to Abraham Lincoln, Mr. Williams tries to reveal the experience of great men in the Americas since the advent of the whites. History in this book would be a sensuous record of the Americanization of the white men in America, as contrasted with ordinary history, which is a complacent record of the civilization and Europizing (if you can allow the word) of the American continent.

In this record of truly American heroes, then, the author is seeking out not the ideal achievement of great men of the New World but the men themselves, in all the dynamic explosiveness of their energy. This peculiar dynamic energy, this strange yearning and passion and uncanny explosive quality in men derived from Europe, is American, the American element. Seek out *this* American element, O Americans!, is the poet's charge.

All America is now going hundred per cent American. But the only hundred per cent American is the Red Indian, and he can only be canonized when he is finally dead. And not even the most American American can transmogrify into an Indian. Whence, then, the hundred per cent?

It is here that Mr. Williams's—and Poe's—distinction between the *national* and the *local* is useful. Most of the hundred per centism is national, and therefore not American at all. The new one hundred per cent literature is all *about* Americans, in the intensest American vernacular. And yet, in vision, in conception, in the very manner, it still remains ninety-nine per cent European. But for *Ulysses* and Marcel Proust and a few other beetling high-brows, where would the modernist hundred per centers of America have been? Alas, where they are now, save for cutting a few capers.

What then? William Carlos Williams tries to bring into his consciousness America itself, the still-unravished bride of silences. The great continent, its bitterness, its brackish quality, its vast glamour, its strange cruelty. Find this, Americans, and get it into your bones. The powerful, unyielding breath of the Americas, which Columbus sniffed, even in Europe, and which sent the Conquistadores mad. National America is a gruesome sort of fantasy. But the unravished *local* America still waits vast and virgin as ever, though in process of being murdered.

The author sees the genius of the continent as a woman with exquisite, super-subtle tenderness and recoiling cruelty. It is a myth-woman who will demand of men a sensitive awareness, a supreme sensuous delicacy, and at the same time an infinitely tempered resistance, a power of endurance and of resistance.

To evoke a vision of the essential America is to evoke Americans, bring them into conscious life. To bring a few American citizens into American consciousness–the consciousness at present being all bastardized European–is to form the nucleus of the new race. To have the nucleus of a new race is to have a future: and a true aristocracy. It is to have the germ of an aristocracy in sensitive tenderness and diamond-like resistance.

A man, in America, can only *begin* to be American. After five hundred years there are no *racial* white Americans. They are only national, woebegone, or strident. After five hundred years more there may be the developing nucleus of a true American race. If only men, some few, trust the American passion that is in them, and pledge themselves to it.

But the passion is not national. No man who doesn't feel the last anguish of tragedy–*and beyond that*–will ever know America, or begin, even at the beginning's beginning, to be American.

There are two ways of being American: and the chief, says Mr. Williams, is by recoiling into individual smallness and insentience, and gutting the great continent in frenzies of mean fear. It is the Puritan way. The other is by *touch;* touch America as she is; dare to touch her! And this is the heroic way.

And this, this sensitive touch upon the unseen America, is to be the really great adventure in the New World. Mr. Williams's book contains his adventure; and, therefore, for me, has a fascination. There are very new and profound glimpses into life: the strength of insulated smallness in the New Englanders, the fascination of "being nothing" in the Negroes, the *spell-bound* quality of men like Columbus, De Soto, Boone. It is a glimpse of what the vast America *wants men to be,* instead of another strident assertion of what men have made, do make, will make, can make, out of the murdered territories of the New World.

It would be easy enough to rise, in critical superiority, as a critic always feels he must, superior to his author, and find fault. The modernist style is sometimes irritating. Was Tenochtitlan really so wonderful? (See Adolf Bandelier's *The Golden Man.*) Does not Mr. Williams mistake Poe's agony of *destructive penetration,* through all the horrible bastard-Europe alluvium of his 1840 America, for the positive America itself?

But if an author rouses my deeper sympathy he can have as many faults as he likes, I don't care. And if I disagree with him a bit, heaven save me from feeling superior just because I have a chance to snarl. I am only too thankful that Mr. Williams wrote his book.

Heat, by Isa Glenn

Heat is the title of a novel by an American authoress, Isa Glenn, a name quite unfamiliar. The cover-notice says "Miss Glenn," but the book is, in the life sense, mature, and seems at least like the work of a married woman. I don't think any married woman would have written *Jane Eyre*, nor either *The Constant Nymph*. In those books there is a certain naïve attitude to men which would hardly survive a year of married life. But the authoress of *Heat* is not naïve about her men. She is kindly, rather sisterly and motherly, and a trifle contemptuous. Affectionate contempt, coupled with yearning, is the note of the feeling towards the officers in the American army out there in the Philippines, and to the American fortune-hunting business men. The authoress, or rather, let us say the heroine, Charlotte, is evidently quite a good sport, from the man's point of view. She doesn't let you down. And so the men are quite good sports to her. They like her; and she likes them. But she feels a little contempt for them, amid her liking: and at the same time a yearning after some man who will call her his own. The men, for their part, feel very honourable and kindly towards Miss Charlotte, but they are a little afraid of her. They have to respect her just a bit too much. No man could feel tenderly possessive towards the Statue of Liberty. And Charlotte is, in the way of independence and honesty and thinking for herself, just a bit of a Statue of Liberty.

She is not so liberal, though, about the women, the wives of the officers out there in Manila. They are to her just repellent, even if not repulsive. She sees them with that utter cold antipathy with which women often regard other women—especially when the other women are elderly, physically unattractive, and full of flirtatious grimaces. To a man, there is something strange and disconcerting in the attitude of a woman like Charlotte towards other women, in particular her married seniors. She seems to be able to eye them with such complete cold understanding, that it takes one into quite another world of life. It is how a slim silvery fish in a great tank may eye the shapeless, greyish, groping-fishes that float heavily past her.

The story is laid in the Philippines, those islands belonging to the United States far away in the steaming hot Pacific, towards China: islands bought from Spain with good American dollars. A forlorn, unholily hot, lost remnant of the world belonging, really, to the age of the ichthyosaurus, not to our day.

To Manila, then, goes Charlotte, to be a school-teacher to the brown native children: a school-teacher, of course, with high missionary fervour. On the same boat, a transport, goes Tom Vernay, young lieutenant in the American army, fresh from the military school of West Point. There is also a big blond heavy American, Saulsbury, out to make a fortune in cement: modern cement buildings for the Philippines.

This is before the war: twenty years ago, or so. The whole of the first half of the book, at least, is written with the pre-war outlook. Maybe it was actually written before the war.

Charlotte, of course, loves Tom Vernay. But "loves" can mean so many things. She is thrilled by a certain purity in him, and by his intense, but vague, romantic yearning. He is an American who is "different": he has poetry in him. So Charlotte can feel intensely practical and "wise," hence a little protective and superior. She adores him. But at the same time, she feels a little protectively superior.

And he? At moments he adores her. At moments, he falls within her spell. He always likes her. He always, unconsciously, relies on her in the background. But! There is always a but! She is beautiful, with her fine gold hair and her girl's boyish figure. But!

But what, then?

Well, she is not exactly romantic. Going out to be a school-teacher, to "uplift" brown Filipinos! Going out alone, unprotected too, very capable of looking after herself, and looking after him too! Going out with a great idea that natives and niggers are as good as you are, if they are only educated up to your level. We're all alike under the skin, only our education is unequal. So let's level up the education. That kind of thing!

Yes! It was generous and democratic, and he approved of it in an admiring sort of way. But!

Another but! What is it this time?

This time, it is that his music simply won't play. With the key of her fine democratic spirit she only locks up the flow of her passion tighter, locks it up dead. It needs another key altogether to release the music of his desire.

He is romantic. Manila, shut up tight and tortuous, steaming hot and smelly within the ponderous Spanish fortifications, fascinates him with the allure of the haughty and passionate past. Let it steam and smell! so long as the powerfully sweet flower, the Dama de la Noche, also perfumes the nights, and guitars tinkle in unseen patios, and the love-song scrapes and yearns and sinks in the Spanish throat. Romance! he wants romance.

And as the months pass by, and the heat soaks into his brain, and the strange reptilian moisture of heat goes through his very bones, he wants romance more and more.

Charlotte, poor thing, in a cheap, half-breed lodging-house, spending her days trying to teach insolent brown native children whose heads are rancid with coconut oil, and whose nauseating sexual knowingness seems to be born with them, as a substitute for any other kind of knowledge, does not get so much romance out of it. She is kind to her pupils, she goes to the huts of their parents, and is purely charitable. For which reason, the lizard-like natives jeer at her with a subtle but fathomless contempt. She is only the "ticher," she is, to put it orientally, their servant, their white bondwoman. And as such they treat her, with infinite subtle disresprect, and that indescribable derision of the East.

Poor Charlotte doesn't like it at all. A well-born, well-educated American girl, she is accustomed to all the respect in the world. It is *she* who feels privileged to hold a little contempt for others, not quite as clear and sure as herself. And now, these dirty little sexual natives give off silent and sometimes audible mockery at her, because she is kind instead of bullying, and clean instead of impure. Her sort of sexual cleanness makes the little brown women scream with derision: to them it is raw, gawky, incredible incompetence, if not a sort of impotence; the ridiculous female eunuch.

And there must be a grain of truth in it: for she cannot keep her Vernay in her spell. He has fallen wildly, romantically in love with a mysterious Spanish beauty. Romance, this time laid on with a trowel. The oldest, haughtiest family on the island, selling out to retire to Spain, from under the authority of these dogs of Americans! —a fat, waddling, insolent, black-moustached Spanish mother, with her rasping Castilian speech! and a daughter, ah! a Dolores! small and dusky and hidden in a mantilla!—about to be carried off to Spain to be married to some elderly Spaniard who will throw his hands in the air when he is excited!—Dolores, who has a fancy for the blue eyes and the white uniform of the American officers!

Tom Vernay has blue eyes and a white uniform, and is tall. One glimpse of the nose-tip of Dolores, from under her mantilla, does what all the intimacy with Charlotte could not do: it starts his music wildly playing. He is enamoured, and enamoured of Dolores. Through a little brother, a meeting is brought about. Then there is the daily clandestine stroll upon the unfrequented wall. In all the heat! Dolores Ayala! Ah, heaven of romance! Ah, Tom! He feels himself a Don at last! Don Tomás!

And Charlotte, very much in the background, losing her good looks and the fine brightness of her hair, going thin and raky and bitter in the heat and insult of the islands where already she has sweated for three years, must even now defend Vernay from the officers' wives.

The love-affair works up. The Ayalas are about to depart. Tom Vernay must marry Dolores. Against her parents' will, he must marry her clandestinely, in the American church. But he must resign his commission in the army first, for there will be a great scandal, and he must not expose his country to odium.

So, he resigns his commission. The Ayalas are almost ready to sail. A great buzz goes up among the officers' wives, when the news comes out that Tom Vernay has sent in his resignation. The colonel's wife is giving a dinner-party at the Army Club: one of the endless perspiring parties. Charlotte is there, because they want to pump her; otherwise they don't ask her: she is merely the "ticher" of the natives, the school-teacher, shrivelling in the heat, becoming an old maid. Vernay is not present.

As the party moves from the table to go to dance, Vernay, white and strained, appears and murmurs to Charlotte that she must come to his room for a moment. Resentfully, she goes. To find–ah, to find the mousy, muffled-up Dolores there, all thrilled with herself for having escaped the family vigilance and arranged a rendezvous.

Tom Vernay, the romantic, is absolutely unequal to the occasion. Dolores, laughing, throws herself on Tom's breast, kissing his mouth. Tom, who has honourable intentions, can't stand it, holds her off and turns her to Charlotte–poor Charlotte! "Listen, dear, you must go home tonight with Miss Carson. And tomorrow morning we can get the chaplain to marry us."–"Why?" cries Dolores. "I can never marry you! Didn't you understand?"–"We will talk about that in the morning. Go home now with Miss Carson, like a good girl." Dolores, instead of being the "good girl," looks at poor Charlotte. And Dolores refuses to be taken off. "I got here so easily," she laughed. "I can do this wicked thing often and often, before we sail for Spain. I shall have to crawl on my knees to the Stations in penance. But is it not worth it–your eyes are so blue!"

It isn't what Dolores would say in real Spanish, but the gist is all right. Tom insists that she go home with poor Charlotte, who by no means enjoys this scene in his bedroom at the Club. He gives Dolores to understand that he has resigned his commission in order to marry her: marry her in the morning.

This is too much for Dolores. She loathes being put off. She loathes the other woman, the very school-teacher, dragged in on her. She never intended to marry him, and have heretic babies, and be carted off to the United States. Not she! But this wicked thing! Ah! But now, without a uniform, she doesn't intend even to love him. Adios!

The faithful Charlotte smuggles her out of the Club, unseen, as she smuggled herself in. Home goes Dolores. The book, the biggest, romantic part, is finished.

The second part opens some years later. Vernay, his commission gone, has deteriorated rapidly in civilian life, till now he is a mere whisky-lapper, a derelict in smelly clothes, gone native. Charlotte, who has still been teaching school, but far away in a lonely island, returns and determines to find him, to rescue him.

She finds him: but he is beyond rescue. She finds him in a squalid native quarter, down by the ill-smelling river, in a region of broken bottles. He is vague and corrupted, and his reptilian little native wife is big with his second child. It is enough. The book ends.

Poor Charlotte! There is nothing more to be done.

What was there ever to be done? The kind of attraction he wanted in a woman she hadn't got, and would have despised herself for having. She shuddered at the sexual little beasts of native women, working men up with snaky caresses. Ah, yes, she had to admit it, poor thing, that these native women had a power, a strange and hideous power over men. But it was a power she would loathe to possess.

And lacking it, she lost her Vernay, and went on being a faded school-teacher. We can call it the man's fault: the man's imbecility and perversity. But in the long run, a man will succumb to the touch of the woman who, touching him, will start his music playing. And the woman whom he esteems and even cherishes, but who, touching him, leaves him musicless and passionless, he will ultimately abandon. That is, if he gets the chance.

Gifts of Fortune, by H. M. Tomlinson

Gifts of Fortune is not a travel-book. It is not even, as the jacket describes it, a book of travel memories. Travel in this case is a stream of reflections, where images intertwine with dark thoughts and obscure emotion, and the whole flows on turbulent and deep and transitory. It is reflection, thinking back on travel and on life, and in the mirror sense, throwing back snatches of image.

Mr. Tomlinson's own title: *Gifts of Fortune: With Some Hints to Those About to Travel* is a little grimly misleading. Those about to travel, in the quite commonplace sense of the word, will find very few encouraging hints in the long essay which occupies a third of this book, and is entitled, "Hints to Those About to Travel." The chief hint they would hear would be, perhaps, the sinister suggestion that they had better stay at home.

There are travellers and travellers, as Mr. Tomlinson himself makes plain. There are scientific ones, game-shooting ones, Thomas Cook ones, thrilled ones, and bored ones. And none of these, as such, will find a single "hint" in all the sixty-six hinting pages, which will be of any use to them.

Mr. Tomlinson is travelling in retrospect, in soul rather than in the flesh, and his hints are to other souls. To travelling bodies he says little.

The sea tempts one to travel. But what is the nature of the temptation? To what are we tempted? Mr. Tomlinson gives us the hint, for his own case. "What draws us to the sea is the light over it," etc.

There you have the key to this book. Coasts of illusion! "There are other worlds." A man who has travelled this world in the flesh travels again, sails once more wilfully along coasts of illusion, and wilfully steers into other worlds. Take then the illusion, accept the gifts of fortune, "that passes as a shadow on the wall."

"My journeys have all been the fault of books, though Lamb would never have called them that." Mr. Tomlinson is a little weary of books, though he has here written another. A talk with seamen in the forecastle of a ship has meant more to him than any book. So he says. But that is how a man feels, at times. As a matter of fact, from these essays it is obvious that books like Bates's *Amazon,* Conrad's *Nigger of the Narcissus,* and Melville's *Moby Dick* have gone deeper into him than any talk with seamen in forecastles of steamers.

How could it be otherwise? Seamen see few coasts of illusion. They see very little of anything. And what is Mr. Tomlinson after? What are we all after, if it comes to that? It is our yearning to land on the coasts of illusion, it is our passion for other worlds that carries us on. And with Bates or Conrad or Melville we are already away over the intangible seas. As Mr. Tomlinson makes very plain, a P. & O. liner will only take us from one hotel to another. Which isn't what we set out for, at all. *That* is not crossing seas.

And this is the theme of the Hints to Those. We travel in order to cross seas and land on other coasts. We do not travel in order to go from one hotel to another, and see a few side-shows. We travel, perhaps, with a secret and absurd hope of setting foot on the Hesperides, of running our boat up a little creek and landing in the Garden of Eden.

This hope is always defeated. There is no Garden of Eden, and the Hesperides never were. Yet, in our very search for them, we touch the coasts of illusion, and come into contact with other worlds.

This world remains the same, wherever we go. Every ship is a money-investment, and must be made to pay. The earth exists to be exploited, and is exploited. Malay head-hunters are now playing football instead of hunting heads. The voice of the gramophone is heard in the deepest jungle.

That is the world of disillusion. Travel, and you'll know it. It is just as well to know it. Our world is a world of disillusion, whether it's Siam or Kamchatka or Athabaska: the same exploitation, the same mechanical lifelessness.

But travelling through our world of disillusion until we are finally and bitterly disillusioned, we come home at last, after the long voyage, home to the rain and the dismalness of England. And how marvellously well Mr. Tomlinson gives the feeling of a ship at the end of the voyage, coming in at night, in the rain, the engines slowed down, then stopped: and in the unspeakable emptiness and blankness of silent engines and rain and nothingness, the passengers wait for the tug, staring out upon utter emptiness, from a ship that has gone suddenly quite dead! It is the end of the voyage of disillusion.

But behold, in the morning, England, England, in her own wan sun, her strange, quiet Englishmen, so silent and intent and self-resourceful! It is the coast of illusion, the other world itself.

This is the gist of the Hints to Those About to Travel. You'll never find what you look for. There are no happy lands. But you'll come upon coasts of illusion when you're not expecting them.

Following the Hints come three sketches which are true travel memories, one on the Amazon, one in the Malay States, one in Borneo. They are old memories, and they gleam with illusion, with the iridescence of illusion and disillusion at once. Far off, we are in the midst of exploitation and mechanical civilization, just the same. Far off, in the elysium of a beautiful spot in Borneo, the missionary's wife sits and weeps for home, when she sees an outgoing ship. Far off, there is the mad Rajah, whom we turned out, with all kinds of medals and number-plates on his breast, thinking himself grander than ever, though he is a beggar.

And all the same, far off, there is that other world, or one of those other worlds, that give the lie to those realities we are supposed to accept.

The rest of the book is all England. There is a sketch: "Conrad Is Dead." And another, an appreciation of *Moby Dick*. But for the rest, it is the cruel disillusion, and then the infinitely soothing illusion of this world of ours.

Mr. Tomlinson has at the back of his mind, for ever, the grisly vision of his war experience. In itself, this is a horror of disillusion in the world of man. We cannot get away from it, and we have no business to. Man has turned the world into a thing of horror. What we have to do is to face the fact.

And facing it, accept other values and make another world. "We now open a new volume on sport," says Mr. Tomlinson, "with an antipathy we never felt for Pawnees, through the reading of a recent narrative by an American who had been collecting in Africa for an American museum. He confessed he would have felt some remorse when he saw the infant still clinging to the breast of its mother, a gorilla, whom he had just murdered; so he shot the infant without remorse, because he was acting scientifically. As a corpse, the child added to the value of its dead mother."

We share Mr. Tomlinson's antipathy to such sportsmen and such scientists absolutely. And it is not mere pity on our part for the gorilla. It is an absolute detestation of the *insentience* of armed, bullying men, in face of living, sentient things. Surely the most beastly offence against life is this degenerate insentience. It is not cruelty, exactly, which makes such a sportsman. It is crass insentience, a crass stupidity and deadness of fibre. Such overweening fellows, called men, are barren of the feeling for life. A gorilla is a live thing, with a strange unknown life of its own. Even to get a glimpse of its weird life, one little gleam of insight, makes our own life so much the wider, more vital. As a dead thing it can only depress us. We *must* have a feeling for life itself.

And this Mr. Tomlinson conveys: the strangeness and the beauty of life. Once be disillusioned with the man-made world, and you still see the magic, the beauty, the delicate realness of all the other life. Mr. Tomlinson sees it in flashes of great beauty. It comes home to him even in the black moth he caught. "It was quiet making a haze," etc. He sees the strange terror of the world of insects. "A statue to St. George killing a mosquito instead of a dragon would look ridiculous. But it was lucky for the Saint he had only a dragon to overcome."

Life! Life exists: and perhaps men do not truly exist. "And for a wolf who runs up and down his cage, sullenly ignoring our overtures, and behaving as though we did not exist, we begin to feel there is something to be said."

"And consider the fascination of the octopus!"

"I heard a farmer," etc.

"At sunrise today," etc.

"Perhaps the common notion," etc.

One gradually gets a new vision of the world, if one goes through the disillusion absolutely. It is a world where all things are alive, and where the life of strange creatures and beings flickers on us and makes it take strange new developments. "But in this estuary," etc. And it is exactly so. The earth is a planet, and we are inhabitants of the planet, along with many other strange creatures. Life is a strange planetary phenomenon, all interwoven.

Mr. Tomlinson gives us glimpses of a new vision, what we might call the planetary instead of the mundane vision. The glimpses are of extreme beauty, so sensitive to the other life in things. And how grateful we ought to be to a man who sets new visions, new feelings sensitively quivering in us.

The World of William Clissold, by H. G. Wells

The World of William Clissold is, we are told, a novel. We are assured it is a novel, and nothing but a novel. We are not allowed to think of it even as a "mental autobiography" of Mr. Wells. It is a novel.

Let us hope so. For, having finished this first volume, nothing but hope of finding something in the two volumes yet to appear will restrain us from asserting, roundly and flatly, that this is simply not good enough to be called a novel. If *Tono-Bungay* is a novel, then this is not one.

We have with us the first volume of *The World of William Clissold.* The second volume will appear on October 1st, the third on November 1st. We may still hope, then, if we wish to.

This first volume consists of "A Note before the Title-Page," in which we are forbidden to look on this book as anything but a novel, and especially forbidden to look on it as a *roman à clef:* which means we mustn't identify the characters with any living people such as, for instance, Mr. Winston Churchill or the Countess of Oxford and Asquith; which negative command is very easy to obey, since, in this first volume, at least, there are no created characters at all: it is all words, words, words, about Socialism and Karl Marx, bankers and cave-men, money and the superman. One would welcome any old scarecrow of a character on this dreary, flinty hillside of abstract words.

The next thing is the title-page: "The World of William Clissold: A Novel from a New Angle"—whatever that pseudo-scientific phrase may mean.

Then comes Book I: "The Frame of the Picture." All right, we think! If we must get the frame first, and the picture later, let's make the best of the frame.

The frame consists of William Clissold informing us that he is an elderly gentleman of fifty-nine, and that he is going to tell us all about himself. He is quite well off, having made good in business, so that now he has retired and has bought a house near Cannes, and is going to tell us everything, absolutely everything about himself: insisting rather strongly that he is and always has been a somewhat scientific gentleman with an active mind, and that his mental activities have been more important than any other activity in his life. In short, he is not a "mere animal," he is an animal with a ferocious appetite for "ideas," and enormous thinking powers.

Again, like a submissive reader, we say: "Very well! Proceed!" and we sit down in front of this mental gentleman. William Clissold immediately begins to tell us what he believes, what he always has believed, and what he hasn't always believed, and what he won't believe, and we feel how superior he is to other people who believe other mere things. He talks about God, is very uneasy because of Roman Catholics—like an Early Victorian—and is naughtily funny about Mr. G.—which can mean either Mr. Gladstone or Mr. God.

But we bear up. After all, God, or Mr. G., is only the frame for William Clissold. We must put up with a frame of some sort. And God turns out to be Humanity in its nobler or disinterestedly scientific aspect: or the Mind of Men collectively: in short, William Clissold himself, in a home-made halo. Still, after all, it is only a frame. Let us get on to the picture.

Mr. Clissold, being somewhat of an amateur at making a self-portrait and framing it, has got bits of the picture stuck on to the frame, and great angular sections of the frame occupying the space where the picture should be. But patience! It is a sort of futuristic interpenetration, perhaps.

The first bit of the story is a little boy at a country house, sitting in a boat and observing the scientific phenomena of refraction and reflection. He also observes some forget-me-nots on the bank, and rather likes the look of them. So, scrambling carefully down through mud and sedges, he clutches a handful of the blue flowers, only to find his legs scratched and showing blood, from the sedges. "Oh! Oh! I cried in profound dismay. . . . Still do I remember most vividly my astonishment at the treachery of that golden, flushed, and sapphire-eyed day.—That it should turn on me!"

This "section" is called "The Treacherous Forget-me-nots." But since, after all, the forget-me-nots had never asked the boy to gather them, wherein lay the treachery?

But they represent poetry. And perhaps William Clissold means to convey that, scrambling after poetry, he scratched his legs, and fell to howling, and called the poetry treacherous.

As for a child thinking that the sapphire-eyed day had turned on him—what a dreary old-boy of a child, if he did! But it is elderly-gentleman psychology, not childish.

The story doesn't get on very fast, and is extremely sketchy. The elderly Mr. Clissold is obviously bored by it himself. Two little boys, their mother and father, move from Bexhill to a grand country house called Mowbray. In the preface we are assured that Mowbray does not exist on earth, and we can well believe it. After a few years, the father of the two boys, a mushroom city magnate, fails, is arrested as a swindler, convicted, and swallows potassium cyanide. We have no vital glimpse of him. He never says anything, except "Hello, Sonny!" And he does ask the police to have some *déjeuner* with him, when he is arrested. The boys are trailed round Belgium by a weeping mother, who also is not created, and with whom they are only bored. The mother marries again: the boys go to the London University: and the story is lost again in a vast grey drizzle of words.

William Clissold, having in "The Frame" written a feeble résumé of Mr. Wells's *God the Invisible King,* proceeds in The Story, Book II, to write a much duller résumé of Mr. Wells's *Outline of History.* Cave-men, nomads, patriarchs, tribal Old Men, out they all come again, in the long march of human progress. Mr. Clissold, who holds forth against "systems," cannot help systematizing us all into a gradual and systematic uplift from the ape. There is also a complete *exposé* of Socialism and Karl Marxism and finance, and a denunciation of Communism. There is a little feeble praise of the pure scientist who does physical research in a laboratory, and a great contempt of professors and dons who lurk in holes and study history. Last, and not least, there is a contemptuous sweeping of the temple, of all financiers, bankers, and money-men: they are all unscientific, untrained semi-idiots monkeying about with things they know nothing of.

And so, rather abruptly, end of Vol. I.

Except, of course, William Clissold has been continually taking a front seat in the picture, aged fifty-nine, in the villa back of Cannes. There is a slim slip of a red-haired Clem, who ruffles the old gentleman's hair.

" 'It's no good!' she said. 'I can't keep away from you today.' And she hasn't! She has ruffled my hair, she has also ruffled my mind"—much more important, of course, to William C.

This is the young Clementina: "She has a mind like one of those water-insects that never get below the surface of anything. . . . She professes an affection for me that is altogether monstrous"—I should say so—"and she knows no more about my substantial self than the water-insect knows of the deeps of the pond. . . . She knows as little about the world."

Poor Clementina, that lean, red-haired slip of a young thing. She is no more to him than an adoring sort of mosquito. But oh! wouldn't we like to hear all she *does* know about him, this sexagenarian bore, who says of her: "the same lean, red-haired Clem, so absurdly insistent that she idolizes me, and will have no other man but me, invading me whenever she dares, and protecting me," etc.

Clementina, really, sounds rather nice. What a pity *she* didn't herself write *The World of William Clissold:* it would have been a novel, then. But she wouldn't even look at the framework of that world, says Clissold. And we don't blame her.

What is the elderly gentleman doing with her at all? Is it his "racial urge," as he calls it, still going on, rather late in life? We imagine the dear little bounder saying to her: "You are the mere object of my racial urge." To which, no doubt, she murmurs in the approved Clissold style: "My King!"

But it is altogether a poor book: the effusion of a peeved elderly gentleman who has nothing to grumble at, but who peeves at everything, from Clem to the High Finance, and from God, or Mr. G., to Russian Communism. His effective self is disgruntled, his ailment is a peevish, ashy indifference to *everything,* except himself, himself as centre of the universe. There is not one gleam of sympathy with anything in all the book, and not one breath of passionate rebellion. Mr. Clissold is too successful and wealthy to rebel and too hopelessly peeved to sympathize.

What has got him into such a state of peevishness is a problem: unless it is his insistence on the Universal Mind, which he, of course exemplifies. The emotions are to him irritating aberrations. Yet even he admits that even thought must be preceded by some obscure physical happenings, some kind of confused sensation or emotion which is the necessary coarse body of thought and from which thought, living thought, arises or sublimates.

This being so, we wonder that he so insists on the Universal or racial *mind* of man, as the only hope or salvation. If the mind is fed from the obscure sensations, emotions, physical happenings inside us, if the mind is really no more than an exhalation of these, is it not obvious that without a full and subtle emotional life the mind itself must wither: or that it must turn itself into an automatic sort of grind-mill, grinding upon itself?

And in that case the superficial Clementina no doubt knows far more about the "deeps of the pond" of Mr. Clissold than that tiresome gentleman knows himself. He grinds on and on at the stale bones of sociology, while his actual living goes to pieces, falls into a state of irritable peevishness which makes his "mental autobiography" tiresome. His scale of values is all wrong.

So far, anyhow, this work is not a novel, because it contains none of the passionate and emotional reactions which are at the root of all thought, and which must be conveyed in a novel. This book is all chewed-up newspaper, and chewed-up scientific reports, like a mouse's nest. But perhaps the novel will still come: in Vols. II and III.

For, after all, Mr. Wells is not Mr. Clissold, thank God! And Mr. Wells has given us such brilliant and such very genuine novels that we can only hope the Clissold "angle" will straighten out in Vol. II.

Saïd the Fisherman, by Marmaduke Pickthall

Since the days of Lady Hester Stanhope and her romantic pranks, down to the exploits of Colonel T. E. Lawrence in the late war, there seems always to have been some more or less fantastic Englishman, or woman, Arabizing among the Arabs. Until we feel we know the desert and the Bedouin better than we know Wales or our next-door neighbour.

Perhaps there is an instinctive sympathy between the Semite Arab and the Anglo-Saxon. If so, it must have its root way down in the religious make-up of both peoples. The Arab is intensely a One-God man, and so is the Briton.

But the Briton is mental and critical in his workings, the Arab uncritical and impulsive. In the Arab, the Englishman sees himself with the lid off.

T. E. Lawrence distinguishes two kinds of Englishmen in the East: the kind that goes native, more or less like Sir Richard Burton, and takes on native dress, speech, manners, morals, and women; then the other kind, that penetrates to the heart of Arabia, like Charles M. Doughty, but remains an Englishman in the fullest sense of the word. Doughty, in his rags and misery, his blond beard, his scrupulous honesty, with his Country for ever behind him, is indeed the very pith of England, dwelling in the houses of hair.

Marmaduke Pickthall, I am almost sure, remained an Englishman and a gentleman in the Near East. Only in imagination he goes native. And that thoroughly.

We are supposed to get inside the skin of Saïd the Fisherman, to hunger, fear, lust, enjoy, suffer, and dare as Saïd does, and to see the world through Saïd's big, dark, shining Arab eyes.

It is not easy. It is not easy for a man of one race entirely to identify himself with a man of another race, of different culture and religion. When the book opens, Saïd is a fisherman naked on the coast of Syria, living with his wife Hasneh in a hut by the sands. Saïd is young, strong-bodied, and lusty: Hasneh is beginning to fade.

The first half of the novel is called: The Book of his Luck; the second half: The Book of his Fate. We are to read into the word Fate the old meaning, of revenge of the gods.

Saïd's savings are treacherously stolen by his partner. The poor fisherman wails, despairs, rouses up, and taking a hint about evil genii, packs himself and his scraps on an ass, and lets Hasneh run behind, and sets off to Damascus.

The Book of his Luck is a curious mixture of *Arabian Nights* and modern realism. I think, on the whole, Scheherazade's influence is strongest. The poor fisherman suddenly becomes one of the lusty Sinbad sort, and his luck is stupendous. At the same time, he is supposed to remain the simple man Saïd, with ordinary human responsibilities.

We are prepared to go gaily on with Saïd, his sudden glory of impudence and luck, when straight away we get a hit below the belt. Saïd, the mere man, abandons the poor, faithful, devoted Hasneh, his wife, in circumstances of utter meanness. We double up, and for the time being completely lose interest in the lucky and lusty fisherman. It takes an incident as sufficiently realistic and as amusing as that of the missionary's dressing-gown, to get us up again. Even then we have cold feet because of the impudent Saïd; he looks vulgar, common. And we resent a little the luck and the glamour of him, the fact that we have to follow him as a hero. A picaresque novel is all very well, but the one quality demanded of a picaro, to make him more than a common sneak, is a certain reckless generosity.

Saïd is reckless enough, but, as shown by Mr. Pickthall, with impudence based on meanness, the sort of selfishness that is mongrel, and a bit sneaking. Yet Mr. Pickthall still continues to infuse a certain glamour into him, and to force our sympathy for him.

It is the thing one most resents in a novel: having one's sympathy *forced* by the novelist, towards some character we should never naturally sympathize with.

Saïd is a handsome, strong, lusty scoundrel, impudent, with even a certain dauntlessness. We could get on with him very well indeed, if every now and then we didn't get another blow under the belt, by a demonstration of his cold, gutter-snipe callousness.

One almost demands revenge on him. The revenge comes, and again we are angry.

The author hasn't treated us fairly. He has identified himself too closely with his hero: he can't see wood for trees. Because, of course, inside the skin of Saïd, Mr. Pickthall is intensely a good, moral Englishman, and intensely uneasy.

So with an Englishman's over-scrupulous honesty, he has had to show us his full reactions to Saïd. Marmaduke Pickthall, Englishman, is fascinated by Saïd's lustiness, his reckless, impudent beauty, his immoral, or non-moral nature. We hope it is non-moral. We are shown it is immoral. Marmaduke Pickthall loathes the mean immorality of Saïd, and has to punish him for it, in the Book of his Fate.

All very well, but it's a risky thing to hold the scales for a man whose moral nature is not your own. Mr. Pickthall's moral values are utilitarian and rational: Saïd's are emotional and sensual. The fact that Saïd's moral values are emotional and sensual makes Saïd so lusty and handsome, gives him such glamour for Mr. Pickthall. Mr. Pickthall resents the spell, and brings a charge of immorality. Then the Fates and the Furies get their turn.

The two charges against Saïd are his abandonment of the poor Hasneh, and his indifference to his faithful friend Selim.

As to Hasneh, she had been his wife for six years and borne him no children, and during these years he had lived utterly poor and vacant. But he was a man of energy. The moment he leaves the seashore, he becomes another fellow, wakes up.

The poor lout he was when he lived with Hasneh is transformed. Ca-Ca-Caliban. Get a new mistress, be a new man! Saïd had no tradition of sexual fidelity. His aim in living—or at least a large part of his aim in living—was sensual gratification; and this was not against his religion. His newly released energy, the new man he was, needed a new mistress, many new mistresses. It was part of his whole tradition. Because all Hasneh's service and devotion did not stimulate his energies, rather deadened them. She was a weight round his neck. And her prostrate devotion, while pathetic, was *not* admirable. It was a dead weight. He needed a subtler mistress.

Here the judgment of Marmaduke Pickthall is a white man's judgment on a dark man. The Englishman sympathizes with the poor abandoned woman at the expense of the energetic man. The sympathy is false. If the woman were alert and kept her end up, she would neither be poor nor abandoned. But it was easier for her to fall at Saïd's feet than to stand on her own.

If you ride a mettlesome horse you mind the bit, or you'll get thrown. It's a law of nature.

Saïd was mean, in that he did not send some sort of help to Hasneh, when he could. But that is the carelessness of a sensual nature, rather than villainy. Out of sight, out of mind, is true of those who have not much mind: and Saïd had little.

No, our quarrel with him is for being a fool, for not being on the alert: the same quarrel we had with Hasneh. If he had not been a slack fool his Christian wife would not have ruined him so beautifully. And if he had been even a bit wary and cautious, he would not have let himself in for his last adventure.

It is this adventure which sets us quarrelling with Mr. Pickthall and his manipulation of our sympathy. With real but idiotic courage Saïd swims out to an English steamer off Beirut. He is taken to London: falls into the nightmare of that city: loses his reason for ever, but, a white-haired handsome imbecile, is restored to his faithful ones in Alexandria.

We would fain think this ghastly vengeance fell on him because of his immorality. But it didn't. Not at all. It was merely because of his foolish, impudent leaping before he'd looked. He wouldn't realize his own limitations, so he went off the deep end.

It is a summing-up of the Damascus Arab by a sympathetic, yet outraged Englishman. One feels that Mr. Pickthall gave an extra shove to the mills of God. Perfectly gratuitous!

Yet one is appalled, thinking of Saïd in London. When one does come out of the open sun into the dank dark autumn of London, one almost loses one's reason, as Saïd does. And then one wonders: can the backward civilizations show us anything half so ghastly and murderous as we show them, and with pride?

Pedro de Valdivia, by R. B. Cunninghame Graham

This book will have to go on the history shelf; it has no chance among the memoirs or the lives. There is precious little about Valdivia himself. There is, however, a rather scrappy chronicle of the early days of Chile, a meagre account of its conquest and settlement under Pedro de Valdivia.

Having read Mr. Graham's preface, we suddenly come upon another title-page, and another title—"*Pedro de Valdivia, Conqueror of Chile*. Being a Short Account of his Life, Together with his Five Letters to Charles V." So? We are to get Valdivia's own letters! Interminable epistles of a Conquistador, we know more or less what to expect. But let us look where they are.

It is a serious-looking book, with 220 large pages, and costing fifteen shillings net. The Short Account we find occupies the first 123 pages, the remaining 94 are occupied by the translation of the five letters. So! Nearly half the book is Valdivia's; Mr. Graham only translates him. And we shall have a lot of Your-Sacred-Majestys to listen to, that we may be sure of.

When we have read both the Short Account and the Letters, we are left in a state of irritation and disgust. Mr. Cunninghame Graham steals all his hero's gunpowder. He deliberately—or else with the absent-mindedness of mere egoism—picks all the plums out of Valdivia's cake, puts them in his own badly-kneaded dough, and then has the face to serve us up Valdivia whole, with the plums which we have already eaten sitting as large as life in their original position. Of course, all Valdivia's good bits in his own letters read like the shamelessest plagiarism. Haven't we just read them in Mr. Graham's Short Account? Why should we have to read them again? Why does that uninspired old Conquistador try to fob them off on us?

Poor Valdivia! That's what it is to be a Conquistador and a hero to Mr. Graham. He puts himself first, and you are so much wadding to fill out the pages.

The Spanish Conquistadores, famous for courage and endurance, are by now notorious for insentience and lack of imagination. Even Bernal Diaz, after a few hundred pages, makes one feel one could yell, he is so doggedly, courageously unimaginative, visionless, really *sightless:* sightless, that is, with the living eye of living discernment. Cortés, strong man as he is, is just as tough and visionless in *his* letters to His-Most-Sacred-Majesty. And Don Cunninghame, alas, struts feebly in the conquistadorial footsteps. Not only does he write without imagination, without imaginative insight or sympathy, without colour, and without real feeling, but he seems to pride himself on the fact. He is being conquistadorial.

We, however, refuse entirely to play the part of poor Indians. We are not frightened of old Dons in caracoling armchairs. We are not even amused by their pretence of being on horse-back. A horse is a four-legged sensitive animal. What a pity the Indians felt so frightened of it! Anyhow, it is too late now for cavalierly conduct.

Mr. Graham's Preface sets the note in the very first words. It is a note of twaddling impertinence, and it runs through all the work. "Commentators tell us [do they, though?] that most men are savages at heart, and give more admiration to the qualities of courage, patience in hardships, and contempt of death than they accord to the talents of the artist, man of science, or the statesman. [Funny sort of commentators Mr. Graham reads.]

"If this is true of men, they say it is doubly true of women, who would rather be roughly loved by a tall fellow of his hands [hands, forsooth!] even though their physical and moral cuticle [sic] suffer some slight abrasion, than inefficiently wooed by a philanthropist. [Ah, ladies, you who are inefficiently wooed by philanthropists, is there never a tall fellow of his hands about?]

"This may be so [continues Mr. Graham], and, if it is, certainly Pedro de Valdivia was an archetype [! !–] of all the elemental qualities nature implants in a man. [He usually had some common Spanish wench for his kept woman, though we are not told concerning her cuticle.]

"Brave to a fault [chants Mr. Graham], patient and enduring to an incredible degree, of hardships under which the bravest might have quailed [what's a quail got to do with it?], loyal to king and country [Flemish Charles V] and a stout man-at-arms, he had yet no inconsiderable talents of administration, talents not so conspicuous today among the Latin race. [Dear-dear!]

"Thus–and I take all the above for granted–etc."

Mr. Graham has shown us, not Valdivia, but himself. He lifts a swash-buckling fountain pen, and off he goes. The result is a shoddy, scrappy, and not very sincere piece of work. The Conquistadores were damned by their insensitiveness to life, which we call lack of imagination. And they let a new damnation into the America they conquered. But they couldn't help it. It was the educational result of Spanish struggle for existence against the infidel Moors. The Conquistadores were good enough instruments, but they were not good enough men for the miserable and melancholy work of conquering a continent. Yet, at least, they never felt themselves *too good* for their job, as some of the inky conquerors did even then, and do still.

Mr. Graham does not take Valdivia very seriously. He tells us almost nothing about him: save that he was born in Estremadura (who cares!) and had served in the Italian and German wars, had distinguished himself in the conquest of Venezuela, and, in 1532, accompanied Pizarro to Peru. Having thrown these few facts at us, off goes Mr. Graham to the much more alluring, because much better known, story of the Pizarros, and we wonder where Valdivia comes in. We proceed with Pizarro to Peru, and so, apparently, did Valdivia, and we read a little piece of the story even Prescott has already told us. Then we get a glimpse of Almagro crossing the Andes to Chile, and very impressive little quotations from Spanish writers. After which Valdivia begins to figure, in some unsubstantial remote regions with Indian names, as a mere shadow of a colonizer. We never see the country, we never meet the man, we get no feeling of the Indians. There is nothing dramatic, no Incas, no temples and treasures and tortures, only remote colonization going on in a sort of nowhere. Valdivia becomes a trifle more real when he comes again into Peru, to fight on the loyal side against Gonzalo Pizarro and old Carvajal, but this is Peruvian history, with nothing new to it. Valdivia returns to Chile and vague colonizing; there are vague mentions of the Magellan Straits; there is a Biobio River, but to one who has never been to Chile, it might just as well be Labrador. There is a bit of a breath of life in the extracts of Valdivia's own letters. And there are strings of names of men who are nothing but names, and continual mention of Indians who also remain merely nominal. Till the very last pages, when we do find out, after he is killed, that Valdivia was a big man, fat now he is elderly, of a hearty disposition, good-natured as far as he has enough imagination, and rather commonplace save for his energy as a colonizing instrument.

It is all thrown down, in bits and scraps, as Mr. Graham comes across it in Garcilaso's book, or in Gómara. And it is interlarded with Mr. Graham's own comments, of this nature: "Christians seemed to have deserved their name in those days, for faith and faith alone could have enabled them to endure such misery, and yet be always ready at the sentinel's alarm to buckle on their swords." Oh, what clichés! Faith in the proximity of gold, usually. "Cavalry in those days played the part now played by aeroplanes," says Mr. Graham suavely. He himself seems to have got into an aeroplane, by mistake, instead of onto a conquistadorial horse, for his misty bird's-eye views are just such confusion.

The method followed, for the most part, seems to be that of sequence of time. All the events of each year are blown together by Mr. Graham's gustiness, and you can sort them out. At the same time, great patches of Peruvian history suddenly float up out of nowhere, and at the end, when Valdivia is going to get killed by the Indians, suddenly we are swept away on a biographical carpet, and forced to follow the life of the poet Ercilla, who wrote his Araucana poem about Valdivia's Indians, but who never came to Chile till Valdivia was dead. After which, we are given a feeble account of a very striking incident, the death of Valdivia. And there the Short Account dies also, abruptly, and Chile is left to its fate.

Then follow the five letters. They are moderately interesting, the best, of course, belonging to Peruvian story, when Valdivia helped the mean La Gasca against Gonzalo Pizarro. For the rest, the "loyalty" seems a little overdone, and we are a little tired of the bluff, manly style of soldiers who have not imagination enough to see the things that really matter. Men of action are usually deadly failures in the long run. Their precious energy makes them uproot the tree of life, and leave it to wither, and their stupidity makes them proud of it. Even in Valdivia, and he seems to have been as human as any Conquistador, the stone blindness to any mystery or meaning in the Indians themselves, the utter unawareness of the fact that they might have a point of view, the abject insensitiveness to the strange, eerie atmosphere of that America he was proceeding to exploit and to ruin, puts him at a certain dull level of intelligence which we find rather nauseous. The world has suffered so cruelly from these automatic men of action. Valdivia was not usually cruel, it appears. But he cut off the hands and noses of two hundred "rebels," Indians who were fighting for their own freedom, and he feels very pleased about it. It served to cow the others. But imagine deliberately chopping off one slender brown Indian hand after another! Imagine taking a dark-eyed Indian by the hair, and cutting off his nose! Imagine seeing man after man, in the prime of life, with his mutilated face streaming blood, and his wrist-stump a fountain of blood, and tell me if the men of action don't need absolutely to be held in leash by the intelligent being who *can* see these things as monstrous, root cause of endless monstrosity! We, who suffer from the bright deeds of the men of action of the past, may well keep an eye on the "tall fellows of their hands" of our own day.

Prescott never went to Mexico nor to Peru, otherwise he would have sung a more scared tune. But Mr. Graham is supposed to know his South America. One would never believe it. The one thing he could have done, re-created the landscape of Chile for us, and made us feel those Araucanians as men of flesh and blood, he never does, not for a single second. He might as well never have left Scotland; better, for perhaps he would not have been so glib about unseen lands. All he can say of the Araucanians today is that they are "as hard-featured a race as any upon earth."

Mr. Graham is trivial and complacent. There is, in reality, a peculiar dread horror about the conquest of America, the story is always dreadful, more or less. Columbus, Pizarro, Cortés, Quesada, De Soto, the Conquistadores seem all like men of doom. Read a man like Adolf Bandelier, who knows the *inside* of his America, read his *Golden Man*—El Dorado—and feel the reverberation within reverberation of horror the Conquistadores left behind them.

Then we have Mr. Graham as a translator. In the innumerable and sometimes quite fatuous and irritating footnotes—they are sometimes interesting—our author often gives the original Spanish for the phrase he has translated. And even here he is peculiarly glib and unsatisfactory: " 'God knows the trouble it cost,' he says pathetically." Valdivia is supposed to say this "pathetically." The footnote gives Valdivia's words: *"Un bergantin y el trabajo que costó, Dios lo sabe."*—"A brigantine, and the work it cost, God knows." Why *trouble* for *trabajo?* And why pathetically? Again, the proverb: *"A Dios rogando, y con la maza dando,"* is translated: "Praying to God, and battering with the mace." But why *battering* for *dando,* which means merely *donnant,* and might be rendered *smiting,* or *laying on,* but surely not *battering!* Again, Philip II is supposed to say to Ercilla, who stammered so much as to be unintelligible: *"Habladme por escrito, Don Alonso!"* Which is: "Say it to me in writing, Don Alonso!" Mr. Graham, however, translates it: "Write to me, Don Alonso!" . . . These things are trifles, but they show the peculiar laziness or insensitiveness to language which is so great a vice in a translator.

The motto of the book is:

El más seguro don de la fortuna
Es no lo haber tenido vez alguna.

Mr. Graham puts it: "The best of fortune's gifts is never to have had good luck at all." Well, Ercilla may have meant this. The literal sense of the Spanish, anybody can make out: "The most sure gift of fortune, is not to have had it not once." Whether one would be justified in changing the "don de la fortuna" of the first line into "good luck" in the second is a point we must leave to Mr. Graham. Anyhow, he seems to have blest his own book in this equivocal fashion.

Nigger Heaven, by Carl Van Vechten; *Flight*, by Walter White; *Manhattan Transfer*, by John Dos Passos; *In Our Time*, by Ernest Hemingway

Nigger Heaven is one of the Negro names for Harlem, that dismal region of hard stone streets way up Seventh Avenue beyond One Hundred and Twenty-Fifth Street, where the population is all coloured, though not much of it is real black. In the daytime, at least, the place aches with dismalness and a loose-end sort of squalor, the stone of the streets seeming particularly dead and stony, obscenely stony.

Mr. Van Vechten's book is a nigger book, and not much of a one. It opens and closes with nigger cabaret scenes in feeble imitation of Cocteau or Morand, second-hand attempts to be wildly lurid, with background effects of black and vermilion velvet. The middle is a lot of stuffing about high-brow niggers, the heroine being one of the old-fashioned school-teacherish sort, this time an assistant in a public library; and she has only one picture in her room, a reproduction of the Mona Lisa, and on her shelves only books by James Branch Cabell, Anatole France, Jean Cocteau, etc.; in short, the literature of disillusion. This is to show how refined she is. She is just as refined as any other "idealistic" young heroine who earns her living, and we have to be reminded continually that she is golden-brown.

Round this heroine goes on a fair amount of "race" talk, nigger self-consciousness which, if it didn't happen to mention it was black, would be taken for merely another sort of self-conscious grouch. There is a love-affair–a rather palish-brown–which might go into any feeble American novel whatsoever. And the whole coloured thing is peculiarly colourless, a second-hand dish barely warmed up.

The author seems to feel this, so he throws in a highly-spiced nigger in a tartan suit, who lives off women–rather in the distance–and two perfect red-peppers of nigger millionairesses who swim in seas of champagne and have lovers and fling them away and sniff drugs; in short, altogether the usual old bones of hot stuff, warmed up with all the fervour the author can command–which isn't much.

It is a false book by an author who lingers in nigger cabarets hoping to heaven to pick up something to write about and make a sensation–and, of course, money.

Flight is another nigger book; much more respectable, but not much more important. The author, we are told, is himself a Negro. If we weren't told, we should never know. But there is rather a call for coloured stuff, hence we had better be informed when we're getting it.

The first part of *Flight* is interesting—the removal of Creoles, just creamy-coloured old French-Negro mixture, from the Creole quarter of New Orleans to the Negro quarter of Atlanta. This is real, as far as life goes, and external reality: except that to me, the Creole quarter of New Orleans is dead and lugubrious as a Jews' burying ground, instead of highly romantic. But the first part of *Flight* is good Negro *data*.

The culture of Mr. White's Creoles is much more acceptable than that of Mr. Van Vechten's Harlem golden-browns. If it is only skin-deep, that is quite enough, since the pigmentation of the skin seems to be the only difference between the Negro and the white man. If there be such a thing as a Negro soul, then that of the Creole is very very French-American, and that of the Harlemite is very very Yankee-American. In fact, there seems no blackness about it at all. Reading Negro books, or books about Negroes written from the Negro standpoint, it is absolutely impossible to discover that the nigger is any blacker inside than we are. He's an absolute white man, save for the colour of his skin: which, in many cases, is also just as white as a Mediterranean white man's.

It is rather disappointing. One likes to cherish illusions about the race soul, the eternal Negroid soul, black and glistening and touched with awfulness and with mystery. One is not allowed. The nigger is a white man through and through. He even sees himself as white men see him, blacker than he ought to be. And his soul is an Edison gramophone on which one puts the current records: which is what the white man's soul is, just the same, a gramophone grinding over the old records.

New York is the melting-pot which melts even the nigger. The future population of this melting-pot will be a pale-greyish-brown in colour, and its psychology will be that of Mr. White or Byron Kasson, which is the psychology of a shrewd mixture of English, Irish, German, Jewish, and Negro. These are the grand ingredients of the melting-pot, and the amalgam, or alloy, whatever you call it, will be a fine mixture of all of them. Unless the melting-pot gets upset.

Apparently there is only one feeling about the Negro, wherein he differs from the white man, according to Mr. White; and this is the feeling of warmth and humanness. But *we* don't feel even that. More mercurial, but not by any means warmer or more human, the nigger seems to be: even in nigger books. And he sees in himself a talent for life which the white man has lost. But remembering glimpses of Harlem and Louisiana, and the down-at-heel greyness of the colourless Negro *ambiente,* myself I don't feel even that.

But the one thing the Negro *knows* he can do, is sing and dance. He knows it, because the white man has pointed it out to him so often. There, again, however, disappointment! About one nigger in a thousand amounts to anything in song or dance: the rest are just as songful and limber as the rest of Americans.

Mimi, the pale-biscuit heroine of *Flight,* neither sings nor dances. She is rather cultured and makes smart dresses and passes over as white, then marries a well-to-do white American, but leaves him because he is not "live" enough, and goes back to Harlem. It is just what Nordic wives do, just how they feel about their husbands. And if they don't go to Harlem, they go somewhere else. And then they come back. As Mimi will do. Three months of Nigger Heaven will have her fed up, and back she'll be over the white line, settling again in the Washington Square region, and being "of French extraction." Nothing is more monotonous than these removals.

All these books might as well be called *Flight*. They give one the impression of swarms of grasshoppers hopping big hops, and buzzing occasionally on the wing, all from nowhere to nowhere, all over the place. What's the point of all this flight, when they start from nowhere and alight on nowhere? For the Nigger Heaven is as sure a nowhere as anywhere else.

Manhattan Transfer is still a greater ravel of flights from nowhere to nowhere. But at least the author knows it, and gets a kind of tragic significance into the fact. John Dos Passos is a far better writer than Mr. Van Vechten or Mr. White, and his book is a far more real and serious thing. To me, it is the best modern book about New York that I have read. It is an endless series of glimpses of people in the vast scuffle of Manhattan Island, as they turn up again and again and again, in a confusion that has no obvious rhythm, but wherein at last we recognize the systole-diastole of success and failure, the end being all failure, from the point of view of life; and then another flight towards another nowhere.

If you set a blank record revolving to receive all the sounds, and a film-camera going to photograph all the motions of a scattered group of individuals, at the points where they meet and touch in

New York, you would more or less get Mr. Dos Passos's method. It is a rush of disconnected scenes and scraps, a breathless confusion of isolated moments in a group of lives, pouring on through the years, from almost every part of New York. But the order of time is more or less kept. For half a page you are on the Lackawanna ferry-boat–or one of the ferry-boats–in the year 1900 or somewhere there–the next page you are in the Brevoort a year later–two pages ahead it is Central Park, you don't know when–then the wharves–way up Hoboken–down Greenwich Village–the Algonquin Hotel–somebody's apartment. And it seems to be different people, a different girl every time. The scenes whirl past like snowflakes. Broadway at night–whizz! gone!–a quick-lunch counter! gone!–a house on Riverside Drive, the Palisades, night–gone! But, gradually, you get to know the faces. It is like a movie picture with an intricacy of different stories and no close-ups and no writing in between. Mr. Dos Passos leaves out the writing in between.

But if you are content to be confused, at length you realize that the confusion is genuine, not affected; it is life, not a pose. The book becomes what life is, a stream of different things and different faces rushing along in the consciousness, with no apparent direction save that of time, from past to present, from youth to age, from birth to death, and no apparent goal at all. But what makes the rush so swift, one gradually realizes, is the wild, strange frenzy for success: egoistic, individualistic success.

This very complex film, of course, does not pretend to film *all* New York. Journalists, actors and actresses, dancers, unscrupulous lawyers, prostitutes, Jews, out-of-works, politicians, labour agents–that kind of gang. It is on the whole a gang, though we do touch respectability on Riverside Drive now and then. But it is a gang, the vast loose gang of strivers and winners and losers which seems to be the very pep of New York, the city itself an inordinately vast gang.

At first it seems too warm, too passionate. One thinks: this is much too healthily lusty for the present New York. Then we realize we are away before the war, when the place was steaming and alive. There is sex, fierce, ranting sex, real New York: sex as the prime stimulus to business success. One realizes what a lot of financial success has been due to the reckless speeding-up of the sex dynamo. Get hold of the right woman, get absolutely rushed out of yourself loving her up, and you'll be able to rush a success in the city. Only, both to the man and woman, the sex must be the stimulant to success; otherwise it stimulates towards suicide, as it does with the one character whom the author loves, and who was "truly male."

The war comes, and the whole rhythm collapses. The war ends. There are the same people. Some have got success, some haven't. But success and failure alike are left irritable and inert. True, everybody is older, and the fire is dying down into spasmodic irritability. But in all the city the fire is dying down. The stimulant is played out, and you have the accumulating irritable restlessness of New York of today. The old thrill has gone, out of socialism as out of business, out of art as out of love, and the city rushes on ever faster, with more maddening irritation, knowing the apple is a Dead Sea shiner.

At the end of the book, the man who was a little boy at the beginning of the book, and now is a failure of perhaps something under forty, crosses on the ferry from Twenty-third Street, and walks away into the gruesome ugliness of the New Jersey side. He is making another flight into nowhere, to land upon nothingness.

"Say, will you give me a lift?" he asks the red-haired man at the wheel (of a furniture-van).

"How fur ye goin'?"

"I dunno . . . Pretty far."

The End.

He might just as well have said "nowhere!"

In Our Time is the last of the four American books, and Mr. Hemingway has accepted the goal. He keeps on making flights, but he has no illusion about landing anywhere. He knows it will be nowhere every time.

In Our Time calls itself a book of stories, but it isn't that. It is a series of successive sketches from a man's life, and makes a fragmentary novel. The first scenes, by one of the big lakes in America—probably Superior—are the best; when Nick is a boy. Then come fragments of war—on the Italian front. Then a soldier back home, very late, in the little town way west in Oklahoma. Then a young American and wife in post-war Europe; a long sketch about an American jockey in Milan and Paris; then Nick is back again in the Lake Superior region, getting off the train at a burnt-out town, and tramping across the empty country to camp by a trout-stream. Trout is the one passion life has left him—and this won't last long.

It is a short book: and it does not pretend to be about one man. But it is. It is as much as we need know of the man's life. The sketches are short, sharp, vivid, and most of them excellent. (The "mottoes" in front seem a little affected.) And these few sketches are enough to create the man and all his history: we need know no more.

Nick is a type one meets in the more wild and woolly regions of the United States. He is the remains of the lone trapper and cowboy. Nowadays he is educated, and through with everything. It is a state of *conscious,* accepted indifference to everything except freedom from work and the moment's interest. Mr. Hemingway does it extremely well. Nothing matters. Everything happens. One wants to keep oneself loose. Avoid one thing only: getting connected up. Don't get connected up. If you get held by anything, break it. Don't be held. Break it, and get away. Don't get away with the idea of getting somewhere else. Just get away, for the sake of getting away. Beat it! "Well, boy, I guess I'll beat it." Ah, the pleasure in saying that!

Mr. Hemingway's sketches, for this reason, are excellent: so short, like striking a match, lighting a brief sensational cigarette, and it's over. His young love-affair ends as one throws a cigarette-end away. "It isn't fun any more."—"Everything's gone to hell inside me."

It is really honest. And it explains a great deal of sentimentality. When a thing has gone to hell inside you, your sentimentalism tries to pretend it hasn't. But Mr. Hemingway is through with the sentimentalism. "It isn't fun any more. I guess I'll beat it."

And he beats it, to somewhere else. In the end he'll be a sort of tramp, endlessly moving on for the sake of moving away from where he is. This is a negative goal, and Mr. Hemingway is really good, because he's perfectly straight about it. He is like Krebs, in that devastating Oklahoma sketch: he doesn't love anybody, and it nauseates him to have to pretend he does. He doesn't even *want* to love anybody; he doesn't want to go anywhere, he doesn't want to do anything. He wants just to lounge around and maintain a healthy state of nothingness inside himself, and an attitude of negation to everything outside himself. And why shouldn't he, since that is exactly and sincerely what he feels? If he really *doesn't* care, then why should he care? Anyhow, he doesn't.

Solitaria, by V. V. Rozanov

We are told on the wrapper of this book that Prince Mirsky considered Rozanov "one of the greatest Russians of modern times . . . Rozanov is the greatest revelation of the Russian mind yet to be shown to the West."

We become diffident, confronted with these superlatives. And when we have read E. Gollerbach's long "Critico-Biographical Study," forty-three pages, we are more suspicious still, in spite of the occasionally profound and striking quotations from *Solitaria* and from the same author's *Fallen Leaves*. But there we are; we've got another of these morbidly introspective Russians, morbidly wallowing in adoration of Jesus, then getting up and spitting in His beard, or in His back hair, at least; characters such as Dostoievsky has familiarized us with, and of whom we are tired. Of these self-divided, *gamin*-religious Russians who are so absorbedly concerned with their own dirty linen and their own piebald souls we have had a little more than enough. The contradictions in them are not so very mysterious, or edifying, after all. They have a spurting, *gamin* hatred of civilization, of Europe, of Christianity, of governments, and of everything else, in their moments of energy; and in their inevitable relapses into weakness, they make the inevitable recantation; they whine, they humiliate themselves, they seek unspeakable humiliation for themselves, and call it Christ-like, and then with the left hand commit some dirty little crime or meanness, and call it the mysterious complexity of the human soul. It's all masturbation, half-baked, and one gets tired of it. One gets tired of being told that Dostoievsky's *Legend of the Grand Inquisitor* "is the most profound declaration which ever was made about man and life." As far as I'm concerned, in proportion as a man gets more profoundly and personally interested in himself, so does my interest in him wane. The more Dostoievsky gets worked up about the tragic nature of the human soul, the more I lose interest. I have read the *Grand Inquisitor* three times, and never can remember what it's really about. This I make as a confession, not as a vaunt. It always seems to me, as the Germans say, *mehr Schrei wie Wert*.

And in Rozanov one fears one has got a pup out of the Dostoievsky kennel. *Solitaria* is a sort of philosophical work, about a hundred pages, of a kind not uncommon in Russia, consisting in fragmentary jottings of thoughts which occurred to the author, mostly during the years 1910 and 1911, apparently, and scribbled down where they came, in a cab, in the train, in the w.c., on the sole of a bathing-slipper. But the thought that came in a cab might just as well have come in the w.c. or "examining my coins," so what's the odds? If Rozanov wanted to give the physical context to the thought, he'd have to create the scene. "In a cab," or "examining my coins" means nothing.

Then we get a whole lot of bits, some of them interesting, some not; many of them to be classified under the heading of: To Jesus or not to Jesus! if we may profanely parody Hamlet's To be or not to be. But it is the Russian's own parody. Then you get a lot of self-conscious personal bits: "The only *masculine* thing about you—is your trousers": which was said to Rozanov by a girl; though, as it isn't particularly true, there was no point in his repeating it. However, he has that "self-probing" nature we have become acquainted with. "Teaching is form, and I am formless. In teaching there must be order and a system, and I am systemless and even disorderly. There is duty—and to me any duty at the bottom of my heart always seemed comical, and on any duty, at the bottom of my heart, I always wanted to play a trick (except tragic duty). . . ."

Here we have the pup of the Dostoievsky kennel, a so-called nihilist: in reality, a Mary-Mary-quite-contrary. It is largely tiresome contrariness, even if it is spontaneous and not self-induced.

And, of course, in Mary-Mary-quite-contrary we have the ever-recurrent whimper: *I* want to be good! I *am* good: Oh, I am *so* good, I'm better than anybody! I love Jesus and all the saints, and above all, the blessed Virgin! Oh, how I love purity!—and so forth. Then they give a loud *crepitus ventris* as a punctuation.

Dostoievsky has accustomed us to it, and we are hard-boiled. Poor Voltaire, if he recanted, he only recanted once, when his strength had left him, and he was neither here nor there. But these Russians are for ever on their death-beds, and neither here nor there.

Rozanov's talk about "lovely faces and dear souls" of children, and "for two years I have been 'in Easter,' in the pealing of bells," truly "arrayed in white raiment," just makes me feel more hard-boiled than ever. It's a cold egg.

Yet, in *Solitaria* there are occasional profound things. "I am not such a scoundrel yet as to think about morals"—"Try to crucify the Sun, and you will see which is God"—and many others. But to me, self-conscious personal revelations, touched with the gutter-snipe and the actor, are not very interesting. One has lived too long.

So that I come to the end of Gollerbach's "Critico-Biographical Study" sick of the self-fingering sort of sloppiness, and I have very much the same feeling at the end of *Solitaria,* though occasionally Rozanov hits the nail on the head and makes it jump.

Then come twenty pages extracted from Rozanov's *The Apocalypse of Our Times,* and at once the style changes, at once you have a real thing to deal with. The *Apocalypse* must be a far more important book than *Solitaria,* and we wish to heaven we had been given it instead. Now at last we see Rozanov as a real thinker, and "the greatest revelation of the Russian mind yet to be shown to the West."

Rozanov had a real man in him, and it is true, what he says of himself, that he did not feel in himself that touch of the criminal which Dostoievsky felt in *himself*. Rozanov was not a criminal. Somewhere, he was integral, and grave, and a seer, a true one, not a *gamin*. We see it all in his *Apocalypse*. He is not really a Dostoievskian. That's only his Russianitis.

The book is an attack on Christianity, and as far as we are given to see, there is no canting or recanting in it. It is passionate, and suddenly valid. It is not jibing or criticism or pulling to pieces. It is a real passion. Rozanov has more or less recovered the genuine pagan vision, the phallic vision, and with those eyes he looks, in amazement and consternation, on the mess of Christianity.

For the first time we get what we have got from no Russian, neither Tolstoi nor Dostoievsky nor any of them, a real, positive view on life. It is as if the pagan Russian had wakened up in Rozanov, a kind of Rip van Winkle, and was just staggering at what he saw. His background is the vast old pagan background, the phallic. And in front of this, the tortured complexity of Christian civilization—what else can we call it?—is a kind of phantasmagoria to him.

He is the first Russian, as far as I am concerned, who has ever said anything to me. And his vision is full of passion, vivid, valid. He is the first to see that immortality is in the vividness of life, not in the loss of life. The butterfly becomes a whole revelation to him: and to us.

When Rozanov is wholly awake, and a new man, a risen man, the living and resurrected pagan, then he is a great man and a great seer, and perhaps, as he says himself, the first Russian to emerge. Speaking of Tolstoi and Leontiev and Dostoievsky, Rozanov says:

"I speak straight out what they dared not even suspect. I speak because after all I am more of a thinker than they. That is all." . . . "But the problem (in the case of Leontiev and Dostoievsky) is and was about anti-Christianity, about the victory over the very essence of Christianity, over that terrible avitalism. Whereas from him, from the phallus everything flows."

When Rozanov is in this mood, and in this vision, he is not dual, nor divided against himself. He is one complete thing. His vision and his passion are positive, non-tragical.

Then again he starts to Russianize, and he comes in two. When he becomes aware of himself, and personal, he is often ridiculous, sometimes pathetic, sometimes a bore, and almost always "dual." Oh, how they love to be dual, and divided against themselves, these Dostoievskian Russians! It is as good as a pose: always a Mary-Mary-quite-contrary business. "The great horror of the human soul consists in this, that while thinking of the Madonna it at the same time does not cease thinking of Sodom and of its sins; and the still greater horror is that even in the very midst of Sodom it does not forget the Madonna, it yearns for Sodom and the Madonna, and this at one and the same time, without any discord."

The answer to that is, that Sodom and Madonna-ism are two halves of the same movement, the mere tick-tack of lust and asceticism, pietism and pornography. If you're not pious, you won't be pornographical, and *vice versa*. If there are no saints, there'll be no sinners. If there were no ascetics, there'd be no lewd people. If you divide the human psyche into two halves, one half will be white, the other black. It's the division itself which is pernicious. The swing to one extreme causes the swing to the other. The swing towards Immaculate Madonna-ism inevitably causes the swing back to the whore of prostitution, then back again to the Madonna, and so *ad infinitum*. But you can't blame the soul for this. All you have to blame is the craven, cretin human intelligence, which is always seeking to get away from its own centre.

But Rozanov, when he isn't Russianizing, is the first Russian really to see it, and to recover, if unstably, the old human wholeness.

So that this book is extremely interesting, and really important. We get impatient with the Russianizing. And yet, with Gollerbach's Introduction and the letters at the end, we do get to know all we want to know about Rozanov, personally. It is not of vast importance, what he was personally. If he behaved perversely, he was never, like Dostoievsky, inwardly perverse, and when he says he was not "born rightly," he is only yelping like a Dostoievsky pup.

It is the voice of the new man in him, not the Dostoievsky whelp, that means something. And it means a great deal. We shall wait for a full translation of *The Apocalypse of Our Times,* and of *Oriental Motifs*. Rozanov matters, for the future.

The Peep Show, by Walter Wilkinson

When I was a budding author, just before the war, I used to hear Ford Hueffer asserting that every man could write *one* novel, and hinting that he ought to be encouraged to do it. The novel, of course, would probably be only a human document. Nevertheless, it would be worth while, since every life is a life.

There was a subtle distinction drawn, in those halcyon days of talk "about" things, between literature and the human documents. The latter was the real thing, mind you, but it wasn't art. The former was art, you must know, but—but—it wasn't the raw beefsteak of life, it was the dubious steak-and-kidney pie. Now you must choose: the raw beefsteak of life, or the suspicious steak-and-kidney pie of the public restaurant of art.

Perhaps that state of mind and that delicate stomach for art has passed away. To me, literary talk was always like a rattle that literary men spun to draw attention to themselves. But *The Peep Show* reminds me of the old jargon. They would have called it "A charming human document," and have descanted on the naïve niceness of the unsophisticated author. It used to seem so delightful, to the latter-day *littérateur,* to discover a book that was not written by a writer. "Oh, he's not a writer, you know! That's what makes it so delightful!"

The Peep Show is a simple and unpretentious account of a young man who made his own puppets and went round for a few weeks in Somerset and Devon, two or three years ago, in the holiday season, giving puppet shows. It wasn't Punch and Judy, because the showman, though not exactly a high-brow, was neither exactly a low-brow. He believed in the simple life: which means nuts, vegetables, no meat, tents, fresh air, nature, and niceness. Now this puppet showman was *naturally* vegetarian, and *naturally* nice, with the vices *naturally* left out: a nice modern young fellow, who had enjoyed William Morris's *News from Nowhere* immensely, as a boy. One might say, a grandson of the William Morris stock, but a much plainer, more unpretentious fellow than his cultural forebears. And really "of the people." And really penniless.

But he is not a high-brow: has hardly heard of Dostoievsky, much less read him: and the "Works of William Shakespeare, in one volume," which accompanied the puppet show for the first week, is just a standing joke to the showman. As if anybody ever *did* read Shakespeare, actually! That's the farce of it. Bill Shakespeare! "Where's the works of the immortal William?— Say, are you sitting on Big Bill in one vol.?"

The author has very little to do with culture, whether in the big sense or the little! But he is a simple lifer. And as a simple lifer he sets out, with much trepidation, to make his living by showing his "reformed" puppets: not so brutal, beery, and beefy, as Punch; more suitable to the young, in every way. Still, they actually *are* charming puppets.

The book is an absolutely simple and unaffected account of the two months' or six-weeks' tour, from the Cotswolds down through Ilfracombe to Bideford, then back inland, by Taunton and Wells. It was mostly a one-man show: the author trundled his "sticks" before him, on a pair of old bath-chair wheels.

And, curiously, the record of those six weeks makes a book. Call it a human document, call it literature, I don't know the difference. The style is, in a sense, amateur: yet the whole attempt was amateur, that whole Morris aspect of life is amateur. And therefore the style is perfect: even, in the long run, poignant. The very banalities at last have the effect of the *mot juste*. "It is an exquisite pleasure to find oneself so suddenly in the sweet morning air, to tumble out of bed, to clamber over a stone wall and scramble across some rushy dunes down to the untrodden seashore, there to take one's bath in the lively breakers."

That is exactly how the cleverest youth writes, in an essay on the seaside, at night school. There is an inevitability about its banality, the "exquisite pleasure," the "sweet morning air," to "tumble out of bed"—which in actuality was carefully crawling out of a sleeping sack—; the "clamber over a stone wall," the "scramble across some rushy [sic] dunes" to the "untrodden shore," the "bath" in the "lively breakers": it is almost a masterpiece of clichés. It is the way thousands and thousands of the cleverest of the "ordinary" young fellows write, who have had just a touch more than our "ordinary" education, and who have a certain limpidity of character, and not much of the old Adam in them. It is what the "ordinary" young man, who is "really nice," does write. You have to have something vicious in you to be a creative writer. It is the something vicious, old-adamish, incompatible to the "ordinary" world, inside a man, which gives an edge to his awareness, and makes it impossible for him to talk of a "bath" in "lively breakers."

The puppet showman has not got this something vicious, so his perceptions lack fine edge. He can't help being "nice." And niceness is negative only too often. But, still, he is not *too* nice.

So the book is a book. It is not insipid. It is not banal. All takes place in the banal world: nature is banal, all the people are banal, save, perhaps, the very last "nobber": and all the philosophy is banal. And yet it is all *just*. "If I were a philosopher expounding a new theory of living, inventing a new 'ism,' I should call myself a holidayist, for it seems to me that the one thing the world needs to put it right is a holiday. There is no doubt whatever about the sort of life nice people want to lead. Whenever they get the chance, what do they do but go away to the country or the seaside, take off their collars and ties and have a good time playing at childish games and contriving to eat some simple [sic] food very happily without all the encumbrances of chairs and tables. This world might be quite a nice place if only simple people would be content to be simple and be proud of it; if only they would turn their backs on these pompous politicians and ridiculous Captains of Industry who, when you come to examine them, turn out to be very stupid, ignorant people, who are simply suffering from an unhappy mania of greediness; who are possessed with perverse and horrible devils which make them stick up smoking factories in glorious Alpine valleys, or spoil some simple country by digging up and exploiting its decently buried mineral resources; or whose moral philosophy is so patently upside down when they attempt to persuade us that quarrelling, and fighting, and wars, or that these ridiculous accumulations of wealth are the most important, instead of the most undesirable things in life. If only simple people would ignore them and behave always in the jolly way they do on a seashore what a nice world we might have to live in.

"Luckily Nature has a way with her, and we may rest assured that this wretched machine age will be over in a few years' time. It has grown up as quickly as a mushroom, and like a mushroom it has no stability. It will die."

But this is just "philosophy," and by the way. It is the apotheosis of ordinariness. The narrative part of the book is the succinct revelation of ordinariness, as seen from the puppet showman's point of view. And, owing to the true limpidity and vicelessness of the author, ordinariness becomes almost vivid. The book is a book. It is not something to laugh at. It is so curiously *true*. And it has therefore its own touch of realization of the tragedy of human futility:

the futility even of ordinariness. It contains the ordinary man's queer little bitter disappointment in life, because life, the life of people, is more ordinary than even he had imagined. The puppet showman is a bit of a pure idealist, in a fairly ordinary sense. He *really* doesn't want money. He *really* is not greedy. He *really* is shy of trespassing on anybody. He *really* is nice. He starts out by being too nice.

What is his experience? He struggles and labours, and is lucky if he can make five shillings in a day's work. When it rains, when there's no crowd, when it's Sunday, when the police won't allow you to show, when the local authorities won't allow you to pitch the sticks–then there is nothing doing. Result–about fifteen shillings a week earnings. That is all the great and noble public will pay for a puppet show. And you can live on it.

It is enough to embitter any man, to see people gape at a show, then melt away when the hat comes around. Not even a penny that they're not *forced* to pay. Even on their holidays. Yet they give shillings to go to the dirty kinema.

The puppet showman, however, refuses to be embittered. He remembers those who do pay, and pay heartily: sixpence the maximum. People are on the whole "nice" to him. Myself, I should want to spit on such niceness. The showman, however, accepts it. He is cheery by determination. When I was a boy among the miners, the question that would have been flung at the puppet showman would have been: "Lad, wheer'st keep thy ba's?" For his unfailing forbearance and meekness! It is admirable, but . . . Anyhow, what's the good of it? They just trod on him, all the same: all those masses of ordinary people more vulgar than he was; because there is a difference between vulgarity and ordinariness. Vulgarity is low and greedy. The puppet showman is never that. He is at least pure, in the ordinary sense of the word: never greedy nor base.

And if he is not embittered, the puppet showman is bitterly disappointed and chagrined. No, he has to decide that the world is not *altogether* a nice place to show puppets in. People are "nice," but by jove, they are tight. They don't want puppets. They don't want anything but chars-à-bancs and kinemas, girlies and curlies and togs and a drink. Callous, vulgar, less than human the ordinary world looks, full of "nice" people, as one reads this book. And that holiday region of Ilfracombe and Bideford, those country lanes of Devonshire reeling with chars-à-bancs and blurting blind dust and motor-horns, or mud and motor-horns, all August: that is hell! England my England! Who would be a holidayist? Oh, people are "nice"! But you've got to be vulgar, as well as ordinary, if you're going to stand them.

To me, a book like *The Peep Show* reveals England better than twenty novels by clever young ladies and gentlemen. Be absolutely decent in the ordinary sense of the word, be a "holidayist" and a firm believer in niceness; and then set out into the world of all those nice people, putting yourself more or less at their mercy. Put yourself at the mercy of the nice holiday-making crowd. Then come home, absolutely refusing to have your tail between your legs, but—"singing songs in praise of camping and tramping and the stirring life we jolly showmen lead." Because absolutely nobody has been *really nasty to you*. They've all been quite nice. Oh, quite! Even though you *are* out of pocket on the trip.

All the reader can say, at the end of this songful, cheerful book is: God save me from the nice, ordinary people, and from ever having to make a living out of them. God save me from being "nice."

The Social Basis of Consciousness, by Trigant Burrow

Dr. Trigant Burrow is well known as an independent psychologist through the essays and addresses he has published in pamphlet form from time to time. These have invariably shown the spark of original thought and discovery. The gist of all these essays now fuses into this important book, the latest addition to the International Library of Psychology, Philosophy and Scientific Method.

Dr. Burrow is that rare thing among psychiatrists, a humanly honest man. Not that practitioners are usually dishonest. They are intellectually honest, professionally honest: all that. But that other simple thing, human honesty, does not enter in, because it is primarily subjective; and subjective honesty, which means that a man is honest about his own inward experiences, is perhaps the rarest thing, especially among professionals. Chiefly, of course, because men, and especially men with a theory, don't know anything about their own inward experiences.

Here Dr. Burrow is a rare and shining example. He set out, years ago, as an enthusiastic psychoanalyst and follower of Freud, working according to the Freudian method, in America. And gradually the sense that something was wrong, vitally wrong, in the theory and in the practice of psychoanalysis both, invaded him. Like any truly honest man, he turned and asked himself what it was that was wrong, with himself, with his methods, and with the theory according to which he was working.

This book is the answer, a book for every man interested in the human consciousness to read carefully. Because Dr. Burrow's conclusions, sincere, almost naïve in their startled emotion, are far-reaching, and vital.

First, in the criticism of the Freudian method, Dr. Burrow found, in his clinical experiences, that he was always applying a *theory*. Patients came to be analysed, and the analyst was there to examine with open mind. But the mind could not be open, because the patient's neurosis, all the patient's experience, *had* to be fitted to the Freudian theory of the inevitable incest-motive.

And gradually Dr. Burrow realized that to fit life every time to a theory is in itself a mechanistic process, a process of unconscious repression, a process of image-substitution. All theory that has to be applied to life proves at last just another of these unconscious images which the repressed psyche uses as a substitute for life, and against which the psychoanalyst is fighting. The analyst wants to break all this image business, so that life can flow freely. But it is useless to try to do so by replacing in the unconscious another image —this time, the image, the fixed motive of the incest-complex.

Theory as theory is all right. But the moment you apply it to *life,* especially to the subjective life, the theory becomes mechanistic, a substitute for life, a factor in the vicious unconscious. So that while the Freudian theory of the unconscious and of the incest-motive is valuable as a *description* of our psychological condition, the moment you begin to *apply* it, and make it master of the living situation, you have begun to substitute one mechanistic or unconscious illusion for another.

In short, the analyst is just as much fixed in his vicious unconscious as is his neurotic patient, and the will to apply a mechanical incest-theory to every neurotic experience is just as sure an evidence of neurosis, in Freud or in the practitioner, as any psychologist could ask.

So much for the criticism of the psychoanalytic method.

If, then, Dr. Burrow asks himself, it is not sex-repression which is at the root of the neurosis of modern life, what is it? For certainly, according to his finding, sex-repression is not the root of the evil.

The question is a big one, and can have no single answer. A single answer would only be another "theory." But Dr. Burrow has struggled through years of mortified experience to come to some conclusion nearer the mark. And his finding is surely much deeper and more vital, and, also, much less spectacular than Freud's.

The real trouble lies in the inward sense of "separateness" which dominates every man. At a certain point in his evolution, man became cognitively conscious: he bit the apple: he began to know. Up till that time his consciousness flowed unaware, as in the animals. Suddenly, his consciousness split.

"It would appear that in his separativeness man has inadvertently fallen a victim to the developmental exigencies of his own consciousness. Captivated by the phylogenetically new and unwonted spectacle of his own image, it would seem he has been irresistibly arrested before the mirror of his own likeness and that in the present self-conscious phase of his mental evolution he is still standing spellbound before it. That such is the case with man is not remarkable. For the appearance of the phenomenon of consciousness marked a complete severance from all that was his past. Here was broken the chain of evolutionary events whose links extended back through the nebulous æons of our remotest ancestry, and in the first moment of his consciousness man stood, for the first time, *alone*. It was in this moment that he was 'created,' as the legend runs, 'in the image and likeness of God.' For, breaking with the teleological traditions of his age-long biology, man now became suddenly *aware*."

Consciousness is self-consciousness. "That is, consciousness in its inception entails the fallacy of *a self as over against other selves*."

Suddenly aware of himself, and of other selves over against him, man is a prey to the division inside himself. Helplessly he must strive for more consciousness, which means, also, a more intensified aloneness, or individuality; and at the same time he has a horror of his own aloneness, and a blind, dim yearning for the old togetherness of the far past, what Dr. Burrow calls the preconscious state.

What man really wants, according to Dr. Burrow, is a sense of togetherness with his fellow-men, which shall balance the secret but overmastering sense of separateness and aloneness which now dominates him. And therefore, instead of the Freudian method of personal analysis, in which the personality of the patient is pitted against the personality of the analyst in the old struggle for dominancy, Dr. Burrow would substitute a method of group analysis, wherein the reactions were distributed over a group of people, and the intensely personal element eliminated as far as possible. For it is only in the intangible reaction of several people, or many people together, on one another that you can really get the loosening and breaking of the me-and-you tension and contest, the inevitable contest of two individualities brought into connexion. What must be broken is the egocentric absolute of the individual. We are all such hopeless little absolutes to ourselves. And if we are sensitive, it hurts us, and we complain, we are called neurotic. If we are complacent, we enjoy our own petty absolutism, though we hide it and pretend to be quite meek and humble. But in secret, we are absolute and perfect to ourselves, and nobody could be better than we are. And this is called being normal.

Perhaps the most interesting part of Dr. Burrow's book is his examination of normality. As soon as man became aware of himself, he made a picture of himself. Then he began to live according to the picture. Mankind at large made a picture of itself, and every man had to conform to the picture: the ideal.

This is the great image or idol which dominates our civilization, and which we worship with mad blindness. The idolatry of self.

Consciousness should be a flow from within outwards. The organic necessity of the human being should flow into spontaneous action and spontaneous awareness, consciousness.

But the moment man became aware of himself he made a picture of himself, and began to live from the picture: that is, from without inwards. This is truly the reversal of life. And this is how we live. We spend all our time over the picture. All our education is but the elaborating of the picture. "A good little girl"–"a brave boy"–"a noble woman"–"a strong man"–"a productive society"–"a progressive humanity"–it is all the picture. It is all living from the outside to the inside. It is all the death of spontaneity. It is all, strictly, automatic. It is all the vicious unconscious which Freud postulated.

If we could once get into our heads–or if we once dare admit to one another–that we are *not* the picture, and the picture is not what we are, then we might lay a new hold on life. For the picture is really the death, and certainly the neurosis, of us all. We have to live from the outside in, idolatrously. And the picture of ourselves, the picture of humanity which has been elaborated through some thousands of years, and which we are still adding to, is just a huge idol. It is not real. It is a horrible compulsion set over us.

Individuals rebel: and these are the neurotics, who show some sign of health. The mass, the great mass, goes on worshipping the idol, and behaving according to the picture: and this is the normal. Freud tried to force his patients back to the normal, and almost succeeded in shocking them into submission, with the incest-bogy. But the bogy is nothing compared to the actual idol.

As a matter of fact, the mass is more neurotic than the individual patient. This is Dr. Burrow's finding. The mass, the normals, never live a life of their own. They cannot. They live entirely according to the picture. And according to the picture, each one is a little absolute unto himself; there is none better than he. Each lives for his own self-interest. The "normal" activity is to push your own interest with every atom of energy you can command. It is "normal" to get on, to get ahead, at whatever cost. The man who does disinterested work is abnormal. Every Johnny must look out for himself: that is normal. Luckily for the world, there still is a minority of individuals who do disinterested work, and are made use of by the "normals." But the number is rapidly decreasing.

And then the normals betray their utter abnormality in a crisis like the late war. There, there indeed the uneasy individual can look into the abysmal insanity of the normal masses. The same holds good of the Bolshevist hysteria of today: it is hysteria, incipient social insanity. And the last great insanity of all, which is going to tear our civilization to pieces, the insanity of class hatred, is almost entirely a "normal" thing, and a "social" thing. It is a state of fear, of ghastly collective fear. And it is absolutely a mark of the normal. To say that class hatred *need not exist* is to show abnormality. And yet it is true. Between man and man, class hatred hardly exists. It is an insanity of the mass, rather than of the individual.

But it is part of the picture. The picture says it is horrible to be poor, and splendid to be rich, and in spite of all individual experience to the contrary, we accept the terms of the picture, and thereby accept class war as inevitable.

Humanity, society has a picture of itself, and lives accordingly. The individual likewise has a private picture of himself, which fits into the big picture. In this picture he is a little absolute, and nobody could be better than he is. He must look after his own self-interest. And if he is a man, he must be very male. If she is a woman, she must be very female.

Even sex, today, is only part of the picture. Men and women alike, when they are being sexual, are only acting up. They are living according to the picture. If there is any dynamic, it is that of self-interest. The man "seeketh his own" in sex, and the woman seeketh her own: in the bad, egoistic sense in which St. Paul used the words. That is, the man seeks himself, the woman seeks herself, always, and inevitably. It is inevitable, when you live according to the picture, that you seek only yourself in sex. Because the picture is your own image of yourself: your *idea* of yourself. If you are quite normal, you don't have any true self, which "seeketh not her own, is not puffed up." The true self, in sex, would seek a *meeting,* would seek to meet the other. This would be the true flow: what Dr. Burrow calls the "societal consciousness," and what I would call the human consciousness, in contrast to the social, or image consciousness.

But today, all is image consciousness. Sex does not exist; there is only sexuality. And sexuality is merely a greedy, blind self-seeking. Self-seeking is the real motive of sexuality. And therefore, since the thing sought is the same, the self, the mode of seeking is not very important. Heterosexual, homosexual, narcissistic, normal, or incest, it is all the same thing. It is just sexuality, not sex. It is one of the universal forms of self-seeking. Every man, every woman just seeks his own self, her own self, in the sexual experience. It is the picture over again, whether in sexuality or self-sacrifice, greed or charity, the same thing, the self, the image, the idol, the image of me, and norm!

The true self is not aware that it is a self. A bird, as it sings, sings itself. But not according to a picture. It has no idea of itself.

And this is what the analyst must try to do: to liberate his patient from his own image, from his horror of his own isolation and the horror of the "stoppage" of his real vital flow. To do it, it is no use rousing sex bogies. A man is not neurasthenic or neurotic because he loves his mother. If he desires his mother, it is because he is neurotic, and the desire is merely a symptom. The cause of the neurosis is further to seek.

And the cure? For myself, I believe Dr. Burrow is right: the cure would consist in bringing about a state of honesty and a certain trust among a *group* of people, or many people—if possible, all the people in the world. For it is only when we can get a man to fall back into his true relation to other men, and to women, that we can give him an opportunity to be himself. So long as men are inwardly dominated by their own isolation, their own absoluteness, which after all is but a picture or an idea, nothing is possible but insanity more or less pronounced. Men must get back into *touch.* And to do so they must forfeit the vanity and the *noli me tangere* of their own absoluteness: also they must utterly break the present great picture of a normal humanity: shatter that mirror in which we all live grimacing: and fall again into true relatedness.

I have tried more or less to give a *résumé* of Dr. Burrow's book. I feel there is a certain impertinence in giving these *résumés.* But not more than in the affectation of "criticizing" and being superior. And it is a book one should read and assimilate, for it helps a man in his own inward life.

The Station: Athos, Treasures and Men, by Robert Byron; *England and the Octopus*, by Clough Williams-Ellis; *Comfortless Memory*, by Maurice Baring; *Ashenden*, by W. Somerset Maugham

Athos is an old place, and Mr. Byron is a young man. The combination for once is really happy. We can imagine ourselves being very bored by a book on ancient Mount Athos and its ancient monasteries with their ancient rule. Luckily Mr. Byron belongs to the younger generation, even younger than the Sitwells, who have shown him the way to be young. Therefore he is not more than becomingly impressed with ancientness. He never gapes in front of it. He settles on it like a butterfly, tastes it, is perfectly honest about the taste, and flutters on. And it is charming.

We confess that we find this youthful revelation of ancient Athos charming. It is all in the butterfly manner. But the butterfly, airy creature, is by no means a fool. And its interest is wide. It is amusing to watch a spangled beauty settle on the rose, then on a spat-out cherry-stone, then with a quiver of sunny attention, upon a bit of horse-droppings in the road. The butterfly tries them all, with equal concern. It is neither shocked nor surprised, though sometimes, if thwarted, it is a little exasperated. But it is still a butterfly, graceful, charming, and ephemeral. And, of course, the butterfly on its careless, flapping wings is just as immortal as some hooting and utterly learned owl. Which is to say, we are thankful Mr. Byron is no more learned and serious than he is, and his description of Athos is far more vitally convincing than that, for example, of some heavy Gregorovius.

The four young men set out from England with a purpose. The author wants to come into closer contact with the monks and monasteries, which he has already visited; and to write a book about it. He definitely sets out with the intention of writing a book about it. He has no false shame. David, the archæologist, wants to photograph the Byzantine frescoes in the monastery buildings. Mark chases and catches insects. And Reinecker looks at art and old pots. They are four young gentlemen with the echoes of Oxford still in their ears, light and frivolous as butterflies, but with an underneath tenacity of purpose and almost a grim determination *to do something*.

The butterfly and the Sitwellian manner need not deceive us. These young gentlemen are not simply gay. They are grimly in earnest to get something done. They are not young sports amusing themselves. They are young earnests making their mark. They are stoics rather than frivolous, and epicureans truly in the deeper sense, of undergoing suffering in order to achieve a higher pleasure.

For the monasteries of Mount Athos are no Paradise. The food which made the four young men shudder makes us shudder. The vermin in the beds are lurid. The obstinacy and grudging malice of some of the monks, whose one pleasure seems to have been in thwarting and frustrating the innocent desires of the four young men, make our blood boil too. We know exactly what sewage is like, spattering down from above on to leaves and rocks. And the tortures of heat and fatigue are very real indeed.

It is as if the four young men expected to be tormented at every hand's turn. Which is just as well, for tormented they were. Monks apparently have a special gift of tormenting people: though of course some of the monks were charming. But it is chiefly out of the torments of the young butterflies, always humorously and gallantly told, that we get our picture of Athos, its monasteries and its monks. And we are left with no desire at all to visit the holy mountain, unless we could go disembodied, in such state that no flea could bite us, and no stale fish could turn our stomachs.

Then, disembodied, we should like to go and see the unique place, the lovely views, the strange old buildings, the unattractive monks, the paintings, mosaics, frescoes of that isolated little Byzantine world.

For everything artistic is there purely Byzantine. Byzantine is to Mr. Byron what Baroque is to the Sitwells. That is to say, he has a real feeling for it, and finds in it a real kinship with his own war-generation mood. Also, it is his own special elegant stone to sling at the philistine world.

Perhaps, in a long book like this, the unfailing humoresque of the style becomes a little tiring. Perhaps a page or two here and there of honest-to-God simplicity might enhance the high light of the author's facetious impressionism. But then the book might have been undertaken by some honest-to-God professor, and we so infinitely prefer Mr. Byron.

When we leave Mr. Byron we leave the younger generation for the elder; at least as far as style and manner goes. Mr. Williams-Ellis has chosen a thankless subject: *England and the Octopus:* the

Octopus being the millions of little streets of mean little houses that are getting England in their grip, and devouring her. It is a depressing theme, and the author rubs it in. We see them all, those millions of beastly little red houses spreading like an eruption over the face of rural England. Look! Look! says Mr. Williams-Ellis, till we want to shout: Oh, shut up! What's the good of our looking! We've looked and got depressed too often. Now leave us alone.

But Mr. Williams-Ellis is honestly in earnest and has an honest sense of responsibility. This is the difference between the attitude of the younger and the older generations. The younger generation can't take anything very seriously, and refuses to feel responsible for humanity. The younger generation says in effect: I didn't make the world. I'm not responsible. All I can do is to make my own little mark and depart. But the elder generation still feels responsible for all humanity.

And Mr. Williams-Ellis feels splendidly responsible for poor old England: the face of her, at least. As he says: You can be put in prison for uttering a few mere swear-words to a policeman, but you can disfigure the loveliest features of the English country-side, and probably be called a public benefactor. And he wants to alter all that.

And he's quite right. His little book is excellent: sincere, honest, and even passionate, the well-written, humorous book of a man who knows what he's writing about. Everybody ought to read it, whether we know all about it beforehand or not. Because in a question like this, of the utter and hopeless disfigurement of the English country-side by modern industrial encroachment, the point is not whether we can do anything about it or not, all in a hurry. The point is, that we should all become acutely conscious of what is happening, and of what has happened; and as soon as we are really awake to this, we can begin to arrange things differently.

Mr. Williams-Ellis makes us conscious. He wakes up our age to our own immediate surroundings. He makes us able to look intelligently at the place we live in, at our own street, our own post-office or pub or bank or petrol pump-station. And when we begin to look around us critically and intelligently, it is fun. It is great fun. It is like analysing a bad picture and seeing how it could be turned into a good picture.

Mr. Williams-Ellis's six questions which should be asked of every building ought to be printed on a card and distributed to every individual in the nation. Because, as a nation, it is our intuitive faculty for seeing beauty and ugliness which is lying dead in us. As a nation we are dying of ugliness.

Let us open our eyes, or let Mr. Williams-Ellis open them for us, to houses, streets, railways, railings, paint, trees, roofs, petrol-pumps, advertisements, tea-shops, factory-chimneys, let us open our eyes and see them as they are, beautiful or ugly, mean and despicable, or grandiose, or pleasant. People who live in mean, despicable surroundings become mean and despicable. The chief thing is to become properly conscious of our environment.

But if some of the elder generation really take things seriously, some others only pretend. And this *pretending* to take things seriously is a vice, a real vice, and the young know it.

Mr. Baring's book *Comfortless Memory* is, thank heaven, only a little book, but it is sheer pretence of taking seriously things which its own author can never for a moment consider serious. That is, it is faked seriousness, which is utterly boring. I don't know when Mr. Baring wrote this slight novel. But he ought to have published it at least twenty years ago, when faked seriousness was more in the vogue. Mr. Byron, the young author, says that progress is the appreciation of Reality. Mr. Baring, the elderly author, offers us a piece of portentous unreality larded with Goethe, Dante, Heine, hopelessly out of date, and about as exciting as stale restaurant cake.

A dull, stuffy elderly author makes faked love to a bewitching but slightly damaged lady who has "lived" with a man she wasn't married to!! She is an enigmatic lady: very! For she falls in love, violently, virginally, deeply, passionately and exclusively, with the comfortably married stuffy elderly author. The stuffy elderly author himself tells us so, much to his own satisfaction. And the lovely, alluring, enigmatic, experienced lady actually expires, in her riding-habit, out of sheer love for the comfortably married elderly author. The elderly author assures us of it. If it were not quite so stale it would be funny.

Mr. Somerset Maugham is even more depressing. His Mr. Ashenden is also an elderly author, who becomes an agent in the British Secret Service during the War. An agent in the Secret Service is a sort of spy. Spying is a dirty business, and Secret Service altogether is a world of under-dogs, a world in which the meanest passions are given play.

And this is Mr. Maugham's, or at least Mr. Ashenden's world. Mr. Ashenden is an elderly author, so he takes life seriously, and takes his fellow-men seriously, with a seriousness already a little out of date. He has a sense of responsibility towards humanity. It would be much better if he hadn't. For Mr. Ashenden's sense of responsibility oddly enough is inverted. He is almost passionately concerned with proving that all men and all women are either dirty dogs or imbeciles. If they are clever men or women, they are crooks, spies, police-agents, and tricksters "making good," living in the best hotels because they know that in a humble hotel they'll be utterly declassé, and showing off their base cleverness, and being dirty dogs, from Ashenden himself, and his mighty clever colonel, and the distinguished diplomat, down to the mean French porters.

If, on the other hand, you get a decent, straight individual, especially an individual capable of feeling love for another, then you are made to see that such a person is a despicable fool, encompassing his own destruction. So the American dies for his dirty washing, the Hindu dies for a blowsy woman who wants her wrist-watch back, the Greek merchant is murdered by mistake, and so on. It is better to be a live dirty dog than a dead lion, says Mr. Ashenden. Perhaps it is, to Mr. Ashenden.

But these stories, being "serious," are faked. Mr. Maugham is a splendid observer. He can bring before us persons and places most excellently. But as soon as the excellently observed characters have to move, it is a fake. Mr. Maugham gives them a humorous shove or two. We find they are nothing but puppets, instruments of the author's pet prejudice. The author's pet prejudice being "humour," it would be hard to find a bunch of more ill-humoured stories, in which the humour has gone more rancid.

Fallen Leaves, by V. V. Rozanov

Rozanov is now acquiring something of a European reputation. There is a translation in French, and one promised in German, and the advanced young writers in Paris and Berlin talk of him as one of the true lights. Perhaps *Solitaria* is more popular than *Fallen Leaves:* but then, perhaps it is a little more sensational: *Fallen Leaves* is not sensational: it is on the whole quiet and sad, and truly Russian.

The book was written, apparently, round about 1912: and the author died a few years later. So that, from the western point of view, Rozanov seems like the last of the Russians. Post-revolution Russians are something different.

Rozanov is the last of the Russians, after Chekhov. It is the true Russian voice, become very plaintive now. Artzybashev, Gorky, Merejkovski are his contemporaries, but they are all three a little bit off the tradition. But Rozanov is right on it. His first wife had been Dostoievsky's mistress: and somehow his literary spirit showed the same kind of connexion: a Dostoievskian flicker that steadied and became a legal and orthodox light; yet always, of course, suspect. For Rozanov had been a real and perverse liar before he reformed and became a pious, yet suspected conservative. Perhaps he was a liar to the end: who knows? Yet *Solitaria* and *Fallen Leaves* are not lies, not so much lies as many more esteemed books.

The *Fallen Leaves* are just fragments of thought jotted down anywhere and anyhow. As to the importance of the where or how, perhaps it *is* important to keep throwing the reader out into the world, by means of the: At night: At work: In the tram: In the w.c.–which is sometimes printed after the reflections. Perhaps, to avoid any appearance of systematization, or even of philosophic abstraction, these little *addenda* are useful. Anyhow, it is Russian, and deliberate, done with the intention of keeping the reader–or Rozanov himself–in contact with the *moment,* the actual time and place. Rozanov says that with *Solitaria* he introduced a new *tone* into literature, the tone of manuscript, a manuscript being unique and personal, coming from the individual alone direct to the reader. And "the secret (bordering on madness) that I am talking to myself: so constantly and attentively and *passionately,* that apart from this

I practically hear nothing"—this is the secret of his newness, and of his book.

The description is just: and fortunately, on the whole, Rozanov talks sincerely to himself; he really does, on the whole, refrain from performing in front of himself. Of course he is self-conscious: he knows it and accepts it and tries to make it a stark-naked self-consciousness, between himself and himself as between himself and God. "Lord, preserve in me that chastity of the writer: not to look in the glass." From a professional liar it is a true and sincere prayer. "I am coquetting like a girl before the whole world, hence my constant agitation." "A writer must suppress the writer in himself (authorship, literariness)."

He is constantly expressing his hatred of literature, as if it poisoned life for him, as if he felt he did not live, he was only *literary*. "The *most happy* moments of life I remember were those when I saw (heard) people in a state of happiness. Stakha and A.P.P-va, 'My Friend's' story of her first love and marriage (the culminating point of my life). From this I conclude that I was born a contemplator, not an actor. I came into the world in order to *see,* and not to *accomplish.*" There is his trouble, that he felt he was always looking on at life, rather than partaking in it. And he felt this as a humiliation: and in his earlier days, it had made him act up, as the Americans say. He had acted up as if he were a real actor on life's stage. But it was too theatrical: his "lying," his "evil" were too much acted up. A liar and an evil bird he no doubt was, because the lies and the acting up to evil, whether they are "pose" or spontaneous, have a vile effect. But he never got any real satisfaction even out of that. He never felt he had really been evil. He had only acted up, like all the Stavrogins, or Ivan Karamazovs of Dostoievsky. Always acting up, trying to *act* feelings because you haven't really got any. That was the condition of the Russians at the end: even Chekhov. Being terribly emotional, terribly full of feeling, terribly good and pathetic or terribly evil and shocking, just to *make* yourself have feelings, when you have none. This was very Russian—and is very modern. A great deal of the world is like it today.

Rozanov left off "acting up" and became quiet and decent, except, perhaps, for little bouts of hysteria, when he would be perfectly vicious towards a friend, or make a small splash of "sin." As far as a man who *has* no real fount of emotion can love he loved his second wife, "My Friend." He tried very, very hard to love her, and no doubt he succeeded. But there was always the taint of pity, and she, poor thing, must have been terribly emotionally overwrought, as a woman is with an emotional husband who has no real virile emotion or compassion, only "pity." "European civilization will perish through compassion," he says: but then goes on to say, profoundly, that it is not compassion but pseudo-compassion, with an element of perversity in it. This is very Dostoievskian: and this pseudo-compassion tainted even Rozanov's love for his wife. There is somewhere an element of mockery. And oh, how Rozanov himself would have liked to escape it, and just to feel simple affection. But he couldn't. " 'Today' was completely absent in Dostoievsky," he writes. Which is a very succinct way of saying that Dostoievsky never had any immediate feelings, only "projected" ones, which are bound to destroy the immediate object, the actual "today," the very body which is "today." So poor Rozanov saw his wife dying under his eyes with a paralysis due to a disease of the brain. She was his "today," and he could not help, somewhere, jeering at her. But he suffered, and suffered deeply. At the end, one feels his suffering *was* real: his grief over his wife *was* real. So he had gained that much reality: he really grieved for her, and that was love. It was a great achievement, after all, for the most difficult thing in the world is to achieve real feeling, especially real sympathy, when the sympathetic centres seem, from the very start, as in Rozanov, dead. But Rozanov knew his own nullity, and tried very hard to come through to real honest feeling. And in his measure, he succeeded. After all the Dostoievskian hideous "impurity" he did achieve a certain final purity, or genuineness, or true individuality, towards the end. Even at the beginning of *Fallen Leaves* he is often sentimental and false, repulsive.

And one cannot help feeling a compassion for the Russians of the old regime. They were such healthy barbarians in Peter the Great's time. Then the whole accumulation of western ideas, ideals, and inventions was poured in a mass into their hot and undeveloped consciousness, and worked like wild yeast. It produced a century of literature, from Pushkin to Rozanov, and then the wild working of this foreign leaven had ruined, for the time being, the very constitution of the Russian psyche. It was as if they had taken too violent a drug, or been injected with too strong a vaccine. The affective and effective centres collapsed, the control went all wrong, the energy died down in a rush, the nation fell, for the time being completely ruined. Too sudden civilization always kills. It kills the South Sea Islanders: it killed the Russians, more slowly, and perhaps even more effectually. Once the idea and the ideal become too strong for the spontaneous emotion in the individual, the civilizing influence ceases to be civilizing and becomes very harmful, like powerful drugs which ruin the balance and destroy the control of the organism.

Rozanov knew this well. What he says about revolution and democracy leaves nothing to be said. And what he says of "officialdom" is equally final. I believe Tolstoi would be absolutely amazed if he could come back and see the Russia of today. I believe Rozanov would feel no surprise. He knew the inevitability of it. His attitude to the Jews is extraordinary, and shows uncanny penetration. And his sort of "conservatism," which would be Fascism today, was only a hopeless attempt to draw back from the way things were going.

But the disaster was inside himself already; there was no drawing back. Extraordinary is his note on his "dreaminess." "At times I am aware of something monstrous in myself. And that monstrous thing is my dreaminess. Then nothing can penetrate the circle traced by it.

"I am all stone.

"And a stone is a monster.

"For one must love and be aflame.

"From that dreaminess have come all my misfortunes in life (my former work in the Civil Service), the mistake of my whole proceedings (only when 'out of myself' was I attentive to My Friend [his wife]–and her pains), and also my sins.

"In my dreaminess I could do nothing.

"And on the other hand I could do anything ['sin'].

"Afterwards I was sorry: but it was too late. Dreaminess has devoured me, and everything round me."

There is the clue to the whole man's life: this "dreaminess" when he is like stone, insentient, and can do nothing, yet can do "anything." Over this dreaminess he has no control, nor over the stoniness. But what seemed to him dreaminess and stoniness seemed to others, from his actions, vicious malice and depravity. So that's that. It is one way of being damned.

And there we have the last word of the Russian, before the great *débâcle*. Anyone who understands in the least Rozanov's state of soul, in which, apparently, he was born, born with this awful insentient stoniness somewhere in him, must sympathize deeply with his real suffering and his real struggle to get back a positive self, a feeling self: to overcome the "dreaminess," to dissolve the stone. How much, and how little, he succeeded we may judge from this book: and from his harping on the beauty of procreation and fecundity: and from his strange and self-revealing statements concerning Weininger. Rozanov is modern, terribly modern. And if he does not put the fear of God into us, he puts a real fear of destiny, or of doom: and of "civilization" which does not come from within, but which is poured over the mind, by "education."

Art Nonsense and Other Essays, by Eric Gill *

Art Nonsense and Other Essays, reads the title of this expensive, handsomely printed book. Instinctively the eye reads: *Art Nonsense and Other Nonsense,* especially as the letter "O" in Mr. Gill's type rolls so large and important, in comparison with the other vowels.

But it isn't really fair. "Art Nonsense" is the last essay in the book, and not the most interesting. It is the little essays at the beginning that cut most ice. Then in one goes, with a plunge.

Let us say all the bad things first. Mr. Gill is not a born writer: he is a crude and crass amateur. Still less is he a born thinker, in the reasoning and argumentative sense of the word. He is again a crude and crass amateur: crass is the only word: maddening, like a tiresome uneducated workman arguing in a pub–*argefying* would describe it better–and banging his fist. Even, from his argument, one would have to conclude that Mr. Gill is not a born artist. A born craftsman, rather. He deliberately takes up the craftsman's point of view, argues about it like a craftsman, like a man in a pub, and really has a craftsman's dislike of the fine arts. He has, *au fond,* the man-in-a-pub's *moral* mistrust of art, though he tries to get over it.

So that there is not really much about art in this book. There is what Mr. Gill feels and thinks as a craftsman, shall we say as a medieval craftsman? We start off with a two-page "Apology": bad. Then comes an essay on "Slavery and Freedom" (1918), followed by "Essential Perfection" (1918), "A Grammar of Industry" (1919), "Westminster Cathedral" (1920), "Dress" (1920), "Songs without Clothes" (1921), "Of Things Necessary and Unnecessary" (1921), "Quæ ex Veritate et Bono" (1921), on to the last essay, the twenty-fourth, on "Art Nonsense," written in 1929. The dates are interesting: the titles are interesting. What is "Essential Perfection"? and what are "Songs without Clothes"? and why these tags of Latin? and what is a "Grammar of Industry," since industry has nothing to do with words? So much of it is jargon, like a workman in a pub.

So much of it is jargon. Take the blurb on the wrapper, which is extracted from Mr. Gill's "Apology." "Two primary ideas run

* First published in the *Book Collector's Quarterly,* this review was accompanied by a note from Mrs. Lawrence to this effect: "Lawrence wrote this unfinished review a few days before he died. The book interested him, and he agreed with much in it. Then he got tired of writing and I persuaded him not to go on. It is the last thing he wrote."

through all the essays of this book: that 'art is simply the well making of what needs making' and that 'art is collaboration with God in creating.' "

Could anything, I ask you, be worse? "Art is *simply* the well making of what needs making." There's a sentence for you! So simple! Imagine that a song like "Sally in our Alley"—which is art—should be "simply the well making of what needs making." Or that it should be "collaboration with God in creating." What a nasty, conceited, American sort of phrase! And how one dislikes this modern hob-nobbing with God, or giving Him the go-by.

But if one once begins to quarrel with Mr. Gill, one will never leave off. His trick of saying, over and over, "upon the contrary" instead of "on the contrary," his trick of firing off phrases, as in the essay on "Essential Perfection," which opens: "God is Love. That is not to say merely that God is loving or lovable, but that He *is* Love. In this, Love is an absolute, not a relative term. The Love of God is man's Essential Perfection. The Essential Perfection of man is not in his physical functions—the proper material exercise of his organs—but in his worship of God, and the worship of God is perfect in Charity"—all of which means really nothing: even his trick of printing a line under a word, for emphasis, instead of using italics—an untidy proceeding; if he doesn't like italics, why not space wider, in the Continental fashion?—all this is most irritating. Irritating like an uneducated workman in a pub holding forth and showing off, making a great noise with a lot of clichés, and saying nothing at all.

Then we learn that Mr. Gill is a Roman Catholic: surely a convert. And we know these new English Catholics. They are the last words in Protest. They are Protestants protesting against Protestantism, and so becoming Catholics to Protestants, they have protested against every absolute. As Catholics, therefore, they will swallow all the old absolutes whole, swallow the pill without looking at it, and call that Faith. The big pill being God, and little pills being terms like Charity and Chastity and Obedience and Humility. Swallow them whole, and you are a good Catholic; lick at them and see what they taste like, and you are a queasy Protestant. Mr. Gill is a Catholic, so he uses terms like "Holy Church" and "a good R.C." quite easily, at first; but as the years go by, more rarely. The mere function of swallowing things whole becomes tedious.

That is a long preamble, and perhaps an unkind one. But Mr.

Gill is so bad at the mere craft of language, that he sets a real writer's nerves on edge all the time.

Now for the good side of the book. Mr. Gill is primarily a craftsman, a workman, and he has looked into his own soul deeply to know what he feels about work. And he has seen a truth which, in my opinion, is a great truth, an invaluable truth for humanity, and a truth of which Mr. Gill is almost the discoverer. The gist of it lies in the first two paragraphs of the first essay, "Slavery and Freedom."

"That state is a state of Slavery in which a man does what he likes to do in his spare time and in his working time that which is required of him. This state can only exist when what a man likes to do is to please himself.

"That state is a state of Freedom in which a man does what he likes to do in his working time and in his spare time that which is required of him. This state can only exist when what a man likes to do is to please God."

It seems to me there is more in those two paragraphs than in all Karl Marx or Professor Whitehead or a dozen other philosophers rolled together. True, we have to swallow whole the phrase "to please God," but when we think of a man happily working away in concentration on the job he is doing, if it is only soldering a kettle, then we know what living state it refers to. "To please God" in this sense only means happily doing one's best at the job in hand, and being livingly absorbed in an activity which makes one in touch with—with the heart of all things; call it God. It is a state which any man or woman achieves when busy and concentrated on a job which calls forth real skill and attention, or devotion. It is a state of absorption into the creative spirit, which is God.

Here, then, is a great truth which Mr. Gill has found in his living experience, and which he flings in the teeth of modern industrialism. Under present conditions, it is useless to utter such truth: and that is why none of the clever blighters do utter it. But it is only the truth that is useless which really matters.

"The test of a man's freedom is his responsibility as a workman. Freedom is not incompatible with discipline, it is only incompatible with irresponsibility. He who is free is responsible for his work. He who is not responsible for his work is not free."

"There is nothing to be said for freedom except that it is the will of God.

"The Service of God is perfect freedom."

Here, again, the "service of God" is only that condition in which we feel ourselves most truly alive and vital, and the "will of God" is the inrush of pure life to which we gladly yield ourselves.

It all depends what you make of the word God. To most of us today it is a fetish-word, dead, yet useful for invocation. It is not a question of Jesus. It is a question of God, Almighty God. We have to square ourselves with the very words. And to do so, we must rid them of their maddening moral import, and give them back—Almighty God—the old vital meaning: strength and glory and honour and might and beauty and wisdom. These are the continual attributes of Almighty God, in the far past. And the same today, the god who enters us and imbues us with his strength and glory and might and honour and beauty and wisdom, this is a god we are eager to worship. And this is the god of the craftsman who makes things well, so that the presence of the god enters into the thing made. The workman making a pair of shoes with happy absorption in skill is imbued with the god of strength and honour and beauty, undeniable. Happy, intense absorption in any work, which is to be brought as near to perfection as possible, this is a state of being with God, and the men who have not known it have missed life itself.

This is what Mr. Gill means, I take it, and it is an enormously important truth. It is a truth on which a true civilization might be established. But first, you must give men back their belief in God, and then their free responsibility in work. For belief, Mr. Gill turns to the Catholic Church. Well, it is a great institution, and we all like to feel romantic about it. But the Catholic Church needs to be born again, quite as badly as the Protestant. I cannot feel there is much more belief in God in Naples or Barcelona, than there is in Liverpool or Leeds. Yet they are truly Catholic cities. No, the Catholic Church has fallen into the same disaster as the Protestant: of preaching a *moral* God, instead of Almighty God, the God of strength and glory and might and wisdom: a "good" God, instead of a vital and magnificent God. And we no longer any of us *really* believe in an exclusively "good" God. The Catholic Church in the cities is as dead as the Protestant Church. Only in the country, among peasants, where the old ritual of the seasons lives on in its beauty, is there still some living, instinctive "faith" in the God of Life.

Mr. Gill has two main themes: "work done well," and "beauty" —or rather "Beauty." He is almost always good, simple and profound, truly a prophet, when he is speaking of work done well. And he is nearly always tiresome about Beauty. Why, oh why, will people keep on trying to define words like Art and Beauty and God, words which represent deep emotional states in us, and are therefore incapable of definition? Why bother about it? "Beauty is absolute, loveliness is relative," says Mr. Gill. Yes, yes, but really, what does it matter? Beauty is beauty, loveliness is loveliness, and if Mr. Gill thinks that Beauty ought really to have a subtly moral character, while loveliness is merely casual, or equivalent for prettiness —well, why not? But other people don't care.

STUDY OF THOMAS HARDY

CHAPTER I

Of Poppies and Phœnixes and the Beginning of the Argument

Man has made such a mighty struggle to feel at home on the face of the earth, without even yet succeeding. Ever since he first discovered himself exposed naked betwixt sky and land, belonging to neither, he has gone on fighting for more food, more clothing, more shelter; and though he has roofed-in the world with houses and though the ground has heaved up massive abundance and excess of nutriment to his hand, still he cannot be appeased, satisfied. He goes on and on. In his anxiety he has evolved nations and tremendous governments to protect his person and his property; his strenuous purpose, unremitting, has brought to pass the whole frantic turmoil of modern industry, that he may have enough, enough to eat and wear, that he may be safe. Even his religion has for the systole of its heart-beat, propitiation of the Unknown God who controls death and the sources of nourishment.

But for the diastole of the heart-beat, there is something more, something else, thank heaven, than this unappeased rage of self-preservation. Even the passion to be rich is not merely the greedy wish to be secure within triple walls of brass, along with a huge barn of plenty. And the history of mankind is not altogether the history of an effort at self-preservation which has at length become over-blown and extravagant.

Working in contradiction to the will of self-preservation, from the very first man wasted himself begetting children, colouring himself and dancing and howling and sticking feathers in his hair, in scratching pictures on the walls of his cave, and making graven images of his unutterable feelings. So he went on wildly and with gorgeousness taking no thought for the morrow, but, at evening, considering the ruddy lily.

In his sleep, however, it must have come to him early that the lily is a wise and housewifely flower, considerate of herself, laying up secretly her little storehouse and barn, well under the ground, well tucked with supplies. And this providence on the part of the lily, man laid to heart. He went out anxiously at dawn to kill the largest mammoth, so that he should have a huge hill of meat, that he could never eat his way through.

And the old man at the door of the cave, afraid of the coming winter with its scant supplies, watching the young man go forth, told impressive tales to the children of the ant and the grasshopper; and praised the thrift and husbandry of that little red squirrel, and drew a moral from the gaudy, fleeting poppy.

"Don't, my dear children," continued the ancient paleolithic man as he sat at the door of his cave, "don't behave like that reckless, shameless scarlet flower. Ah, my dears, you little know the amount of labour, the careful architecture, all the chemistry, the weaving and the casting of energy, the business of day after day and night after night, yon gaudy wreck has squandered. Pfff!—and it is gone, and the place thereof shall know it no more. Now, my dear children, don't be like that."

Nevertheless, the old man watched the last poppy coming out, the red flame licking into sight; watched the blaze at the top clinging around a little tender dust, and he wept, thinking of his youth. Till the red flag fell before him, lay in rags on the earth. Then he did not know whether to pay homage to the void, or to preach.

So he compromised, and made a story about a phœnix. "Yes, my dears, in the waste desert, I know the green and graceful tree where the phœnix has her nest. And there I have seen the eternal phœnix escape away into flame, leaving life behind in her ashes. Suddenly she went up in to red flame, and was gone, leaving life to rise from her ashes."

"And did it?"

"Oh, yes, it rose up."

"What did it do then?"

"It grew up, and burst into flame again."

And the flame was all the story and all triumph. The old man knew this. It was this he praised, in his innermost heart, the red outburst at the top of the poppy that had no fear of winter. Even the latent seeds were secondary, within the fire. No red; and there was just a herb, without name or sign of poppy. But he had seen the flower in all its evanescence and its being.

When his educated grandson told him that the red was there to bring the bees and the flies, he knew well enough that more bees and flies and wasps would come to a sticky smear round his grandson's mouth, than to yards of poppy-red.

Therefore his grandson began to talk about the excess which always accompanies reproduction. And the old man died during this talk, and was put away. But his soul was uneasy, and came back from the shades to have the last word, muttering inaudibly in the cave door, "If there is always excess accompanying reproduction, how can you call it excess? When your mother makes a pie, and has too much paste, then that is excess. So she carves a paste rose with her surplus, and sticks it on the top of the pie. That is the flowering of the excess. And children, if they are young enough, clap their hands at this blossom of pastry. And if the pie bloom not too often with the rose of excess, they eat the paste blossom-shaped lump with reverence. But soon they become sophisticated, and know that the rose is no rose, but only excess, surplus, a counterfeit, a lump, unedifying and unattractive, and they say, 'No, thank you, mother; no rose.'

"Wherefore, if you mean to tell me that the red of my shed poppy was no more than the rose of the paste on the pie, you are a fool. You mean to say that young blood had more stuff than he knew what to do with. He knocked his structure of leaves and stalks together, hammered the poppy-knob safe on top, sieved and bolted the essential seeds, shut them up tight, and then said 'Ah!' And whilst he was dusting his hands, he saw a lot of poppy-stuff to spare. 'Must do something with it—must do something with it—mustn't be wasted!' So he just rolled it out into red flakes, and dabbed it round the knobby seed-box, and said, 'There, the simple creature will take it in, and I've got rid of it.'

"My dear child, that is the history of the poppy and of the excess which accompanied his reproduction, is it? That's all you can say of him, when he makes his red splash in the world?—that he had a bit left over from his pie with the five-and-twenty blackbirds in, so he put a red frill round? My child, it is good you are young, for you are a fool."

So the shade of the ancient man passed back again, to foregather with all the shades. And it shook its head as it went, muttering, "Conceit, conceit of self-preservation and of race-preservation, conceit!" But he had seen the heart of his grandson, with the wasteful red peeping out, like a poppy-bud. So he chuckled.

Why, when we are away for our holidays, do we exclaim with rapture, "What a splendid field of poppies!"—or "Isn't the poppy sweet, a red dot among the camomile flowers!"—only to go back on it all, and when the troubles come in, and we walk forth in heaviness, taking ourselves seriously, later on, to cry, in a harsh and bitter voice: "Ah, the gaudy treason of those red weeds in the corn!"—or when children come up with nosegays, "Nasty red flowers, poison, darling, make baby go to sleep," or when we see the scarlet flutter in the wind: "Vanity and flaunting vanity," and with gusto watch the red bits disappear into nothingness, saying: "It is well such scarlet vanity is cast to nought."

Why are we so rarely away on our holidays? Why do we persist in taking ourselves seriously, in counting our money and our goods and our virtues? We are down in the end. We rot and crumble away. And that without ever bursting the bud, the tight economical bud of caution and thrift and self-preservation.

The phœnix grows up to maturity and fulness of wisdom, it attains to fatness and wealth and all things desirable, only to burst into flame and expire in ash. And the flame and the ash are the be-all and the end-all, and the fatness and wisdom and wealth are but the fuel spent. It is a wasteful ordering of things, indeed, to be sure: but so it is, and what must be must be.

But we are very cunning. If we cannot carry our goods and our fatness, at least our goodness can be stored up like coin. And if we are not sure of the credit of the bank, we form ourselves into an unlimited liability company to run the future. We must have an obvious eternal deposit in which to bank our effort. And because the red of the poppy and the fire of the phœnix are contributed to no store, but are spent with the day and disappear, we talk of vanity and foolish mortality.

The phoenix goes gadding off into flame and leaves the future behind, unprovided for, in its ashes. There is no prodigal poppy left to return home in repentance, after the red is squandered in a day. Vanity, and vanity, and pathetic transience of mortality. All that is left us to call eternal is the tick-tack of birth and death, monotonous as time. The vain blaze flapped away into space and is gone, and what is left but the tick-tack of time, of birth and death?

But I will chase that flamy phœnix that gadded off into nothingness. Whoop and halloo and away we go into nothingness, in hot pursuit. Say, where are the flowers of yester-year? *Où sont les neiges d'antan?* Where's Hippolyta, where's Thaïs, each one loveliest among women? Who knows? Where are the snows of yester-year?

That is all very well, but they must be somewhere. They may not be in any bank or deposit, but they are not lost for ever. The virtue of them is still blowing about in nothingness and in somethingness. I cannot walk up and say, "How do you do, Dido?" as Æneas did in the shades. But Dido–Dido!–the robin cocks a scornful tail and goes off, disgusted with the noise. You might as well look for your own soul as to look for Dido. "Didon dina dit-on du dos d'un dodu dindon," comes rapidly into my mind, and a few frayed scraps of Virgil, and a vision of fair, round, half-globe breasts and blue eyes with tears in them; and a tightness comes into my heart: all forces rushing into me through my consciousness. But what of Dido my unconsciousness has, I could not tell you. Something, I am sure, and something that has come to me without my knowledge, something that flew away in the flames long ago, something that flew away from that pillar of fire, which was her body, day after day whilst she lived, flocking into nothingness to make a difference there. The reckoning of her money and her mortal assets may be discoverable in print. But what she is in the roomy space of somethingness, called nothingness, is all that matters to me.

She is something, I declare, even if she were utterly forgotten. How could any new thing be born unless it had a new nothingness to breathe? A new creature breathing old air, or even renewed air: it is terrible to think of. A new creature must have new air, absolutely brand-new air to breathe. Otherwise there is no new creature, and birth and death are a tick-tack.

What was Dido was new, absolutely new. It had never been before, and in Dido it *was*. In its own degree, the prickly sow-thistle I have just pulled up *is*, for the first time in all time. It is itself, a new thing. And most vividly it is itself in its yellow little disc of a flower: most vividly. In its flower it is. In its flower it issues something to the world that never was issued before. Its like has been before, its exact equivalent never. And this richness of new being is richest in the flowering yellow disc of my plant.

What then of this excess that accompanies reproduction? The excess is the thing itself at its maximum of being. If it had stopped short of this excess, it would not have been at all. If this excess were missing, darkness would cover the face of the earth. In this excess, the plant is transfigured into flower, it achieves at last itself. The aim, the culmination of all is the red of the poppy, this flame of the phœnix, this extravagant being of Dido, even her so-called waste.

But no, we dare not. We dare not fulfil the last part of our programme. We linger into inactivity at the vegetable, self-preserving stage. As if we preserved ourselves merely for the sake of remaining as we are. Yet there we remain, like the regulation cabbage, hide-bound, a bunch of leaves that may not go any farther for fear of losing a market value. A cabbage seen straddling up into weakly fiery flower is a piteous, almost an indecent sight to us. Better be a weed, and noxious. So we remain tight shut, a bunch of leaves, full of greenness and substance.

But the rising flower thrusts and pushes at the heart of us, strives and wrestles, while the static will hold us immovable. And neither will relent. But the flower, if it cannot beat its way through into being, will thrash destruction about itself. So the bound-up cabbage is beaten rotten at the heart.

Yet we call the poppy "vanity" and we write it down a weed. It is humiliating to think that, when we are taking ourselves seriously, we are considering our own self-preservation, or the greater scheme for the preservation of mankind. What is it that really matters? For the poppy, that the poppy disclose its red: for the cabbage, that it run up into weakly fiery flower: for Dido, that she be Dido, that she become herself, and die as fate will have it. Seed and fruit and produce, these are only a minor aim: children and good works are a minor aim. Work, in its ordinary meaning, and all effort for the public good, these are labour of self-preservation, they are only means to the end. The final aim is the flower, the fluttering, singing nucleus which is a bird in spring, the magical spurt of being which is a hare all explosive with fulness of self, in the moonlight; the real passage of a man down the road, no sham, no shadow, no counterfeit, whose eyes shine blue with his own reality, as he moves amongst things free as they are, a being; the flitting under the lamp of a woman incontrovertible, distinct from everything and from everybody, as one who is herself, of whom Christ said, "to them that have shall be given."

The final aim of every living thing, creature, or being is the full achievement of itself. This accomplished, it will produce what it will produce, it will bear the fruit of its nature. Not the fruit, however, but the flower is the culmination and climax, the degree to be striven for. Not the work I shall produce, but the real Me I shall achieve, that is the consideration; of the complete Me will come the complete fruit of me, the work, the children.

And I know that the common wild poppy has achieved so far its complete poppy-self, unquestionable. It has uncovered its red. Its light, its self, has risen and shone out, has run on the winds for a moment. It is splendid. The world is a world because of the poppy's red. Otherwise it would be a lump of clay. And I am I as well, since the disclosure. What it is, I breathe it and snuff it up, it is about me and upon me and of me. And I can tell that I do not know it all yet. There is more to disclose. What more, I do not know. I tremble at the inchoate infinity of life when I think of that which the poppy has to reveal, and has not as yet had time to bring forth. I make a jest of it. I say to the flower, "Come, you've played that red card long enough. Let's see what else you have got up your sleeve." But I am premature and impertinent. My impertinence makes me ashamed. He has not played his red card long enough to have outsatisfied me.

Yet we must always hold that life is the great struggle for self-preservation, that this struggle for the means of life is the essence and whole of life. As if it would be anything so futile, so ingestive. Yet we ding-dong at it, always hammering out the same phrase, about the struggle for existence, the right to work, the right to the vote, the right to this and the right to that, all in the struggle for existence, as if any external power could give us the right to ourselves. That we have within ourselves. And if we have it not, then the remainder that we do possess will be taken away from us. "To them that have shall be given, and from them that have not shall be taken away even that which they have."

CHAPTER II

Still Introductory: About Women's Suffrage, and Laws, and the War, and the Poor, with Some Fanciful Moralizing

It is so sad that the earnest people of today serve at the old, second-rate altar of self-preservation. The woman-suffragists, who are certainly the bravest, and, in the old sense, most heroic party amongst us, even they are content to fight the old battles on the old ground, to fight an old system of self-preservation to obtain a more advanced system of preservation. The vote is only a means, they admit. A means to what? A means to making better laws, laws which shall protect the unprotected girl from a vicious male, which shall protect the sweated woman-labourer from the unscrupulous greed of the capitalist, which shall protect the interest of women in the State. And surely this is worthy and admirable.

Yet it is like protecting the well-being of a cabbage in the cabbage-patch, while the cabbage is rotting at the heart for lack of power to run out into blossom. Could you make any law in any land, empowering the poppy to flower? You might make a law refusing it liberty to bloom. But that is another thing. Could any law put into being something which did not before exist? It could not. Law can only modify the conditions, for better or worse, of that which already exists.

But law is a very, very clumsy and mechanical instrument, and we people are very, very delicate and subtle beings. Therefore I only ask that the law shall leave me alone as much as possible. I insist that no law shall have immediate power over me, either for my good or for my ill. And I would wish that many laws be unmade, and no more laws made. Let there be a parliament of men and women for the careful and gradual unmaking of laws.

If it were for this purpose that women wanted the vote, I should be glad, and the opposition would be vital and intense, instead of just flippantly or exasperatedly static. Because then the woman's movement would be a living human movement. But even so, the claiming of a vote for the purpose of unmaking the laws would be rather like taking a malady in order to achieve a cure.

The women, however, want the vote in order to make more laws. That is the most lamentable and pathetic fact. They will take this clumsy machinery to make right the body politic. And, pray, what is the sickness of the body politic? Is it that some men are sex-mad or sex-degraded, and that some, or many, employers are money-degraded? And if so, will you, by making laws for putting in prison the sex-degraded, and putting out of power the money-degraded, thereby make whole and clean the State? Wherever you put them, will not the degradation exist, and continue? And is the State, then, merely an instrument for weeding the public of destructive members? And is this, then, the crying necessity for more thorough weeding?

Whence does the degradation or perversion arise? Is there any great sickness in the body politic? Then where and what is it? Am I, or your suffragist woman, or your voting man, sex-whole and money-healthy, are we sound human beings? Have we achieved to true individuality and to a sufficient completeness in ourselves? Because, if not—then, physician, heal thyself.

That is no taunt, but the finest and most damning criticism ever passed: "Physician, heal thyself." No amount of pity can blind us to the inexorable reality of the challenge.

Where is the source of all money-sickness, and the origin of all sex-perversion? That is the question to answer. And no cause shall come to life unless it contain an answer to this question. Laws, and all State machinery, these only regulate the sick, separate the sick and the whole, clumsily, oh, so clumsily that it is worse than futile. Who is there who searches out the origin of the sickness, with a hope to quench the malady at its source?

It lies in the heart of man, and not in the conditions—that is obvious, yet always forgotten. It is not a malaria which blows in through the window and attacks us when we are healthy. We are each one of us a swamp, we are like the hide-bound cabbage going rotten at the heart. And for the same reason that, instead of producing our flower, instead of continuing our activity, satisfying our true desire, climbing and clambering till, like the poppy, we lean on the sill of all the unknown, and run our flag out there in the colour and shine of being, having surpassed that which has been before, we hang back, we dare not even peep forth, but, safely shut up in bud, safely and darkly and snugly enclosed, like the regulation cabbage, we remain secure till our hearts go rotten, saying all the while how safe we are.

No wonder there is a war. No wonder there is a great waste and squandering of life. Anything, anything to prove that we are not altogether sealed in our own self-preservation as dying chrysalides. Better the light be blown out, wilfully, recklessly, in the wildest wind, than remain secure under the bushel, saved from every draught.

So we go to war to show that we can throw our lives away. Indeed, they have become of so little value to us. We cannot live, we cannot *be*. Then let us tip-cat with death, let us rush, throwing our lives away. Then, at any rate, we shall have a sensation—and "perhaps," after all, the value of life is in death.

What does the law matter? What does money, power, or public approval matter? All that matters is that each human being shall *be* in his own fulness. If something obstruct us, we break it or put it aside, as the shoots of the trees break even through the London pavements. That is, if life is strong enough in us. If not, we are glad to fight with death. Does not the war show us how little, under all our carefulness, we count human life and human suffering, how little we value ourselves at bottom, how we hate our own security? We have many hospitals and many laws and charities for the poor. And at the same time, we send ourselves to be killed and torn and tortured, we spread grief and desolation, and then, only then, we are somewhat satisfied. For have we not proved that we can transcend our own self-preservation, that we do not care so much for ourselves, after all? Indeed, we almost hate ourselves.

Indeed, well may we talk about a just and righteous war against Germany, but against ourselves also, our own self-love and caution. It is no war for the freedom of man from militarism or the Prussian yoke; it is a war for freedom of the bonds of our own cowardice and sluggish greed of security and well-being; it is a fight to regain ourselves out of the grip of our own caution.

Tell me no more we care about human life and suffering. We are, every one of us, revelling at this moment in the squandering of human life as if it were something we needed. And it is shameful. And all because that, to *live,* we are afraid to [risk] ourselves. We can only die.

Let there be an end, then, of all this welter of pity, which is only self-pity reflected onto some obvious surface. And let there be an end of this German hatred. We ought to be grateful to Germany that she still has the power to burst the bound hide of the cabbage. Where do I meet a man or a woman who does not draw deep and thorough satisfaction from this war? Because of pure shame that we should have seemed such poltroons living safe and atrophied, not daring to take one step to life. And this is the only good that can result from the "world disaster": that we realize once more that self-preservation is not the final goal of life; that we realize that we can still squander life and property and inflict suffering wholesale. That will free us, perhaps, from the bushel we cower under, from the paucity of our lives, from the cowardice that will not let us *be,* which will only let us exist in security, unflowering, unreal, fat, under the cosy jam-pot of the State, under the shelter of the social frame.

And we must be prepared to fight, after the war, a renewed rage of activity for greater self-preservation, a renewed outcry for a stronger bushel to shelter our light. We must also undertake the incubus of crippled souls that will come home, and of crippled souls that will be left behind: men in whom the violence of war shall have shaken the life-flow and broken or perverted the course; women who will cease to live henceforth, yet will remain existing in the land, fixed at some lower point of fear or brutality.

Yet if we are left maimed and halt, if you die or I die, it will not matter, so long as there is alive in the land some new sense of what is and what is not, some new courage to let go the securities, and to *be,* to risk ourselves in a forward venture of life, as we are willing to risk ourselves in a rush of death.

Nothing will matter so long as life shall sprout up again strong after this winter of cowardice and well-being, sprout into the unknown. Let us only have had enough of pity: pity that stands before the glass and weeps for ever over the sight of its own tears. This is what we have made of Christ's Commandment: "Thou shalt love thy neighbour as thyself"–a mirror for the tears of self-pity. How do we love our neighbour? By taking to heart his poverty, his small wage, and the attendant evils thereof. And is that how we love our neighbour as *ourselves?* Do I, then, think of myself as a moneyed thing enjoying advantages, or a non-moneyed thing suffering from disadvantages? Evidently I do. Then why the tears? They must rise from the inborn knowledge that neither money or non-money, advantages or disadvantages, matter supremely: what matters is the light under the bushel, the flower fighting under the safeguard of the leaves. I am weeping over my denied self. And I am very sorry for myself, held in the grip of some stronger force. Where can I find an image of myself? Ah, in the poor, in my poor neighbour labouring in the grip of an unjust system of capitalism. Let me look at him, let my heart be wrung, let me give myself to his service. Poor fellow, poor image, he is so badly off. Alas and alas, I do love my neighbour as myself: I am as anxious about his pecuniary welfare as I am about myself. I am so sorry for him, the poor X. He is a man like me. So I lie to myself and to him. For I do not care about him and his poverty: I care about my own unsatisfied soul. But I sidetrack to him, my poor neighbour, to vent on him my self-pity.

It is as if a poppy, when he is grown taller than his neighbours, but has not come to flower, should look down and, because he can get no further, say: "Alas, for those poor dwindlers down there: they don't get half as much rain as I do." He grows no more, and his non-growing makes him sad, and he tries to crouch down so as not to be any taller than his neighbour, thinking his sorrow is for his neighbour; and his neighbour struggles weakly into flower, after his fight for the sunshine. But the rich young poppy crouches, gazing down, nor even once lifts up his head to blossom. He is so afraid of giving himself forth, he cannot move on to expose his new nakedness, up there to confront the horrific space of the void, he is afraid of giving himself away to the unknown. He stays within his shell.

Which is the parable of the rich poppy. The *truth* about him is, he grows as fast as he can, though he devours no man's substance, because he has neither storehouse nor barn to devour them with, and neither a poppy nor a man can devour much through his own mouth. He grows as fast as he can, and from his innermost self he shuttles the red fire out, bit by bit, a little further, till he has brought it together and up to bud. There he hangs his head, hesitates, halts, reflects a moment, shrinking from the great climax when he lets off his fire. He ought to perceive now his neighbours, and to stand arrested, crying, "Alas, those poor dwindlers!" But his fire breaks out of him, and he lifts his head, slowly, subtly, tense in an ecstasy of fear overwhelmed by joy, submits to the issuing of his flame and his fire, and there it hangs at the brink of the void, scarlet and radiant for a little while, immanent on the unknown, a signal, an outpost, an advance-guard, a forlorn, splendid flag quivering from the brink of the unfathomed void, into which it flutters silently, satisfied, whilst a little ash, a little dusty seed remains behind on the solid ledge of earth.

And the day is richer for a poppy, the flame of another phœnix is filled in to the universe, something is, which was not.

That is the whole point: something is which was not. And I wish it were true of us. I wish we were all like kindled bonfires on the edge of space, marking out the advance-posts. What is the aim of self-preservation, but to carry us right out to the firing-line; there, what *is* is in contact with what is not. If many lives be lost by the way, it cannot be helped, nor if much suffering be entailed. I do not go out to war in the intention of avoiding all danger or discomfort: I go to fight for myself. Every step I move forward into being brings a newer, juster proportion into the world, gives me less need of storehouse and barn, allows me to leave all, and to take what I want by the way, sure that it will always be there; allows me in the end to fly the flag of myself, at the extreme tip of life.

He who would save his life must lose it. But why should he go on and waste it? Certainly let him cast it upon the waters. Whence and how and whither it will return is no matter, in terms of values. But like a poppy that has come to bud, when he reaches the shore, when he has traversed his known and come to the beach to meet the unknown, he must strip himself naked and plunge in, and pass out: if he dare. And the rest of his life he will be a stirring at the unknown, cast out upon the waters. But if he dare not plunge in, if he dare not take off his clothes and give himself naked to the flood, then let him prowl in rotten safety, weeping for pity of those he imagines worse off than himself. He dare not weep aloud for his own cowardice. And weep he must. So he will find him objects of pity.

CHAPTER III

Containing Six Novels and the Real Tragedy

This is supposed to be a book about the people in Thomas Hardy's novels. But if one wrote everything they give rise to, it would fill the Judgment Book.

One thing about them is that none of the heroes and heroines care very much for money, or immediate self-preservation, and all of them are struggling hard to come into being. What exactly the struggle into being consists in, is the question. But most obviously, from the Wessex novels, the first and chiefest factor is the struggle into love and the struggle with love: by love, meaning the love of a man for a woman and a woman for a man. The *via media* to being, for man or woman, is love, and love alone. Having achieved and accomplished love, then the man passes into the unknown. He has become himself, his tale is told. Of anything that is complete there is no more tale to tell. The tale is about becoming complete, or about the failure to become complete.

It is urged against Thomas Hardy's characters that they do unreasonable things—quite, quite unreasonable things. They are always going off unexpectedly and doing something that nobody would do. That is quite true, and the charge is amusing. These people of Wessex are always bursting suddenly out of bud and taking a wild flight into flower, always shooting suddenly out of a tight convention, a tight, hide-bound cabbage state into something quite madly personal. It would be amusing to count the number of special marriage licenses taken out in Hardy's books. Nowhere, except perhaps in Jude, is there the slightest development of personal action in the characters: it is all explosive. Jude, however, does see more or less what he is doing, and acts from choice. He is more consecutive. The rest explode out of the convention. They are people each with a real, vital, potential self, even the apparently wishy-washy heroines of the earlier books, and this self suddenly bursts the shell of manner and convention and commonplace opinion, and acts independently, absurdly, without mental knowledge or acquiescence.

And from such an outburst the tragedy usually develops. For there does exist, after all, the great self-preservation scheme, and in it we must all live. Now to live in it after bursting out of it was the problem these Wessex people found themselves faced with. And they never solved the problem, none of them except the comically, insufficiently treated Ethelberta.

This because they must subscribe to the system in themselves. From the more immediate claims of self-preservation they could free themselves: from money, from ambition for social success. None of the heroes or heroines of Hardy cared much for these things. But there is the greater idea of self-preservation, which is formulated in the State, in the whole modelling of the community. And from this idea, the heroes and heroines of Wessex, like the heroes and heroines of almost anywhere else, could not free themselves. In the long run, the State, the Community, the established form of life remained, remained intact and impregnable, the individual, trying to break forth from it, died of fear, of exhaustion, or of exposure to attacks from all sides, like men who have left the walled city to live outside in the precarious open.

This is the tragedy of Hardy, always the same: the tragedy of those who, more or less pioneers, have died in the wilderness, whither they had escaped for free action, after having left the walled security, and the comparative imprisonment, of the established convention. This is the theme of novel after novel: remain quite within the convention, and you are good, safe, and happy in the long run, though you never have the vivid pang of sympathy on your side: or, on the other hand, be passionate, individual, wilful, you will find the security of the convention a walled prison, you will escape, and you will die, either of your own lack of strength to bear the isolation and the exposure, or by direct revenge from the community, or from both. This is the tragedy, and only this: it is nothing more metaphysical than the division of a man against himself in such a way: first, that he is a member of the community, and must, upon his honour, in no way move to disintegrate the community, either in its moral or its practical form; second, that the convention of the community is a prison to his natural, individual desire, a desire that compels him, whether he feel justified or not, to break the bounds of the community, lands him outside the pale, there to stand alone, and say: "I was right, my desire was real and inevitable; if I was to be myself I must fulfil it, convention or no convention," or else, there to stand alone, doubting, and saying: "Was I right, was I wrong? If I was wrong, oh, let me die!"—in which case he courts death.

The growth and the development of this tragedy, the deeper and deeper realization of this division and this problem, the coming towards some conclusion, is the one theme of the Wessex novels.

And therefore the books must be taken chronologically, to reveal the development and to advance towards the conclusion.

1. *Desperate Remedies.*

Springrove, the dull hero, fast within convention, dare not tell Cytherea that he is already engaged, and thus prepares the complication. Manston, represented as fleshily passionate, breaks the convention and commits murder, which is very extreme, under compulsion of his desire for Cytherea. He is aided by the darkly passionate, lawless Miss Aldclyffe. He and Miss Aldclyffe meet death, and Springrove and Cytherea are united to happiness and success.

2. *Under the Greenwood Tree.*

After a brief excursion from the beaten track in the pursuit of social ambition and satisfaction of the imagination, figured by the Clergyman, Fancy, the little school-mistress, returns to Dick, renounces imagination, and settles down to steady, solid, physically satisfactory married life, and all is as it should be. But Fancy will carry in her heart all her life many unopened buds that will die unflowered; and Dick will probably have a bad time of it.

3. *A Pair of Blue Eyes.*

Elfride breaks down in her attempt to jump the first little hedge of convention, when she comes back after running away with Stephen. She cannot stand even a little alone. Knight, his conventional ideas backed up by selfish instinct, cannot endure Elfride when he thinks she is not virgin, though now she loves him beyond bounds. She submits to him, and owns the conventional idea entirely right, even whilst she is innocent. An aristocrat walks off with her whilst the two men hesitate, and she, poor innocent victim of passion not vital enough to overthrow the most banal conventional ideas, lies in a bright coffin, while the three confirmed lovers mourn, and say how great the tragedy is.

4. *Far from the Madding Crowd.*

The unruly Bathsheba, though almost pledged to Farmer Boldwood, a ravingly passionate, middle-aged bachelor pretendant, who has suddenly started in mad pursuit of some unreal conception of woman, personified in Bathsheba, lightly runs off and marries Sergeant Troy, an illegitimate aristocrat, unscrupulous and yet sensitive in taking his pleasures. She loves Troy, he does not love her. All the time she is loved faithfully and persistently by the good Gabriel, who is like a dog that watches the bone and bides the time. Sergeant Troy treats Bathsheba badly, never loves her, though he is the only man in the book who knows anything about her. Her pride helps her to recover. Troy is killed by Boldwood; exit the unscrupulous, but discriminative, almost cynical young soldier and the mad, middle-aged pursuer of the Fata Morgana; enter the good, steady Gabriel, who marries Bathsheba because he will make her a good husband, and the flower of imaginative first love is dead for her with Troy's scorn of her.

5. *The Hand of Ethelberta.*

Ethelberta, a woman of character and of brilliant parts, sets out in pursuit of social success, finds that Julius, the only man she is inclined to love, is too small for her, hands him over to the good little Picotee, and she herself, sacrificing almost cynically what is called her heart, marries the old scoundrelly Lord Mountclerc, runs him and his estates and governs well, a sound, strong pillar of established society, now she has nipped off the bud of her heart. Moral: it is easier for the butler's daughter to marry a lord than to find a husband with her love, if she be an exceptional woman.

The Hand of Ethelberta is the one almost cynical comedy. It marks the zenith of a certain feeling in the Wessex novels, the zenith of the feeling that the best thing to do is to kick out the craving for "Love" and substitute commonsense, leaving sentiment to the minor characters.

This novel is a shrug of the shoulders, and a last taunt to hope, it is the end of the happy endings, except where sanity and a little cynicism again appear in *The Trumpet Major,* to bless where they despise. It is the hard, resistant, ironical announcement of personal failure, resistant and half-grinning. It gives way to violent, angry passions and real tragedy, real killing of beloved people, self-killing. Till now, only Elfride among the beloved, has been killed; the good men have always come out on top.

6. *The Return of the Native.*

This is the first tragic and important novel. Eustacia, dark, wild, passionate, quite conscious of her desires and inheriting no tradition which would make her ashamed of them, since she is of a novelistic Italian birth, loves, first, the unstable Wildeve, who does not satisfy her, then casts him aside for the newly returned Clym, whom she marries. What does she want? She does not know, but it is evidently some form of self-realization; she wants to be herself, to attain herself. But she does not know how, by what means, so romantic imagination says, Paris and the *beau monde*. As if that would have stayed her unsatisfaction.

Clym has found out the vanity of Paris and the *beau monde*. What, then, does he want? He does not know; his imagination tells him he wants to serve the moral system of the community, since the material system is despicable. He wants to teach little Egdon boys in school. There is as much vanity in this, easily, as in Eustacia's Paris. For what is the moral system but the ratified form of the material system? What is Clym's altruism but a deep, very subtle cowardice, that makes him shirk his own being whilst apparently acting nobly; which makes him choose to improve mankind rather than to struggle at the quick of himself into being. He is not able to undertake his own soul, so he will take a commission for society to enlighten the souls of others. It is a subtle equivocation. Thus both Eustacia and he sidetrack from themselves, and each leaves the other unconvinced, unsatisfied, unrealized. Eustacia, because she moves outside the convention, must die; Clym, because he identified himself with the community, is transferred from Paris to preaching. He had never become an integral man, because when faced with the demand to produce himself, he remained under cover of the community and excused by his altruism.

His remorse over his mother is adulterated with sentiment; it is exaggerated by the push of tradition behind it. Even in this he does not ring true. He is always according to pattern, producing his feelings more or less on demand, according to the accepted standard. Practically never is he able to act or even feel in his original self; he is always according to the convention. His punishment is his final loss of all his original self: he is left preaching, out of sheer emptiness.

Thomasin and Venn have nothing in them turbulent enough to push them to the bounds of the convention. There is always room for them inside. They are genuine people, and they get the prize within the walls.

Wildeve, shifty and unhappy, attracted always from outside and never driven from within, can neither stand with nor without the established system. He cares nothing for it, because he is unstable, has no positive being. He is an eternal assumption.

The other victim, Clym's mother, is the crashing-down of one of the old, rigid pillars of the system. The pressure on her is too great. She is weakened from the inside also, for her nature is non-conventional; it cannot own the bounds.

So, in this book, all the exceptional people, those with strong feelings and unusual characters, are reduced; only those remain who are steady and genuine, if commonplace. Let a man will for himself, and he is destroyed. He must will according to the established system.

The real sense of tragedy is got from the setting. What is the great, tragic power in the book? It is Egdon Heath. And who are the real spirits of the Heath? First, Eustacia, then Clym's mother, then Wildeve. The natives have little or nothing in common with the place.

What is the real stuff of tragedy in the book? It is the Heath. It is the primitive, primal earth, where the instinctive life heaves up. There, in the deep, rude stirring of the instincts, there was the reality that worked the tragedy. Close to the body of things, there can be heard the stir that makes us and destroys us. The heath heaved with raw instinct. Egdon, whose dark soil was strong and crude and organic as the body of a beast. Out of the body of this crude earth are born Eustacia, Wildeve, Mistress Yeobright, Clym, and all the others. They are one year's accidental crop. What matters if some are drowned or dead, and others preaching or married: what matter, any more than the withering heath, the reddening berries, the seedy furze, and the dead fern of one autumn of Egdon? The Heath persists. Its body is strong and fecund, it will bear many more crops beside this. Here is the sombre, latent power that will go on producing, no matter what happens to the product. Here is the deep, black source from whence all these little contents of lives are drawn. And the contents of the small lives are spilled and wasted. There is savage satisfaction in it: for so much more remains to come, such a black, powerful fecundity is working there that what does it matter?

Three people die and are taken back into the Heath; they mingle their strong earth again with its powerful soil, having been broken off at their stem. It is very good. Not Egdon is futile, sending forth life on the powerful heave of passion. It cannot be futile, for it is eternal. What is futile is the purpose of man.

Man has a purpose which he has divorced from the passionate purpose that issued him out of the earth into being. The Heath threw forth its shaggy heather and furze and fern, clean into being. It threw forth Eustacia and Wildeve and Mistress Yeobright and Clym, but to what purpose? Eustacia thought she wanted the hats and bonnets of Paris. Perhaps she was right. The heavy, strong soil of Egdon, breeding original native beings, is under Paris as well as under Wessex, and Eustacia sought herself in the gay city. She thought life there, in Paris, would be tropical, and all her energy and passion out of Egdon would there come into handsome flower. And if Paris real had been Paris as she imagined it, no doubt she was right, and her instinct was soundly expressed. But Paris real was not Eustacia's imagined Paris. Where was her imagined Paris, the place where her powerful nature could come to blossom? Beside some strong-passioned, unconfined man, her mate.

Which mate Clym might have been. He was born out of passionate Egdon to live as a passionate being whose strong feelings moved him ever further into being. But quite early his life became narrowed down to a small purpose: he must of necessity go into business, and submit his whole being, body and soul as well as mind, to the business and to the greater system it represented. His feelings, that should have produced the man, were suppressed and contained, he worked according to a system imposed from without. The dark struggle of Egdon, a struggle into being as the furze struggles into flower, went on in him, but could not burst the enclosure of the idea, the system which contained him. Impotent to *be,* he must transform himself, and live in an abstraction, in a generalization, he must identify himself with the system. He must live as Man or Humanity, or as the Community, or as Society, or as Civilization. "An inner strenuousness was preying on his outer symmetry, and they rated his look as singular. . . . His countenance was overlaid with legible meanings. Without being thought-worn, he yet had certain marks derived from a perception of his surroundings, such as are not infrequently found on man at the end of the four or five years of endeavour which follow the close of placid pupilage. He already showed that thought is a disease of the flesh, and indirectly bore evidence that ideal physical beauty is incompatible with emotional development and a full recognition of the coil of things. Mental luminousness must be fed with the oil of life, even if there is already a physical seed for it; and the pitiful sight of two demands on one supply was just showing itself here."

But did the face of Clym show that thought is a disease of flesh, or merely that in his case a dis-ease, an un-ease, of flesh produced thought? One does not catch thought like a fever: one produces it. If it be in any way a disease of flesh, it is rather the rash that indicates the disease than the disease itself. The "inner strenuousness" of Clym's nature was not fighting against his physical symmetry, but against the limits imposed on his physical movement. By nature, as a passionate, violent product of Egdon, he should have loved and suffered in flesh and in soul from love, long before this age. He should have lived and moved and had his being, whereas he had only his business, and afterwards his inactivity. His years of pupilage were past, "he was one of whom something original was expected," yet he continued in pupilage. For he produced nothing original in being or in act, and certainly no original thought. None of his ideas were original. Even he himself was not original. He was over-taught, had become an echo. His life had been arrested, and his activity turned into repetition. Far from being emotionally developed, he was emotionally undeveloped, almost entirely. Only his mental faculties were developed. And, hid, his emotions were obliged to work according to the label he put upon them: a ready-made label.

Yet he remained for all that an original, the force of life was in him, however much he frustrated and suppressed its natural movement. "As is usual with bright natures, the deity that lies ignominiously chained within an ephemeral human carcass shone out of him like a ray." But was the deity chained within his ephemeral human carcass, or within his limited human consciousness? Was it his blood, which rose dark and potent out of Egdon, which hampered and confined the deity, or was it his mind, that house built of extraneous knowledge and guarded by his will, which formed the prison?

He came back to Egdon—what for? To re-unite himself with the strong, free flow of life that rose out of Egdon as from a source? No—"to preach to the Egdon eremites that they might rise to a serene comprehensiveness without going through the process of enriching themselves." As if the Egdon eremites had not already far more serene comprehensiveness than ever he had himself, rooted as they were in the soil of all things, and living from the root! What did it matter how they enriched themselves, so long as they kept this strong, deep root in the primal soil, so long as their instincts moved out to action and to expression? The system was big enough for them, and had no power over their instincts. They should have taught him rather than he them.

And Egdon made him marry Eustacia. Here was action and life, here was a move into being on his part. But as soon as he got her, she became an idea to him, she had to fit in his system of ideas. According to his way of living, he knew her already, she was labelled and classed and fixed down. He had got into this way of living, and he could not get out of it. He had identified himself with the system, and he could not extricate himself. He did not know that Eustacia had her being beyond his. He did not know that she existed untouched by his system and his mind, where no system had sway and where no consciousness had risen to the surface. He did not know that she was Egdon, the powerful, eternal origin seething with production. He thought he knew. Egdon to him was the tract of common land, producing familiar rough herbage, and having some few unenlightened inhabitants. So he skated over heaven and hell, and having made a map of the surface, thought he knew all. But underneath and among his mapped world, the eternal powerful fecundity worked on heedless of him and his arrogance. His preaching, his superficiality made no difference. What did it matter if he had calculated a moral chart from the surface of life? Could that affect life, any more than a chart of the heavens affects the stars, affects the whole stellar universe which exists beyond our knowledge? Could the sound of his words affect the working of the body of Egdon, where in the unfathomable womb was begot and conceived all that would ever come forth? Did not his own heart beat far removed and immune from his thinking and talking? Had he been able to put even his own heart's mysterious resonance upon his map, from which he charted the course of lives in his moral system? And how much more completely, then, had he left out, in utter ignorance, the dark, powerful source whence all things rise into being, whence they will always continue to rise, to struggle forward to further being? A little of the static surface he could see, and map out. Then he thought his map was the thing itself. How blind he was, how utterly blind to the tremendous movement carrying and producing the surface. He did not know that the greater part of every life is underground, like roots in the dark in contact with the beyond. He preached, thinking lives could be moved like hen-houses from here to there. His blindness indeed brought on the calamity. But what matter if Eustacia or Wildeve or Mrs. Yeobright died: what matter if he himself became a mere rattle of repetitive words–what did it matter? It was regrettable; no more. Egdon, the primal impulsive body, would go on producing all that was to be produced, eternally, though the will of man should destroy the blossom yet in bud, over and over again. At last he must learn what it is to be at one, in his mind and will, with the primal impulses that rise in him. Till then, let him perish or preach. The great reality on which the little tragedies enact themselves cannot be detracted from. The will and words which militate against it are the only vanity.

This is a constant revelation in Hardy's novels: that there exists a great background, vital and vivid, which matters more than the people who move upon it. Against the background of dark, passionate Egdon, of the leafy, sappy passion and sentiment of the woodlands, of the unfathomed stars, is drawn the lesser scheme of lives: *The Return of the Native, The Woodlanders,* or *Two on a Tower.* Upon the vast, incomprehensible pattern of some primal morality greater than ever the human mind can grasp, is drawn the little, pathetic pattern of man's moral life and struggle, pathetic, almost ridiculous. The little fold of law and order, the little walled city within which man has to defend himself from the waste enormity of nature, becomes always too small, and the pioneers venturing out with the code of the walled city upon them, die in the bonds of that code, free and yet unfree, preaching the walled city and looking to the waste.

This is the wonder of Hardy's novels, and gives them their beauty. The vast, unexplored morality of life itself, what we call the immorality of nature, surrounds us in its eternal incomprehensibility, and in its midst goes on the little human morality play, with its queer frame of morality and its mechanized movement; seriously, portentously, till some one of the protagonists chances to look out of the charmed circle, weary of the stage, to look into the wilderness raging round. Then he is lost, his little drama falls to pieces, or becomes mere repetition, but the stupendous theatre outside goes on enacting its own incomprehensible drama, untouched. There is this quality in almost all Hardy's work, and this is the magnificent irony it all contains, the challenge, the contempt. Not the deliberate ironies, little tales of widows or widowers, contain the irony of human life as we live it in our self-aggrandized gravity, but the big novels, *The Return of the Native,* and the others.

And this is the quality Hardy shares with the great writers, Shakespeare or Sophocles or Tolstoi, this setting behind the small action of his protagonists the terrific action of unfathomed nature; setting a smaller system of morality, the one grasped and formulated by the human consciousness within the vast, uncomprehended and incomprehensible morality of nature or of life itself, surpassing human consciousness. The difference is, that whereas in Shakespeare or Sophocles the greater, uncomprehended morality, or fate, is actively transgressed and gives active punishment, in Hardy and Tolstoi the lesser, human morality, the mechanical system is actively transgressed, and holds, and punishes the protagonist, whilst the greater morality is only passively, negatively transgressed, it is represented merely as being present in background, in scenery, not taking any active part, having no direct connexion with the protagonist. Œdipus, Hamlet, Macbeth set themselves up against, or find themselves set up against, the unfathomed moral forces of nature, and out of this unfathomed force comes their death. Whereas Anna Karenina, Eustacia, Tess, Sue, and Jude find themselves up against the established system of human government and morality, they cannot detach themselves, and are brought down. Their real tragedy is that they are unfaithful to the greater unwritten morality, which would have bidden Anna Karenina be patient and wait until she, by virtue of greater right, could take what she needed from society; would have bidden Vronsky detach himself from the system, become an individual, creating a new colony of morality with Anna; would have bidden Eustacia fight Clym for his own soul, and Tess take and claim her Angel, since she had the greater light; would have bidden Jude and Sue endure for very honour's sake, since one must bide by the best that one has known, and not succumb to the lesser good.

Had Œdipus, Hamlet, Macbeth been weaker, less full of real, potent life, they would have made no tragedy; they would have comprehended and contrived some arrangement of their affairs, sheltering in the human morality from the great stress and attack of the unknown morality. But being, as they are, men to the fullest capacity, when they find themselves, daggers drawn, with the very forces of life itself, they can only fight till they themselves are killed, since the morality of life, the greater morality, is eternally unalterable and invincible. It can be dodged for some time, but not opposed. On the other hand, Anna, Eustacia, Tess or Sue–what was there in their position that was necessarily tragic? Necessarily painful it was, but they were not at war with God, only with Society. Yet they were all cowed by the mere judgment of man upon them, and all the while by their own souls they were right. And the judgment of men killed them, not the judgment of their own souls or the judgment of Eternal God.

Which is the weakness of modern tragedy, where transgression against the social code is made to bring destruction, as though the social code worked our irrevocable fate. Like Clym, the map appears to us more real than the land. Shortsighted almost to blindness, we pore over the chart, map out journeys, and confirm them: and we cannot see life itself giving us the lie the whole time.

CHAPTER IV

An Attack on Work and the Money Appetite and on the State

There is always excess, the biologists say, a brimming-over. For they have made the measure, and the supply must be made to fit. They have charted the course, and if at the end of it there is a jump beyond the bounds into nothingness: well, there is always excess, for they have charted the journey aright.

There is always excess, a brimming-over. At spring-time a bird brims over with blue and yellow, a glow-worm brims over with a drop of green moonshine, a lark flies up like heady wine, with song, an errand-boy whistles down the road, and scents brim over the measure of the flower. Then we say, It is spring.

When is a glow-worm a glow-worm? When she's got a light on her tail. What is she when she hasn't got a light on her tail? Then she's a mere worm, an insect.

When is a man a man? When he is alight with life. Call it excess? If it is missing, there is no man, only a creature, a clod, undistinguished.

With man it is always spring—or it may be; with him every day is a blossoming day, if he will. He is a plant eternally in flower, he is an animal eternally in rut, he is a bird eternally in song. He has his excess constantly on his hands, almost every day. It is not with him a case of seasons, spring and autumn and winter. And happy man if his excess come out in blue and gold and singing, if it be not like the paste rose on the pie, a burden, at last a very sickness.

The wild creatures are like fountains whose sources gather their waters until spring-time, when they leap their highest. But man is a fountain that is always playing, leaping, ebbing, sinking, and springing up. It is not for him to gather his waters till spring-time, when his fountain, rising higher, can at last flow out flower-wise in mid-air, teeming awhile with excess, before it falls spent again.

His rhythm is not so simple. A pleasant little stream of life is a bud at autumn and winter, fluttering in flocks over the stubble, the fallow, rustling along. Till spring, when many waters rush in to the sources, and each bird is a fountain playing.

Man, fortunate or unfortunate, is rarely like an autumn bird, to enjoy his pleasant stream of life flowing at ease. Some men are like that, fortunate and delightful. But those men or women will not read this book. Why should they?

The sources of man's life are over-full, they receive more than they give out. And why? Because a man is a well-head built over a strong, perennial spring and enclosing it in, a well-head whence the water may be drawn at will, and under which the water may be held back indefinitely. Sometimes, and in certain ways, according to certain rules, the source may bubble and spring out, but only at certain times, always under control. And the fountain cannot always bide for the permission, the suppressed waters strain at the well-head, and hence so much sadness without cause. *Weltschmerz* and other unlocalized pains, where the source presses for utterance.

And how is it given utterance? In sheer play of being free? That cannot be. It shall be given utterance in work, the conscious mind has unanimously decreed. And the door is held holy. My life is to be utilized for work, first and foremost—and this in spite of Mary of Bethany.

Only, or very largely, in the work I do, must I live, must my life take movement. And why do I work? To eat—is the original answer. When I have earned enough to eat, what then? Work for more, to provide for the future. And when I have provided for the future? Work for more to provide for the poor. And when I have worked to provide for the poor, what then? Keep on working, the poor are never provided for, the poor have ye always with you.

That is the best that man has been able to do.

But what a ghastly programme! I do not want to work. You must, comes the answer. But nobody wants to work, originally. Yet everybody works, because he must—it is repeated. And what when he is not working? Let him rest and amuse himself, and get ready for tomorrow morning.

Oh, my God, work is the great body of life, and sleep and amusement like two wings, bent only to carry it along. Is this, then, all?

And Carlyle gets up and says, It is all, and mankind goes on in grim, serious approval, more than acquiescent, approving, thinking itself religiously right.

But let us pull the tail out of the mouth of this serpent. Eternity is not a process of eternal self-inglutination. We must work to eat, and eat to work—that is how it is given out. But the real problem is quite different. "We must work to eat, and eat to–what?" Don't say "work," it is so unoriginal.

In Nottingham we boys began learning German by learning proverbs. "Mann muss essen um zu leben, aber Mann muss nicht leben um zu essen," was the first. "One must eat to live, but one must not live to eat." A good German proverb according to the lesson-book. Starting a step further back, it might be written, "One must work to eat, but one must not eat to work." Surely that is just, because the second proverb says, "One must eat to live."

"One must work to eat, and eat to live," is the result.

Take this vague and almost uninterpretable word "living." To how great a degree are "to work" and "to live" synonymous? That is the question to answer, when the highest flight that our thought can take, for the sake of living, is to say that we must return to the medieval system of handicrafts, and that each man must become a labouring artist, producing a complete article.

Work is, simply, the activity necessary for the production of a sufficient supply of food and shelter: nothing more holy than that. It is the producing of the means of self-preservation. Therefore it is obvious that it is not the be-all and the end-all of existence. We work to provide means of subsistence, and when we have made provision, we proceed to live. But all work is only the making provision for that which is to follow.

It may be argued that work has a fuller meaning, that man lives most intensely when he works. That may be, for some few men, for some few artists whose lives are otherwise empty. But for the mass, for the 99.9 per cent of mankind, work is a form of non-living, of non-existence, of submergence.

It is necessary to produce food and clothing. Then, under necessity, the thing must be done as quickly as possible. Is not the highest recommendation for a labourer the fact that he is quick? And how does any man become quick, save through finding the shortest way to his end, and by repeating one set of actions? A man who can repeat certain movements accurately is an expert, if his movements are those which produce the required result.

And these movements are the calculative or scientific movements of a machine. When a man is working perfectly, he is the perfect machine. Aware of certain forces, he moves accurately along the line of their resultant. The perfect machine does the same.

All work is like this, the approximation to a perfect mechanism, more or less intricate and adjustable. The doctor, the teacher, the lawyer, just as much as the farm labourer or the mechanic, when working most perfectly, is working with the utmost of mechanical, scientific precision, along a line calculated from known fact, calculated instantaneously.

In this work, man has a certain definite, keen satisfaction. When he is utterly impersonal, when he is merely the mode where certain mechanical forces meet to find their resultant, then a man is something perfect, the perfect instrument, the perfect machine.

It is a state which, in his own line, every man strives and longs for. It is a state which satisfies his moral craving, almost the deepest craving within him. It is a state when he lies in line with the great force of gravity, partakes perfectly of its subtlest movement and motion, even to psychic vibration.

But it is a state which every man hopes for release from. The dream of every man is that in the end he shall have to work no more. The joy of every man is, when he is released from his labour, having done his share for the time being.

What does he want to be released from, and what does he want to be released unto? A man is not a machine: when he has finished work, he is not motionless, inert. He begins a new activity. And what?

It seems to me as if a man, in his normal state, were like a palpitating leading-shoot of life, where the unknown, all unresolved, beats and pulses, containing the quick of all experience, as yet unrevealed, not singled out. But when he thinks, when he moves, he is retracing some proved experience. He is as the leading-shoot which, for the moment, remembers only that which is behind, the fixed wood, the cells conducting towards their undifferentiated tissue of life. He moves as it were in the trunk of the tree, in the channels long since built, where the sap must flow as in a canal. He takes knowledge of all this past experience upon which the new tip rides quivering, he becomes again the old life, which has built itself out in the fixed tissue, he lies in line with the old movement, unconscious of where it breaks, at the growing plasm, into something new, unknown. He is happy, all is known, all is finite, all is established, and knowledge can be perfect here in the trunk of the tree, which life built up and climbed beyond.

Such is a man at work, safe within the proven, deposited experience, thrilling as he traverses the fixed channels and courses of life; he is only matter of some of the open ways which life laid down for its own passage; he has only made himself one with what has been, travelling the old, fixed courses, through which life still passes, but which are not in themselves living.

And in the end, this is always a prison to him, this proven, deposited experience which he must explore, this past of life. For is he not in himself a growing tip, is not his own body a quivering plasm of what will be, and has never yet been? Is not his own soul a fighting-line, where what is and what will be separates itself off from what has been? Is not this his purest joy of movement, the indistinguishable, complex movement of being? And is not this his deepest desire, to be himself, to be this quivering bud of growing tissue which he is? He may find knowledge by retracing the old courses, he may satisfy his moral sense by working within the known, certain of what he is doing. But for real, utter satisfaction, he must give himself up to complete quivering uncertainty, to sentient non-knowledge.

And this is why man is always crying out for freedom, to be free. He wants to be free to be himself. For this reason he has always made a heaven where no work need be done, where to *be* is all, where to *be* comprises all that has been done, is perfect knowledge, and where that which will be done is so swift as to be a sleep, a Nirvana, an absorption.

So there is this deepest craving of all, to be free from the necessity to work. It is obvious in all mankind. "Must I become one with the old, habitual movements?" says man. "I must, to satisfy myself that the new is new and the old is old, that all is one like a tree, though I am no more than the tiniest cell in the tree." So he becomes one with the old, habitual movement: he is the perfect machine, the perfect instrument: he works. But, satisfied for the time being of that which has been and remains now finite, he wearies for his own limitless being, for the unresolved, quivering, infinitely complex and indefinite movement of new living, he wants to be free.

And ever, as his knowledge of what is past becomes greater, he wants more and more liberty to be himself. There is the necessity for self-preservation, the necessity to submerge himself in the utter mechanical movement. But why so much: why repeat so often the mechanical movement? Let me not have so much of this work to do, let me not be consumed overmuch in my own self-preservation, let me not be imprisoned in this proven, finite experience all my days.

This has been the cry of humanity since the world began. This is the glamour of kings, the glamour of men who had opportunity to *be,* who were not under compulsion to do, to serve. This is why kings were chosen heroes, because they were the beings, the producers of new life, not servants of necessity, repeating old experience.

And humanity has laboured to make work shorter, so we may all be kings. True, we have the necessity to work, more or less, according as we are near the growing tip, or further away. Some men are far from the growing tip. They have little for growth in them, only the power for repeating old movement. They will always find their own level. But let those that have life, live.

So there has been produced machinery, to take the place of the human machine. And the inventor of the labour-saving machine has been hailed as a public benefactor, and we have rejoiced over his discovery. Now there is a railing against the machine, as if it were an evil thing. And the thinkers talk about the return to the medieval system of handicrafts. Which is absurd.

As I look round this room, at the bed, at the counterpane, at the books and chairs and the little bottles, and think that machines made them, I am glad. I am very glad of the bedstead, of the white enamelled iron with brass rail. As it stands, I rejoice over its essential simplicity. I would not wish it different. Its lines are straight and parallel, or at right angles, giving a sense of static motionlessness. Only that which is necessary is there, whittled down to the minimum. There is nothing to hurt me or to hinder me; my wish for something to serve my purpose is perfectly fulfilled.

Which is what a machine can do. It can provide me with the perfect mechanical instrument, a thing mathematically and scientifically correct. Which is what I want. I like the books, on the whole, I can scarcely imagine them more convenient to me, I like the common green-glass smelling-salts, and the machine-turned feet of the common chest of drawers. I hate the machine-carving on a chair, and the stamped pattern on a rug. But I have no business to ask a machine to make beautiful things for me. I can ask it for perfect accommodating utensils or articles of use, and I shall get them.

Wherefore I do honour to the machine and to its inventor. It will produce what we want, and save us the necessity of much labour. Which is what it was invented for.

But to what pitiable misuse is it put! Do we use the machine to produce goods for our need, or is it used as a muck-rake for raking together heaps of money? Why, when man, in his godly effort, has produced a means to freedom, do we make it a means to more slavery?

Why?—because the heart of man is crude and greedy. Why is a labourer willing to work ten hours a day for a mere pittance? Because he is serving a system for the enrichment of the individual, a system to which he subscribes, because he might himself be that individual, and, since his one ideal is to be rich, he owes his allegiance to the system established for the raking of riches into heaps, a system that satisfies his imagination. Why try to alter the present industrial system on behalf of the working-man, when his imagination is satisfied only by such a system?

The poor man and the rich, they are the head and tail of the same penny. Stand them naked side by side, and which is better than the other? The rich man, probably, for he is likely to be the sadder and the wiser.

The universal ideal, the one conscious ideal of the poor people, is riches. The only hope lies in those people, who, in fact or imagination, have experienced wealth, and have appetites accordingly.

It is not true, that, before we can get over our absorbing passion to be rich, we must each one of us know wealth. There are sufficient people with sound imagination and normal appetite to put away the whole money tyranny of England today.

There is no evil in money. If there were a million pounds under my bed, and I did not know of it, it would make no difference to me. If there were a million pounds under my bed, and I did know of it, it would make a difference, perhaps, to the form of my life, but to the living me, and to my individual purpose, it could make no difference, since I depend neither on riches nor on poverty for my being.

Neither poverty nor riches obsesses me. I would not be like a begging friar to forswear all owing and having. For I would not admit myself so weak that either I must abstain totally from wealth, or succumb to the passion for possessions.

Have I not a normal money appetite, as I have a normal appetite for food? Do I want to kill a hundred bison, to satisfy the imaginative need of my stomach, as the Red Indian did? Then why should I want a thousand pounds, when ten are enough? "Thy eyes are bigger than thy belly," says the mother of the child who takes more than he can eat. "Your pocket is bigger than your breeches," one could say to a man greedy to get rich.

It is only greediness. But it is very wearisome. There are plenty of people who are not greedy, who have normal money appetites. They need a certain amount, and they know they need it. It is no honour to be a pauper. It is only decent that every man should have enough and a little to spare, and every self-respecting man will see he gets it. But why can't we really grow up, and become adult with regard to money as with regard to food? Why can't we know when we have enough, as we know when we have had enough to eat?

We could, of course, if we had any real sense of values. It is all very well to leave, as Christianity tries to leave, the dinner to be devoured by the glutton, whilst the Christian draws off in disgust, and fasts. But we each have our place at the board, as we well know, and it is indecent to withdraw before the glutton, leaving the earth to be devoured.

Can we not stay at the board? We must eat to live. And living is not simply not-dying. It is the only real thing, it is the aim and end of all life. Work is only a means to subsistence. The work done, the living earned, how then to go on to enjoy it, to fulfil it, that is the question. How shall a man live? What do we mean by living?

Let every man answer for himself. We only know, we want the freedom to live, the freedom of leisure and means. But there are ample means, there is half an eternity of pure leisure for mankind to take, if he would, if he did not think, at the back of his mind, that riches are the means of freedom. Riches would be the means of freedom, if there were no poor, if there were equal riches everywhere. Till then, riches and poverty alike are bonds and prisons, for every man must live in the ring of his own defences, to defend his property. And this ring is the surest of prisons.

So cannot we see, rich and poor alike, how we have circumscribed, hampered, imprisoned ourselves within the limits of our poor-and-rich system, till our life is utterly pot-bound? It is not that some of us want more money and some of us less. It is that our money is like walls between us, we are immured in gold, and we die of starvation or etiolation.

A plant has strength to burst its pot. The shoots of London trees have force to burst through the London pavements. Is there not life enough in us to break out of this system? Let every man take his own, and go his own way, regardless of system and State, when his hour comes. Which is greater, the State or myself? Myself, unquestionably, since the State is only an arrangement made for my convenience. If it is not convenient for me, I must depart from it. There is no need to break laws. The only need is to be a law unto oneself.

And if sufficient people came out of the walled defences, and pitched in the open, then very soon the walled city would be a mere dependent on the free tents of the wilderness. Why should we care about bursting the city walls? We can walk through the gates into the open world. Those State educations with their ideals, their armaments of aggression and defence, what are they to me? They must fight out their own fates. As for me, I would say to every decent man whose heart is straining at the enclosure, "Come away from the crowd and the community, come away and be separate in your own soul, and live. Your business is to produce your own real life, no matter what the nations do. The nations are made up of individual men, each man will know at length that he must single himself out, nor remain any longer embedded in the matrix of his nation, or community, or class. Our time has come; let us draw apart. Let the physician heal himself."

And outside, what will it matter save that a man is a man, is himself? If he must work, let him work a few hours a day, a very few, whether it be at wheeling bricks, or shovelling coal into a furnace, or tending a machine. Let him do his work, according to his kind, for some three or four hours a day. That will produce supplies in ample sufficiency. Then let him have twenty hours for being himself, for producing himself.

CHAPTER V

Work and the Angel and the Unbegotten Hero

It is an inherent passion, this will to work, it is a craving to produce, to create, to be as God. Man turns his back on the unknown, on that which is yet to be, he turns his face towards that which has been, and he sees, he rediscovers, he becomes again that which has been before. But this time he is conscious, he knows what he is doing. He can at will reproduce the movement life made in its initial passage, the movement life still makes, and will continue to make, as a habit, the movement already made so unthinkably often that rather than a movement it has become a state, a condition of all life; it has become matter, or the force of gravity, or cohesion, or heat, or light. These old, old habits of life man rejoices to rediscover in all their detail.

Long, long ago life first rolled itself into seed, and fell to earth, and covered itself up with soil, slowly. And long, long ago man discovered the process, joyfully, and, in this wise as God, repeated it. He found out how soil is shifted. Proud as a needy God, he dug the ground, and threw the little, silent fragments of life under the dust. And was he not doing what life itself had initiated, was he not, in this particular, even greater than life, more definite?

Still further back, in an unthinkable period long before chaos, life formed the habit we call gravitation. This was almost before any differentiation, before all those later, lesser habits, which we call matter or such a thing as centrifugal force, were formed. It was a habit of the great mass of life, not of any part in particular. Therefore it took man's consciousness much longer to apprehend, and even now we have only some indications of it, from various parts. But we rejoice in that which we know. Long, long ago, one surface of matter learned to roll on a rolling motion across another surface, as the tide rolls up the land. And long ago man saw this motion, and learned a secret, and made the wheel, and rejoiced.

So, facing both ways, like Janus, face forward, in the quivering, glimmering fringe of the unresolved, facing the unknown, and looking backward over the vast rolling tract of life which follows and represents the initial movement, man is given up to his dual business, of being, in blindness and wonder and pure godliness, the living stuff of life itself, unrevealed; and of knowing, with unwearying labour and unceasing success, the manner of that which has been, which is revealed.

And work is the repetition of some one of those rediscovered movements, the enacting of some part imitated from life, the attaining of a similar result as life attained. And this, even if it be only shovelling coal onto a fire, or hammering nails into a shoe-sole, or making accounts in ledgers, is what work is, and in this lies the initial satisfaction of labour. The motive of labour, that of obtaining wages, is only the overcoming of inertia. It is not the real driving force. When necessity alone compels man, from moment to moment, to work, then man rebels and dies. The driving force is the pleasure in doing something, the living will to work.

And man must always struggle against the *necessity* to work, though the necessity to work is one of the inevitable conditions of man's existence. And no man can continue in any piece of work, out of sheer necessity, devoid of any essential pleasure in that work.

It seems as if the great aim and purpose in human life were to bring all life into the human consciousness. And this is the final meaning of work: the extension of human consciousness. The lesser meaning of work is the achieving of self-preservation. From this lesser, immediate necessity man always struggles to be free. From the other, greater necessity, of extending the human consciousness, man does not struggle to be free.

And to the immediate necessity for self-preservation man must concede, but always having in mind the other, greater necessity, to which he would hasten.

But the bringing of life into human consciousness is not an aim in itself, it is only a necessary condition of the progress of life itself. Man is himself the vivid body of life, rolling glimmering against the void. In his fullest living he does not know what he does, his mind, his consciousness, unacquaint, hovers behind, full of extraneous gleams and glances, and altogether devoid of knowledge. Altogether devoid of knowledge and conscious motive is he when he is heaving into uncreated space, when he is actually living, becoming himself.

And yet, that he may go on, may proceed with his living, it is necessary that his mind, his consciousness, should extend behind him. The mind itself is one of life's later-developed habits. *To know* is a force, like any other force. Knowledge is only one of the conditions of this force, as combustion is one of the conditions of heat. *To will* is only a manifestation of the same force, as expansion may be a manifestation of heat. And this knowing is now an inevitable habit of life's, developed late; it is a force active in the immediate rear of life, and the greater its activity, the greater the forward, unknown movement ahead of it.

It seems as though one of the conditions of life is, that life shall continually and progressively differentiate itself, almost as though this differentiation were a Purpose. Life starts crude and unspecified, a great Mass. And it proceeds to evolve out of that mass ever more distinct and definite particular forms, an ever-multiplying number of separate species and orders, as if it were working always to the production of the infinite number of perfect individuals, the individual so thorough that he should have nothing in common with any other individual. It is as if all coagulation must be loosened, as if the elements must work themselves free and pure from the compound.

Man's consciousness, that is, his mind, his knowledge, is his greater manifestation of individuality. With his consciousness he can perceive and know that which is not himself. The further he goes, the more extended his consciousness, the more he realizes the things that are not himself. Everything he perceives, everything he knows, everything he feels, is something extraneous to him, is not himself, and his perception of it is like a cell-wall, or more, a real space separating him. I see a flower, because it is not me. I know a melody, because it is not me. I feel cold, because it is not me. I feel joy when I kiss, because it is not me, the kiss, but rather one of the bounds or limits where I end. But the kiss is a closer division of me from the mass than a sense of cold or heat. It whittles the more keenly naked from the gross.

And the more that I am driven from admixture, the more I am singled out into utter individuality, the more this intrinsic me rejoices. For I am as yet a gross impurity, I partake of everything. I am still rudimentary, part of a great, unquickened lump.

In the origin, life must have been uniform, a great, unmoved, utterly homogeneous infinity, a great not-being, at once a positive and negative infinity: the whole universe, the whole infinity, one motionless homogeneity, a something, a nothing. And yet it can never have been utterly homogeneous: mathematically, yes; actually, no. There must always have been some reaction, infinitesimally faint, stirring somehow through the vast, homogeneous inertia.

And since the beginning, the reaction has become extended and intensified; what was one great mass of individual constituency has stirred and resolved itself into many smaller, characteristic parts; what was an utter, infinite neutrality, has become evolved into still rudimentary, but positive, orders and species. So on and on till we get to naked jelly, and from naked jelly to enclosed and separated jelly, from homogeneous tissue to organic tissue, on and on, from invertebrates to mammals, from mammals to man, from man to tribesman, from tribesman to me: and on and on, till, in the future, wonderful, distinct individuals, like angels, move about, each one being himself, perfect as a complete melody or a pure colour.

Now one craves that his life should be more individual, that I and you and my neighbour should each be distinct in clarity from each other, perfectly distinct from the general mass. Then it would be a melody if I walked down the road; if I stood with my neighbour, it would be a pure harmony.

Could I, then, being my perfect self, be selfish? A selfish person is an impure person, one who wants that which is not himself. Selfishness implies admixture, grossness, unclarity of being. How can I, a pure person incapable of being anything but myself, detract from my neighbour? That which is mine is singled out to me from the mass, and to each man is left his own. And what can any man want for, except that which is his own, if he be himself? If he have that which is not his own, it is a burden, he is not himself. And how can I help my neighbour except by being utterly myself? That gives him into himself: which is the greatest gift a man can receive.

And necessarily accompanying this more perfect being of myself is the more extended knowledge of that which is not myself. That is, the finer, more distinct the individual, the more finely and distinctly is he aware of all other individuality. It needs a delicate, pure soul to distinguish between the souls of others; it needs a thing which is purely itself to see other things in their purity or their impurity.

Yet in life, so often, one feels that a man who is, by nature, intrinsically an individual, is by practice and knowledge an impurity, almost a nonentity. To each individuality belongs, by nature, its own knowledge. It would seem as if each soul, detaching itself from the mass, the matrix, should achieve its own knowledge. Yet this is not so. Many a soul which we feel should have detached itself and become distinct, remains embedded, and struggles with knowledge that does not pertain to it. It reached a point of distinctness and a degree of personal knowledge, and then became confused, lost itself.

And then, it sought for its whole being in work. By re-enacting some old movement of life's, a struggling soul seeks to detach itself, to become pure. By gathering all the knowledge possible, it seeks to receive the stimulus which shall help it to continue to distinguish itself.

"Ye must be born again," it is said to us. Once we are born, detached from the flesh and blood of our parents, issued separate, as distinct creatures. And later on, the incomplete germ which is a young soul must be fertilized, the parent womb which encloses the incomplete individuality must conceive, and we must be brought forth to ourselves, distinct. This is at the age of twenty or thirty.

And we, who imagine we live by knowledge, imagine that the impetus for our second birth must come from knowledge, that the germ, the sperm impulse, can come out of some utterance only. So, when I am young, at eighteen, twenty, twenty-three, when the anguish of desire comes upon me, as I lie in the womb of my times, to receive the quickening, the impetus, I send forth all my calls and call hither and thither, asking for the Word, the Word which is the spermatozoon which shall come and fertilize me and set me free. And it may be the word, the idea exists which shall bring me forth, give me birth. But it may also be that the word, the idea, has never yet been uttered.

Shall I, then, be able, with all the knowledge in the world, to produce my being, if the knowledge be not extant? I shall not.

And yet we believe that only the Uttered Word can come into us and give us the impetus to our second birth. Give us a religion, give us something to believe in, cries the unsatisfied soul embedded in the womb of our times. Speak the quickening word, it cries, that will deliver us into our own being.

So it searches out the Spoken Word, and finds it, or finds it not. Possibly it is not yet uttered. But all that will be uttered lies potent in life. The fools do not know this. They think the fruit of knowledge is found only in shops. They will go anywhere to find it, save to the Tree. For the Tree is so obvious, and seems so played out.

Therefore the unsatisfied soul remains unsatisfied, and chooses Work, maybe Good Works, for its incomplete action. It thinks that in work it has being, in knowledge it has gained its distinct self.

Whereas all amount of clumsy distinguishing ourselves from other things will not make us thus become ourselves, and all amount of repeating even the most complex motions of life will not produce one new motion.

We start the wrong way round: thinking, by learning what we are not, to know what we as individuals are: whereas the whole of the human consciousness contains, as we know, not a tithe of what *is*, and therefore it is hopeless to proceed by a method of elimination; and thinking, by discovering the motion life has made, to be able therefrom to produce the motion it will make: whereas we know that, in life, the new motion is not the resultant of the old, but something quite new, quite other, according to our perception.

So we struggle mechanically, unformed, unbegotten, unborn, repeating some old process of life, unable to become ourselves, unable to produce anything new.

Looking over the Hardy novels, it is interesting to see which of the heroes one would call a distinct individuality, more or less achieved, which an unaccomplished potential individuality, and which an impure, unindividualized life embedded in the matrix, either achieving its own lower degree of distinction, or not achieving it.

In *Desperate Remedies* there are scarcely any people at all, particularly when the plot is working. The tiresome part about Hardy is that, so often, he will neither write a morality play nor a novel. The people of the first book, as far as the plot is concerned, are not people: they are the heroine, faultless and white; the hero, with a small spot on his whiteness; the villainess, red and black, but more red than black; the villain, black and red; the Murderer, aided by the Adulteress, obtains power over the Virgin, who, rescued at the last moment by the Virgin Knight, evades the evil clutch. Then the Murderer, overtaken by vengeance, is put to death, whilst Divine Justice descends upon the Adulteress. Then the Virgin unites with the Virgin Knight, and receives Divine Blessing.

That is a morality play, and if the morality were vigorous and original, all well and good. But, between-whiles, we see that the Virgin is being played by a nice, rather ordinary girl.

In *The Laodicean,* there is all the way through a *prédilection d'artiste* for the aristocrat, and all the way through a moral condemnation of him, a substituting the middle or lower-class personage with bourgeois virtues into his place. This was the root of Hardy's pessimism. Not until he comes to Tess and Jude does he ever sympathize with the aristocrat—unless it be in *The Mayor of Casterbridge,* and then he sympathizes only to slay. He always, always represents them the same, as having some vital weakness, some radical ineffectuality. From first to last it is the same.

Miss Aldclyffe and Manston, Elfride and the sickly lord she married, Troy and Farmer Boldwood, Eustacia Vye and Wildeve, de Stancy in *The Laodicean,* Lady Constantine in *Two on a Tower,* the Mayor of Casterbridge and Lucetta, Mrs. Charmond and Dr. Fitzpiers in *The Woodlanders,* Tess and Alec d'Urberville, and, though different, Jude. There is also the blond, passionate, yielding man: Sergeant Troy, Wildeve, and, in spirit, Jude.

These are all, in their way, the aristocrat-characters of Hardy. They must every one die, every single one.

Why has Hardy this *prédilection d'artiste* for the aristocrat, and why, at the same time, this moral antagonism to him?

It is fairly obvious in *The Laodicean,* a book where, the spirit being small, the complaint is narrow. The heroine, the daughter of a famous railway engineer, lives in the castle of the old de Stancys. She sighs, wishing she were of the de Stancy line: the tombs and portraits have a spell over her. "But," says the hero to her, "have you forgotten your father's line of ancestry: Archimedes, Newcomen, Watt, Tylford, Stephenson?"—"But I have a *prédilection d'artiste* for ancestors of the other sort," sighs Paula. And the hero despairs of impressing her with the list of his architect ancestors: Phidias, Ictinus and Callicrates, Chersiphron, Vitruvius, Wilars of Cambray, William of Wykeham. He deplores her marked preference for an "animal pedigree."

But what is this "animal pedigree"? If a family pedigree of her ancestors, working-men and burghers, had been kept, Paula would not have gloried in it, animal though it were. Hers was a *prédilection d'artiste.*

And this because the aristocrat alone has occupied a position where he could afford to *be,* to be himself, to create himself, to live as himself. That is his eternal fascination. This is why the preference for him is a *prédilection d'artiste.* The preference for the architect line would be a *prédilection de savant,* the preference for the engineer pedigree would be a *prédilection d'economiste.*

The *prédilection d'artiste*—Hardy has it strongly, and it is rooted deeply in every imaginative human being. The glory of mankind has been to produce lives, to produce vivid, independent, individual men, not buildings or engineering works or even art, not even the public good. The glory of mankind is not in a host of secure, comfortable, law-abiding citizens, but in the few more fine, clear lives, beings, individuals, distinct, detached, single as may be from the public.

And these the artist of all time has chosen. Why, then, must the aristocrat always be condemned to death, in Hardy? Has the community come to consciousness in him, as in the French Revolutionaries, determined to destroy all that is not the average? Certainly in the Wessex novels, all but the average people die. But why? Is there the germ of death in these more single, distinguished people, or has the artist himself a bourgeois taint, a jealous vindictiveness that will now take revenge, now that the community, the average, has gained power over the aristocrat, the exception?

It is evident that both is true. Starting with the bourgeois morality, Hardy makes every exceptional person a villain, all exceptional or strong individual traits he holds up as weaknesses or wicked faults. So in *Desperate Remedies, Under the Greenwood Tree, Far from the Madding Crowd, The Hand of Ethelberta, The Return of the Native* (but in *The Trumpet-Major* there is an ironical dig in the ribs to this civic communal morality), *The Laodicean, Two on a*

Tower, The Mayor of Casterbridge, and *Tess,* in steadily weakening degree. The blackest villain is Manston, the next, perhaps, Troy, the next Eustacia, and Wildeve, always becoming less villainous and more human. The first show of real sympathy, nearly conquering the bourgeois or commune morality, is for Eustacia, whilst the dark villain is becoming merely a weak, pitiable person in Dr. Fitzpiers. In *The Mayor of Casterbridge* the dark villain is already almost the hero. There is a lapse in the maudlin, weak but not wicked Dr. Fitzpiers, duly condemned, Alec d'Urberville is not unlikable, and Jude is a complete tragic hero, at once the old Virgin Knight and Dark Villain. The condemnation gradually shifts over from the dark villain to the blond bourgeois virgin hero, from Alec d'Urberville to Angel Clare, till in Jude they are united and loved, though the preponderance is of a dark villain, now dark, beloved, passionate hero. The condemnation shifts over at last from the dark villain to the white virgin, the bourgeois in soul: from Arabella to Sue. Infinitely more subtle and sad is the condemnation at the end, but there it is: the virgin knight is hated with intensity, yet still loved; the white virgin, the beloved, is the arch-sinner against life at last, and the last note of hatred is against her.

It is a complete and devastating shift-over, it is a complete *volte-face* of moralities. Black does not become white, but it takes white's place as good; white remains white, but it is found bad. The old, communal morality is like a leprosy, a white sickness: the old, anti-social, individualist morality is alone on the side of life and health.

But yet, the aristocrat must die, all the way through: even Jude. Was the germ of death in him at the start? Or was he merely at outs with his times, the times of the Average in triumph? Would Manston, Troy, Farmer Boldwood, Eustacia, de Stancy, Henchard, Alec d'Urberville, Jude have been real heroes in heroic times, without tragedy? It seems as if Manston, Boldwood, Eustacia, Henchard, Alec d'Urberville, and almost Jude, might have been. In an heroic age they might have lived and more or less triumphed. But Troy, Wildeve, de Stancy, Fitzpiers, and Jude have something fatal in them. There is a rottenness at the core of them. The failure, the misfortune, or the tragedy, whichever it may be, was inherent in them: as it was in Elfride, Lady Constantine, Marty South in *The Woodlanders,* and Tess. They have all passionate natures, and in them all failure is inherent.

So that we have, of men, the noble Lord in *A Pair of Blue Eyes,*

Sergeant Troy, Wildeve, de Stancy, Fitzpiers, and Jude, all passionate, aristocratic males, doomed by their very being, to tragedy, or to misfortune in the end.

Of the same class among women are Elfride, Lady Constantine, Marty South, and Tess, all aristocratic, passionate, yet necessarily unfortunate females.

We have also, of men, Manston, Farmer Boldwood, Henchard, Alec d'Urberville, and perhaps Jude, all passionate, aristocratic males, who fell before the weight of the average, the lawful crowd, but who, in more primitive times, would have formed romantic rather than tragic figures.

Of women in the same class are Miss Aldclyffe, Eustacia, Lucetta, Mrs. Charmond.

The third class, of bourgeois or average hero, whose purpose is to live and have his being in the community, contains the successful hero of *Desperate Remedies,* the unsuccessful but not very much injured two heroes of *A Pair of Blue Eyes,* the successful Gabriel Oak, the unsuccessful, left-preaching Clym, the unsuccessful but not very much injured astronomer of *Two on a Tower,* the successful Scotchman of Casterbridge, the unsuccessful and expired Giles Winterborne of *The Woodlanders,* the arch-type, Angel Clare, and perhaps a little of Jude.

The companion women to these men are: the heroine of *Desperate Remedies,* Bathsheba, Thomasin, Paula, Henchard's daughter, Grace in *The Woodlanders,* and Sue.

This, then, is the moral conclusion drawn from the novels:

1. The physical individual is in the end an inferior thing which must fall before the community: Manston, Henchard, etc.

2. The physical and spiritual individualist is a fine thing which must fall because of its own isolation, because it is a sport, not in the true line of life: Jude, Tess, Lady Constantine.

3. The physical individualist and spiritual bourgeois or communist is a thing, finally, of ugly, undeveloped, non-distinguished or perverted physical instinct, and must fall physically. Sue, Angel Clare, Clym, Knight. It remains, however, fitted into the community.

4. The undistinguished, bourgeois or average being with average or civic virtues usually succeeds in the end. If he fails, he is left practically uninjured. If he expire during probation, he has flowers on his grave.

By individualist is meant, not a selfish or greedy person, anxious to satisfy appetites, but a man of distinct being, who must act in his own particular way to fulfil his own individual nature. He is a man who, being beyond the average, chooses to rule his own life to his own completion, and as such is an aristocrat.

The artist always has a predilection for him. But Hardy, like Tolstoi, is forced in the issue always to stand with the community in condemnation of the aristocrat. He cannot help himself, but must stand with the average against the exception, he must, in his ultimate judgment, represent the interests of humanity, or the community as a whole, and rule out the individual interest.

To do this, however, he must go against himself. His private sympathy is always with the individual against the community: as is the case with the artist. Therefore he will create a more or less blameless individual and, making him seek his own fulfilment, his highest aim, will show him destroyed by the community, or by that in himself which represents the community, or by some close embodiment of the civic idea. Hence the pessimism. To do this, however, he must select his individual with a definite weakness, a certain coldness of temper, inelastic, a certain inevitable and inconquerable adhesion to the community.

This is obvious in Troy, Clym, Tess, and Jude. They have naturally distinct individuality but, as it were, a weak life-flow, so that they cannot break away from the old adhesion, they cannot separate themselves from the mass which bore them, they cannot detach themselves from the common. Therefore they are pathetic rather than tragic figures. They have not the necessary strength: the question of their unfortunate end is begged in the beginning.

Whereas Œdipus or Agamemnon or Clytemnestra or Orestes, or Macbeth or Hamlet or Lear, these are destroyed by their own conflicting passions. Out of greed for adventure, a desire to be off, Agamemnon sacrifices Iphigenia: moreover he has his love-affairs outside Troy: and this brings on him death from the mother of his daughter, and from his pledged wife. Which is the working of the natural law. Hamlet, a later Orestes, is commanded by the Erinyes of his father to kill his mother and his uncle: but his maternal filial feeling tears him. It is almost the same tragedy as Orestes, without any goddess or god to grant peace.

In these plays, conventional morality is transcended. The action is between the great, single, individual forces in the nature of Man, not between the dictates of the community and the original passion. The Commandment says: "Thou shalt not kill." But doubtless Macbeth had killed many a man who was in his way. Certainly Hamlet suffered no qualms about killing the old man behind the curtain. Why should he? But when Macbeth killed Duncan, he divided himself in twain, into two hostile parts. It was all in his own soul and blood: it was nothing outside himself: as it was, really, with Clym, Troy, Tess, Jude. Troy would probably have been faithful to his little unfortunate person, had she been a lady, and had he not felt himself cut off from society in his very being, whilst all the time he cleaved to it. Tess allowed herself to be condemned, and asked for punishment from Angel Clare. Why? She had done nothing particularly, or at least irrevocably, unnatural, were her life young and strong. But she sided with the community's condemnation of her. And almost the bitterest, most pathetic, deepest part of Jude's misfortune was his failure to obtain admission to Oxford, his failure to gain his place and standing in the world's knowledge, in the world's work.

There is a lack of sternness, there is a hesitating betwixt life and public opinion, which diminishes the Wessex novels from the rank of pure tragedy. It is not so much the eternal, immutable laws of being which are transgressed, it is not that vital life-forces are set in conflict with each other, bringing almost inevitable tragedy—yet not necessarily death, as we see in the most splendid Æschylus. It is, in Wessex, that the individual succumbs to what is in its shallowest, public opinion, in its deepest, the human compact by which we live together, to form a community.

CHAPTER VI

The Axle and the Wheel of Eternity

It is agreed, then, that we will do a little work—two or three hours a day—labouring for the community, to produce the ample necessities of life. Then we will be free.

Free for what? The terror of the ordinary man is lest leisure should come upon him. His eternal, divine instinct is to free himself from the labour of providing what we call the necessities of life, in the common sense. And his personal horror is of finding himself with nothing to do.

What does a flower do? It provides itself with the necessities of life, it propagates itself in its seeds, and it has its fling all in one. Out from the crest and summit comes the fiery self, the flower, gorgeously.

This is the fall into the future, like a waterfall that tumbles over the edge of the known world into the unknown. The little, individualized river of life issues out of its source, its little seed, its well-head, flows on and on, making its course as it goes, establishing a bed of green tissue and stalks, flows on, and draws near the edge where all things disappear. Then the stream divides. Part hangs back, recovers itself, and lies quiescent, in seed. The rest flows over, the rest dips into the unknown, and is gone.

The same with man. He has to build his own tissue and form, serving the community for the means wherewithal, and then he comes to the climax. And at the climax, simultaneously, he begins to roll to the edge of the unknown, and, in the same moment, lays down his seed for security's sake. That is the secret of life: it contains the lesser motions in the greater. In love, a man, a woman, flows on to the very furthest edge of known feeling, being, and out beyond the furthest edge: and taking the superb and supreme risk, deposits a security of life in the womb.

Am I here to deposit security, continuance of life in the flesh? Or is that only a minor function in me? Is it not merely a preservative measure, procreation? It is the same for me as for any man or woman. That she bear children is not a woman's significance. But that she bear herself, that is her supreme and risky fate: that she drive on to the edge of the unknown, and beyond. She may leave children behind, for security. It is arranged so.

It is so arranged that the very act which carries us out into the unknown shall probably deposit seed for security to be left behind. But the act, called the sexual act, is not for the depositing of the seed. It is for leaping off into the unknown, as from a cliff's edge, like Sappho into the sea.

It is so plain in my plant, the poppy. Out of the living river, a fine silver stream detaches itself, and flows through a green bed which it makes for itself. It flows on and on, till it reaches the crest beyond which is ethereal space. Then, in tiny, concentrated pools, a little hangs back, in reservoirs that shall later seal themselves up as quick but silent sources. But the whole, almost the whole, splashes splendidly over, is seen in red just as it drips into darkness, and disappears.

So with a man in the act of love. A little of him, a very little, flows into the tiny quick pool to start another source. But the whole spills over in waste to the beyond.

And only at high flood should the little hollows fill to make a new source. Only when the whole rises to pour in a great wave over the edge of all that has been, should the little seed-wells run full. In the woman lie the reservoirs. And when there comes the flood-tide, then the dual stream of woman and man, as the whole two waves meet and break to foam, bursting into the unknown, these wells and fountain heads are filled.

Thus man and woman pass beyond this Has-Been and this is when the two waves meet in flood and heave over and out of Time, leaving their dole to Time deposited. It is for this man needs liberty, and to prepare him for this he must use his leisure.

Always so that the wave of his being shall meet the other wave, that the two shall make flood which shall flow beyond the face of the earth, must a man live. Always the dual wave. Where does my poppy spill over in red, but there where the two streams have flowed and clasped together, where the pollen stream clashes into the pistil stream, where the male clashes into the female, and the two heave out in utterance. There, in the seethe of male and female, seeds are filled as the flood rises to pour out in a red fall. There, only there, where the male seethes against the female, comes the transcendent flame and the filling of seeds.

In plants where the male stream and the female stream flow separately, as in dog's mercury or in the oak tree, where is the flame? It is not. But in my poppy, where at the summit the two streams, which till now have run deviously, scattered down many ways, at length flow concentrated together, and the pure male stream meets the pure female stream in a heave and an overflowing: there, there is the flower indeed.

And this is happiness: that my poppy gather his material and build his tissue till he has led the stream of life in him on and on to the end, to the whirlpool at the summit, where the male seethes and whirls in incredible speed upon the pivot of the female, where the two are one, as axle and wheel are one, and the motions travel out to infinity. There, where he is a complete full stream, travelling with and upon the other complete female stream, the twain make a flood over the face of all the earth, which shall pass away from the earth. And since I am a man with a body of flesh, I shall contain the seed to make sure this continuing of life in this body of flesh, I shall contain the seed for the woman of flesh in whom to beget my children.

But this is an incorporate need: it is really no separate or distinct need. The clear, full, inevitable need in me is that I, the male, meet the female stream which shall carry mine so that the two run to fullest flood, to furthest motion. It is no primary need of the begetting of children. It is the arriving at my highest mark of activity, of being; it is her arrival at her intensest self.

Why do we consider the male stream and the female stream as being only in the flesh? It is something other than physical. The physical, what we call in its narrowest meaning, the sex, is only a definite indication of the great male and female duality and unity. It is that part which is settled into an almost mechanized system of detaining some of the life which otherwise sweeps on and is lost in the full adventure.

There is female apart from Woman, as we know, and male apart from Man. There is male and female in my poppy plant, and this is neither man nor woman. It is part of the great twin river, eternally each branch resistant to the other, eternally running each to meet the other.

It may be said that male and female are terms relative only to physical sex. But this is the consistent indication of the greater meaning. Do we for a moment believe that a man is a man and a woman a woman, merely according to, and for the purpose of, the begetting of children? If there were organic reproduction of children, would there be no distinction between man and woman? Should we all be asexual?

We know that our view is partial. Man is man, and woman is woman, whether no children be born any more for ever. As long as time lasts, man is man. In eternity, where infinite motion becomes rest, the two may be one. But until eternity man is man. Until eternity, there shall be this separateness, this interaction of man upon woman, male upon female, this suffering, this delight, this imperfection. In eternity, maybe, the action may be perfect. In infinity, the spinning of the wheel upon the hub may be a frictionless whole, complete, an unbroken sleep that is infinite, motion that is utter rest, a duality that is sheerly one.

But except in infinity, everything of life is male or female, distinct. But the consciousness, that is of both: and the flower, that is of both. Every impulse that stirs in life, every single impulse, is either male or female, distinct, except the being of the complete flower, of the complete consciousness, which is two in one, fused. These are infinite and eternal. The consciousness, what we call the truth, is eternal, beyond change or motion, beyond time or limit.

But that which is not conscious, which is Time, and Life, that is our field.

CHAPTER VII

Of Being and Not-Being

In life, then, no new thing has ever arisen, or can arise, save out of the impulse of the male upon the female, the female upon the male. The interaction of the male and female spirit begot the wheel, the plough, and the first utterance that was made on the face of the earth.

As in my flower, the pistil, female, is the centre and swivel, the stamens, male, are close-clasping the hub, and the blossom is the great motion outwards into the unknown, so in a man's life, the female is the swivel and centre on which he turns closely, producing his movement. And the female to a man is the obvious form, a woman. And normally, the centre, the turning pivot, of a man's life is his sex-life, the centre and swivel of his being is the sexual act. Upon this turns the whole rest of his life, from this emanates every motion he betrays. And that this should be so, every man makes his effort. The supreme effort each man makes, for himself, is the effort to clasp as a hub the woman who shall be the axle, compelling him to true motion, without aberration. The supreme desire of every man is for mating with a woman, such that the sexual act be the closest, most concentrated motion in his life, closest upon the axle, the prime movement of himself, of which all the rest of his motion is a continuance in the same kind. And the vital desire of every woman is that she shall be clasped as axle to the hub of the man, that his motion shall portray her motionlessness, convey her static being into movement, complete and radiating out into infinity, starting from her stable eternality, and reaching eternity again, after having covered the whole of time.

This is complete movement: man upon woman, woman within man. This is the desire, the achieving of which, frictionless, is impossible, yet for which every man will try, with greater or less intensity, achieving more or less success.

This is the desire of every man, that his movement, the manner of his walk, and the supremest effort of his mind, shall be the pulsation outwards from stimulus received in the sex, in the sexual act, that the woman of his body shall be the begetter of his whole life, that she, in her female spirit, shall beget in him his idea, his motion, himself. When a man shall look at the work of his hands, that has succeeded, and shall know that it was begotten in him by the woman of his body, then he shall know what fundamental happiness is. Just as when a woman shall look at her child, that was begotten in her by the man of her spirit, she shall know what it is to be happy, fundamentally. But when a woman looks at her children that were begotten in her by a strange man, not the man of her spirit, she must know what it is to be happy with anguish, and to love with pain. So with a man who looks at his work which was not begotten in him by the woman of his body. He rejoices, troubles, and suffers an agony like death which contains resurrection.

For while, ideally, the soul of the woman possesses the soul of the man, procreates it and makes it big with new idea, motion, in the sexual act, yet, most commonly, it is not so. Usually, sex is only functional, a matter of relief or sensation, equivalent to eating or drinking or passing of excrement.

Then, if a man must produce work, he must produce it to some other than the woman of his body: as, in the same case, if a woman produce children, it must be to some other than the man of her desire.

In this case, a man must seek elsewhere than in woman for the female to possess his soul, to fertilize him and make him try with increase. And the female exists in much more than his woman. And the finding of it for himself gives a man his vision, his God.

And since no man and no woman can get a perfect mate, nor obtain complete satisfaction at all times, each man according to his need must have a God, an idea, that shall compel him to the movement of his own being. And then, when he lies with his woman, the man may concurrently be with God, and so get increase of his soul. Or he may have communion with his God apart and averse from the woman.

Every man seeks in woman for that which is stable, eternal. And if, under his motion, this break down in her, in the particular woman, so that she be no axle for his hub, but be driven away from herself, then he must seek elsewhere for his stability, for the centre to himself.

Then either he must seek another woman, or he must seek to

make conscious his desire to find a symbol, to create and define in his consciousness the object of his desire, so that he may have it at will, for his own complete satisfaction.

In doing this latter, he seeks with his desire the female elsewhere than in the particular woman. Since everything that is, is either male or female or both, whether it be clouds or sunshine or hills or trees or a fallen feather from a bird, therefore in other things and in such things man seeks for his complement. And he must at last always call God the unutterable and the inexpressible, the unknowable, because it is his unrealized complement.

But all gods have some attributes in common. They are the unexpressed Absolute: eternal, infinite, unchanging. Eternal, Infinite, Unchanging: the High God of all Humanity is this.

Yet man, the male, is essentially a thing of movement and time and change. Until he is stirred into thought, he is complete in movement and change. But once he thinks, he must have the Absolute, the Eternal, Infinite, Unchanging.

And Man is stirred into thought by dissatisfaction, or unsatisfaction, as heat is born of friction. Consciousness is the same effort in male and female to obtain perfect frictionless interaction, perfect as Nirvana. It is the reflex both of male and female from defect in their dual motion. Being reflex from the dual motion, consciousness contains the two in one, and is therefore in itself Absolute.

And desire is the admitting of deficiency. And the embodiment of the object of desire reveals the original defect or the defaulture. So that the attributes of God will reveal that which man lacked and yearned for in his living. And these attributes are always, in their essence, Eternality, Infinity, Immutability.

And these are the qualities man feels in woman, as a principle. Let a man walk alone on the face of the earth, and he feels himself like a loose speck blown at random. Let him have a woman to whom he belongs, and he will feel as though he had a wall to back up against; even though the woman be mentally a fool. No man can endure the sense of space, of chaos, on four sides of himself. It drives him mad. He must be able to put his back to the wall. And this wall is his woman.

From her he has a sense of stability. She supplies him with the feeling of Immutability, Permanence, Eternality. He himself is a raging activity, change potent within change. He dare not even conceive of himself, save when he is sure of the woman permanent beneath him, beside him. He dare not leap into the unknown save from the sure stability of the unyielding female. Like a wheel, if he turn without an axle, his motion is wandering neutrality.

So always, the fear of a man is that he shall find no axle for his motion, that no woman can centralize his activity. And always, the fear of a woman is that she can find no hub for her stability, no man to convey into motion her full stability. Either the particular woman breaks down before the stress of the man, becomes erratic herself, no stay, no centre; or else the man is insufficiently active to carry out the static principle of his female, of his woman.

So life consists in the dual form of the Will-to-Motion and the Will-to-Inertia, and everything we see and know and are is the resultant of these two Wills. But the One Will, of which they are dual forms, that is as yet unthinkable.

And according as the Will-to-Motion predominates in race, or the Will-to-Inertia, so must that race's conception of the One Will enlarge the attributes which are lacking or deficient in the race.

Since there is never to be found a perfect balance or accord of the two Wills, but always one triumphs over the other, in life, according to our knowledge, so must the human effort be always to recover balance, to symbolize and so to possess that which is missing. Which is the religious effort of Man.

There seems to be a fundamental, insuperable division, difference, between man's artistic effort and his religious effort. The two efforts are mixed with each other, as they are revealed, but all the while they remain two, not one, all the while they are separate, single, never compounded.

The religious effort is to conceive, to symbolize that which the human soul, or the soul of the race, lacks, that which it is not, and which it requires, yearns for. It is the portrayal of that complement to the race-life which is known only as a desire: it is the symbolizing of a great desire, the statement of the desire in terms which have no meaning apart from the desire.

Whereas the artistic effort is the effort of utterance, the supreme effort of expressing knowledge, that which has been for once, that which was enacted, where the two wills met and intersected and left their result, complete for the moment. The artistic effort is the portraying of a moment of union between the two wills, according to knowledge. The religious effort is the portrayal or symbolizing of the eternal union of the two wills, according to aspiration. But in this eternal union, the features of one or the other Will are always salient.

The dual Will we call the Will-to-Motion and the Will-to-Inertia. These cause the whole of life, from the ebb and flow of a wave, to the stable equilibrium of the whole universe, from birth and being and knowledge to death and decay and forgetfulness. And the Will-to-Motion we call the male will or spirit, the Will-to-Inertia the female. This will to inertia is not negative, and the other positive. Rather, according to some conception, is Motion negative and Inertia, the static, geometric idea, positive. That is according to the point of view.

According to the race-conception of God, we can see whether in that race the male or the female element triumphs, becomes predominant.

But it must first be seen that the division into male and female is arbitrary, for the purpose of thought. The rapid motion of the rim of a wheel is the same as the perfect rest at the centre of the wheel. How can one divide them? Motion and rest are the same, when seen completely. Motion is only true of things outside oneself. When I am in a moving train, strictly, the land moves under me, I and the train are still. If I were both land and train, if I were large enough, there would be no motion. And if I were very very small, every fibre of the train would be in motion for me, the point of rest would be infinitely reduced.

How can one say, there is motion and rest? If all things move together in one infinite motion, that is rest. Rest and motion are only two degrees of motion, or two degrees of rest. Infinite motion and infinite rest are the same thing. It is obvious. Since, if motion were infinite, there would be no standing-ground from which to regard it as motion. And the same with rest.

It is easier to conceive that there is no such thing as rest. For a thing to us at rest is only a thing travelling at our own rate of motion: from another point of view, it is a thing moving at the lowest rate of motion we can recognize. But this table on which I write, which I call at rest, I know is really in motion.

So there is no such thing as rest. There is only infinite motion. But infinite motion must contain every degree of rest. So that motion and rest are the same thing. Rest is the lowest speed of motion which I recognize under normal conditions.

So how can one speak of a Will-to-Motion or a Will-to-Inertia, when there is no such thing as rest or motion? And yet, starting from any given degree of motion, and travelling forward in ever-increasing degree, one comes to a state of speed which covers the whole of space instantaneously, and is therefore rest, utter rest. And starting from the same speed and reducing the motion infinitely, one reaches the same condition of utter rest. And the direction or method of approach to this infinite rest is different to our conception. And only travelling upon the slower, does the swifter reach the infinite rest of inertia: which is the same as the infinite rest of speed, the two things having united to surpass our comprehension.

So we may speak of Male and Female, of the Will-to-Motion and of the Will-to-Inertia. And so, looking at a race, we can say whether the Will-to-Inertia or the Will-to-Motion has gained the ascendancy, and in which direction this race tends to disappear.

For it is as if life were a double cycle, of men and women, facing opposite ways, travelling opposite ways, revolving upon each other, man reaching forward with outstretched hand, woman reaching forward with outstretched hand, and neither able to move till their hands have grasped each other, when they draw towards each other from opposite directions, draw nearer and nearer, each travelling in his separate cycle, till the two are abreast, and side by side, until even they pass on again, away from each other, travelling their opposite ways to the same infinite goal.

Each travelling to the same goal of infinity, but entering it from the opposite ends of space. And man, remembering what lies behind him, how the hands met and grasped and tore apart, utters his tragic art. Then moreover, facing the other way into the unknown, conscious of the tug of the goal at his heart, he hails the woman coming from the place whither he is travelling, searches in her for signs, and makes his God from the suggestion he receives, as she advances.

Then she draws near, and he is full of delight. She is so close, that they touch, and then there is a joyful utterance of religious art. They are torn apart, and he gives the cry of tragedy, and goes on remembering, till the dance slows down and breaks, and there is only a crowd.

It is as if this cycle dance where the female makes the chain with the male becomes ever wider, ever more extended, and the further they get from the source, from the infinity, the more distinct and individual do the dancers become. At first they are only figures. In the Jewish cycle, David, with his hand stretched forth, cannot recognize the woman, the female. He can only recognize some likeness of himself. For both he and she have not danced very far from the source and origin where they were both one. Though she is in the gross utterly other than he, yet she is not very distinct from him. And he hails her Father, Almighty, God, Beloved, Strength, hails her in his own image. And with hand outstretched, fearful and passionate, he reaches to her. But it is Solomon who touches her hand, with rapture and joy, and cries out his gladness in the Song of Songs. Who is the Shulamite but God come close, for a moment, into physical contact? The Song may be a drama: it is still religious art. It is the development of the Psalms. It is utterly different from the Book of Job, which is remembrance.

Always the threefold utterance: the declaring of the God seen approaching, the rapture of contact, the anguished joy of remembrance, when the meeting has passed into separation. Such is religion, religious art, and tragic art.

But the chain is not broken by the letting-go of hands. It is broken by the overbearing of one cycle by the other. David, when he lay with a woman, lay also with God; Solomon, when he lay with a woman, knew God and possessed Him and was possessed by Him. For in Solomon and in the Woman, the male clasped hands with the female.

But in the terrible moment when they should break free again, the male in the Jew was too weak, the female overbore him. He remained in the grip of the female. The force of inertia overpowered him, and he remained remembering. But very true had been David's vision, and very real Solomon's contact. So that the living thing was conserved, kept always alive and powerful, but restrained, restricted, partial.

For centuries, the Jew knew God as David had perceived Him, as Solomon had known Him. It was the God of the body, the rudimentary God of physical laws and physical functions. The Jew lived on in physical contact with God. Each of his physical functions he shared with God; he kept his body always like the body of a bride ready to serve the bridegroom. He had become the servant of his God, the female, passive. The female in him predominated, held him passive, set utter bounds to his movement, to his roving, kept his mind as a slave to guard intact the state of sensation wherein he found himself. Which persisted century after century, the secret, scrupulous voluptuousness of the Jew, become almost self-voluptuousness, engaged in the consciousness of his own physique, or in the extracted existence of his own physique. His own physique included the woman, naturally, since the man's body included the woman's, the woman's the man's. His religion had become a physical morality, deep and fundamental, but entirely of one sort. Its living element was this scrupulous physical voluptuousness, wonderful and satisfying in a large measure.

The conscious element was a resistance to the male or active principle. Being female, occupied in self-feeling, in realization of the age, in submission to sensation, the Jewish temper was antagonistic to the active male principle, which would deny the age and refuse sensation, seeking ever to make transformation, desiring to be an instrument of change, to register relationships. So this race recognized only male sins: it conceived only sins of commission, sins of change, of transformation. In the whole of the Ten Commandments, it is the female who speaks. It is natural to the male to make the male God a God of benevolence and mercy, susceptible to pity. Such is the male conception of God. It was the female spirit which conceived the saying: "For I, the Lord thy God, am a jealous God, visiting the iniquities of the fathers upon the children unto the third and fourth generation of them that hate me, and showing mercy unto thousands of them that love me."

It was a female conception. For is not man the child of woman? Does she not see in him her body, even more vividly than in her own? Man is more her body to her even than her own body. For the whole of flesh is hers. Woman knows that she is the fountain of all flesh. And her pride is that the body of man is of her issue. She can see the man as the One Being, for she knows he is of her issue.

It were a male conception to see God with a manifold Being, even though He be One God. For man is ever keenly aware of the multiplicity of things, and their diversity. But woman, issuing from the other end of infinity, coming forth as the flesh, manifest in sensation, is obsessed by the oneness of things, the One Being, undifferentiated. Man, on the other hand, coming forth as the desire to single out one thing from another, to reduce each thing to its intrinsic self by process of elimination, cannot but be possessed by the infinite diversity and contrariety in life, by a passionate sense of isolation, and a poignant yearning to be at one.

That is the fundamental of female conception: that there is but One Being: this Being necessarily female. Whereas man conceives a manifold Being, the supreme of which is male. And owing to the complete Monism of the female, which is essentially static, self-sufficient, the expression of God has been left always to the male, so that the supreme God is forever He.

Nevertheless, in the God of the Ancient Jew, the female has triumphed. That which was born of Woman, that is indeed the God of the Old Testament. So utterly is he born of Woman that he scarcely needs to consider Woman: she is there unuttered.

And the Jewish race, continued in this Monism, stable, circumscribed, utterly unadventurous, utterly self-preservative, yet very deeply living, until the present century.

But Christ rose from the suppressed male spirit of Judea, and uttered a new commandment: Thou shalt love thy neighbour as thyself. He repudiated Woman: "Who is my mother?" He lived the male life utterly apart from woman.

"Thou shalt love thy neighbour as thyself"–that is the great utterance against Monism, and the compromise with Monism. It does not say "Thou shalt love thy neighbour because he is thyself," as the ancient Jew would have said. It commands "Thou shalt recognize thy neighbour's distinction from thyself, and allow his separate being, because he also is of God, even though he be almost a contradiction to thyself."

Such is the cry of anguish of Christianity: that man is separate from his brother, separate, maybe, even, in his measure, inimical to him. This the Jew had to learn. The old Jewish creed of identity, that Eve was identical with Adam, and all men children of one single parent, and therefore, in the absolute, identical, this must be destroyed.

Cunning and according to female suggestion is the story of the Creation: that Eve was born from the single body of Adam, without intervention of sex, both issuing from one flesh, as a child at birth seems to issue from one flesh of its mother. And the birth of Jesus is the retaliation to this: a child is born, not to the flesh, but to the spirit: and you, Woman, shall conceive, not to the body, but to the Word. "In the beginning was the Word," says the New Testament.

The great assertion of the Male was the New Testament, and, in its beauty, the Union of Male and Female. Christ was born of Woman, begotten by the Holy Spirit. This was why Christ should be called the Son of Man. For He was born of Woman. He was born to the Spirit, the Word, the Man, the Male.

And the assertion entailed the sacrifice of the Son of Woman. The body of Christ must be destroyed, that of Him which was Woman must be put to death, to testify that He was Spirit, that He was Male, that He was Man, without any womanly part.

So the other great camp was made. In the creation, Man was

driven forth from Paradise to labour for his body and for the woman. All was lost for the knowledge of the flesh. Out of the innocence and Nirvana of Paradise came, with the Fall, the consciousness of the flesh, the body of man and woman came into very being.

This was the first great movement of Man: the movement into the conscious possession of a body. And this consciousness of the body came through woman. And this knowledge, this possession, this enjoyment, was jealously guarded. In spite of all criticism and attack, Job remained true to this knowledge, to the utter belief in his body, in the God of his body. Though the Woman herself turned tempter, he remained true to it.

The senses, sensation, sensuousness, these things which are incontrovertibly Me, these are my God, these belong to God, said Job. And he persisted, and he was right. They issue from God on the female side.

But Christ came with His contradiction: That which is Not-Me, that is God. All is God, except that which I know immediately as Myself. First I must lose Myself, then I find God. Ye must be born again.

Unto what must man be born again? Unto knowledge of his own separate existence, as in Woman he is conscious of his own incorporate existence. Man must be born unto knowledge of his own distinct identity, as in woman he was born to knowledge of his identification with the Whole. Man must be born to the knowledge, that in the whole being he is nothing, as he was born to know that in the whole being he was all. He must be born to the knowledge that other things exist beside himself, and utterly apart from all, and before he can exist himself as a separate identity, he must allow and recognize their distinct existence. Whereas previously, on the more female Jewish side, it had been said: "All that exists is as Me. We are all one family, out of one God, having one being."

With Christ ended the Monism of the Jew. God, the One God, became a Trinity, three-fold. He was the Father, the All-containing; He was the Son, the Word, the Changer, the Separator; and He was the Spirit, the Comforter, the Reconciliator between the Two.

And according to its conditions, Christianity has, since Christ, worshipped the Father or the Son, the one more than the other. Out of an over-female race came the male utterance of Christ. Throughout Europe, the suppressed, inadequate male desire, both in men and women, stretched to the idea of Christ, as a woman should stretch out her hands to a man. But Greece, in whom the female was overridden and neglected, became silent. So through the Middle Ages went on in Europe this fight against the body, against the senses, against this continual triumph of the senses. The worship of Europe, predominantly female, all through the medieval period, was to the male, to the incorporeal Christ, as a bridegroom, whilst the art produced was the collective, stupendous, emotional gesture of the Cathedrals, where a blind, collective impulse rose into concrete form. It was the profound, sensuous desire and gratitude which produced an art of architecture, whose essence is in utter stability, of movement resolved and centralized, of absolute movement, that has no relationship with any other form, that admits the existence of no other form, but is conclusive, propounding in its sum the One Being of All.

There was, however, in the Cathedrals, already the denial of the Monism which the Whole uttered. All the little figures, the gargoyles, the imps, the human faces, whilst subordinated within the Great Conclusion of the Whole, still, from their obscurity, jeered their mockery of the Absolute, and declared for multiplicity, polygeny. But all medieval art has the static, architectural, absolute quality, in the main, even whilst in detail it is differentiated and distinct. Such is Dürer, for example. When his art succeeds, it conveys the sense of Absolute Movement, movement proper only to the given form, and not relative to other movements. It portrays the Object, with its Movement content, and not the movement which contains in one of its moments the Object.

It is only when the Greek stimulus is received, with its addition of male influence, its addition of relative movement, its revelation of movement driving the object, the highest revelation which had yet been made, that medieval art became complete Renaissance art, that there was the union and fusion of the male and female spirits, creating a perfect expression for the time being.

During the medieval times, the God had been Christ on the Cross, the Body Crucified, the flesh destroyed, the Virgin Chastity combating Desire. Such had been the God of the Aspiration. But the God of Knowledge, of that which they acknowledged as themselves, had been the Father, the God of the Ancient Jew.

But now, with the Renaissance, the God of Aspiration became in accord with the God of Knowledge, and there was a great outburst of joy, and the theme was not Christ Crucified, but Christ born of Woman, the Infant Saviour and the Virgin; or of the Annunciation, the Spirit embracing the flesh in pure embrace.

This was the perfect union of male and female, in this the hands met and clasped, and never was such a manifestation of Joy. This Joy reached its highest utterance perhaps in Botticelli, as in his *Nativity of the Saviour,* in our National Gallery. Still there is the architectural composition, but what an outburst of movement from the source of motion. The Infant Christ is a centre, a radiating spark of movement, the Virgin is bowed in Absolute Movement, the earthly father, Joseph, is folded up, like a clod or a boulder, obliterated, whilst the Angels fly round in ecstasy, embracing and linking hands.

The bodily father is almost obliterated. As balance to the Virgin Mother he is there, presented, but silenced, only the movement of his loin conveyed. He is not the male. The male is the radiant infant, over which the mother leans. They two are the ecstatic centre, the complete origin, the force which is both centrifugal and centripetal.

This is the joyous utterance of the Renaissance, to which we listen for ever. Perhaps there is a melancholy in Botticelli, a pain of Woman mated to the Spirit, a nakedness of the Aphrodite issued exposed to the clear elements, to the fleshlessness of the male. But still it is joy transparent over pain. It is the utterance of complete, perfect religious art, unwilling, perhaps, when the true male and the female meet. In the Song of Solomon, the female was preponderant, the male was impure, not single. But here the heart is satisfied for the moment, there is a moment of perfect being.

And it seems to be so in other religions: the most perfect moment centres round the mother and the male child, whilst the physical male is deified separately, as a bull, perhaps.

After Botticelli came Correggio. In him the development from gesture to articulate expression was continued, unconsciously, the movement from the symbolic to the representation went on in him, from the object to the animate creature. The Virgin and Child are no longer symbolic, in Correggio: they no longer belong to religious art, but are distinctly secular. The effort is to render the living person, the individual perceived, and not the great aspiration, or an idea. Art now passes from the naïve, intuitive stage to the state of knowledge. The female impulse, to feel and to live in feeling, is now embraced by the male impulse–to know, and almost carried off by knowledge. But not yet. Still Correggio is unconscious, in his art; he is in that state of elation which represents the marriage of male and female, with the pride of the male perhaps predominant. In the *Madonna with the Basket,* of the National Gallery, the Madonna is most thoroughly a wife, the child is most triumphantly a man's child. The Father is the origin. He is seen labouring in the distance, the true support of this mother and child. There is no Virgin worship, none of the mystery of woman. The artist has reached to a sufficiency of knowledge. He knows his woman. What he is now concerned with is not her great female mystery, but her individual character. The picture has become almost lyrical–it is the woman as known by the man, it is the woman as he has experienced her. But still she is also unknown, also she is the mystery. But Correggio's chief business is to portray the woman of his own experience and knowledge, rather than the woman of his aspiration and fear. The artist is now concerned with his own experience rather than with his own desire. The female is now more or less within the power and reach of the male. But still she is there, to centralize and control his movement, still the two react and are not resolved. But for the man, the woman is henceforth part of a stream of movement, she is herself a stream of movement, carried along with himself. He sees everything as motion, retarded perhaps by the flesh, or by the stable being of this life in the body. But still man is held and pivoted by the object, even if he tend to wear down the pivot to a nothingness.

Thus Correggio leads on to the whole of modern art, where the male still wrestles with the female, in unconscious struggle, but where he gains ever gradually over her, reducing her to nothing. Ever there is more and more vibration, movement, and less and less stability, centralization. Ever man is more and more occupied with his own experience, with his own overpowering of resistance, ever less and less aware of any resistance in the object, less and less aware of any stability, less and less aware of anything unknown, more and more preoccupied with that which he knows, till his knowledge tends to become an abstraction, because it is limited by no unknown.

It is the contradiction of Dürer, as the Parthenon Frieze was the contradiction of Babylon and Egypt. To Dürer woman did not exist; even as to a child at the breast, woman does not exist separately. She is the overwhelming condition of life. She was to Dürer that which possessed him, and not that which he possessed. Her being overpowered him, he could only see in her terms, in terms of stability and of stable, incontrovertible being. He is overpowered by the vast assurance at whose breasts he is suckled, and, as if astounded, he grasps at the unknown. He knows that he rests within some great stability, and, marvelling at his own power for movement, touches the objects of this stability, becomes familiar with them. It is a question of the starting-point. Dürer starts with a sense of that which he does not know and would discover; Correggio with the sense of that which he has known, and would re-create.

And in the Renaissance, after Botticelli, the motion begins to divide in these two directions. The hands no longer clasp in perfect union, but one clasp overbears the other. Botticelli develops to Correggio and to Andrea del Sarto, develops forward to Rembrandt, and Rembrandt to the Impressionists, to the male extreme of motion. But Botticelli, on the other hand, becomes Raphael, Raphael and Michelangelo.

In Raphael we see the stable, architectural developing out further, and becoming the geometric: the denial or refusal of all movement. In the *Madonna degli Ansidei* the child is drooping, the mother stereotyped, the picture geometric, static, abstract. When there is any union of male and female, there is no goal of abstraction: the abstract is used in place, as a means of a real union. The goal of the male impulse is the announcement of motion, endless motion, endless diversity, endless change. The goal of the female impulse is the announcement of infinite oneness, of infinite stability. When the two are working in combination, as they must in life, there is, as it were, a dual motion, centrifugal for the male, fleeing abroad, away from the centre, outward to infinite vibration, and centripetal for the female, fleeing in to the eternal centre of rest. A combination of the two movements produces a sum of motion and stability at once, satisfying. But in life there tends always to be more of one than the other. The Cathedrals, Fra Angelico, frighten us or [bore] us with their final annunciation of centrality and stability. We want to escape. The influence is too female for us.

In Botticelli, the architecture remains, but there is the wonderful movement outwards, the joyous, if still clumsy, escape from the centre. His religious pictures tend to be stereotyped, resigned. The Primavera herself is static, melancholy, a stability become almost a negation. It is as if the female, instead of being the great, unknown Positive, towards which all must flow, became the great Negative, the centre which denied all motion. And the Aphrodite stands there not as a force, to draw all things unto her, but as the naked, almost unwilling pivot, as the keystone which endured all thrust and remained static. But still there is the joy, the great motion around her, sky and sea, all the elements and living, joyful forces.

Raphael, however, seeks and finds nothing there. He goes to the centre to ask: "What is this mystery we are all pivoted upon?" To Fra Angelico it was the unknown Omnipotent. It was a goal, to which man travelled inevitably. It was the desired, the end of the long horizontal journey. But to Raphael it was the negation. Still he is a seeker, an aspirant, still his art is religious art. But the Virgin, the essential female, was to him a negation, a neutrality. Such must have been his vivid experience. But still he seeks her. Still he desires the stability, the positive keystone which grasps the arch together, not the negative keystone neutralizing the thrust, itself a neutrality. And reacting upon his own desire, the male reacting upon itself, he creates the Abstraction, the geometric conception of life. The fundament of all is the geometry of all. Which is the Plato conception. And the desire is to formulate the complete geometry.

So Raphael, knowing that his desire reaches out beyond the range of possible experience, sensible that he will not find satisfaction in any one woman, sensible that the female impulse does not, or cannot unite in him with the male impulse sufficiently to create a stability, an eternal moment of truth for him, of realization, closes his eyes and his mind upon experience, and abstracting himself, reacting upon himself, produces the geometric conception of the fundamental truth, departs from religion, from any God idea, and becomes philosophic.

Raphael is the real end of Renaissance in Italy; almost he is the real end of Italy, as Plato was the real end of Greece. When the God-idea passes into the philosophic or geometric idea, then there is a sign that the male impulse has thrown the female impulse, and has recoiled upon itself, has become abstract, asexual.

Michelangelo, however, too physically passionate, containing too much of the female in his body ever to reach the geometric abstraction, unable to abstract himself, and at the same time, like Raphael, unable to find any woman who in her being should resist him and reserve still some unknown from him, strives to obtain his own physical satisfaction in his art. He is obsessed by the desire of the body. And he must react upon himself to produce his own bodily satisfaction, aware that he can never obtain it through woman. He must seek the moment, the consummation, the keystone, the pivot, in his own flesh. For his own body is both male and female.

Raphael and Michelangelo are men of different nature placed in the same position and resolving the same question in their several ways. Socrates and Plato are a parallel pair, and, in another degree, Tolstoi and Turgeniev, and, perhaps, St. Paul and St. John the Evangelist, and, perhaps, Shakespeare and Shelley.

The body it is which attaches us directly to the female. Sex, as we call it, is only the point where the dual stream begins to divide, where it is nearly together, almost one. An infant is of no very determinate sex: that is, it is of both. Only at adolescence is there a real differentiation, the one is singled out to predominate. In what we call happy natures, in the lazy, contented people, there is a fairly equable balance of sex. There is sufficient of the female in the body of such a man as to leave him fairly free. He does not suffer the torture of desire of a more male being. It is obvious even from the physique of such a man that in him there is a proper proportion between male and female, so that he can be easy, balanced, and without excess. The Greek sculptors of the "best" period, Phidias and then Sophocles, Alcibiades, then Horace, must have been fairly well-balanced men, not passionate to any excess, tending to voluptuousness rather than to passion. So also Victor Hugo and Schiller and Tennyson. The real voluptuary is a man who is female as well as male, and who lives according to the female side of his nature, like Lord Byron.

The pure male is himself almost an abstraction, almost bodiless, like Shelley or Edmund Spenser. But, as we know humanity, this condition comes of an omission of some vital part. In the ordinary sense, Shelley never lived. He transcended life. But we do not want to transcend life, since we are of life.

Why should Shelley say of the skylark:

"Hail to thee, blithe Spirit!—bird thou never wert!—"? Why should he insist on the bodilessness of beauty, when we cannot know of any save embodied beauty? Who would wish that the skylark were not a bird, but a spirit? If the whistling skylark were a spirit, then we should all wish to be spirits. Which were impious and flippant.

I can think of no being in the world so transcendently male as Shelley. He is phenomenal. The rest of us have bodies which contain the male and the female. If we were so singled out as Shelley, we should not belong to life, as he did not belong to life. But it were impious to wish to be like the angels. So long as mankind exists it must exist in the body, and so long must each body pertain both to the male and the female.

In the degree of pure maleness below Shelley are Plato and Raphael and Wordsworth, then Goethe and Milton and Dante, then Michelangelo, then Shakespeare, then Tolstoi, then St. Paul.

A man who is well balanced between male and female, in his own nature, is, as a rule, happy, easy to mate, easy to satisfy, and content to exist. It is only a disproportion, or a dissatisfaction, which makes the man struggle into articulation. And the articulation is of two sorts, the cry of desire or the cry of realization, the cry of satisfaction, the effort to prolong the sense of satisfaction, to prolong the moment of consummation.

A bird in spring sings with the dawn, ringing out from the moment of consummation in wider and wider circles. Dürer, Fra Angelico, Botticelli, all sing of the moment of consummation, some of them still marvelling and lost in the wonder at the other being, Botticelli poignant with distinct memory. Raphael too sings of the moment of consummation. But he was not lost in the moment, only sufficiently lost to know what it was. In the moment, he was not completely consummated. He must strive to complete his satisfaction from himself. So, whilst making his great acknowledgment to the Woman, he must add to her to make her whole, he must give her his completion. So he rings her round with pure geometry, till she becomes herself almost of the geometric figure, an abstraction. The picture becomes a great ellipse crossed by a dark column. This is the *Madonna degli Ansidei*. The Madonna herself is almost insignificant. She and the child are contained within the shaft thrust across the ellipse.

This column must always stand for the male aspiration, the arch or ellipse for the female completeness containing this aspiration. And the whole picture is a geometric symbol of the consummation of life.

What we call the Truth is, in actual experience, that momentary state when in living the union between the male and the female is consummated. This consummation may be also physical, between the male body and the female body. But it may be only spiritual, between the male and female spirit.

And the symbol by which Raphael expresses this moment of consummation is by a dark, strong shaft or column leaping up into, and almost transgressing a faint, radiant, inclusive ellipse.

To express the same moment Botticelli uses no symbol, but builds up a complicated system of circles, of movements wheeling in their horizontal plane about their fixed centres, the whole builded up dome-shape, and then the dome surpassed by another singing cycle in the open air above.

This is Botticelli always: different cycles of joy, different moments of embrace, different forms of dancing round, all contained in one picture, without solution. He has not solved it yet.

And Raphael, in reaching the pure symbolic solution, has surpassed art and become almost mathematics. Since the business of art is never to solve, but only to declare.

There is no such thing as solution. Nietzsche talks about the *Ewige Wiederkehr*. It is like Botticelli singing cycles. But each cycle is different. There is no real recurrence.

And to single out one cycle, one moment, and to exclude from this moment all context, and to make this moment timeless, this is what Raphael does, and what Plato does. So that their absolute Truth, their geometric Truth, is only true in timelessness.

Michelangelo, on the other hand, seeks for no absolute Truth. His desire is to realize in his body, in his feeling, the moment-consummation which is for Man the perfect truth-experience. But he knows of no embrace. For him, personally, woman does not exist. For Botticelli she existed as the Virgin-Mother, and as the Primavera, and as Aphrodite. She existed as the pure origin of life on the female side, as the bringer of light and delight, and as the passionately Desired of every man, as the Known and Unknown in one: to Raphael she existed either as a minor part of his experience, having nothing to do with his aspiration, or else his aspiration merely used her as a statement included within the Great Abstraction.

To Michelangelo the female scarcely existed outside his own physique. There he knew of her and knew the desire of her. But Raphael, in his passion to be self-complete, roused his desire for consummation to a white-hot pitch, so that he became incandescent, reacting on himself, consuming his own flesh and his own bodily life, to reach the pitch of perfect abstraction, the resisting body holding back the raging stream of outward force, till the two formed a stable incandescence, a luminous geometric conception of permanence and inviolability. Meanwhile his body burned away, overpowered, in this state of incandescence.

Michelangelo's will was different. The body in him, that which knew of the female and therefore was the female, was stronger and more insistent. His desire for consummation was desire for the satisfying moment when the male and female spirits touch in closest embrace, vivifying each other, not one destroying the other, but still are two. He knew that for Man consummation is a temporal state. The pure male spirit must ever conceive of timelessness, the pure female of the moment. And Michelangelo, more mixed than Raphael, must always rage within the limits of time and of temporal forms. So he reacted upon himself, sought the female in himself, aggrandized it, and so reached a wonderful momentary stability of flesh exaggerated till it became tenuous, but filled and balanced by the outward-pressing force. And he reached his consummation in that way, reached the perfect moment, when he realized and revealed his figures in all their marvellous equilibrium. The Jewish tradition, with its great physical God, source of male and female, attracted him. By turning towards the female goal, of utter stability and permanence in Time, he arrived at his consummation. But only by reacting on himself, by withdrawing his own mobility. Thus he made his great figures, the Moses, static and looming, announcing, like the Jewish God, the magnificence and eternality of the physical law; the David, young, but with too much body for a young figure, the physique exaggerated, the clear, outward-leaping, essential spirit of the young man smothered over, the real maleness cloaked, so that the statue is almost a falsity. Then the slaves, heaving in body, fastened in bondage that refuses them movement; the motionless Madonna, no Virgin but Woman in the flesh, not the pure female conception, but the spouse of man, the mother of bodily children. The men are not male, nor the women female, to any degree.

The Adam can scarcely stir into life. That large body of almost transparent, tenuous texture is not established enough for motion. It is not that it is too ponderous: it is too unsubstantial, unreal. It is not motion, life, he craves, but body. Give him but a firm, concentrated physique. That is the cry of all Michelangelo's pictures.

But, powerful male as he was, he satisfies his desire by insisting upon and exaggerating the body in him, he reaches the point of consummation in the most marvellous equilibrium which his figures show. To attain this equilibrium he must exaggerate and exaggerate and exaggerate the flesh, make it ever more tenuous, keeping it really in true ratio. And then comes the moment, the perfect stable poise, the perfect balance between object and movement, the perfect combination of male and female in one figure.

It is wonderful, and peaceful, this equilibrium, once reached. But it is reached through anguish and self-battle and self-repression, therefore it is sad. Always, Michelangelo's pictures are full of joy, of self-acceptance and self-proclamation. Michelangelo fought and arrested the mobile male in him; Raphael was proud in the male he was, and gave himself utter liberty, at the female expense.

And it seems as though Italy had ever since the Renaissance been possessed by the Raphaelesque conception of the ultimate geometric basis of life, the geometric essentiality of all things. There is in the Italian, at the very bottom of all, the fundamental, geometric conception of absolute static combination. There is the shaft enclosed in the ellipse, as a permanent symbol. There exists no shaft, no ellipse separately, but only the whole complete thing; there is neither male nor female, but an absolute interlocking of the two in one, an absolute combination, so that each is gone in the complete identity. There is only the geometric abstraction of the moment of consummation, a moment made timeless. And this conception of a long, clinched, timeless embrace, this overwhelming conception of timeless consummation, of which there is no beginning nor end, from which there is no escape, has arrested the Italian race for three centuries. It is the source of its indifference and its fatalism and its positive abandon, and of its utter incapacity to be sceptical, in the Russian sense.

This conception contains also, naturally, as part of the same idea, Aphrodite-worship and Phallic-worship. But these are subordinate, and belong to a sort of initiatory period. The real conception, for the individual, is marriage, inviolable marriage, which always was and always has been, no matter what apparent aberrations there may or may not be. And the manifestation of divinity is the child. In marriage, in utter, interlocked marriage, man and woman cease to be two beings and become one, one and one only, not two in one as with us, but absolute One, a geometric absolute, timeless, the Absolute, the Divine. And the child, as issue of this divine and timeless state, is hailed with love and joy.

But the Italian is now beginning to withdraw from his clinched and timeless embrace, from his geometric abstraction, into the northern conception of himself and the woman as two separate identities, which meet, combine, but always must withdraw again.

So that the Futurist Boccioni now makes his sculpture, *Development of a Bottle through Space,* try to express the withdrawal, and at the same time he must adhere to the conception of this same interlocked state of marriage between centripetal and centrifugal forces, the geometric abstraction of the bottle. But he can neither do one thing nor the other. He wants to re-state the real abstraction.

And at the same time he has an unsatisfied desire to satisfy. He must insist on the centrifugal force, and so destroy at once his abstraction. He must insist on the male spirit of motion outwards, because, during three static centuries, there has necessarily come to pass a preponderance of the female in the race, so that the Italian is rather more female than male now, as is the whole Latin race rather voluptuous than passionate, too much aware of their utter lockedness male with female, and too hopeless, as males, to act, to be passionate. So that when I look at Boccioni's sculpture, and see him trying to state the timeless abstract being of a bottle, the pure geometric abstraction of the bottle, I am fascinated. But then, when I see him driven by his desire for the male complement into portraying motion, simple motion, trying to give expression to the bottle in terms of mechanics, I am confused. It is for science to explain the bottle in terms of force and motion. Geometry, pure mathematics, is very near to art, and the vivid attempt to render the bottle as a pure geometric abstraction might give rise to a work of art because of the resistance of the medium, the stone. But a representation in stone of the lines of force which create that state of rest called a bottle, that is a model in mechanics.

And the two representations require two different states of mind in the appreciator, so that the result is almost nothingness, mere confusion. And the portraying of a state of mind is impossible. There can only be made scientific diagrams of states of mind. A state of mind is a resultant between an attack and a resistance. And how can one produce a resultant without first causing the collision of the originating forces?

The attitude of the Futurists is the scientific attitude, as the attitude of Italy is mainly scientific. It is the forgetting of the old, perfect Abstraction, it is the departure of the male from the female, it is the act of withdrawal: the denying of consummation and the starting afresh, the learning of the alphabet.

CHAPTER VIII

The Light of the World

The climax that was reached in Italy with Raphael has never been reached in like manner in England. There has never been, in England, the great embrace, the surprising consummation, which Botticelli recorded and which Raphael fixed in a perfect Abstraction.

Correggio, Andrea del Sarto, both men of less force than those other supreme three, continued the direct line of development, turning no curve. They still found women whom they could not exhaust: in them, the male still reacted upon the incontrovertible female. But ever there was a tendency to greater movement, to a closer characterization, a tendency to individualize the human being, and to represent him as being embedded in some common, divine matrix.

Till after the Renaissance, supreme God had always been God the Father. The Church moved and had its being in Almighty God, Christ was only the distant, incandescent gleam towards which humanity aspired, but which it did not know.

Raphael and Michelangelo were both servants of the Father, of the Eternal Law, of the Prime Being. Raphael, faced with the question of Not-Being, when it was forced upon him that he would never accomplish his own being in the flesh, that he would never know completeness, the momentary consummation, in the body, accomplished the Geometrical Abstraction, which is the abstraction from the Law, which is the Father.

There was, however, Christ's great assertion of Not-Being, of No-Consummation, of life after death, to reckon with. It was after the Renaissance, Christianity began to exist. It had not existed before.

In God the Father we are all one body, one flesh. But in Christ we abjure the flesh, there is no flesh. A man must lose his life to save it. All the natural desires of the body, these a man must be able to deny, before he can live. And then, when he lives, he shall live in the knowledge that he is himself, so that he can always say: "I am I."

In the Father we are one flesh, in Christ we are crucified, and rise again, and are One with Him in Spirit. It is the difference between Law and Love. Each man shall live according to the Law, which changeth not, says the old religion. Each man shall live according to Love, which shall save us from death and from the Law, says the new religion.

But what is Love? What is the deepest desire Man has yet known? It is always for this consummation, this momentary contact or union of male with female, of spirit with spirit and flesh with flesh, when each is complete in itself and rejoices in its own being, when each is in himself or in herself complete and single and essential. And love is the great aspiration towards this complete consummation and this joy; it is the aspiration of each man that all men, that all life, shall know it and rejoice. Since, until all men shall know it, no man shall fully know it. Since, by the Law, we are all one flesh. So that Love is only a closer vision of the Law, a more comprehensive interpretation: "Think not I come to destroy the Law, or the Prophets: I come not to destroy, but to fulfil. For verily I say unto you, till heaven and earth pass, one jot or one tittle shall in no wise pass from the Law, till all be fulfilled."

In Christ I must save my soul through love, I must lose my life, and thereby find it. The Law bids me preserve my life to the Glory of God. But Love bids me lose my life to the Glory of God. In Christ, when I shall have overcome every desire I know in myself, so that I adhere to nothing, but am loosed and set free and single, then, being without fear, and having nothing that I can lose, I shall know what I am, I, transcendent, intrinsic, eternal.

The Christian commandment: "Thou shalt love thy neighbour as thyself" is a more indirect and moving, a more emotional form of the Greek commandment "Know thyself." This is what Christianity says, indirectly: "Know thyself, and each man shall thereby know himself."

Now in the Law, no man shall know himself, save in the Law. And the Law is the immediate law of the body. And the necessity of each man to know himself, to achieve his own consummation, shall be satisfied and fulfilled in the body. God, Almighty God, is the father, and in fatherhood man draws nearest to him. In the act of love, in the act of begetting, Man is with God and of God. Such is the Law. And there shall be no other God devised. That is the great obstructive commandment.

This is the old religious leap down, absolutely, even if not in direct statement. It is the Law. But through Christ it was at last declared that in the physical act of love, in the begetting of children, man does not necessarily know himself, nor become Godlike, nor satisfy his deep, innate desire to BE. The physical act of love may be a complete disappointment, a nothing, and fatherhood may be the least significant attribute to a man. And physical love may fail utterly, may prove a sterility, a nothingness. Is a man then duped, and is his deepest desire a joke played on him?

There is a law, beyond the known law, there is a new Commandment. There is love. A man shall find his consummation the crucifixion of the body and the resurrection of the spirit.

Christ, the Bridegroom, or the Bride, as may be, awaits the desiring soul that shall seek Him, and in Him shall all men find their consummation, after their new birth. It is the New Law; the old Law is revoked.

"This is my Body, take, and eat," says Christ, in the Communion, the ritual representing the Consummation. "Come unto Me all ye that labour and are heavy-laden, and I will give you rest."

For each man there is the bride, for each woman the bridegroom, for all, the Mystic Marriage. It is the New Law. In the mystic embrace of Christ each man shall find fulfilment and relief, each man shall become himself, a male individual, tried, proved, completed, and satisfied. In the mystic embrace of Christ each man shall say, "I am myself, and Christ is Christ"; each woman shall be proud and satisfied, saying, "It is enough."

So, by the New Law, man shall satisfy this his deepest desire. "In the body ye must die, even as I died, on the cross," says Christ, "that ye may have everlasting life." But this is a real contradiction of the Old Law, which says, "In the life of the body we are one with the Father." The Old Law bids us live: it is the old, original commandment, that we shall live in the Law, and not die. So that the new Christian preaching of Christ Crucified is indeed against the Law. "And when ye are dead in the body, ye shall be one with the spirit, ye shall know the Bride, and be consummate in Her Embrace, in the Spirit," continues the Christian Commandment.

It is a larger interpretation of the Law, but, also, it is a breach of the Law. For by the Law, Man shall in no wise injure or deny or desecrate his living body of flesh, which is of the Father. Therefore, though Christ gave the Holy Ghost, the Comforter; though He bowed before the Father; though He said that no man should be forgiven the denial of the Holy Spirit, the Reconciler between the Father and the Son; yet did the Son deny the Father, must he deny the Father?

"Ye are my Spirit, in the Spirit ye know Me, and in marriage of the Spirit I am fulfilled of you," said the Son.

And it is the Unforgivable Sin to declare that these two are contradictions one of the other, though contradictions they are. Between them is linked the Holy Spirit, as a reconciliation, and whoso shall speak hurtfully against the Holy Spirit shall find no forgiveness.

So Christ, up in arms against the Father, exculpated Himself and bowed to the Father. Yet man must insist either on one or on the other: either he must adhere to the Son or to the Father. And since the Renaissance, disappointed in the flesh, the northern races have sought the consummation through Love; and they have denied the Father.

The greatest and deepest human desire, for consummation, for Self-Knowledge, has sought a different satisfaction. In Love, in the act of love, that which is mixed in me becomes pure, that which is female in me is given to the female, that which is male in her draws into me, I am complete, I am pure male, she is pure female; we rejoice in contact perfect and naked and clear, singled out unto ourselves, and given the surpassing freedom. No longer we see through a glass, darkly. For she is she, and I am I, and, clasped together with her, I know how perfectly she is not me, how perfectly I am not her, how utterly we are two, the light and the darkness, and how infinitely and eternally not-to-be-comprehended by either of us is the surpassing One we make. Yet of this One, this incomprehensible, we have an inkling that satisfies us.

And through Christ Jesus, I know that I shall find my Bride, when I have overcome the impurity of the flesh. When the flesh in me is put away, I shall embrace the Bride, and I shall know as I am known.

But why the Schism? Why shall the Father say "Thou shalt have no other God before Me"? Why is the Lord our God a jealous God? Why, when the body fails me, must I still adhere to the Law, and give it praise as the perfect Abstraction, like Raphael, announce it as the Absolute? Why must I be imprisoned within the flesh, like Michelangelo, till I must stop the voice of my crying out, and be satisfied with a little where I wanted completeness?

And why, on the other hand, must I lose my life to save it? Why must I die, before I can be born again? Can I not be born again, save out of my own ashes, save in resurrection from the dead? Why must I deny the Father, to love the Son? Why are they not One God to me, as we always protest they are?

It is time that the schism ended, that man ceased to oppose the Father to the Son, the Son to the Father. It is time that the Protestant Church, the Church of the Son, should be one again with the Roman Catholic Church, the Church of the Father. It is time that man shall cease, first to live in the flesh, with joy, and then, unsatisfied, to renounce and to mortify the flesh, declaring that the Spirit alone exists, that Christ He is God.

If a man find incomplete satisfaction in the body, why therefore shall he renounce the body and say it is of the devil? And why, at the start, shall a man say, "The body, that is all, and the consummation, that is complete in the flesh, for me."

Must it always be that a man set out with a worship of passion and a blindness to love, and that he end with a stern commandment to love and a renunciation of passion?

Does not a youth now know that he desires the body as the *via media,* that consummation is consummation of body and spirit, both?

How can a man say, "I am this body," when he will desire beyond the body tomorrow? And how can a man say, "I am this spirit," when his own mouth gives lie to the words it forms?

Why is a race, like the Italian race, fundamentally melancholy, save that it has circumscribed its consummation within the body? And the Jewish race, for the same reason, has become now almost hollow, with a pit of emptiness and misery in their eyes.

And why is the English race neutral, indifferent, like a thing that eschews life, save that it has said so insistently: "I am this spirit. This body, it is not me, it is unworthy"? The body at last begins to wilt and become corrupt. But before it submits, half the life of the English race must be a lie. The life of the body, denied by the professed adherence to the spirit, must be something disowned, corrupt, ugly.

Why should the worship of the Son entail the denial of the Father?

Since the Renaissance, northern humanity has sought for consummation in the spirit, it has sought for the female apart from woman. "I am I, and the Spirit is the Spirit; in the Spirit I am myself," and this has been the utterance of our art since Raphael.

There has been the ever-developing dissolution of form, the dissolving of the solid body within the spirit. He began to break the clear outline of the object, to seek for further marriage, not only between body and body, not the perfect, stable union of body with body, not the utter completeness and accomplishment of architectural form, with its recurrent cycles, but the marriage between body and spirit, or between spirit and spirit.

It is no longer the Catholic exultation "God is God," but the

Christian annunciation, "Light is come into the world." No longer has a man only to obey, but he has to die and be born again; he has to close his eyes upon his own immediate desires, and in the darkness receive the perfect light. He has to know himself in the spirit, he has to follow Christ to the Cross, and rise again in the light of the life.

And, in this light of life, he will see his Bride, he will embrace his complement and his fulfilment, and achieve his consummation. "It is the spirit that quickeneth; the flesh forgetteth nothing; the words I speak unto you, they are the spirit, and they are life."

And though in the Gospel, according to John particularly, Jesus constantly asserts that the Father has sent Him, and that He is of the Father, yet there is always the spirit of antagonism to the Father.

"And it came to pass, as He spake these things, a certain woman of the company lifted up her voice and said unto Him: 'Blessed is the womb that bare thee, and the paps thou hast sucked.'

"But He said, Yea, rather, blessed are they that hear the word of God, and keep it."

And the woman who heard this knew that she was denied of the honour of her womb, and that the blessing of her breasts was taken away.

Again He said: "And there be those that were born eunuchs, and there be those that were made eunuchs by men, and there be eunuchs which have made themselves eunuchs for the kingdom of heaven's sake. He that is able to receive it, let him receive it." But before the Father a eunuch is blemished, even a childless man is without honour.

So that the spirit of Jesus is antagonistic to the spirit of the Father. And St. John enhances this antagonism. But in St. John there is the constant insistence on the Oneness of Father and Son, and on the Holy Spirit.

Since the Renaissance there has been the striving for the Light, and the escape from the Flesh, from the Body, the Object. And sometimes there has been the antagonism to the Father, sometimes reconciliation with Him. In painting, the Spirit, the Word, the Love, all that was represented by John, has appeared as light. Light is the constant symbol of Christ in the New Testament. It is light, actual sunlight or the luminous quality of day, which has infused more and more into the defined body, fusing away the outline, absolving the concrete reality, making a marriage, an embrace between the two things, light and object.

In Rembrandt there is the first great evidence of this, the new exposition of the commandment "Know thyself." It is more than the "Hail, holy Light!" of Milton. It is the declaration that light is our medium of existence, that where the light falls upon our darkness, there we *are:* that I am but the point where light and darkness meet and break upon one another.

There is now a new conception of life, an utterly new conception, of duality, of two-fold existence, light and darkness, object and spirit two-fold, and almost inimical.

The old desire, for movement about a centre of rest, for stability, is gone, and in its place rises the desire for pure ambience, pure spirit of change, free from all laws and conditions of being.

Henceforward there are two things, and not one. But there is journeying towards the one thing again. There is no longer the One God Who contains us all, and in Whom we live and move and have our being, and to Whom belongs each one of our movements. I am no longer a child of the Father, brother of all men. I am no longer part of the great body of God, as all men are part of it. I am no longer consummate in the body of God, identified with it and divine in the act of marriage.

The conception has utterly changed. There is the Spirit, and there is Myself. I exist in contact with the Spirit, but I am not the Spirit. I am other, I am Myself. Now I am become a man, I am no more a child of the Father. I am a man. And there are many men. And the Father has lost his importance. We are multiple, manifold men, we own only one Hope, one Desire, one Bride, one Spirit.

At last man insists upon his own separate Self, insists that he has a distinct, inconquerable being which stands apart even from Spirit, which exists other than the Spirit, and which seeks marriage with the Spirit.

And he must study himself and marvel over himself in the light of the Spirit, he must become lyrical: but he must glorify the Spirit, above all. Since that is the Bride. So Rembrandt paints his own portrait again and again, sees it again and again within the light.

He has no hatred of the flesh. That he was not completed in the flesh, even in the marriage of the body, is inevitable. But he is married in the flesh, and his wife is with him in the body, he loves his body, which she gave him complete, and he loves her body, which is not himself, but which he has known. He has known and rejoiced in the earthly bride, he will adhere to her always. But there is the Spirit beyond her: there is his desire which transcends her, there is the Bride still he craves for and courts. And he knows, this is the Spirit, it is not the body. And he paints it as the light. And he paints himself within the light. For he has a deep desire to know himself in the embrace of the spirit. For he does not know himself, he is never consummated.

In the Old Law, fulfilled in him, he is not appeased, he must transcend the Law. The Woman is embraced, caught up, and carried forward, the male spirit, passing on half satisfied, must seek a new bride, a further consummation. For there is no bride on earth for him.

To Dürer, the whole earth was as a bride, unknown and unaccomplished, offering satisfaction to him. And he sought out the earth endlessly, as a man seeks to know a bride who surpasses him. It was all: the Bride.

But to Rembrandt the bride was not to be found, he must react upon himself, he must seek in himself for his own consummation. There was the Light, the Spirit, the Bridegroom. But when Rembrandt sought the complete Bride, sought for his own consummation, he knew it was not to be found, he knew she did not exist in the concrete. He knew, as Michelangelo knew, that there was not on the earth a woman to satisfy him, to be his mate. He must seek for the Bride beyond the physical woman; he must seek for the great female principle in an abstraction.

But the abstraction was not the geometric abstraction, created from knowledge, a state of Absolute Remembering, making Absolute of the Consummation which had been, as in Raphael. It was the desired Unknown, the goodly Unknown, the Spirit, the Light. And with this Light Rembrandt must seek even the marriage of the body. Everything he did approximates to the Consummation, but never can realize it. He paints always faith, belief, hope; never Raphael's terrible, dead certainty.

To Dürer, every moment of his existence was occupied. He existed within the embrace of the Bride, which embrace he could never fathom nor exhaust.

Raphael knew and outraged the Bride, but he harked back, obsessed by the consummation which had been.

To Rembrandt, woman was only the first acquaintance with the Bride. Of woman he obtained and expected no complete satisfaction. He knew he must go on, beyond the woman. But though the flesh could not find its consummation, still he did not deny the flesh. He was an artist, and in his art no artist ever could blaspheme the Holy Spirit, the Reconciler. Only a dogmatist could do that. Rembrandt did not deny the flesh, as so many artists try to do. He went on from her to the fuller knowledge of the Bride, in true progression. Which makes the wonderful beauty of Rembrandt.

But, like Michelangelo, owning the flesh, and a northern Christian being bent on personal salvation, personal consummation in the flesh, such as a Christian feels with us when he receives the Sacrament and hears the words "This is My Body, take, and eat," Rembrandt craved to marry the flesh and the Spirit, to achieve consummation in the flesh through marriage with the Spirit.

Which is the great northern confusion. For the flesh is of the flesh, and the Spirit of the Spirit, and they are two, even as the Father and the Son are two, and not One.

Raphael conceived the two as One, thereby revoking Time. Michelangelo would have created the bridal Flesh, to satisfy himself. Rembrandt would have married his own flesh to the Spirit, taken the consummate Kiss of the Light upon his fleshly face.

Which is a confusion. For the Father cannot know the Son, nor the Son the Father. So, in Rembrandt, the marriage is always imperfect, the embrace is never close nor consummate, as it is in Botticelli or in Raphael, or in Michelangelo. There is an eternal non-marriage betwixt flesh and spirit. They are two; they are never Two-in-One. So that in Rembrandt there is never complete marriage betwixt the Light and the Body. They are contiguous, never.

This has been the confusion and the error of the northern countries, but particularly of Germany, this desire to have the spirit mate with the flesh, the flesh with the spirit. Spirit can mate with spirit, and flesh with flesh, and the two matings can take place separately, flesh with flesh, or spirit with spirit. But to try to mate flesh with spirit makes confusion.

The bride I mate with my body may or may not be the Bride in whom I find my consummation. It may be that, at times, the great female principle does not abide abundantly in woman: that, at certain periods, woman, in the body, is not the supreme representative of the Bride. It may be the Bride is hidden from Man, as the Light, or as the Darkness, which he can never know in the flesh.

It may be, in the same way, that the great male principle is only weakly evidenced in man during certain periods, that the Bridegroom be hidden away from woman, for a century or centuries, and that she can only find Him as the voice, or the Wind. So I think it was with her during the medieval period; that the greatest women of the period knew that the Bridegroom did not exist for them in the body, but as the Christ, the Spirit.

And, in times of the absence of the bridegroom from the body, then woman in the body must either die in the body, or, mating in the body, she must mate with the Bridegroom in the Spirit, in a separate marriage. She cannot mate her body with the Spirit, nor mate her spirit with the Body. That is confusion. Let her mate the man in body, and her spirit with the Spirit, in a separate marriage. But let her not try to mate her spirit with the body of the man, that does not mate her Spirit.

The effort to mate spirit with body, body with spirit, is the crying confusion and pain of our times.

Rembrandt made the first effort. But art has developed to a clarity since then. It reached its climax in our own Turner. He did not seek to mate body with spirit. He mated his body easily, he did not deny it. But what he sought was the mating of the Spirit. Ever, he sought the consummation in the Spirit, and he reached it at last. Ever, he sought the Light, to make the light transfuse the body, till the body was carried away, a mere bloodstain, became a ruddy stain of red sunlight within white sunlight. This was perfect consummation in Turner, when, the body gone, the ruddy light meets the crystal light in a perfect fusion, the utter dawn, the utter golden sunset, the extreme of all life, where all is One, One-Being, a perfect glowing Oneness.

Like Raphael, it becomes an abstraction. But this, in Turner, is the abstraction from the spiritual marriage and consummation, the final transcending of all the Law, the achieving of what is to us almost a nullity. If Turner had ever painted his last picture, it would have been a white, incandescent surface, the same whiteness when he finished as when he began, proceeding from nullity to nullity, through all the range of colour.

Turner is perfect. Such a picture as his *Norham Castle, Sunrise,* where only the faintest shadow of life stains the light, is the last word that can be uttered, before the blazing and timeless silence.

He sought, and he found, perfect marriage in the spirit. It was apart from woman. His Bride was the Light. Or he was the bride himself, and the Light–the Bridegroom. Be that as it may, he became one and consummate with the Light, and gave us the consummate revelation.

Corot, also, nearer to the Latin tradition of utter consummation in the body, made a wonderful marriage in the spirit between light and darkness, just tinctured with life. But he contained more of the two consummations together, the marriage in the body, represented in geometric form, and the marriage in the spirit, represented by shimmering transfusion and infusion of light through darkness.

But Turner is the crisis in this effort: he achieves pure light, pure and singing. In him the consummation is perfect, the perfect marriage in the spirit.

In the body his marriage was other. He never attempted to mingle the two. The marriage in the body, with the woman, was apart from, completed away from the marriage in the Spirit, with the Bride, the Light.

But I cannot look at a later Turner picture without abstracting myself, without denying that I have limbs, knees and thighs and breast. If I look at the Norham Castle, and remember my own knees and my own breast, then the picture is a nothing to me. I must not know. And if I look at Raphael's *Madonna degli Ansidei,* I am cut off from my future, from aspiration. The gate is shut upon me, I can go no further. The thought of Turner's *Sunrise* becomes magic and fascinating, it gives the lie to this completed symbol. I know I am the other thing as well.

So that, whenever art or any expression becomes perfect, it becomes a lie. For it is only perfect by reason of abstraction from that context by which and in which it exists as truth.

So Turner is a lie, and Raphael is a lie, and the marriage in the spirit is a lie, and the marriage in the body is a lie, each is a lie without the other. Since each excludes the other in these instances, they are both lies. If they were brought together, and reconciled, then there were a jubilee. But where is the Holy Spirit that shall reconcile Raphael and Turner?

There must be marriage of body in body, and of spirit in spirit, and Two-in-One. And the marriage in the body must not deny the marriage in the spirit, for that is blasphemy against the Holy Ghost; and the marriage in the spirit shall not deny the marriage in the body, for that is blasphemy against the Holy Ghost. But the two must be for ever reconciled, even if they must exist on occasions apart one from the other.

For in Botticelli the dual marriage is perfect, or almost perfect, body and spirit reconciled, or almost reconciled, in a perfect dual consummation. And in all art there is testimony to the wonderful dual marriage, the true consummation. But in Raphael, the marriage in the spirit is left out so much that it is almost denied, so that the picture is almost a lie, almost a blasphemy. And in Turner, the marriage in the body is almost denied in the same way, so that his picture is almost a blasphemy. But neither in Raphael nor in Turner is the denial positive: it is only an over-affirmation of the one at the expense of the other.

But in some men, in some small men, like bishops, the denial of marriage in the body is positive and blasphemous, a sin against the Holy Ghost. And in some men, like Prussian army officers, the denial of marriage in the spirit is an equal blasphemy. But which of the two is a greater sinner, working better for the destruction of his fellow-man, that is for the One God to judge.

CHAPTER IX

A Nos Moutons

Most fascinating in all artists is this antinomy between Law and Love, between the Flesh and the Spirit, between the Father and the Son.

For the moralist it is easy. He can insist on that aspect of the Law or Love which is in the immediate line of development for his age, and he can sternly and severely exclude or suppress all the rest.

So that all morality is of temporary value, useful to its times. But Art must give a deeper satisfaction. It must give fair play all round.

Yet every work of art adheres to some system of morality. But if it be really a work of art, it must contain the essential criticism on the morality to which it adheres. And hence the antinomy, hence the conflict necessary to every tragic conception.

The degree to which the system of morality, or the metaphysic, of any work of art is submitted to criticism within the work of art makes the lasting value and satisfaction of that work. Æschylus, having caught the oriental idea of Love, correcting the tremendous Greek conception of the Law with this new idea, produces the intoxicating satisfaction of the Orestean trilogy. The Law, and Love, they are here the Two-in-One in all their magnificence. But Euripides, with his aspiration towards Love, Love the supreme, and his almost hatred of the Law, Law the Triumphant but Base Closer of Doom, is less satisfactory, because of the very fact that he holds

Love always Supreme, and yet must endure the chagrin of seeing Love perpetually transgressed and overthrown. So he makes his tragedy: the higher thing eternally pulled down by the lower. And this unfairness in the use of terms, higher and lower, but above all, the unfairness of showing Love always violated and suffering, never supreme and triumphant, makes us disbelieve Euripides in the end. For we have to bring in pity, we must admit that Love is at a fundamental disadvantage before the Law, and cannot therefore ever hold its own. Which is weak philosophy.

If Æschylus has a metaphysic to his art, this metaphysic is that Love and Law are Two, eternally in conflict, and eternally being reconciled. This is the tragic significance of Æschylus.

But the metaphysic of Euripides is that the Law and Love are two eternally in conflict, and unequally matched, so that Love must always be borne down. In Love a man shall only suffer. There is also a Reconciliation, otherwise Euripides were not so great. But there is always the unfair matching, this disposition insisted on, which at last leaves one cold and unbelieving.

The moments of pure satisfaction come in the choruses, in the pure lyrics, when Love is put into true relations with the Law, apart from knowledge, transcending knowledge, transcending the metaphysic, where the aspiration to Love meets the acknowledgment of the Law in a consummate marriage, for the moment.

Where Euripides adheres to his metaphysic, he is unsatisfactory. Where he transcends his metaphysic, he gives that supreme equilibrium wherein we know satisfaction.

The adherence to a metaphysic does not necessarily give artistic form. Indeed the over-strong adherence to a metaphysic usually destroys any possibility of artistic form. Artistic form is a revelation of the two principles of Love and the Law in a state of conflict and yet reconciled: pure motion struggling against and yet reconciled with the Spirit: active force meeting and overcoming and yet not overcoming inertia. It is the conjunction of the two which makes form. And since the two must always meet under fresh conditions, form must always be different. Each work of art has its own form, which has no relation to any other form. When a young painter studies an old master, he studies, not the form, that is an abstraction which does not exist: he studies maybe the method of the old great artist: but he studies chiefly to understand how the old great artist suffered in himself the conflict of Love and Law, and brought them to a reconciliation. Apart from artistic method, it is not Art that the young man is studying, but the State of Soul of the great old artist, so that he, the young artist, may understand his own soul and gain a reconciliation between the aspiration and the resistant

It is most wonderful in poetry, this sense of conflict contained within a reconciliation:

Hail to thee, blithe Spirit!
  Bird thou never wert,
That from Heaven, or near it,
  Pourest thy full heart
In profuse strains of unpremeditated art.

Shelley wishes to say, the skylark is a pure, untrammelled spirit, a pure motion. But the very "Bird thou never wert" admits that the skylark *is* in very fact a bird, a concrete, momentary thing. If the line ran, "Bird thou never art," that would spoil it all. Shelley wishes to say, the song is poured out of heaven: but "or near it," he admits. There is the perfect relation between heaven and earth. And the last line is the tumbling sound of a lark's singing, the real Two-in-One.

The very adherence to rhyme and regular rhythm is a concession to the Law, a concession to the body, to the being and requirements of the body. They are an admission of the living, positive inertia which is the other half of life, other than the pure will to motion. In this consummation, they are the resistance and response of the Bride in the arms of the Bridegroom. And according as the Bride and Bridegroom come closer together, so is the response and resistance more fine, indistinguishable, so much the more, in this act of consummation, is the movement that of Two-in-One, indistinguishable each from the other, and not the movement of two brought together clumsily.

So that in Swinburne, where almost all is concession to the body, so that the poetry becomes almost a sensation and not an experience or a consummation, justifying Spinoza's "Amor est titillatio, concomitante idea causae externae," we find continual adherence to the body, to the Rose, to the Flesh, the physical in everything, in the sea, in the marshes; there is an overbalance in the favour of Supreme Law; Love is not Love, but passion, part of the Law; there is no Love, there is only Supreme Law. And the poet sings the Supreme Law to gain rebalance in himself, for he hovers always on the edge of death, of Not-Being, he is always out of reach of the Law, bodiless, in the faintness of Love that has triumphed and denied the Law, in the dread of an over-developed, over-sensitive soul which exists always on the point of dissolution from the body.

But he is not divided against himself. It is the novelists and dramatists who have the hardest task in reconciling their metaphysic, their theory of being and knowing, with their living sense of being. Because a novel is a microcosm, and because man in viewing the universe must view it in the light of a theory, therefore every novel must have the background or the structural skeleton of some theory of being, some metaphysic. But the metaphysic must always subserve the artistic purpose beyond the artist's conscious aim. Otherwise the novel becomes a treatise.

And the danger is, that a man shall make himself a metaphysic to excuse or cover his own faults or failure. Indeed, a sense of fault or failure is the usual cause of a man's making himself a metaphysic, to justify himself.

Then, having made himself a metaphysic of self-justification, or a metaphysic of self-denial, the novelist proceeds to apply the world to this, instead of applying this to the world.

Tolstoi is a flagrant example of this. Probably because of profligacy in his youth, because he had disgusted himself in his own flesh, by excess or by prostitution, therefore Tolstoi, in his metaphysic, renounced the flesh altogether, later on, when he had tried and had failed to achieve complete marriage in the flesh. But above all things, Tolstoi was a child of the Law, he belonged to the Father. He had a marvellous sensuous understanding, and very little clarity of mind.

So that, in his metaphysic, he had to deny himself, his own being, in order to escape his own disgust of what he had done to himself, and to escape admission of his own failure.

Which made all the later part of his life a crying falsity and shame. Reading the reminiscences of Tolstoi, one can only feel shame at the way Tolstoi denied all that was great in him, with vehement cowardice. He degraded himself infinitely, he perjured himself far more than did Peter when he denied Christ. Peter repented. But Tolstoi denied the Father, and propagated a great system of his recusancy, elaborating his own weakness, blaspheming his own strength. "What difficulty is there in writing about how an officer fell in love with a married woman?" he used to say of his *Anna Karenina;* "there's no difficulty in it, and, above all, no good in it."

Because he was mouthpiece to the Father in uttering the law of passion, he said there was no difficulty in it, because it came naturally to him. Christ might just as easily have said, there was no difficulty in the Parable of the Sower, and no good in it, either, because it flowed out of him without effort.

And Thomas Hardy's metaphysic is something like Tolstoi's. "There is no reconciliation between Love and the Law," says Hardy. "The spirit of Love must always succumb before the blind, stupid, but overwhelming power of the Law."

Already as early as *The Return of the Native* he has come to this theory, in order to explain his own sense of failure. But before that time, from the very start, he has had an overweening theoretic antagonism to the Law. "That which is physical, of the body, is weak, despicable, bad," he said at the very start. He represented his fleshy heroes as villains, but very weak and maundering villains. At its worst, the Law is a weak, craven sensuality: at its best, it is a passive inertia. It is the gap in the armour, it is the hole in the foundation.

Such a metaphysic is almost silly. If it were not that man is much stronger in feeling than in thought, the Wessex novels would be sheer rubbish, as they are already in parts. *The Well-Beloved* is sheer rubbish, fatuity, as is a good deal of *The Dynasts* conception.

But it is not as a metaphysician that one must consider Hardy. He makes a poor show there. For nothing in his work is so pitiable as his clumsy efforts to push events into line with his theory of being, and to make calamity fall on those who represent the principle of Love. He does it exceedingly badly, and owing to this effort his form is execrable in the extreme.

His feeling, his instinct, his sensuous understanding is, however, apart from his metaphysic, very great and deep, deeper than that, perhaps, of any other English novelist. Putting aside his metaphysic, which must always obtrude when he thinks of people, and turning to the earth, to landscape, then he is true to himself.

Always he must start from the earth, from the great source of the Law, and his people move in his landscape almost insignificantly, somewhat like tame animals wandering in the wild. The earth is the manifestation of the Father, of the Creator, Who made us in the Law. God still speaks aloud in His Works, as to Job, so to Hardy, surpassing human conception and the human law. "Dost thou know the balancings of the clouds, the wondrous works of him which is perfect in knowledge? How thy garments are warm, when he quieteth the earth by the south wind? Hast thou with him spread out the sky, which is strong?"

This is the true attitude of Hardy—"With God is terrible majesty." The theory of knowledge, the metaphysic of the man, is much smaller than the man himself. So with Tolstoi.

"Knowest thou the time when the wild goats of the rock bring forth? Or canst thou mark when the hinds do calve? Canst thou number the months that they fulfil? Or knowest thou the time when they bring forth? They bow themselves, they bring forth their young ones, they cast out their sorrows. Their young ones are good in liking, they grow up with corn; they go forth, and return not unto them."

There is a good deal of this in Hardy. But in Hardy there is more than the concept of Job, protesting his integrity. Job says in the end: "Therefore have I uttered that I understood not; things too wonderful for me, which I knew not.

"I have heard of thee by hearing of the ear; but now mine eye seeth thee.

"Wherefore I abhor myself, and repent in dust and ashes."

But Jude ends where Job began, cursing the day and the services of his birth, and in so much cursing the act of the Lord, "Who made him in the womb."

It is the same cry all through Hardy, this curse upon the birth in the flesh, and this unconscious adherence to the flesh. The instincts, the bodily passions are strong and sudden in all Hardy's men. They are too strong and sudden. They fling Jude into the arms of Arabella, years after he has known Sue, and against his own will.

For every man comprises male and female in his being, the male always struggling for predominance. A woman likewise consists in male and female, with female predominant.

And a man who is strongly male tends to deny, to refute the female in him. A real "man" takes no heed for his body, which is the more female part of him. He considers himself only as an instrument, to be used in the service of some idea.

The true female, on the other hand, will eternally hold herself superior to any idea, will hold full life in the body to be the real happiness. The male exists in doing, the female in being. The male lives in the satisfaction of some purpose achieved, the female in the satisfaction of some purpose contained.

In Æschylus, in the *Eumenides,* there is Apollo, Loxias, the Sun God, the prophet, the male: there are the Erinyes, daughters of primeval Mother Night, representing here the female risen in retribution for some crime against the flesh; and there is Pallas, unbegotten daughter of Zeus, who is as the Holy Spirit in the Christian religion, the spirit of wisdom.

Orestes is bidden by the male god, Apollo, to avenge the murder of his father, Agamemnon, by his mother: that is, the male, murdered by the female, must be avenged by the male. But Orestes is child of his mother. He is in himself female. So that in himself the conscience, the madness, the violated part of his own self, his own body, drives him to the Furies. On the male side, he is right; on the female, wrong. But peace is given at last by Pallas, the Arbitrator, the spirit of wisdom.

And although Æschylus in his consciousness makes the Furies hideous, and Apollo supreme, yet, in his own self and in very fact, he makes the Furies wonderful and noble, with their tremendous hymns, and makes Apollo a trivial, sixth-form braggart and ranter. Clytemnestra also, wherever she appears, is wonderful and noble. Her sin is the sin of pride: she was the first to be injured. Agamemnon is a feeble thing beside her.

So Æschylus adheres still to the Law, to Right, to the Creator who created man in His Own Image, and in His Law. What he has learned of Love, he does not yet quite believe.

Hardy has the same belief in the Law, but in conceipt of his own understanding, which cannot understand the Law, he says that the Law is nothing, a blind confusion.

And in conceipt of understanding, he deprecates and destroys both women and men who would represent the old primeval Law, the great Law of the Womb, the primeval Female principle. The Female shall not exist. Where it appears, it is a criminal tendency, to be stamped out.

This in Manston, Troy, Boldwood, Eustacia, Wildeve, Henchard, Tess, Jude, everybody. The women approved of are not Female in any real sense. They are passive subjects to the male, the re-echo from the male. As in the Christian religion, the Virgin worship is no real Female worship, but worship of the Female as she is passive and subjected to the male. Hence the sadness of Botticelli's Virgins.

Thus Tess sets out, not as any positive thing, containing all purpose, but as the acquiescent complement to the male. The female in her has become inert. Then Alec d'Urberville comes along, and possesses her. From the man who takes her Tess expects her own consummation, the singling out of herself, the addition of the male complement. She is of an old line, and has the aristocratic quality of respect for the other being. She does not see the other person as an extension of herself, existing in a universe of which she is the centre and pivot. She knows that other people are outside her. Therein she is an aristocrat. And out of this attitude to the other person came her passivity. It is not the same as the passive quality in the other little heroines, such as the girl in *The Woodlanders,* who is passive because she is small.

Tess is passive out of self-acceptance, a true aristocratic quality, amounting almost to self-indifference. She knows she is herself incontrovertibly, and she knows that other people are not herself. This is a very rare quality, even in a woman. And in a civilization so unequal, it is almost a weakness.

Tess never tries to alter or to change anybody, neither to alter nor to change nor to divert. What another person decides, that is his decision. She respects utterly the other's right to be. She is herself always.

But the others do not respect her right to be. Alec d'Urberville sees her as the embodied fulfilment of his own desire: something, that is, belonging to him. She cannot, in his conception, exist apart from him nor have any being apart from his being. For she is the embodiment of his desire.

This is very natural and common in men, this attitude to the world. But in Alec d'Urberville it applies only to the woman of his desire. He cares only for her. Such a man adheres to the female like a parasite.

It is a male quality to resolve a purpose to its fulfilment. It is the male quality, to seek the motive power in the female, and to convey this to a fulfilment; to receive some impulse into his senses, and to transmit it into expression.

Alec d'Urberville does not do this. He is male enough, in his way; but only physically male. He is constitutionally an enemy of the principle of self-subordination, which principle is inherent in every man. It is this principle which makes a man, a true male, see his job through, at no matter what cost. A man is strictly only himself when he is fulfilling some purpose he has conceived: so that the principle is not of self-subordination, but of continuity, of development. Only when insisted on, as in Christianity, does it become self-sacrifice. And this resistance to self-sacrifice on Alec d'Urberville's part does not make him an individualist, an egoist, but rather a non-individual, an incomplete, almost a fragmentary thing.

There seems to be in d'Urberville an inherent antagonism to any progression in himself. Yet he seeks with all his power for the source of stimulus in woman. He takes the deep impulse from the female. In this he is exceptional. No ordinary man could really have betrayed Tess. Even if she had had an illegitimate child to another man, to Angel Clare, for example, it would not have shattered her as did her connexion with Alec d'Urberville. For Alec d'Urberville could reach some of the real sources of the female in a woman, and draw from them. Troy could also do this. And, as a woman instinctively knows, such men are rare. Therefore they have a power over a woman. They draw from the depth of her being.

And what they draw, they betray. With a natural male, what he draws from the source of the female, the impulse he receives from the source he transmits through his own being into utterance, motion, action, expression. But Troy and Alec d'Urberville, what they received they knew only as gratification in the senses; some perverse will prevented them from submitting to it, from becoming instrumental to it.

Which was why Tess was shattered by Alec d'Urberville, and why she murdered him in the end. The murder is badly done, altogether the book is botched, owing to the way of thinking in the author, owing to the weak yet obstinate theory of being. Nevertheless, the murder is true, the whole book is true, in its conception.

Angel Clare has the very opposite qualities to those of Alec d'Urberville. To the latter, the female in himself is the only part of himself he will acknowledge: the body, the senses, that which he shares with the female, which the female shares with him. To Angel Clare, the female in himself is detestable, the body, the senses, that which he will share with a woman, is held degraded. What he wants really is to receive the female impulse other than through the body. But his thinking has made him criticize Christianity, his deeper instinct has forbidden him to deny his body any further, a deadlock in his own being, which denies him any purpose, so that he must take to hand, labour out of sheer impotence to resolve himself, drives him unwillingly to woman. But he must see her only as the Female Principle, he cannot bear to see her as the Woman in the Body. Her he thinks degraded. To marry her, to have a physical marriage with her, he must overcome all his ascetic revulsion, he must, in his own mind, put off his own divinity, his pure maleness, his singleness, his pure completeness, and descend to the heated welter of the flesh. It is objectionable to him. Yet his body, his life, is too strong for him.

Who is he, that he shall be pure male, and deny the existence of the female? This is the question the Creator asks of him. Is then the male the exclusive whole of life?—is he even the higher or supreme part of life? Angel Clare thinks so: as Christ thought.

Yet it is not so, as even Angel Clare must find out. Life, that is Two-in-One, Male and Female. Nor is either part greater than the other.

It is not Angel Clare's fault that he cannot come to Tess when he finds that she has, in his words, been defiled. It is the result of generations of ultra-Christian training, which had left in him an inherent aversion to the female, and to all in himself which pertained to the female. What he, in his Christian sense, conceived of as Woman, was only the servant and attendant and administering spirit to the male. He had no idea that there was such a thing as positive Woman, as the Female, another great living Principle counterbalancing his own male principle. He conceived of the world as consisting of the One, the Male Principle.

Which conception was already gendered in Botticelli, whence the melancholy of the Virgin. Which conception reached its fullest in Turner's pictures, which were utterly bodiless; and also in the great scientists or thinkers of the last generation, even Darwin and Spencer and Huxley. For these last conceived of evolution, of one spirit or principle starting at the far end of time, and lonelily traversing Time. But there is not one principle, there are two, travelling always to meet, each step of each one lessening the distance between the two of them. And Space, which so frightened Herbert Spencer, is as a Bride to us. And the cry of Man does not ring out into the Void. It rings out to Woman, whom we know not.

This Tess knew, unconsciously. An aristocrat she was, developed through generations to the belief in her own self-establishment. She could help, but she could not be helped. She could give, but she could not receive. She could attend to the wants of the other person, but no other person, save another aristocrat—and there is scarcely such a thing as another aristocrat—could attend to her wants, her deepest wants.

So it is the aristocrat alone who has any real and vital sense of "the neighbour," of the other person; who has the habit of submerging himself, putting himself entirely away before the other person: because he expects to receive nothing from the other person. So that now he has lost much of his initiative force, and exists almost isolated, detached, and without the surging ego of the ordinary man, because he has controlled his nature according to the other man, to exclude him.

And Tess, despising herself in the flesh, despising the deep Female she was, because Alec d'Urberville had betrayed her very source, loved Angel Clare, who also despised and hated the flesh. She did not hate d'Urberville. What a man did, he did, and if he did it to her, it was her look-out. She did not conceive of him as having any human duty towards her.

The same with Angel Clare as with Alec d'Urberville. She was very grateful to him for saving her from her despair of contamination, and from her bewildered isolation. But when he accused her, she could not plead or answer. For she had no right to his goodness. She stood alone.

The female was strong in her. She was herself. But she was out of place, utterly out of her element and her times. Hence her utter bewilderment. This is the reason why she was so overcome. She was outwearied from the start, in her spirit. For it is only by receiving from all our fellows that we are kept fresh and vital. Tess was herself, female, intrinsically a woman.

The female in her was indomitable, unchangeable, she was utterly constant to herself. But she was, by long breeding, intact from mankind. Though Alec d'Urberville was of no kin to her, yet, in the book, he has always a quality of kinship. It was as if only a kinsman, an aristocrat, could approach her. And this to her undoing. Angel Clare would never have reached her. She would have abandoned herself to him, but he would never have reached her. It needed a physical aristocrat. She would have lived with her husband, Clare, in a state of abandon to him, like a coma. Alec d'Urberville forced her to realize him, and to realize herself. He came close to her, as Clare could never have done. So she murdered him. For she was herself.

And just as the aristocratic principle had isolated Tess, it had isolated Alec d'Urberville. For though Hardy consciously made the young betrayer a plebeian and an impostor, unconsciously, with the supreme justice of the artist, he made him the same as de Stancy, a true aristocrat, or as Fitzpiers, or Troy. He did not give him the tiredness, the touch of exhaustion necessary, in Hardy's mind, to an aristocrat. But he gave him the intrinsic qualities.

With the men as with the women of old descent: they have nothing to do with mankind in general, they are exceedingly personal.

For many generations they have been accustomed to regard their own desires as their own supreme laws. They have not been bound by the conventional morality: this they have transcended, being a code unto themselves. The other person has been always present to their imagination, in the spectacular sense. He has always existed to them. But he has always existed as something other than themselves.

Hence the inevitable isolation, detachment of the aristocrat. His one aim, during centuries, has been to keep himself detached. At last he finds himself, by his very nature, cut off.

Then either he must go his own way, or he must struggle towards reunion with the mass of mankind. Either he must be an incomplete individualist, like de Stancy, or like the famous Russian nobles, he must become a wild humanitarian and reformer.

For as all the governing power has gradually been taken from the nobleman, and as, by tradition, by inherent inclination, he does not occupy himself with profession other than government, how shall he use that power which is in him and which comes into him?

He is, by virtue of breed and long training, a perfect instrument. He knows, as every pure-bred thing knows, that his root and source is in his female. He seeks the motive power in the woman. And, having taken it, has nothing to do with it, can find, in this democratic, plebeian age, no means by which to transfer it into action, expression, utterance. So there is a continual gnawing of unsatisfaction, a constant seeking of another woman, still another woman. For each time the impulse comes fresh, everything seems all right.

It may be, also, that in the aristocrat a certain weariness makes him purposeless, vicious, like a form of death. But that is not necessary. One feels that in Manston, and Troy, and Fitzpiers, and Alec d'Urberville, there is good stuff gone wrong. Just as in Angel Clare, there is good stuff gone wrong in the other direction.

There can never be one extreme of wrong, without the other extreme. If there had never been the extravagant Puritan idea, that the Female Principle was to be denied, cast out by man from his soul, that only the Male Principle, of Abstraction, of Good, of Public Good, of the Community, embodied in "Thou shalt love thy neighbour as thyself," really existed, there would never have been produced the extreme Cavalier type, which says that only the Female Principle endures in man, that all the Abstraction, the Good, the Public Elevation, the Community, was a grovelling cowardice, and that man lived by enjoyment, through his senses, enjoyment which ended in his senses. Or perhaps better, if the extreme Cavalier type had never been produced, we should not have had the Puritan, the extreme correction.

The one extreme produces the other. It is inevitable for Angel Clare and for Alec d'Urberville mutually to destroy the woman they both loved. Each does her the extreme of wrong, so she is destroyed.

The book is handled with very uncertain skill, botched and bungled. But it contains the elements of the greatest tragedy: Alec d'Urberville, who has killed the male in himself, as Clytemnestra symbolically for Orestes killed Agamemnon; Angel Clare, who has killed the female in himself, as Orestes killed Clytemnestra: and Tess, the Woman, the Life, destroyed by a mechanical fate, in the communal law.

There is no reconciliation. Tess, Angel Clare, Alec d'Urberville, they are all as good as dead. For Angel Clare, though still apparently alive, is in reality no more than a mouth, a piece of paper, like Clym left preaching.

There is no reconciliation, only death. And so Hardy really states his case, which is not his consciously stated metaphysic, by any means, but a statement how man has gone wrong and brought death on himself: how man has violated the Law, how he has supererogated himself, gone so far in his male conceit as to supersede the Creator, and win death as a reward. Indeed, the works of supererogation of our male assiduity help us to a better salvation.

Jude is only Tess turned round about. Instead of the heroine containing the two principles, male and female, at strife within her one being, it is Jude who contains them both, whilst the two women with him take the place of the two men to Tess. Arabella is Alec d'Urberville, Sue is Angel Clare. These represent the same pair of principles.

But, first, let it be said again that Hardy is a bad artist. Because he must condemn Alec d'Urberville, according to his own personal creed, therefore he shows him a vulgar intriguer of coarse lasses, and as ridiculous convert to evangelism. But Alec d'Urberville, by the artist's account, is neither of these. It is, in actual life, a rare man who seeks and seeks among women for one of such character and intrinsic female being as Tess. The ordinary sensualist avoids such characters. They implicate him too deeply. An ordinary sensualist would have been much too common, much too afraid, to turn to Tess. In a way, d'Urberville was her mate. And his subsequent passion for her is in its way noble enough. But whatever his passion, as a male, he must be a betrayer, even if he had been the most faithful husband on earth. He betrayed the female in a woman, by taking her, and by responding with no male impulse from himself. He roused her, but never satisfied her. He could never satisfy her. It was like a soul-disease in him: he was, in the strict though not the technical sense, impotent. But he must have wanted, later on, not to be so. But he could not help himself. He was spiritually impotent in love.

Arabella was the same. She, like d'Urberville, was converted by an evangelical preacher. It is significant in both of them. They were not just shallow, as Hardy would have made them out.

He is, however, more contemptuous in his personal attitude to the woman than to the man. He insists that she is a pig-killer's daughter; he insists that she drag Jude into pig-killing; he lays stress on her false tail of hair. That is not the point at all. This is only Hardy's bad art. He himself, as an artist, manages in the whole picture of Arabella almost to make insignificant in her these pig-sticking, false-hair crudities. But he must have his personal revenge on her for her coarseness, which offends him, because he is something of an Angel Clare.

The pig-sticking and so forth are not so important in the real picture. As for the false tail of hair, few women dared have been so open and natural about it. Few women, indeed, dared have made Jude marry them. It may have been a case with Arabella of "fools rush in." But she was not such a fool. And her motives are explained in the book. Life is not, in the actual, such a simple affair of getting a fellow and getting married. It is, even for Arabella, an affair on which she places her all. No barmaid marries anybody, the first man she can lay hands on. She cannot. It must be a personal thing to her. And no ordinary woman would want Jude. Moreover, no ordinary woman could have laid her hands on Jude.

It is an absurd fallacy this, that a small man wants a woman bigger and finer than he is himself. A man is as big as his real desires. Let a man, seeing with his eyes a woman of force and being, want her for his own, then that man is intrinsically an equal of that woman. And the same with a woman.

A coarse, shallow woman does not want to marry a sensitive, deep-feeling man. She feels no desire for him, she is not drawn to him, but repelled, knowing he will contemn her. She wants a man to correspond to herself: that is, if she is a young woman looking for a mate, as Arabella was.

What an old, jaded, yet still unsatisfied woman or man wants is another matter. Yet not even one of these will take a young creature of real character, superior in force. Instinct and fear prevent it.

Arabella was, under all her disguise of pig-fat and false hair, and vulgar speech, in character somewhat an aristocrat. She was, like Eustacia, amazingly lawless, even splendidly so. She believed in herself and she was not altered by any outside opinion of herself. Her fault was pride. She thought herself the centre of life, that all which existed belonged to her in so far as she wanted it.

In this she was something like Job. His attitude was "I am strong and rich, and, also, I am a good man." He gave out of his own sense of bounty, and felt no indebtedness. Arabella was almost the same. She felt also strong and abundant, arrogant in her hold on life. She needed a complement; and the nearest thing to her satisfaction was Jude. For as she, intrinsically, was a strong female, by far overpowering her Annies and her friends, so was he a strong male.

The difference between them was not so much a difference of quality, or degree, as a difference of form. Jude, like Tess, wanted full consummation. Arabella, like Alec d'Urberville, had that in her which resisted full consummation, wanted only to enjoy herself in contact with the male. She would have no transmission.

There are two attitudes to love. A man in love with a woman says either: "I, the man, the male, am the supreme, I am the one, and the woman is administered unto me, and this is her highest function, to be administered unto me." This was the conscious attitude of the Greeks. But their unconscious attitude was the reverse: they were in truth afraid of the female principle, their vaunt was empty, they went in deep, inner dread of her. So did the Jews, so do the Italians. But after the Renaissance, there was a change. Then began conscious Woman-reverence, and a lack of instinctive reverence, rather only an instinctive pity. It is according to the balance between the Male and Female principles.

The other attitude of a man in love, besides this of "she is administered unto my maleness," is, "She is the unknown, the undiscovered, into which I plunge to discovery, losing myself."

And what we call real love has always this latter attitude.

The first attitude, which belongs to passion, makes a man feel proud, splendid. It is a powerful stimulant to him, the female administered to him. He feels full of blood, he walks the earth like a Lord. And it is to this state Nietzsche aspires in his *Wille zur Macht*. It is this the passionate nations crave.

And under all this there is, naturally, the sense of fear, transition, and the sadness of mortality. For, the female being herself an independent force, may she not withdraw, and leave a man empty, like ash, as one sees a Jew or an Italian so often?

This first attitude, too, of male pride receiving the female administration may, and often does, contain the corresponding intense fear and reverence of the female, as of the unknown. So that, starting from the male assertion, there came in the old days the full consummation; as often there comes the full consummation now.

But not always. The man may retain all the while the sense of himself, the primary male, receiving gratification. This constant reaction upon himself at length dulls his senses and his sensibility, and makes him mechanical, automatic. He grows gradually incapable of receiving any gratification from the female, and becomes a *roué,* only automatically alive, and frantic with the knowledge thereof.

It is the tendency of the Parisian–or has been–to take this attitude to love, and to intercourse. The woman knows herself all the while as the primary female receiving administration of the male. So she becomes hard and external, and inwardly jaded, tired out. It is the tendency of English women to take this attitude also. And it is this attitude of love, more than anything else, which devitalizes a race, and makes it barren.

It is an attitude natural enough to start with. Every young man must think that it is the highest honour he can do to a woman, to receive from her her female administration to his male being, whilst he meanwhile gives her the gratification of himself. But intimacy usually corrects this, love, or use, or marriage: a married man ceases to think of himself as the primary male: hence often his dullness. Unfortunately, he also fails in many cases to realize the gladness of a man in contact with the unknown in the female, which gives him a sense of richness and oneness with all life, as if, by being part of life, he were infinitely rich. Which is different from the sense of power, of dominating life. The *Wille zur Macht* is a spurious feeling.

For a man who dares to look upon, and to venture within the unknown of the female, losing himself, like a man who gives himself to the sea, or a man who enters a primeval, virgin forest, feels, when he returns, the utmost gladness of singing. This is certainly the gladness of a male bird in his singing, the amazing joy of return from the adventure into the unknown, rich with addition to his soul, rich with the knowledge of the utterly illimitable depth and breadth of the unknown; the ever-yielding extent of the unacquired, the unattained; the inexhaustible riches lain under unknown skies over unknown seas, all the magnificence that *is,* and yet which is unknown to any of us. And the knowledge of the reality with which it awaits me, the male, the knowledge of the calling and struggling of all the unknown, illimitable Female towards me, unembraced as yet, towards those men who will endlessly follow me, who will endlessly struggle after me, beyond me, further into this calling, unrealized vastness, nearer to the outstretched, eager, advancing unknown in the woman.

It is for this sense of All the magnificence that is unknown to me, of All that which stretches forth arms and breast to the Inexhaustible Embrace of all the ages, towards me, whose arms are outstretched, for this moment's embrace which gives me the inkling of the Inexhaustible Embrace that every man must and does yearn. And whether he be a *roué,* and vicious, or young and virgin, this is the bottom of every man's desire, for the embrace, for the advancing into the unknown, for the landing on the shore of the undiscovered half of the world, where the wealth of the female lies before us.

What is true of men is so of women. If we turn our faces west, towards nightfall and the unknown within the dark embrace of a wife, they turn their faces east, towards the sunrise and the brilliant, bewildering, active embrace of a husband. And as we are dazed with the unknown in her, so is she dazed with the unknown in us. It is so. And we throw up our joy to heaven like towers and spires and fountains and leaping flowers, so glad we are.

But always, we are divided within ourselves. Is it not that I am wonderful? Is it not a gratification for me when a stranger shall land on my shores and enjoy what he finds there? Shall I not also enjoy it? Shall I not enjoy the strange motion of the stranger, like a pleasant sensation of silk and warmth against me, stirring unknown fibres? Shall I not take this enjoyment without venturing out in dangerous waters, losing myself, perhaps destroying myself seeking the unknown? Shall I not stay at home, and by feeling the swift, soft airs blow out of the unknown upon my body, shall I not have rich pleasure of myself?

And, because they were afraid of the unknown, and because they wanted to retain the full-veined gratification of self-pleasure, men have kept their women tightly in bondage. But when the men were no longer afraid of the unknown, when they deemed it exhausted, they said, "There are no women; there are only daughters of men" —as we say now, as the Greeks tried to say. Hence the "Virgin" conception of woman, the passionless, passive conception, progressing from Fielding's Amelia to Dickens's Agnes, and on to Hardy's Sue.

Whereas Arabella in *Jude the Obscure* has what one might call the selfish instinct for love, Jude himself has the other, the unselfish. She sees in him a male who can gratify her. She takes him, and is gratified by him. Which makes a man of him. He becomes a grown, independent man in the arms of Arabella, conscious of having met, and satisfied, the female demand in him. This makes a man of any youth. He is proven unto himself as a male being, initiated into the freedom of life.

But Arabella refused his purpose. She refused to combine with him in one purpose. Just like Alec d'Urberville, she had from the outset an antagonism to the submission to any change in herself, to any development. She had the will to remain where she was, static, and to receive and exhaust all impulse she received from the male, in her senses. Whereas in a normal woman, impulse received from the male drives her on to a sense of joy and wonder and glad freedom in touch with the unknown of which she is made aware, so that she exists on the edge of the unknown half in rapture. Which is the state the writers wish to portray in "Amelia" and "Agnes," but particularly in the former; which Reynolds wishes to portray in his pictures of women.

To all this Arabella was antagonistic. It seems like a perversion in her, as if she played havoc with the stuff she was made of, as Alec d'Urberville did. Nevertheless she remained always unswervable female, she never truckled to the male idea, but was self-responsible, without fear. It is easier to imagine such a woman, out of one's desires, than to find her in real life. For, where a half-criminal type, a reckless, dare-devil type resembling her, may be found on the outskirts of society, yet these are not Arabella. Which criminal type, or reckless, low woman, would want to marry Jude? Arabella wanted Jude. And it is evident she was not too coarse for him, since she made no show of refinement from the first. The female in her, reckless and unconstrained, was strong enough to draw him after her, as her male, right to the end. Which other woman could have done this? At least let acknowledgment be made to her great female force of character. Her coarseness seems to me exaggerated to make the moralist's case good against her.

Jude could never hate her. She did a great deal for the true making of him, for making him a grown man. She gave him to himself.

And there was danger at the outset that he should never become a man, but that he should remain incorporeal, smothered out under his idea of learning. He was somewhat in Angel Clare's position. Not that generations of particular training had made him almost rigid and paralysed to the female: but that his whole passion was concentrated away from woman to reinforce in him the male impulse towards extending the consciousness. His family was a difficult family to marry. And this because, whilst the men were physically vital, with a passion towards the female from which no moral training had restrained them, like a plant tied to a stick and diverted, they had at the same time an inherent complete contempt of the female, valuing only that which was male. So that they were strongly divided against themselves, with no external hold, such as a moral system, to grip to.

It would have been possible for Jude, monkish, passionate, medieval, belonging to woman yet striving away from her, refusing to know her, to have gone on denying one side of his nature, adhering to his idea of learning, till he had stultified the physical impulse of his being and perverted it entirely. Arabella brought him to himself, gave him himself, made him free, sound as a physical male.

That she would not, or could not, combine her life with him for the fulfilment of a purpose was their misfortune. But at any rate, his purpose of becoming an Oxford don was a cut-and-dried purpose which had no connexion with his living body, and for which probably no woman could have united with him.

No doubt Arabella hated his books, and hated his whole attitude to study. What had he, a passionate, emotional nature, to do with learning for learning's sake, with mere academics? Any woman must know it was ridiculous. But he persisted with the tenacity of all perverseness. And she, in this something of an aristocrat, like Tess, feeling that she had no right to him, no right to receive anything from him, except his sex, in which she felt she gave and did not receive, for she conceived of herself as the primary female, as that which, in taking the male, conferred on him his greatest boon, she left him alone. Her attitude was, that he would find all he desired in coming to her. She was occupied with herself. It was not that she wanted *him*. She wanted to have the sensation of herself in contact with him. His being she refused. She allowed only her own being.

Therefore she scarcely troubled him, when he earned little money and took no notice of her. He did not refuse to take notice of her because he hated her, or was deceived by her, or disappointed in her. He was not. He refused to consider her seriously because he adhered with all his pertinacity to the idea of study, from which he excluded her.

Which she saw and knew, and allowed. She would not force him to notice her, or to consider her seriously. She would compel him to nothing. She had had a certain satisfaction of him, which would be no more if she stayed for ever. For she was non-developing. When she knew him in her senses she knew the end of him, as far as she was concerned. That was all.

So she just went her way. He did not blame her. He scarcely missed her. He returned to his books.

Really, he had lost nothing by his marriage with Arabella: neither innocence nor belief nor hope. He had indeed gained his manhood. She left him the stronger and completer.

And now he would concentrate all on his male idea, of arresting himself, of becoming himself a non-developing quality, an academic mechanism. That was his obsession. That was his craving: to have nothing to do with his own life. This was the same as Tess when she turned to Angel Clare. She wanted life merely in the secondary, outside form, in the consciousness.

It was another form of the disease, or decay of old family, which possessed Alec d'Urberville; a different form, but closely related. D'Urberville wanted to arrest all his activity in his senses. Jude Fawley wanted to arrest all his activity in his mind. Each of them wanted to become an impersonal force working automatically. Each of them wanted to deny, or escape the responsibility and trouble of living as a complete person, a full individual.

And neither was able to bring it off. Jude's real desire was, not to live in the body. He wanted to exist only in his mentality. He was as if bored, or *blasé,* in the body, just like Tess. This seems to be the result of coming of an old family, that had been long conscious, long self-conscious, specialized, separate, exhausted.

This drove him to Sue. She was his kinswoman, as d'Urberville was kinsman to Tess. She was like himself in her being and her desire. Like Jude, she wanted to live partially, in the consciousness, in the mind only. She wanted no experience in the senses, she wished only to know.

She belonged, with Tess, to the old woman-type of witch or prophetess, which adhered to the male principle, and destroyed the female. But in the true prophetess, in Cassandra, for example, the denial of the female cost a strong and almost maddening effect. But in Sue it was done before she was born.

She was born with the vital female atrophied in her: she was almost male. Her *will* was male. It was wrong for Jude to take her physically, it was a violation of her. She was not the virgin type, but the witch type, which has no sex. Why should she be forced into intercourse that was not natural to her?

It was not natural for her to have children. It is inevitable that her children die. It is not natural for Tess nor for Angel Clare to have children, nor for Arabella nor for Alec d'Urberville. Because none of these wished to give of themselves to the lover, none of them wished to mate: they only wanted their own experience. For Jude alone it was natural to have children, and this in spite of himself.

Sue wished to identify herself utterly with the male principle. That which was female in her she wanted to consume within the male force, to consume it in the fire of understanding, of giving utterance. Whereas an ordinary woman knows that she *contains* all understanding, that she is the unutterable which man must for ever continue to try to utter, Sue felt that all must be uttered, must be given to the male, that, in truth, only Male existed, that everything was the Word, and the Word was everything.

Sue is the production of the long selection by man of the woman in whom the female is subordinated to the male principle. A long line of Amelias and Agneses, those women who submitted to the man-idea, flattered the man, and bored him, the Gretchens and the Turgeniev heroines, those who have betrayed the female and who therefore only seem to exist to be betrayed by their men, these have produced at length a Sue, the pure thing. And as soon as she is produced she is execrated.

What Cassandra and Aspasia became to the Greeks, Sue has become to the northern civilization. But the Greeks never pitied Woman. They did not show her that highest impertinence—not even Euripides.

But Sue is scarcely a woman at all, though she is feminine enough.

Cassandra submitted to Apollo, and gave him the Word of affiance, brought forth prophecy to him, not children. She received the embrace of the spirit, He breathed His Grace upon her: and she conceived and brought forth a prophecy. It was still a marriage. Not the marriage of the Virgin with the Spirit, but the marriage of the female spirit with the male spirit, bodiless.

With Sue, however, the marriage was no marriage, but a submission, a service, a slavery. Her female spirit did not wed with the male spirit: she could not prophesy. Her spirit submitted to the male spirit, owned the priority of the male spirit, wished to become the male spirit. That which was female in her, resistant, gave her only her critical faculty. When she sought out the physical quality in the Greeks, that was her effort to make even the unknowable physique a part of knowledge, to contain the body within the mind.

One of the supremest products of our civilization is Sue, and a product that well frightens us. It is quite natural that, with all her mental alertness, she married Phillotson without ever considering the physical quality of marriage. Deep instinct made her avoid the consideration. And the duality of her nature made her extremely liable to self-destruction. The suppressed, atrophied female in her, like a potent fury, was always there, suggesting to her to make the fatal mistake. She contained always the rarest, most deadly anarchy in her own being.

It needed that she should have some place in society where the clarity of her mental being, which was in itself a form of death, could shine out without attracting any desire for her body. She needed a refinement on Angel Clare. For she herself was a more specialized, more highly civilized product on the female side, than Angel Clare on the male. Yet the atrophied female in her would still want the bodily male.

She attracted to herself Jude. His experience with Arabella had for the time being diverted his attention altogether from the female. His attitude was that of service to the pure male spirit. But the physical male in him, that which knew and belonged to the female, was potent, and roused the female in Sue as much as she wanted it roused, so much that it was a stimulant to her, making her mind the brighter.

It was a cruelly difficult position. She must, by the constitution of her nature, remain quite physically intact, for the female was atrophied in her, to the enlargement of the male activity. Yet she wanted some quickening for this atrophied female. She wanted even kisses.

That the new rousing might give her a sense of life. But she could only *live* in the mind.

Then, where could she find a man who would be able to feed her with his male vitality, through kisses, proximity, without demanding the female return? For she was such that she could only receive quickening from a strong male, for she was herself no small thing. Could she then find a man, a strong, passionate male, who would devote himself entirely to the production of the mind in her, to the production of male activity, or of female activity critical to the male?

She could only receive the highest stimulus, which she must inevitably seek, from a man who put her in constant jeopardy. Her essentiality rested upon her remaining intact. Any suggestion of the physical was utter confusion to her. Her principle was the ultra-Christian principle–of living entirely according to the Spirit, to the One, male spirit, which knows, and utters, and shines, but exists beyond feeling, beyond joy or sorrow, or pain, exists only in Knowing. In tune with this, she was herself. Let her, however, be turned under the influence of the other dark, silent, strong principle, of the female, and she would break like a fine instrument under discord.

Yet, to live at all in tune with the male spirit, she must receive the male stimulus from a man. Otherwise she was as an instrument without a player. She must feel the hands of a man upon her, she must be infused with his male vitality, or she was not alive.

Here then was her difficulty: to find a man whose vitality could infuse her and make her live, and who would not, at the same time, demand of her a return, the return of the female impulse into him. What man could receive this drainage, receiving nothing back again? He must either die, or revolt.

One man had died. She knew it well enough. She knew her own fatality. She knew she drained the vital, male stimulus out of a man, producing in him only knowledge of the mind, only mental clarity: which man must always strive to attain, but which is not life in him, rather the product of life.

Just as Alec d'Urberville, on the other hand, drained the female vitality out of a woman, and gave her only sensation, only experience in the senses, a sense of herself, nothing to the soul or spirit, thereby exhausting her.

Now Jude, after Arabella, and following his own *idée fixe,* haunted this mental clarity, this knowing, above all. What he contained in himself, of male and female impulse, he wanted to bring forth, to draw into his mind, to resolve into understanding, as a plant resolves that which it contains into flower.

This Sue could do for him. By creating a vacuum, she could cause the vivid flow which clarified him. By rousing him, by drawing from him his turgid vitality, made thick and heavy and physical with Arabella, she could bring into consciousness that which he contained. For he was heavy and full of unrealized life, clogged with untransmuted knowledge, with accretion of his senses. His whole life had been till now an indrawing, ingestion. Arabella had been a vital experience for him, received into his blood. And how was he to bring out all this fulness into knowledge or utterance? For all the time he was being roused to new physical desire, new life-experience, new sense-enrichening, and he could not perform his male function of transmitting this into expression, or action. The particular form his flowering should take, he could not find. So he hunted and studied, to find the call, the appeal which should call out of him that which was in him.

And great was his transport when the appeal came from Sue. She wanted, at first, only his words. That of him which could come to her through speech, through his consciousness, her mind, like a bottomless gulf, cried out for. She wanted satisfaction through the mind, and cried out for him to satisfy her through the mind.

Great, then, was his joy at giving himself out to her. He gave, for it was more blessed to give than to receive. He gave, and she received some satisfaction. But where she was not satisfied, there he must try still to satisfy her. He struggled to bring it all forth. She was, as himself, asking himself what he was. And he strove to answer, in a transport.

And he answered in a great measure. He singled himself out from the old matrix of the accepted idea, he produced an individual flower of his own.

It was for this he loved Sue. She did for him quickly what he would have done for himself slowly, through study. By patient, diligent study, he would have used up the surplus of that turgid energy in him, and would, by long contact with old truth, have arrived at the form of truth which was in him. What he indeed wanted to get from study was, not a store of learning, nor the vanity of education, a sort of superiority of educational wealth, though this also gave him pleasure. He wanted, through familiarity with the true thinkers and poets, particularly with the classic and theological thinkers, because of their comparative sensuousness, to find conscious expression for that which he held in his blood. And to do this, it was necessary for him to resolve and to reduce his blood, to overcome the female sensuousness in himself, to transmute his sensuous being into another state, a state of clarity, of consciousness. Slowly, laboriously, struggling with the Greek and the Latin, he would have burned down his thick blood as fuel, and have come to the true light of himself.

This Sue did for him. In marriage, each party fulfils a dual function with regard to the other: exhaustive and enrichening. The female at the same time exhausts and invigorates the male, the male at the same time exhausts and invigorates the female. The exhaustion and invigoration are both temporary and relative. The male, making the effort to penetrate into the female, exhausts himself and invigorates her. But that which, at the end, he discovers and carries off from her, some seed of being, enrichens him and exhausts her. Arabella, in taking Jude, accepted very little from him. She absorbed very little of his strength and vitality into herself. For she only wanted to be aware of herself in contact with him, she did not want him to penetrate into her very being, till he moved her to her very depths, till she loosened to him some of her very self for his enrichening. She was intrinsically impotent, as was Alec d'Urberville.

So that in her Jude went very little further in Knowledge, or in Self-Knowledge. He took only the first steps: of knowing himself sexually, as a sexual male. That is only the first, the first necessary, but rudimentary, step.

When he came to Sue, he found her physically impotent, but spiritually potent. That was what he wanted. Of Knowledge in the blood he had a rich enough store: more than he knew what to do with. He wished for the further step, of reduction, of essentializing into Knowledge. Which Sue gave to him.

So that his experience with Arabella, plus his first experience of trembling intimacy and incandescent realization with Sue made one complete marriage: that is, the two women added together made One Bride.

When Jude had exhausted his surplus self, in spiritual intimacy with Sue, when he had gained through her all the wonderful understanding she could evoke in him, when he was clarified to himself, then his marriage with Sue was over. Jude's marriage with Sue was over before he knew her physically. She had, physically, nothing to give him.

Which, in her deepest instinct, she knew. She made no mistake in marrying Phillotson. She acted according to the pure logic of her nature. Phillotson was a man who wanted no marriage whatsoever with the female. Sexually, he wanted her as an instrument through which he obtained relief, and some gratification: but, really, relief. Spiritually, he wanted her as a thing to be wondered over and delighted in, but quite separately from himself. He knew quite well he could never marry her. He was a human being as near to mechanical function as a human being can be. The whole process of digestion, masticating, swallowing, digesting, excretion, is a sort of super-mechanical process. And Phillotson was like this. He was an organ, a function-fulfilling organ, he had no separate existence. He could not create a single new movement or thought or expression. Everything he did was a repetition of what had been. All his study was a study of what had been. It was a mechanical, functional process. He was a true, if small, form of the *Savant*. He could understand only the functional laws of living, but these he understood honestly. He was true to himself, he was not overcome by any cant or sentimentalizing. So that in this he was splendid. But it is a cruel thing for a complete, or a spiritual, individuality to be submitted to a functional organism.

The Widow Edlin said that there are some men no woman of any feeling could touch, and Phillotson was one of them. If the Widow knew this, why was Sue's instinct so short?

But Mrs. Edlin was a full human being, creating life in a new form through her personality. She must have known Sue's deficiency. It was natural for Sue to read and to turn again to:

> Thou hast conquered, O pale Galilean!
> The world has grown grey from Thy breath.

In her the pale Galilean had indeed triumphed. Her body was as insentient as hoar-frost. She knew well enough that she was not alive in the ordinary human sense. She did not, like an ordinary woman, receive all she knew through her senses, her instincts, but through her consciousness. The pale Galilean had a pure disciple in her: in her He was fulfilled. For the senses, the body, did not exist in her; she existed as a consciousness. And this is so much so, that she was almost an Apostate. She turned to look at Venus and Apollo. As if she could know either Venus or Apollo, save as ideas. Nor Venus nor Aphrodite had anything to do with her, but only Pallas and Christ.

She was unhappy every moment of her life, poor Sue, with the knowledge of her own non-existence within life. She felt all the time the ghastly sickness of dissolution upon her, she was as a void unto herself.

So she married Phillotson, the only man she could, in reality, marry. To him she could be a wife: she could give him the sexual relief he wanted of her, and supply him with the transcendence which was a pleasure to him; it was hers to seal him with the seal which made an honourable human being of him. For he felt, deep within himself, something a reptile feels. And she was his guarantee, his crown.

Why does a snake horrify us, or even a newt? Why was Phillotson like a newt? What is it, in our life or in our feeling, to which a newt corresponds? Is it that life has the two sides, of growth and of decay, symbolized most acutely in our bodies by the semen and the excreta? Is it that the newt, the reptile, belong to the putrescent activity of life; the bird, the fish to the growth activity? Is it that the newt and the reptile are suggested to us through those sensations connected with excretion? And was Phillotson more or less connected with the decay activity of life? Was it his function to reorganize the life-excreta of the ages? At any rate, one can honour him, for he was true to himself.

Sue married Phillotson according to her true instinct. But being almost pure Christian, in the sense of having no physical life, she had turned to the Greeks, and with her mind was an Aphrodite-worshipper. In craving for the highest form of that which she lacked, she worshipped Aphrodite. There are two sets of Aphrodite-worshippers: daughters of Aphrodite and the almost neutral daughters of Mary of Bethany. Sue was, oh, cruelly far from being a daughter of Aphrodite. She was the furthest alien from Aphrodite. She might excuse herself through her Venus Urania—but it was hopeless.

Therefore, when she left Phillotson, in whose marriage she consummated her own crucifixion, to go to Jude, she was deserting the God of her being for the God of her hopeless want. How much could she become a living, physical woman? But she would get away from Phillotson.

She went to Jude to continue the spiritual marriage, bodiless. That was all very well, if he had been satisfied. If he had been satisfied, they might have lived in this spiritual intimacy, without physical contact, for the rest of their lives, so strong was her true instinct for herself.

He, however, was not satisfied. He reached the point where he was clarified, where he had reduced from his blood into his consciousness all that was uncompounded before. He had become himself as far as he could, he had fulfilled himself. All that he had gathered in his youth, all that he had gathered from Arabella, was assimilated now, fused and transformed into one clear Jude.

Now he wants that which is necessary for him if he is to go on. He wants, at its lowest, the physical, sexual relief. For continually baulked sexual desire, or necessity, makes a man unable to live freely, scotches him, stultifies him. And where a man is roused to the fullest pitch, as Jude was roused by Sue, then the principal connexion becomes a necessity, if only for relief. Anything else is a violation.

Sue ran away to escape physical connexion with Phillotson, only to find herself in the arms of Jude. But Jude wanted of her more than Phillotson wanted. This was what terrified her to the bottom of her nature. Whereas Phillotson always only wanted sexual relief of her, Jude wanted the consummation of marriage. He wanted that deepest experience, that penetrating far into the unknown and undiscovered which lies in the body and blood of man and woman, during life. He wanted to receive from her the quickening, the primitive seed and impulse which should start him to a new birth. And for this he must go back deep into the primal, unshown, unknown life of the blood, the thick source-stream of life in her.

And she was terrified lest he should find her out, that it was wanting in her. This was her deepest dread, to see him inevitably disappointed in her. She could not bear to be put into the balance, wherein she knew she would be found wanting.

For she knew in herself that she was cut off from the source and origin of life. For her, the way back was lost irrevocably. And when Jude came to her, wanting to retrace with her the course right back to the springs and the welling-out, she was more afraid than of death. For she could not. She was like a flower broken off from the tree, that lives a while in water, and even puts forth. So Sue lived sustained and nourished by the rarefied life of books and art, and by the inflow from the man. But, owing to centuries and centuries of weaning away from the body of life, centuries of insisting upon the supremacy and bodilessness of Love, centuries of striving to escape the conditions of being and of striving to attain the condition of Knowledge, centuries of pure Christianity, she had gone too far. She had climbed and climbed to be near the stars. And now, at last, on the topmost pinnacle, exposed to all the horrors and the magnificence of space, she could not go back. Her strength had fallen from her. Up at that great height, with scarcely any foothold, but only space, space all round her, rising up to her from beneath, she was like a thing suspended, supported almost at the point of extinction by the density of the medium. Her body was lost to her, fallen away, gone. She existed there as a point of consciousness, no more, like one swooned at a great height, held up at the tip of a fine pinnacle that drove upwards into nothingness.

Jude rose to that height with her. But he did not die as she died. Beneath him the foothold was more, he did not swoon. There came a time when he wanted to go back, down to earth. But she was fastened like Andromeda.

Perhaps, if Jude had not known Arabella, Sue might have persuaded him that he too was bodiless, only a point of consciousness. But she was too late; another had been before her and given her the lie.

Arabella was never so jealous of Sue as Sue of Arabella. How shall the saint that tips the pinnacle, Saint Simon Stylites thrust on the highest needle that pricks the heavens, be envied by the man who walks the horizontal earth? But Sue was cruelly anguished with jealousy of Arabella. It was only this, this knowledge that Jude wanted Arabella, which made Sue give him access to her own body.

When she did that, she died. The Sue that had been till then, the glimmering, pale, star-like Sue, died and was revoked on the night when Arabella called at their house at Aldbrickham, and Jude went out in his slippers to look for her, and did not find her, but came back to Sue, who in her anguish gave him then the access to her body. Till that day, Sue had been, in her will and in her very self, true to one motion, to Love, to Knowledge, to the Light, to the upward motion. Phillotson had not altered this. When she had suffered him, she had said: "He does not touch me; I am beyond him."

But now she must give her body to Jude. At that moment her light began to go out, all she had lived for and by began to turn into a falseness, Sue began to nullify herself.

She could never become physical. She could never return down to earth. But there, lying bound at the pinnacle-tip, she had to pretend she was lying on the horizontal earth, prostrate with a man.

It was a profanation and a pollution, worse than the pollution of Cassandra or of the Vestals. Sue had her own form: to break this form was to destroy her. Her destruction began only when she said to Jude, "I give in."

As for Jude, he dragged his body after his consciousness. His instinct could never have made him actually desire physical connexion with Sue. He was roused by an appeal made through his consciousness. This appeal automatically roused his senses. His consciousness desired Sue. So his senses were forced to follow his consciousness.

But he must have felt, in knowing her, the *frisson* of sacrilege, something like the Frenchman who lay with a corpse. Her body, the body of a Vestal, was swooned into that state of bloodless ecstasy wherein it was dead to the senses. Or it was the body of an insane woman, whose senses are directed from the disordered mind, whose mind is not subjected to the senses.

But Jude was physically undeveloped. Altogether he was medieval. His senses were vigorous but not delicate. He never realized what it meant to *him,* his taking Sue. He thought he was satisfied.

But if it was death to her, or profanation, or pollution, or breaking, it was unnatural to him, blasphemy. How could he, a living, loving man, warm and productive, take with his body the moonlit cold body of a woman who did not live to him, and did not want him? It was monstrous, and it sent him mad.

She knew it was wrong, she knew it should never be. But what else could she do? Jude loved her now with his will. To have left him to Arabella would have been to destroy him. To have shared him with Arabella would have been possible to Sue, but impossible to him, for he had the strong, purist idea that a man's body should follow and be subordinate to his spirit, his senses should be subordinate to and subsequent to his mind. Which idea is utterly false.

So Jude and Sue are damned, partly by their very being, but chiefly by their incapacity to accept the conditions of their own and each other's being. If Jude could have known that he did not want Sue physically, and then have made his choice, they might not have wasted their lives. But he could not know.

If he could have known, after a while, after he had taken her many times, that it was wrong, still they might have made a life. He must have known that, after taking Sue, he was depressed as she was depressed. He must have known worse than that. He must have felt the devastating sense of the unlivingness of life, things must have ceased to exist for him, when he rose from taking Sue, and he must have felt that he walked in a ghastly blank, confronted just by space, void.

But he would acknowledge nothing of what he felt. He must feel according to his idea and his will. Nevertheless, they were too truthful ever to marry. A man as real and personal as Jude cannot, from his deeper religious sense, marry a woman unless indeed he can marry her, unless with her he can find or approach the real consummation of marriage. And Sue and Jude could not lie to themselves, in their last and deepest feelings. They knew it was no marriage; they knew it was wrong, all along; they knew they were sinning against life, in forcing a physical marriage between themselves.

How many people, man and woman, live together, in England, and have children, and are never, never asked whether they have been through the marriage ceremony together? Why then should Jude and Sue have been brought to task? Only because of their own uneasy sense of wrong, of sin, which they communicated to other people. And this wrong or sin was not against the community, but against their own being, against life. Which is why they were, the pair of them, instinctively disliked.

They never knew happiness, actual, sure-footed happiness, not for a moment. That was incompatible with Sue's nature. But what they knew was a very delightful but poignant and unhealthy condition of lightened consciousness. They reacted on each other to stimulate the consciousness. So that, when they went to the flower-show, her sense of the roses, and Jude's sense of the roses, would be most, most poignant. There is always this pathos, this poignancy, this trembling on the verge of pain and tears, in their happiness.

"Happy?" he murmured. She nodded.

The roses, how the roses glowed for them! The flowers had more being than either he or she. But as their ecstasy over things sank a little, they felt, the pair of them, as if they themselves were wanting in real body, as if they were too unsubstantial, too thin and evanescent in substance, as if the other solid people might jostle right through them, two wandering shades as they were.

This they felt themselves. Hence their uncertainty in contact with other people, hence their abnormal sensitiveness. But they had their own form of happiness, nevertheless, this trembling on the verge of ecstasy, when, the senses strongly roused to the service of the consciousness, the things they contemplated took flaming being, became flaming symbols of their own emotions to them.

So that the real marriage of Jude and Sue was in the roses. Then, in the third state, in the spirit, these two beings met upon the roses and in the roses were symbolized in consummation. The rose is the symbol of marriage-consummation in its beauty. To them it is more than a symbol, it is a fact, a flaming experience.

They went home tremblingly glad. And then the horror when, because of Jude's unsatisfaction, he must take Sue sexually. The flaming experience became a falsity, or an *ignis fatuus* leading them on.

They exhausted their lives, he in the consciousness, she in the body. She was glad to have children, to prove she was a woman. But in her it was a perversity to wish to prove she was a woman. She was no woman. And her children, the proof thereof, vanished like hoar-frost from her.

It was not the stone-masonry that exhausted him and weakened him and made him ill. It was this continuous feeding of his consciousness from his senses, this continuous state of incandescence of the consciousness, when his body, his vital tissues, the very protoplasm in him, was being slowly consumed away. For he had no life in the body. Every time he went to Sue, physically, his inner experience must have been a shock back from life and from the form of outgoing, like that of a man who lies with a corpse. He had no life in the senses: he had no inflow from the source to make up for the enormous wastage. So he gradually became exhausted, burned more and more away, till he was frail as an ember.

And she, her body also suffered. But it was in the mind that she had had her being, and it was in the mind she paid her price. She tried and tried to receive and to satisfy Jude physically. She bore him children, she gave herself to the life of the body.

But as she was formed she was formed, and there was no altering it. She needed all the life that belonged to her, and more, for the supplying of her mind, since such a mind as hers is found only, healthily, in a person of powerful vitality. For the mind, in a common person, is created out of the surplus vitality, or out of the remainder after all the sensuous life has been fulfilled.

She needed all the life that belonged to her, for her mind. It was her form. To disturb that arrangement was to make her into somebody else, not herself. Therefore, when she became a physical wife and a mother, she forswore her own being. She abjured her own mind, she denied it, took her faith, her belief, her very living away from it.

It is most probable she lived chiefly in her children. They were her guarantee as a physical woman, the being to which she now laid claim. She had forsaken the ideal of an independent mind.

She would love her children with anguish, afraid always for their safety, never certain of their stable existence, never assured of their real reality. When they were out of her sight, she would be uneasy, uneasy almost as if they did not exist. There would be a gnawing at her till they came back. She would not be satisfied till she had them crushed on her breast. And even then, she would not be sure, she would not be sure. She could not be sure, in life, of anything. She could only be sure, in the old days, of what she saw with her mind. Of that she was absolutely sure.

Meanwhile Jude became exhausted in vitality, bewildered, aimless, lost, pathetically nonproductive.

Again one can see what instinct, what feeling it was which made Arabella's boy bring about the death of the children and of himself. He, sensitive, so bodiless, so selfless as to be a sort of automaton, is very badly suggested, exaggerated, but one can see what is meant. And he feels, as any child will feel, as many children feel today, that they are really anachronisms, accidents, fatal accidents, unreal, false notes in their mothers' lives, that, according to her, they have no being: that, if they have being, then she has not. So he takes away all the children.

And then Sue ceases to be: she strikes the line through her own existence, cancels herself. There exists no more Sue Fawley. She cancels herself. She wishes to cease to exist, as a person, she wishes to be absorbed away, so that she is no longer self-responsible.

For she denied and forsook and broke her own real form, her own independent, cool-lighted mind-life. And now her children are not only dead, but self-slain, those pledges of the physical life for which she abandoned the other.

She has a passion to expiate, to expiate, to expiate. Her children should never have been born: her instinct always knew this. Now their dead bodies drive her mad with a sense of blasphemy. And she blasphemed the Holy Spirit, which told her she is guilty of their birth and their death, of the horrible nothing which they are. She is even guilty of their little, palpitating sufferings and joys of mortal life, now made nothing. She cannot bear it—who could? And she wants to expiate, doubly expiate. Her mind, which she set up in her conceit, and then forswore, she must stamp it out of existence, as one stamps out fire. She would never again think or decide for herself. The world, the past, should have written every decision for her. The last act of her intellect was the utter renunciation of her mind and the embracing of utter orthodoxy, where every belief, every thought, every decision was made ready for her, so that she did not exist self-responsible. And then her loathed body, which had committed the crime of bearing dead children, which had come to life only to spread nihilism like a pestilence, that too should be scourged out of existence. She chose the bitterest penalty in going back to Phillotson.

There was no more Sue. Body, soul, and spirit, she annihilated herself. All that remained of her was the will by which she annihilated herself. That remained fixed, a locked centre of self-hatred, life-hatred so utter that it had no hope of death. It knew that life is life, and there is no death for life.

Jude was too exhausted himself to save her. He says of her she was not worth a man's love. But that was not the point. It was not a question of her worth. It was a question of her being. If he had said she was not capable of receiving a man's love as he wished to bestow it, he might have spoken nearer the truth. But she practically told him this. She made it plain to him what she wanted, what she could take. But he overrode her. She tried hard to abide by her own form. But he forced her. He had no case against her, unless she made the great appeal for him, that he should flow to her, whilst at the same time she could not take him completely, body and spirit both.

She asked for what he could not give—what perhaps no man can give: passionate love without physical desire. She had no blame for him: she had no love for him. Self-love triumphed in her when she first knew him. She almost deliberately asked for more, far more, than she intended to give. Self-hatred triumphed in the end. So it had to be.

As for Jude, he had been dying slowly, but much quicker than she, since the first night she took him. It was best to get it done quickly in the end.

And this tragedy is the result of over-development of one principle of human life at the expense of the other; an over-balancing; a laying of all the stress on the Male, the Love, the Spirit, the Mind, the Consciousness; a denying, a blaspheming against the Female, the Law, the Soul, the Senses, the Feelings. But she is developed to the very extreme, she scarcely lives in the body at all. Being of the feminine gender, she is yet no woman at all, nor male; she is almost neuter. He is nearer the balance, nearer the centre, nearer the wholeness. But the whole human effort, towards pure life in the spirit, towards becoming pure Sue, drags him along; he identifies himself with this effort, destroys himself and her in his adherence to this identification.

But why, in casting off one or another form of religion, has man ceased to be religious altogether? Why will he not recognize Sue and Jude, as Cassandra was recognized long ago, and Achilles, and the Vestals, and the nuns, and the monks? Why must being be denied altogether?

Sue had a being, special and beautiful. Why must not Jude recognize it in all its speciality? Why must man be so utterly irreverent, that he approaches each being as if it were no-being? Why must it be assumed that Sue is an "ordinary" woman—as if such a thing existed? Why must she feel ashamed if she is specialized? And why must Jude, owing to the conception he is brought up in, force her to act as if she were his "ordinary" abstraction, a woman?

She was not a woman. She was Sue Bridehead, something very particular. Why was there no place for her? Cassandra had the Temple of Apollo. Why are we so foul that we have no reverence for that which we are and for that which is amongst us? If we had reverence for our life, our life would take at once religious form. But as it is, in our filthy irreverence, it remains a disgusting slough, where each one of us goes so thoroughly disguised in dirt that we are all alike and indistinguishable.

If we had reverence for what we are, our life would take real form, and Sue would have a place, as Cassandra had a place; she would have a place which does not yet exist, because we are all so vulgar, we have nothing.

CHAPTER X

It seems as if the history of humanity were divided into two epochs: the Epoch of the Law and the Epoch of Love. It seems as though humanity, during the time of its activity on earth, has made two great efforts: the effort to appreciate the Law and the effort to overcome the Law in Love. And in both efforts it has succeeded. It has reached and proved the Two Complementary Absolutes, the Absolute of the Father, of the Law, of Nature, and the Absolute of the Son, of Love, of Knowledge. What remains is to reconcile the two.

In the beginning, Man said: "What am I, and whence is this world around me, and why is it as it is?" Then he proceeded to explore and to personify and to deify the Natural Law, which he called

Father. And having reached the point where he conceived of the Natural Law in its purity, he had finished his journey, and was arrested.

But he found that he could not remain at rest. He must still go on. Then there was to discover by what principle he must proceed further than the Law. And he received an inkling of Love. All over the world the same, the second great epoch started with the incipient conception of Love, and continued until the principle of Love was conceived in all its purity. Then man was again at an end, in a cul-de-sac.

The Law it is by which we exist. It was the Father, the Law-Maker, Who said: "Let there be Light": it was He Who breathed life into the handful of dust and made man. "Thus have I made man, in mine own image. I have ordered his outgoing and his incoming, and have cast the line whereby he shall walk." So said the Father. And man went out and came in according to the ordering of the Lord; he walked by the line of the Lord and did not deviate. Till the path was worn barren, and man knew all the way, and the end seemed to have drawn nigh.

Then he said: "I will leave the path. I will go out as the Lord hath not ordained, and come in when my hour is fulfilled. For it is written, a man shall eat and drink with the Lord: but I will neither eat nor drink, I will go hungry, yet I will not die. It is written, a man shall take himself a wife and beget him seed unto the glory of God. But I will not take me a wife, nor beget seed, but I will know no woman. Yet will I not die. And it is written, a man shall save his body from harm, and preserve his flesh from hurt, for he is made in the image and likeness of the Father. But I will deliver up my body to hurt, and give my flesh unto the dust, yet will I not die, but live. For man does not live by bread alone, nor by the common law of the Father. Beyond this common law, I am I. When my body is destroyed and my bones have perished, then I am I. Yes, not until my body is consumed and my bones have mingled with the dust, not until then am I whole, not until then do I live. But I die in Christ, and rise again. And when I am risen again, I live in the spirit. Neither hunger nor cold can lay hold on me, nor desire lay hands on me. When I am risen again, then I shall *know*. Then I shall live in the ineffable bliss of knowledge. When the sun goes forth in the morning, I shall know the glory of God, who passes the sun from His left hand to His right, in the peace of His Understanding. As the night comes in her divers shadows, I know the peace that passeth all understanding. For God knoweth. Neither does He Will nor Command nor desire nor act, but exists perfect in the peace of knowledge."

If a man must live still and act in the body, then let his action be to the recognizing of the life in other bodies. Each man is to himself the Natural Law. He can only conceive of the Natural Law as he knows it in himself. The hardest thing for any man to do is for him to recognize and to know that the natural law of his neighbour is other than, and maybe even hostile to, his own natural law, and yet is true. This hard lesson Christ tried to instil in the doctrine of the other cheek. Orestes could not conceive that it was the natural law of Clytemnestra's nature that she should murder Agamemnon for sacrificing her daughter, and for leaving herself abandoned in the pride of her womanhood, unmated because he wanted the pleasure of war, and for his unfaithfulness to her with other women; Clytemnestra could not understand that Orestes should want to kill her for fulfilling the law of her own nature. The law of the mother's nature was other than the law of the son's nature. This they could neither of them see: hence the killing. This Christianity would teach them: to recognize and to admit the law of the other person, outside and different from the law of one's own being. It is the hardest lesson of love. And the lesson of love learnt, there must be learned the next lesson, of reconciliation between different, maybe hostile, things. That is the final lesson. Christianity ends in submission, in recognizing and submitting to the law of the other person. "Thou shalt love thy enemy."

Therefore, since by the law man must act or move, let his motion be the utterance of the God of Peace, of the perfect, unutterable Peace of Knowledge.

And man has striven this way, to utter the Universal Peace of God. And, striving on, he has passed beyond the limits of utterance, and has reached once more the silence of the beginning.

After Sue, after Dostoievsky's *Idiot,* after Turner's latest pictures, after the symbolist poetry of Mallarmé and the others, after the music of Debussy, there is no further possible utterance of the peace that passeth all understanding, the peace of God which is Perfect Knowledge. There is only silence beyond this.

Just as after Plato, after Dante, after Raphael, there was no further utterance of the Absoluteness of the Law, of the Immutability of the Divine Conception.

So that, as the great pause came over Greece, and over Italy, after the Renaissance, when the Law had been uttered in its absoluteness, there comes over us now, over England and Russia and France, the pause of finality, now we have seen the purity of Knowledge, the great, white, uninterrupted Light, infinite and eternal.

But that is not the end. The two great conceptions, of Law and of Knowledge or Love, are not diverse and accidental, but complementary. They are, in a way, contradictions each of the other. But they are complementary. They are the Fixed Absolute, the Geometric Absolute, and they are the radiant Absolute, the Unthinkable Absolute of pure, free motion. They are the perfect Stability, and they are the perfect Mobility. They are the fixed condition of our being, and they are the transcendent condition of knowledge in us. They are our Soul, and our Spirit, they are our Feelings, and our Mind. They are our Body and our Brain. They are Two-in-One.

And everything that has ever been produced has been produced by the combined activity of the two, in humanity, by the combined activity of soul and spirit. When the two are acting together, then Life is produced, then Life, or Utterance, Something, is *created*. And nothing is or can be created save by combined effort of the two principles, Law and Love.

All through the medieval times, Law and Love were striving together to give the perfect expression to the Law, to arrive at the perfect conception of the Law. All through the rise of the Greek nation, to its culmination, the Law and Love were working in that nation to attain the perfect expression of the Law. They were driven by the Unknown Desire, the Holy Spirit, the Unknown and Unexpressed. But the Holy Spirit is the Reconciler and the Originator. Him we do not know.

The greatest of all Utterance of the Law has given expression to the Law as it is in relation to Love, both ruled by the Holy Spirit. Such is the Book of Job, such Æschylus in the Trilogy, such, more or less, is Dante, such is Botticelli. Those who gave expression to the Law after these suppressed the contact, and achieved an abstraction. Plato, Raphael.

The greatest utterance of Love has given expression to Love as it is in relation to the Law: so Rembrandt, Shakespeare, Shelley, Wordsworth, Goethe, Tolstoi. But beyond these there have been Turner, who suppressed the context of the Law; also there have been Dostoievsky, Hardy, Flaubert. These have shown Love in conflict with the Law, and only Death the resultant, no Reconciliation.

So that humanity does not continue for long to accept the conclusions of these writers, nor even of Euripides and Shakespeare always. These great tragic writers endure by reason of the truth of the conflict they describe, because of its completeness, Law, Love, and Reconciliation, all active. But with regard to their conclusions, they leave the soul finally unsatisfied, unbelieving.

Now the aim of man remains to recognize and seek out the Holy Spirit, the Reconciler, the Originator, He who drives the twin principles of Law and of Love across the ages.

Now it remains for us to know the Law and to know the Love, and further to seek out the Reconciliation. It is time for us to build our temples to the Holy Spirit, and to raise our altars to the Holy Ghost, the Supreme, Who is beyond us but is with us.

We know of the Law, and we know of Love, and to that little we know of each of these we have given our full expression. But have not completed one perfect utterance, not one. Small as is the circle of our knowledge, we are not able to cast it complete. In Æschylus's *Eumenides,* Apollo is foolish, Athena mechanical. In Shakespeare's *Hamlet* the conclusion is all foolish. If we had conceived each party in his proper force, if Apollo had been equally potent with the Furies and no Pallas had appeared to settle the question merely by dropping a pebble, how would Æschylus have solved his riddle? He could not work out the solution he knew must come, so he forced it.

And so it has always been, always: either a wrong conclusion, or one forced by the artist, as if he put his thumb in the scale to equalize a balance which he could not make level. Now it remains for us to seek the true balance, to give each party, Apollo and the Furies, Love and the Law, his due, and so to seek the Reconciler.

Now the principle of the Law is found strongest in Woman, and the principle of Love in Man. In every creature, the mobility, the law of change, is found exemplified in the male; the stability, the conservatism is found in the female. In woman man finds his root and establishment. In man woman finds her exfoliation and florescence. The woman grows downwards, like a root, towards the centre and the darkness and the origin. The man grows upwards, like the stalk, towards discovery and light and utterance.

Man and Woman are, roughly, the embodiment of Love and the Law: they are the two complementary parts. In the body they are most alike, in genitals they are almost one. Starting from the connexion, almost unification, of the genitals, and travelling towards the feelings and the mind, there becomes ever a greater difference and a finer distinction between the two, male and female, till at last, at the other closing in the circle, in pure utterance, the two are really one again, so that any pure utterance is a perfect unity, the two as one, united by the Holy Spirit.

We start from one side or the other, from the female side or the male, but what we want is always the perfect union of the two. That is the Law of the Holy Spirit, the law of Consummate Marriage. That every living thing seeks, individually and collectively. Every man starts with his deepest desire, a desire for consummation of marriage between himself and the female, a desire for completeness, that completeness of being which will give completeness of satisfaction and completeness of utterance. No man can as yet find perfect consummation of marriage between himself and the Bride, be the bride either Woman or an Idea, but he can approximate to it, and every generation can get a little nearer.

But it needs that a man shall first know in reverence and submit to the Natural Law of his own individual being: that he shall also know that he is but contained within the great Natural Law, that he is but a Child of God, and not God himself: that he shall then poignantly and personally recognize that the law of another man's nature is different from the law of his own nature, that it may be even hostile to him, and yet is part of the great Law of God, to be admitted: this is the Christian action of "loving thy neighbour," and of dying to be born again: lastly, that a man shall know that between his law and the law of his neighbour there is an affinity, that all is contained in one, through the Holy Spirit.

It needs that a man shall know the natural law of his own being, then that he shall seek out the law of the female, with which to join himself as complement. He must know that he is half, and the woman is the other half: that they are two, but that they are two-in-one.

He must with reverence submit to the law of himself: and he must with suffering and joy know and submit to the law of the woman: and he must know that they two together are one within the Great Law, reconciled within the Great Peace. Out of this final knowledge shall come his supreme art. There shall be the art which recognizes and utters his own law; there shall be the art which recognizes his own and also the law of the woman, his neighbour, utters the glad embraces and the struggle between them, and the submission of one; there shall be the art which knows the struggle between the two conflicting laws, and knows the final reconciliation, where both are equal, two in one, complete. This is the supreme art, which yet remains to be done. Some men have attempted it, and left us the results of efforts. But it remains to be fully done.

But when the two clasp hands, a moment, male and female, clasp hands and are one, the poppy, the gay poppy flies into flower again; and when the two fling their arms about each other, the moonlight runs and clashes against the shadow; and when the two toss back their hair, all the larks break out singing; and when they kiss on the mouth, a lovely human utterance is heard again–and so it is.

SURGERY FOR THE NOVEL—OR A BOMB

You talk about the future of the baby, little cherub, when he's in the cradle cooing; and it's a romantic, glamorous subject. You also talk, with the parson, about the future of the wicked old grandfather who is at last lying on his death-bed. And there again you have a subject for much vague emotion, chiefly of fear this time.

How do we feel about the novel? Do we bounce with joy thinking of the wonderful novelistic days ahead? Or do we grimly shake our heads and hope the wicked creature will be spared a little longer? Is the novel on his death-bed, old sinner? Or is he just toddling round his cradle, sweet little thing? Let us have another look at him before we decide this rather serious case.

There he is, the monster with many faces, many branches to him, like a tree: the modern novel. And he is almost dual, like Siamese twins. On the one hand, the pale-faced, high-browed, earnest novel, which you have to take seriously; on the other, that smirking, rather plausible hussy, the popular novel.

Let us just for the moment feel the pulses of *Ulysses* and of Miss Dorothy Richardson and M. Marcel Proust, on the earnest side of Briareus; on the other, the throb of *The Sheik* and Mr. Zane Grey, and, if you will, Mr. Robert Chambers and the rest. Is *Ulysses* in his cradle? Oh, dear! What a grey face! And *Pointed Roofs,* are they a gay little toy for nice little girls? And M. Proust? Alas! You can hear the death-rattle in their throats. They can hear it themselves. They are listening to it with acute interest, trying to discover whether the intervals are minor thirds or major fourths. Which is rather infantile, really.

So there you have the "serious" novel, dying in a very long-drawn-out fourteen-volume death-agony, and absorbedly, childishly interested in the phenomenon. "Did I feel a twinge in my little toe, or didn't I?" asks every character of Mr. Joyce or of Miss Richardson or M. Proust. Is my aura a blend of frankincense and orange pekoe and boot-blacking, or is it myrrh and bacon-fat and Shetland tweed? The audience round the death-bed gapes for the answer. And when, in a sepulchral tone, the answer comes at length, after hundreds of pages: "It is none of these, it is abysmal chloro-coryambasis," the audience quivers all over, and murmurs: "That's just how I feel myself."

Which is the dismal, long-drawn-out comedy of the death-bed of the serious novel. It is self-consciousness picked into such fine bits that the bits are most of them invisible, and you have to go by smell. Through thousands and thousands of pages Mr. Joyce and Miss Richardson tear themselves to pieces, strip their smallest emotions to the finest threads, till you feel you are sewed inside a wool mattress that is being slowly shaken up, and you are turning to wool along with the rest of the woolliness.

It's awful. And it's childish. It really is childish, after a certain age, to be absorbedly self-conscious. One has to be self-conscious at seventeen: still a little self-conscious at twenty-seven; but if we are going it strong at thirty-seven, then it is a sign of arrested development, nothing else. And if it is still continuing at forty-seven, it is obvious senile precocity.

And there's the serious novel: senile-precocious. Absorbedly, childishly concerned with *what I am*. "I am this, I am that, I am the other. My reactions are such, and such, and such. And, oh, Lord, if I liked to watch myself closely enough, if I liked to analyse my feelings minutely, as I unbutton my gloves, instead of saying crudely I unbuttoned them, then I could go on to a million pages instead of a thousand. In fact, the more I come to think of it, it is gross, it is uncivilized bluntly to say: I unbuttoned my gloves. After all, the absorbing adventure of it! Which button did I begin with?" etc.

The people in the serious novels are so absorbedly concerned with themselves and what they feel and don't feel, and how they react to every mortal button; and their audience as frenziedly absorbed in the application of the author's discoveries to their own reactions: "That's me! That's exactly it! I'm just finding myself in this book!" Why, this is more than death-bed, it is almost post-mortem behaviour.

Some convulsion or cataclysm will have to get this serious novel out of its self-consciousness. The last great war made it worse. What's to be done? Because, poor thing, it's really young yet. The novel has never become fully adult. It has never quite grown to years of discretion. It has always youthfully hoped for the best, and felt rather sorry for itself on the last page. Which is just childish. The childishness has become very long-drawn-out. So very many adolescents who drag their adolescence on into their forties and their fifties and their sixties! There needs some sort of surgical operation, somewhere.

Then the popular novels—the *Sheiks* and *Babbitts* and Zane Grey novels. They are just as self-conscious, only they do have more illusions about themselves. The heroines do think they are lovelier, and more fascinating, and purer. The heroes do see themselves more heroic, braver, more chivalrous, more fetching. The mass of the populace "find themselves" in the popular novels. But nowadays it's a funny sort of self they find. A Sheik with a whip up his sleeve, and a heroine with weals on her back, but adored in the end, adored, the whip out of sight, but the weals still faintly visible.

It's a funny sort of self they discover in the popular novels. And the essential moral of *If Winter Comes,* for example, is so shaky. "The gooder you are, the worse it is for you, poor you, oh, poor you. Don't you be so blimey good, it's not good enough." Or *Babbitt:* "Go on, you make your pile, and then pretend you're too good for it. Put it over the rest of the grabbers that way. They're only pleased with themselves when they've made their pile. You go one better."

Always the same sort of baking-powder gas to make you rise: the soda counteracting the cream of tartar, and the tartar counteracted by the soda. Sheik heroines, duly whipped, wildly adored. Babbitts with solid fortunes, weeping from self-pity. Winter-Comes heroes as good as pie, hauled off to jail. *Moral:* Don't be too good, because you'll go to jail for it. *Moral:* Don't feel sorry for yourself till you've made your pile and don't need to feel sorry for yourself. *Moral:* Don't let him adore you till he's whipped you into it. Then you'll be partners in mild crime as well as in holy matrimony.

Which again is childish. Adolescence which *can't* grow up. Got into the self-conscious rut and going crazy, quite crazy in it. Carrying on their adolescence into middle age and old age, like the looney Cleopatra in *Dombey and Son,* murmuring "Rose-coloured curtains" with her dying breath.

The future of the novel? Poor old novel, it's in a rather dirty, messy tight corner. And it's either got to get over the wall or knock a hole through it. In other words, it's got to grow up. Put away childish things like: "Do I love the girl, or don't I?"—"Am I pure and sweet, or am I not?"—"Do I unbutton my right glove first, or my left?"—"Did my mother ruin my life by refusing to drink the cocoa which my bride had boiled for her?" These questions and their answers don't really interest me any more, though the world still goes sawing them over. I simply don't care for any of these things now, though I used to. The purely emotional and self-analytical stunts are played out in me. I'm finished. I'm deaf to the whole band. But I'm neither *blasé* nor cynical, for all that. I'm just interested in something else.

Supposing a bomb were put under the whole scheme of things, what would we be after? What feelings do we want to carry through into the next epoch? What feelings will carry us through? What is the underlying impulse in us that will provide the motive power for a new state of things, when this democratic-industrial-lovey-dovey-darling-take-me-to-mamma state of things is bust?

What next? That's what interests me. "What now?" is no fun any more.

If you wish to look into the past for what-next books, you can go back to the Greek philosophers. Plato's Dialogues are queer little novels. It seems to me it was the greatest pity in the world, when philosophy and fiction got split. They used to be one, right from the days of myth. Then they went and parted, like a nagging married couple, with Aristotle and Thomas Aquinas and that beastly Kant. So the novel went sloppy, and philosophy went abstract-dry. The two should come together again–in the novel.

You've got to find a new impulse for new things in mankind, and it's really fatal to find it through abstraction. No, no; philosophy and religion, they've both gone too far on the algebraical tack: Let X stand for sheep and Y for goats: then X minus Y equals Heaven, and X plus Y equals Earth, and Y minus X equals Hell. Thank you! But what coloured shirt does X have on?

The novel has a future. It's got to have the courage to tackle new propositions without using abstractions; it's got to present us with new, really new feelings, a whole line of new emotion, which will get us out of the emotional rut. Instead of snivelling about what is and has been, or inventing new sensations in the old line, it's got to break a way through, like a hole in the wall. And the public will scream and say it is sacrilege: because, of course, when you've been jammed for a long time in a tight corner, and you get really used to its stuffiness and its tightness, till you find it suffocatingly cozy; then, of course, you're horrified when you see a new glaring hole in what was your cosy wall. You're horrified. You back away from the cold stream of fresh air as if it were killing you. But gradually, first one and then another of the sheep filters through the gap, and finds a new world outside.

ART AND MORALITY

It is a part of the common claptrap that "art is immoral." Behold, everywhere, artists running to put on jazz underwear, to demoralize themselves; or, at least, to *débourgeoiser* themselves.

For the bourgeois is supposed to be the fount of morality. Myself, I have found artists far more morally finicky.

Anyhow, what has a water-pitcher and six insecure apples on a crumpled tablecloth got to do with bourgeois morality? Yet I notice that most people, who have not learnt the trick of being arty, feel a real moral repugnance for a Cézanne still-life. They think it is not *right*.

For them, it isn't.

Yet how can they feel, as they do, that it is subtly *immoral?*

The very same design, if it was humanized, and the tablecloth was a draped nude and the water-pitcher a nude semi-draped, weeping over the draped one, would instantly become highly moral. Why?

Perhaps from painting better than from any other art we can realize the subtlety of the distinction between what is dumbly *felt* to be moral, and what is felt to be immoral. The moral instinct in the man in the street.

But instinct is largely habit. The moral instinct of the man in the street is largely an emotional defence of an old habit.

Yet what can there be in a Cézanne still-life to rouse the aggressive moral instinct of the man in the street? What ancient habit in man do these six apples and a water-pitcher succeed in hindering?

A water-pitcher that isn't so very much like a water-pitcher, apples that aren't very appley, and a tablecloth that's not particularly much of a tablecloth. I could do better myself!

Probably! But then, why not dismiss the picture as a poor attempt? Whence this anger, this hostility? The derisive resentment?

Six apples, a pitcher, and a tablecloth can't suggest improper *behaviour*. They don't–not even to a Freudian. If they did, the man in the street would feel much more at home with them.

Where, then, does the immorality come in? Because come in it does.

Because of a very curious habit that civilized man has been forming down the whole course of civilization, and in which he is now hard-boiled. The slowly formed habit of seeing just as the photographic camera sees.

You may say, the object reflected on the retina is *always* photographic. It may be. I doubt it. But whatever the image on the retina may be, it is rarely, even now, the photographic image of the object which is actually *taken in* by the man who sees the object. He does not, even now, see for himself. He sees what the Kodak has taught him to see. And man, try as he may, is not a Kodak.

When a child sees a man, what does the child *take in,* as an impression? Two eyes, a nose, a mouth of teeth, two straight legs, two straight arms: a sort of hieroglyph which the human child has used through all the ages to represent man. At least, the old hieroglyph was still in use when I was a child.

Is this what the child actually *sees?*

If you mean by seeing, consciously registering, then this is what the child actually sees. The photographic image may be there all right, upon the retina. But there the child leaves it: outside the door, as it were.

Through many ages, mankind has been striving to register the image on the retina *as it is:* no more glyphs and hieroglyphs. We'll have the real objective reality.

And we have succeeded. As soon as we succeed, the Kodak is invented, to prove our success. Could lies come out of a black box, into which nothing but light had entered? Impossible! It takes life to tell a lie.

Colour also, which primitive man cannot really *see,* is now seen by us, and fitted to the spectrum.

Eureka! We have seen it, with our own eyes.

When we see a red cow, we see a red cow. We are quite sure of it, because the unimpeachable Kodak sees exactly the same.

But supposing we had all of us been born blind, and had to get our image of a red cow by touching her, and smelling her, hearing her moo, and "feeling" her? Whatever should we think of her? Whatever sort of image should we have of her, in our dark minds? Something very different, surely!

As vision developed towards the Kodak, man's idea of himself developed towards the snapshot. Primitive man simply didn't know *what* he was: he was always half in the dark. But we have learned to see, and each of us has a complete Kodak idea of himself.

You take a snap of your sweetheart, in the field among the buttercups, smiling tenderly at the red cow with a calf, and dauntlessly offering a cabbage-leaf.

Awfully nice, and absolutely "real." There is your sweetheart, complete in herself, enjoying a sort of absolute objective reality: complete, perfect, all her surroundings contributing to her, incontestable. She is really a "picture."

This is the habit we have formed: of visualizing *everything*. Each man to himself is a picture. That is, he is a complete little objective reality, complete in himself, existing by himself, absolutely, in the middle of the picture. All the rest is just setting, background. To every man, to every woman, the universe is just a setting to the absolute little picture of himself, herself.

This has been the development of the conscious ego in man, through several thousand years: since Greece first broke the spell of "darkness." Man has learnt to *see* himself. So now, he *is* what he sees. He makes himself in his own image.

Previously, even in Egypt, men had not learnt to *see straight*. They fumbled in the dark, and didn't quite know where they were, or what they were. Like men in a dark room, they only *felt* their own existence surging in the darkness of other creatures.

We, however, have learned to see ourselves for what we are, as the sun sees us. The Kodak bears witness. We see as the All-Seeing Eye sees, with the universal vision. And we *are* what is seen: each man to himself an identity, an isolated absolute, corresponding with a universe of isolated absolutes. A picture! A Kodak snap, in a universal film of snaps.

We have achieved universal vision. Even god could not see *differently* from what we see: only more extensively, like a telescope, or more intensively, like a microscope. But the same vision. A vision of images which are real, and each one limited to itself.

We behave as if we had got to the bottom of the sack, and seen the Platonic Idea with our own eyes, in all its photographically developed perfection, lying in the bottom of the sack of the universe. Our own ego!

The identifying of ourselves with the visual image of ourselves has become an instinct; the habit is already old. The picture of me, the me that is *seen*, is me.

As soon as we are supremely satisfied about it, somebody starts to upset us. Comes Cézanne with his pitcher and his apples, which not only are not life-like, but are a living lie. The Kodak will prove it.

The Kodak will take all sorts of snaps, misty, atmospheric, sun-dazed, dancing–all quite different. Yet the image is *the* image. There is only more or less sun, more or less vapour, more or less light and shade.

The All-Seeing Eye sees with every degree of intensity and in every possible kind of mood: Giotto, Titian, El Greco, Turner, all so different, yet all the true image in the All-Seeing Eye.

This Cézanne still-life, however, is *contrary* to the All-Seeing Eye. Apples, to the eye of God, could not look like that, nor could a tablecloth, nor could a pitcher. So, it is *wrong*.

Because man, since he grew out of a personal God, has taken over to himself all the attributes of the Personal Godhead. It is the all-seeing human eye which is now the Eternal Eye.

And if apples don't *look* like that, in any light or circumstance, or under any mood, then they shouldn't be painted like that.

Oh, *là-là-là!* The apples *are* just like that, to me! cries Cézanne. They *are* like that, no matter what they look like.

Apples are always apples! says Vox Populi, Vox Dei.

Sometimes they're a sin, sometimes they're a knock on the head, sometimes they're a bellyache, sometimes they're part of a pie, sometimes they're sauce for the goose.

And you can't see a bellyache, neither can you see a sin, neither can you see a knock on the head. So paint the apple in these aspects, and you get—probably, or approximately—a Cézanne still-life.

What an apple looks like to an urchin, to a thrush, to a browsing cow, to Sir Isaac Newton, to a caterpillar, to a hornet, to a mackerel who finds one bobbing on the sea, I leave you to conjecture. But the All-Seeing must have mackerel's eyes, as well as man's.

And this is the immorality in Cézanne: he begins to see more than the All-Seeing Eye of humanity can possibly see, Kodak-wise. If you can see in the apple a bellyache and a knock on the head, and paint these in the image, among the prettiness, then it is the death of the Kodak and the movies, and must be immoral.

It's all very well talking about decoration and illustration, significant form, or tactile values, or plastique, or movement, or space-composition, or colour-mass relations, afterwards. You might as well force your guest to eat the menu card, at the end of the dinner.

What art has got to do, and will go on doing, is to reveal things in their different relationships. That is to say, you've got to see in the apple the bellyache, Sir Isaac's knock on the cranium, the vast, moist wall through which the insect bores to lay her eggs in the middle, and the untasted, unknown quality which Eve saw hanging on a tree. Add to this the glaucous glimpse that the mackerel gets as he comes to the surface, and Fantin-Latour's apples are no more to you than enamelled rissoles.

The true artist doesn't substitute immorality for morality. On the contrary, he *always* substitutes a finer morality for a grosser. And as soon as you see a finer morality, the grosser becomes relatively immoral.

The universe is like Father Ocean, a stream of all things slowly moving. We move, and the rock of ages moves. And since we move and move for ever, in no discernible direction, there is no centre to the movement, to us. To us, the centre shifts at every moment. Even the pole-star ceases to sit on the pole. *Allons!* there is no road before us!

There is nothing to do but to maintain a true relationship to the things we move with and amongst and against. The apple, like the moon, has still an unseen side. The movement of Ocean will turn it round to us, or us to it.

There is nothing man can do but maintain himself in true relationship to his contiguous universe. An ancient Rameses can sit in stone absolute, absolved from visual contact, deep in the silent ocean of sensual contact. Michelangelo's Adam can open his eyes for the first time, and see the old man in the skies, objectively. Turner can tumble into the open mouth of the objective universe of light, till we see nothing but his disappearing heels. As the stream carries him, each in his own relatedness, each one differently, so a man must go through life.

Each thing, living or unliving, streams in its own odd, intertwining flux, and nothing, not even man nor the God of man, nor anything that man has thought or felt or known, is fixed or abiding. All moves. And nothing is true, or good, or right, except in its own living relatedness to its own circumambient universe; to the things that are in the stream with it.

Design, in art, is a recognition of the relation between various things, various elements in the creative flux. You can't *invent* a design. You recognize it, in the fourth dimension. That is, with your blood and your bones, as well as with your eyes.

Egypt had a wonderful relation to a vast living universe, only dimly visual in its reality. The dim eye-vision and the powerful blood-feeling of the Negro African, even today, gives us strange images, which our eyes can hardly see, but which we know are surpassing. The big silent statue of Rameses is like a drop of water, hanging through the centuries in dark suspense, and never static. The African fetish-statues have no movement, visually represented. Yet one little motionless wooden figure stirs more than all the Parthenon frieze. It sits in the place where no Kodak can snap it.

As for us, we have our Kodak-vision, all in bits that group or jig. Like the movies, that jerk but never move. An endless shifting and rattling together of isolated images, "snaps," miles of them, all of them jigging, but each one utterly incapable of movement or change, in itself. A kaleidoscope of inert images, mechanically shaken.

And this is our vaunted "consciousness," made up, really, of inert visual images and little else: like the cinematograph.

Let Cézanne's apples go rolling off the table for ever. They live by their own laws, in their own *ambiente,* and not by the laws of the Kodak—or of man. They are casually related to man. But to those apples, man is by no means the absolute.

A new relationship between ourselves and the universe means a new morality. Taste the unsteady apples of Cézanne, and the nailed-down apples of Fantin-Latour are apples of Sodom. If the *status quo* were paradise, it would indeed be a sin to taste the new apples; but since the *status quo* is much more prison than paradise, we can go ahead.

MORALITY AND THE NOVEL

The business of art is to reveal the relation between man and his circumambient universe, at the living moment. As mankind is always struggling in the toils of old relationships, art is always ahead of the "times," which themselves are always far in the rear of the living moment.

When van Gogh paints sunflowers, he reveals, or achieves, the vivid relation between himself, as man, and the sunflower, as sunflower, at that quick moment of time. His painting does not represent the sunflower itself. We shall never know what the sunflower itself is. And the camera will *visualize* the sunflower far more perfectly than van Gogh can.

The vision on the canvas is a third thing, utterly intangible and inexplicable, the offspring of the sunflower itself and van Gogh himself. The vision on the canvas is for ever incommensurable with the canvas, or the paint, or van Gogh as a human organism, or the sunflower as a botanical organism. You cannot weigh nor measure nor even describe the vision on the canvas. It exists, to tell the truth, only in the much-debated fourth dimension. In dimensional space it has no existence.

It is a revelation of the perfected relation, at a certain moment, between a man and a sunflower. It is neither man-in-the-mirror nor flower-in-the-mirror, neither is it above or below or across anything. It is in between everything, in the fourth dimension.

And this perfected relation between man and his circumambient universe is life itself, for mankind. It has the fourth-dimensional quality of eternity and perfection. Yet it is momentaneous.

Man and the sunflower both pass away from the moment, in the process of forming a new relationship. The relation between all things changes from day to day, in a subtle stealth of change. Hence art, which reveals or attains to another perfect relationship, will be for ever new.

At the same time, that which exists in the non-dimensional space of pure relationship is deathless, lifeless, and eternal. That is, it gives us the *feeling* of being beyond life or death. We say an Assyrian lion or an Egyptian hawk's head "lives." What we really mean is that it is beyond life, and therefore beyond death. It gives us that feeling. And there is something inside us which must also be beyond life and beyond death, since that "feeling" which we get from an Assyrian lion or an Egyptian hawk's head is so infinitely precious to us. As the evening star, that spark of pure relation between night and day, has been precious to man since time began.

If we think about it, we find that our life *consists in* this achieving of a pure relationship between ourselves and the living universe about us. This is how I "save my soul" by accomplishing a pure relationship between me and another person, me and other people, me and a nation, me and a race of men, me and the animals, me and the trees or flowers, me and the earth, me and the skies and sun and stars, me and the moon: an infinity of pure relations, big and little, like the stars of the sky: that makes our eternity, for each one of us, me and the timber I am sawing, the lines of force I follow; me and the dough I knead for bread, me and the very motion with which I write, me and the bit of gold I have got. This, if we knew it, is our life and our eternity: the subtle, perfected relation between me and my whole circumambient universe.*

And morality is that delicate, for ever trembling and changing *balance* between me and my circumambient universe, which precedes and accompanies a true relatedness.

Now here we see the beauty and the great value of the novel. Philosophy, religion, science, they are all of them busy nailing things down, to get a stable equilibrium. Religion, with its nailed-down One God, who says *Thou shalt, Thou shan't,* and hammers home every time; philosophy, with its fixed ideas; science with its "laws": they, all of them, all the time, want to nail us on to some tree or other.

But the novel, no. The novel is the highest example of subtle inter-relatedness that man has discovered. Everything is true in its own time, place, circumstance, and untrue outside of its own place, time, circumstance. If you try to nail anything down, in the novel, either it kills the novel, or the novel gets up and walks away with the nail.

Morality in the novel is the trembling instability of the balance. When the novelist puts his thumb in the scale, to pull down the balance to his own predilection, that is immorality.

The modern novel tends to become more and more immoral, as

* As an inscription discovered in a copy of James Mason's *Fra Angelico,* this paragraph was published separately under the title "The Universe and Me" by the Powgen Press, New York, 1935.

the novelist tends to press his thumb heavier and heavier in the pan: either on the side of love, pure love: or on the side of licentious "freedom."

The novel is not, as a rule, immoral because the novelist has any dominant *idea,* or *purpose.* The immorality lies in the novelist's helpless, unconscious predilection. Love is a great emotion. But if you set out to write a novel, and you yourself are in the throes of the great predilection for love, love as the supreme, the only emotion worth living for, then you will write an immoral novel.

Because *no* emotion is supreme, or exclusively worth living for. *All* emotions go to the achieving of a living relationship between a human being and the other human being or creature or thing he becomes purely related to. All emotions, including love and hate, and rage and tenderness, go to the adjusting of the oscillating, unestablished balance between two people who amount to anything. If the novelist puts his thumb in the pan, for love, tenderness, sweetness, peace, then he commits an immoral act: he *prevents* the possibility of a pure relationship, a pure relatedness, the only thing that matters: and he makes inevitable the horrible reaction, when he lets his thumb go, towards hate and brutality, cruelty and destruction.

Life is so made that opposites sway about a trembling centre of balance. The sins of the fathers are visited on the children. If the fathers drag down the balance on the side of love, peace, and production, then in the third or fourth generation the balance will swing back violently to hate, rage, and destruction. We must balance as we go.

And of all the art forms, the novel most of all demands the trembling and oscillating of the balance. The "sweet" novel is more falsified, and therefore more immoral, than the blood-and-thunder novel.

The same with the smart and smudgily cynical novel, which says it doesn't matter what you do, because one thing is as good as another, anyhow, and prostitution is just as much "life" as anything else.

This misses the point entirely. A thing isn't life just because somebody does it. This the artist ought to know perfectly well. The ordinary bank clerk buying himself a new straw hat isn't "life" at all: it is just existence, quite all right, like everyday dinners: but not "life."

By life, we mean something that gleams, that has the fourth-dimensional quality. If the bank clerk feels really piquant about his hat, if he establishes a lively relation with it, and goes out of the shop with the new straw on his head, a changed man, be-aureoled, then that is life.

The same with the prostitute. If a man establishes a living relation to her, if only for one moment, then it is life. But if it *doesn't:* if it is just money and function, then it is not life, but sordidness, and a betrayal of living.

If a novel reveals true and vivid relationships, it is a moral work, no matter what the relationships may consist in. If the novelist *honours* the relationship in itself, it will be a great novel.

But there are so many relationships which are not real. When the man in *Crime and Punishment* murders the old woman for sixpence, although it is *actual* enough, it is never quite real. The balance between the murderer and the old woman is gone entirely; it is only a mess. It is actuality, but it is not "life," in the living sense.

The popular novel, on the other hand, dishes up a réchauffé of old relationships: *If Winter Comes.* And old relationships dished up are likewise immoral. Even a magnificent painter like Raphael does nothing more than dress up in gorgeous new dresses relationships which have already been experienced. And this gives a gluttonous kind of pleasure to the mass: a voluptuousness, a wallowing. For centuries, men say of their voluptuously ideal woman: "She is a Raphael Madonna." And women are only just learning to take it as an insult.

A new relation, a new relatedness hurts somewhat in the attaining; and will always hurt. So life will always hurt. Because real voluptuousness lies in re-acting old relationships, and at the best, getting an alcoholic sort of pleasure out of it, slightly depraving.

Each time we strive to a new relation, with anyone or anything, it is bound to hurt somewhat. Because it means the struggle with and the displacing of old connexions, and this is never pleasant. And moreover, between living things at least, an adjustment means also a fight, for each party, inevitably, must "seek its own" in the other, and be denied. When, in the two parties, each of them seeks his own, her own, absolutely, then it is a fight to the death. And this is true of the thing called "passion." On the other hand, when, of the two parties, one yields utterly to the other, this is called sacrifice, and it also means death. So the Constant Nymph died of her eighteen months of constancy.

It isn't the nature of nymphs to be constant. She should have been constant in her nymph-hood. And it is unmanly to accept sacrifices. He should have abided by his own manhood.

There is, however, the third thing, which is neither sacrifice nor fight to the death: when each seeks only the true relatedness to the other. Each must be true to himself, herself, his own manhood, her own womanhood, and let the relationship work out of itself. This means courage above all things: and then discipline. Courage to accept the life-thrust from within oneself, and from the other person. Discipline, not to exceed oneself any more than one can help. Courage, when one has exceeded oneself, to accept the fact and not whine about it.

Obviously, to read a really new novel will *always* hurt, to some extent. There will always be resistance. The same with new pictures, new music. You may judge of their reality by the fact that they do arouse a certain resistance, and compel, at length, a certain acquiescence.

The great relationship, for humanity, will always be the relation between man and woman. The relation between man and man, woman and woman, parent and child, will always be subsidiary.

And the relation between man and woman will change for ever, and will for ever be the new central clue to human life. It is the *relation itself* which is the quick and the central clue to life, not the man, nor the woman, nor the children that result from the relationship, as a contingency.

It is no use thinking you can put a stamp on the relation between man and woman, to keep it in the *status quo*. You can't. You might as well try to put a stamp on the rainbow or the rain.

As for the bond of love, better put it off when it galls. It is an absurdity, to say that men and women *must love*. Men and women will be for ever subtly and changingly related to one another; no need to yoke them with any "bond" at all. The only morality is to have man true to his manhood, woman to her womanhood, and let the relationship form of itself, in all honour. For it is, to each, *life itself*.

If we are going to be moral, let us refrain from driving pegs through anything, either through each other or through the third thing, the relationship, which is for ever the ghost of both of us. Every sacrificial crucifixion needs five pegs, four short ones and a long one, each one an abomination. But when you try to nail down the relationship itself, and write over it *Love* instead of *This is the King of the Jews,* then you can go on putting in nails for ever. Even Jesus called it the Holy Ghost, to show you that you can't lay salt on its tail.

The novel is a perfect medium for revealing to us the changing rainbow of our living relationships. The novel can help us to live, as nothing else can: no didactic Scripture, anyhow. If the novelist keeps his thumb out of the pan.

But when the novelist *has* his thumb in the pan, the novel becomes an unparalleled perverter of men and women. To be compared only, perhaps, to that great mischief of sentimental hymns, like "Lead, Kindly Light," which have helped to rot the marrow in the bones of the present generation.

WHY THE NOVEL MATTERS

We have curious ideas of ourselves. We think of ourselves as a body with a spirit in it, or a body with a soul in it, or a body with a mind in it. *Mens sana in corpore sano*. The years drink up the wine, and at last throw the bottle away, the body, of course, being the bottle.

It is a funny sort of superstition. Why should I look at my hand, as it so cleverly writes these words, and decide that it is a mere nothing compared to the mind that directs it? Is there really any huge difference between my hand and my brain? Or my mind? My hand is alive, it flickers with a life of its own. It meets all the strange universe in touch, and learns a vast number of things, and knows a vast number of things. My hand, as it writes these words, slips gaily along, jumps like a grasshopper to dot an *i*, feels the table rather cold, gets a little bored if I write too long, has its own rudiments of thought, and is just as much *me* as is my brain, my mind, or my soul. Why should I imagine that there is a *me* which is more *me* than my hand is? Since my hand is absolutely alive, me alive.

Whereas, of course, as far as I am concerned, my pen isn't alive at all. My pen *isn't me* alive. Me alive ends at my finger-tips.

Whatever is me alive is me. Every tiny bit of my hands is alive, every little freckle and hair and fold of skin. And whatever is me alive is me. Only my finger-nails, those ten little weapons between me and an inanimate universe, they cross the mysterious Rubicon between me alive and things like my pen, which are not alive, in my own sense.

So, seeing my hand is all alive, and me alive, wherein is it just a bottle, or a jug, or a tin can, or a vessel of clay, or any of the rest of that nonsense? True, if I cut it it will bleed, like a can of cherries. But then the skin that is cut, and the veins that bleed, and the bones that should never be seen, they are all just as alive as the blood that flows. So the tin can business, or vessel of clay, is just bunk.

And that's what you learn, when you're a novelist. And that's what you are very liable *not* to know, if you're a parson, or a philosopher, or a scientist, or a stupid person. If you're a parson, you talk about souls in heaven. If you're a novelist, you know that paradise is in the palm of your hand, and on the end of your nose, because both are alive; and alive, and man alive, which is more than you can say, for certain, of paradise. Paradise is after life, and I for one am not keen on anything that is *after* life. If you are a philosopher, you talk about infinity, and the pure spirit which knows all things. But if you pick up a novel, you realize immediately that infinity is just a handle to this self-same jug of a body of mine; while as for knowing, if I find my finger in the fire, I know that fire burns, with a knowledge so emphatic and vital, it leaves Nirvana merely a conjecture. Oh, yes, my body, me alive, *knows,* and knows intensely. And as for the sum of all knowledge, it can't be anything more than an accumulation of all the things I know in the body, and you, dear reader, know in the body.

These damned philosophers, they talk as if they suddenly went off in steam, and were then much more important than they are when they're in their shirts. It is nonsense. Every man, philosopher included, ends in his own finger-tips. That's the end of his man alive. As for the words and thoughts and sighs and aspirations that fly from him, they are so many tremulations in the ether, and not alive at all. But if the tremulations reach another man alive, he may receive them into his life, and his life may take on a new colour, like a chameleon creeping from a brown rock on to a green leaf. All very well and good. It still doesn't alter the fact that the so-called spirit, the message or teaching of the philosopher or the saint, isn't alive at all, but just a tremulation upon the ether, like a radio message. All this spirit stuff is just tremulations upon the ether. If you, as man alive, quiver from the tremulation of the ether into new life, that is because you are man alive, and you take sustenance and stimulation into your alive man in a myriad ways. But to say that the message, or the spirit which is communicated to you, is more important than your living body, is nonsense. You might as well say that the potato at dinner was more important.

Nothing is important but life. And for myself, I can absolutely see life nowhere but in the living. Life with a capital L is only man alive. Even a cabbage in the rain is cabbage alive. All things that are alive are amazing. And all things that are dead are subsidiary to the living. Better a live dog than a dead lion. But better a live lion than a live dog. *C'est la vie!*

It seems impossible to get a saint, or a philosopher, or a scientist, to stick to this simple truth. They are all, in a sense, renegades. The saint wishes to offer himself up as spiritual food for the multitude. Even Francis of Assisi turns himself into a sort of angel-cake, of which anyone may take a slice. But an angel-cake is rather less than man alive. And poor St. Francis might well apologize to his body, when he is dying: "Oh, pardon me, my body, the wrong I did you through the years!" It was no wafer, for others to eat.

The philosopher, on the other hand, because he can think, decides that nothing but thoughts matter. It is as if a rabbit, because he can make little pills, should decide that nothing but little pills matter. As for the scientist, he has absolutely no use for me so long as I am man alive. To the scientist, I am dead. He puts under the microscope a bit of dead me, and calls it me. He takes me to pieces, and says first one piece, and then another piece, is me. My heart, my liver, my stomach have all been scientifically me, according to the scientist; and nowadays I am either a brain, or nerves, or glands, or something more up-to-date in the tissue line.

Now I absolutely flatly deny that I am a soul, or a body, or a mind, or an intelligence, or a brain, or a nervous system, or a bunch of glands, or any of the rest of these bits of me. The whole is greater than the part. And therefore, I, who am man alive, am greater than my soul, or spirit, or body, or mind, or consciousness, or anything else that is merely a part of me. I am a man, and alive. I am man alive, and as long as I can, I intend to go on being man alive.

For this reason I am a novelist. And being a novelist, I consider myself superior to the saint, the scientist, the philosopher, and the poet, who are all great masters of different bits of man alive, but never get the whole hog.

The novel is the one bright book of life. Books are not life. They are only tremulations on the ether. But the novel as a tremulation can make the whole man alive tremble. Which is more than poetry, philosophy, science, or any other book-tremulation can do.

The novel is the book of life. In this sense, the Bible is a great confused novel. You may say, it is about God. But it is really about man alive. Adam, Eve, Sarai, Abraham, Isaac, Jacob, Samuel, David, Bath-Sheba, Ruth, Esther, Solomon, Job, Isaiah, Jesus, Mark, Judas, Paul, Peter: what is it but man alive, from start to finish? Man alive, not mere bits. Even the Lord is another man alive, in a burning bush, throwing the tablets of stone at Moses's head.

I do hope you begin to get my idea, why the novel is supremely important, as a tremulation on the ether. Plato makes the perfect ideal being tremble in me. But that's only a bit of me. Perfection is only a bit, in the strange make-up of man alive. The Sermon on the Mount makes the selfless spirit of me quiver. But that, too, is only a bit of me. The Ten Commandments set the old Adam shivering in me, warning me that I am a thief and a murderer, unless I watch it. But even the old Adam is only a bit of me.

I very much like all these bits of me to be set trembling with life and the wisdom of life. But I do ask that the whole of me shall tremble in its wholeness, some time or other.

And this, of course, must happen in me, living.

But as far as it can happen from a communication, it can only happen when a whole novel communicates itself to me. The Bible—but *all* the Bible—and Homer, and Shakespeare: these are the supreme old novels. These are all things to all men. Which means that in their wholeness they affect the whole man alive, which is the man himself, beyond any part of him. They set the whole tree trembling with a new access of life, they do not just stimulate growth in one direction.

I don't want to grow in any one direction any more. And, if I can help it, I don't want to stimulate anybody else into some particular direction. A particular direction ends in a *cul-de-sac*. We're in a *cul-de-sac* at present.

I don't believe in any dazzling revelation, or in any supreme Word. "The grass withereth, the flower fadeth, but the Word of the Lord shall stand for ever." That's the kind of stuff we've drugged ourselves with. As a matter of fact, the grass withereth, but comes up all the greener for that reason, after the rains. The flower fadeth, and therefore the bud opens. But the Word of the Lord, being man-uttered and a mere vibration on the ether, becomes staler and staler, more and more boring, till at last we turn a deaf ear and it ceases to exist, far more finally than any withered grass. It is grass that renews its youth like the eagle, not any Word.

We should ask for no absolutes, or absolute. Once and for all and for ever, let us have done with the ugly imperialism of any absolute. There is no absolute good, there is nothing absolutely right. All things flow and change, and even change is not absolute. The whole is a strange assembly of apparently incongruous parts, slipping past one another.

Me, man alive, I am a very curious assembly of incongruous parts. My yea! of today is oddly different from my yea! of yesterday. My tears of tomorrow will have nothing to do with my tears of a year ago. If the one I love remains unchanged and unchanging, I shall cease to love her. It is only because she changes and startles me into change and defies my inertia, and is herself staggered in her inertia by my changing, that I can continue to love her. If she stayed put, I might as well love the pepper-pot.

In all this change, I maintain a certain integrity. But woe betide me if I try to put my finger on it. If I say of myself, I am this, I am that!–then, if I stick to it, I turn into a stupid fixed thing like a lamp-post. I shall never know wherein lies my integrity, my individuality, my me. I *can* never know it. It is useless to talk about my ego. That only means that I have made up an *idea* of myself, and that I am trying to cut myself out to pattern. Which is no good. You can cut your cloth to fit your coat, but you can't clip bits off your living body, to trim it down to your idea. True, you can put yourself into ideal corsets. But even in ideal corsets, fashions change.

Let us learn from the novel. In the novel, the characters can do nothing but *live*. If they keep on being good, according to pattern, or bad, according to pattern, or even volatile, according to pattern, they cease to live, and the novel falls dead. A character in a novel has got to live, or it is nothing.

We, likewise, in life have got to live, or we are nothing.

What we mean by living is, of course, just as indescribable as what we mean by *being*. Men get ideas into their heads, of what they mean by Life, and they proceed to cut life out to pattern. Sometimes they go into the desert to seek God, sometimes they go into the desert to seek cash, sometimes it is wine, woman, and song, and again it is water, political reform, and votes. You never know what it will be next: from killing your neighbour with hideous bombs and gas that tears the lungs, to supporting a Foundlings Home and preaching infinite Love, and being co-respondent in a divorce.

In all this wild welter, we need some sort of guide. It's no good inventing Thou Shalt Nots!

What then? Turn truly, honourably to the novel, and see wherein you are man alive, and wherein you are dead man in life. You may love a woman as man alive, and you may be making love to a woman as sheer dead man in life. You may eat your dinner as man alive, or as a mere masticating corpse. As man alive you may have a shot at your enemy. But as a ghastly simulacrum of life you may be firing bombs into men who are neither your enemies nor your friends, but just things you are dead to. Which is criminal, when the things happen to be alive.

To be alive, to be man alive, to be whole man alive: that is the point. And at its best, the novel, and the novel supremely, can help you. It can help you not to be dead man in life. So much of a man walks about dead and a carcass in the street and house, today: so much of women is merely dead. Like a pianoforte with half the notes mute.

But in the novel you can see, plainly, when the man goes dead, the woman goes inert. You can develop an instinct for life, if you will, instead of a theory of right and wrong, good and bad.

In life, there is right and wrong, good and bad, all the time. But what is right in one case is wrong in another. And in the novel you see one man becoming a corpse, because of his so-called goodness, another going dead because of his so-called wickedness. Right and wrong is an instinct: but an instinct of the whole consciousness in a man, bodily, mental, spiritual at once. And only in the novel are *all* things given full play, or at least, they may be given full play, when we realize that life itself, and not inert safety, is the reason for living. For out of the full play of all things emerges the only thing that is anything, the wholeness of a man, the wholeness of a woman, man alive, and live woman.

JOHN GALSWORTHY

Literary criticism can be no more than a reasoned account of the feeling produced upon the critic by the book he is criticizing. Criticism can never be a science: it is, in the first place, much too personal, and in the second, it is concerned with values that science ignores. The touchstone is emotion, not reason. We judge a work of art by its effect on our sincere and vital emotion, and nothing else. All the critical twiddle-twaddle about style and form, all this pseudo-scientific classifying and analysing of books in an imitation-botanical fashion, is mere impertinence and mostly dull jargon.

A critic must be able to *feel* the impact of a work of art in all its complexity and its force. To do so, he must be a man of force and complexity himself, which few critics are. A man with a paltry, impudent nature will never write anything but paltry, impudent criticism. And a man who is *emotionally* educated is rare as a phœnix. The more scholastically educated a man is generally, the more he is an emotional boor.

More than this, even an artistically and emotionally educated man must be a man of good faith. He must have the courage to admit what he feels, as well as the flexibility to *know* what he feels. So Sainte-Beuve remains, to me, a great critic. And a man like Macaulay, brilliant as he is, is unsatisfactory, because he is not honest. He is emotionally very alive, but he juggles his feelings. He prefers a fine effect to the sincere statement of the æsthetic and emotional reaction. He is quite intellectually capable of giving us a true account of what he feels. But not morally. A critic must be emotionally alive in every fibre, intellectually capable and skilful in essential logic, and then morally very honest.

Then it seems to me a good critic should give his reader a few standards to go by. He can change the standards for every new critical attempt, so long as he keeps good faith. But it is just as well to say: This and this is the standard we judge by.

Sainte-Beuve, on the whole, set up the standard of the "good man." He sincerely believed that the great man was essentially the good man in the widest range of human sympathy. This remained his universal standard. Pater's standard was the lonely philosopher of pure thought and pure æsthetic truth. Macaulay's standard was tainted by a political or democratic bias, he must be on the side of the weak. Gibbon tried a purely moral standard, individual morality.

Reading Galsworthy again—or most of him, for all is too much—one feels oneself in need of a standard, some conception of a real man and a real woman, by which to judge all these Forsytes and their contemporaries. One cannot judge them by the standard of the good man, nor of the man of pure thought, nor of the treasured humble nor the moral individual. One would like to judge them by the standard of the human being, but what, after all, is that? This is the trouble with the Forsytes. They are human enough, since anything in humanity is human, just as anything in nature is natural. Yet not one of them seems to be a really vivid human being. They are social beings. And what do we mean by that?

It remains to define, just for the purpose of this criticism, what we mean by a social being as distinct from a human being. The necessity arises from the sense of dissatisfaction which these Forsytes give us. Why can't we admit them as human beings? Why can't we have them in the same category as Sairey Gamp for example, who is satirically conceived, or of Jane Austen's people, who are social enough? We can accept Mrs. Gamp or Jane Austen's characters or even George Meredith's Egoist as human beings in the same category as ourselves. Whence arises this repulsion from the Forsytes, this refusal, this emotional refusal, to have them identified with our common humanity? Why do we feel so instinctively that they are inferiors?

It is because they seem to us to have lost caste as human beings, and to have sunk to the level of the social being, that peculiar creature that takes the place in our civilization of the slave in the old civilizations. The human individual is a queer animal, always changing. But the fatal change today is the collapse from the psychology of the free human individual into the psychology of the social being, just as the fatal change in the past was a collapse from the freeman's psyche to the psyche of the slave. The free moral and the slave moral, the human moral and the social moral: these are the abiding antitheses.

While a man remains a man, a true human individual, there is at the core of him a certain innocence or naïveté which defies all analysis, and which you cannot bargain with, you can only deal with it in good faith from your own corresponding innocence or naïveté. This does not mean that the human being is nothing but naïve or innocent. He is Mr. Worldly Wiseman also to his own degree. But in his essential core he is naïve, and money does not touch him. Money, of course, with every man living goes a long way. With the alive human being it may go as far as his penultimate feeling. But in the last naked him it does not enter.

With the social being it goes right through the centre and is the controlling principle no matter how much he may pretend, nor how much bluff he may put up. He may give away all he has to the poor and still reveal himself as a social being swayed finally and helplessly by the money-sway, and by the social moral, which is inhuman.

It seems to me that when the human being becomes too much divided between his subjective and objective consciousness, at last something splits in him and he becomes a social being. When he becomes too much aware of objective reality, and of his own isolation in the face of a universe of objective reality, the core of his identity splits, his nucleus collapses, his innocence or his naïveté perishes, and he becomes only a subjective-objective reality, a divided thing hinged together but not strictly individual.

While a man remains a man, before he falls and becomes a social individual, he innocently feels himself altogether within the great continuum of the universe. He is not divided nor cut off. Men may be against him, the tide of affairs may be rising to sweep him away. But he is one with the living continuum of the universe. From this he cannot be swept away. Hamlet and Lear feel it, as does Œdipus or Phædra. It is the last and deepest feeling that is in a man while he remains a man. It is there the same in a deist like Voltaire or a scientist like Darwin: it is there, imperishable, in every great man: in Napoleon the same, till material things piled too much on him and he lost it and was doomed. It is the essential innocence and naïveté of the human being, the sense of being at one with the great universe-continuum of space-time-life, which is vivid in a great man, and a pure nuclear spark in every man who is still free.

But if man loses his mysterious naïve assurance, which is his innocence; if he gives *too* much importance to the external objective reality and so collapses in his natural innocent pride, then he becomes obsessed with the idea of objectives or material assurance; he wants to *insure* himself, and perhaps everybody else: universal insurance. The impulse rests on fear. Once the individual loses his naïve at-oneness with the living universe he falls into a state of fear and tries to insure himself with wealth. If he is an altruist he wants to insure everybody, and feels it is the tragedy of tragedies if this can't be done. But the whole necessity for thus materially insuring oneself with wealth, money, arises from the state of fear into which a man falls who has lost his at-oneness with the living universe, lost his peculiar nuclear innocence and fallen into fragmentariness. Money, material salvation is the only salvation. What is salvation is God. Hence money is God. The social being may rebel even against this god, as do many of Galsworthy's characters. But that does not give them back their innocence. They are only anti-materialists instead of positive materialists. And the anti-materialist is a social being just the same as the materialist, neither more nor less. He is castrated just the same, made a neuter by having lost his innocence, the bright little individual spark of his at-oneness.

When one reads Mr. Galsworthy's books it seems as if there were not on earth one single human individual. They are all these social beings, positive and negative. There is not a free soul among them, not even Pendyce, or June Forsyte. If money does not actively determine their being, it does negatively. Money, or property, which is the same thing. Mrs. Pendyce, lovable as she is, is utterly circumscribed by property. Ultimately, she is not lovable at all, she is part of the fraud, she is prostituted to property. And there is nobody else. Old Jolyon is merely a sentimental materialist. Only for one moment do we see a man, and that is the road-sweeper in *Fraternity* after he comes out of prison and covers his face. But even *his* manhood has to be explained away by a wound in the head: an abnormality.

Now it looks as if Mr. Galsworthy set out to make that very point: to show that the Forsytes were not full human individuals, but social beings fallen to a lower level of life. They have lost that bit of free manhood and free womanhood which makes men and women. *The Man of Property* has the elements of a very great novel, a very great satire. It sets out to reveal the social being in all his strength and inferiority. But the author has not the courage to carry it through. The greatness of the book rests in its new and sincere and amazingly profound satire. It is the ultimate satire on modern humanity, and done from the inside, with really consummate skill and sincere creative passion, something quite new. It seems to be a real effort to show up the social being in all his weirdness. And then it fizzles out.

Then, in the love affair of Irene and Bosinney, and in the sentimentalizing of old Jolyon Forsyte, the thing is fatally blemished. Galsworthy had not quite enough of the superb courage of his satire. He faltered, and gave in to the Forsytes. It is a thousand pities. He might have been the surgeon the modern soul needs so badly, to cut away the proud flesh of our Forsytes from the living body of men who are fully alive. Instead, he put down the knife and laid on a soft, sentimental poultice, and helped to make the corruption worse.

Satire exists for the very purpose of killing the social being, showing him what an inferior he is and, with all his parade of social honesty, how subtly and corruptly debased. Dishonest to life, dishonest to the living universe on which he is parasitic as a louse. By ridiculing the social being, the satirist helps the true individual, the real human being, to rise to his feet again and go on with the battle. For it is always a battle, and always will be.

Not that the majority are necessarily social beings. But the majority is only *conscious* socially: humanly, mankind is helpless and unconscious, unaware even of the thing most precious to any human being, that core of manhood or womanhood, naïve, innocent at-oneness with the living universe-continuum, which alone makes a man individual and, as an individual, *essentially* happy, even if he be driven mad like Lear. Lear was essentially happy, even in his greatest misery. A happiness from which Goneril and Regan were excluded as lice and bugs are excluded from happiness, being social beings, and, as such, parasites, fallen from true freedom and independence.

But the tragedy today is that men are only materially and socially conscious. They are unconscious of their own manhood, and so they let it be destroyed. Out of free men we produce social beings by the thousand every week.

The Forsytes are all parasites, and Mr. Galsworthy set out, in a really magnificent attempt, to let us see it. They are parasites upon the thought, the feelings, the whole body of life of really living individuals who have gone before them and who exist alongside with them. All they can do, having no individual life of their own, is out of fear to rake together property, and to feed upon the life that has been given by living men to mankind. They have no life, and so they live for ever, in perpetual fear of death, accumulating property to ward off death. They can keep up convention, but they cannot carry on a tradition. There is a tremendous difference between the two things. To carry on a tradition you must add something to the tradition. But to keep up a convention needs only the monotonous persistency of a parasite, the endless endurance of the craven, those who fear life because they are not alive, and who cannot die because they cannot live—the social beings.

As far as I can see, there is nothing but Forsyte in Galsworthy's books: Forsyte positive or Forsyte negative, Forsyte successful or Forsyte *manqué*. That is, every single character is determined by money: either the getting it, or the having it, or the wanting it, or the utter lacking it. Getting it are the Forsytes as such; having it are the Pendyces and patricians and Hilarys and Biancas and all that lot; wanting it are the Irenes and Bosinneys and young Jolyons; and utterly lacking it are all the charwomen and squalid poor who from the background—the shadows of the "having" ones, as old Mr. Stone says. This is the whole Galsworthy gamut, all absolutely determined by money, and not an individual soul among them. They are all fallen, all social beings, a castrated lot.

Perhaps the overwhelming numerousness of the Forsytes frightened Mr. Galsworthy from utterly damning them. Or perhaps it was something else, something more serious in him. Perhaps it was his utter failure to see what you were when you *weren't* a Forsyte. What was there *besides* Forsytes in all the wide human world? Mr. Galsworthy looked, and found nothing. Strictly and truly, after his frightened search, he had found nothing. But he came back with Irene and Bosinney, and offered us that. Here! he seems to say. Here is the anti-Forsyte! Here! Here you have it! Love! Pa-assion! PASSION.

We look at this love, this PASSION, and we see nothing but a doggish amorousness and a sort of anti-Forsytism. They are the *anti* half of the show. Runaway dogs of these Forsytes, running in the back garden and furtively and ignominiously copulating—this is the effect, on me, of Mr. Galsworthy's grand love affairs, Dark Flowers or Bosinneys, or Apple Trees or George Pendyce—whatever they be. About every one of them something ignominious and doggish, like dogs copulating in the street, and looking round to see if the Forsytes are watching.

Alas! this is the Forsyte trying to be freely sensual. He can't do it; he's lost it. He can only be doggishly messy. Bosinney is not only a Forsyte, but an anti-Forsyte, with a vast grudge against property. And the thing a man has a vast grudge against is the man's determinant. Bosinney is a property hound, but he has run away from the kennels, or been born outside the kennels, so he is a rebel. So he goes sniffing round the property bitches, to get even with the successful property hounds that way. One cannot help preferring Soames Forsyte, in a choice of evils.

Just as one prefers June or any of the old aunts to Irene. Irene seems to me a sneaking, creeping, spiteful sort of bitch, an anti-Forsyte, absolutely living off the Forsytes—yes, to the very end; absolutely living off their money and trying to do them dirt. She is like Bosinney, a property mongrel doing dirt in the property kennels. But she is a real property prostitute, like the little model in *Fraternity*. Only she is *anti!* It is a type recurring again and again in Galsworthy: the parasite upon the parasites, "Big fleas have little fleas, etc." And Bosinney and Irene, as well as the vagabond in *The Island Pharisees,* are among the little fleas. And as a tramp loves his own vermin, so the Forsytes and the Hilarys love these, their own particular body parasites, their *antis*.

It is when he comes to sex that Mr. Galsworthy collapses finally. He becomes nastily sentimental. He wants to make sex important, and he only makes it repulsive. Sentimentalism is the working off on yourself of feelings you haven't really got. We all *want* to have certain feelings: feelings of love, of passionate sex, of kindliness, and so forth. Very few people really feel love, or sex passion, or kindliness, or anything else that goes at all deep. So the mass just fake these feelings inside themselves. Faked feelings! The world is all gummy with them. They are better than real feelings, because you can spit them out when you brush your teeth; and then to-morrow you can fake them afresh.

Shelton, in *The Island Pharisees,* is the first of Mr. Galsworthy's lovers, and he might as well be the last. He is almost comical. All we know of his passion for Antonia is that he feels at the beginning a "hunger" for her, as if she were a beefsteak. And towards the end he once kisses her, and expects her, no doubt, to fall instantly at his feet overwhelmed. He never for a second feels a moment of gentle sympathy with her. She is class-bound, but she doesn't seem to have been inhuman. The inhuman one was the lover. He can gloat over her in the distance, as if she were a dish of pig's trotters, *pieds truffés:* she can be an angelic *vision* to him a little way off, but when the poor thing has to be just a rather ordinary middle-class girl to him, quite near, he hates her with a comical, rancorous hate. It is most queer. He is helplessly *anti*. He hates her for even existing as a woman of her own class, for even having her own existence. Apparently she should just be a floating female sex-organ, hovering round to satisfy his little "hungers," and then *basta*. Anything of the real meaning of sex, which involves the whole of a human being, never occurs to him. It is a function, and the female is a sort of sexual appliance, no more.

And so we have it again and again, on this low and bastard level, all the human correspondence lacking. The sexual level is extraordinarily low, like dogs. The Galsworthy heroes are all weirdly in love with themselves, when we know them better, afflicted with chronic narcissism. They know just three types of women: the Pendyce mother, prostitute to property; the Irene, the essential *anti* prostitute, the floating, flaunting female organ; and the social woman, the mere lady. All three are loved and hated in turn by the recurrent heroes. But it is all on the debased level of property, positive or *anti*. It is all a doggy form of prostitution. Be quick and have done.

One of the funniest stories is *The Apple Tree*. The young man finds, at a lonely Devon farm, a little Welsh farm-girl who, being a Celt and not a Saxon, at once falls for the Galsworthian hero. This young gentleman, in the throes of narcissistic love for his marvellous self, falls for the maid because she has fallen so utterly and abjectly for him. She doesn't call him "My King," not being Wellsian; she only says: "I can't live away from you. Do what you like with me. Only let me come with you!" The proper prostitutional announcement!

For this, of course, a narcissistic young gentleman just down from Oxford falls at once. Ensues a grand pa-assion. He goes to buy her a proper frock to be carried away in, meets a college friend with a young lady sister, has jam for tea and stays the night, and the grand pa-assion has died a natural death by the time he spreads the marmalade on his bread. He has returned to his own class, and nothing else exists. He marries the young lady, true to his class. But to fill the cup of his vanity, the maid drowns herself. It is funny that maids only seem to do it for these narcissistic young gentlemen who, looking in the pool for their own image, desire the added satisfaction of seeing the face of drowned Ophelia there as well; saving them the necessity of taking the narcissus plunge in person. We have gone one better than the myth. Narcissus, in Mr. Galsworthy, doesn't drown himself. He asks Ophelia, or Megan, kindly to drown herself instead. And in this fiction she actually does. And he feels so *wonderful* about it!

Mr. Galsworthy's treatment of passion is really rather shameful.

The whole thing is doggy to a degree. The man has a temporary "hunger"; he is "on the heat" as they say of dogs. The heat passes. It's done. Trot away, if you're not tangled. Trot off, looking shamefacedly over your shoulder. People have been watching! Damn them! But never mind, it'll blow over. Thank God, the bitch is trotting in the other direction. She'll soon have another trail of dogs after her. That'll wipe out my traces. Good for that! Next time I'll get properly married and do my doggishness in my own house.

With the fall of the individual, sex falls into a dog's heat. Oh, if only Mr. Galsworthy had had the strength to satirize this too, instead of pouring a sauce of sentimental savouriness over it. Of course, if he had done so he would never have been a popular writer, but he would have been a great one.

However, he chose to sentimentalize and glorify the most doggy sort of sex. Setting out to satirize the Forsytes, he glorifies the *anti,* who is one worse. While the individual remains real and unfallen, sex remains a vital and supremely important thing. But once you have the fall into social beings, sex becomes disgusting, like dogs on the heat. Dogs are social beings, with no true canine individuality. Wolves and foxes don't copulate on the pavement. Their sex is wild and in act utterly private. Howls you may hear, but you will never see anything. But the dog is tame–and he makes excrement and he copulates on the pavement, as if to spite you. He is the Forsyte *anti.*

The same with human beings. Once they become tame they become, in a measure, exhibitionists, as if to spite everything. They have no real feelings of their own. Unless somebody "catches them at it" they don't really feel they've felt anything at all. And this is how the mob is today. It is Forsyte *anti.* It is the social being spiting society.

Oh, if only Mr. Galsworthy had satirized *this* side of Forsytism, the anti-Forsyte posturing of the "rebel," the narcissus and the exhibitionist, the dogs copulating on the pavement! Instead of that, he glorified it, to the eternal shame of English literature.

The satire, which in *The Man of Property* really had a certain noble touch, soon fizzles out, and we get that series of Galsworthian "rebels" who are, like all the rest of the modern middle-class rebels, not in rebellion at all. They are merely social beings behaving in an anti-social manner. They worship their own class, but they pretend to go one better and sneer at it. They are Forsyte *antis,* feeling snobbish about snobbery. Nevertheless, they want to attract attention and make money. That's why they are *anti.* It is the vicious circle of Forsytism. Money means more to them than it does to a Soames Forsyte, so they pretend to go one better, and despise it, but they will do anything to have it—things which Soames Forsyte would not have done.

If there is one thing more repulsive than the social being positive, it is the social being negative, the mere *anti.* In the great debacle of decency this gentleman is the most indecent. In a subtle way Bosinney and Irene are more dishonest and more indecent than Soames and Winifred, but they are *anti,* so they are glorified. It is pretty sickening.

The introduction to *The Island Pharisees* explains the whole show: "Each man born into the world is born to go a journey, and for the most part he is born on the high road. . . . As soon as he can toddle, he moves, by the queer instinct we call the love of life, along this road: . . . his fathers went this way before him, they made this road for him to tread, and, when they bred him, passed into his fibre the love of doing things as they themselves had done them. So he walks on and on. . . . Suddenly, one day, without intending to, he notices a path or opening in the hedge, leading to right or left, and he stands looking at the undiscovered. After that he stops at all the openings in the hedge; one day, with a beating heart, he tries one. And this is where the fun begins."—Nine out of ten get back to the broad road again, and sidetrack no more. They snuggle down comfortably in the next inn, and think where they might have been. "But the poor silly tenth is faring on. Nine times out of ten he goes down in a bog; the undiscovered has engulfed him." But the tenth time he gets across, and a new road is opened to mankind.

It is a class-bound consciousness, or at least a hopeless social consciousness which sees life as a high road between two hedges. And the only way out is gaps in the hedge and excursions into naughtiness! These little *anti* excursions, from which the wayfarer slinks back to solid comfort nine times out of ten; an odd one goes down in a bog; and a very rare one finds a way across and opens out a new road.

In Mr. Galsworthy's novels we see the nine, the ninety-nine, the nine hundred and ninety-nine slinking back to solid comfort; we see an odd Bosinney go under a bus, because he hadn't guts enough to do something else, the poor *anti!* but that rare figure sidetracking into the unknown we do *not* see. Because, as a matter of fact, the whole figure is faulty at that point. If life is a great highway, then it must forge on ahead into the unknown. Sidetracking gets nowhere. That is mere *anti.* The tip of the road is always unfinished, in the wilderness. If it comes to a precipice and a cañon—well, then, there is need for some exploring. But we see Mr. Galsworthy, after *The Country House,* very safe on the old highway, very secure in comfort, wealth, and renown. He at least has gone down in no bog, nor lost himself striking new paths. The hedges nowadays are ragged with gaps, anybody who likes strays out on the little trips of "unconventions." But the Forsyte road has not moved on at all. It has only become dishevelled and sordid with excursionists doing the *anti* tricks and being "unconventional," and leaving tin cans behind.

In the three early novels, *The Island Pharisees, The Man of Property, Fraternity,* it looked as if Mr. Galsworthy might break through the blind end of the highway with the dynamite of satire, and help us out on to a new lap. But the sex ingredient of his dynamite was damp and muzzy, the explosion gradually fizzled off in sentimentality, and we are left in a worse state than before.

The later novels are purely commercial, and, if it had not been for the early novels, of no importance. They are popular, they sell well, and there's the end of them. They contain the explosive powder of the first books in minute quantities, fizzling as silly squibs. When you arrive at *To Let,* and the end, at least the *promised* end, of the Forsytes, what have you? Just money! Money, money, money and a certain snobbish silliness, and many more *anti* tricks and poses. Nothing else. The story is feeble, the characters have no blood and bones, the emotions are faked, faked, faked. It is one great fake. Not necessarily of Mr. Galsworthy. The characters fake their own emotions. But that doesn't help us. And if you look closely at the characters, the meanness and low-level vulgarity are very distasteful. You have all the Forsyte meanness, with none of the energy. Jolyon and Irene are meaner and more treacherous to their son than the older Forsytes were to theirs. The young ones are of a limited, mechanical, vulgar egoism far surpassing that of Swithin or James, their ancestors. There is in it all a vulgar sense of being rich, and therefore we do as we like: an utter incapacity for anything like *true* feeling, especially in the women, Fleur, Irene, Annette, June: a glib crassness, a youthful spontaneity which is just impertinence and lack of feeling; and all the time, a creeping, "having" sort of vulgarity of money and self-will, money and self-will, so that we wonder sometimes if Mr. Galsworthy is not treating his public in real bad faith, and being cynical and rancorous under his rainbow sentimentalism.

Fleur he destroys in one word: she is "having." It is perfectly true. We don't blame the young Jon for clearing out. Irene he destroys in a phrase out of Fleur's mouth to June: "Didn't she spoil your life too?"—and it is precisely what she did. Sneaking and mean, Irene prevented June from getting her lover. Sneaking and mean, she prevents Fleur. She is the bitch in the manger. She is the sneaking *anti*. Irene, the most beautiful woman on earth! And Mr. Galsworthy, with the cynicism of a successful old sentimentalist, turns it off by making June say: "Nobody can spoil a life, my dear. That's nonsense. Things happen, but we bob up."

This is the final philosophy of it all. "Things happen, but we bob up." Very well, then, write the book in that key, the keynote of a frank old cynic. There's no point in sentimentalizing it and being a sneaking old cynic. Why pour out masses of feelings that pretend to be genuine and then turn it all off with: "Things happen, but we bob up"?

It is quite true, things happen, and we bob up. If we are vulgar sentimentalists, we bob up just the same, so nothing has happened and nothing can happen. All is vulgarity. But it pays. There is money in it.

Vulgarity pays, and cheap cynicism smothered in sentimentalism pays better than anything else. Because nothing *can* happen to the degraded social being. So let's pretend it does, and then bob up!

It is time somebody began to spit out the jam of sentimentalism, at least, which smothers the "bobbing-up" philosophy. It is time we turned a straight light on this horde of rats, these younger Forsyte sentimentalists whose name is legion. It is sentimentalism which is stifling us. Let the social beings keep on bobbing up while ever they can. But it is time an effort was made to turn a hosepipe on the sentimentalism they ooze over everything. The world is one sticky mess, in which the little Forsytes indeed may keep on bobbing still, but in which an honest feeling can't breathe.

But if the sticky mess gets much deeper, even the little Forsytes won't be able to bob up any more. They'll be smothered in their own slime along with everything else. Which is a comfort.

INTRODUCTION TO THESE PAINTINGS

The reason the English produce so few painters is not that they are, as a nation, devoid of a genuine feeling for visual art: though to look at their productions, and to look at the mess which has been made of actual English landscape, one might really conclude that they were, and leave it at that. But it is not the fault of the God that made them. They are made with æsthetic sensibilities the same as anybody else. The fault lies in the English attitude to life.

The English, and the Americans following them, are paralysed by fear. That is what thwarts and distorts the Anglo-Saxon existence, this paralysis of fear. It thwarts life, it distorts vision, and it strangles impulse: this overmastering fear. And fear of what, in heaven's name? What is the Anglo-Saxon stock today so petrified with fear about? We have to answer that before we can understand the English failure in the visual arts: for, on the whole, it is a failure.

It is an old fear, which seemed to dig in to the English soul at the time of the Renaissance. Nothing could be more lovely and fearless than Chaucer. But already Shakespeare is morbid with fear, fear of consequences. That is the strange phenomenon of the English Renaissance: this mystic terror of the consequences, the consequences of action. Italy, too, had her reaction, at the end of the sixteenth century, and showed a similar fear. But not so profound, so overmastering. Aretino was anything but timorous: he was bold as any Renaissance novelist, and went one better.

What appeared to take full grip on the northern consciousness at the end of the sixteenth century was a terror, almost a horror of sexual life. The Elizabethans, grand as we think them, started it. The real "mortal coil" in Hamlet is all sexual; the young man's horror of his mother's incest, sex carrying with it a wild and nameless terror which, it seems to me, it had never carried before. Œdipus and Hamlet are very different in this respect. In Œdipus there is no recoil in horror from sex itself: Greek drama never shows us that. The horror, when it is present in Greek tragedy, is against *destiny,* man caught in the toils of destiny. But with the Renaissance itself, particularly in England, the horror is sexual. Orestes is dogged by destiny and driven mad by the Eumenides. But Hamlet is overpowered by horrible revulsion from his physical connexion with his mother, which makes him recoil in similar revulsion from Ophelia, and almost from his father, even as a ghost. He is horrified at the merest suggestion of physical connexion, as if it were an unspeakable taint.

This, no doubt, is all in the course of the growth of the "spiritual-mental" consciousness, at the expense of the instinctive-intuitive consciousness. Man came to have his own body in horror, especially in its sexual implications: and so he began to suppress with all his might his instinctive-intuitive consciousness, which is so radical, so physical, so sexual. Cavalier poetry, love poetry, is already devoid of body. Donne, after the exacerbated revulsion-attraction excitement of his earlier poetry, becomes a divine. "Drink to me only with thine eyes," sings the cavalier: an expression incredible in Chaucer's poetry. "I could not love thee, dear, so much, loved I not honour more," sings the Cavalier lover. In Chaucer the "dear" and the "honour" would have been more or less identical.

But with the Elizabethans the grand rupture had started in the human consciousness, the mental consciousness recoiling in violence away from the physical, instinctive-intuitive. To the Restoration dramatist sex is, on the whole, a dirty business, but they more or less glory in the dirt. Fielding tries in vain to defend the Old Adam. Richardson with his calico purity and his underclothing excitements sweeps all before him. Swift goes mad with sex and excrement revulsion. Sterne flings a bit of the same excrement humorously around. And physical consciousness gives a last song in Burns, then is dead. Wordsworth, Keats, Shelley, the Brontës, all are post-mortem poets. The essential instinctive-intuitive body is dead, and worshipped in death—all very unhealthy. Till Swinburne and Oscar Wilde try to start a revival from the mental field. Swinburne's "white thighs" are purely mental.

Now, in England—and following, in America—the physical self was not just fig-leafed over or suppressed in public, as was the case in Italy and on most of the Continent. In England it excited a strange horror and terror. And this extra morbidity came, I believe, from the great shock of syphilis and the realization of the consequences of the disease. Wherever syphilis, or "pox," came from, it was fairly new in England at the end of the fifteenth century. But by the end of the sixteenth, its ravages were obvious, and the shock of them had just penetrated the thoughtful and the imaginative consciousness. The royal families of England and Scotland were syphilitic; Edward VI and Elizabeth born with the inherited consequences of the disease. Edward VI died of it, while still a boy. Mary died childless and in utter depression. Elizabeth had no eyebrows, her teeth went rotten; she must have felt herself, somewhere, utterly unfit for marriage, poor thing. That was the grisly horror that lay behind the glory of Queen Bess. And so the Tudors died out: and another syphilitic-born unfortunate came to the throne, in the person of James I. Mary Queen of Scots had no more luck than the Tudors, apparently. Apparently Darnley was reeking with the pox, though probably at first she did not know it. But when the Archbishop of St. Andrews was christening her baby James, afterwards James I of England, the old clergyman was so dripping with pox that she was terrified lest he should give it to the infant. And she need not have troubled, for the wretched infant had brought it into the world with him, from that fool Darnley. So James I of England slobbered and shambled, and was the wisest fool in Christendom, and the Stuarts likewise died out, the stock enfeebled by the disease.

With the royal families of England and Scotland in this condition, we can judge what the noble houses, the nobility of both nations, given to free living and promiscuous pleasure, must have been like. England traded with the East and with America; England, unknowing, had opened her doors to the disease. The English aristocracy travelled and had curious taste in loves. And pox entered the blood of the nation, particularly of the upper classes, who had more chance of infection. And after it had entered the blood, it entered the consciousness, and hit the vital imagination.

It is possible that the effects of syphilis and the conscious realization of its consequences gave a great blow also to the Spanish psyche, precisely at this period. And it is possible that Italian society, which was on the whole so untravelled, had no connexion with America, and was so privately self-contained, suffered less from the disease. Someone ought to make a thorough study of the effects of "pox" on the minds and the emotions and imaginations of the various nations of Europe, at about the time of our Elizabethans.

The apparent effect on the Elizabethans and the Restoration wits is curious. They appear to take the whole thing as a joke. The common oath, "Pox on you!" was almost funny. But how common the oath was! How the word "pox" was in every mind and in every mouth. It is one of the words that haunt Elizabethan speech. Taken very manly, with a great deal of Falstaffian bluff, treated as a huge joke! Pox! Why, he's got the pox! Ha-ha! What's he been after?

There is just the same attitude among the common run of men

today with regard to the minor sexual diseases. Syphilis is no longer regarded as a joke, according to my experience. The very word itself frightens men. You could joke with the word "pox." You can't joke with the word "syphilis." The change of word has killed the joke. But men still joke about *clap!* which is a minor sexual disease. They pretend to think it manly, even, to have the disease, or to have had it. "What! never had a shot of clap!" cries one gentleman to another. "Why, where have you been all your life?" If we change the word and insisted on "gonorrhœa," or whatever it is, in place of "clap," the joke would die. And anyhow I have had young men come to me green and quaking, afraid they've caught a "shot of clap."

Now, in spite of all the Elizabethan jokes about pox, pox was no joke to them. A joke may be a very brave way of meeting a calamity, or it may be a very cowardly way. Myself, I consider the Elizabethan pox joke a purely cowardly attitude. They didn't think it funny, for by God it *wasn't* funny. Even poor Elizabeth's lack of eyebrows and her rotten teeth were not funny. And they all knew it. They may not have known it was the direct result of pox: though probably they did. This fact remains, that no man can contract syphilis, or any deadly sexual disease, without feeling the most shattering and profound terror go through him, through the very roots of his being. And no man can look without a sort of horror on the effects of a sexual disease in another person. We are so constituted that we are all at once horrified and terrified. The fear and dread has been so great that the pox joke was invented as an evasion, and following that, the great hush! hush! was imposed. Man was *too* frightened: that's the top and bottom of it.

But now, with remedies discovered, we need no longer be *too* frightened. We can begin, after all these years, to face the matter. After the most fearful damage has been done.

For an overmastering fear is poison to the human psyche. And this overmastering fear, like some horrible secret tumour, has been poisoning our consciousness ever since the Elizabethans, who first woke up with dread to the entry of the original syphilitic poison into the blood.

I know nothing about medicine and very little about diseases, and my facts are such as I have picked up in casual reading. Nevertheless I am convinced that the secret awareness of syphilis, and the utter secret terror and horror of it, has had an enormous and incalculable effect on the English consciousness and on the American. Even when the fear has never been formulated, there it has lain, potent and overmastering. I am convinced that *some* of Shakespeare's horror and despair, in his tragedies, arose from the shock of his consciousness of syphilis. I don't suggest for one moment Shakespeare ever contracted syphilis. I have never had syphilis myself. Yet I know and confess how profound is my fear of the disease, and more than fear, my horror. In fact, I don't think I am so very much afraid of it. I am more horrified, inwardly and deeply, at the idea of its existence.

All this sounds very far from the art of painting. But it is not so far as it sounds. The appearance of syphilis in our midst gave a fearful blow to our sexual life. The real natural innocence of Chaucer was impossible after that. The very sexual act of procreation might bring as one of its consequences a foul disease, and the unborn might be tainted from the moment of conception. Fearful thought! It is truly a fearful thought, and all the centuries of getting used to it won't help us. It remains a fearful thought, and to free ourselves from this fearful dread we should use all our wits and all our efforts, not stick our heads in the sand of some idiotic joke, or still more idiotic don't-mention-it. The fearful thought of the consequences of syphilis, or of any sexual disease, upon the unborn gives a shock to the impetus of fatherhood in any man, even the cleanest. Our consciousness is a strange thing, and the knowledge of a certain fact may wound it mortally, even if the fact does not touch us directly. And so I am certain that *some* of Shakespeare's father-murder complex, *some* of Hamlet's horror of his mother, of his uncle, of all old men came from the feeling that fathers may transmit syphilis, or syphilis-consequences, to children. I don't know even whether Shakespeare was actually aware of the consequences to a child born of a syphilitic father or mother. He may not have been, though most probably he was. But he certainly was aware of the effects of syphilis itself, especially on men. And this awareness struck at his deep sex imagination, at his instinct for fatherhood, and brought in an element of terror and abhorrence there where men should feel anything but terror and abhorrence, into the procreative act.

The terror-horror element which had entered the imagination with regard to the sexual and procreative act was at least partly responsible for the rise of Puritanism, the beheading of the king-father Charles, and the establishment of the New England colonies. If America really sent us syphilis, she got back the full recoil of the horror of it, in her puritanism.

But deeper even than this, the terror-horror element led to the crippling of the consciousness of man. Very elementary in man is his sexual and procreative being, and on his sexual and procreative being depend many of his deepest instincts and the flow of his intuition. A deep instinct of kinship joins men together, and the kinship of flesh-and-blood keeps the warm flow of intuitional awareness streaming between human beings. Our true awareness of one another is intuitional, not mental. Attraction between people is really instinctive and intuitional, not an affair of judgment. And in mutual attraction lies perhaps the deepest pleasure in life, mutual attraction which may make us "like" our travelling companion for the two or three hours we are together, then no more; or mutual attraction that may deepen to powerful love, and last a life-time.

The terror-horror element struck a blow at our feeling of physical communion. In fact, it almost killed it. We have become ideal beings, creatures that exist in idea, to one another, rather than flesh-and-blood kin. And with the collapse of the feeling of physical, flesh-and-blood kinship, and the substitution of our ideal, social or political oneness, came the failing of our intuitive awareness, and the great unease, the *nervousness* of mankind. We are *afraid* of the instincts. We are *afraid* of the intuition within us. We suppress the instincts, and we cut off our intuitional awareness from one another and from the world. The reason being some great shock to the procreative self. Now we know one another only as ideal or social or political entities, fleshless, bloodless, and cold, like Bernard Shaw's creatures. Intuitively we are dead to one another, we have all gone cold.

But by intuition alone can man *really* be aware of man, or of the living, substantial world. By intuition alone can man live and know either woman or world, and by intuition alone can he bring forth again images of magic awareness which we call art. In the past men brought forth images of magic awareness, and now it is the convention to admire these images. The convention says, for example, we must admire Botticelli or Giorgione, so Baedeker stars the pictures, and we admire them. But it is all a fake. Even those that get a thrill, even when they call it ecstasy, from these old pictures are only undergoing cerebral excitation. Their deeper responses, down in the intuitive and instinctive body, are not touched. They cannot be, because they are dead. A dead intuitive body stands there and gazes at the corpse of beauty: and usually it is completely and honestly bored. Sometimes it feels a mental coruscation which it calls an ecstasy or an æsthetic response.

Modern people, but particularly English and Americans, *cannot* feel anything with the whole imagination. They can see the living body of imagery as little as a blind man can see colour. The imaginative vision, which includes physical, intuitional perception, they *have not got*. Poor things, it is dead in them. And they stand in front of a Botticelli Venus, which they know as conventionally "beautiful," much as a blind man might stand in front of a bunch of roses and pinks and monkey-musk, saying: "Oh, do tell me which is red; let me feel red! Now let me feel white! Oh, let me feel it! What is this I am feeling? Monkey-musk? Is it white? Oh, do you say it is yellow blotched with orange-brown? Oh, but I can't feel it! What *can* it be? Is white velvety, or just silky?"

So the poor blind man! Yet he may have an acute perception of alive beauty. Merely by touch and scent, his intuitions being alive, the blind man may have a genuine and soul-satisfying experience of imagery. But not pictorial images. These are for ever beyond him.

So those poor English and Americans in front of the Botticelli Venus. They stare so hard; they do so *want* to see. And their eyesight is perfect. But all they can see is a sort of nude woman on a sort of shell on a sort of pretty greenish water. As a rule they rather dislike the "unnaturalness" or "affectation" of it. If they are high-brows they may get a little self-conscious thrill of æsthetic excitement. But real imaginative awareness, which is so largely physical, is denied them. *Ils n'ont pas de quoi,* as the Frenchman said of the angels, when asked if they made love in heaven.

Ah, the dear high-brows who gaze in a sort of ecstasy and get a correct mental thrill! Their poor high-brow bodies stand there as dead as dust-bins, and can no more feel the sway of complete imagery upon them than they can feel any other real sway. *Ils n'ont pas de quoi.* The instincts and the intuitions are so nearly dead in them, and they fear even the feeble remains. Their fear of the instincts and intuitions is even greater than that of the English Tommy who calls: "Eh, Jack! Come an' look at this girl standin' wi' no clothes on, an' two blokes spittin' at 'er." That is his vision of Botticelli's Venus. It is, for him, complete, for he is void of the image-seeing imagination. But at least he doesn't have to work up a cerebral excitation, as the high-brow does, who is really just as void.

All alike, cultured and uncultured, they are still dominated by that unnamed, yet overmastering dread and hate of the instincts deep in the body, dread of the strange intuitional awareness of the body, dread of anything but ideas, which *can't* contain bacteria. And the dread all works back to a dread of the procreative body, and is partly traceable to the shock of the awareness of syphilis.

The dread of the instincts included the dread of intuitional awareness. "Beauty is a snare"–"Beauty is but skin-deep"–"Handsome is as handsome does"–"Looks don't count"–"Don't judge by appearances"–if we only realized it, there are thousands of these vile proverbs which have been dinned into us for over two hundred years. They are all of them false. Beauty is not a snare, nor is it skin-deep, since it always involves a certain loveliness of modelling, and handsome doers are often ugly and objectionable people, and if you ignore the look of the thing you plaster England with slums and produce at last a state of spiritual depression that is suicidal, and if you don't judge by appearances, that is, if you can't trust the impression which things make on you, you are a fool. But all these base-born proverbs, born in the cash-box, hit direct against the intuitional consciousness. Naturally, man gets a great deal of his life's satisfaction from beauty, from a certain sensuous pleasure in the look of the thing. The old Englishman built his hut of a cottage with a childish joy in its appearance, purely intuitional and direct. The modern Englishman has a few borrowed ideas, simply doesn't know *what* to feel, and makes a silly mess of it: though perhaps he is improving, hopefully, in this field of architecture and house-building. The intuitional faculty, which alone relates us in direct awareness to physical things and substantial presences, is atrophied and dead, and we don't know *what* to feel. We know we ought to feel something, but what?–Oh, tell us what! And this is true of all nations, the French and Italians as much as the English. Look at new French suburbs! Go through the crockery and furniture departments in the *Dames de France* or any big shop. The blood in the body stands still, before such *crétin* ugliness. One has to decide that the modern bourgeois is a *crétin*.

This movement against the instincts and the intuition took on a moral tone in all countries. It started in hatred. Let us never forget that modern morality has its roots in hatred, a deep, evil hate of the instinctive, intuitional, procreative body. This hatred is made more virulent by fear, and an extra poison is added to the fear by unconscious horror of syphilis. And so we come to modern bourgeois consciousness, which turns upon the secret poles of fear and hate. That is the real pivot of all bourgeois consciousness in all countries: fear and hate of the instinctive, intuitional, procreative body in man or woman. But of course this fear and hate had to take on a righteous appearance, so it became moral, said that the instincts, intuitions and all the activities of the procreative body were evil, and promised a *reward* for their suppression. That is the great clue to bourgeois psychology: the reward business. It is screamingly obvious in Maria Edgeworth's tales, which must have done unspeakable damage to ordinary people. Be good, and you'll have money. Be wicked, and you'll be utterly penniless at last, and the good ones will have to offer you a little charity. This is sound working morality in the world. And it makes one realize that, even to Milton, the true hero of *Paradise Lost* must be Satan. But by this baited morality the masses were caught and enslaved to industrialism before ever they knew it; the good got hold of the goods, and our modern "civilization" of money, machines, and wage-slaves was inaugurated. The very pivot of it, let us never forget, being fear and hate, the most intimate fear and hate, fear and hate of one's own instinctive, intuitive body, and fear and hate of every other man's and every other woman's warm, procreative body and imagination.

Now it is obvious what result this will have on the plastic arts, which depend entirely on the representation of substantial bodies, and on the intuitional perception of the *reality* of substantial bodies. The reality of substantial bodies can only be perceived by the imagination, and the imagination is a kindled state of consciousness in which intuitive awareness predominates. The plastic arts are all imagery, and imagery is the body of our imaginative life, and our imaginative life is a great joy and fulfilment to us, for the imagination is a more powerful and more comprehensive flow of consciousness than our ordinary flow. In the flow of true imagination we know in full, mentally and physically at once, in a greater, enkindled awareness. At the maximum of our imagination we are religious. And if we deny our imagination, and have no imaginative life, we are poor worms who have never lived.

In the seventeenth and eighteenth centuries we have the deliberate denial of intuitive awareness, and we see the results on the arts. Vision became more optical, less intuitive and painting began to flourish. But what painting! Watteau, Ingres, Poussin, Chardin have some real imaginative glow still. They are still somewhat free. The puritan and the intellectual has not yet struck them down with his fear and hate obsession. But look at England! Hogarth, Reynolds, Gainsborough, they all are already bourgeois. The coat is really more important than the man. It is amazing how important clothes suddenly become, how they *cover* the subject. An old Reynolds colonel in a red uniform is much more a uniform than an individual, and as for Gainsborough, all one can say is: What a lovely dress and hat! What really expensive Italian silk! This painting of garments continued in vogue, till pictures like Sargent's seem to be nothing but yards and yards of satin from the most expensive shops, having some pretty head popped on the top. The imagination is quite dead. The optical vision, a sort of flashy coloured photography of the eye, is rampant.

In Titian, in Velasquez, in Rembrandt the people are there inside their clothes all right, and the clothes are imbued with the life of the individual, the gleam of the warm procreative body comes through all the time, even if it be an old, half-blind woman or a weird, ironic little Spanish princess. But modern people are nothinging inside their garments, and a head sticks out at the top and hands stick out of the sleeves, and it is a bore. Or, as in Lawrence or Raeburn, you have something very pretty but almost a mere cliché, with very little instinctive or intuitional perception to it.

After this, and apart from landscape and water-colour, there is strictly no English painting that exists. As far as I am concerned, the pre-Raphaelites don't exist; Watts doesn't, Sargent doesn't, and none of the moderns.

There is the exception of Blake. Blake is the only painter of imaginative pictures, apart from landscape, that England has produced. And unfortunately there is so little Blake, and even in that little the symbolism is often artificially imposed. Nevertheless, Blake paints with real intuitional awareness and solid instinctive feeling. He dares handle the human body, even if he sometimes makes it a mere ideograph. And no other Englishman has even dared handle it with alive imagination. Painters of composition-pictures in England, of whom perhaps the best is Watts, never quite get beyond the level of cliché, sentimentalism, and *funk*. Even Watts is a failure, though he made some sort of try: even Etty's nudes in York fail imaginatively, though they have some feeling for flesh. And the rest, the Leightons, even the moderns don't really do anything. They never get beyond studio models and clichés of the nude. The image never gets across to us, to seize us intuitively. It remains merely optical.

Landscape, however, is different. Here the English exist and hold their own. But, for me, personally, landscape is always waiting for something to occupy it. Landscape seems to be *meant* as a background to an intenser vision of life, so to my feeling painted landscape is background with the real subject left out.

Nevertheless, it can be very lovely, especially in water-colour, which is a more bodiless medium, and doesn't aspire to very substantial existence, and is so small that it doesn't try to make a very deep seizure on the consciousness. Water-colour will always be more of a statement than an experience.

And landscape, on the whole, is the same. It doesn't call up the more powerful responses of the human imagination, the sensual, passional responses. Hence it is the favourite modern form of expression in painting. There is no deep conflict. The instinctive and intuitional consciousness is called into play, but lightly, superficially. It is not confronted with any living, procreative body.

Hence the English have delighted in landscape, and have succeeded in it well. It is a form of escape for them, from the actual human body they so hate and fear, and it is an outlet for their perishing æsthetic desires. For more than a century we have produced delicious water-colours, and Wilson, Crome, Constable, Turner are all great landscape-painters. Some of Turner's landscape compositions are, to my feelings, among the finest that exist. They still satisfy me more even than van Gogh's or Cézanne's landscapes, which make a more violent assault on the emotions, and repel a little for that reason. Somehow I don't want landscape to make a violent assault on my feelings. Landscape is background with the figures left out or reduced to minimum, so let it stay back. Van Gogh's surging earth and Cézanne's explosive or rattling planes worry me. Not being profoundly interested in landscape, I prefer it to be rather quiet and unexplosive.

But, of course, the English delight in landscape is a delight in escape. It is always the same. The northern races are so innerly afraid of their own bodily existence, which they believe fantastically to be an evil thing—you could never find them feel anything but uneasy shame, or an equally shameful gloating, over the fact that a man was having intercourse with his wife, in his house next door—that all they cry for is an escape. And, especially, art must provide that escape.

It is easy in literature. Shelley is pure escape: the body is sublimated into sublime gas. Keats is more difficult—the body can still be *felt* dissolving in waves of successive death—but the death-business is very satisfactory. The novelists have even a better time. You can get some of the lasciviousness of Hetty Sorrell's "sin," and you can enjoy condemning her to penal servitude for life. You can thrill to Mr. Rochester's *passion,* and you can enjoy having his eyes burnt out. So it is, all the way: the novel of "passion"!

But in paint it is more difficult. You cannot paint Hetty Sorrell's sin or Mr. Rochester's passion without being really shocking. And you *daren't* be shocking. It was this fact that unsaddled Watts and Millais. Both might have been painters if they hadn't been Victorians. As it is, each of them is a wash-out.

Which is the poor, feeble history of art in England, since we can lay no claim to the great Holbein. And art on the continent, in the last century? It is more interesting, and has a fuller story. An artist *can* only create what he really religiously *feels* is truth, religious truth really *felt,* in the blood and the bones. The English could never think anything connected with the body *religious*—unless it were the eyes. So they painted the social appearance of human beings, and hoped to give them wonderful eyes. But they *could* think landscape religious, since it had no sensual reality. So they felt religious about it and painted it as well as it could be painted, maybe, from their point of view.

And in France? In France it was more or less the same, but with a difference. The French, being more rational, decided that the body had its place, but that it should be rationalized. The Frenchman of today has the most reasonable and rationalized body possible. His conception of sex is basically hygienic. A certain amount of copulation is good for you. *Ça fait du bien au corps!* sums up the physical side of a Frenchman's idea of love, marriage, food, sport, and all the rest. Well, it is more sane, anyhow, than the Anglo-Saxon terrors. The Frenchman is afraid of syphilis and afraid of the procreative body, but not quite so deeply. He has known for a long time that you can take precautions. And he is not profoundly imaginative.

Therefore he has been able to paint. But his tendency, just like that of all the modern world, has been to get away from the body, while still paying attention to its hygiene, and still not violently quarrelling with it. Puvis de Chavannes is really as sloppy as all the other spiritual sentimentalizers. Renoir is jolly: *ça fait du bien au corps!* is his attitude to the flesh. If a woman didn't have buttocks and breasts, she wouldn't be paintable, he said, and he was right. *Ça fait du bien au corps!* What do you paint with, Maître?—With my penis, and be damned! Renoir didn't try to get away from the body. But he had to dodge it in some of its aspects, rob it of its natural terrors, its natural demonishness. He is delightful, but a trifle banal. *Ça fait du bien au corps!* Yet how infinitely much better he is than any English equivalent.

Courbet, Daumier, Degas, they all painted the human body. But Daumier satirized it, Courbet saw it as a toiling thing, Dégas saw it as a wonderful instrument. They all of them deny it its finest qualities, its deepest instincts, its purest intuitions. They prefer, as it were, to industrialize it. They deny it the best imaginative existence.

And the real grand glamour of modern French art, the real outburst of delight came when the body was at last dissolved of its substance, and made part and parcel of the sunlight-and-shadow scheme. Let us say what we will, but the real grand thrill of modern French art was the discovery of light, the discovery of light, and all the subsequent discoveries of the impressionists, and of the post-impressionists, even Cézanne. No matter how Cézanne may have reacted from the impressionists, it was they, with their deliriously joyful discovery of light and "free" colour, who really opened his eyes. Probably the most joyous moment in the whole history of painting was the moment when the incipient impressionists discovered light, and with it, colour. Ah, then they made the grand, grand escape into freedom, into infinity, into light and delight. They escaped from the tyranny of solidity and the menace of mass-form. They escaped, they escaped from the dark procreative body which so haunts a man, they escaped into the open air, *plein air* and *plein soleil:* light and almost ecstasy.

Like every other human escape, it meant being hauled back later with the tail between the legs. Back comes the truant, back to the old doom of matter, of corporate existence, of the body sullen and stubborn and obstinately refusing to be transmuted into pure light, pure colour, or pure anything. It is not concerned with purity. Life isn't. Chemistry and mathematics and ideal religion are, but these are only small bits of life, which is itself bodily, and hence neither pure nor impure.

After the grand escape into impressionism and pure light, pure colour, pure bodilessness—for what is the body but a shimmer of lights and colours!—poor art came home truant and sulky, with its tail between its legs. And it is this return which now interests us. We know the escape was illusion, illusion, illusion. The cat had to come back. So now we despise the "light" blighters too much. We haven't a good word for them. Which is nonsense, for they too are wonderful, even if their escape was into *le grand néant,* the great nowhere.

But the cat came back. And it is the home-coming tom that now has our sympathy: Renoir, to a certain extent, but mostly Cézanne, the sublime little grimalkin, who is followed by Matisse and Gauguin and Derain and Vlaminck and Braque and all the host of other defiant and howling cats that have come back, perforce, to form and substance and *thereness,* instead of delicious nowhereness.

Without wishing to labour the point, one cannot help being amused at the dodge by which the impressionists made the grand escape from the body. They metamorphosed it into a pure assembly of shifting lights and shadows, all coloured. A web of woven, luminous colour was a man, or a woman—and so they painted her, or him: a web of woven shadows and gleams. Delicious! and quite true as far as it goes. A purely optical, *visual* truth: which paint is supposed to be. And they painted delicious pictures: a little too delicious. They bore us, at the moment. They bore people like the very modern critics intensely. But very modern critics need not be so intensely bored. There is something very lovely about the good impressionist pictures. And ten years hence critics will be bored by the present run of post-impressionists, though not so passionately bored, for these post-impressionists don't move us as the impressionists moved our fathers. We have to persuade ourselves, and we have to persuade one another to be impressed by the post-impressionists, on the whole. On the whole, they rather depress us. Which is perhaps good for us.

But modern art criticism is in a curious hole. Art has suddenly gone into rebellion, against all the canons of accepted religion, accepted good form, accepted everything. When the cat came back from the delicious impressionist excursion, it came back rather tattered, but bristling and with its claws out. The glorious escape was all an illusion. There *was* substance still in the world, a thousand times be damned to it! There *was* the body, the great lumpy body. There it was. You had it shoved down your throat. What really existed was lumps, lumps. Then paint 'em. Or else paint the thin "spirit" with gaps in it and looking merely dishevelled and "found out." Paint had found the spirit out.

This is the sulky and rebellious mood of the post-impressionists. They still hate the body—hate it. But, in a rage, they admit its existence, and paint it as huge lumps, tubes, cubes, planes, volumes, spheres, cones, cylinders, all the "pure" or mathematical forms of substance. As for landscape, it comes in for some of the same rage. It has also suddenly gone lumpy. Instead of being nice and ethereal and non-sensual, it was discovered by van Gogh to be heavily, overwhelmingly substantial and sensual. Van Gogh took up landscape in heavy spadefuls. And Cézanne had to admit it. Landscape, too, after being, since Claude Lorrain, a thing of pure luminosity and floating shadow, suddenly exploded, and came tumbling back on to the canvases of artists in lumps. With Cézanne, landscape "crystallized," to use one of the favourite terms of the critics, and it has gone on crystallizing into cubes, cones, pyramids, and so forth ever since.

The impressionists brought the world at length, after centuries of effort, into the delicious oneness of light. At last, at last! Hail, holy Light! the great natural One, the universal, the universalizer! We are not divided, all one body we—one in Light, lovely light! No sooner had this pæan gone up than the post-impressionists, like Judas, gave the show away. They exploded the illusion, which fell back to the canvas of art in a chaos of lumps.

This new chaos, of course, needed new apologists, who therefore rose up in hordes to apologize, almost, for the new chaos. They felt a little guilty about it, so they took on new notes of effrontery, defiant as any Primitive Methodists, which, indeed, they are: the Primitive Methodists of art criticism. These evangelical gentlemen at once ran up their chapels, in a Romanesque or Byzantine shape, as was natural for a primitive and a methodist, and started to cry forth their doctrines in the decadent wilderness. They discovered once more that the æsthetic experience was an ecstasy, an ecstasy granted only to the chosen few, the elect, among whom said critics were, of course, the arch-elect. This was outdoing Ruskin. It was almost Calvin come to art. But let scoffers scoff, the æsthetic ecstasy was vouchsafed only to the few, the elect, and even then only when they had freed their minds of false doctrine. They had renounced the mammon of "subject" in pictures, they went whoring no more after the Babylon of painted "interest," nor did they hanker after the flesh-pots of artistic "representation." Oh, purify yourselves, ye who would know the æsthetic ecstasy, and be lifted up to the "white peaks of artistic inspiration." Purify yourselves of all base hankering for a tale that is told, and of all low lust for likenesses. Purify yourselves, and know the one supreme way, the way of Significant

Form. I am the revelation and the way! I am Significant Form, and my unutterable name is Reality. Lo, I am Form and I am Pure, behold, I am Pure Form. I am the revelation of Spiritual Life, moving behind the veil. I come forth and make myself known, and I am Pure Form, behold, I am Significant Form.

So the prophets of the new era in art cry aloud to the multitude, in exactly the jargon of the revivalists, for revivalists they are. They will revive the Primitive Method-brethren, the Byzantines, the Ravennese, the early Italian and French primitives (which ones, in particular, we aren't told); these were Right, these were Pure, these were Spiritual, these were Real! And the builders of early Romanesque churches, O my brethren! these were holy men, before the world went a-whoring after Gothic. Oh, return, my brethren, to the Primitive Method. Lift up your eyes to Significant Form, and be saved.

Now myself, brought up a nonconformist as I was, I just was never able to understand the language of salvation. I never knew what they were talking about, when they raved about being saved, and safe in the arms of Jesus, and Abraham's bosom, and seeing the great light, and entering into glory: I just was puzzled, for what did it *mean?* It seemed to work out as a getting rather drunk on your own self-importance, and afterwards coming dismally sober again and being rather unpleasant. That was all I could see in actual experience of the entering-into-glory business. The term itself, like something which ought to mean something but somehow doesn't, stuck on my mind like an irritating bur, till I decided that it was just an artificial stimulant to the individual self-conceit. How could I enter into glory, when glory is just an abstraction of a human state, and not a separate reality at all? If glory means anything at all, it means the thrill a man gets when a great many people look up to him with mixed awe, reverence, delight. Today, it means Rudolph Valentino. So that the cant about entering into glory is just used fuzzily to enhance the individual sense of self-importance —one of the rather cheap cocaine-phrases.

And I'm afraid "æsthetic ecstasy" sounds to me very much the same, especially when accompanied by exhortations. It so sounds like another great uplift into self-importance, another apotheosis of personal conceit; especially when accompanied by a lot of jargon about the pure world of reality existing behind the veil of this vulgar world of accepted appearances, and of the entry of the elect through the doorway of visual art. Too evangelical altogether, too much chapel and Primitive Methodist, too obvious a trick for advertising one's own self-glorification. The ego, as an American says, shuts itself up and paints the inside of the walls sky-blue, and thinks it is in heaven.

And then the great symbols of this salvation. When the evangelical says: Behold the lamb of God!—what on earth does he want one to behold? Are we invited to look at a lamb, with woolly, muttony appearance, frisking and making its little pills? Awfully nice, but what *has* it got to do with God or my soul? Or the cross? What *do* they expect us to see in the cross? A sort of gallows? Or the mark we use to cancel a mistake?—cross it out! That the cross by itself was supposed to *mean* something always mystified me. The same with the Blood of the Lamb.—Washed in the Blood of the Lamb! always seemed to me an extremely unpleasant suggestion. And when Jerome says: He who has once washed in the blood of Jesus need never wash again!—I feel like taking a hot bath at once, to wash off even the suggestion.

And I find myself equally mystified by the cant phrases like Significant Form and Pure Form. They are as mysterious to me as the Cross and the Blood of the Lamb. They are just the magic jargon of invocation, nothing else. If you want to invoke an æsthetic ecstasy, stand in front of a Matisse and whisper fervently under your breath: "Significant Form! Significant Form!"—and it will come. It sounds to me like a form of masturbation, an attempt to make the body react to some cerebral formula.

No, I am afraid modern criticism has done altogether too much for modern art. If painting survives this outburst of ecstatic evangelicism, which it will, it is because people do come to their senses, even after the silliest vogue.

And so we can return to modern French painting, without having to quake before the bogy, or the Holy Ghost of Significant Form: a bogy which doesn't exist if we don't mind leaving aside our self-importance when we look at a picture.

The actual fact is that in Cézanne modern French art made its first tiny step back to real substance, to objective substance, if we may call it so. Van Gogh's earth was still subjective earth, himself projected into the earth. But Cézanne's apples are a real attempt to let the apple exist in its own separate entity, without transfusing it with personal emotion. Cézanne's great effort was, as it were, to shove the apple away from him, and let it live of itself. It seems a small thing to do: yet it is the first real sign that man has made for several thousands of years that he is willing to admit that matter *actually* exists. Strange as it may seem, for thousands of years, in short, ever since the mythological "Fall," man has been preoccupied with the constant preoccupation of the denial of the existence of matter, and the proof that matter is only a form of spirit. And then, the moment it is done, and we realize finally that matter is only a form of energy, whatever that may be, in the same instant matter rises up and hits us over the head and makes us realize that it exists absolutely, since it is compact energy itself.

Cézanne felt it in paint, when he felt for the apple. Suddenly he felt the tyranny of mind, the white, worn-out arrogance of the spirit, the mental consciousness, the enclosed ego in its sky-blue heaven self-painted. He felt the sky-blue prison. And a great conflict started inside him. He was dominated by his old mental consciousness, but he wanted terribly to escape the domination. He wanted to *express* what he suddenly, convulsedly knew! the existence of matter. He terribly wanted to paint the real existence of the body, to make it artistically palpable. But he couldn't. He hadn't got there yet. And it was the torture of his life. He wanted to be himself in his own procreative body—and he couldn't. He was, like all the rest of us, so intensely and exclusively a mental creature, or a spiritual creature, or an egoist, that he could no longer identify himself with his intuitive body. He wanted to, terribly. At first he determined to do it by sheer bravado and braggadocio. But no good; it couldn't be done that way. He had, as one critic says, to become humble. But it wasn't a question of becoming humble. It was a question of abandoning his cerebral conceit and his "willed ambition" and coming down to brass tacks. Poor Cézanne, there he is in his self-portraits, even the early showy ones, peeping out like a mouse and saying: I *am* a man of flesh, am I not? For he was not quite, as none of us are. The man of flesh has been slowly destroyed through centuries, to give place to the man of spirit, the mental man, the ego, the self-conscious I. And in his artistic soul Cézanne knew it, and wanted to rise in the flesh. He couldn't do it, and it embittered him. Yet, with his apple, he did shove the stone from the door of the tomb.

He wanted to be a man of flesh, a real man: to get out of the sky-blue prison into real air. He wanted to live, really live in the body, to know the world through his instincts and his intuitions, and to be himself in his procreative blood, not in his mere mind and spirit. He wanted it, he wanted it terribly. And whenever he tried, his mental consciousness, like a cheap fiend, interfered. If he wanted to paint a woman, his mental consciousness simply overpowered him and wouldn't let him paint the woman of flesh, the first Eve who lived before any of the fig-leaf nonsense. He couldn't do it. If he wanted to paint people intuitively and instinctively, he couldn't do it. His mental concepts shoved in front, and these he *wouldn't* paint–mere representations of what the *mind* accepts, not what the intuitions gather–and they, his mental concepts, wouldn't let him paint from intuition; they shoved in between all the time, so he painted his conflict and his failure, and the result is almost ridiculous.

Woman he was not allowed to know by intuition; his mental self, his ego, that bloodless fiend, forbade him. Man, other men, he was likewise not allowed to know–except by a few, few touches. The earth likewise he was not allowed to know: his landscapes are mostly acts of rebellion against the mental concept of landscape. After a fight tooth-and-nail for forty years, he did succeed in knowing an apple, fully; and, not quite as fully, a jug or two. That was all he achieved.

It seems little, and he died embittered. But it is the first step that counts, and Cézanne's apple is a great deal, more than Plato's Idea. Cézanne's apple rolled the stone from the mouth of the tomb, and if poor Cézanne couldn't unwind himself from his cerements and mental winding-sheet, but had to lie still in the tomb, till he died, still he gave us a chance.

The history of our era is the nauseating and repulsive history of the crucifixion of the procreative body for the glorification of the spirit, the mental consciousness. Plato was an arch-priest of this crucifixion. Art, that handmaid, humbly and honestly served the vile deed, through three thousand years at least. The Renaissance put the spear through the side of the already crucified body, and syphilis put poison into the wound made by the imaginative spear. It took still three hundred years for the body to finish: but in the eighteenth century it became a corpse, a corpse with an abnormally active mind: and today it stinketh.

We, dear reader, you and I, we were born corpses, and we are corpses. I doubt if there is even one of us who has ever known so much as an apple, a whole apple. All we know is shadows, even of apples. Shadows of everything, of the whole world, shadows even of ourselves. We are inside the tomb, and the tomb is wide and shadowy like hell, even if sky-blue by optimistic paint, so we think it is all the world. But our world is a wide tomb full of ghosts, replicas. We are all spectres, we have not been able to touch even so much as an apple. Spectres we are to one another. Spectre you are to me, spectre I am to you. Shadow you are even to yourself. And by shadow I mean idea, concept, the abstracted reality, the ego. We are not solid. We don't live in the flesh. Our instincts and intuitions are dead, we live wound round with the winding-sheet of abstraction. And the touch of anything solid hurts us. For our instincts and intuitions, which are our feelers of touch and knowing through touch, they are dead, amputated. We walk and talk and eat and copulate and laugh and evacuate wrapped in our winding-sheets, all the time wrapped in our winding-sheets.

So that Cézanne's apple hurts. It made people shout with pain. And it was not till his followers had turned him again into an abstraction that he was ever accepted. Then the critics stepped forth and abstracted his good apple into Significant Form, and henceforth Cézanne was saved. Saved for democracy. Put safely in the tomb again, and the stone rolled back. The resurrection was postponed once more.

As the resurrection will be postponed *ad infinitum* by the good bourgeois corpses in their cultured winding-sheets. They will run up a chapel to the risen body, even if it is only an apple, and kill it on the spot. They are wide awake, are the corpses, on the alert. And a poor mouse of a Cézanne is alone in the years. Who else shows a spark of awakening life, in our marvellous civilized cemetery? All is dead, and dead breath preaching with phosphorescent effulgence about æsthetic ecstasy and Significant Form. If only the dead would bury their dead. But the dead are not dead for nothing. Who buries his own sort? The dead are cunning and alert to pounce on any spark of life and bury *it,* even as they have already buried Cézanne's apple and put up to it a white tombstone of Significant Form.

For who of Cézanne's followers does anything but follow at the triumphant funeral of Cézanne's achievement? They follow him in order to bury him, and they succeed. Cézanne is deeply buried under all the Matisses and Vlamincks of his following, while the critics read the funeral homily.

It is quite easy to accept Matisse and Vlaminck and Friesz and all the rest. They are just Cézanne abstracted again. They are all just tricksters, even if clever ones. They are all mental, mental, egoists, egoists, egoists. And therefore they are all acceptable now to the enlightened corpses of connoisseurs. You needn't be afraid of Matisse and Vlaminck and the rest. They will never give your corpse-anatomy a jar. They are just shadows, minds mountebanking and playing charades on canvas. They may be quite amusing charades, and I am all for the mountebank. But of course it is all games inside the cemetery, played by corpses and *hommes d'esprit,* even *femmes d'esprit, like* Mademoiselle Laurencin. As for *l'esprit,* said Cézanne, I don't give a fart for it. Perhaps not! But the connoisseurs will give large sums of money. Trust the dead to pay for their amusement, when the amusement is deadly!

The most interesting figure in modern art, and the only really interesting figure, is Cézanne: and that, not so much because of his achievement as because of his struggle. Cézanne was born at Aix in Provence in 1839: small, timorous, yet sometimes bantam defiant, sensitive, full of grand ambition, yet ruled still deeper by a naïve, Mediterranean sense of truth or reality, imagination, call it what you will. He is not a big figure. Yet his struggle is truly heroic. He was a bourgeois, and one must never forget it. He had a moderate bourgeois income. But a bourgeois in Provence is much more real and human than a bourgeois in Normandy. He is much nearer the actual people, and the actual people are much less subdued by awe of his respectable bourgeois money.

Cézanne was naïve to a degree, but not a fool. He was rather insignificant, and grandeur impressed him terribly. Yet still stronger in him was the little flame of life where he *felt* things to be true. He didn't betray himself in order to get success, because he couldn't: to his nature it was impossible: he was too pure to be able to betray his own small real flame for immediate rewards. Perhaps that is the best one can say of a man, and it puts Cézanne, small and insignificant as he is, among the heroes. He would *not* abandon his own vital imagination.

He was terribly impressed by physical splendour and flamboyancy, as people usually are in the lands of the sun. He admired terribly the splendid virtuosity of Paul Veronese and Tintoretto, and even of later and less good baroque painters. He wanted to be like that —terribly he wanted it. And he tried very, very hard, with bitter effort. And he always failed. It is a cant phrase with the critics to say "he couldn't draw." Mr. Fry says: "With all his rare endowments, he happened to lack the comparatively common gift of illustration, the gift that any draughtsman for the illustrated papers learns in a school of commercial art."

Now this sentence gives away at once the hollowness of modern criticism. In the first place, can one learn a "gift" in a school of commercial art, or anywhere else? A gift surely is given, we tacitly assume, by God or Nature or whatever higher power we hold responsible for the things we have no choice in.

Was, then, Cézanne devoid of this gift? Was he simply incapable of drawing a cat so that it would look like a cat? Nonsense! Cézanne's work is full of accurate drawing. His more trivial pictures, suggesting copies from other masters, are perfectly well drawn—that is, conventionally: so are some of the landscapes, so even is that portrait of M. Geffroy and his books, which is, or was, so famous. Why these cant phrases about not being able to draw? Of course Cézanne could draw, as well as anybody else. And he had learned everything that was necessary in the art-schools.

He *could* draw. And yet, in his terrifically earnest compositions in the late Renaissance or baroque manner, he drew so badly. Why? Not because he couldn't. And not because he was sacrificing "significant form" to "insignificant form," or mere slick representation, which is apparently what artists themselves mean when they talk about drawing. Cézanne knew all about drawing: and he surely knew as much as his critics do about significant form. Yet he neither succeeded in drawing so that things looked right, nor combining his shapes so that he achieved real form. He just failed.

He failed, where one of his little slick successors would have succeeded with one eye shut. And why? Why did Cézanne fail in his early pictures? Answer that, and you'll know a little better what art is. He didn't fail because he understood nothing about drawing or significant form or æsthetic ecstasy. He knew about them all, and didn't give a spit for them.

Cézanne failed in his earlier pictures because he was trying with his mental consciousness to do something which his living Provençal body didn't want to do, or couldn't do. He terribly wanted to do something grand and voluptuous and sensuously satisfying, in the Tintoretto manner. Mr. Fry calls that his "willed ambition," which is a good phrase, and says he had to learn humility, which is a bad phrase.

The "willed ambition" was more than a mere willed ambition—it was a genuine desire. But it was a desire that thought it would be satisfied by ready-made baroque expressions, whereas it needed to achieve a whole new marriage of mind and matter. If we believed in reincarnation, then we should have to believe that after a certain number of new incarnations into the body of an artist, the soul of Cézanne *would* produce grand and voluptuous and sensually rich pictures—but not at all in the baroque manner. Because the pictures he actually did produce with undeniable success are the first steps in that direction, sensual and rich, with not the slightest hint of baroque, but new, the man's new grasp of substantial reality.

There was, then, a certain discrepancy between Cézanne's *notion* of what he wanted to produce, and his other, intuitive knowledge of what he *could* produce. For whereas the mind works in possibilities, the intuitions work in actualities, and what you *intuitively* desire, that is possible to you. Whereas what you mentally or "consciously" desire is nine times out of ten impossible: hitch your wagon to a star, and you'll just stay where you are.

So the conflict, as usual, was not between the artist and his medium, but between the artist's *mind* and the artist's *intuition* and *instinct*. And what Cézanne had to learn was not humility—cant word! —but honesty, honesty with himself. It was not a question of any gift or significant form or æsthetic ecstasy: it was a question of Cézanne being himself, just Cézanne. And when Cézanne is himself he is not Tintoretto, nor Veronese, nor anything baroque at all. Yet he is something *physical*, and even sensual: qualities which he had identified with the masters of virtuosity.

In passing, if we think of Henri Matisse, a real virtuoso, and imagine him possessed with a "willed ambition" to paint grand and flamboyant baroque pictures, then we know at once that he would not have to "humble" himself at all, but that he would start in and paint with great success grand and flamboyant modern-baroque pictures. He would succeed because he has the gift of virtuosity. And the gift of virtuosity simply means that you don't have to humble yourself, or even be honest with yourself, because you are a clever mental creature who is capable at will of making the intuitions and instincts subserve some mental concept: in short, you can prostitute your body to your mind, your instincts and intuitions you can prostitute to your "willed ambition," in a sort of masturbation process, and you can produce the impotent glories of virtuosity. But Veronese and Tintoretto are real painters; they are not mere *virtuosi*, as some of the later men are.

The point is very important. Any creative act occupies the whole consciousness of a man. This is true of the great discoveries of science as well as of art. The truly great discoveries of science and real works of art are made by the whole consciousness of man working together in unison and oneness: instinct, intuition, mind, intellect all fused into one complete consciousness, and grasping what we may call a complete truth, or a complete vision, a complete revelation in sound. A discovery, artistic or otherwise, may be more or less intuitional, more or less mental; but intuition will have entered into it, and mind will have entered too. The whole consciousness is concerned in every case.—And a painting requires the activity of the whole imagination, for it is made of imagery, and the imagination is that form of complete consciousness in which predominates the intuitive awareness of forms, images, the *physical* awareness.

And the same applies to the genuine appreciation of a work of art, or the *grasp* of a scientific law, as to the production of the same. The whole consciousness is occupied, not merely the mind alone, or merely the body. The mind and spirit alone can never really grasp a work of art, though they may, in a masturbating fashion, provoke the body into an ecstasized response. The ecstasy will die out into ash and more ash. And the reason we have so many trivial scientists promulgating fantastic "facts" is that so many modern scientists likewise work with the mind alone, and *force* the intuitions and instincts into a prostituted acquiescence. The very statement that water is H_2O is a mental *tour de force*. With our bodies we know that water is *not* H_2O, our intuitions and instincts both know it is not so. But they are bullied by the impudent mind. Whereas if we said that water, under certain circumstances, produces two volumes of hydrogen and one of oxygen, then the intuitions and instincts would agree entirely. But that water *is composed* of two volumes of hydrogen to one of oxygen we cannot physically believe. It needs something else. Something is missing. Of course, alert science does not ask us to believe the commonplace assertion of: *water* is H_2O, but school children have to believe it.

A parallel case is all this modern stuff about astronomy, stars, their distances and speeds and so on, talking of billions and trillions of miles and years and so forth: it is just occult. The mind is revelling in words, the intuitions and instincts are just left out, or prostituted into a sort of ecstasy. In fact, the sort of ecstasy that lies in absurd figures such as 2,000,000,000,000,000,000,000,000,000 miles or years or tons, figures which abound in modern *scientific* books on astronomy, is just the sort of æsthetic ecstasy that the over-mental critics of art assert they experience today from Matisse's pictures.

It is all poppycock. The body is either stunned to a corpse, or prostituted to ridiculous thrills, or stands coldly apart.

When I read how far off the suns are, and what they are made of, and so on, and so on, I believe all I am *able* to believe, with the true imagination. But when my intuition and instinct can grasp no more, then I call my mind to a halt. I am not going to accept mere mental asseverations. The mind can assert anything, and pretend it has proved it. My beliefs I test on my body, on my intuitional consciousness, and when I get a response there, then I accept. The same is true of great scientific "laws," like the law of evolution. After years of acceptance of the "laws" of evolution–rather desultory or "humble" acceptance–now I realize that my vital imagination makes great reservations. I find I can't, with the best will in the world, believe that the species have "evolved" from one common life-form. I just can't feel it, I have to violate my intuitive and instinctive awareness of something else, to make myself believe it. But since I know that my intuitions and instincts may still be held back by prejudice, I seek in the world for someone to make me intuitively and instinctively feel the truth of the "law"–and I don't find anybody. I find scientists, just like artists, asserting things they are *mentally* sure of, in fact cocksure, but about which they are much too egoistic and ranting to be *intuitively, instinctively* sure. When I find a man, or a woman, intuitively and instinctively sure of anything, I am all respect. But for scientific or artistic braggarts how can one have respect? The intrusion of the egoistic element is a sure proof of intuitive uncertainty. No man who is sure by instinct and intuition *brags,* though he may fight tooth and nail for his beliefs.

Which brings us back to Cézanne, why he couldn't draw, and why he couldn't paint baroque masterpieces. It is just because he was real, and could only believe in his own expression when it expressed a moment of wholeness or completeness of consciousness in himself. He could not prostitute one part of himself to the other. He *could* not masturbate, in paint or words. And that is saying a very great deal, today; today, the great day of the masturbating consciousness, when the mind prostitutes the sensitive responsive body, and just forces the reactions. The masturbating consciousness produces all kinds of novelties, which thrill for the moment, then go very dead. It cannot produce a single genuinely new utterance.

What we have to thank Cézanne for is not his humility, but for his proud, high spirit that refused to accept the glib utterances of his facile mental self. He wasn't poor-spirited enough to be facile—nor humble enough to be satisfied with visual and emotional clichés. Thrilling as the baroque masters were to him in themselves, he realized that as soon as he reproduced them he produced nothing but cliché. The mind is full of all sorts of memory, visual, tactile, emotional memory, memories, groups of memories, systems of memories. A cliché is just a worn-out memory that has no more emotional or intuitional root, and has become a habit. Whereas a novelty is just a new grouping of clichés, a new arrangement of accustomed memories. That is why a novelty is so easily accepted: it gives the little shock or thrill of surprise, but it does not *disturb* the emotional and intuitive self. It forces you to see nothing new. It is only a novel compound of clichés. The work of most of Cézanne's successors is just novel, just a new arrangement of clichés, soon growing stale. And the clichés are Cézanne clichés, just as in Cézanne's own earlier pictures the clichés were all, or mostly, baroque clichés.

Cézanne's early history as a painter is a history of his fight with his own cliché. His consciousness wanted a new realization. And his ready-made mind offered him all the time a ready-made expression. And Cézanne, far too inwardly proud and haughty to accept the ready-made clichés that came from his mental consciousness, stocked with memories, and which appeared mocking at him on his canvas, spent most of his time smashing his own forms to bits. To a true artist, and to the living imagination, the cliché is the deadly enemy. Cézanne had a bitter fight with it. He hammered it to pieces a thousand times. And still it reappeared.

Now again we can see why Cézanne's drawing was so bad. It was bad because it represented a smashed, mauled cliché, terribly knocked about. If Cézanne had been willing to accept his own baroque cliché, his drawing would have been perfectly conventionally "all right," and not a critic would have had a word to say about it. But when his drawing was conventionally all right, to Cézanne himself it was mockingly all wrong, it was cliché. So he flew at it and knocked all the shape and stuffing out of it, and when it was so mauled that it was all wrong, and he was exhausted with it, he let it go; bitterly, because it still was not what he wanted. And here comes in the comic element in Cézanne's pictures. His rage with the cliché made him distort the cliché sometimes into parody, as we see in pictures like *The Pasha* and *La Femme*. "You *will* be cliché, will you?" he gnashes. "Then *be* it!" And he shoves it in a frenzy of exasperation over into parody. And the sheer exasperation makes the parody still funny; but the laugh is a little on the wrong side of the face.

This smashing of the cliché lasted a long way into Cézanne's life; indeed, it went with him to the end. The way he worked over and over his forms was his nervous manner of laying the ghost of his cliché, burying it. Then when it disappeared perhaps from his forms themselves, it lingered in his composition, and he had to fight with the *edges* of his forms and contours, to bury the ghost there. Only his colour he knew was not cliché. He left it to his disciples to make it so.

In his very best pictures, the best of the still-life compositions, which seem to me Cézanne's greatest achievement, the fight with the cliché is still going on. But it was in the still-life pictures he learned his final method of *avoiding* the cliché: just leaving gaps through which it fell into nothingness. So he makes his landscape succeed.

In his art, all his life long, Cézanne was tangled in a twofold activity. He wanted to express something, and before he could do it he had to fight the hydra-headed cliché, whose last head he could never lop off. The fight with the cliché is the most obvious thing in his pictures. The dust of battle rises thick, and the splinters fly wildly. And it is this dust of battle and flying of splinters which his imitators still so fervently imitate. If you give a Chinese dressmaker a dress to copy, and the dress happens to have a darned rent in it, the dressmaker carefully tears a rent in the new dress, and darns it in exact replica. And this seems to be the chief occupation of Cézanne's disciples, in every land. They absorb themselves reproducing imitation mistakes. He let off various explosions in order to blow up the stronghold of the cliché, and his followers make grand firework imitations of the explosions, without the faintest inkling of the true attack. They do, indeed, make an onslaught on representation, true-to-life representation: because the explosion in Cézanne's pictures blew them up. But I am convinced that what Cézanne himself wanted *was* representation. He *wanted* true-to-life representation. Only he wanted it *more* true to life. And once you have got photography, it is a very, very difficult thing to get representation *more* true-to-life: which it has to be.

Cézanne was a realist, and he wanted to be true to life. But he would not be content with the optical cliché. With the impressionists, purely optical vision perfected itself and fell *at once* into cliché, with a startling rapidity. Cézanne saw this. Artists like Courbet and Daumier were not purely optical, but the other element in these two painters, the intellectual element, was cliché. To the optical vision they added the concept of force-pressure, almost like an hydraulic brake, and this force-pressure concept is mechanical, a cliché, though still popular. And Daumier added mental satire, and Courbet added a touch of a sort of socialism: both cliché and unimaginative.

Cézanne wanted something that was neither optical nor mechanical nor intellectual. And to introduce into our world of vision something which is neither optical nor mechanical nor intellectual-psychological requires a real revolution. It was a revolution Cézanne began, but which nobody, apparently, has been able to carry on.

He wanted to touch the world of substance once more with the intuitive touch, to be aware of it with the intuitive awareness, and to express it in intuitive terms. That is, he wished to displace our present mode of mental-visual consciousness, the consciousness of mental concepts, and substitute a mode of consciousness that was predominantly intuitive, the awareness of touch. In the past the primitives painted intuitively, but *in the direction* of our present mental-visual, conceptual form of consciousness. They were working away from their own intuition. Mankind has never been able to trust the intuitive consciousness, and the decision to accept that trust marks a very great revolution in the course of human development.

Without knowing it, Cézanne, the timid little conventional man sheltering behind his wife and sister and the Jesuit father, was a pure revolutionary. When he said to his models: "Be an apple! Be an apple!" he was uttering the foreword to the fall not only of Jesuits and the Christian idealists altogether, but to the collapse of our whole way of consciousness, and the substitution of another way. If the human being is going to be primarily an apple, as for Cézanne it was, then you are going to have a new world of men: a world which has very little to say, men that can sit still and just be physically there, and be truly non-moral. That was what Cézanne meant with his: "Be an apple!" He knew perfectly well that the moment the model began to intrude her personality and her "mind," it would be cliché and moral, and he would have to paint cliché. The only part of her that was not banal, known *ad nauseam,* living cliché, the only part of her that was not living cliché was her appleyness. Her body, even her very sex, was known, nauseously:

connu, connu! the endless chance of known cause-and-effect, the infinite web of the hated cliché which nets us all down in utter boredom. He knew it all, he hated it all, he refused it all, this timid and "humble" little man. He knew, as an artist, that the only bit of a woman which nowadays escapes being ready-made and ready-known cliché is the appley part of her. Oh, be an apple, and leave out all your thoughts, all your feelings, all your mind and all your personality, which we know all about and find boring beyond endurance. Leave it all out—and be an apple! It is the appleyness of the portrait of Cézanne's wife that makes it so permanently interesting: the appleyness, which carries with it also the feeling of knowing the other side as well, the side you don't see, the hidden side of the moon. For the intuitive apperception of the apple is so *tangibly* aware of the apple that it is aware of it *all round,* not only just of the front. The eye sees only fronts, and the mind, on the whole, is satisfied with fronts. But intuition needs all-aroundness, and instinct needs insideness. The true imagination is for ever curving round to the other side, to the back of presented appearance.

So to my feeling the portraits of Madame Cézanne, particularly the portrait in the red dress, are more interesting than the portrait of M. Geffroy, or the portraits of the housekeeper or the gardener. In the same way the *Card-Players* with two figures please me more than those with four.

But we have to remember, in his figure-paintings, that while he was painting the appleyness he was also deliberately painting *out* the so-called humanness, the personality, the "likeness," the physical cliché. He had deliberately to paint it out, deliberately to make the hands and face rudimentary, and so on, because if he had painted them in fully they would have been cliché. He *never* got over the cliché denominator, the intrusion and interference of the ready-made concept, when it came to people, to men and women. Especially to women he could only give a cliché response—and that maddened him. Try as he might, women remained a known, ready-made cliché object to him, and he *could not* break through the concept obsession to get at the intuitive awareness of her. Except with his wife—and in his wife he did at least know the appleyness. But with his housekeeper he failed somewhat. She was a bit cliché, especially the face. So really is M. Geffroy.

With men Cézanne often dodged it by insisting on the clothes, those stiff cloth jackets bent into thick folds, those hats, those blouses, those curtains. Some of the *Card-Players,* the big ones with four figures, seem just a trifle banal, so much occupied with painted stuff, painted clothing, and the humanness a bit cliché. Nor good colour, nor clever composition, nor "planes" of colour, nor anything else will save an emotional cliché from being an emotional cliché, though they may, of course, garnish it and make it more interesting.

Where Cézanne did sometimes escape the cliché altogether and really give a complete intuitive interpretation of actual objects is in some of the still-life compositions. To me these good still-life scenes are purely representative and quite true to life. Here Cézanne did what he wanted to do: he made the things quite real, he didn't deliberately leave anything out, and yet he gave us a triumphant and rich intuitive vision of a few apples and kitchen pots. For once his intuitive consciousness triumphed, and broke into utterance. And here he is inimitable. His imitators imitate his accessories of tablecloths folded like tin, etc.—the unreal parts of his pictures—but they don't imitate the pots and apples, because they can't. It's the real appleyness, and you can't imitate it. Every man must create it new and different out of himself: new and different. The moment it looks "like" Cézanne, it is nothing.

But at the same time Cézanne was triumphing with the apple and appleyness he was still fighting with the cliché. When he makes Madame Cézanne most *still,* most appley, he starts making the universe slip uneasily about her. It was part of his desire: to make the human form, the *life* form, come to rest. Not static—on the contrary. Mobile but come to rest. And at the same time he set the unmoving material world into motion. Walls twitch and slide, chairs bend or rear up a little, cloths curl like burning paper. Cézanne did this partly to satisfy his intuitive feeling that nothing is really *statically* at rest—a feeling he seems to have had strongly—as when he watched the lemons shrivel or go mildewed, in his still-life group, which he left lying there so long so that he *could* see that gradual flux of change: and partly to fight the cliché, which says that the inanimate world *is* static, and that walls *are* still. In his fight with the cliché he denied that walls are still and chairs are static. In his intuitive self he *felt* for their changes.

And these two activities of his consciousness occupy his later landscapes. In the best landscapes we are fascinated by the mysterious *shiftiness* of the scene under our eyes; it shifts about as we watch it. And we realize, with a sort of transport, how intuitively *true* this is of landscape. It is *not* still. It has its own weird anima, and to our wide-eyed perception it changes like a living animal under our gaze. This is a quality that Cézanne sometimes got marvellously.

Then again, in other pictures he seems to be saying: Landscape is not like this and not like this and not like this and not . . . etc.—and every *not* is a little blank space in the canvas, defined by the remains of an assertion. Sometimes Cézanne builds up a landscape essentially out of omissions. He puts fringes on the complicated vacuum of the cliché, so to speak, and offers us that. It is interesting in a *repudiative* fashion, but it is not the new thing. The appleyness, the intuition has gone. We have only a mental repudiation. This occupies many of the later pictures: and ecstasizes the critics.

And Cézanne was bitter. He had never, as far as his *life* went, broken through the horrible glass screen of the mental concepts, to the actual *touch* of life. In his art he had touched the apple, and that was a great deal. He had intuitively known the apple and intuitively brought it forth on the tree of his life, in paint. But when it came to anything beyond the apple, to landscape, to people, and above all to nude woman, the cliché had triumphed over him. The cliché had triumphed over him, and he was bitter, misanthropic. How not to be misanthropic when men and women are just clichés to you, and you hate the cliché? Most people, of course, love the cliché—because most people *are* the cliché. Still, for all that, there is perhaps more appleyness in man, and even in nude woman, than Cézanne was able to get at. The cliché obtruded, so he just abstracted away from it. Those last water-colour landscapes are just abstractions from the cliché. They are blanks, with a few pearly-coloured sort of edges. The blank is vacuum, which was Cézanne's last word against the cliché. It is a vacuum, and the edges are there to assert the vacuity.

And the very fact that we can reconstruct almost instantly a whole landscape from the few indications Cézanne gives, shows what a cliché the landscape is, how it exists already, ready-made, in our minds, how it exists in a pigeon-hole of the consciousness, so to speak, and you need only be given its number to be able to get it out, complete. Cézanne's last water-colour landscapes, made up of a few touches on blank paper, are a satire on landscape altogether. *They leave so much to the imagination!*—that immortal cant phrase, which means they give you the clue to a cliché and the cliché comes. That's what the cliché exists for. And that sort of imagination is just a rag-bag memory stored with thousands and thousands of old and really worthless sketches, images, etc., clichés.

We can see what a fight it means, the escape from the domination of the ready-made mental concept, the mental consciousness stuffed full of clichés that intervene like a complete screen between us and life. It means a long, long fight, that will probably last for ever. But Cézanne did get as far as the apple. I can think of nobody else who has done anything.

When we put it in personal terms, it is a fight in a man between his own ego, which is his ready-made mental self which inhabits either a sky-blue, self-tinted heaven or a black, self-tinted hell, and his other free intuitive self. Cézanne never freed himself from his ego, in his life. He haunted the fringes of experience. "I who am so feeble in life"—but at least he knew it. At least he had the greatness to feel bitter about it. Not like the complacent bourgeois who now "appreciate" him!

So now perhaps it is the English turn. Perhaps this is where the English will come in. They have certainly stayed out very completely. It is as if they had received the death-blow to their instinctive and intuitive bodies in the Elizabethan age, and since then they have steadily died, till now they are complete corpses. As a young English painter, an intelligent and really modest young man, said to me: "But I do think we ought to begin to paint good pictures, now that we know pretty well all there is to know about how a picture should be made. You do agree, don't you, that technically we know almost all there is to know about painting?"

I looked at him in amazement. It was obvious that a new-born babe was as fit to paint pictures as he was. He knew technically all there was to know about pictures: all about two-dimensional and three-dimensional composition, also the colour-dimension and the dimension of values in that view of composition which exists apart from form: all about the value of planes, the value of the angle in planes, the different values of the same colour on different planes: all about edges, visible edges, tangible edges, intangible edges: all about the nodality of form-groups, the constellating of mass-centres: all about the relativity of mass, the gravitation and the centrifugal force of masses, the resultant of the complex impinging of masses, the isolation of a mass in the line of vision: all about pattern, line pattern, edge pattern, tone pattern, colour pattern, and the pattern of moving planes: all about texture, impasto, surface, and what happens at the edge of the canvas: also which is the æsthetic centre of the canvas, the dynamic centre, the effulgent centre, the kinetic centre, the mathematical centre, and the Chinese centre: also the points of departure in the foreground, and the points of disappearance in the background, together with the various routes between these points, namely, as the crow flies, as the cow walks, as the mind intoxicated with knowledge reels and gets there: all about spotting, what you spot, which spot, on the spot, how many spots, balance of spots, recedence of spots, spots on the explosive vision and spots on the co-ordinative vision: all about literary interest and how to hide it successfully from the policeman: all about photographic representation, and which heaven it belongs to, and which hell: all about the sex-appeal of a picture, and when you can be arrested for solicitation, when for indecency: all about the psychology of a picture, which section of the mind it appeals to, which mental state it is intended to represent, how to exclude the representation of all other states of mind from the one intended, or how, on the contrary, to give a hint of complementary states of mind fringing the state of mind portrayed: all about the chemistry of colours, when to use Winsor & Newton and when not, and the relative depth of contempt to display for Lefranc: on the history of colour, past and future, whether cadmium will really stand the march of ages, whether viridian will go black, blue, or merely greasy, and the effect on our great-great-grandsons of the flake white and zinc white and white lead we have so lavishly used: on the merits and demerits of leaving patches of bare, prepared canvas, and which preparation will bleach, which blacken: on the mediums to be used, the vice of linseed oil, the treachery of turps, the meanness of gums, the innocence or the unspeakable crime of varnish: on allowing your picture to be shiny, on insisting that it should be shiny, on weeping over the merest suspicion of gloss and rubbing it with a raw potato: on brushes, and the conflicting length of the stem, the best of the hog, the length of bristle most to be desired on the many varying occasions, and whether to slash in one direction only: on the atmosphere of London, on the atmosphere of Glasgow, on the atmosphere of Rome, on the atmosphere of Paris, and the peculiar action of them all upon vermilion, cinnabar, pale cadmium yellow, mid-chrome, emerald green, Veronese green, linseed oil, turps, and Lyall's perfect medium: on quality, and its relation to light, and its ability to hold its own in so radical a change of light as that from Rome to London—all these things the young man knew—and out of it, God help him, he was going to make pictures.

Now, such innocence and such naïveté, coupled with true mod-

V

Education

EDUCATION OF THE PEOPLE

EDUCATION OF THE PEOPLE

I

What is education all about? What is it doing? Does anybody know? It doesn't matter so much for people with money. For them social intercourse is an end in itself, a sort of charming game for which they need a little polish of manner, a trifle of social grace, and a certain amount of accomplishments, mental and otherwise. Even supposing they look on life as a serious affair, it only means they intend, in some way or other, to devote themselves to the service of the nation. And the service of the nation, though an important matter surely, is by now a somewhat cut-and-dried business.

The point is, the nation which is served. And what is the nation? Without attempting a high-flown definition, it is the people. And who are the people? Why, they are the proletariat. For according to the modern democratic ideal under which we still march, *ideally,* the upper classes exist only for the purpose of devoting themselves to the good of the people. Everything works back to the people, to the proletariat, strictly. If a man justifies his existence nowadays—and what man doesn't?—he proclaims that he is a servant and benefactor of the people, the vast proletariat. From the King downwards, this is so.

And the people, the proletariat. What about them and their education? They are the be-all and the end-all. To them everything is *ideally* devoted (mind, we are only writing now of education as it exists for us as an ideal, or an idea). There is not an idealist, or a man of ideas living who does not ostensibly come forward, like the Pope in Holy Week, with a basin and a towel to bathe the feet of the poor. And the poor sit aloft while their feet are laved. And then what? What *are* the poor, actually?

Because, before you can educate the people, you must know what the people are. We know well enough they are the proletariat, the human implements of industry. But that, we argue, is in their utilitarian aspect only. They have a higher reality. Their proletarian or laborious nature is their mundane nature. When the Pope washes the feet of the poor men, it is not because the poor men have been shunting trucks on the railway and got their feet hot and dirty.

Not at all. He washes their feet as an act of symbolic recognition of the divine nature which is alive in each of these poor men. In this world, we are content to recognize divinity only in those that serve. The whole world screams *Ich dien.* Heaven knows *what* it serves! And yet, if we go back to the Pope, we shall realize that it is not in the *service,* the *labour* that he recognizes the divinity, but in the actual nature of the *servant,* the labourer, the humble individual. He washes the feet of the humble, not the feet of trades-unionistic, strike-menacing truck-shunters.

The man and his job. You've got to make a distinction between the two. If Louis Quatorze was content to be a State, we can't allow (ideally, at least) our dustman Jim Shepherd to regard himself as the apotheosis of dustbins. When Louis Quatorze said that He was the State, or the State was Him, he belittled himself really. For after all, it is a much rarer and more difficult thing to be oneself than to be either a State or a dustbin. At his best, a man is himself; his job, even if it be State-swaying, comes a long way after. For almost anybody could sway a State or swing a dust tub. But no man can take on another man's self. If you want to be unique, be yourself. And the spark of divinity in each being, however humble, is what the Pope recognizes in Holy Week.

The job is not by any means holy: and the man, in some degree, is. No doubt here we shall raise the wind of opposition from labour units and employer's units. But we don't care. We represent the true idealists who even now sit on the Board of Education and foggily but fervently enact their ideals. The job is not at all divine, the labour in some measure *is.* So let technical education remain apart.

But here comes the first dilemma. Because, however cloistral our elementary schools may be, sheltering the eternal flame of the high ideal of human existence, Jimmy Shepherd, aged twelve, and Nancy Shepherd, aged thirteen, know very well that the eternal flame of the high ideal is all my-eye. It's all toffee, my dear sirs. What you've got to do is to *get a job,* and when you've got your job then you must *make a decent screw.* First and last, this is the state of man. So says little Jimmy Shepherd, and so says his sister Nancy. She's got her thirteen-year-old eye on a laundry, and he's got his twelve-year-old eye on a bottle-factory. Headmaster and headmistress and all the teachers know perfectly well that the high goal of all *their* endeavours is the laundry and the bottle-factory. They try to stunt a bit sometimes about the high ideal of human existence, the dignity of human life or the nobility of labour. But if they *really* want to put the fear of the Lord into Jimmy or Nancy they say: "You'll break more bottles than you'll make, my young genius," or else "You'll burn more shirt-fronts than you'll brighten, my girl: and *then* you'll know what you're in for, at the week-end." This mystic week-end is not the sacred Sabbath of Holy Communion. It is *pay-day,* and nothing else.

The high idealists up in Whitehall may preserve some illusion around themselves. But there is absolutely no illusion for the elementary school-teachers. They know what the end will be. And they know that they've got to keep their *own* job, and they've got to struggle for a head-ship. And between the disillusion of their scholars' destiny, on the one hand, and the disillusion of their own mean and humiliating destiny, on the other, they haven't much breath left for the fanning of the high flame of noble human existence.

If ever there is a poor devil on the face of the earth it is the elementary school-teacher. He is invested with a wretched idealist sort of authority over a pack of children, an authority which parents jeer at and despise. For they know the teacher is under *their* thumb. "*I* pay for you, I'll let you know, out of the rates. *I'm* your employer. And therefore you'll treat my child properly, or I'm going up to the Town Hall." All of which Jimmy and Nancy exultingly hear, and the teacher, guardian of the high flame of human divinity, quakes because he knows his job is in danger. He is insulted from above and from below. Comes along an inspector of schools, a university man himself, with no respect for the sordid promiscuity of the elementary school. For elementary schools know no remoteness and dignity of the rostrum. The teacher is on a level with the scholars, or inferior to them. And an elementary school knows no code of honour, no *esprit de corps*. There is the profound cynicism of the laundry and the bottle-factory at the bottom of everything. How should a refined soul down from Oxford fail to find it a little sordid and common?

The elementary school-teacher is in a vile and false position. Set up as representative of an ideal which is all toffee, invested in an authority which has absolutely no base except in the teacher's own isolate will, he is sneered at by the idealists above and jeered at by the materialists below, and ends by being a mongrel who is neither a wage-earner nor a professional, neither a head-worker nor a hand-worker, neither living by his brain nor by his physical toil, but a bit of both, and despised for both. He is caught between the upper and nether millstones of idealism and materialism, and every shred of natural pride is ground out of him, so that he has to die or to cultivate some unpleasant *suffisance* which makes him objectionable for ever.

Yet who dare say that the idealists are wrong? And who dare say the materialists are right? The elementary school is where the two meet, like millstones. And teacher and scholars are ground between the two.

It is absolutely fatal for the manhood of the teacher. And it is bitterly detrimental for the scholars. You can hardly keep a boy for ten years in the elementary schools, "educating him" to be himself, "educating him" up to the high ideal of human existence, with the bottle-factory outside the gate all the time, without producing a state of cynicism in the child's soul. Children are wonderfully subtle at dodging a hateful conclusion. If they are going to live, they must keep some illusions. But alas, they know the shoddiness of their illusions. What boy of fourteen, in an elementary school, but is a subtle cynic about all ideals?

What is wrong, then? The system. But when you've said that you've said nothing. The system, after all, is only the outcome of the human psyche, the human desires. We shout and blame the machine. But who on earth makes the machine, if we don't? And any alterations in the system are only modifications in the machine. The system is *in us,* it is not something external to us. The machine is in us, or it would never come out of us. Well then, there's nothing to blame but ourselves, and there's nothing to change except inside ourselves.

For instance, you may exclude technical training from the elementary schools; you may prolong the school years to the age of sixteen–or to the age of twenty, if you like. And what then? At the gate of the school lies the sphinx who puts this question to every emerging scholar, boy or girl: "How are you going to make your living?" And every boy or girl must answer or die: so the poor things believe.

We call this the system. It isn't, really. The trouble lies in us who are so afraid of this particular sphinx. "My dear sphinx, my wants are very small, my needs still smaller. I wonder you trouble yourself about so trivial a matter. I am going to get a job in a bottle-factory, where I shall have to spend a certain number of hours a day. But that is the least of my concerns. My dear sphinx, you are a kitten at riddles. If you'd asked me, now, what I'm going to do with my life, apart from the bottle-factory, you might have frightened me. As it is, really, every smoky tall chimney is an answer to you."

Curious that when the toothless old sphinx croaks "How are you going to get your living?" our knees give way beneath us. What has happened to us, that we are so frightened by that toothless old lion of *want?* Do we really think we might not be able to earn our bread and butter?–bread and margarine, at the worst? Why are we so frightened? Out of fifty million people, about ten thousand can't obtain their bread and butter without the workhouse or some such aid. But what's the odds? The odds against your earning your living are one in five thousand. There are not so many odds against your dying of typhoid or being killed in a street-accident. Yet you don't really care a snap about street-accidents or typhoid. Then why are you so afraid of dying of starvation? You'll never die of starvation, anyhow. So what *are* you afraid of?

The fear of penury is very curious, in our age. In really poor ages, men did not fear penury. They didn't care. But we are abjectly terrified of it. Why? It isn't any such awful thing, if you don't care about keeping up appearances.

There is no cure for this craven terror of poverty save in human courage and insouciance. A sphinx has you by your cravenness. Œdipus and all those before him might just have easily answered the sphinx by saying, "Oh, my dear sphinx, that's quite easy. A Borogove, of course. What, don't you know what a Borogove is? My dear sphinx, go to school, go to school. I knew all about Borogoves before I was out of the cradle, and here you are, heaven knows how old, propounding silly riddles to which Borogove is the answer, and you admit you've never heard of one. I absolutely refuse to concern myself with *your* solution, if you know nothing of mine." Exit the sphinx with its tail between its legs.

And so with the sphinx of our material existence. She'll never go off with her tail between her legs till we simply jeer at her. "Earn my living, you crazy old bitch? Why, I'm going Jimmy-Shepherding. No, not sheep at all. *Jimmishepherding*. You don't understand. Worse luck for you, old bird."

You can set up State Aid and Old Age Pensions and Young Age Pensions till you're black in the face. But if you can't cure people of being frightened for their own existence, you'll educate them in vain. You may as well let a frightened little Jimmy Shepherd go bottle-blowing at the age of four. If he's frightened for his own existence, he'll never do more than keep himself assertively materially alive. And that's the end of it. So he might just as well start young, and avoid those lying years of idealistic education.

So that the first thing to be done, in the education of the people, is to cure them of the fear of not earning their own living. This won't be easy. The fear goes deep, in our nervous age. Men will go through all the agonies of war, and come out more frightened still of not being able to earn their living. It is a mystery. They will face guns and shells and unspeakable horrors, almost with equanimity. After all, that's merely death. It's not life. Life is the thing to be afraid of–and having enough money to live on is the anguished soul-problem. It has become an *idée fixe,* the idea of earning, or not earning, a living. And we are all monomaniacs in it.

And yet, the only way to solve the whole problem is to cure mankind, from the inside, of the fear. And this is the business of our reformed education. At present, we are all in the boat because our idealists are just as terrified of not earning their living as are the materialists. Even more.

That's the point. The idealists are more terrified than the materialists about not being able to earn their living. The materialists are brutal about it. They don't have to excuse themselves. They handle the tools and do the graft. But the idealists, those that sit in the Olympus of Whitehall, for example? It is they who tremble. They are earning their living tooth-and-nail, by promulgating up there in the clouds. But the material world cocks its eye on them. It keeps them as a luxury, as the Greeks kept their Olympic gods. After all, the idealists butter our motives with fair words and their own parsnips. When we have at last decided that our motives are none the better for the fair-word buttering of idealism, then the idealists will have to eat their Olympic parsnips very dry. Which is what they are afraid of. So they churn fair words, up there, and the proletariat churns margarine and a little butter down below, and so far there is an exchange. But as the price of butter rises the price of fair words depreciates, till the idealists are in a fair way of doing no trade at all, up on Olympus. Which is what they are afraid of. So they churn phrases like mad, hoping to bring out something that will catch the market.

And there we are. Between the idealists and the materialists our poor "elementary" children have their education shaken into them. Which is a shame. It is a shame to treat children as we treat them in school, to a lot of highfalutin and lies, and to a lot of fear and humiliation. Instead of putting the fear of the Lord into them we put the fear of the job. After which the job rises up and gives us a nasty knock in the eye; we get strikes and Labour menaces, and idealism is in a fair way of being kicked off Olympus altogether. Materialism threatens to sit aloft. And Olympus fawns and cringes, and is terrified, because it doesn't know how it will earn its living.

Idealism would be all right if it weren't frightened. But it *is* frightened: frightened to death. It is terrified that it won't be able to butter its parsnips. It is terrified that it won't be able to make a living. Curious thing, but rich people are inwardly more terrified of poverty, want, destitution, even than poor people. Even the proletariat is not so agonized with fear of not being able to make a living as are millionaires and dukes. The more the money the more intense the fear.

So there we are, all living in an agony and nightmare of fear of not being able to make a living. But we actually *are* the living. We live, and therefore everything is ours. Whence, then, the fear? Just a sort of irrational mob-panic.

Idealism *must* get over its fright. It is most to blame. There it sits in a fog, promulgating ideas and ideals, and all the time in a mad panic for fear of losing its job. There it sits decreeing that our children shall be educated pure from the taint of materialism and industrialism, and all the time it is fawning and cringing before industrialism and materialism, and having throes and spasms of agony about its own salary. Certainly even idealists must have a salary. But why are they in such agonies of fear lest it be not forthcoming? After all, if they draw a salary, it is because they are *not* frightened. Their salary is the tithe due to their living fearlessness. And so, cadging their screw in panic, they are a swindle. And they cause our children to be educated to the tune of their swindlery.

And then no wonder that our children, the children of the people, look down their nose at ideals. It is no wonder the young workmen sneer at all idealism, all idealists, and at everything higher than wages and short hours. They are having their own back on the lie, and on the liars, that educated them in school. They've been educated in the lie, and therefore they also can spout idealism at will. But by their deeds ye shall know them: both parties.

Here's the end, then, of the first word on Education. Idealism is no good without fearlessness. To follow a high aim, you must be fearless of the consequences. To promulgate a high aim, and to be fearful of the consequences–as our idealists today–is much worse than leaving high aims alone altogether. Teach the three R's and leave the children to look out for their own aims. That's the very best thing we can do at the moment, since we are all cowards.

But later, when we've plucked a bit of our courage up, we'll embark on a new course of education, and *vogue la galère*. Those of us that are going to starve, why, we'll take our chance. Who has wits, and *guts,* doesn't starve: neither does he care about starving. *Courage, mes amis.*

II

Elementary Education today assumes two responsibilities. It has in its hands the moulding of the nation. And elementary schoolteachers are taught that they are to mould the young nation to two ends. They are to strive to produce in the child under their charge: (1) The perfect citizen; (2) The perfect individual.

Unfortunately the teachers are not enlightened as to what we mean by a perfect citizen and a perfect individual. When they are, during their training, instructed and lectured upon the teaching of history, they are told that the examples of history teach us the virtues of citizenship: and when drawing and painting and literary compositon are under discussion, these subjects are supposed to teach the child self-expression.

Citizenship has been an indefinite Fata Morgana to the elementary school-teacher: but self-expression has been a worse. Before the war we sailed serene under this flag of self-expression. Each child was to *express himself:* why, nobody thought necessary to explain. But infants were to express themselves, and nothing but themselves. Here was a pretty task for a teacher: he was to make his pupil *express himself*. Which *self* was left vague. A child was to be given a lump of soft clay and told to express himself, presumably in the pious hope that he might model a Tanagra figure or a Donatello plaque, all on his little lonely-o.

Now it is obvious that every boy's first act of self-expression would be to throw the lump of soft clay at something: preferably at the teacher. This impulse is to be suppressed. On what grounds, metaphysically? since the soft clay was given for self-expression. To this just question there is no answer. Self-expression in infants means, presumably, incipient Tanagra figurines and Donatello plaques, incipient *Iliads* and *Macbeths* and "Odes to the Nightingale": a world of infant prodigies, in short. And the responsibility for all this foolery was heaped on the shoulders of that public clown, the elementary school-teacher.

The war, however, brought us to our senses a little, and we ran the flag of citizenship up above the flag of self-expression. This was much easier for the teacher. At least, now, the ideal was *service,* not self-expression. "Work, and learn how to serve your country." Service means authority: while self-expression means pure negation of all authority. So that teaching became a somewhat simpler matter under the ideal of national service.

However, the war is over, and there is a slump in national service. The public isn't inspired by the ideal of serving its country any more: it has had its whack. And the idealists, who must run to give the public the inspiration it fancies at the moment, are again coming forward with trayfuls of infant prodigies and "self-expression."

Now citizenship and self-expression are all right, as ideals for the education of the people, if only we knew what we meant by the two terms. The interpretation we give them is just ludicrous. Self-sacrifice in time of need: disinterested nobility of heart to enable each one to vote properly at a general election: an understanding of what is meant by income-tax and money interest: all vague and fuzzy. Nobody pretends to enlighten the teacher as to the mysteries of citizenship. Nobody attempts to instruct *him* in the relationship of the individual to the community. Nothing at all. There is a little gas about *esprit de corps* and national interest—but it is all gas.

None of which would matter if we would just leave the ideals out of our educational system. If we were content to teach a child to read and write and do his modicum of arithmetic, just as at an earlier stage his mother teaches him to walk and to talk, so that he may toddle his little way upon the face of the earth by himself, it would be all right. It would be a thousand times better, as things stand, to chuck overboard all your drawing and painting and music and modelling and pseudo-science and "graphic" history and "graphic" geography and "self-expression," all the lot. Pitch them overboard, teach the three R's, and then proceed with a certain amount of technical instruction, in preparation for the coming job. For all the rest, for all that concerns the child himself, leave him alone. If he likes to learn, the means of learning are in his hands. Brilliant scholars could be drafted into secondary schools. If he doesn't like to learn, it is his affair. The quality of learning is not strained. Is not radical *unlearnedness* just as true a form of self-expression, and just as desirable a state, for many natures (even the bulk), as learnedness? Here we talk of free self-expression, and we proceed to force all natures into ideal and æsthetic expression. We talk about individuality, and try to drag up every weed into a rose-bush. If a nettle likes to be a nettle, if it likes to have no flowers to speak of, why, that's the nettle's affair. Why should we force some poor devil of an elementary school-teacher to sting his fingers to bits trying to graft the obstreperous nettle-stem with rose and vine? We, who sail under the flag of freedom, are bullies such as the world has never known before: idealist bullies: bullying idealism, which will allow nothing except in terms of itself.

Every teacher knows that it is worse than useless trying to educate at least fifty per cent of his scholars. Worse than useless: it is dangerous: perilously dangerous. What is the result of it? Drag a lad who has no capacity for true learning or understanding through the processes of education, and what do you produce in him, in the end? A profound contempt for education, and for all educated people. It has meant nothing to him but irritation and disgust. And that which a man finds irritating and disgusting he finds odious and contemptible.

And this is the point to which we are bringing the nation, inevitably. Everybody is educated: and what is education? A sort of *unmanliness*. Go down in the hearts of the masses of the people and this is what you'll find: the cynical conviction that every educated man is unmanly, less manly than an uneducated man. Every little Jimmy Shepherd has dabbled his bit in pseudo-science and in the arts; he has seen a test-tube and he has handled plasticine and a camel's-hair brush; he knows that $a + a + b = 2a + b$. What more is there for him to know? Nothing. Pfui to your learning.

A little learning *is* a dangerous thing: how dangerous we are likely to be finding out. A man who has not the soul, or the spirit, to learn and to *understand,* he whose whole petty education consists in the acquiring of a few tricks, will inevitably, in the end, come to regard all educated or understanding people as tricksters. And once *that* happens, what becomes of your State? It is inevitably at the mercy of your bottle-washing Jimmy Shepherds and his parallel Nancys. For the uninstructible outnumber the instructible by a very large majority. Behold us then in the grimy fist of Jimmy Shepherd, the uninstructible Brobdingnag. Fools we are, we've put ourselves there: so if he pulls all our heads off, serves us right. He is Brobdingnagian because he is legion. Whilst we poor instructible mortals are Lilliputian in comparison. And the one power we had, the power of commanding reverence or respect in the Brobdingnag, a power God-given to us, we ourselves have squandered and degraded. On our own heads be it.

For a sensible system of education, then. Begin at the age of seven—five is too soon—and teach reading, writing, arithmetic as the only necessary mental subjects: reading to include geography, map-practice, history, and so on. Three hours a day is enough for these. Another hour a day might be devoted to physical and domestic training. Leave a child alone for the rest: out of sight and out of mind.

At the age of twelve, make a division. Teachers, schoolmasters, school-inspectors, and parents will carefully decide what children shall be educated further. These shall be drafted to secondary schools, where an extended curriculum includes Latin or French, and some true science. Secondary scholars will remain till the age of sixteen.

The children who will not be drafted to the secondary schools will, at the age of twelve, have their "mental" education reduced to two hours, whilst three hours will be devoted to physical and domestic training: that is, martial exercises and the rudiments of domestic labour, such as boot-mending, plumbing, soldering, painting and paper-hanging, gardening—all those minor trades on which domestic life depends, and in which every working man should have some proficiency. This is to continue for three years.

Then on the completion of the fourteenth year, these scholars will be apprenticed half-time to some trade to which they are judged fitting, by a consensus of teachers and parents and the scholars themselves. For two years these half-timers shall spend the morning at their own trade, and some two hours in the afternoon at martial exercises and reading and at what we call domestic training, boot-mending, etc. At the age of sixteen they enter on their regular labours, as artisans.

The secondary scholars shall for two years, from the age of twelve to the age of fourteen, follow the curriculum of the secondary school for four hours a day, but shall put in one hour a day at the workshops and at physical training. At the completion of the fourteenth year a division shall be made among these secondary scholars. Those who are apparently "complete," as far as mental education can make them, according to their own nature and capacity, shall be drafted into some apprenticeship for some sort of semi-profession, such as school-teaching, and all forms of clerking. Like the elementary scholars, however, all secondary scholars put in two hours in the afternoon at reading and in the workshops or at physical training: one hour for the mental education, one hour for the physical. At the age of sixteen, clerks, school-teachers, etc., shall enter their regular work, or the regular training for their work.

The remaining scholars, of the third or highest class, shall at the age of sixteen be drafted into colleges. Those that have scientific bent shall be trained scientifically, those that incline to the liberal arts shall be educated according to their inclination, and those that have gifts in the pure arts or in the technical arts shall find artistic training. But an hour a day shall be devoted to some craft, and to physical training. Every man shall have a craft at which finally he is expert—or two crafts if he choose—even if he be destined for professional activity as a doctor, a lawyer, a priest, a professor, and so on.

The scholars of the third class shall remain in their colleges till the age of twenty, receiving there a general education as in our colleges today, although emphasis is laid on some particular branch of the education. At the age of twenty these scholars shall be drafted for their years of final training—as doctors, lawyers, priests, artists and so on. At the age of twenty-two they shall enter the world.

All education should be State education. All children should start together in the elementary schools. From the age of seven to the age of twelve boys and girls of every class should be educated together in the elementary schools. This will give us a common human basis, a common radical understanding. All children, boys and girls, should receive a training in the respective male and female domestic crafts. Every man should finally be expert at some craft, and should be a trained *free* soldier, no matter what his profession. Every woman also should have her chosen, expert craft, so that each individual is master of some kind of work.

Of course a great deal will depend on teachers and headmasters. The elementary teachers will not be so terribly important, but they will be carefully selected for their power to control and instruct children, not for their power to pass examinations. Headmasters will always be men of the highest education, invested with sound authority. A headmaster, once established, will be like a magistrate in a community.

Because one of the most important parts in this system of education will be the judging of the scholars. Teachers, masters, inspectors and parents will all of them unite to decide the next move for the child. The child will be consulted–but the last decision will be left to the headmaster and the inspector–the final word to the inspector.

Again, no decision will be final. If at any time it shall become apparent that a child is unfit for the group he occupies, then, after a proper consultation, he shall be removed to his own natural group. Again, if a child has no capacity for arithmetic, we shall not persist for five years in drilling arithmetic into him. Some form of useful manual work will be substituted for the arithmetic lesson: and so on.

Such is a brief sketch of a sensible system of education for a civilized people. It may be argued that it puts too much power into the hands of schoolmasters and school-inspectors. But better there than in the hands of factory-owners and trades unions. The position of masters and inspectors will be discussed later.

Again, it may be argued that there is too much rule and government here. As a matter of fact, we are all limited to our own natures. And the aim above all others in this system is to recognize the true nature in each child, and to give each its natural chance. If we want to be free, we cannot be free to do otherwise than follow our own soul, our own true nature, to its fulfilment. And for this purpose primarily the suggested scheme would exist. Each individual is to be helped, wisely, reverently, towards his own natural fulfilment. Children can't choose for themselves. They are not sufficiently conscious. A choice is made, even if nobody makes it. The bungle of circumstance decrees the fate of almost every child today. Which is why most men hate their fates, circumstantial and false as they are.

And then, as to cost: which is always important. Our present system of education is extravagantly expensive, and simply dangerous to our social existence. It turns out a lot of half-informed youth who despise the whole business of understanding and wisdom, and who realize that in a world like ours nothing but money matters. Our system of education tacitly grants that nothing but money matters, but puts up a little parasol of human ideals under which human divinity can foolishly masquerade for a few hours during school life, and on Sundays. Coming from under this parasol, little Jimmy Shepherd knows that he's quite as divine as anybody else. He's quite as much a little god as anybody else, because he's been told so in school from the age of five till the age of fifteen, so he ought to know. Nobody's any better than he is: he's quite as good as anybody else, and, because he's a poor dustman's son, even more acceptable in the eyes of God. And therefore why hasn't he got as much money? since money is all that he can make any use of. His own human divinity is no more use to him than anybody else's human divinity, and once it comes to fighting for shillings he's absolutely not going to be put off by any toffee about ideals. And there we are with little Jimmy Shepherd, aged fifteen. He's a right dangerous little party, all of our own making: and his name is legion.

Our system of education today threatens our whole social existence tomorrow. We should be wise if by decree we shut up all elementary schools at once, and kept them shut. Failing that, we must look round for a better system, one that will work.

But if we try a new system, we must know what we're about. No good floundering into another muddle. While education was strictly a religious process, it had a true goal. While it existed for governing classes, it had a goal. And *universal elementary* education has had a goal. But a fatal one.

We have assumed that we could educate Jimmy Shepherd and make him a Shelley or an Isaac Newton. At the very least we were sure we could make him a highly intelligent being. And we're just beginning to find our mistake. We can't make a highly intelligent being out of Jimmy Shepherd. Why should we, if the Lord created him only moderately intelligent? Why do we want always to go one better than the Creator?

So now, having gone a very long way downhill on a very dangerous road, and having got ourselves thoroughly entangled in a vast mob which may at any moment start to bolt down to the precipice Gadarene-wise, why, the best we can do is to try to steer uphill.

We've got first to find which way *is* uphill. We've got to shape our course by some just idea. We shaped it by a faulty idea of equality and the perfectibility of man. Now for the true idea: either that or the precipice edge.

III

It is obvious that the old ideal of Equality won't do. It is landing us daily deeper in a mess. And yet no idea which has passionately swayed mankind can be altogether wrong: not even the most fallacious-seeming. Therefore, before we can dispose of the equality ideal, the ideal that all men are essentially equal, we have got to find how far it is true.

In no sense whatever are men actually equal. Physically, some are big and some are small, some weak, some strong; mentally, some are intelligent, some are not, and the degrees of difference are infinite;

spiritually, some are rare and fine, some are vulgar; morally, some are repulsive and some attractive. True, all men have noses, mouths, stomachs, and so on. But then this is a mere abstraction. Every nose, every stomach is different, actually, from every other nose and stomach. It is all according to the individual. Noses and stomachs are not interchangeable. You might perhaps graft the end of one man's nose on the nose of another man. But the grafted gentleman would not thereby have a dual identity. His essential self would remain the same: a little disfigured, perhaps, but not metamorphosed. Whatever tricks you may perform, of grafting one bit of an individual on another, you don't produce a new individual, a new type. You only produce a disfigured, patched-up old individual. It isn't like grafting roses. You couldn't graft bits of Lord Northcliffe on a thousand journalists and produce a thousand Napoleons of the Press. Every journalist would remain himself: a little disfigured or mutilated, maybe.

It is quite sickening to hear scientists rambling on about the interchange of tissue and members from one individual to another. They have at last reached the old alchemistic fantasy of producing the homunculus. They hope to take the hind leg of a pig and by happy grafting produce a marvellous composite individual, a fused erection of living tissue which will at last prove that man can *make* man, and that therefore he isn't divine at all, he is a purely human marvel, only so extraordinarily clever and marvellous that the sun will stop still to look at him.

When science begins to generalize from its own performances it is puerile as the alchemists were, at last. The truth about man, before he falls into imbecility, is that each one is just himself. That's the first, the middle truth. Every man has his own identity, which he preserves till he falls into imbecility or worse. Upon this clue of his own identity every man is fashioned. And the clue of a man's own identity is a man's own self or soul, that which is incommutable and incommunicable in him. Every man, while he remains a man and does not lapse into disintegration, becoming a lump of chaos, is truly himself, only himself, no matter how many fantastic attitudes he may assume. True it is that man goes and gets a host of ideas in his head, and proceeds to reconstruct himself according to those ideas. But he never actually succeeds in this business of reconstructing himself out of his own head, until he has gone cracked. And then he may prance on all fours like Nebuchadnezzar, or do as he likes. But whilst he remains sane the buzzing ideas in his head will never allow him to change or metamorphose his own identity: modify, yes; but never change. While a man remains sane he remains himself and nothing but himself, no matter how fantastically he may attitudinize according to some pet idea. For example, this of equality. St. Francis was ready to fall in rapture at the feet of the peasant. But he wasn't ready to take the muck-rake from the peasant's hands and start spreading manure at twopence a day, an insignificant and forgotten nobody, a serf. Not at all. St. Francis kept his disciples and was a leader of men, in spite of all humility, poverty, and equality. Quite right, because St. Francis was by nature a leader of men, and what has any creed or theory of equality to do with it? He was born such: it was his own intrinsic being. In his soul he was a leader. Where does equality come in? Why, by his poverty, St. Francis wished to prove his own intrinsic superiority, not his equality. And if a man is a born leader, what does it matter if he hasn't got twopence, or if he has got two million? His own nature is his destiny, not his purse.

All a man can be, at the very best, is himself. At the very worst he can be something a great deal less than himself, a money-grubber, a millionaire, a State, like Louis Quatorze, a self-conscious ascetic, a spiritual prig, a grass-chewing Nebuchadnezzar.

So where does equality come in? Men are palpably unequal in *every* sense except the mathematical sense. Every man counts one: and this is the root of all equality: here, in a pure intellectual abstraction.

The moment you come to compare them, men are unequal, and their inequalities are infinite. But supposing you *don't* compare them. Supposing, when you meet a man, you have the pure decency not to compare him either with yourself or with anything else. Supposing you can meet a man with this same singleness of heart. What then? Is the man your equal, your inferior, your superior? He can't be, if there is no comparison. If there is no comparison, he is the incomparable. He is the incomparable. He is single. He is himself. When I am single-hearted, I don't compare myself with my neighbour. He is immediate to me, I to him. He is not my *equal,* because this presumes comparison. He is incomparably himself, I am incomparably myself. We behold each other in our pristine and simple being. And this is the first, the finest, the perfect way of human intercourse.

And on this great first-truth of the pristine incomparable nature of every individual soul is founded, mistakenly, the theory of equality. Every man, when he is incontestably himself, is single, incomparable, beyond compare. But to deduce from this that all men are equal is a sheer false deduction: a simple *non sequitur*. Let every man be himself, purely himself. And then, in the evil hour when you *do* start to compare, you will see the endless inequality between men.

In the perfect human intercourse, a relation establishes itself happily and spontaneously. No two men meet one another direct without a spontaneous equilibrium taking place. Doubtless there is inequality between the two. But there is no *sense* of inequality. The give-and-take is perfect; without knowing, each is adjusted to the other. It is as the stars fall into their place, great and small. The small are as perfect as the great, because each is itself and in its own place. But the great are none the less the great, the small the small. And the joy of each is that it is so.

The moment I begin to pay direct mental attention to my neighbour, however; the moment I begin to scrutinize him and attempt to set myself over against him, the element of comparison enters. Immediately I am aware of the inequalities between us. But even so, it is inequalities and not inequality. There is *never* either any equality or any inequality between me and my neighbour. Each of us is himself, and as such is single, alone in the universe, and not to be compared. Only in our parts are we comparable. And our parts are vastly unequal.

Which finishes equality for ever, as an ideal. Finishes also fraternity. For fraternity implies a consanguinity which is almost the same as equality. Men are not equal, neither are they brothers. They are themselves. Each one is himself, and each one is essentially, starrily responsible for himself. Any assumption by one person of responsibility for another person is an interference, and a destructive tyranny. No person is responsible for the *being* of any other person. Each one is starrily single, starrily self-responsible, not to be blurred or confused.

Here then is the new ideal for society: not that all men are equal, but that each man is himself: "one is one and all alone and ever more shall be so." Particularly this is the ideal for a new system of education. Every man shall be himself, shall have every opportunity to come to his own intrinsic fullness of being. There are unfortunately many individuals to whom these words mean nothing: mere verbiage. We must have a proper contempt and defiance of these individuals, though their name be legion.

How are we to obtain that a man shall come to his own fullness of being; that a child shall grow up true to his own essential self? It is no use just letting the child do as it likes. Because the human being, more than any other living thing, is susceptible to falsification. We alone have mental consciousness, speech, and thought. And this mental consciousness is our greatest peril.

A child in the bath sees the soap, and wants it, and won't be happy till he gets it. When he gets it he rubs it into his eyes and sucks it, and is in a far more unhappy state. Why? To see the soap and to want it is a natural act on the part of any young animal, a sign of that wonderful naïve curiosity which is so beautiful in young life. But the "he won't be happy till he gets it" quality is, alas, purely human. A young animal, if diverted, would forget the piece of soap at once. It is only an accident in his horizon. Or, given the piece of soap, he would sniff it, perhaps turn it over, and then merely abandon it. Beautiful to us is the pure nonchalance of a young animal which *forgets* the piece of soap the moment it has sniffed it and found it no good. Only the intelligent human baby proceeds to fill its mouth, stomach, and eyes with acute pain, on account of the piece of soap. Why? Because the poor little wretch got an idea, an incipient idea into its little head. The rabbit never gets an idea into its head, so it can sniff the soap and turn away. But a human baby, poor, tormented little creature, *can't help* getting an idea into his young head. And then he *can't help* acting on his idea: no matter what the consequences. And this bit of soap shows us what a bitter responsibility our mental consciousness is to us, and how it leads astray even the infant in his bath. Poor innocent: we like to imagine him a spontaneous, unsophisticated little creature. But what do we mean by sophistication? We mean that a being is at the mercy of some idea which it has got into its head, and which has no true relation to its actual desire or need. Witness the piece of soap. The baby saw the piece of soap, and got an idea into its head that the soap was immeasurably desirable. Acting on this simple idea, it nearly killed itself, and filled an hour or so of its young life with horrid misery.

It is only when we grow up that we learn not to be run away with by ideas which we get in our heads and which don't correspond to any true natural desire or need. At least, education and growing-up is supposed to be a process of learning to escape the automatism of ideas, to live direct from the spontaneous, vital centre of oneself.

Anyhow, it is criminal to expect children to "express themselves" and to bring themselves up. They will eat the soap and pour the treacle on their hair and put their fingers in the candle-flame, in the acts of physical self-expression, and in the wildness of spiritual self-expression they will just go to pieces. All because, really, they have enough mental intelligence to obliterate their instinctive intelligence and to send them to destruction. A little animal that can crawl will manage to live, if abandoned. Abandon a child of five years and it won't merely die, it will almost certainly maim and kill itself. This mental consciousness we are born with is the most double-edged blessing of all, and grown-ups must spend years and years guarding their children from the disastrous effects of this blessing.

Now let us go back to the maxim that every human being must come to the fullness of himself. It is part of our sentimental and trashy creed today that a little child is most purely himself, and that growing up perverts him away from himself. We assume he starts as a spontaneous little soul, limpid, purely self-expressive, and grows up to be a sad, sophisticated machine. Which is all very well, and might easily be so, if the mind of the little innocent didn't start to work so soon, and to interfere with all his little spontaneity. Nothing is so subject to small, but fatal automatization as a child: some little thing it sets its *mind* on, and the game is up. And a child is always setting its little mind on something, usually something which doesn't at all correspond with the true and restless desire of its living soul. And then, which will win, the little mind or the little soul? We all know, to our sorrow. When a child sets its little mind on the soap, its little soul, not to speak of its little eyes and stomach, is thrown to the winds. And yet the desire for the soap is only the misdirection of the eternally yearning, desirous soul of an infant.

Here we are, then. Instead of waiting for the wisdom out of the mouths of babes and sucklings, let us see that we keep the soap-tablet out of the same mouths. We've got to educate our children, and it's no light responsibility. We've got to try to educate them to that point where at last there will be a perfect correspondence between the spontaneous, yearning, impulsive-desirous soul and the automatic *mind* which runs on little wheels of ideas. And this is the hardest job we could possibly set ourselves. For man just doesn't know how to interpret his own soul-promptings, and therefore he sets up a complicated arrangement of ideas and ideals and works himself automatically till he works himself into the grave or the lunatic-asylum.

We've got to educate our children. Which means, we've got to decide for them: day after day, year after year, we've got to go on deciding for our children. It's not the slightest use asking little Jimmy "What would you like, dear?" because little Jimmy doesn't know. And if he *thinks* he knows, it's only because, as a rule, he's got some fatal little idea into his head, like the soap-tablet. Yet listen to the egregious British parent solemnly soliciting his young son: "What would you like to be, dear? A doctor or a clergyman?"—"An engine-driver," replies Jimmy, and the comedy of babes-and-sucklings continues.

We've got to decide for our children: for years and years we have to make their decisions. And we've got to take the responsibility on to ourselves, as a community. It's no good feeding our young with a sticky ideal education till they are fourteen years old, then pitching them out, pap-fed, into the whirling industrial machine and the warren of back streets. It's no good expecting parents to do anything. Parents don't know how to decide; they go to little Jimmy as if he were the godhead. And even if they did know how to decide, they can do nothing in face of the factory and the trades union and the back streets.

We, the educators, have got to decide for the children: decide the steps of their young fates, seriously and reverently. It is a sacred business, and unless we can act from our deep, believing souls, we'd best not act at all, but leave it to Northcliffe and trades unions.

We must choose, with this end in view. We want quality of life, not quantity. We don't want swarms and swarms of people in back streets. We want distinct individuals, and these are incompatible with swarms and masses. A small, choice population, not a horde of hopeless units.

And every man to be himself, to come to his own fullness of being. Not every man a little wonder of cleverness or high ideals. Every man himself, according to his true nature. And those who are comparatively non-mental can form a vigorous, passionate proletariat of indomitable individuals: and those who will work as clerks to be free and energetic, not humiliated as they are now, but fierce with their own freedom of beings: and the *man* will be always more than his job; the job will be a minor business.

We must have an ideal. So let our ideal be living, spontaneous individuality in every man and woman. Which living, spontaneous individuality, being the hardest thing of all to come at, will need most careful rearing. Educators will take a grave responsibility upon themselves. They will be the priests of life, deep in the wisdom of life. They will be the life-priests of the new era. And the leaders, the inspectors, will be men deeply initiated into the mysteries of life, adepts in the dark mystery of living, fearing nothing but life itself, and subject to nothing but their own reverence for the incalculable life-gesture.

IV

It is obvious that a system of education such as the one we so briefly sketched out in our second chapter will inevitably produce distinct classes of society. The basis is the great class of workers. From this class will rise also the masters of industry, and, probably, the leading soldiers. Second comes the clerkly caste, which will include elementary teachers and minor professionals, and which will produce the local government bodies. Thirdly we have the class of the higher professions, legal, medical, scholastic: and this class will produce the chief legislators. Finally, there is the small class of the supreme judges: not merely legal judges, but judges of the destiny of the nation.

These classes will not arise accidentally, through the accident of money, as today. They will not derive through heredity, as the great oriental castes. There will be no automatism. A man will not be chosen to a class, or a caste, because he is exceptionally fitted for a particular job. If a child shows an astonishing aptitude, let us say, for designing clocks, and at the same time has a profound natural life-understanding, then he will pass on to the caste of professional masters, or even to that of supreme judges, and his skill in clocks will only be one of his accomplishments, his *private* craft. The whole business of educators will be to estimate, not the particular faculty of the child for some particular job: not at all; nor even a specific intellectual capacity; the whole business will be to estimate the profound life-quality, the very nature of the child, that which makes him ultimately what he is, his soul-strength and his soul-wisdom, which cause him to be a natural master of life. Technical capacity is all the time subsidiary. The highest quality is living understanding—not intellectual understanding. Intellectual understanding belongs to the technical activities. But vital understanding belongs to the masters of life. And all the professionals in our new world are not mere technical experts: they are life-directors. They combine with their soul-power some great technical skill. But the first quality will be the soul-quality, the quality of being, and the power for the directing of life itself.

Hence we shall see that the system is primarily religious, and only secondarily practical. Our supreme judges and our master professors will be primarily *priests.* Let us not take fright at the word. The true religious faculty is the most powerful and the highest faculty in man, once he exercises it. And by the religious faculty we mean the inward worship of the creative life-mystery: the implicit knowledge that life is unfathomable and unsearchable in its motives, not to be described, having no ascribable goal save the bringing-forth of an ever-changing, ever-unfolding creation: that new creative being and impulse surges up all the time in the deep fountains of the soul, from some great source which the world has known as God; that the business of man is to become so spontaneous that he shall utter at last direct the act and the *state* which arises in him from his deep being: and finally, that the mind with all its great powers is only the servant of the inscrutable, unfathomable soul. The *idea* or the *ideal* is only instrumental in the unfolding of the soul of man, a tool, not a goal. Always simply a tool.

We should have the courage to refrain from dogma. Dogma is the translation of the religious impulse into an intellectual term. An intellectual term is a finite, fixed, mechanical thing. We must be content for ever to live from the undescribed and indescribable impulse. Our god is the Unnamed, the Veiled, and any attempt to give names, or to remove veils, is just a mental impertinence which ends in nothing but futility and impertinencies.

So, the new system will be established upon the living religious faculty in men. In some men this faculty has a more direct expression in consciousness than in other men. Some men are aware of the deep troublings of the creative sources of their own souls, they are aware, they find speech or utterance in act, they come forth in consciousness. In other men the troublings are dumb, they will never come forth in expression, unless they find a mediator, a minister, an interpreter.

And this is how the great castes naturally arrange themselves. Those whose souls are alive and strong but whose voices are unmodulated, and whose thoughts unformed and slow, these constitute the great base of all peoples at all times: and it will always be so. For the creative soul is for ever charged with the potency of still unborn speech, still unknown thoughts. It is the everlasting source which surges everlastingly with the massive, subterranean fires of creation, new creative being: and whose fires find issue in pure jets and bubblings of unthinkable newness only here and there, in a few, or comparatively few, individuals.

It must always be so. We cannot imagine the deep fires of the earth rushing out everywhere, in a myriad myriad jets. The great volcanoes stand isolate. And at the same time the life-issues concentrate in certain individuals. Why it is so, we don't know. But why should we know? We are, after all, *only* individuals, we are not the eternal life-mystery itself.

And therefore there will always be the vast, living masses of mankind, incoherent and almost expressionless by themselves, carried to perfect expression in the great individuals of their race and time. As the leaves of a tree accumulate towards blossom, so will the great bulk of mankind at all time accumulate towards its leaders. We don't want to turn every leaf of an apple tree into a flower. And so why should we want to turn every individual human being into a unit of complete expression? Why should it be our goal to turn every coal-miner into a Shelley or a Parnell? We can't do either. Coal-miners are consummated in a Parnell, and Parnells are consummated in a Shelley. That is how life takes its way: rising as a volcano rises to an apex, not in a countless multiplicity of small issues.

Time to recognize again this great truth of human life, and to put it once more into practice. Democracy is gone beyond itself. The true democracy is that in which a people gradually cumulate, from the vast base of the populace upwards through the zones of life and understanding to the summit where the great man, or the most perfect utterer, is alone. The false democracy is that wherein every issue, even the highest, is dragged down to the lowest issue, the myriad-multiple lowest human issue: today, the wage.

Mankind may have a perverse, self-wounding satisfaction in this reversal of the life-course. But it is a poor, spiteful, ignominious satisfaction.

In its living periods mankind accumulates upwards, through the zones of life-expression and passionate consciousness, upwards to the supreme utterer, or utterers. In its disintegrating periods the reverse is the case. Man accumulates downwards, down to the lowest issue. And the great men of the downward development are the men who symbolize the gradually sinking zones of being, till the final symbol, the great man who represents the wage-reality rises up and is hailed as the supreme. No doubt he is the material, mechanical universal of mankind, a unit of automatized existence.

It is a pity that democracy should be identified with this downward tendency. We who believe that every man's soul is single and incomparable, we thought we were democrats. But evidently democracy is a question of the integral wage, not the integral soul. If everything comes down to the wage, then down it comes. When it is a question of the human soul, the direction must be a cumulation upwards: upwards from the very roots, in the vast Demos, up to the very summit of the supreme judge and utterer, the first of men. There is a first of men: and there is the vast, basic Demos: always, at every age in every continent. The people is an organic whole, rising from the roots, through trunk and branch and leaf, to the perfect blossom. This is the tree of human life. The supreme blossom utters the whole tree, supremely. Roots, stem, branch, these have their own being. But their perfect climax is in the blossom which is beyond them, and which yet is organically one with them.

We see mankind through countless ages trying to express this truth. There is the rising up through degrees of aristocracy up to kings or emperors; there is a rising up through degrees of church dignity, to the pope; there is a rising up through zones of priestly and military elevation, to the Egyptian King-God; there is the strange accumulation of caste.

And what is the fault mankind has had to find with all these great systems? The fact that *somewhere,* the individual soul was discounted, abrogated. And when? Usually at the bottom. The slave, the serf, the vast populace, had no soul. It has been left to our era to put the populace in possession of its own soul. But no populace will ever know, by itself, what to do with its own soul. Left to itself, it will never do more than demand a pound a day, and so on. The populace finds its living soul-expression cumulatively through the rising up of the classes above it, towards pure utterance or expression or being. And the populace has its supreme satisfaction in the up-flowing of the sap of life, from its vast roots and trunk, up to the perfect blossom. The populace partakes of the flower of life: but it can never *be* the supreme, lofty flower of life: only leaves of grass. And shall we hew down the Tree of Life for the sake of the leaves of grass?

It is time to start afresh. And we need system. Those who cry out against our present system, blame it for all evils of modern life, call it the Machine which devours us all, and demand the abolition of all systems, these people confuse the issue. They actually desire the disintegration of mankind into amorphousness and oblivion: like the parched dust of Babylon. Well, that is a goal, for those that want it.

As a matter of fact, all life is organic. You can't have the merest speck of rudimentary life, without organic differentiation. And men who are collectively active in organic life-production must be organized. Men who are active purely in material production must be mechanized. There is the duality.

Obviously a system which is established for the purposes of pure material production, as ours today, is in its very nature a mechanism, a social machine. In this system we live and die. But even such a system as the great popes tried to establish was palpably not a machine, but an organization, a social organism. There is nothing at all to be gained from disunion, disintegration, and amorphousness. From mechanical systematization there is vast material productivity to be gained. But from an organic system of human life we shall produce the real blossoms of life and being.

There must be a system; there *must* be classes of men; there *must* be differentiation: either that, or amorphous nothingness. The true choice is not between system and no-system. The choice is between system and system, mechanical or organic.

We have blamed the great aristocratic system of the past, because of the automatic principle of heredity upon which they were established. A great man does not necessarily have a son at all great. We have blamed the great ecclesiastical system of the Church of Rome for the automatic principle of mediation on which it was established; we blame the automatism of caste, and of dogma. And then what? What do we put in place of all these semi-vital principles? The utterly non-vital, completely automatized system of material production. The ghosts of the great dead must turn on us.

What good is our intelligence to us, if we will not use it in the greatest issues? Nothing will excuse us from the responsibility of living: even death is no excuse. We have to live. So we may as well live fully. We are doomed to live. And therefore it is not the smallest use running into *pis allers* and trying to shirk the responsibility of living. We can't get out of it.

And therefore the only thing to do is to undertake the responsibility with good grace. What responsibility? The responsibility of establishing a new system: a new, organic system, free as far as ever it can be from automatism or mechanism: a system which depends on the profound spontaneous soul of men.

How to begin? Is it any good having revolutions and cataclysms? Who knows? Revolutions and cataclysms may be inevitable. But they are merely hopeless and catastrophic unless there come to life the germ of a new mode. And the new mode must be incipient somewhere. And therefore, let us start with education.

Let us start at once with a new system of education: a system which will cost us no more, nay, less than the dangerous present system. At least we shall produce capable individuals. Let us first of all have compulsory instruction of all teachers in the new idea. Then let us begin with the schools. Life can go on just the same. It is not a cataclysmic revolution. It is a forming of new buds upon the tree, under the harsh old foliage.

What do we want? We want to produce the new society of the future, gradually, livingly. It will be a slow job, but why not? We cut down the curriculum for the elementary school at once. We abolish all the smatterings. The smatterings of science, drawing, painting and music are only the absolute death-blow to real science and song and artistic capacity. Folk-song lives till we have schools; and then it is dead, and the shrill shriek of self-conscious scholars is supposed to take its place.

Away with all smatterings. Away with the imbecile pretence of culture in the elementary schools. Remember the back streets, remember that the souls of the working people are only rendered neurasthenic by your false culture. We want to keep the young populace robust and sufficiently nonchalant. Teach a boy to read, to write, and to do simple sums, and you have opened the door of all culture to him, if he wants to go through.

Even if we do no more, let us do so much. Away with all smatterings. Three hours a day of reading, writing and arithmetic, and that's the lot of mental education, until the age of twelve. When we say three hours a day, we mean the three hours of the morning. What it will amount to will be two hours of work: two intervals of absolutely free play, twenty minutes each interval: and twenty minutes for assembly and clearing-up and dismissal.

In the afternoon, actual *martial* exercises, swimming, and games, actual gymnasium *games,* but no Swedish drill. None of that physical-exercise business, that meaningless, vicious self-automatization; no athleticism. Never let physical movement be didactic, didactically performed from the mind.

Thus doing, we shall reduce the cost of our schools hugely, and we can hope to get some children, not the smirking, self-conscious, nervous little creatures we do produce. If we dare to have workshops, let us convert some of our schools into genuine work-sheds, where boys learn to mend boots and do joinering and carpentry and plumbing such as they will need in their own homes; other schools into kitchens, sculleries, and sewing-rooms for the girls. But let this be definite technical instruction for practical use, not some nonsense of fancy wood-carving and model churches. And let the craft-instructors be actual craftsmen, not school-teachers. Separate the workshop entirely from the school. Let there be no connexion. Avoid all "correlation," it is most vicious. Craftsmanship is a physical spontaneous intelligence, quite apart from *ideal* intelligence, and ruined by the introduction of the deliberate mental act.

And all the time, watch the *being* in each scholar. Let the schoolmaster and the crafts-master and the games-master all watch the individual lads, to find out the living nature in each child, so that, ultimately, a man's destiny shall be shaped into the natural form of that man's being, not as now, where children are rammed down into ready-made destinies, like so much canned fish.

You can cut down the expenses of the morning school to one-half. Big classes will not matter. The *personal* element, personal supervision is of no moment.

V

State Education has a dual aim: (1) The production of the desirable citizen; (2) The development of the individual.

You can obtain one kind of perfect citizen by suppressing individuality and cultivating the public virtues: which has been the invariable tendency of reform, and of social idealism in modern days. A real individual has a spark of danger in him, a menace to society. Quench this spark and you quench the individuality, you obtain a social unit, not an integral man. All modern progress has tended, and still tends, to the production of quenched social units: dangerless beings, ideal creatures.

On the other hand, by the over-development of the individualistic qualities, you produce a disintegration of all society. This was the Greek danger, as the quenching of the individual in the social unit was the Roman danger.

You must have a harmony and an inter-relation between the two modes. Because, though man is first and foremost an individual being, yet the very accomplishing of his individuality rests upon his fulfilment in social life. If you isolate an individual you deprive him of his life: if you leave him no isolation you deprive him of himself. And there it is! Life consists in the interaction between a man and his fellows, from the individual, integral love in each.

And upon what does human relationship rest? It rests upon our accepted attitude to life, our belief in the life-aims, and in our conception of right and wrong. No matter how we may pretend, for example, to be free from moral dogma, every one of our actions, and even our emotions, is under the influence of our ingrown moral creed. We cannot act without moral bias. Still more, we are influenced by our conception of the nature of man. We believe that, being men and women, we are therefore such and such and such. Without formulating or putting into any conscious expression what our idea of a man and a woman, a white man and a white woman *is,* we still have a large, potent idea, accumulated in our psyche through the course of ages. And according to this *idea* of what we ourselves are, and of what our neighbour is, we take up our attitude to the world, and we model all our behaviour. Lastly, though we express it or not, we believe that life has some great goal, of happiness and peace and harmony, and all our judgments are biased by this belief.

Here we are, then, born and swaddled in fixed beliefs, no matter how we may deny our beliefs, with lip-denial. There they are, in our very tissue. And they are not to be ousted save by new beliefs.

Such is man: a creature of beliefs and of foregone conclusion. As a matter of fact, we should never put one foot before the other, save for the foregone conclusion that we shall find the earth beneath the outstretched foot. Man travels a long journey through time. And the nature of his travels varies from time to time. Sometimes even he discovers himself upon the brink of a precipice, on the shore of a sea. Remains then to adopt a new conclusion, to take a new direction, to put the foot down differently. When we pass from Arabia Felix to Arabia Petrea, it needs must be with a different tread. Man *must* walk. And to walk he must believe that he will find the ground there under his feet at every stride. That is, he must have beliefs and foregone conclusions, and conceptions of what the nature of life is, and the goal thereof. Only, as the land changes, his beliefs must change. It is no use charging on over the edge of a precipice. It is no use plunging on from stony ground into soft sand, and keeping the same hob-nailed boots on. Man is given mental intelligence in order that he may effect quick changes, quick readjustments, preserving himself alive and integral through a myriad environments and adverse circumstances which would exterminate a non-adaptable animal.

So now that the human soul is drawing near the conclusion of one of its great phases: now it has suddenly blundered out of Arabia Felix into Arabia Deserta, and is passing beyond the zone of grass and green trees altogether into the magic of the sands, it behoves us all to readjust ourselves. We can't go back to the fleshpots of the old fat peace, because the old fat peace is not within us. Let us go on, then, and adjust ourselves to the new stage.

We have got to discover a new mode of human relationship—for man is the world to man. We have blundered blind into a new world, and we don't know how to get on. It behoves us to find out.

We have got to discover a new mode of human relationship. Which means, incidentally, that we have got to get a new conception of man and of ourselves. And we have then to establish a new morality.

It is useless to think that we can get along without a conception of what man is, and without a belief in ourselves, and without the morality to support this belief. The only point is that our conception, our belief, and our morality, though valid for the time being, is valid only for the time being. We are a million things which we don't know we are. Now and again we make new and shocking discoveries in ourselves: our right hand suddenly becomes a new and monstrous-seeming member to us, our right eye has the iniquity to see those things which were never before seen. Hence a dilemma. We have either to cut off the hand and pluck out the eye, and remain virtuously *in statu quo*. Or we have to accept the eye and accept the hand, and admit that our virtue has lost its validity. In this latter issue, we must grow a new virtue as a snake grows a new skin. Which we can do, if we will, with much éclat.

Now the good old creed we have been suckled in teaches us that man is *essentially* and *finally* an ideal being: essentially and finally a pure spirit, an abstraction, a term of abstract consciousness. As such he has his immortality and his identity with the infinite. This identity with the infinite is the goal of life. And it is reached through love, self-abandoning love. All that is truly love is good and holy; all that is not truly love is evil.

There is the creed, in a nutshell. And any creed which is to be found in a nutshell is a creed which has dropped off the Tree of Life, and is finished.

Now it is according to this creed that we proceed, at present, to educate our children. Sentimentally, we like to assume that a child is a little pure spirit arrived out of the infinite and clothed in innocent, manna-like flesh. This pure little spirit only needs to be fed on beauty, truth, and light, and it will grow up into a creature so near the angels that we'd best not mention it. Little stories full of love and sacrifice, little acts full of grace, little productions, little models in plasticine more spiritual than Donatello, little silver-point drawings more ethereal than Botticelli, little water-colour blobs that will suggest the world's dawn: all these things we quite seriously expect of small children, and in this expectation Whitehall gravely elaborates the educational system.

Ideal and innocent little beings, their minds only need to be *led* into the Canaan of their promise, and we shall have a world of *blameless* Shelleys and *superior* Botticellis. The degree of blamelessness and ideal superiority we set out to attain, in educating our children, is unimaginable. Pure little spirits, unblemished darlings! So sad that as they grow up some of the grossness of the world creeps in! *How* it creeps in, heaven knows, unless it is through the Irish stew and rice pudding at dinner. Or perhaps *somewhere* there are evil communications to corrupt good manners: time itself seems the great corrupter.

Whatever the end may be—and the end is bathos—our children *must* be regarded as ideal little beings, and their little minds must be *led* into blossom. Of course their little bodies are important: most important. Because, of course, their little bodies are the instruments of their dear little minds. And therefore you can't have a good sweet mind without a sweet healthy body. Give *every* attention to the body, for it is the sacred ark, the holy vessel which contains the holy of holies, the *mind* of the ideal little creature. *Mens sana in corpore sano.*

And therefore the child is taught to cherish its own little body, to do its little exercises and its little drill, so that it can become a fine man, or a fine woman. Let it only turn its *mind* to its own physique, and it will produce a physique that would shame Phidias. Let only the mind take up the body, and it will produce a body as a show gardener produces carrots, something to take your breath away. For the mind, the ideal reality, this is omnipotent and everything. The body is but a lower extension from the mind, diminishing in virtue as it descends. What is noble is near the brain: the ignoble is near the earth. A child is an ideal little creature, a term of ideal consciousness, pure spirit.

Any ideal, once it is really established, becomes ridiculous, so ridiculous that we begin to feel a certain mistrust of mankind's collective sense of humour. A man is never half such a fool as mankind makes of him. Mankind is a sententious imbecile without misgiving. When an individual reaches this stage, we put him away.

Well, our ideal little darlings, our innocents from the infinite, our sweet and unspoiled little natures, our little spirits straight from the hands of the Maker, our idealized little children, what are we making of them, as we lead their pure little minds into the Canaan of promise, as we educate them up to all that is pure and spiritual and ideal? What are we making of them? Fools, bitter fools. Bitter fools. If you want to know, ask them.

What is a child? A breath of the spirit of God? Well then, the breath of the spirit of God is something that still needs defining. It isn't like the waft of a handkerchief perfumed with *Ess-Bouquet.*

But, seriously, before we can dream of pretending to educate a child, we must get a different notion of the nature of children. When we see a seed putting forth its fat cotyledon, do we rhapsodize about the pure beauty of the divine issue? When we see a foal on stalky legs creaking after its mother, are we smitten with dazzled revelation of the hidden God? If we want to be dazzled with revelation, look at a mature tree in full blossom, a mature stallion in the full pride of spring. Look at a man or a woman in the magnificence of their full-grown powers, not at a tubby infant.

What is an infant? What is its holy little mind? An infant is a new clue to an as-yet-unformed human being, and its little mind is a pulp of undistinguished memory and cognition. A little child has one clue to itself, central within itself. For the rest, it is new pulp, busy with differentiation towards the great goal of fulfilled being. Instead of worshipping the child, and seeing in it a divine emission which time will stale, we ought to realize that here is a new little clue to a human being, laid soft and vulnerable on the face of the earth. Here is our responsibility, to see that this unformed thing shall come to its own final form and fullness, both physical and mental.

Which is a long and difficult business. We have to feed the little creature in more ways than one: not only its little stomach and its little mind, but its little passions and will, its senses. Long experience has taught us that a baby should be fed on milk and pap: though we're not *quite* sure even now whether carrot-water wouldn't be better. Our ancient creed makes us insist on awaking the little "mind." We are all quite agreed that we have serious responsibilities with regard to the infant stomach and the infant mind. But we don't even know, yet, that there is anything else.

We think that all the reaction goes on within the stomach and the little brain. All that is wonderful, under the soft little skull; all that is tiresome, under the tubby wall of the abdomen. A set of organs which *ought* to work beautifully and automatically, considering the care we take: and a marvellous little mind which, we are sure, is full of invisible celestial blossoms of consciousness.

Poor baby: no wonder it is queer. That self-same little stomach isn't half so automatic as we and our precious doctors would like to have it. The "instrument" of the human body isn't half so instrumental as it might be. Imagine a kettle, for instance, suddenly refusing to sit on the fire, and not to be persuaded. Think of a sewing-machine that insisted on sewing cushions, nothing but cushions, and would not be pacified. What a world! And yet we go on expecting the baby's stomach to cook the food and boil the water automatically, as if it were a kettle. And when it refuses, we still talk to it as if it *were* a kettle. Anything rather than depart from our foregone conclusion that the human body is a complicated instrument, a sort of system of retorts and generators which will finally produce the electric messages of ideas.

The body is not an instrument, but a living organism. And the goal of life is not the idea, the mental consciousness is not the sum and essence of a human being. Human consciousness is not only ideal; cognition, or knowing, is not only a mental act. Acts of emotion and volition are acts of primary cognition and may be almost entirely non-mental.

Even apart from this, it is obvious to anyone who handles a baby that the vital activity is neither mental nor stomachic. Wherein lies the mystery of a baby, for us adults? From what has grown the legend of the adoration of the infant? From the fact that in the infant the great affective centres, volitional and emotional, act direct and spontaneous, without mental cognition or interference. When mental cognition starts, it only puts a spoke in the wheel of the great affective centres. This for ever baffles us. We can see that it is not mental reaction which constitutes the true consciousness of a baby. Neither perception nor apperception, nor conception, nor any form of cognition, such as is recognized by our psychology, is to be ascribed to the infant mind. And yet there *is* consciousness, and even cognition: here, as in the mindless animals.

What kind of consciousness is it? We must look to the great affective centres, emotional and volitional. And we shall find that in the tiny infant there are two emotional centres primal and intensely active, with two corresponding volitional centres. We need go through no tortures of scientific psychology to get at the truth. We need only take direct heed of the infant.

And then we shall realize that the busy business of consciousness is not taking place beneath the soft little skull, but beneath the little navel, and in the midst of the little breast. Here are the two great affective centres of the so-called emotional consciousness. Which emotional consciousness, according to our idealistic psychology, is only some sort of *force,* like imagination, heat, or electric current. This force which arises and acts from the primal emotional-affective centres is supposed to be impersonal, general, truly a mechanical universal force, like electricity or heat or any kinetic force.

Impersonal, and having nothing to do with the individual. The personal and the individual element does not enter until we reach mental consciousness. Personality, individuality, depends on mentality. So our psychology assumes. In the *mind,* a child is personal and individual, it is itself. Outside the mind, it is an instrument, a dynamo, if you like, a unit of difficult kinetic force betraying a sort of automatic consciousness, the same in every child, undifferentiated. In the same way, according to our psychology, animals have no personality and no individuality, because they have no mental cognition. They have a certain psyche which they hold in common. What is true of one rabbit is true of another. All we can speak of is "the psychology of the rabbit," one rabbit having just the same psyche as another. Why? Because it has no recognizable cognition: it has only instinct.

We know this is all wrong, because, having met a rabbit or two, we have seen quite clearly that each separate rabbit was a separate, distinct rabbit–individual, with a specific nature of his own. We should be sorry to attribute a *mind* to him. But he has consciousness, and quite an individual consciousness too. It is notorious that human beings see foreigners all alike. To an English sailor the faces of a crowd of Chinese are all alike. But that is because the English sailor doesn't *see* the difference, not because the difference doesn't exist. Why, each fat domestic sheep, mere clod as it seems, has a distinct individual nature of its own, known to a shepherd after a very brief acquaintance.

So here we are with the great affective centres, volitional and emotional. The two chief emotional centres in the baby are the solar plexus of the abdomen and the cardiac plexus of the breast. The corresponding ganglia of the volitional system are the lumbar ganglion and the thoracic ganglion.

And we may as well leave off at once regarding these great affective centres as merely instrumental, like little dynamos and accumulators and so on. Nonsense. They are primary, integral mind-centres, each of a specific nature. There is a specific form of *knowing* takes place at each of these centres, without any mental reference at all. And the specific form of knowing at each of the great affective centres in the infant is of an individual and personal nature, peculiar to the very soul and being of that infant.

That is, at the great solar plexus an infant *knows,* in primary, mindless knowledge; and from this centre he acts and reacts directly, individually, and self-responsibly. The same from the cardiac plexus, and the two corresponding ganglia, lumbar and thoracic. The brain at first acts only as a switchboard which keeps these great active centres in circuit of communication. The process of idealization, mental consciousness, is a subsidiary process. It is a second form of conscious activity. Mental activity, final cognition, ideation, is only set up secondarily from the perfect interaction and inter-communication of the primary affective centres, which remain all the time our dynamic first-minds.

VI

How to begin to educate a child. First rule, leave him alone. Second rule, leave him alone. Third rule, leave him alone. That is the whole beginning.

Which doesn't mean we are to let him starve, or put his fingers in the fire, or chew broken glass. That is mere neglect. As a little organism, he must have his proper environment. As a little individual he has his place and his limits: we also are individuals, and as such cannot allow him to make an unlimited nuisance of himself. But as a little person and a little mind, if you please, he does not exist. Personality and mind, like moustaches, belong to a certain age. They are a deformity in a child.

It is in this respect that we repeat, *leave him alone.* Leave his sensibilities, his emotions, his spirit, and his mind severely alone. There is the devil in mothers, that they must try to provoke *personal* recognition and *personal* response from their infants. They might as well start rubbing *Tatcho* on the tiny chin, to provoke a beard. Except that the *Tatcho* provocation will have no effect, unless perhaps a blister: whereas the emotional or psychic provocation has, alas, only too much effect.

For this reason babies should invariably be taken away from their modern mothers and given, not to yearning and maternal old maids, but to rather stupid fat women who can't be bothered with them. There should be a league for the prevention of maternal love, as there is a society for the prevention of cruelty to animals. The stupid fat woman may not guard so zealously against germs. But all the germs in the list of bacteriology are not so dangerous for a child as mother-love.

And why? Not for any thrilling Freudian motive, but because our now deadly idealism insists on idealizing every human relationship, but particularly that of mother and child. Heaven, how we all prostrate ourselves before the mother-child relationship, in all the grovelling degeneracy of Mariolatry! Highest, purest, most ideal of relationships, mother and child!

What nasty drivel! The mother-child relationship is certainly deep and important, but to make it high, or pure, or ideal is to make a nauseous perversion of it. A healthy, natural child has no high nature, no purity, and no ideal being. To stimulate these qualities in the infant is to produce psychic deformity, just as ugly as if we stimulated the growth of a beard on the baby face.

As far as all these high and personal matters go, *leave the child alone.* Personality and spiritual being mean with us our *mental consciousness* of our *own self.* A mother is to a high degree, alas, mentally conscious of her own self, her own exaltedness, her own mission, in these miserable days. And she wants her own mental consciousness reciprocated in the child. The child must *recognize* and respond. Alas, that the child cannot give her the greatest smack in the eye, every time she smirks and yearns for recognition and response. If we are to save the ultimate sanity of our children, it is *down with mothers! A bas les mères!*

Down to the right level. Pull them down from their exalted perches. No more of this Madonna smirking and yearning. No more soul. A mother should have ten strokes with the birch every time she "comes over" with soul or yearning love or aching responsibility. Ten hard, keen, stinging strokes on her bare back, each time. Be cause White Slave Traffic is a cup of tea compared with yearning mother-love. It should be knocked out of her, for it is a vice which threatens the ultimate sanity of our race.

The relation between mother and child is not personal at all, until it becomes perverted. Personal means mental consciousness of self. And a child has *no* mental consciousness and *no* self, and ten times less than no mental consciousness of self until that fiend, its mother, followed by a string of personally affected females, proceeds to provoke this mental consciousness in the small psyche. Worst luck of all, the emotional female fiends succeed. Sometimes they produce an *obvious* derangement in the psyche of the infant, and then they receive all the pity in the world, instead of a good barbaric thrashing. Usually the derangement is only incipient, due to develop later as morbid self-consciousness and neurosis. How can we help being neurotic when our mothers provoked self-consciousness in us at the breast: provoked our self-conscious reciprocity, in order to satisfy their own spiritual and ideal lust for communion in self-consciousness?

Down with exalted mothers, and down with the exaltation of motherhood, for it threatens the sanity of our race. The relation of mother and child, while it remains natural, is non-personal, non-ideal, non-spiritual. It is effective at the great primary centres, the solar plexus and the cardiac plexus, and from these centres it acts *direct,* without the so-called conscious knowledge: that is, without any transfer into the mind. Nothing is so strange as the remote look of recognition, remote, heavy, and potent, which is seen in the eyes of an infant. This wonderful remote look should be magic and sacred to a mother. Her whole instinct should revolt against disturbing it.

But no creature so perverse as the human mother today. No creature so delights in the traducing of the deepest instincts. Show me a woman who can be satisfied with the remote, deep, far-off baby-recognition. Show me the woman who can rest without provoking the look of *present* recognition in the eyes of a baby; that winsome, pathetic smile of infant recognition which is murder to a child so young. Why, even in the eyes of a child of seven the look of recognition is still remote and impersonal; it has a certain heavy far-offness which is its beauty. The self does not stand fully present in the eyes until maturity, look does not actually meet look until then.

The old, instinctive mother instinctively cast off her personal consciousness in her communication with her child, and entered into that state of deep, unformed or untranslated consciousness, non-mental, on a lower, more primal plane. For this the idealists despised her, and hence the idealizing, the making mental and self-conscious of the naturally non-mental, spontaneous state of motherhood.

Remains now for the perverted, idealized mother deliberately to cast off her ideal, self-conscious motherhood, to return to the old deeps. Or else man must drag her ideal robes off her, by force. But back she must go, to the old mindlessness, the old unconsciousness, the despised animality of motherhood. Our spiritualizing processes have been sheer perversion, when they have influenced the basic human affections.

The true relation between mother and child is established between the primary affective centres in each, without mental, self-conscious intervention. At the primary centres, the solar plexus and the cardiac plexus, the dynamic individual consciousness stirs and flushes and seeks an object. The primary dynamic consciousness is like a living force which moves from its own polarized centre seeking an object, the object being chiefly some other corresponding pole of vitality in another living being. So from the solar plexus of the infant sympathetic system moves a pristine conscious-force, seeking an object, a corresponding pole. This corresponding pole is found in the solar plexus of the mother.

As a matter of fact, the first polarity between the essential clue of the infant and the essential clue of the mother, located in the solar plexus, was established long before birth, at the moment of conception. But during all the period of gestation, the infant had no actual separate existence. It is only after birth, after the break of the navel-string, that the child's polar vitality becomes separate and distinct.

And at the same time, as soon as the child is liberated into separate and distinct existence, it craves at once for the readjustment of the old connexion, the fitting together of the wound of the navel with its origin in the mother. We don't mean that the child has any idea of what has happened. We don't mean that it summons its little wits to effect the desired restitution.

What actually happens is that, once the child is born and divided into separate existence, then at the solar plexus there surges a current of free vital consciousness, like a wave of electricity seeking its correspondent pole. The correspondent pole is found naturally in the great affective centre, the solar plexus of the mother. But failing the mother, the corresponding pole may be found in another being, or even, as in the legend, in a she-wolf. Suffice it that the two great dynamic centres, the solar plexus in the infant and the solar plexus in some external being, are seized into correspondence, and a vital circuit set up.

The vital circuit, we remark, is set up between two extraneous and individual beings, each separately existing. Yet the circuit embraces the two in a perfectly balanced unison. The mother and child are on the same plane. The mother is one in vital correspondence with the child. That is, in all her direct intercourse with the child she is as rudimentary as the child itself, her dynamic consciousness is as undeveloped and non-mental as the child's.

Herein we have the true mother: she who corresponds with her child on the deep, rudimentary plane of the first dynamic consciousness. This correspondence is a sightless, mindless correspondence of touch and sound. The two dark poles of vital being must be kept constant in mother and infant, so that the flow is uninterrupted. This constancy is preserved by intimacy of contact, physical immediacy. But this physical immediacy does not make the two beings any less distinct and separate. It makes them more so. The child develops its own single, incipient self at its own primary centre; the mother develops her own separate, matured female self. The circuit of dynamic polarity which keeps the two equilibrized also produces each of them, produces the infant's developing body and psyche, produces the perfected womanhood of the mother.

All this, so long as the circuit is not broken, the flow perverted. The circuit, the flow is kept as the child lies against the bosom of its mother, just as the circle of magnetic force is kept constant in a magnet, by the "keeper" which unites the two poles. The child which sleeps in its mother's arms, the child which sucks its mother's breast, the child which screams and kicks on its mother's knee is established in a vital circuit with its parent, out of which circuit its being arises and develops. From pole to pole, direct, the current flows: from the solar plexus in the abdomen of the child to the solar plexus in the abdomen of the mother, from the cardiac plexus in the breast of the child to the cardiac plexus in the breast of the mother. The mouth which sucks, the little voice which calls and cries, both issue from the deep centres of the breast and bowels, giving expression from these centres, and not from the brain. The baby is not mentally vocal. It utters itself from the great affective centres. And this is why it has such power to charm or to madden us. The mother in her response utters herself from the same affective centres; her coos and callings also are unintelligible. Not the mind speaks, but the deep, happy bowels, the lively breast.

Introduce one grain of self-consciousness into the mother, as she chuckles and coos to her baby, and what then? The good life-flow instantly breaks. The sounds change. She begins to produce them deliberately, under mental control. And what then? The deep affective centre in the baby is suddenly robbed, as when the mouth still sucking is suddenly snatched from the full breast. The vital flow is suddenly interrupted, and a new stimulus is applied to the child. There is a new provocation, a provocation for mental response from the infantile self-consciousness. And what then? The child either howls, or turns pale and makes this convulsed effort at mental-conscious, or self-conscious response. After which it is probably sick.

The same with the baby's eyes. They do not see, mentally. Mentally, they are sightless and dark. But they have the remote, deep vision of the deep affective centres. And so a mother, laughing and clapping to her baby, has the same half-sightless, glaucous look in her eyes, vision non-mental and non-critical, the primary affective centres corresponding through the eyes, void of idea or mental cognition.

But rouse the devil of a woman's self-conscious will, and she, clapping and cooing and laughing apparently just as before, will try to force a personal, *conscious* recognition into the eyes of the baby. She will try and try and try, fiendishly. And the child will blindly, instinctively resist. But with the cunning of seven legions of devils and the persistency of hell's most hellish fiend, the cooing, clapping, devilish modern mother traduces the child into the personal mode of consciousness. She succeeds, and starts this hateful "personal" love between herself and her excited child, and the unspoken but unfathomable hatred between the violated infant and her own assaulting soul, which together make the bane of human life, and give rise to all the neurosis and neuritis and nervous troubles we are all afflicted with.

With children we must absolutely leave out the self-conscious and personal note. Communication must be remote and impersonal, a correspondence direct between the deep affective centres. And this is the reason why we must kick out all the personal fritter from the elementary schools. Stories must be *tales,* fables. They may have a flat *moral* if you like. But they must never have a personal, self-conscious note, the little-Mary-who-dies-and-goes-to-heaven touch, or the little-Alice-who-saw-a-fairy. This is the most vicious element in our canting infantile education today. "And you will all see fairies, dears, if you know how to look for them."

It is perversion of the infant mind at the start. This continual introduction of a little child-heroine or -hero, with whom the little girl or the little boy can self-consciously identify herself or himself, stultifies all development at the true centres. Fairies are not a personal, *mental* reality. Alice Jenkinson, who lives in "The Laburnums," Leslie Road, Brixton, knows quite well that fairies are all "my-eye." But she is quite content to smirk self-consciously and say, "Yes, miss," when teacher asks her if she'd like to see a fairy. It's all very well playing games of pretence, so long as you enter right into the game, robustly, and forget your own pretensive self. But when, like the little Alices of today, you keep a constant self-conscious smirk on your nose all the time you're "playing fairies," then to hell with you and your fairies. And ten times to hell with the smirking, self-conscious "teacher" who encourages you. A hateful, self-tickling, self-abusive affair, the whole business.

And this is what is wrong, first and foremost, with our education: this attempt deliberately to provoke reactions in the great affective centres and to dictate these reactions from the mind. Fairies are true embryological realities of the human psyche. They are true and real for the great affective centres, which see as through a glass, darkly, and which have direct correspondence with living and naturalistic influences in the surrounding universe, correspondence which cannot have mental, rational utterance, but must express itself, if it be expressed, in preternatural forms. Thus fairies are true, and Little Red Riding Hood is most true.

But they are not true for Alice Jenkinson, smirking little minx. Because Alice Jenkinson is an incurably self-conscious little piece of goods, and she *cannot* act direct from the great affective centres, she *can* only act perversely, by reflection, from her *personal* consciousness. And therefore, for her, all fairies and princesses and Peters and Wendys should be put on the fire, and she should be spanked and transported to Newcastle, to have some of her self-consciousness taken out of her.

An inspector should be sent round *at once* to burn all pernicious Little Alice and Little Mary literature in the elementary schools, and empowered to cut down to one-half the salary of any teacher found smirking or smuggling or indulging in any other form of pretty self-consciousness and personal grace. Abolish all the bunkum, go back to the three R's. Don't cultivate any more imagination at all in children: it only means pernicious self-consciousness. Let us, for heaven's sake, have children without imagination and without "nerves," for the two are damnably inseparable.

Down with imagination in school, down with self-expression. Let us have a little severe hard work, good, clean, well-written exercises, well-pronounced words, well-set-down sums: and as far as head-work goes, no more. No more self-conscious dabblings and smirkings and lispings of "The silver birch is a dainty lady" (so is little Alice, of course). The silver birch must be finely downcast to see itself transmogrified into a smirky little Alice. The owl and the pussy-cat may have gone to sea in the pea-green boat, and the little girl may well have said: "What long teeth you've got, Grandmother!" This is well within the bounds of natural pristine experience. But that dainty-lady business is only self-conscious smirking.

It will be a long time before we know how to act or speak again from the deep affective centres, without self-conscious perversion. And therefore, in the interim, whilst we learn, let us abolish all pretence at naïveté and childish self-expression. Let us have a bit of solid, hard, tidy work. And for the rest, *leave the children alone*. Pitch them out into the street or the playgrounds, and take no notice of them. Drive them savagely away from their posturings.

There must be an end to the self-conscious attitudinizing of our children. The self-consciousness and all the damned high-flownness must be taken out of them, and their little personalities must be nipped in the bud. Children shall be regarded as young *creatures*, not as young affected persons. Creatures, not persons.

VII

As a matter of fact, our private hope is that by a sane system of education we may release the coming generation from our own nasty disease of self-consciousness: a disease quite as rampant among the working-classes as among the well-to-do classes; and perhaps even more malignant there, because, having fewer forms of expression, it tends to pivot in certain ideas, which fix themselves in the psyche and become little less than manias. The wage is the mania of the moment: the working-man consciousness of himself as a working-man, which has now become an *idée fixe*, excluding any possibility of his remaining a lively human being.

What do we mean by self-consciousness? If we will realize that all spontaneous life, desire, impulse, and first-hand individual consciousness arises and is effective at the great nerve-centres of the body, and *not* in the brain, we shall begin to understand. The great nerve-centres are in pairs, sympathetic and volitional. Again, they are polarized in upper and lower duality, above and below the diaphragm. Thus the solar plexus of the abdomen is the first great affective centre, sympathetic, and the lumbar ganglion, volitional, is its partner. At these two great centres arises our first consciousness, our primary impulses, desires, motives. These are our primal minds, here located in the dual great affective centres below the diaphragm. But immediately above the diaphragm we have the cardiac plexus and the thoracic ganglion, another great pair of conjugal affective centres, acting in immediate correspondence with the two lower centres. And these four great nerve-centres establish the first field of our consciousness, the first plane of our vital being. They are the four corner-stones of our psyche, the four powerful vital poles which, flashing darkly in polarized interaction one with another, form the fourfold issue of our individual life. At these great centres, primarily, we live and move and have our being. Thought and idea do not enter in. The motion arises spontaneous, we know not how, and is emitted in dark vibrations. The vibration goes forth, seeks its object, returns, establishing a life-circuit. And this life-circuit, established internally between the four first poles, and established also externally between the primal affective centres in two different beings or creatures, this complex life-circuit or system of circuits constitutes in itself our profound primal consciousness, and contains all our radical knowledge, knowledge non-ideal, non-mental, yet still knowledge, primary cognition, individual and potent.

The mental cognition or consciousness is, as it were, distilled or telegraphed from the primal consciousness into a sort of written, final script, in the brain. If we imagine the infinite currents and meaningful vibrations in the world's atmosphere, and if we realize how some of these, at the great wireless stations, are ticked off and written down in fixed script, we shall form some sort of inkling of how the primary consciousness centralized in the great affective centres, and circulating in vital circuits of primary cognition, is captured by the supremely delicate registering apparatus in the brain and registered there like some strange code, the newly rising mental consciousness. The brain itself, no doubt, is a very tissue of memory, every smallest cell is a vast material memory which only needs to be roused, quickened by the vibration coming from the primary centres, only needs the new fertilization of a new quiver of experience, to blossom out as a mental conception, an idea. This power for the transfer of the pure affective experience, the primary consciousness, into final mental experience, ideal consciousness, varies extremely according to individuals. It would seem as if, in Negroes for example, the primary affective experience, the affective consciousness is profound and intense, but the transfer into mental consciousness is comparatively small. In ourselves, in modern educated Europeans, on the other hand, the primal experience, the vital consciousness grows weaker and weaker, the mind fixes the control and limits the life-activity. For, let us realize once and for all that the whole mental consciousness and the whole sum of the mental content of mankind is never, and can never be more than a mere tithe of all the vast surging primal consciousness, the affective consciousness of mankind.

Yet we presume to limit the potent spontaneous consciousness to the poor limits of the mental consciousness. In us, instead of our life issuing spontaneously at the great affective centres, the mind, the mental consciousness, grown unwieldy, turns round upon the primary affective centres, seizes control, and proceeds to evoke our primal motions and emotions, didactically. The mind subtly, without knowing, provokes and dictates our own feelings and impulses. That is to say, a man helplessly and unconsciously *causes* from his mind every one of his own important reactions at the great affective centres. He can't help himself. It isn't his own fault. The old polarity has broken down. The primal centres have collapsed from their original spontaneity, they have become subordinate, neuter, negative, waiting for the mind's provocation, waiting to be worked according to some secondary idea. Thus arises our pseudo-spontaneous modern living.

We are in the toils of helpless self-consciousness. We can't help ourselves. It is like being in a boat with no oars. What can we do but drift? We know we are drifting, but we don't know how or where. Because there is no primary *resistance* in us, nothing that resists the helpless but fatal flux of ideas which streams us away. The resistant spontaneous centres have broken down in us.

Why does this happen? Because we have become too conscious? Not at all. Merely because we have become too fixedly conscious. We have limited our consciousness, tethered it to a few great ideas, like a goat to a post. We insist over and over again on what we know from one mere centre of ourselves, the mental centre. We insist that we are essentially spirit, that we are ideal beings, conscious personalities, mental creatures. As far as ever possible we have resisted the independence of the great affective centres. We have struggled for some thousands of years, not only to get our passions under control, but absolutely to eliminate certain passions, and to give all passions an ideal nature.

And so, at last, we succeed. We do actually give all our passions an ideal nature. Our passions at last are nothing more or less than ideas auto-suggested into practice. We try to persuade ourselves that it is all fine and grand and flowing. And for quite a long time we manage to take ourselves in. But we can't continue, *ad infinitum,* this life of self-satisfied auto-suggestion.

Because, if you think of it, everything which is provoked or originated *by an idea* works automatically or mechanically. It works by principle. So that even our wickedness today, being ideal in its origin, a sort of deliberate reaction to the *accepted* ideal, amounts to the same mechanism. It is an ideal working of the affective centres in the *opposite direction* from the accepted direction: opposite and opposite and opposite, till murder itself becomes an ideal at last. But it is all auto-affective. No matter which way you *work* the affective centres, once you work them from the mental consciousness you automatize them. And the human being craves for change in his automatism. Sometimes it seems to him horrible that he must, in a fixed routine, get up in the morning and put his clothes on, day in, day out. He can't bear his automatism. He is beside himself in his self-consciousness. But he is a damned little Oliver Twist: nothing but twist, and always wanting "more." He doesn't want to drop his self-consciousness. He wants more, always more. The damned little ideal being, he wants to work his own little psyche till the end of time, like a clever little god-in-the-machine that he is. And he despises any real spontaneity with all the street-arab insolence of depraved idealism. Man would rather be the ideal god inside his own automaton than anything else on earth. And woman is ten times worse. Woman as the goddess in the machine of the human psyche is a heroine who will drive us, like a female chauffeur, through all the avenues of hell, till she pitches us eventually down the bottomless pit. And even then she'll save herself, she'll kilt her skirts and look round for new passengers. She has a million more dodges for automatic self-stimulation than man has. When man has finished, woman can still cadge a million more sensational reactions out of herself and her co-respondent.

Man is accursed once he falls into the trick of ideal self-automatism. But he is infinitely conceited about it. He really works his own psyche! He really *is* the god of his own creation! Isn't this enough to puff him out? Here he is, tricky god and creator of himself at last! And he's not going to be ousted from his at-last-acquired godhead. Not he! The triumphant little god sits in the machine of his own psyche and turns on the petrol. It is like a story by H. G. Wells—too true to life, alas. There sits every man ensconced upon the engine of his own psyche, turning on the ideal taps and opening the ideal valves of his own nature, and so proud of himself, it's a wonder he hasn't set off to fly to the sun in one of his aeroplanes, like a new Icarus. But he lacks the fine boldness for such a flight. He wants to sit tight in his little hobby machine, near enough to his little hearth and home, this tubby, domestic little mechanical godhead.

A curse on idealism! A million curses on self-conscious automatic humanity, men and women both. Curses on their auto-suggestive self-reactions, from which they derive such inordinate self-gratification. Most curses of all upon the women, the self-conscious provokers of infinite sensations, of which man is the instrument. Let there be a fierce new Athanasian creed, to damn and blast all idealists. But let spiritual, ideal self-conscious woman be the most damned of all. Men, after all, don't get much more than aeroplane thrills and political thrills out of their god-in-the-machine reactions. But women get soul-thrills and sexual thrills, they float and squirm on clouds of self-glorification, with a lot of knock-kneed would-be saints and apostles of the male sort goggling sanctified eyes upwards at them, as in some sickening Raphael picture.

It is enough to send a sane person mad, to see this goggling, squirming, self-glorifying idealized humanity carrying on its self-conscious little games. And how it loves its little games. Just heaven, how it wallows in them, ideally!

What is to be done? We talk about new systems of education, and here we have a civilized mankind sucking its fingers avidly, as if its own fingers were so many sticks of juicy barley-sugar. It loves itself so much, this ideal self-conscious humanity, that it could verily eat itself. And so it nibbles gluttishly at itself.

Is it the slightest good doing anything but joining in with the sucking and self-nibbling? Probably not. We'll throw stones at them none the less, even if every stone boomerangs back in our own teeth. Perhaps once we shall catch humanity one in the eye.

The question is, don't our children get this self-conscious, self-nibbling habit, in the very womb of their travesty mothers, before they are even born? We are afraid it is so. Our miserable offspring, churned in the abdomen of insatiable self-conscious woman, woman self-consciously every moment seeking and watching her own reactions, her own pregnancy and her own everything, grinding all her sensations from her head and reflecting them all back into her head, all her physical churnings ground exceeding small in the hateful self-conscious mills of her female mind, ideal and unremitting; do not our miserable offspring issue from the ovens of such a womb writhing and crisping with self-conscious morbid hunger of self? Alas and alack, to all appearance they do. The self-conscious devil is in them, either smirking and smarming, or preening and prancing, or irritably self-nibbling and sentimentalizing, or stolidly *sufficient,* or hostile. But there it is, the hateful devil of self-conscious self-importance born with them, simmered into them in the acid-seething, irritable womb.

What's to be done? Why, of course, keep the game up. Tickle the poor little wretches into ecstasies of self-consciousness. Gather round them and stare at them and mouth over them and sentimentalize and rhapsodize over them. Get the doctor to paw them, the nurse to expose them naked to a horde of ideal prurient females, get the parson to preach over them and roll his eyes to heaven over their sanctity. Then send them to school to "express themselves," in the hopes that they'll turn out infant prodigies. For, oh, dear me! *what* a feather in the cap of a mortal mother is an infant prodigy!

If *one* healthily sensitive mother in these days bore one healthy-souled, simple child she'd pick him up and bolt for her life from the mobs of our ghoulish "charming" women, and the mobs of goggling adoring men. She'd run, poor Hagar, to some desert with her Ishmael. And there she'd give him to a she-wolf, or a she-bear, or a she-lion to suckle. She'd never trust herself. Verily, she'd have more faith in a rattlesnake, as far as motherhood is concerned.

Would God a she-wolf had suckled me, and stood over me with her paps, and kicked me back into a rocky corner when she'd had enough of me. It might have made a man of me.

But it's no use sighing. Romulus and Remus had all the luck. We see now why they bred a great, great race: because they had no mother: a race of men. Christians have no fathers: only these ogling woman-worshipping saints, and the self-conscious friction of exalted mothers.

Let us rail—why shouldn't we? It is subject enough for railing.

But what about these infants? Alas, there isn't a wild she-wolf in the length and breadth of Britain. There isn't a crevice in the British Isles where you could suckle a brat undisturbed by the village constable. And therefore, no hope with us of heroic twins.

What are we going to do? Presumably, nothing: except carry on the pretty process of smirking and goggling which we call education. The sense of futility overwhelms us. The thought of all the exalted mothers of England, and of all the knock-kneed smug God-besprinkled fathers is too much for us: all the hosts of the sentimental, self-conscious ones, the sensational self-conscious ones, the free-and-easy self-conscious ones, the downright no-nonsense-about-me self-conscious ones, the elegant self-conscious ones, the would-be dissolute self-conscious ones, the very-very-naughty self-conscious ones, the *chic* self-conscious ones, and spiritual self-conscious ones, and the *nuancy* self-conscious ones (those full of *nuances*), and the self-sacrificial self-conscious ones, and the do-all-you-can-for-others self-conscious ones, the do-your-bit self-conscious ones, the yearning, the aspiring, the sighing, the leering, the tip-the-winking self-conscious ones, females and so-called men: all the lot of them: *ad nauseam* and *ad nauseissimam:* they are too much for me. All of them like so many little barrel-organs grinding their own sensations, nay, their own very natures, out of their own little heads: and become so automatic at it they don't even know they're doing it. They think they are fine spontaneous angels, these little automata. And they are automata, self-turning little barrel-organs, all of them, from the millionaire down to the dustman. The dustman grinds himself off according to his own dustman-ideal prescription.

VIII

We've got to get on to a different tack: snap! off the old tack and veer on to a new one. No more seeing ourselves as others see us. No more seeing ourselves at all. A fig for such sights.

The primary conscious centres, the very first and deepest, are in the lower body. A button for your brain, whoever you are. If you are not darkly potent below the belt, you are nothing.

Let go the upper consciousness. Switch it off for a time. Release the cramped and tortured lower consciousness. Drop this loving and merging business. Fall back into your own isolation and the insuperable pride thereof. Break off the old polarity, the merging into oneness with others, with everything. Snap the old connexions.

Break clean away from the old yearning navel-string of love, which unites us to the body of everything. Break it, and be born. Fall apart into your own isolation; set apart single and potent in singularity for ever. One is one and all alone and ever more shall be so. Exult in it. Exult in the fact that you are yourself, and alone for ever. Exult in your own dark being. Across the gulf are strangers, myriad-faced dancing strangers like midges and like Pleiades. One draws near; there is a thrill and a fiery contact. But never a merging. A withdrawal, a bond of knowledge, but no identification. Recognition across space: across a dark and bottomless space: two beings who recognize each other across the chasm, who occasionally cross and meet in a fiery contact, but who find themselves invariably withdrawn afterwards, with dark, dusky-glowing faces glancing across the insuperable chasm which intervenes between two beings.

Have done; let go the old connexions. Fall apart, fall asunder, each into his own unfathomable dark bath of isolation. Break up the old incorporation. Finish for ever the old unison with homogeneity. Let every man fall apart into a fathomless, single isolation of being, exultant at his own core, and apart. Then, dancing magnificent in our own space, as the spheres dance in space, we can set up the extra-individual communication. Across the space comes the thrill of communication. There is an approach, a flash and blaze of contact, and then the sheer fiery purity of a purer isolation, a more exultant singleness. Not a mass of homogeneity, like sunlight, but a fathomless multiplicity, like the stars at night, each one isolate in the darkly singing space. This symbol of Light, the homogeneous and universal Day, the daylight, symbolizes our universal mental consciousness, which we have in common. But our *being* we have in integral separateness, as the stars at night. To think of lumping the stars together into one mass is hideous. Each one separate, each one his own peculiar ray. So the universe is made up.

And the sun only hides all this. Imagine, if the sun shone all the time, we should never know there was anything but ourselves in the universe. Everything would be limited to the plane superficies of ourself and our own mundane nature. Everything would be as we see it and as we think it.

Which is what ails us. Living as we do entirely in the light of the mental consciousness, we think everything is as we see it and as we think it. Which is a vast illusion. Imagine a man who all his life has been shut up in a hermetically dark room, between sundown and sunrise, and let out only when light was full in the heavens.

He would imagine that everything, all the time, was light, that the firmament was a vast blue space screened from us sometimes by our own vapours, but otherwise a blue, unblemished void occupied by ourselves and the sun, one blue unchanging blaze of eternal light, with ourselves for the only inhabitants, under the sun.

Which, in spite of Galileo, that star-master, is what we actually do think. If we proceed to imagine other worlds, we cook up a few distortions of our own world and scatter them into space. A Martian may have long ears and horns on his forehead, but he is only ourselves dressed up, busy making super-zeppelins. We are convinced, as a matter of fact, that the stars and ourselves are all seed of one sort.

And what holds true cosmologically holds much more true psychologically. The man sealed up during twilight and night-time would have a rare shock the first time he was taken out under the stars. To see all the blue heavens crumpled and shrivelled away! To see the pulsation of myriad orbs proudly moving in the endless darkness, insouciant, sunless, taking a stately path we know not whither or how. Ha, the day-time man would feel his heart and brain burst to a thousand shivers, he would feel himself falling like a seed into space. All that he counted *himself* would be suddenly dispelled. All that he counted eternal, infinite, *Everything,* suddenly shrivelled like a vast, burnt roof of paper, or a vast paper lantern: the eternal light gone out: and behold, multiplicity, twinkling, proud multiplicity, utterly indifferent of oneness, proud far-off orbs taking their lonely way beyond the bounds of knowledge, emitting their own unique and untransmutable rays, pulsing with their own isolate pulsation.

This is what must happen to us. We have kept up a false daylight all through our nights. Our sophistry has intervened like a lamp between us and the slow-stepping stars, we have turned our cheap lanterns on the dark and wizard face of Galileo, till lo and behold, his words are as harmless as butterflies. Of course the orbs are manifold: we admit it easily. But *light* is one and universal and infinite.

Put it in human terms: men are manifold, but Wisdom and Understanding are one and universal. Men are manifold, but the Spirit, the consciousness, is one, as sunlight is one. And therefore, because the consciousness of mankind is really one and universal, mankind is one and universal. Therefore each individual is a term of the Infinite.

A pretty bit of sophistry. Because the sunlight covers all the stars, therefore the stars are one, each is a homogeneous bit of light. Behold, how oneness achieves its ridiculous triumph, by self-deception. It is a famous dodge, this of self-deception. The popes couldn't squash Galileo. But clever mankind has succeeded in smearing out his star-shine, by a trick of the psyche.

Mankind is an ostrich with its head in the bush of the infinite. This doesn't prevent the stars all trooping past with a superb smile at the rump of the bird.

We don't find fault with the mental consciousness, the daylight consciousness of mankind. Not at all. We only find fault with the One-and-Allness which is attributed to it. It isn't One-and-All, any more than the sun is one and all. Has it never occurred to us that the sun serves no more than as a great lantern and bonfire to the ambulating intermediary world? Has it never occurred to us that the sun is not *superior* to our little earth, and to the other little stars, but just instrumental, a bonfire and a lamp and an axle-tree? After all, it is the little spheres which *live,* and the great sun is instrumental to their living, even as the powerful arc-lamps high over Piccadilly only serve to illuminate the little feet of foot-passengers.

So there we are. All our Oneness and our infinite, which does but mount up to the sum-total of human mentality or consciousness, is merely instrumental to the small individual consciousness of individual beings. Bigness as a rule means departure from life. Things which are vividly living are never so very big. Vastness is a term which applies to the non-vital universe. The moment we consider the vital universe, vastness and extensiveness cease to be terms of merit, and become terms of demerit. Whatever is vast and extensive in the *living* world is less quick, less alive than that which creates no impression of superlative size. In the *living* world, appreciation is intensive, not extensive. A small fowl like a lark or a kestrel is more to us than a flock of rooks or an ostrich or a condor. One is one and all alone and ever more shall be so.

Hence the little stellar orbs, living as we feel they must be, are more than the great sun they hover round: just as the shadowy human men are more than the great fire round which they squat and move in the dark camp. So, the universe is a great living camp squatted round the sun. We warm ourselves and prepare our food at the fire. But, after all, the fire is only the means to our living. So the sun. It is but the means to the living of the little mid-way spheres, the great fire camped in the middle of the sky, at which they warm themselves and prepare their meat.

And so with human beings. One is one, and as such, always more than an aggregation. Vitally, intensively, one human being is always more than six collective human beings. Because, in the collectivity, what is gained in bulk or number is lost in intrinsic being. The *quick* of any collective group is some consciousness they have in common. But the quick of the individual is the integral soul, for ever indescribable and unstateable. That which is *in common* is never any more than some mere property of the vital, individual soul.

Away then with the old system of valuation, that many is more than one. In the static material world it is so. But in the living world, the opposite is true. One is more than many. The Japanese know that one flower is lovelier than many flowers. Alone, one flower lives and has its own integral wonder. Massed with other flowers, it has a being-in-common, and this being-in-common is always inferior to the single aloneness of one creature. Being-in-common means the summing-up of one element held in common by many individuals. But this one common element, however many times multiplied, is never more than one mere part in any individual, and therefore much *less* than any individual. The more common the element, the smaller is its part in the individual, and hence the greater its vital insignificance. So with humanity, or mankind, or the infinite, as compared with one individual.

All of which is not mere verbal metaphysic, but an attempt to get in human beings a new attitude to life. Instead of finding our highest reality in an ever-extending aggregation with the rest of men, we shall realize at last that the highest reality for every living creature is in its purity of singleness and its perfect solitary integrity, and that everything else should be but a means to this end. All communion, all love, and all communication, which is all consciousness, are but a means to the perfected singleness of the individual being.

Which doesn't mean anarchy and disorder. On the contrary, it means the most delicately and inscrutably established order, delicate, intricate, complicate as the stars in heaven, when seen in their strange groups and goings. Neither does it mean what is nowadays called individualism. The so-called individualism is no more than a cheap egotism, every self-conscious little ego assuming unbounded rights to display his self-consciousness. We mean none of this. We mean, in the first place, the recognition of the exquisite arresting *manifoldness* of being, multiplicity, plurality, as the stars are plural in their starry singularity. Lump the green flashing Sirius with red Mars, and what will you get? A muddy orb. Aggregate them, and what then? A mere smudgy cloudy nebula. One is one and all alone and ever more shall be so. Enveloped each one in its fathomless abyss of isolation. Magically, vitally alone, flashing with singleness.

Towards *this,* then, we are to educate our children and ourselves. Not towards any infinitely extended consciousness. Not towards any vastness or unlimitedness of any sort. Not towards any inordinate range of understanding or consciousness. Not towards any merging in any whole whatsoever. But delicately, through all the processes of communion and communication, love and consciousness, to the perfect singleness of a full and flashing, orb-like maturity.

And if this is the goal of all our striving and effort, then let us take the first stride by *leaving the child alone,* in his own soul. Take all due care of him, materially; give him all love and tenderness and wrath which the spontaneous soul emits: but always, always, at the very quick, leave him alone. Leave him alone. He is not you and you are not he. He is never to be merged into you nor you into him. Though you love him and he love you, this is but a communion in unfathomable difference, not an identification into oneness. There is *no* living oneness for two people: only a deadly oneness, of merged human beings.

Leave the child *alone*. Alone! That is the great word and world. Suppose the moon went through the sky, loving all the stars, hugging them to her breast, and crushing them into one beam with her. O vile thought! Like a swollen leper the dead moon would roll out of a void and corpse-like sky. Supposing she even caught the star Sirius as he passes low, and embraced him into oneness with herself, so that he merged amorphous into her. Immediately Orion would fall to pieces in the ruined heavens, the planets would drop from their orbits, a vast cataclysm and a rain of ruin in the cosmos.

Sirius must move and flash in his own circumambient space, single. Who knows what strange relation and intercommunion he has with Aldebaran, with the Pole Star, even with ourselves? But whatever his intercommunion, he is never raped from his own singleness, he never falls from his own isolate self.

The same for the child. After the navel-string breaks, he is alone in the aura of his own exquisite and mystic solitariness, and there must be no trespass into this solitariness. He is alone. *Leave* him alone. Never forget. Never forget to leave him alone, within his own soul's inviolability.

Do not be afraid, either, to *drive* him into his own soul's inviolable singleness. A child will trespass. It is born nowadays with an irritable craving to trespass into the nature of its mother. Nay, the parent-child relationship in these nervous days resolves itself into one series of trespasses across the confines of the two natures, till there is some unholy arrest.

Now the *seeking* centres of the human system are the great sympathetic centres. It is from these, and primarily from the solar plexus, that the individual goes forth seeking communion with another being or creature or thing. At the solar plexus the child yearns avidly for the mother, for contact, for unison, for absorption even. A nervous child yearns and frets ceaselessly for complete identification. It wants to merge, to merge back into the mother, with the ceaseless craving of morbid love.

What are we to do when a child a few weeks old is so smitten, nervously craving for the mother and for re-identification with her? What on earth are we to do?

It is quite simple. *Break* the spell. Set up the activity of the volitional centres. For at the volitional centres a creature keeps itself apart, integral, centred in its own isolation. Living as we have done in one mode only, the mode of love, praising as we have done the single mode of unification and identification through love with the beloved, and with all the rest of the universe, we have used all the strength of the upper, mentally directed *will* to break the power of these dark, proud, integral volitional centres of the lower body. And we have almost succeeded. So that human life is born now creeping, parasitic in its tendency. The proud volitional centres of the lower body, those which maintain a human being integral and distinct, these have collapsed, so that the whole individual crawls helplessly and parasitically from the sympathetic centres, to establish himself in a permanent life-oneness with another being, usually the mother. And the mother, too, rejoices in this horrible parasitism of her child, she feels exalted, like God, now she is the host of the parasite.

Break the horrible circle of this lust. Break it. Seize babies away from their mothers, with hard, fierce, terrible hands. Send the volts of fierce anger and severing force violently into the child. Volts of hard, violent anger, that shock the feeble volitional centres into life again. Smack the whimpering child. Smack it sharp and fierce on its small buttocks. With all the ferocity of a living, healthy anger, spank the little tail, till at last the powerful dynamic centres of the spinal system vibrate into life, out of their atrophied torture. It is not too late. Quick, quick, mothers of England, spank your wistful babies. Good God, spank their little bottoms; with sharp, red anger spank them and make men of them. Drive them back. Drive them back from their yearning, loving parasitism; startle them for ever out of their pseudo-angelic wistfulness; cure them with a quick wild yell of all their wonder-child spirituality. Sharp, sharp, before it is too late. Be *fierce* with the little darling, and put hell's temper into its soft little soul. Quick, before we are lost.

Let us get this wide, wistful look out of our children's eyes—this oh-so-spiritual look, varied by an oh-so-spiteful look. Let us cure them of their inordinate sensitiveness and consciousness. Kick the cat out of the room when the cat is a nuisance, and let the baby see you do it. And if the baby whimpers, kick the baby after the cat. In just mercy, do it. And then maybe you'll have a slim-muscled, independent cat that can walk with a bit of moon-devilish defiance, instead of the ravel of knitting-silk with a full belly and a sordid *meeau* which is "Pussy" of our dear domestic hearth. More important than the cat, you'll get a healthily reacting human infant, animal and fierce and not-to-be-coddled, the first signs of a proud man whose neck won't droop like a weak lily, nor reach forward for ever like a puppy reaching to suck, and whose knees won't be aching all his life with a luscious, loose desire to slip into some woman's lap, dear darling, and feel her caress his brow.

This instant moment we've got to start to put some fire into the backbones of our children. Do you know what the backbone is? It is the long sword of the vivid, proud, *dark* volition of man, something primal and creative. Not that miserable mental obstinacy which goes in the name of *will* nowadays. Not a will-to-power or a will-to-goodness or a will-to-love or a will-*to* anything else. All these wills to this, that, and the other are only so many obstinate mechanical directions given to some chosen mental idea. You may choose the idea of power, and fix your mechanical little will on that, as the Germans did; or the idea of love, and fix your equally mechanical and still more obstinate little will on *that,* as we do, privately. And all you'll get is some neurotic automaton or parasite, materialistic as hell. You must be automatic and materialistic once you substitute an ideal pivot for the spontaneous centres.

But at the centres of the primal will, situate in the spinal system, the great volitional centres, here a man arises in his own dark pride and singleness, his own sensual magnificence in single being. Here the flashing indomitable man himself takes rise. It is not any tuppenny mechanical instrumental thing, a will-to-this or a will-to-that.

And these, these great centres of primal proud volition, these, especially in the lower body, are the life-centres that have gone soft and rotten in us. Here we need sharp, fierce reaction: sharp discipline, rigour; fierce, fierce severity. We, who are willing to operate surgically on our physical sick, my God, we must be quick and operate psychically on our psychic sick, or they are done for.

Whipping, beating, yes, these alone will thunder into the moribund centres and bring them to life. Sharp, stinging whipping, keen, fierce smacks, and all the roused fury of reaction in the child, these alone will restore us to psychic health. Away with all mental punishments and reprobation. You *must* rouse the powerful physical reaction of anger, dark flushing anger in the child. You must. You *must* fight him, tooth and nail, if you're going to keep him healthy and alive. And if you're going to be able to love him with warm, rich bowels of love, my heaven, how you must fight him, how openly and fiercely and with no nonsense about it.

Rouse the powerful volitional centres at the base of the spine, and those between the shoulders. Even with stinging rods, rouse them.

IX

In the early years a child's education should be entirely non-mental. Instead of trying to attract an infant's attention, trying to arouse its *notice,* to make it *perceive,* the mother or nurse should mindlessly put it into contact with the physical universe. What is the first business of the baby? To ascertain the physical reality of its own context, even of its own very self. It has to learn to wave its little hands and feet. To a baby it is for a long time a startling thing, to find its own hand waving. It does not know what is moving, nor how it moves. It is quite unconscious of having inaugurated the motion, as a cat is unconscious of what makes the shadow after which it darts, or in what its own elusive tail-tip consists. So a baby marvels over the transit of this strange *something* which moves again and again across its own little vision. Behold, it is only the small fist. So it watches and watches. What is it doing?

When a baby absorbedly, almost painfully watches its own vagrant and spasmodic fist, is it trying to form a concept of that fist? Is it trying to formulate a little idea? "That is *my* fist: it is *I* who move it: I wave it *so,* and *so!*"–Not at all. The concept of *I* is quite late in forming. Some children do not realize that they are themselves until they are four or five years old. They are something objective to themselves: "Jackie wants it"–"Baby wants it"–and not "*I* want it." In the same way with the hand or the foot. A child for some years has no *conception* of its own foot as part of itself. It is "*the* foot." In most languages it is always "the foot, the hand," and not "my foot, my hand." But in English the ego is very insistent. We put it self-consciously in possession as soon as possible.

None the less, it is some time before a child is possessed of its own ego. A baby watches its little fist waving through the air, perilously near its nose. What is it doing, thinking about the fist? NO! It is establishing the *rapport* or connexion between the primary affective centres which controls the fist. From the deep sympathetic plexus leaps out an impulse. The fist waves, wildly, to the peril of the little nose. It waves, does it! It leaps, it moves! And from the fountain of impulse deep in the little breast, it moves. But there is also a quiver of fear because of this spasmodic, convulsive motion. Fear! And the first volitional centre of the upper body struggles awake, between the shoulders. It moves, the arm moves, ah, convulsively, wildly, wildly! Ah, look, beyond control it moves, spurting from the wild source of impulse. Fear and ecstasy! Fear and ecstasy! But the other dawning power obtrudes. Shall it move, the wildly waving little arm? Then look, it shall move smoothly, it shall not flutter abroad. So! And so! Such a swing means such a balance, such an explosion of force means a leap in such and such a direction.

The volitional centre in the shoulders establishes itself bit by bit in relation to the sympathetic plexus in the breast, and forms a circuit of spontaneous-voluntary intelligence. The volitional centres are those which put us primarily into line with the earth's gravity. The wildly waving infant fist does not know how to swing attuned to the earth's gravity, the omnipresent force of gravity. Life flutters broadcast in the baby's arm. But at the thoracic ganglion acts a new vital power, which gradually seizes the motor energy that comes explosive from the sympathetic centre, and ranges it in line with all kinetic force, in line with the mysterious, omnipresent centre-pull of the earth's great gravity. There is a true circuit now between the earth's centre and the centre of ebullient energy in the child. Everything depends on these true, polarized or orbital circuits. There is no disarray, no haphazard.

Once the flux of life from the spontaneous centres is put into its true kinetic relation with the earth's centre, adjusted to the force of gravity; once the gravitation of the baby's hand is spontaneously accepted and realized in the primary affective centres of the baby's psyche, then that little hand can take true and voluntary direction. The volitional centre is the pole that relates us, kinetically, to the earth's centre. The sympathetic plexus is the source whence the movement-impulse leaps out. Connect the two centres into a perfect circuit, and then, the moment the baby's fist leaps out for the tassel on its cradle, the volitional ganglion swings the leaping fist truly to its goal.

But this requires practice, for a baby. And in the course of the practice the infant bangs its own nose and swings its arm too far, so that it hurts, and brings a fair amount of trouble upon itself. But in the end, the fluttering, palpitating movement of the first days becomes a true and perfect flight, a gesture, a motion.

Has the mind got anything to do with all this? Does there enter any *idea* of movement into the baby's head, does the child form any conception of what it is doing? NONE. This whole range of activity and consciousness is non-mental, effective at the primary centres. It is not mere automatism. Far from it. It is *spontaneous consciousness,* effective and perfect in itself.

And it is in this spontaneous consciousness that education arises. One of the reasons why uneducated peasant nurses are on the whole so much better for infants than over-conscious mothers is that an uneducated nurse does not introduce any *idea* into her attitude towards the child. When she claps her hands before the child, again and again, nods, smiles, coos, and claps again, she is stimulating the infant to motion, pure, mindless motion. She wants the child to clap too. She wants its one little hand to find the other little hand, she wants to start the quick touch-and-go in the little shoulders. When you see her, time after time, making a fierce, wild gesture with her arm, before the eyes of the baby, and the baby laughing and chuckling, she is rousing the infant to the same fierce, free, reckless *geste*. Fierce, free, wild, reckless *geste!* How it excites the child to a quaint reckless chuckle! How it wakes in him the desire, the impulse for free, sheer motion! It starts the proud *geste* of independence.

This is the clue to early education: movement, physical motion, the attuning of the kinetic energy of the motor centres to the vast sway of the earth's centre. Without this we are nothing: clumsy, mechanical clowns, or pinched little automata.

But if you are going to make use of this form of education you must find teachers full of physical life and zest, of fine, physical, motor intelligence, and mentally rather stupid, or at least quiescent. Above all things, the *idea,* like a strangling worm, must not creep into the motor centres. It must be excluded. If we move, we must move primarily like a bird in the sky, which swings in supreme adjustment to the multiple forces of the winds of heaven and the pull of earth, mindless, idea-less, a speck of perfect physical animation. That is the whole point of real physical life: its joy in spontaneous mindless animation, in motion sheer and superb, like a leaping fish or a hovering hawk or a deer which bounds away, creatures which have never known the pride and the blight of the idea. The idea is a glorious thing in its place. But interposed in all our living, interpolated into our every gesture, it is like some fatal mildew crept in, some vile blight.

Let children be taught the pride of clear, clean movement. If it only be putting a cup on the table, or a book on a shelf, let it be a fine pure motion, not a slovenly shove. Parents and teachers should be keen as hawks, watching their young in motion. Do we imagine that a young hawk learns to fly and stoop, does a young swallow learn to skim, or a hare to dash uphill, or a hound to turn and seize him in full course, without long, keen pain of learning? Where there is no pain of effort there is a wretched, drossy degeneration, like the hateful cluttered sheep of our lush pastures. Look at the lambs, how they explode with new life, and skip up into the air. Already a *little* bit gawky! And then look at their mothers. Whereas a wild sheep is a fleet, fierce thing, leaping and swift like the sun.

So with our children. We, parents and teachers, must prevent their degenerating into physical cloddishness or mechanical affectation or fluttered nervousness. We must be after them, fiercely, sharpen and chasten their movements, their bearing, their walk. If a boy slouches out of a door, throw a book at him, like lightning. That will make him jump into keen and handsome alertness. And if a girl comes creeping, whining in, seize her by her pigtail and run her out again, full speed. That will bring the fire to her eyes and the poise to her head: if she's got any fire in her: and if she hasn't, why, give her a good knock to see if you can drive some in.

Anything, anything rather than the nervous, twisting, wistful, pathetic, centreless children we are cursed with: or the fat and self-satisfied, sheep-in-the-pasture children who are becoming more common: or the impudent, I'm-as-good-as-anybody smirking children who are far too numerous. But it's all our own fault. We're afraid to *fight* with our children, and so we let them degenerate. Poor loving parents *we* are!

There must be a fight. There must be an element of danger, always. How do the wild animals get their grace, their beauty, their allure? Through being on the *qui vive,* always on the *qui vive.* A lark on a sand-dune springs up to heaven in song. She leaps up in a pure, fine strength. She trills out in triumph, she is beside herself in mid-heaven. But let her mind her p's and q's. In the first place, if she doesn't flick her wings finely and rapidly, with exquisite skilful energy, she'll come a cropper to earth. Let her mind the winds of heaven, in the first place. And in the second, let her mind the shadow of Monsieur the kestrel. And in the third place, let her be wary how she drops. And in the fourth place, let her be wary of who sees her dropping. For, the moment she alights on this bristling earth she's got to dart to cover, and cut some secret track to her nest, or she's likely to be in trouble. It's all very well climbing a ladder of song to heaven. But you've got to have your wits about you all the time, even while you're cock-a-lorying on your ladder: and *inevitably* you've got to climb down. Mind you don't give your enemies too good a chance, that's all. And watch it that you don't indicate where your nest is, or your ladder of song will have been a sore business. On the *qui vive,* bright lark!

So with our children. On the *qui vive.* The old-fashioned parents were right, when they made their children watch what they were about. But old-fashioned parents were a bore, dragging in moral and religious justification. If we are to chase our children, and chasten them too, it must be because they make our blood boil, not because some ethical or religious code sanctifies us.

"Miss, if you eat in that piggish, mincing fashion, you shall go without a meal or two."

"Why?"

"Because you're an objectionable sight."

"Well, you needn't look at me."

Here Miss should get a box on the ear.

"Take that! And know that I *need* look at you, since I'm responsible for you. And since I'm responsible for you, I'll watch it you don't behave like a mincing little pig."

Observe, no morals, no "What will people think of you?" or "What would your Daddy say?" or "What if Aunt Lucy saw you now!" or "It's wrong for little girls to be mincing and ugly!" or "You'll be sorry for it when you grow up!" or "I thought you were a good little girl!" or *"Now,* what did teacher say to you in Sunday-school?"—None of all these old dodges for shifting responsibility somewhere else. The plain fact is that parents and teachers *are* responsible for the bearing and developing of their children, so they may as well accept the responsibility flatly, and without dodges.

"I am responsible for the way you grow up, milady, and I'll fulfil my responsibility. So stop pushing your food about on your plate and looking like a self-conscious cockatoo, or leave the table and walk well out of my sight."

This is the tone that any honourable parent would take, seeing his little girl mincing and showing off at dinner. Let us keep the bowels of our compassion alive, and also the bowels of our wrath. No priggish brow-beating and mechanical authority, nor any disapproving superiority, but a plain, open anger when anger is aroused, and pleasure when this is waked.

The parent who sits at table in pained but disapproving silence while the child makes a nuisance of itself, and says: "Dear, I should be *so* glad if you would try to like your pudding: or if you don't like it, have a little bread-and-butter," and who goes on letting the brat be a nuisance, this ideal parent is several times at fault. First she is assuming a pained ideal aloofness which is the worst form of moral bullying, a sort of *Of course I won't interfere, but I am in the right* attitude which is insufferable. If a parent is in the right, then she *must* interfere, otherwise why does she bring up her child at all? If she doesn't interfere, what right has she to assume any virtue of superiority? Then, when she is angry with the child, what right has she to say "Dear," which term implies a state of affectionate communion? This prefixing of the ideal rebuke with the term "Dear" or "Darling" is a hateful travesty of all good feeling. It is using love or affection as a bullying weapon: which vile, sordid act the idealist is never afraid to commit. It is assuming authority of love, when love, as an emotional relationship, can have no authority. Authority must rest on responsible wisdom, and love must be a spontaneous thing, or nothing: an emotional *rapport*. Love and authority have nothing to do with one another. "Whom the Lord loveth, He chasteneth." True! But the Lord's love is not supposed to be an emotional business, but a sort of divine responsibility and purpose. And so is parental love, a responsibility and a living purpose, not an emotion. To make the *emotion* responsible for the purpose is a fine falsification. One says "Dear" or "Darling" when the heart opens with spontaneous cherishment, not when the brow draws with anger or irritation. But the deep purpose and responsibility of parenthood remains unchanged no matter how the emotions flow. The emotions should flow unfalsified, in the very strength of that purpose.

Therefore parents should *never* seek justification outside themselves. They should never say, "I do this for your good." You *don't* do it for the child's good. Parental responsibility is much deeper than an ideal responsibility. It is a vital connexion. Parent and child are polarized together still, somewhat as before birth. When the child in the womb kicks, it may almost hurt the parent. And the reaction is just as direct during all the course of childhood and parenthood. When a child is loose or ugly it is a direct *hurt* to the parent. The parent reacts and retaliates spontaneously. There is no justification, save the bond of parenthood, and certainly there is no ideal intervention.

We must accept the bond of parenthood primarily as a vital, mindless conjunction, non-ideal, passional. A parent *owes* the child all the natural passional reactions provoked. If a child provokes anger, then to deny it this anger, the open, passional anger, is as bad as to deny it food or love. It causes an atrophy in the child, at the volitional centres, and a perversion of the true life-flow.

Why are we so afraid of anger, of wrath, and clean, fierce rage? What cowardice possesses us? Why would we reduce a child to a nervous, irritable wreck, rather than spank it wholesomely? Why do we make such a fuss about a row? A row, a fierce storm in a family is a natural and healthy thing, which we ought even to have the courage to enjoy and exult in, as we can enjoy and exult in a storm of the elements. What makes us so namby-pamby? We ought all to fight: husbands and wives, parents and children, sisters and brothers and friends, all ought to fight, fiercely, freely, openly: and they ought to enjoy it. It stiffens the backbone and makes the eyes flash. Love without a fight is nothing but degeneracy. But the fight must be spontaneous and natural, without fixities and perversions.

The same with parenthood: spontaneous and natural, without any ideal taint.

And this is the beginning of true education: first, the stimulus to physical motion, physical trueness and *élan*, which is given to the infant. And this is continued during the years of early childhood *not by deliberate instruction,* but by the keen, fierce, unremitting swiftness of the parent, whose warm love opens the valves of glad motion in the child, so that the child plays in delicious security and freedom, and whose fierce, vigilant anger sharpens the child to a trueness and boldness of motion and bearing such as are impossible save in children of strong-hearted parents.

Open the valves of warm love so that your child can play in serene joy by itself, or with others, like young weasels safe in a sunny nook of a wood, or young tiger-cubs whose great parents lie grave and apart, on guard. And open also the sharp valves of wrath, that your child may be alert, keen, proud, and fierce in his turn. Let parenthood and childhood be a spontaneous, animal relationship, non-ideal, swift, a continuous interplay of shadow and light, ever-changing relationship and mood. And, parents, keep in your heart, like tigers, the grave and vivid responsibility of parenthood, remote and natural in you, not fanciful and self-conscious.

X

From earliest childhood, let us have independence, independence, self-dependence. Every child to do all it can for itself, wash and dress itself, clean its own boots, brush and fold its own clothes, fetch and carry for itself, mend its own stockings, boy or girl alike, patch its own garments, and as soon as possible make as well as mend for itself. Man and woman are happy when they are busy, and children the same. But there must be the right motive behind the work. It must not always, for a child, be "Help mother" or "Help father" or "Help somebody." This altruism becomes tiresome, and causes disagreeable reaction. Neither must the motive be the ideal of work. "Work is service, hence work is noble. *Laborare est orare.*" Never was a more grovelling motto than this, that work is prayer. Work is not prayer at all: not in the same category. Work is a practical business, prayer is the soul's yearning and desire. Work is not an ideal, save for slaves. But work is quite a pleasant occupation for a human creature, a natural activity.

And the aim of work is neither the emotional helping of mother and father, nor the ethical-religious service of mankind. Nor is it the greedy piling-up of stupid possessions. An individual works for his own pleasure and independence: but chiefly in the happy pride of personal independence, personal liberty. No man is free who depends on servants. Man can never be quite free. Indeed he doesn't want to be. But in his *personal* immediate life he can be vastly freer than he is.

How? By doing things for himself. Once we wake the quick of personal pride, there is a pleasure in performing our own personal service, every man sweeping his own room, making his own bed, washing his own dishes–or in proportion: just as a soldier does. We have got a mistaken notion of ourselves. We conceive of ourselves as ideal beings, nothing but consciousness, and therefore actual work has become degrading, menial to us. But let us change our notion of ourselves. We are only in part ideal beings. For the rest we are lively physical creatures whose life consists in motion and action. We have two feet which need tending, and which need socks and shoes. This is our own personal affair, and it behoves us to see to it. Let me look after my own socks and shoes, since these are private to me. Let me tend to my own apparel and my own personal service. Every bird builds its own nest and preens its own feathers: save perhaps a cuckoo or a filthy little sparrow which likes to oust a swallow, or a crazy ostrich which squats in the sand. Proud personal privacy, personal liberty, gay individual self-dependence. Awake in a child the gay, proud sense of its own aloof individuality, and it will busy itself about its own affairs happily. It all depends what centre you try to drive from, what motive is at the back of all your movement. It is just as irksome to *have* a servant as to *be* a servant: particularly a personal servant. A servant moving about me, or even anybody moving about me, doing things for me, is a horrible drag on my freedom. I feel it as a sort of prostitution. *Noli me tangere.* It is our motto as it is the motto of a wild wolf or deer. I want about me a clear, cool space across which nobody trespasses. I want to remain intact within my own natural isolation, save at those moments when I am drawn to a rare and significant intimacy. The horrible personal promiscuity of our life is extremely ugly and distasteful. As far as possible, let *nobody* do anything for me, personally, save those who are near and dear to me: and even then as little as possible. Let me be by myself, and leave me my native distance. *Sono io*–and not a thing of public convenience.

Self-dependence is independence. To be free one must be self-sufficient, particularly in small, material, personal matters. In the great business of love, or friendship, or living human intercourse one meets and communes with another free individual; there is no service. Service is degrading, both to the servant and the one served: a promiscuity, a sort of prostitution. No one should do for me that which I can reasonably do for myself. Two individuals may be intimately interdependent on one another, as man and wife, for example. But even in this relation each should be as self-dependent, as self-supporting as ever possible. We should be each as single in our independence as the wild animals are. That is the only true pride. To have a dozen servants is to be twelve times prostituted in human relationship, sold and bought and automatized, divested of individual singleness and privacy.

The actual doing things is in itself a joy. If I wash the dishes I learn a quick, light touch of china and earthenware, the feel of it, the weight and roll and poise of it, the peculiar hotness, the quickness or slowness of its surface. I am at the middle of an infinite complexity of motions and adjustments and quick, apprehensive contacts. Nimble faculties hover and play along my nerves, the primal consciousness is alert in me. Apart from all the moral or practical satisfaction derived from a thing well done, I have the *mindless* motor activity and reaction in primal consciousness, which is a pure satisfaction. If I am to be well and satisfied, as a human being, a large part of my life must pass in mindless motion, quick, busy activity in which I am neither bought nor sold, but acting alone and free from the centre of my own active isolation. Not self-consciously, however. Not watching my own reactions. If I wash dishes, I wash them to get them clean. Nothing else.

Every man must learn to be proud and single and alone, and after that, he will be worth knowing. Mankind has degenerated into a conglomerate mass, where everybody strives to look and to be as much as possible an impersonal, non-individual, abstracted unit, a standard. A high *standard* of perfection: that's what we talk about. As if there could be any *standard* among living people, all of whom are separate and single, each one natively distinguished from every other one. Yet we all wear boots made for the abstract "perfect" or standard foot, and coats made as near as possible for the abstract shoulders of Mr. Everyman.

I object to the abstract Mr. Everyman being clapped over me like an extinguisher. I object to wearing his coat and his boots and his hat. Me, in a pair of "Lotus" boots, and a "Burberry," and "Oxonian" hat, why, I might just as well be anybody else. And I strenuously object. I am myself, and I don't want to be rigged out as a poor specimen of Mr. Everyman. I don't want to be standardized, or even idealized.

If I could, I would make my own boots and my own trousers and coats. I suppose even now I could if I would. But in Rome one must do as Rome does: the bourgeois is not worth my while, I can't demean myself to *épater* him, and I am much too sensitive to my own isolation to want to draw his attention.

Although in Rome one must do as Rome does; and although all the world is Rome today, yet even Rome falls. Rome fell, and Rome will fall again. That is the point.

And it is to prepare for this fall of Rome that we conjure up a new system of education. When I say that every boy shall be taught cobbling and boot-making, it is in the hopes that before long a man will make his own boots to his own fancy. If he likes to have Maltese sandals, why, he'll have Maltese sandals; and if he likes better high-laced buskins, why, he can stalk like an Athenian tragedian. Anyhow he'll sit happily devising his own covering for his own feet, and machine-made boots be hanged. They even hurt him, and give him callosities. And yet, so far, he thinks their machine-made standardized nullity is perfection. But wait till we have dealt with him. He'll be gay-shod to the happiness and vanity of his own toes and to the satisfaction of his own desire. And the same with his trousers. If he fancies his legs, and likes to flutter on his own elegant stem, like an Elizabethan, here's to him. And if he has a hankering after scarlet trunk-hose, I say hurray. *Chacun a son goût:* or ought to have. Unfortunately nowadays nobody has his own taste; everybody is trying to turn himself into a eunuch Mr. Everyman, standardized to his collar-stud. A woman is a little different. She wants to look ultra-smart and *chic* beyond words. And so she knows that if she can set all women bitterly asking "Isn't her dress Paquin?" or "Surely it's Poiret," or Lucile, or Chéruit, or somebody *very* Parisian, why, she's done it. She wants to create an *effect:* not the effect of being just *herself,* her one and only self, as a flower in all its spots and frills is its own candid self. Not at all. A modern woman wants to hit you in the eye with her get-up. She wants to be a picture. She wants to derive her own nature from her accoutrements. Put her in a khaki uniform and she's a man shrilly whistling K-K-K-Katie. Let her wear no bodice at all, but just a row of emeralds and an aigrette, and she's a *cocotte* before she's eaten her hors-d'œuvre, even though she was a Bible worker all her life. She lays it all on from the outside, powders her very soul.

But of course, when the little girls from *our* schools grow up they will really consider the lily, and put forth their flowers from their own roots. See them, the darlings, the women of the future, silent and rapt, spinning their own fabric out of their own instinctive souls—and cotton and linen and silk and wool into the bargain, of course—and delicately unfolding the skirts and bodices, or the loose Turkish trousers and little vests, or whatever else they like to wear, evolving and unfurling them in sensitive form, according to their own instinctive desire. She puts on her clothes as a flower unfolds its petals, as an utterance from her own nature, instinctive and individual.

Oh, if only people can learn to do as they like and to have what they like, instead of madly aspiring to do what everybody likes and to look as everybody would like to look. Fancy everybody looking as everybody else likes, and nobody looking like anybody. It sounds like Alice in Wonderland. A well-dressed woman before her mirror says to herself, if she is satisfied: "Every woman would like to look as I look now. Every woman will envy me."

Which is absurd. Fancy a petunia leaning over to a geranium and saying: "Ah, miss, *wouldn't* you just love to be in mauve and white, like me, instead of that common turkey-red!" To which the geranium: "You! In your cheap material! You don't look more than one-and-a-ha'penny a yard. You'd thank your lucky stars if you had an inch of *chiffon velvet* to your name."

Of course, a petunia is a petunia, and a geranium is a geranium. And I'll bet Solomon in all his glory was not arrayed like one of these. Why? Because he was trying to cut a dash and look like something beyond nature, overloading himself. Without doubt Solomon in all his nakedness was a lovely thing. But one has a terrible misgiving about Solomon in all his glory. David probably unfolded his nakedness into clothes that came naturally from him. But that Jewish glory of Solomon's suggests diamonds in lumps. Though we may be wrong, and Solomon in all his glory may have moved in fabrics that rippled naturally from him as his own hair, and his jewels may have glowed as his soul glowed, intrinsic. Let us hope so, in the name of wisdom.

All of which may seem a long way from the education of the people. But it isn't really. It only means to say, don't set up standards and regulation patterns for people. Don't have criteria. Let every individual be single and self-expressive: not self-expressive in the self-conscious, smirking fashion, but busy making something he *needs* and wants to have just so, according to his own soul's desire. Everyone individually and spontaneously busy, like a bird that builds its own nest and preens its own feathers, busy about its own business, alone and unaware.

The fingers must almost live and think by themselves. It is no good working from the idea, from the fancy: the creation must evolve itself from the vital activity of the fingers. Here's the difference between living evolving work and that ideal mental business we call "handicraft instruction" or "handwork" in school today.

Dozens of high-souled idealists sit today at hand-looms and spiritually weave coarse fabrics. It is a high-brow performance. As a rule it comes to an end. But sometimes it achieves another effect. Sometimes actually the mind is lulled, by the steady repetition of mechanical, productive labour, into a kind of swoon. Gradually the idealism moults away, the high-brow resolves into a busy, unconscious worker, perhaps even a night-and-day slogger, absorbed in the process of work.

One should go to the extremity of any experience. But that one should stay there, and make a habit of the extreme, is another matter. A great part of the life of every human creature should pass in mindless, active occupation. But not all the days. There is a time to work, and a time to be still, a time to think, and a time to forget. And they are all different times.

The point about any handwork is that it should not be mind-work. Supposing we are to learn to solder a kettle. The theory is told in a dozen words. But it is not a question of applying a theory. It is a question of *knowing*, by direct physical contact, your kettle-substance, your kettle-curves, your solder, your soldering-iron, your fire, your resin, and all the fusing, slipping interaction of all these. A question of direct knowing by contact, not a question of understanding. The mental understanding of what is happening is quite unimportant to the job. If you are of an inquiring turn of mind, you can inquire afterwards. But while you are at the job, *know* what you're doing, and don't bother about understanding. Know by immediate sensual contact. Know by the tension and reaction of the muscles, know, know profoundly but for ever untellably, at the spontaneous primary centres. Give yourself in an intense, mindless attention, almost as deep as sleep, but not charged with random dreams, charged with potent effectiveness. Busy, intent, absorbed work, forgetfulness, this is one of the joys of life. Thoughts may be straying through the mind all the time. But there is no attention to them. They stream on like dreams, irrelevant. The soul is attending with joy and active purpose to the kettle and the soldering-iron; the mindless psyche concentrates intent on the unwilling little rivulet of solder which runs grudgingly under the nose of the hot tool. To be or not to be. Being isn't a conscious effort, anyhow.

So we realize that there must be a deep gulf, an oblivion, between pedagogy and handwork. Don't let a pedagogue come fussing about in a workshop. He will only muddle up the instincts.

Not that a schoolmaster is necessarily a pedagogue. Poor devil, he starts by being a man, and it isn't always easy to turn a man into that thing. And therefore many a schoolmaster is a thousand times happier turning a lathe or soldering a kettle than expounding long division. But the two activities are incompatible. Not incompatible in the same individual, but incompatible with each other. So, separate the two activities. Let the pedagogue of the morning disappear in the afternoon. If he appears in a workshop, let it be before children who have not known him as a school-teacher.

And in the workshop, let real jobs be done. Workshops may be mere tin sheds, or wooden sheds. Let the parents send the household kettles, broken chairs, boots and shoes, simple tailoring and sewing and darning and even cooking, to the workshop. Let the family business of this sort be given to the children, who will set off to the work-shed and get the job done, under supervision, in the hours of occupation. A good deal can be done that way, instead of the silly theoretic fussing making fancy knickknacks or specimen parts, such as goes on at present.

What we want is for every child to be *handy:* physically adaptable, and handy. If a boy shows any desire to go forward in any craft, he will have his opportunity. He can go on till he becomes an expert. But he must start by being, like Jack at sea, just a handy man. The same with a girl.

Let the handwork be a part of the family and communal life, an extension of family life. Don't muddle it up with the mindwork. Mindwork at its best is theoretic. Our present attempts to make mindwork "objective" and physical, and to instil theoretic mathematics through carpentry and joinery is silly. If we are teaching arithmetic, let us teach pure arithmetic, without bothering with piles of sham pennies and shillings and pounds of sham sugar. In actual life, when we do our shopping, every one of our calculations is made quickly in abstraction: a pure mental act, everything abstracted. And let our mental acts be pure mental acts, not adulterated with "objects." What ails modern education is that it is trying to cram primal physical experience into mental activity—with the result of mere muddledness. Pure physical experience takes place at the great affective centres, and is *de facto* pre-mental, non-mental. Mental experience on the other hand is pure and different, a process of abstraction, and therefore *de facto* not physical.

If our consciousness is dual, and active in duality; if our human activity is of two incompatible sorts, why try to make a mushy oneness of it? The *rapport* between the mental consciousness and the affective or physical consciousness is always a polarity of contradistinction. The two are never one save in their incomprehensible duality. Leave the two modes of activity separate. What connexion is necessary will be effected spontaneously.

XI

The essence of most games, let us not forget, lies in the element of *contest:* contest in force, contest in skill, contest in wit. The essence of work, on the other hand, lies in single, absorbed, mindless productivity. Now here again we have done our best to muck up the natural order of things. All along the line we have tried to introduce the mean and impoverishing factor of *emulation* into work-activities, and we have tried to make games as little as possible contests, and as much as possible fanciful self-conscious processes.

Work is an absorbed and absorbing process of productivity. Introduce this mean motive of emulation, and you cause a flaw at once in the absorption. You introduce a worm-like *arrière-pensée;* you corrupt the true state. Pah, it makes us sick to think of the glib spuriousness which is doled out to young school-teachers, purporting to be "theory of education." The whole system seems to be a conspiracy to falsify and corrupt human nature, introduce an element of meanness, duplicity, and self-consciousness. Emulation is a dirty spirit, introduced into work, a petty, fostered jealousy and affectation. And this is true whether the work be mental or physical.

On the other hand, rivalry is a natural factor in all sport and in practically all games, simple, natural rivalry, the spirit of contest.

Again let us draw attention to a duality in the human psychic activity. There is the original duality between the physical and the mental psyche. And now there is another duality, a duality of mode and direction chiefly: the natural distinction between productive and contestive activities. The state of soul of a man engaged in productive activity is, when pure, quite distinct from that of the same man engaged in some competitive activity.

Let us note here another fatal defect in our modern system. Having attempted, according to ideals, to convert all life and all living into one mode only, the productive mode, we have been forced to introduce into our productive activities the spirit of contest which is original and ineradicable in us. This spirit of contest takes the form of competition: commercial, industrial, spiritual, educational, and even religious competition.

Was ever anything more humiliating than this spectacle of a mankind active in nothing but productive competition, all idea of pure, single-hearted production lost entirely, and all honest fiery contest condemned and tabooed? Here is the clue to the bourgeois. He will have no honest fiery contest. He will have only the mean, Jewish competition in productivity, in money-making. He won't have any single, absorbed production. All work must be a scramble of contest against some other worker.

Is anything more despicable to be conceived? How make an end of it? By separating the two modes. By realizing that man is in at least one-half of his nature a pure fighter—not a competitor competing for some hideous silver mug, or some pot of money—but a fighter, a contester, a warrior.

We must wake again the flashing centres of volition in the fierce, proud backbone, there where we should be superb and indomitable, where we are actually so soft. We can move in herds of self-sacrificing heroism. But laughing defiance has gone out of our shop-keeping world.

And so for the third part of education, games and physical instruction and drill. We are all on the wrong tack again. In the elementary schools physical instruction is a pitiful business, this Swedish drill business. It is a mere pettifogging attempt to turn the body into a mental instrument, and seems warranted to produce nothing but a certain sulky hatred of physical command, and a certain amount of physical self-consciousness.

Physical training and Sandowism altogether is a ridiculous and puerile business. A man sweating and grunting to get his muscles up is one of the maddest and most comical sights. And the modern athlete parading the self-conscious mechanism of his body, reeking with a degraded physical, muscular self-consciousness and nothing but self-consciousness, is one of the most stupid phenomena mankind has ever witnessed. The physique is all right in itself. But to have your physique in your head, like having sex in the head, is unspeakably repulsive. To have your own physique on your mind all the time: why, it is a semi-pathological state, the exact counterpoise to the querulous, peevish invalid.

To have one's mind full of one's own physical self, and to have one's own physical self pranking and bulging under one's own mental direction is a good old perversion. The athlete is perhaps, of all the self-conscious objects of our day, the most self-consciously objectionable.

It is all wrong to mix up the two modes of consciousness. To the physique belongs the mindless, spontaneous consciousness of the great plexuses and ganglia. To the mind belongs pure abstraction, the *idea*. To drag down the idea into a bulging athletic physique; and to drag the body up into the head, till it becomes an obsession: horror.

Let the two modes of consciousness act in their duality, reciprocal, but polarized in difference, not to be muddled and transfused. If you are going to be physically active, physically strenuous and conscious, then *put off your mental attention,* put off all idea, and become a mindless physical spontaneous Consciousness.

Away with all physical culture. Banish it to the limbo of human prostitutions: self-prostitution as it is: the prostitution of the primary self to the secondary idea.

If you will have the gymnasium: and certainly let us have the gymnasium: let it be to get us ready for the great *contests* and games of skill. Never, never let the motive be self-produced, the act self-induced. It is as bad as masturbation. Let there be the profound motive of *battle*. Battle, battle; let that be the word that rouses us to pure physical efforts.

Not Mons or Ypres, of course. Ah, the horror of machine explosions! But living, naked battle, flesh-to-flesh contest. Fierce, tense struggle of man with man, struggle to the death. That is the spirit of the gymnasium. Fierce, unrelenting, honourable contest.

Let all physical culture be pure *training:* training for the contest, and training for the expressive dance. Let us have a gymnasium as the Greeks had it, and for the same purpose: the purpose of pure, perilous delight in contest, and profound, mystic delight in unified motion. Drop morality. But don't drop morality until you've dropped ideal self-consciousness.

Set the boys one against the other like young bantam cocks. Let them fight. Let them hurt one another. Teach them again to fight with gloves and fists, egg them on, spur them on. Let it be fine balanced contest in skill and fierce pride. Egg them on, and look on the black eye and the bloody nose as insignia of honour, like the Germans of old.

Bring out the foils and teach fencing. Teach fencing, teach wrestling, teach ju-jutsu, every form of fierce hand-to-hand contest. And praise the wounds. And praise the valour that will be killed rather than yield. Better fierce and unyielding death than our degraded creeping life.

We are all fighters. Let us fight. Has it come down to chasing a poor fox and kicking a leather ball? Heaven, what a spectacle we should be to the Lacedaemonian. Rouse the old male spirit again. The male is always a fighter. The human male is a superb and godlike fighter, unless he is contravened in his own nature. In fighting to the death he has one great crisis of his being.

What, are we going to revoke our own being? Are we going to soften and soften in self-sacrificial ardour till we are white worms? Are we going to get our battle out of some wretched competition in trade or profession?

We will have a new education, where a black eye is a sign of honour, and where men strip stark for the fierce business of the fight.

What is the fight? It is a primary physical thing. It is not a horrible obscene ideal process, like our last war. It is not a ghastly and blasphemous translation of ideas into engines, and men into cannon-fodder. Away with such war. A million times away with such obscenity. Let the desire of it die out of mankind.

But let us keep the real war, the real fight. And what is the fight? It is a sheer immediate conflict of physical men: that, and that best of all. What does death matter, if a man die in a flame of passionate conflict? He goes to heaven, as the ancients said: somehow, somewhere his soul is at rest, for death is to him a passional consummation.

But to be blown to smithereens while you are eating a sardine: horrible and monstrous abnormality. The soul should leap fiery into death, a consummation. Then nothing is lost. But our horrible cannon-fodder!–let us go the right way about making an end of it.

And the right way, and the only way, is to rouse new, living, passionate desires and activities in the soul of man. Your universal brotherhood, league-of-nations smoshiness and pappiness is no good. It will end in foul hypocrisy, and nothing can ever prevent its so ending.

It is a sort of idiocy to talk about putting an end to all fighting, and turning all energy into some commercial or trades-union competition. What is a fight? It's not an ideal business. It is a physical business. Perhaps up to now, in our ideal world, war was necessarily a terrific conflict of ideas, engines, and explosives derived out of man's cunning ideas. But now we know we are not ideal beings only: now we know that it is hopeless and wretched to confuse the ideal conscious activity with the primal physical conscious activity: and now we know that true contest belongs to the primal physical self, that ideas, *per se,* are static; why, perhaps we shall have sense enough to fight once more hand-to-hand as fierce, naked men. Perhaps we shall be able to abstain from the unthinkable baseness of pitting one ideal engine against another ideal engine, and supplying human life as the fodder for these ideal machines.

Death is glorious. But to be blown to bits by a machine is mere horror. Death, if it be violent death, should come as a grand passional climax and consummation, and then all is well with the soul of the dead.

The human soul is really capable of honour, once it has a true choice. But when it has a choice only of war with explosive engines and poison-gases, and a universal peace which consists in the most sordid commercial and industrial competition, why, believe me, the human soul will choose war, in the long run, inevitably it will; if only with a remote hope of at last destroying utterly this stinking industrial-competitive humanity.

Man *must* have the choice of war. But, raving, insane idealist as he is, he must no longer have the choice of bombs and poison-gases and Big Berthas. That must not be. Let us beat our soldering-irons into swords, if we will. But let us blow all guns and explosives and poison-gases sky-high. Let us shoot every man who makes one more grain of gunpowder, with his own powder.

After all, we are masters of our own inventions. Are we really so feeble and inane that we cannot get rid of the monsters we have brought forth? Why not? Because we are afraid of somebody else's preserving them? Believe me, there's nothing which every man—except insane criminals, and these we ought to hang right off—there's nothing which every man would be so glad to think had vanished out of the world as guns, explosives, and poison-gases. I don't care when my share in them goes sky-high. I'll take every risk of the Japanese or the Germans having a secret store.

Pah, men are all human, till you drive them mad. And for centuries we have been driving each other mad with our idealism and universal love. Pretty weapons they have spawned, pretty fruits of our madness. But the British people tomorrow could destroy all guns, all explosives, all poison-gases, and all apparatus for the making of these things. Perhaps you might leave one-barrelled pistols: but not another thing. And the world would get on its sane legs the very next day. And we should run no danger at all: danger, perhaps, of the loss of some small property. But nothing at all compared with the great sigh of relief.

It's the only way to do it. Melt down *all* your guns of all sorts. Destroy all your explosives, save what bit you want for quarries and mines. Keep no explosive weapon in England bigger than a one-barrelled pistol, which may live for one year longer. At the end of one year no explosive weapon shall exist.

The world at once starts afresh.–Well, do it. Your confabs and your meetings, your discussions and your international agreements will serve you nothing. League of Nations is all bilberry jam: bilge: and you know it. Put your guns in the fire and drown your explosives, and you've done your share of the League of Nations.

But don't pretend you've abolished war. Send your soldiers to Ireland, if you must send them, armed with swords and shields, but with no *engines* of war. Trust the Irish to come out with swords and shields as well: they'll do it. And then have a rare old lively scrap, such as the heart can rejoice in. But in the name of human sanity, never point another cannon: never. And it lies with Britain to take the lead. Nobody else will.

Then, when all your explosive weapons are destroyed–which may be before Christmas–then introduce a proper system of martial training in the schools. Let every boy and every citizen be a soldier, a fighter. Let him have sword and spear and shield, and know how to use them, Let him be determined to use them, too.

For, what does life consist in? Not in being some ideal little monster, a superman. It consists in remaining inside your own skin, and living inside your own skin, and not pretending you're any bigger than you are. And so, if you've got to go in for a scrap, go in your own skin. Don't turn into some ideal-obscene monster, and invent explosive engines which will blow up an ideal enemy whom you've never set eyes on and probably never will set eyes on. Loathsome and hateful insanity that.

If you have an enemy, even a national enemy, go for him in your own skin. Meet him, see him, come into contact and fierce struggle with him. What good is an enemy if he's only abstract and invisible? That's merely ideal. If he is an enemy he is a flesh-and-blood fellow whom I meet and fight with, to the death. I don't blow bombs into the vast air, hoping to scatter a million bits of indiscriminate flesh. God save us, no more of that.

Let us get back inside our own skins, sensibly and sanely. Let us fight when our dander is up: but hand-to-hand, hand-to-hand, always hand-to-hand. Let us meet a man like a man, not like some horrific idea-born machine.

Let us melt our guns. Let us just simply do it as an act of reckless, defiant sanity. Why be afraid? It is such fear that has caused all the bother. Spit on such fear. After all, it can't do anything so vile as it has done already. Let us have a national holiday, melting the guns and drowning the powder. Let us make a spree of it. Let's have it on the Fifth of November: bushels of squibs and rockets. If we're quick we can have them ready. And as a squib fizzes away, we say, "There goes the guts out of a half-ton bomb."

And then let us be soldiers, hand-to-hand soldiers. Lord, but it is a bitter thing to be born at the end of a rotten, idealistic machine-civilization. Think what we've missed: the glorious bright passion of anger and pride, recklessness and dauntless cock-a-lory.

XII

Our life today is a sort of sliding-scale of shifted responsibility. The man, who is supposed to be the responsible party, as a matter of fact flings himself either at the feet of a woman, and makes her his conscience-keeper; or at the feet of the public. The woman, burdened with the lofty importance of man's conscience and decision, turns to her infant and says: "It is all for you, my sacred child. For *you* are the future!" And the precious baby, saddled with the immediate responsibility of all the years, puckers his poor face and howls: as well he may.

Or the public, meaning the ordinary working-man, being told for the fifty-millionth time that everything is for him, every effort and every move is made for his sake, naturally inquires at length:

"Then why doesn't everything come my way?" To which, under the circumstances, there is no satisfactory answer.

So here we are, grovelling before two gods, the baby-in-arms and the people. In the sliding-scale of shirked responsibility, man puts the golden crown of present importance on the head of the woman, and the nimbus of sanctity round the head of the infant, and then grovels in an ecstasy of worship and self-exoneration before the double idol. A disgusting and shameful sight. After which he gets up and slinks off to his money-making and his commercial competition, and feels holy-holy-holy about it. "It is all for sacred woman and her divine child." The most disillusioning part about woman is that she sits on the Brummagem throne and laps up this worship. The baby, poor wretch, gets a stomach-ache. The other god, poor Demogorgon, the gorgon of the People, is even in a worse state. He sees the idealist kneeling before him, crying: "You are Demos, you are the People, you are the All in All. You have ten million heads and ten million voices and twenty million hands. Ah, how wonderful you are! Hail to you! Hail to you! Hail to you!"

Poor Demogorgon Briareus scratches his ten million heads with ten million of his hands, and feels a bit bothered-like. Because every one of the ten million heads is slow and flustered.

"Do you mean it, though?" he says.

"Ah!" shrieks the idealist. "Listen to the divine voice. Ten million throats, and one message! Divine, divine!"

Unfortunately, each of the ten million throats is a little hoarse, each voice a little clumsy and mistrustful.

"All right, then," mumbles Demogorgon Briareus; "fob out, then."

"Certainly! Certainly! Ah, the bliss with which we sacrifice our all to thee!" And he flings a million farthings at the feet of the many-headed.

Briareus picks up a farthing with one million out of his twenty million hands, turns over the coin, spits on it for luck, and puts it in his pocket. Feels, however, that this isn't everything.

"Now work a little harder for us, Great One, Supreme One," cajoles the idealist.

And Demorgorgon, not knowing any better, but with some misgiving rumbling inside him, sets to for a short spell, whilst the idealist shrills out:

"Behold him, the worker, the producer, the provider! Our Providence, our Great One, our God of gods. Demos! Demogorgon!"

All of which flatters Briareus for a long time, till he realizes once more that if he's as divine as all that he ought to see a few more bradburys fluttering his way. So he strikes, and says: "Look here, what do you mean by it?"

"You're quite right, O Great One," replies the idealist. "You are *always* right, Almighty Demos. Only don't stop working, otherwise the whole universe, which is *yours,* mind you, will stop working too. And *then* where will you be?"

Demos thinks there's something in it, so he slogs at it again. But always with a bee buzzing in his bonnet. Which bee stings him from time to time, and then he jumps, and the world jumps with him.

It's time to get the bee out of the bonnet of Briareus, or he'll be jumping right on top of us, he'll become a real Demogorgon.

"Keep still, Demos, my dear. You've got a nasty wasp in your bowler. Keep still; it's dangerous if it stings you. Let me get it out for you."

And so we begin to remove the lie which the idealist has slipped us.

"You're big, Briareus, my dear fellow. You've got ten million heads. But every one of your ten million heads works rather slowly, and not one of your twenty million eyes sees much further than the end of your nose: which is only about an inch and a half, and not ten-million times an inch and a half. And your great ten-million-times voice, rather rough and indistinct, though of course *very* loud, doesn't really tell me anything, Briareus, Demos, O Democracy. Your wonderful cross which you make with your ten-million hands when you vote, it's a stupid and meaningless little mark. You don't know what you're doing: and anyhow it's only a choice of evils, on whose side you put your little cross. A thing repeated ten million times isn't any more important for the repetition: it's a weary, stupid little thing. Go now; be still, Briareus, and let a better man than yourself think for you, with his one clear head. For you must admit that ten million muddled heads are not better than one muddled head, and have no more right to authority. So just be quiet, Briareus, and listen with your twenty million ears to one clear voice, and one bit of sense, and one word of truth. No, don't ramp and gnash your ten million sets of teeth. You won't come it over us with any of your Demogorgon turns. We shan't turn to stone. We shall think what a fool you are."

The same with the infant.

"My poor, helpless child, let's get this nimbus off, so that you can sleep in comfort. There now, play with your toes and digest your pap in peace; the future isn't yours for many a day. We'll look after the present. And that's all *you* will be able to do. Take care of the present, and the past and future can take care of themselves."

After which, to the woman enthroned:

"I'm sorry to trouble you, my dear, but do you mind coming down? We want that throne for a pigeon-place. And do you mind if I put a bottom in your crown? It'll make a good cake-tin. You can bake a nice dethronement-cake in it. You and I, my dear, we've had enough of this worship farce. You're nothing but a woman, a human female creature, and I'm nothing but a man, a human male creature, and there's absolutely no call for worship on either hand. The fact that you're female doesn't mean that I ought to set about worshipping you, and the fact that I'm male doesn't intend to start you worshipping me. It's all bunkum and lies, this worshipping process, anyhow. We're none of us gods: just two-legged human creatures. You're just yourself, and I'm just myself; we're different, and we'll agree to differ. No more of this puffing-up business. It makes us sick.

"You are yourself, a woman, and I'm myself, a man: and that makes a breach between us. So let's leave the breach, and walk across occasionally on some suspension-bridge. But you live on one side, and I live on the other. Don't let us interfere with each other's side. We can meet and have a chat and swing our legs mid-stream on the bridge. But you live on that side and I on this. You're not a man and I'm not a woman. Don't let's pretend we are. Let us stick to our own side, and meet like the magic foreigners we are. There's much more fun in it. Don't bully me, and I won't bully you.

"I've got most of the thinking, abstracting business to do, and most of the mechanical business, so let me do it. I hate to see a woman trying to be abstract, and being abstract, just as I hate and loathe to see a woman doing mechanical work. You hate me when I'm feminine. So I'll let you be womanly; you let me be manly. You look after the immediate personal life, and I'll look after the further, abstracted, and mechanical life. You remain at the centre, I scout ahead. Let us agree to it, without conceit on either side. We're neither better nor worse than each other; we're an equipoise in difference—but in difference, mind, not in sameness."

And then, beyond this, let the men scout ahead. Let them go

always ahead of their women, in the endless trek across life. Central, with the wagons, travels the woman, with the children and the whole responsibility of immediate, personal living. And on ahead, scouting, fighting, gathering provision, running on the brink of death and at the tip of the life advance, all the time hovering at the tip of life and on the verge of death, the men, the leaders, the outriders.

And between men let there be a new, spontaneous relationship, a new fidelity. Let men realize that their life lies ahead, in the dangerous wilds of advance and increase. Let them realize that they must go beyond their women, projected into a region of greater abstraction, more inhuman activity.

There, in these womanless regions of fight, and pure thought and abstracted instrumentality, let men have a new attitude to one another. Let them have a new reverence for their heroes, a new regard for their comrades: deep, deep as life and death.

Let there be again the old passion of deathless friendship between man and man. Humanity can never advance into the new regions of unexplored futurity otherwise. Men who can only hark back to woman become automatic, static. In the great move ahead, in the wild hope which rides on the brink of death, men go side by side, and faith in each other alone stays them. They go side by side. And the extreme bond of deathless friendship supports them over the edge of the known and into the unknown.

Friendship should be a rare, choice, immortal thing, sacred and inviolable as marriage. Marriage and deathless friendship, both should be inviolable and sacred: two great creative passions, separate, apart, but complementary: the one pivotal, the other adventurous: the one, marriage, the centre of human life; and the other, the leap ahead.

Which is the last word in the education of a people.

VI

Ethics, Psychology, Philosophy

THE REALITY OF PEACE

LIFE

DEMOCRACY

THE PROPER STUDY

ON BEING RELIGIOUS

BOOKS

THINKING ABOUT ONESELF

RESURRECTION

CLIMBING DOWN PISGAH

THE DUC DE LAUZUN

[THE GOOD MAN]

THE NOVEL AND THE FEELINGS

[THE INDIVIDUAL CONSCIOUSNESS
V. THE SOCIAL CONSCIOUSNESS]

INTRODUCTION TO PICTURES

THE REALITY OF PEACE

I

THE TRANSFERENCE

Peace is the state of fulfilling the deepest desire of the soul. It is the condition of flying within the greatest impulse that enters us from the unknown. Our life becomes a mechanical round, and it is difficult for us to know or to admit the new creative desires that come upon us. We cling tenaciously to the old states, we resist our own fulfilment with a perseverance that would almost stop the sun in its course. But in the end we are overborne. If we cannot cast off the old habitual life, then we bring it down over our heads in a blind frenzy. Once the temple becomes our prison, we drag at the pillars till the roof falls crashing down on top of us and we are obliterated.

There is a great systole-diastole of the universe. It has no why or wherefore, no aim or purpose. At all times it is, like the beating of the everlasting heart. What it is, is for ever beyond saying. It is unto itself. We only know that the end is the heaven on earth, like the wild rose in blossom.

We are like the blood that travels. We are like the shuttle that flies from never to for ever, from for ever back to never. We are the subject of the eternal systole-diastole. We fly according to the perfect impulse, and we have peace. We resist, and we have the gnawing misery of nullification which we have known previously.

Who can choose beforehand what the world shall be? All law, all knowledge holds good for that which already exists in the created world. But there is no law, no knowledge of the unknown which is to take place. We cannot know, we cannot declare beforehand. We can only come at length to that perfect state of understanding, of acquiescence, when we sleep upon the living drift of the unknown, when we are given to the direction of creation, when we fly like a shuttle that flies from hand to hand in a line across the loom. The pattern is woven of us without our foreknowing, but not without our perfect unison of acquiescence.

What is will, divorced from the impulse of the unknown? What can we achieve by this insulated self-will? Who can take his way into the unknown by will? We are driven. Subtly and beautifully, we are impelled. It is our peace and bliss to follow the rarest prompting. We sleep upon the impulse; we lapse on the strange incoming tide, which rises now where no tide ever rose; we are conveyed to the new ends. And this is peace when we sleep upon the perfect impulse in the spirit. This is peace even whilst we run the gauntlet of destruction. Still we sleep in peace upon the pure impulse.

When we have become very still, when there is an inner silence as complete as death, then, as in the grave, we hear the rare, superfine whispering of the new direction; the intelligence comes. After the pain of being destroyed in all our old securities that we used to call peace, after the pain and death of our destruction in the old life comes the inward suggestion of fulfilment in the new.

This is peace like a river. This is peace like a river to flow upon the tide of the creative direction, towards an end we know nothing of, but which only fills us with bliss of confidence. Our will is a rudder that steers us and keeps us faithfully adjusted to the current. Our will is the strength that throws itself upon the tiller when we are caught by a wrong current. We steer by the delicacy of adjusted understanding, and our will is the strength that serves us in this. Our will is never tired of adjusting the helm according to our pure understanding. Our will is prompt and ready to shove off from any obstruction, to overcome any impediment. We steer with the subtlety of understanding and the strength of our will sees us through.

But all the while our greatest effort and our supreme aim is to adjust ourselves to the river that carries us, so that we may be carried safely to the end, neither wrecked nor stranded nor clogged in weeds. All the while we are but given to the stream, we are borne upon the surpassing impulse which has our end in view beyond us. None of us knows the way. The way is given on the way.

There is a sacrifice demanded—only one, an old sacrifice that was demanded of the first man, and will be demanded of the last. It is demanded of all created life. I must submit my will and my understanding—all I must submit, not to any other will, not to any other understanding, not to anything that is, but to the exquisitest suggestion from the unknown that comes upon me. This I must attend to and submit to. It is not me, it is upon me.

There is no visible security; pure faith is the only security. There is no given way; there will never be any given way. We have no foreknowledge, no security of chart and regulation; there is no pole-star save only pure faith.

We must give up our assurance, our conceit of final knowledge, our vanity of charted right and wrong. We must give these up for ever. We cannot map out the way. We shall never be able to map out the way to the new. All our maps, all our charts, all our right and wrong are only record from the past. But for the new there is a new and for ever incalculable element.

We must give ourselves and be given, not to anything that has been, but to the river of peace that bears us. We must abide by the incalculable impulse of creation; we must sleep in faith. It will seem to us we are nowhere. We shall be afraid of anarchy and confusion. But, in fact, there is no anarchy so horrid as the anarchy of fixed law, which is mechanism.

We must be given in faith, like sleep. We must lapse upon a current that carries us like repose, and extinguishes in repose our self-insistence and self-will. It will seem to us we are nothing when we are no longer actuated by the stress of self-will. It will seem we have no progression, nothing progressive happens. Yet if we look, we shall see the banks of the old slipping noiselessly by; we shall see a new world unfolding round us. It is pure adventure, most beautiful.

But first it needs the act of courage: that we yield up our will to the unknown, that we deliver our course to the current of the invisible. With what rigid, cruel insistence we clutch the control of our lives; with what a morbid frenzy we try to force our conclusions; with what madness of ghastly persistence we break ourselves under our own will! We think to work everything out mathematically and mechanically, forgetting that peace far transcends mathematics and mechanics.

There is a far sublimer courage than the courage of the indomitable will. It is not the courage of the man smiling contemptuously in the face of death that will save us all from death. It is the courage which yields itself to the perfectest suggestion from within. When a man yields himself implicitly to the suggestion which transcends him, when he accepts gently and honourably his own creative fate, he is beautiful and beyond aspersion.

In self-assertive courage a man may smile serenely amid the most acute pains of death, like a Red Indian of America. He may perform acts of stupendous heroism. But this is the courage of death. The strength to die bravely is not enough.

Where has there been on earth a finer courage of death and endurance than in the Red Indian of America? And where has there been more complete absence of the courage of life? Has not this super-brave savage maintained himself in the conceit and strength of his own will since time began, as it seems? He has held himself aloof from all pure change; he has kept his will intact and insulated from life till he is an automaton—mad, living only in the acute inward agony of a negated impulse of creation. His living spirit is crushed down from him, confined within bonds of an unbreakable will, as the feet of a Chinese woman are bound up and clinched in torment. He only knows that he lives by the piercing of anguish and the thrill of peril. He needs the sharp sensation of peril; he needs the progression through danger and the interchange of mortal hate; he needs the outward torture to correspond with the inward torment of the restricted spirit. For that which happens at the quick of a man's life will finally have its full expression in his body. And the Red Indian finds relief in the final tortures of death, for these correspond at last with the inward agony of the cramped spirit; he is released at last to the pure and sacred readjustment of death.

He has all the fearful courage of death. He has all the repulsive dignity of a static, indomitable will. He has all the noble, sensational beauty of arrestedness, the splendour of insulated changelessness, the pride of static resistance to every impulse of mobile, delicate life. And what is the end? He is benumbed against all life, therefore he needs torture to penetrate him with vital sensation. He is cut off from growth, therefore he finds his fulfilment in the slow and mortal anguish of destruction. He knows no consummation of peace, but falls at last in the great conclusion of death.

Having all the resultant courage of negation, he has failed in the great crisis of life. He had not the courage to yield himself to the unknown that should make him new and vivid, to yield himself, deliberately, in faith. Does any story of martyrdom affect us like the story of the conversion of Paul? In an age of barrenness, where people glibly talk of epilepsy on the road to Damascus, we shy off from the history, we hold back from realizing what is told. We dare not know. We dare to gloat on the crucifixion, but we dare not face the mortal fact of the conversion from the accepted world, to the new world which was not yet conceived, that took place in the soul of St. Paul on the road to Damascus.

It is a passage through a crisis greater than death or martyrdom. It is the passage from the old way of death to the new way of creation. It is a transition out of assurance into peace. It is a change of state from comprehension to faith. It is a submission and allegiance given to the new which approaches us, in place of defiance and self-insistence, insistence on the known, that which lies static and external.

Sappho leaped off into the sea of death. But this is easy. Who dares leap off from the old world into the inception of the new? Who dares give himself to the tide of living peace? Many have gone in the tide of death. Who dares leap into the tide of new life? Who dares to perish from the old static entity, lend himself to the unresolved wonder? Who dares have done with his old self? Who dares have done with himself, and with all the rest of the old-established world; who dares have done with his own righteousness; who dares have done with humanity? It is time to have done with all these, and be given to the unknown which will come to pass.

It is the only way. There is this supreme act of courage demanded from every man who would move in a world of life. Empedocles ostentatiously leaps into the crater of the volcano. But a living man must leap away from himself into the much more awful fires of creation. Empedocles knew well enough where he was going when he leaped into Etna. He was only leaping hastily into death, where he would have to go, whether or not. He merely forestalled himself a little. For we must all die. But we need not all live. We have always the door of death in front of us, and, howsoever our track winds and travels, it comes to that door at last. We *must* die within an allotted term; there is not the least atom of choice allowed us in this.

But we are not compelled to live. We are only compelled to die. We may refuse to live; we may refuse to pass into the unknown of life; we may deny ourselves to life altogether. So much choice we have. There is so much free will that we are perfectly free to forestall our date of death, and perfectly free to postpone our date of life, as long as we like.

We must *choose* life, for life will never compel us. Sometimes we have even no choice; we have no alternative to death. Then, again, life is with us; there is the soft impulse of peace. But this we may deny emphatically and to the end, and it is denied to us. We may reject life completely and finally from ourselves. Unless we submit our will to the flooding of life, there is no life in us.

If a man have no alternative but death, death is his honour and his fulfilment. If he is wintry in discontent and resistance, then winter is his portion and his truth. Why should he be cajoled or bullied into a declaration for life? Let him declare for death with a whole heart. Let every man search in his own soul to find there the quick suggestion, whether his soul be quick for life or quick for death. Then let him act as he finds it. For the greatest of all misery is a lie; and if a man belong to the line of obstinate death, he has at least the satisfaction of pursuing this line simply. But we will not call this peace. There is all the world of difference between the sharp, drug-delicious satisfaction or resignation and self-gratifying humility and the true freedom of peace. Peace is when I accept life; when I accept death I have the hopeless equivalent of peace, which is quiescence and resignation.

Life does not break the self-insistent will. But death does. Death compels us and leaves us without choice. And all comparison whatsoever is death, and nothing but death.

To life we must cede our will, acquiesce and be at one with it, or we stand alone, we are excluded, we are exempt from living. The service of life is voluntary.

This fact of conversion, which has seemed, in its connexion with religion, to smack of unreality, to be, like the miracles, not quite credible, even if demonstrable, is a matter of fact essentially natural and our highest credit. We know what it is to prosecute death with all our strength of soul and body. We know what it is to be fulfilled with the activity of death. We have given ourselves body and soul, altogether, to the making of all the engines and contrivances and inventions of death. We have wanted to compel every man whatsoever to the activity of death. We have wanted to envelop the world in a vast unison of death, to let nothing escape. We have been filled with a frenzy of compulsion; our insistent will has co-ordinated into a monstrous engine of compulsion and death.

So now our fundamental being has come out. True, our banner is ostensible peace. But let us not degrade ourselves with lying. We were filled with the might of death. And this has been gathering in us for a hundred years. Our strength of death-passion has accumulated from our fathers; it has grown stronger and stronger from generation to generation. And in us it is confessed.

Therefore, we are in a position to understand the "phenomenon" of conversion. It is very simple. Let every man look into his own heart and see what is fundamental there. Is there a gnawing and unappeasable discontent? Is there a secret desire that there shall be new strife? Is there a prophecy that the worst is yet to come, is there a subtle thrill in the anticipation of a fearful tearing of the body of life at home, here, between the classes of men in England; a great darkness coming over England; the sound of a great rending of destruction? Is there a desire to partake in this rending, either on one side or the other? Is there a longing to see the masses rise up and make an end of the wrong old order? Is there a will to circumvent these masses and subject them to superior wisdom? Shall we govern them for their own good, strongly?

It does not matter on which side the desire stands, it is the desire of death. If we prophesy a triumph of the people over their degenerate rulers, still we prophesy from the inspiration of death. If we cry out in the name of the subjected herds of mankind against iniquitous tyranny, still we are purely deathly. If we talk of the wise controlling the unwise, this is the same death.

For all strife between things old is pure death. The very division of mankind into two halves, the humble and the proud, is death. Unless we pull off the old badges and become ourselves, single and new, we are divided unto death. It helps nothing whether we are on the side of the proud or the humble.

But if, in our heart of hearts, we can find one spark of happiness that is absolved from strife, then we are converted to the new life the moment we accept this spark as the treasure of our being. This is conversion. If there is a quick, new desire to have new heaven and earth, and if we are given triumphantly to this desire, if we know that it will be fulfilled of us, finally and without fail, we are converted. If we will have a new creation on earth, if our souls are chafing to make a beginning, if our fingers are itching to start the new work of building up a new world, a whole new world with a new open sky above us, then we are transported across the unthinkable chasm, from the old dead way to the beginning of all that is to be.

II

The beginning of spring lies in the awakening from winter. For us, to understand is to overcome. We have a winter of death, of destruction, vivid sensationalism of going asunder, the wintry glory of tragical experience to surmount and surpass. Thrusting through these things with the understanding, we come forth in first flowers of our spring with pale and icy blossoms, like bulb-flowers, the pure understanding of death. When we know the death is in ourselves, we are emerging into the new epoch. For whilst we are in the full flux of death, we can find no bottom of resistance from which to understand. When at last life stands under us, we can know what the flood is, in which we are immersed.

That which is understood by man is surpassed by man. When we understand our extreme being in death, we have surpassed into a new being. Many bitter and fearsome things there are for us to know, that we may go beyond them; they have no power over us any more.

Understanding, however, does not belong to every man, is not incumbent on every man. But it is vital that some men understand, that some few go through this final pain and relief of knowledge. For the rest, they have only to know peace when it is given them. But for the few there is the bitter necessity to understand the death that has been, so that we may pass quite clear of it.

The anguish of this knowledge, the knowledge of what we ourselves, we righteous ones, have been and are within the flux of death, is a death in itself. It is the death of our established belief in ourselves, it is the end of our current self-esteem. Those who live in the mind must also perish in the mind. The mindless are spared this.

We are not only creatures of light and virtue. We are also alive in corruption and death. It is necessary to balance the dark against the light if we are ever going to be free. We must know that we, ourselves, are the living stream of seething corruption, this also, all the while, as well as the bright river of life. We must recover our balance to be free. From our bodies comes the issue of corruption as well as the issue of creation. We must have our being in both, our knowledge must consist in both. The veils of the old temple must be rent, for they are but screens to hide from us our own being in corruption.

It is our self-knowledge that must be torn across before we are whole. The man I know myself to be must be destroyed before the true man I am can exist. The old man in me must die and be put away.

Either we can and will understand the other thing that we are, the flux of darkness and lively decomposition, and so become free and whole, or we fight shy of this half of ourselves, as man has always fought shy of it, and gone under the burden of secret shame and self-abhorrence. For the tide of our corruption is rising higher, and unless we adjust ourselves, unless we come out of our veiled temples, and see and know, and take the tide as it comes, ride upon it and so escape it, we are lost.

Within our bowels flows the slow stream of corruption, to the issue of corruption. This is one direction. Within our veins flows the stream of life, towards the issue of pure creation. This is the other direction. We are of both. We are the watershed from which flow the dark rivers of hell on the one hand, and the shimmering rivers of heaven on the other.

If we are ashamed, instead of covering the shame with a veil, let us accept that thing which makes us ashamed, understand it and be at one with it. If we shrink from some sickening issue of ourselves, instead of recoiling and rising above ourselves, let us go down into ourselves, enter the hell of corruption and putrescence, and rise again, not fouled, but fulfilled and free. If there is a loathsome thought or suggestion, let us not dispatch it instantly with impertinent righteousness; let us admit it with simplicity, let us accept it, be responsible for it. It is no good casting out devils. They belong to us, we must accept them and be at peace with them. For they are of us. We are angels and we are devils, both, in our own proper person. But we are more even than this. We are whole beings, gifted with understanding. A full, undiminished being is complete beyond the angels and the devils.

This is the condition of freedom: that in the understanding, I fear nothing. In the body I fear pain, in love I fear hate, in death I fear life. But in the understanding I fear neither love nor hate nor death nor pain nor abhorrence. I am brave even against abhorrence; even the abhorrent I will understand and be at peace with. Not by exclusion, but by incorporation and unison. There is no hope in exclusion. For whatsoever limbo we cast our devils into will receive us ourselves at last. We shall fall into the cesspool of our own abhorrence.

If there is a serpent of secret and shameful desire in my soul, let me not beat it out of my consciousness with sticks. It will lie beyond, in the marsh of the so-called subconsciousness, where I cannot follow it with my sticks. Let me bring it to the fire to see what it is. For a serpent is a thing created. It has its own *raison d'être*. In its own being it has beauty and reality. Even my horror is a tribute to its reality. And I must admit the genuineness of my horror, accept it, and not exclude it from my understanding.

There is nothing on earth to be ashamed of, nor under the earth, except only the craven veils we hang up to save our appearances. Pull down the veils and understand everything, each man in his own self-responsible soul. Then we are free.

Who made us a judge of the things that be? Who says that the water-lily shall rock on the still pool, but the snake shall not hiss in the festering marshy border? I must humble myself before the abhorred serpent and give him his dues as he lifts his flattened head from the secret grass of my soul. Can I exterminate what is created? Not while the condition of its creation lasts. There is no killing the serpent so long as his principle endures. And his principle moves slowly in my belly; I must disembowel myself to get rid of him. "If thine eye offend thee, pluck it out." But the offence is not in the eye, but in the principle it perceives. And howsoever I may pluck out my eyes, I cannot pluck the principle from the created universe. To this I must submit. And I must adjust myself to that which offends me, I must make my peace with it, and cease, in my delicate understanding, to be offended. Maybe the serpent of my abhorrence nests in my very heart. If so, I can but in honour say to him, "Serpent, serpent, thou art at home." Then I shall know that my heart is a marsh. But maybe my understanding will drain the swampy place, and the serpent will evaporate as his condition evaporates. That is as it is. While there is a marsh, the serpent has his holy ground.

I must make my peace with the serpent of abhorrence that is within me. I must own my most secret shame and my most secret shameful desire. I must say, "Shame, thou art me, I am thee. Let us understand each other and be at peace." Who am I that I should hold myself above my last or worst desire? My desires are me, they are the beginning of me; my stem and branch and root. To assume a better angel is an impertinence. Did I create myself? According to the maximum of my desire is my flower and my blossoming. This is beyond my will for ever. I can only learn to acquiesce.

And there is in me the great desire of creation and the great desire of dissolution. Perhaps these two are pure equivalents. Perhaps the decay of autumn purely balances the putting forth of spring. Certainly the two are necessary each to the other; they are the systole-diastole of the physical universe. But the initial force is the force of spring, as is evident. The undoing of autumn can only follow the putting forth of spring. So that creation is primal and original, corruption is only a consequence. Nevertheless, it is the inevitable consequence, as inevitable as that water flows downhill.

There is in me the desire of creation and the desire of dissolution. Shall I deny either? Then neither is fulfilled. If there is no autumn and winter of corruption, there is no spring and summer. All the time I must be dissolved from my old being. The wheat is put together by the pure activity of creation. It is the bread of pure creation I eat in the body. The fire of creation from out of the wheat passes into my blood, and what was put together in the pure grain now comes asunder, the fire mounts up into my blood, the watery mould washes back down my belly to the underearth. These are the two motions wherein we have our life. Is either a shame to me? Is it a pride to me that in my blood the fire flickers out of the wheaten bread I have partaken of, flickers up to further and higher creation? Then how shall it be a shame that from my blood exudes the bitter sweat of corruption on the journey back to dissolution; how shall it be a shame that in my consciousness appear the heavy marsh-flowers of the flux of putrescence, which have their natural roots in the slow stream of decomposition that flows for ever down my bowels?

There is a natural marsh in my belly, and there the snake is naturally at home. Shall he not crawl into my consciousness? Shall I kill him with sticks the moment he lifts his flattened head on my sight? Shall I kill him or pluck out the eye which sees him? None the less, he will swarm within the marsh.

Then let the serpent of living corruption take his place among us honourably. Come then, brindled abhorrent one, you have your own being and your own righteousness, yes, and your own desirable beauty. Come then, lie down delicately in the sun of my mind, sleep on the bosom of my understanding; I shall know your living weight and be gratified.

But keep to your own ways and your own being. Come in just proportion, there in the grass beneath the bushes where the birds are. For the Lord is the lord of all things, not of some only. And everything shall in its proportion drink its own draught of life. But I, who have the gift of understanding, I must keep most delicately and transcendingly the balance of creation within myself, because now I am taken over into the peace of creation. Most delicately and justly I must bring forth the blossom of my spring and provide for the serpent of my living corruption. But each in its proportion. If I am taken over into the stream of death, I must fling myself into the business of dissolution, and the serpent must writhe at my right hand, my good familiar. But since it is spring with me, the snake must wreathe his way secretly along the paths that belong to him, and when I see him asleep in the sunshine I shall admire him in his place.

I shall accept all my desires and repudiate none. It will be a sign of bliss in me when I am reconciled with the serpent of my own horror, when I am free both from the fascination and the revulsion. For secret fascination is a fearful tyranny. And then my desire of life will encompass my desire of death, and I shall be quite whole, have fulfilment in both. Death will take its place in me, subordinate but not subjected. I shall be fulfilled of corruption within the strength of creation. The serpent will have his own pure place in me and I shall be free.

For there are ultimately only two desires, the desire of life and the desire of death. Beyond these is pure being, where I am absolved from desire and made perfect. This is when I am like a rose, when I balance for a space in pure adjustment and pure understanding. The timeless quality of *being* is understanding; when I understand fully, flesh and blood and bone, and mind and soul and spirit one rose of unison, then I *am*. Then I am unrelated and perfect. In true understanding I am always perfect and timeless. In my utterance of that which I have understood I am timeless as a jewel.

The rose as it bursts into blossom reveals the absolute world before us. The brindled, slim adder, as she lifts her delicate head attentively in the spring sunshine–for they say she is deaf–suddenly throws open the world of unchanging, pure perfection to our startled breast. In our whole understanding, when sense and spirit and mind are consummated into pure unison, then we are free in a world of the absolute. The lark sings in a heaven of pure understanding, she drops back into a world of duality and change.

And it does not matter whether we understand according to death or according to life; the understanding is a consummating of the two in one, and a transcending into absolution. This is true of tragedy and of psalms of praise and of the Sermon on the Mount. It is true of the serpent and of the dove, of the tiger and the fragile, dappled doe. For all things that emerge pure in being from the matrix of chaos are roses of pure understanding; in them death and life are adjusted, darkness is in perfect equilibrium with light. This is the meaning of understanding. This is why the leopard gleams to my eye a blossom of pure significance, whilst a hyena seems only a clod thrown at me in contumely. The leopard is a piece of understanding uttered in terms of fire, the dove is expressed in gurgling watery sound. But in them both there is that perfect conjunction of sun and dew which makes for absolution and the world beyond worlds. Only the leopard starts from the sun and must for ever quench himself with the living soft fire of the fawn; the dove must fly up to the sun like mist drawn up.

We, we are all desire and understanding, only these two. And desire is twofold, desire of life and desire of death. All the time we are active in these two great powers, which are for ever contrary and complementary. Except in understanding, and there we are immune and perfect, there the two are one. Yet even understanding is twofold in its appearance. It comes forth as understanding of life or as understanding of death, in strong, glad words like Paul and David, or in pain like Shakespeare.

All active life is either desire of life or desire of death, desire of putting together or desire of putting asunder. We come forth uttering ourselves in terms of fire, like the rose, or in terms of water, like the lily. We wish to say that we are single in our desire for life and creation and putting together. But it is a lie, since we must eat life to live. We must, like the leopard, drink up the lesser life to bring forth our greater. We wish to conquer death. But it is absurd, since only by death do we live, like the leopard. We wish not to die; we wish for life everlasting. But this is mistaken interpretation. What we mean by immortality is this fulfilment of death with life and life with death in us where we are consummated and absolved into heaven, the heaven on earth.

We can never conquer death; that is folly. Death and the great dark flux of undoing, this is the inevitable half. Life feeds death, death feeds life. If life is just one point the stronger in the long run, it is only because death is inevitably the stronger in the short run of each separate existence. They are like the hare and the tortoise.

It is only in understanding that we pass beyond the scope of this duality into perfection, in actual living equipoise of blood and bone and spirit. But our understanding must be dual, it must be death understood and life understood.

We understand death, and in this there is no death. Life has put together all that is put together. Death is the consequent putting asunder. We have been torn to shreds in the hands of death, like Osiris in the myth. But still within us life lay intact like seeds in winter.

That is how we know death, having suffered it and lived. It is now no mystery, finally. Death is understood in us, and thus we transcend it. Henceforward actual death is a fulfilling of our own knowledge.

Nevertheless, we only transcend death by understanding down to the last ebb the great process of death in us. We can never destroy death. We can only transcend it in pure understanding. We can envelop it and contain it. And then we are free.

By standing in the light we see in terms of shadow. We cannot see the light we stand in. So our understanding of death in life is an act of living.

If we live in the mind, we must die in the mind, and in the mind we must understand death. Understanding is not necessarily mental. It is of the senses and the spirit.

But we live also in the mind. And the first great act of living is to encompass death in the understanding. Therefore the first great activity of the living mind is to understand death in the mind. Without this there is no freedom of the mind, there is no life of the mind, since creative life is the attaining a perfect consummation with death. When in my mind there rises the idea of life, then this idea must encompass the idea of death, and this encompassing is the germination of a new epoch of the mind.

III

We long most of all to belong to life. This primal desire, the desire to come into being, the desire to achieve a transcendent state of existence, is all we shall ever know of a *primum mobile*. But it is enough.

And corresponding with this desire for absolute life, immediately consequent is the desire for death. This we will never admit. We cannot admit the desire of death in ourselves even when it is single and dominant. We must still deceive ourselves with the name of life.

This is the root of all confusion, this inability for man to admit, "Now I am single in my desire for destructive death." When it is autumn in the world, the autumn of a human epoch, then the desire for death becomes single and dominant. I want to kill, I want violent sensationalism, I want to break down, I want to put asunder, I want anarchic revolution—it is all the same, the single desire for death.

We long most of all for life and creation. That is the final truth. But not all life belongs to life. Not all life is progressing to a state of transcendent being. For many who are born and live year after year there is no such thing as coming to blossom. Many are saprophyte, living on the dead body of the past. Many are parasite, living on the old and enfeebled body politic; and many, many more are mere impurities. Many, in these days, most human beings, having come into the world on the impulse of death, find that the impulse is not strong enough to carry them into absolution. They reach a maturity of physical life, and then the advance ends. They have not the strength for the further passage into darkness. They are born short, they wash on a slack tide; they will never be flung into the transcendence of the second death. They are spent before they arrive; their life is a slow lapsing out, a slow inward corruption. Their flood is the flood of decomposition and decay; in this they have their being. They are like the large green cabbages that cannot move on into flower. They attain a fatness and magnificence of leaves, then they rot inside. There is not sufficient creative impulse, they lapse into great corpulence. So with the sheep and the pigs of our domestic life. They frisk into life as if they would pass on to pure being. But the tide fails them. They grow fat; their only *raison d'être* is to provide food for a really living organism. They have only the moment of first youth, then they lapse gradually into nullity. It is given us to devour them.

So with very many human lives, especially in what is called the periods of decadence. They have mouths and stomachs, and an obscene *will* of their own. Yes, they have also prolific procreative wombs whence they bring forth increasing insufficiency. But of the germ of intrinsic creation they have none, neither have they the courage of true death. They never live. They are like the sheep in the fields, that have their noses to the ground, and anticipate only the thrill of increase.

These will never understand, neither life nor death. But they will bleat mechanically about life and righteousness, since this is how they can save their appearances. And in their eyes is the furtive tyranny of nullity. They will understand no word of living death, since death encompasses them. If a man understands the living death, he is a man in the quick of creation.

The quick can encompass death, but the living dead are encompassed. Let the dead bury their dead. Let the living dead attend to the dead dead. What has creation to do with them?

The righteousness of the living dead is an abominable nullity. They, the sheep of the meadow, they eat and eat to swell out their living nullity. They are so many, their power is immense, and the negative power of their nullity bleeds us of life as if they were vampires. Thank God for the tigers and the butchers that will free us from the abominable tyranny of these greedy, negative sheep.

It is very natural that every word about death they will decry as evil. For if death be understood, they are found out. They are multitudes of slow, greedy-mouthed decay.

There are the isolated heroes of passionate and beautiful death: Tristan, Achilles, Napoleon. These are the royal lions and tigers of our life. There are many wonderful initiators into the death for re-birth, like Christ and St. Paul and St. Francis. But there is a ghastly multitude of obscene nullity, flocks of hideous sheep with blind mouths and still blinder crying, and hideous coward's eye of tyranny for the sake of their own bloated nothingness.

These are the enemy and the abomination. And they are so many we shall with difficulty save ourselves from them. Indeed, the word humanity has come to mean only this obscene flock of blind mouths and blinder bleating and most hideous coward's tyranny of negation. Save us, oh, holy death; carry us beyond them, oh, holy life of creation; for how shall we save ourselves against such ubiquitous multitudes of living dead? It needs a faith in that which has created all creation, and will therefore never fall before the blind mouth of nullity.

The sheep, the hideous myrmidons of sheep, all *will* and belly and prolific womb, they have their own absolution. They have the base absolution of the *I*. A vile entity detaches itself and shuts itself off immune from the flame of creation and from the stream of death likewise. They assert a free will. And this free will is a horny, glassy, insentient covering into which they creep, like some tough bugs, and therein remain active and secure from life and death. So they swarm in insulated completeness, obscene like bugs.

We are quite insulated from life. And we think ourselves quite immune from death. But death, beautiful death searches us out, even in our armour of insulated will. Death is within us, while we tighten our will to keep him out. Death, beautiful, clean death, washes slowly within us and carries us away. We have never known life, save, perhaps, for a few moments during childhood. Well may heaven lie about us in our infancy, if our maturity is but the bug-like security of a vast and impervious envelope of insentience, the insentience of the human mass. Heaven lies about us in our consummation of manhood, if we are men. If we are men, we attain to heaven in our achieved manhood, our flowering maturity. But if we are like bugs, our first sight of this good earth may well seem heavenly. For we soon learn not to see. A bug, and a sheep, sees only with its fear and its belly. Its eyes look out in a coward's will not to see, a self-righteous vision.

It is not the will of the overweening individual we have to fear today, but the consenting together of a vast host of null ones. It is no Napoleon or Nero, but the innumerable myrmidons of nothingness. It is not the leopard or the hot tiger, but the masses of rank sheep. Shall I be pressed to death, shall I be suffocated under the slow and evil weight of countless long-faced sheep? This is a fate of ignominy indeed. Who compels us today? The malignant null sheep. Who overwhelms us? The persistent, purblind, bug-like sheep. It is a horrid death to be suffocated under these fat-smelling ones.

There is an egoism far more ghastly than that of the tyrannous individual. It is the egoism of the flock. What if a tiger pull me down? It is straight death. But what if the flock which counts me part of itself compress me and squeeze me with slow malice to death? It cannot be, it shall not be. I cry to the spirit of life, I cry to the spirit of death to save me. I *must* be saved from the vast and obscene self-conceit which is the ruling force of the world that envelops me.

The tiger is sufficient unto himself, a law unto himself. Even the grisly condor sits isolated on the peak. It is the will of the flock that is the obscenity of obscenities. Timeless and clinched in stone is the naked head of the vulture. Timeless as rock, the great condor sits inaccessible on the heights. It is the last brink of deathly life, just alive, just dying, not quite static. It has locked its unalterable will for ever against life and death. It persists in the flux of unclean death. It leans for ever motionless on death. The will is fixed; there shall be no yielding to life, no yielding to death. Yet death gradually steals over the huge obscene bird. Gradually the leaves fall from the rotten branch, the feathers leave naked the too-dead neck of the vulture.

But worse than the fixed and obscene will of the isolated individual is the will of the obscene herd. They cringe, the herd; they shrink their buttocks downward like the hyena. They are one flock. They are a nauseous herd together, keeping up a steady heat in the whole. They have one temperature, one aim, one will, enveloping them into an obscene oneness, like a mass of insects or sheep or carrion-eaters. What do they want? They want to maintain themselves insulated from life and death. Their will has asserted its own absolution. They are the arrogant, immitigable beings who have achieved a secure entity. They are *it*. Nothing can be added to them, nor detracted. Enclosed and complete, they have their completion in the whole herd, they have their wholeness in the whole flock, they have their oneness in their multiplicity. Such are the sheep, such is humanity, an obscene whole which is no whole, only a multiplied nullity. But in their multiplicity they are so strong that they can defy both life and death for a time, existing like weak insects, powerful and horrible because of their countless numbers.

It is in vain to appeal to these ghastly myrmidons. They understand neither the language of life nor the language of death. They are fat and prolific and all-powerful, innumerable. They are in truth nauseous slaves of decay. But now, alas! the slaves have got the upper hand. Nevertheless, it only needs that we go forth with whips, like the old chieftain. Swords will not frighten them, they are too many. At all costs the herd of nullity must be subdued. It is the worst coward. It has triumphed, this slave herd, and its tyranny is the tyranny of a pack of jackals. But it can be frightened back to its place. For its cowardice is as great as its arrogance.

Sweet, beautiful death, come to our help. Break in among the herd, make gaps in its insulated completion. Give us a chance, sweet death, to escape from the herd and gather together against it a few living beings. Purify us with death, O death, cleanse from us the rank stench, the intolerable oneness with a negative humanity. Break for us this foul prison where we suffocate in the reek of the flock of the living dead. Smash, beautiful destructive death, smash the complete will of the hosts of man, the will of the self-absorbed bug. Smash the great obscene unison. Death, assert your strength now, for it is time. They have defied you so long. They have even, in their mad arrogance, begun to deal in death as if it also were subjugated. They thought to use death as they have used life this long time, for their own base end of nullification. Swift death was to serve their end of enclosed, arrogant self-assertion. Death was to help them maintain themselves *in statu quo,* the benevolent and self-righteous bugs of humanity.

Let there be no humanity; let there be a few men. Sweet death, save us from humanity. Death, noble, unstainable death, smash the glassy rind of humanity, as one would smash the brittle hide of the insulated bug. Smash humanity, and make an end of it. Let there emerge a few pure and single men—men who give themselves to the unknown of life and death and are fulfilled. Make an end of our unholy oneness, O death, give us to our single being. Release me from the debased social body, O death, release me at last; let me be by myself, let me be myself. Let me know other men who are single and not contained by any multiple oneness. Let me find a few men who are distinct and at ease in themselves like stars. Let me derive no more from the body of mankind. Let me derive direct from life or direct from death, according to the impulse that is in me.

IV

THE ORBIT

It is no good thinking of the living dead. The thought of them is almost as hurtful as their presence. One cannot fight against them. One can only know them as the great static evil which stands against life and against death; and then one skirts them round as if they were a great gap in existence. It is most fearful to fall into that gap. But it is necessary to move in strength round about it, on the actual fields of life and death. We must ignore the static nullity of the living dead, and speak of life and speak of death.

There are two ways and two goals, as it has always been. And so it will always be. Some are set upon one road, the road of death and undoing, and some are set upon the other road, the road of creation. And the fulfilment of every man is the following his own separate road to its end. No man can cause another man to have the same goal or the same path as himself. All paths lead either to death or to the heaven on earth, ultimately. But the paths are like the degrees of longitude, the lines of longitude drawn on a geographer's globe—they are all separate.

Every man has his goal, and this there is no altering. Except by asserting the free will. A man may choose nullity. He may choose to absolve himself from his fate either of life or death. He may oppose his self-will, his free will, between life and his own small entity, or between true death and himself. He may insulate and cut himself off from the systole-diastole of life and death, either within his own small horny integument of a will, or within the big horny will of the herd of humanity. Humanity is like a mass of beetles:

it is one monstrosity of multiple identical units. It is like the much-vaunted ant-swarms, an insulated oneness made out of myriads of null units, one big, self-absorbed nullity. Such is humanity when it is self-absorbed.

And so much free will have we: if life comes to us like a potentiality of transcendence, we *must* yield our ultimate will to the unknown impulse or remain outside, abide alone, like the corn of wheat, outside the river of life; if death comes to us, the desire to act in strength of death, we *must* have the courage of our desire, and ride deathwards like the knights of the Dark Ages, covered with armour of imperviousness and carrying a spear and a shield by which we are known; we must do this, of our own free will and courage accept the mission of death, or else roll up like a wood-louse enfolded upon our own ego, our own entity, our own self-will, roll up tight on our own free will, and remain outside. So much free will there is. That the free will of humanity can provide a great unified hive of immunity from life, and death does not make us any more intrinsically alone from life and death. That we are many millions cut off from life and death does not make us any less cut off. That we are contained within the vast nullity of humanity does not make us other than null. That we are a vast colony of wood-lice, fabricating elaborate social communities like the bees or the wasps or the ants, does not make us any less wood-lice curled up upon nothingness, immune in a vast and multiple negation. It only shows us that the most perfect social systems are probably the most complete nullities, that all relentless organization is in the end pure negation. Who wants to be like an ant? An ant is a little scavenger; ants, a perfect social system of scavengers.

So much free will there is. There is the free will to choose between submitting the will, and so becoming a spark in a great tendency, or withholding the will, curling up within the will, and so remaining outside, exempt from life or death. That death triumphs in the end, even then, does not alter the fact that we can live exempt in nullity, exerting our free will to negation.

All we can do is to know in singleness of heart *which* is our road, then take it unflinching to the end, having given ourselves over to the road. For the straight road of death has splendour and brave colour; it is emblazoned with passion and adventure, sparkling with running leopards and steel and wounds, laguorous with drenched lilies that glisten cold and narcotic from the corrupt mould of self-sacrifice. And the road of life has the buttercups and wild birds whistling of real spring, magnificent architecture of created dreams. I tread the subtle way of edged hostility, bursting through the glamorous pageant of blood for the undying glory of our gentle Iseult, some delicate dame, some lily unblemished, watered by blood. Or I bring forth an exquisite unknown rose from the tree of my veins, a rose of the living spirit, beyond any woman and beyond any man transcendent. To the null, my rose of glistening transcendence is only a quite small cabbage. When the sheep get into the garden they eat the roses indifferently, but the cabbages with gluttonous absorption. To the null, my pageantry of death is so much mountebank performing; or, if I tilt my spear under the negative nose, it is monstrous, inhuman criminality, to be crushed out and stifled, to be put down with an unanimous hideous bleating of righteousness.

There are two roads and a no-road. We will not concern ourselves with the no-road. Who wants to go down a road which is no road? The proprietor may sit at the end of his no-road, like a cabbage on its blind gut of a stalk.

There are two roads, the no-road forgotten. There are two roads. There is hot sunshine leaping down and interpenetrating the earth to blossom. And there is red fire rushing upward on its path to return, in the coming asunder. Down comes the fire from the sun to the seed, splash into the water of the tiny reservoir of life. Up spurts the foam and stream of greenness, a tree, a fountain of roses, a cloud of steamy pear-blossom. Back again goes the fire, leaves shrivel and roses fall, back goes the fire to the sun, away goes the dim water.

So and such is all life and death—apart from the sluglike sheep. There is swift death, and slow. I set a light to the flowery bush, and the balance overtopples into the road of flame; up rushes the bush on wings of fiery death, away goes the dim water in smoke.

The sheep feed upon the moist, fat grass till they are sodden mounds of scarcely kindled grey mold. Quick, the balance! Quick, the golden lion of wrath, pierce them with flame, drink them up to a superb leonine being. It is the quick way of death. Sheep blaze up in the sun in the golden bonfire of the lion; they trickle to darkness in spilled dark blood. The deer is a trembling flower full of shadow and quenched light, fostered in the immunity of the herd. The self-preservation of the herd is round about the shy doe; she will multiply so that the earth is alive with her offspring—if it were not for the tiger. The tiger, like a brand of fire, leaps upon her to restore the balance. His too-much heat drinks their coolness; he waters his thirst with the moist fawn. And the flame of him goes up in the sun brindled with tongues of smoke; the deer disappear like dark mists into the air and the earth. He is a crackling bush burning back to the sun, and burning not away. They are the mists of morning stealing forth and distilling themselves over the sweet earth. So the uneasy balance of life adjusts itself here with the aid of violent death.

Shall we be all like lambs, pellucid flickerings of shadow? Yes, but for the quick mottled leopard and the all-vivid spark of the sharp steel knife. Shall we be all tigers, brands seized in the burning? It is impossible. For even the mother-tiger is quenched with insuperable tenderness when the milk is in her udder; she lies still, and her dreams are frail like fawns. All is somehow adjusted in a strange, unstable equilibrium.

We are tigers, we are lambs. Yet are we also neither tigers nor lambs, nor immune sluggish sheep. We are beyond all this, this relative life of uneasy balancing. We are roses of pure and lovely being. This we are ultimately, beyond all dark and light. Yes, we are tigers, we are lambs, both in our various hour. We are both these, and more. Because we are both these, because we are lambs, frail and exposed, because we are lions furious and devouring, because we are both, and have the courage to be both, in our separate hour, therefore we transcend both, we pass into a beyond, we are roses of perfect consummation.

Immediately we must be both these, both tigers and lambs, according to the hour and the unknown balance; we must be both in the immediate life, that ultimately we are roses of unfailing glad peace.

Nevertheless, this is the greatest truth: we are neither lions of pride and strength, nor lambs of love and submission. We are roses of perfect being.

It is very great to be a lion of glory, like David or Alexander. But these only exist on the lives they consume, as a fire needs fuel. It is very beautiful to be the lamb of innocence and humility, like St. Francis and St. Clare. But these only shine so star-like because of the darkness of the night on which they have risen, as the lily of light balances herself upon a fountain of unutterable shadow.

Where is there peace, if I take my being from the balance of pure opposition? If all men were Alexanders, what then? And even if all men followed St. Francis or St. Bernard, the race of mankind would be extinct in a generation. Think, if there were no night, we could not bear it; we should have to die. For the half of us is shadow. And if there were no day, we should dissolve in the darkness and be gone, for we are creatures of light.

Therefore, if I assert myself a creature purely of light, it is in opposition to the darkness which is in me. If I vaunt myself a lion of strength, I am merely set over and balanced against the lambs which are gentle and meek. My form and shape in either case depend entirely on the virtue of resistance, my life and my whole being. I am like one of the cells in any organism, the pressure from within and the resistance from without keep me as I am. Either I follow the impulse to power, or I follow the impulse of submission. Whichever it is, I am only half, complemented by my opposite. In a world of petty Alexanders, St. Francis is the star. In a world of sheep the wolf is god. Each, saint or wolf, shines by virtue of opposition.

Where, then, is there peace? If I am a lamb with Christ, I exist in a state of pure tension of opposition to the lion of wrath. Am I the lion of pride? It is my fate for ever to fall upon the lamb of meekness and love. Is this peace, or freedom? Is the lamb devoured more free than the lion devouring, or the lion than the lamb? Where is there freedom?

Shall I expect the lion to lie down with the lamb? Shall I expect such a thing? I might as well hope for the earth to cast no shadow, or for burning fire to give no heat. It is no good; these are mere words. When the lion lies down with the lamb he is no lion, and the lamb, lying down with the lion, is no lamb. They are merely a neutralization, a nothingness. If I mix fire and water, I get quenched ash. And so if I mix the lion and the lamb. They are both quenched into nothingness.

Where, then, is there peace? The lion will never lie down with the lamb; in all reverence let it be spoken. Whilst the lion is lion, he must fall on the lamb, to devour her. This is his lionhood and his peace, in so far as he has any peace. And the peace of the lamb is to be devourable.

Where, then, is there peace? There is no peace of reconciliation. Let that be accepted for ever. Darkness will never be light, neither will the one ever triumph over the other. Whilst there is darkness, there is light; and when there is an end of darkness, there is an end of light. There are lions, and there are lambs; there are lambs, and thus there are lions predicated. If there are no lions feline, we are the devourers, leonine enough. This is our manhood also, that we devour the lambs. Am I in my conceit more than myself? Not more, but less. I lie down with the lamb and eat grass. What, then, I am only the neutralization of a man.

Where, then, is there peace, which we must seek and pursue, since it is the ultimate condition of our nature? It is peace for the lion when he carries the crushed lamb in his jaws. It is peace for the lamb when she quivers light and irresponsible within the strong, supporting apprehension of the lion. Where is the skipping joyfulness of the lamb when the magnificent, strong responsibility of the lion is removed? The lamb need take no thought; the lion is responsible for death in her world.

But let there be no lion, and no exquisite apprehension in the lamb, what does she degenerate into? A clod of stupid weight. Look in the eyes of your sheep, and see there the pitch of tension which holds her against the golden lion of pride. See in the eyes of the sheep the soul of the sheep, giving with coward's jeering malice the lie to the great mystic truth of death. Look at the doe of the fallow deer as she turns back her eyes in apprehension. What does she ask for, what is her helpless passion? Some unutterable thrill in her waits with unbearable acuteness for the leap of the mottled leopard. Not of the conjunction with the hart is she consummated, but of the exquisite laceration of fear as the leopard springs upon her loins, and his claws strike in, and he dips his mouth in her. This is the white-hot pitch of her helpless desire. She cannot save herself. Her moment of frenzied fulfilment is the moment when she is torn and scattered beneath the paws of the leopard, like a quenched fire scattered into the darkness. Nothing can alter it. This is the extremity of her desire, this desire for the fearful fury of the brand upon her. She is balanced over at the extreme edge of submission, balanced against the bright beam of the leopard like a shadow against him. The two exist by virtue of juxtaposition in pure polarity. To destroy the one would be to destroy the other; they would vanish together. And to try to reconcile them is only to bring about their nullification.

Where, then, is there peace if the primary law of all the universe is a law of dual attraction and repulsion, a law of polarity? How does the earth pulse round her orbit save in her overwhelming haste towards the sun and her equivalent rejection back from the sun? She swings in these two, the earth of our habitation, making the systole-diastole of our diurnal, of our yearly life. She pulses in a diurnal leap of attraction and repulsion, she travels in a great rhythm of approach and repulse.

Where, then, is there peace? There is peace in that perfect consummation when duality and polarity is transcended into absorption. In lovely, perfect peace the earth rests on her orbit. She has found the pure resultant of gravitation. She goes on for ever in pure rest, she rests for ever in perfect motion, consummated into absolution from a complete duality. Fulfilled from two, she is transported into the perfection of her orbit.

And this is peace. The lion is but a lion, the lamb is but a lamb, half and half separate. But we are the two halves together. I am a lion of pride and wrath, I am a lamb with Christ in meekness. They live in one landscape of my soul; the roaring and the tremulous bleating of their different voices sound from the distance like pure music.

It is by the rage and strength of the lion, and the white, joyous freedom from strength of the lamb, by the equipoise of these two in perfect conjunction, that I pass from the limitation of a relative world into the glad absolution of the rose. It is when I am drawn by centripetal force into communion with the whole, and when I flee in equivalent centrifugal force away into the splendour of beaming isolation, when these two balance and match each other in mid-space, that suddenly, like a miracle, I find the peace of my orbit. Then I travel neither back nor forth. I hover in the unending delight of a rapid, resultant orbit.

When the darkness of which I am an involved seed, and the light which is involved in me as in a seed, when these two draw from the infinite sources towards me, when they meet and embrace in a perfect kiss and a perfect contest of me, when they foam and mount on their ever-intensifying communion in me until they achieve a resultant absolution of oneness, a rose of being blossoming upon the bush of my mortality, then I have peace.

It is not of love that we are fulfilled, but of love in such intimate equipoise with hate that the transcendence takes place. It is not in pride that we are free, but in pride, so perfectly matched by meekness that we are liberated as into blossom. There is a transfiguration, a rose with glimmering petals, upon a bush that knew no more than the dusk of green leaves heretofore. There is a new heaven on the earth, there is new heaven and new earth, the heaven and earth of the perfect rose.

I am not born fulfilled. The end is not before the beginning. I am born uncreated. I am a mixed handful of life as I issue from the womb. Thenceforth I extricate myself into singleness, the slow-developed singleness of manhood. And then I set out to meet the other, the unknown of womanhood. I give myself to the love that makes me join and fuse towards a universal oneness; I give myself to the hate that makes me detach myself, extricate myself vividly from the other in sharp passion; I am given up into universality of fellowship and communion, I am distinguished in keen resistance and isolation, both so utterly, so exquisitely, that I am and I am not at once; suddenly I lapse out of the duality into a sheer beauty of fulfilment. I am a rose of lovely peace.

LIFE

Midmost between the beginning and the end is Man. He is neither the created nor the creator. But he is the quick of creation. He has on one hand the primal unknown from which all creation issues; on the other hand, the whole created universe, even the world of finite spirits. But between the two man is distinct and other; he is creation itself, that which is perfect.

Man is born unfulfilled from chaos, uncreated, incomplete, a baby, a child, a thing immature and inconclusive. It is for him to become fulfilled, to enter at last the state of perfection, to achieve pure and immitigable being, like a star between day and night, disclosing the other world which has no beginning nor end, the otherworld of utterly completed creation, perfect beyond the creator, and conclusive beyond the thing created, living beyond life itself and deathly beyond death, partaking of both and transcending both.

When he comes into his own, man has being beyond life and beyond death; he is perfect of both. There he comprehends the singing of birds and the silence of the snake.

Yet man cannot create himself, nor can he achieve the finality of a thing created. All his time he hovers in the no-land, hovering till he can enter the otherworld of perfection; he still does not create himself, nor does he arrive at the static finality of a thing created. Why should he, since he has transcended the state of creativity and the state of being created, both?

Midway between the beginning and the end is man, midway between that which creates and that which is created, midway in an otherworld, partaking of both, yet transcending.

All the while man is referred back. He cannot create himself. At no moment can man create himself. He can but submit to the creator, to the primal unknown out of which issues the all. At every moment we issue like a balanced flame from the primal unknown. We are not self-contained or self-accomplished. At every moment we derive from the unknown.

This is the first and greatest truth of our being. Upon this elemental truth all our knowledge rests. We issue from the primal unknown. Behold my hands and feet, where I end upon the created universe! But who can see the quick, the well-head, where I have egress from the primordial creativity? Yet at every moment, like a flame which burns balanced upon a wick, do I burn in pure and transcendent equilibrium upon the wick of my soul, balanced and clipped like a flame corporeal between the fecund darkness of the first unknown and the final darkness of the afterlife, wherein is all that is created and finished.

We are balanced like a flame between the two darknesses, the darkness of the beginning and the darkness of the end. We derive from the unknown, and we result into the unknown. But for us the beginning is not the end, for us the two are not one.

It is our business to burn, pure flame, between the two unknowns. We are to be fulfilled in the world of perfection, which is the world of pure creation. We must come into being in the transcendent otherworld of perfection, consummated in life and death both, two in one.

I turn my face, which is blind and yet which knows, like a blind man turning to the sun, I turn my face to the unknown, which is the beginning, and like a blind man who lifts his face to the sun I know the sweetness of the influx from the source of creation into me. Blind, for ever blind, yet knowing, I receive the gift, I know myself the ingress of the creative unknown. Like a seed which unknowing receives the sun and is made whole, I open onto the great invisible warmth of primal creativity and begin to be fulfilled.

This is the law. We shall never know what is the beginning. We shall never know how it comes to pass that we have form and being. But we may always know how through the doorways of the spirit and the body enters the vivid unknown, which is made known in us. Who comes, who is that we hear outside in the night? Who knocks, who knocks again? Who is that that unlatches the painful door?

Then behold, there is something new in our midst. We blink our eyes, we cannot see. We lift the lamp of previous understanding, we illuminate the stranger with the light of our established knowledge. Then at last we accept the newcomer, he is enrolled among us.

So is our life. How do we become new? How is it we change and develop? Whence comes the newness, the further being, into us? What is added unto us, and how does it come to pass?

There is an arrival in us from the unknown, from the primal unknown whence all creation issues. Did we call for this arrival, did we summon the new being, did we command the new creation of ourselves, the new fulfilment? We did not, it is not of us. We are not created of ourselves. But from the unknown, from the great darkness of the outside that which is strange and new arrives on our threshold, enters and takes place in us. Not of ourselves, it is not of ourselves, but of the unknown which is the outside.

This is the first and greatest truth of our being and of our existence. How do we come to pass? We do not come to pass of ourselves. Who can say, Of myself I will bring forth newness? Not of myself, but of the unknown which has ingress into me.

And how has the unknown ingress into me? The unknown has ingress into me because, whilst I live, I am never sealed and set apart; I am but a flame conducting unknown to unknown, through the bright transition of creation. I do but conduct the unknown of my beginning to the unknown of my end, through the transfiguration of perfect being. What is the unknown of the beginning, and what is the unknown of the end? That I can never answer, save that in my completeness of being the two unknowns are consummated in a oneness, a rose of perfect explanation.

The unknown of my beginning has ingress into me through the spirit. My spirit is troubled, it is uneasy. Far off it hears the approach of footsteps through the night. Who is coming? Ah, let the newcomer arrive, let the newcomer arrive. In my spirit I am lonely and inert. I wait for the newcomer. My spirit aches with misery, dread of the newcomer. But also there is the tension of expectancy. I expect a visit, I expect a newcomer. For oh, I am conceited and unrefreshed, I am alone and barren. Yet still is my spirit alert and chuckling with subtle expectancy, awaiting the visit. It will come to pass. The stranger will come.

I listen, in my spirit I listen and listen. Many sounds there are from the unknown. And surely those are footsteps? In haste I open the door. But, alas! there is no one there. I must wait in patience, wait and always wait up for the stranger. Not of myself, it cannot happen of myself. With this in mind I check my impatience, I learn to wait and to watch.

And at last, out of all my desire and weariness, the door opens and this is the stranger. Ah, now! ah, joy! There is the new creation in me. Ah, beautiful! Ah, delight of delights! I am come to pass from the unknown, the unknown is added on to me. The sources of joy and strength are filled in me. I rise up to a new achievement of being, a new fulfilment in creation, a new rose of roses, new heavens on earth.

This is the story of our coming to pass. There is no other way. I must have patience in my soul, to stand and wait. Above all, it must be said in my soul that I wait for the unknown, for I cannot avail anything of myself. I wait upon the unknown, and from the unknown comes my new beginning. Not of myself, not of myself, but of my insuperable faith, my waiting. I am like a small house on the edge of the forest. Out of the unknown darkness of the forest, in the eternal night of the beginning, comes the spirit of creation towards me. But I must keep the light shining in the window, or how will the spirit see my house? If my house is in darkness of sleep or fear, the angel will pass it by. Above all, I must have no fear. I must watch and wait. Like a blind man looking for the sun, I must lift my face to the unknown darkness of space and wait until the sun lights on me. It is a question of creative courage. It is no good if I crouch over a coal fire. This will never bring me to pass.

Once the new has entered into my spirit, from the beginning, I am glad. No one and nothing can make me sorry any more. For I am potential with a new fulfilment, I am enriched with a new incipient perfection. Now no longer do I hover in the doorway listlessly, seeking for something to make up my life. The quota is made up in me, I can begin. It is conceived in me, the invisible rose of fulfilment, which in the end will shine out in the skies of absolution. So long as it is conceived in me, all labour of travail is joy. If I am in bud with the unseen rose of creation, what is labour to me, and what is pain, but pang after pang of new, strange joy? My heart is always glad like a star. My heart is a vivid, quivering star which will fan itself slowly out in flakes and gains creation, a rose of roses taking place.

Where do I pay homage, whereunto do I yield myself? To the unknown, only to the unknown, the Holy Ghost. I wait for the beginning, when the great and all creative unknown shall take notice of me, shall turn to me and inform me. This is my joy and my delight. And again, I turn to the unknown of the end, the darkness which is final, which will gather me into finality.

Do I fear the strange approach of the creative unknown to my door? I fear it only with pain and with unspeakable joy. And do I fear the invisible dark hand of death plucking me into the darkness, gathering me blossom by blossom from the stem of my life into the unknown of my afterwards? I fear it only in reverence and with strange satisfaction. For this is my final satisfaction, to be gathered blossom by blossom, all my life long, into the finality of the unknown which is my end.

DEMOCRACY

I

THE AVERAGE

Whitman gives two laws or principles for the establishment of Democracy. We may epitomize them as:

(1) The Law of the Average; (2) The Principle of Individualism, or Personalism, or Identity.

The Law of the Average is well known to us. Upon this law rests all the vague dissertation concerning equality and social perfection. Rights of Man, Equality of Man, Social Perfectibility of Man: all these sweet abstractions, once so inspiring, rest upon the fatal little hypothesis of the Average.

What is the Average? As we are well aware, there is no such animal. It is a pure abstraction. It is the reduction of the human being to a mathematical unit. Every human being numbers one, one single unit. That is the grand proposition of the Average.

Let us further examine this mysterious One, this Unit, this Average; let us examine it corporeally. The average human being: put him on the table, the little monster, and let us see what his works are like. He is just a little monster. He has two legs, two eyes, one nose—all exact. He has a stomach and a penis. He is a little organism. He is one very complicated organ, a unit, an identity.

What is he for? If he's an organ, he must have a purpose. If he's an organism, he must have a purpose. The question is premature, yet it shall be answered. Since he has a mouth, he is made for eating. Since he has feet, he is made for walking. Since he has a penis, he is made for reproducing his species. And so on, and so on.

What a loathsome little beast he is, this Average, this Unit, this Homunculus. Yet he has his purposes. He is useful to measure by. That's the purpose of all averages. An average is not invented to be an Archetype. What a really comical mistake we have made about him. He is invented to serve as a standard in the business of comparison. He is invented to serve as a standard, just like any other standard, like the metre, or the gramme, or the English pound sterling. That's what he is for—nothing else. He was never intended to be worshipped. What comical, fetish-smitten savages we are.

We use a foot-rule to tell us how big our house is. We don't proceed to say that the foot-rule is the sceptre which sways the earth and all the stars. Yet we have said as much of this little standardized invention of ours, the Average Man, the man-in-the-street. We have made prime fools of ourselves.

Now let us pull the gilt off the image, and see exactly what it is, and what we want it for. It is a mathematical quantity, like the metre or the foot-rule: a purely arbitrary institution of the human mind. Let us be quite clear about that.

But the human mind has invented the institution for its own purposes. Granted. What are the purposes? Merely for the comparing of one *living* man with another *living* man, in case of necessity: just as money is merely a contrivance for comparing a leg of mutton with a volume of Keats's poems. The money in itself is nothing. It is simply the arbitrary static measure for human desires. We mistake the measure for the thing it measures, and proceed to base our desires on money. It is nonsensical materialism.

Now for the Average Man himself. He is five-feet-six-inches high: and therefore you, John, will take an over-size pair of trousers, reach-me-downs; and you, François, mon cher, will take an under-size. The Average Man also has a mouth and a stomach, which consume two pounds of bread and six ounces of meat per day: and therefore you, Fritz, exceed the normal consumption of food, while you, dear Emily, consume less than your share. The Average Man has also a penis; and therefore all of you, François, Fritz, John, and Giacomo, you may begin begetting children at the average age, let us say, of twenty-five.

The Average Man is somehow very unsatisfactory. He is not sufficiently worked out. It is astonishing that we have not perfected him before. But this is because we have mixed the issues. How could we scientifically establish the Average, whilst he had to stand draped upon a pedestal, as an Ideal? Haul him down at once. He is no Ideal. He is just a Standard, the creature on whom Standard suits and Standard boots are fitted, to whose stomach Standard bread is adjusted, and for whose eyes the Standard Lamps are lighted, the Standard Oil Company is busy refining its gallons. He comes under the Government Weights and Measures Act.

Perfect him quickly: the Average, the Normal, the Man-in-the-street. He is so many inches high, broad, deep; he weighs so many pounds. He must eat so much, and sleep so much, and work so much, and play so much, and love so much, and think so much, and argue so much, and read so many newspapers, and have so many children. Somebody, quick,–some Professor of Social Economy–draw us up a perfect Average, and let us have him before the middle of next week. He is urgently required at the moment.

This is all your Man-in-the-street amounts to: this tailor's dummy of an average. He is the image and effigy of all your equality. Men are not equal, and never were, and never will be, save by the arbitrary determination of some ridiculous human Ideal. But still, in the normal course of things, all men *do* have two eyes and one nose and a stomach and a penis. In the teeth of all opposition we assert it. In the normal course of things, all men *do* hunger and thirst and sleep and laugh and feel miserable and fall in love and ache for coition and ache to escape from the woman again. And the Average Man just represents what all men need and desire, physically, functionally, materially, and socially. *Materially* need: that's the point. The Average Man is the standard of material need in the human being.

Please keep out all Spiritual and Mystical needs. They have nothing to do with the Average. You cannot Average such things. As far as the stomach goes, it is not really true that one man's meat is another man's poison. No. The law of the Average holds good for the stomach. All young mammals suck milk, without exception. But in the free, spontaneous self, one man's meat is truly another man's poison. And therefore you *can't* draw any average. You can't *have* an average: unless you are going to poison everybody.

Now we will settle for ever the Equality of Man, and the Rights of Man. Society means people living together. People *must* live together. And to live together, they must have some Standard, some *Material* Standard. This is where the Average comes in. And this is where Socialism and Modern Democracy come in. For Democracy and Socialism rest upon the Equality of Man, which is the Average. And this is sound enough, so long as the Average represents the real basic material needs of mankind: basic material needs: we insist and insist again. For Society, or Democracy, or any Political State or Community exists not for the sake of the individual, nor should ever exist for the sake of the individual, but simply to establish the Average, in order to make living together possible: that is, to make proper facilities for every man's clothing, feeding, housing himself, working, sleeping, mating, playing, according to his necessity as a common unit, an average. Everything beyond that common necessity depends on himself alone.

The proper adjustment of material means of existence: for this the State exists, but for nothing further. The State is a dead ideal. *Nation* is a dead ideal. Democracy and Socialism are dead ideals. They are one and all just *contrivances* for the supplying of the lowest material needs of a people. They are just vast hotels, or hostels, where every guest does some scrap of the business of the day's routine—if it's only lounging gracefully to give the appearance of ease—and for this contribution gets his suitable accommodation. England, France, Germany—these great nations, they have no vital meaning any more, except as great Food Committees and Housing Committees for a throng of people whose material tastes are somewhat in accord. No doubt they *had* other meanings. No doubt the French individuals of the seventeenth century still felt themselves gloriously expressed in stone, in Versailles. But man loses more and more his faculty for collective self-expression. Nay, the great development in collective expression in mankind has been a progress towards the possibility of purely individual expression. The highest Collectivity has for its true goal the purest individualism, pure individual spontaneity. But once more we have mistaken the means for the end: so that Presidents, those representatives of the collected masses, instead of being accounted the chief machine-section of society, which they are, are revered as ideal beings. The thing to do is not to raise the idea of Nation, or even of Internationalism, higher. The need is to take away every scrap of ideal drapery from nationalism and from internationalism, to show it all as a material contrivance for housing and feeding and conveying innumerable people. The housing and feeding, the method of conveyance and the rules of the road may be as different as you please—just as the methods of one great business house, and even of one hotel, are different from those of another. But that is all it is. Man no longer expresses himself in his form of government, and his President is strictly only his superlative butler. This is the true course of evolution: the great collective activities are at last merely auxiliary to the purely individual activities. Business houses may be magnificent, but there is nothing divine in it. This is why the Kaiser sounded so foolish. He was really only the head of a very great business concern. His God was the most intolerable part of his stock-in-trade. Genuine business houses may quarrel and compete, but they don't go to war. Why? Because they are not ideal concerns. They are just practical material concerns. It is only Ideal concerns which go to war, and slaughter indiscriminately with a feeling of exalted righteousness. But when a business concern masquerades as an ideal concern, and behaves in this fashion, it is really unbearable.

There are two things to do. Strip off at once all the ideal drapery from nationality, from nations, peoples, states, empires, and even from Internationalism and Leagues of Nations. Leagues of Nations should be just flatly and simply committees where representatives of the various business houses, so-called Nations, meet and consult. Consultations, board-meetings of the State business men: no more. *Representatives of Peoples*—who can represent me?—I am myself. I don't intend anybody to represent me.

You, you Cabinet Minister—what are you? You are the arch-grocer, the super-hotel-manager, the foreman over the ships and railways. What else are you? You are the super-tradesman, same paunch, same ingratiating manner, same everything. Governments, what are they? Just board-meetings of big business men. Very useful, too—very thankful we are that somebody *will* look after this business. But Ideal! An Ideal Government? What nonsense. We might as well talk of an Ideal Cook's Tourist Agency, or an Ideal Achille Serre Cleaners and Dyers. Even the ideal Ford of America is only an ideal *average* motor-car. His employees are not spontaneous, nonchalant human beings, à la Whitman. They are just well-tested, well-oiled sections of the Ford automobile.

Politics—what are they? Just another, extra-large, commercial wrangle over buying and selling—nothing else. Very good to have the wrangle. Let us have the buying and selling well done. But *ideal!* Politics *ideal! Political Idealists!* What rank gewgaw and nonsense! We have just enough sense not to talk about Ideal Selfridges or Ideal Krupps or Ideal Heidsiecks. Then let us have enough sense to drop the ideal of England or Europe or anywhere else. Let us be men and women, and keep our house in order. But let us pose no longer as houses, or as England, or as housemaids, or democrats.

Pull the ideal drapery off Governments, States, Nations, and Inter-nations. Show them for what they are: big business concerns for manufacturing and retailing Standard goods. Put up a statue of the Average Man, something like those abominable statues of men in woollen underwear which surmount a shop at the corner of Oxford Street and Tottenham Court Road. Let your statue be grotesque: in fact, borrow those ignominious statues of men in pants and vests: the fat one for Germany, the thin one for England, the middling one for France, the gaunt one for America. Point to these statues, which guard the entrance to the House of Commons, to the Chamber, to the Senate, to the Reichstag–and let every Prime Minister and President know the quick of his own ignominy. Let every bursting politician see himself in his commercial pants. Let every senatorial idealist and saviour of mankind be reminded that his office depends on the quality of the underwear he supplies to the State. Let every fiery and rhetorical Deputy remember that he is only held together by his patent suspenders.

And then, when the people of the world have finally got over the state of giddy idealizing of governments, nations, inter-nations, politics, democracies, empires, and so forth; when they really understand that their collective activities are only cook-housemaid to their sheer individual activities; when they at last calmly accept a business concern for what it is; then, at last, we may actually see free men in the streets.

II

IDENTITY

Let us repeat that Whitman establishes the true Democracy on two bases:

(1) The Average; (2) Individualism, Personalism, or Identity.

The Average is much easier to settle and define than is Individualism or Identity. The Average is the same as the Man-in-the-street, the unit of Humanity. This unit is in the first place just an abstraction, an invention of the human mind. In the first place, the Man-in-the-street is no more than an abstract idea. But in the second place, by application to Tom, Dick, and Harry, he becomes a substantial, material, functioning unit. This is how the ideal world is created. It is invented exactly as man invents machinery. First there is an idea; then the idea is substantiated, the inventor fabricates his machine; and then he proceeds to worship his fabrication, and himself as mouthpiece of the Logos. This is how the world, the universe, was invented from the Logos: exactly as man has invented machinery and the whole ideal of humanity. The vital universe was never created from any Logos; but the ideal universe of man was certainly so invented. Man's overweening mind uttered the Word, and the Word was God. So that the world exists today as a flesh-and-blood-and-iron substantiation of this uttered world. This is all the trouble: that the invented *ideal* world of man is superimposed upon living men and women, and men and women are thus turned into abstracted, functioning, mechanical units. This is all the great ideal of Humanity amounts to: an aggregation of ideally functioning units; never a man or woman possible.

Ideals, all ideals and every ideal, are a trick of the devil. They are a superimposition of the abstracted, automatic, invented universe of man upon the spontaneous creative universe. So much for the Average, the Man-in-the-street, and the great ideal of Humanity: all a little trick men have played on us. But quite a useful little trick—so long as we merely use it as one uses the trick of making cakes or pies or bread, just for feeding purposes, and suchlike.

Let us leave the Average, and look at the second basis of democracy. With the Average we settle the cooking, eating, sleeping, housing, mating, and clothing problem. But Whitman insisted on exalting his Democracy; he would not quite leave it on the cooking-eating-mating level. We cook to eat, we eat to sleep, we sleep to build houses, we build houses in order to beget and bear children in safety, we bear children in order to clothe them, we clothe them in order that they may start the old cycle over again, cook and eat and sleep and house and mate and clothe, and so on *ad infinitum*. That is the Average. It is the business of a government to superintend it.

But Whitman insisted on raising Democracy above government, or even above public service or humanity or love of one's neighbour. Heaven knows what his Democracy is—but something as yet unattained. It is something beyond governments and even beyond Ideals. It must be beyond Ideals, because it has never yet been stated. As an idea it doesn't yet exist. Even Whitman, with all his reiteration, got no further than *hinting:* and frightfully bad hints, many of them.

We've heard the Average hint—enough of that. Now for Individualism, Personalism, and Identity. We catch hold of the tail of the hint, and proceed with Identity.

What has Identity got to do with Democracy? It can't have anything to do with politics and governments. It can't much affect one's love for one's neighbour, or for humanity. Yet, stay—it can. Whitman says there is One Identity in all things. It is only the old dogma. All things emanate from the Supreme Being. All things, being all emanations from the Supreme Being, have One Identity.

Very nice. But we don't like the look of this Supreme Being. It is too much like the Man-in-the-street. This Supreme Being, this Anima Mundi, this Logos was surely just invented to suit the human needs. It is surely the magnified Average, abstracted from men, and then clapped on to them again, like identity-medals on wretched khaki soldiers. But instead of a magnified average-function-unit, we have a magnified unit of Consciousness, or Spirit.

Like the Average, this One Identity is useful enough, if we use it aright. It is not a matter of provisioning the body, this time, but of provisioning the spirit, the consciousness. We are all one, and therefore every bit partakes of all the rest. That is, the Whole is inherent in every fragment. That is, every human consciousness has the same intrinsic value as every other human consciousness, because each is an essential part of the Great Consciousness. This is the One Identity which identifies us all.

It is very nice, theoretically. And it is a very great stimulus to universal comprehension; it leads us all to want to know everything; it even tempts us all to imagine we know everything beforehand, and need make no effort. It is the subtlest means of extending the consciousness. But when you have extended your consciousness, even to infinity, what then? Do you really become God? When in your understanding you embrace everything, then surely you are divine? But no! With a nasty bump you have to come down and realize that, in spite of your infinite comprehension, you are not really any other than you were before: not a bit more divine or superhuman or enlarged. Your *consciousness* is not *you:* that is the sad lesson you learn in your superhuman flight of infinite understanding.

This big bump of falling out of the infinite back into your own old self leads you to suspect that the One Identity is not *the* identity. There is another, little sort of identity, which you can't get away from, except by breaking your neck. The One Identity is very like the Average. It is what you are when you aren't yourself. It is what you are when you imagine you're something hugely big—the Infinite, for example. And the consciousness is really capable of attaining infinity. But there you are! Your consciousness has to fly back to the old tree, to peck the old apples, and sleep under the leaves. It was all only an excursion. It was wearing a magic cap. You yourself invented the cap, and then puffed up your head to fit it. But a swelled head at last begins to ache, and you realize it's only your own old chump after all. All the extended consciousness that ranges the infinite heavens must sleep under the thatch of your hair at night: and you are only you; and your *spirit* is only a bird in your tree, that flies, and then settles, whistles, and then is silent.

Man is a queer beast. He spends dozens of centuries puffing himself up and drawing himself in, and at last he has to be content to be just his own size, neither infinitely big nor infinitely little. Man is tragi-comical. His insatiable desire to be *everything* has made him clean forget that he might be himself. To be everything–to be everything: the history of mankind is only a history of this insane craving in man. You can magnify yourself into a Jehovah and a huge Egyptian king-god: or you can reverse the spy-glass, and dwindle yourself away into a speck, lost in the Infinite of Love, as the later great races have done. But still you'll only be chasing the one mad reward, the reward of infinity: which, when you've got it, bursts like a bubble in your hand, and leaves you looking at your own fingers. Well, and what's wrong with your own fingers?

It is a bubble, the One Identity. But, chasing it, man gets his education. It is his education process, the chance of the All, the extension of the consciousness. He *learns* everything: except the last lesson of all, which he can't learn till the bubble has burst in his fingers.

The last lesson?–Ah, the lesson of his own fingers: himself: the little identity; little, but real. Better, far better, to be oneself than to be any bursting Infinite, or swollen One Identity.

It is a radical passion in man, however, the passion to include *everything* in himself, grasp it all. There are two ways of gratifying this passion. The first is Alexander's way, the way of power, power over the material universe. This is what the alchemists and magicians sought. This is what Satan offered Jesus, in the Temptations: power, mystic and actual, over the material world. And power, we know, is a bubble: a platitudinous bubble.

But Jesus chose the other way: not to *have* all, but to *be* all. Not to *grasp* everything into supreme possession: but to *be* everything, through supreme acceptance. It is the same thing, at the very last. The king-god and the crucified-God hold the same bubble in their hands: the bubble of the All, the Infinite. The king-god extends the dominion of his will and consciousness over all things: the crucified identifies his will and consciousness with all things. But the submission of love is at last a process of pure materialism, like the supreme extension of power. Up to a certain point, both in mastering, which is power, and in submitting, which is love, the soul *learns* and fulfils itself. Beyond a certain point, it merely collapses from its centrality, and lapses out into the material chain of cause and effect. The tyranny of Power is no worse than the tyranny of No-power. Government by the highest is no more fatal than government by the lowest. Let the Average govern, let him be called super butler, let us have a faint but tolerant contempt for him. But let us keep our very self integral, greater than any having or knowing, centrally alive and quick.

The last lesson: the myriad, mysterious identities, no one of which can *comprehend* another. They can only exist side by side, as stars do. The lesson of lessons: not in any oneness with the rest of things do we have our pure being: but in clean, fine singleness. Oneness, and collectiveness, these are our lesser states, inferior: our impurity. They are mere states of consciousness and of having.

It is all very well to talk about a Supreme Being, an Anima Mundi, an Oversoul, an Infinite: but it is all just human invention. Come down to actuality. Where do you see Being?–In individual men and women. Where do you find an Anima?–In living individual creatures. Where would you look for a soul?–In a man, in an animal, in a tree or flower. And all the rest, about Supreme Beings and Anima Mundis and Oversouls, is just abstractions. Show me the very animal!–You can't. It is merely a trick of the human will, trying to get power over everything, and therefore making the wish father of the thought. The cart foals the horse, and there you are: a Logos, a Supreme Being, a What-not.

But there are two sorts of individual identity. Every factory-made pitcher has its own little identity, resulting from a certain mechanical combination of Matter with Forces. These are the material identities. They sum up to the material Infinite.

The true identity, however, is the identity of the living self. If we look for God, let us look in the bush where he sings. That is, in living creatures. Every living creature is single in itself, a *ne plus ultra* of creative reality, *fons et origo* of creative manifestation. Why go further? Why begin to abstract and generalize and include? There you have it. Every single living creature is a single creative unit, a unique, incommutable self. Primarily, in its own spontaneous reality, it knows no law. It is a law unto itself. Secondarily, in its material reality, it submits to all the laws of the material universe. But the primal, spontaneous self in any creature has ascendance, truly, over the material laws of the universe; it uses these laws and converts them in the mystery of creation.

This then is the true identity: the inscrutable, single self, the little unfathomable well-head that bubbles forth into being and doing. We cannot analyse it. We can only know it is there. It is not by any means a Logos. It precedes any knowing. It is the fountain-head of everything: the quick of the self.

Not people melted into a oneness: that is not the new Democracy. But people released into their single, starry identity, each one distinct and incommutable. This will never be an ideal; for of the living self you cannot make an idea, just as you have not been able to turn the individual "soul" into an idea. Both are impossible to idealize. An idea is an abstraction from reality, a generalization. And you can't generalize the incommutable.

So the Whitman One Identity, the *En-Masse,* is a horrible nullification of true identity and being. At the best, our *en masse* activities can be but servile, serving the free soul. At the worst, they are sheer self-destruction. Let us put them in their place. Let us get over our rage of social activity, public being, universal self-estimation, republicanism, bolshevism, socialism, empire—all these mad manifestations of *En Masse* and One Identity. They are all self-betrayed. Let our Democracy be in the singleness of the clear, clean self, and let our *En Masse* be no more than an arrangement for the liberty of this self. Let us drop looking after our neighbour. It only robs him of his chance of looking after himself. Which is robbing him of his freedom, with a vengeance.

III

PERSONALITY

> One's-self I sing, a simple separate person,
> Yet utter the word Democratic, the word En-Masse.

Such are the opening words of *Leaves of Grass.* It is Whitman's whole *motif,* the key to all his Democracy. First and last he sings of "the great pride of man in himself." First and last he is Chanter of Personality. If it is not Personality, it is Identity; and if not Identity, it is the Individual: and along with these, Democracy and *En Masse.*

In Whitman, at all times, the true and the false are so near, so interchangeable, that we are almost inevitably left with divided feelings. The Average, one of his greatest idols, we flatly refuse to worship. Again, when we come to do real reverence to identity, we never know whether we shall be taking off our hats to that great mystery, the unique individual self, distinct and primal in every separate man, or whether we shall be saluting that old great idol of the past, the Supreme One which swallows up all true identity.

And now for Personality. What meaning does "person" really carry? A *person* is given in the dictionary as an *individual human being*. But surely the words *person* and *individual* suggest very different things. It is not at all the same to have personality as to have individuality, though you may not be able to define the difference. And the distinction between a person and a human being is perhaps even greater. Some "persons" hardly seem like human beings at all.

The derivation this time helps. *Persona,* in Latin, is a player's mask, or a character in a play: and perhaps the word is cognate with *sonare,* to sound. An *individual* is that which is not divided or not dividable. A *being* we shall not attempt to define, because it is indefinable.

So now, there must be a radical difference between something which was originally a player's mask, or a transmitted sound, and something which means "the undivided." The old meaning lingers in *person,* and is almost obvious in *personality*. A person is a human being *as he appears to others;* and personality is that which is transmitted from the person to his audience: the transmissible effect of a man.

A good actor can assume a personality; he can never assume an individuality. Either he has his own, or none. So that personality is something much more superficial, or at least more volatile than individuality. This volatile quality is the one we must examine.

Let us take a sentence from an American novel: "My *ego* had played a trick on me, and made me think I wanted babies, when I only wanted the man." This is a perfectly straight and lucid statement. But what is the difference between the authoress's *ego* and her *me?* The *ego* is obviously a sort of second self, which she carries about with her. It is her body of accepted consciousness, which she has inherited more or less ready-made from her father and grandfathers. This secondary self is very pernicious, dictating to her issues which are quite false to her true, deeper, spontaneous self, her creative identity.

Nothing in the world is more pernicious than the *ego* or spurious self, the conscious entity with which every individual is saddled. He receives it almost *en bloc* from the preceding generation, and spends the rest of his life trying to drag his spontaneous self from beneath the horrible incubus. And the most fatal part of the incubus, by far, is the dead, leaden weight of handed-on ideals. So that every individual is born with a mill-stone of ideals round his neck, and, whether he knows it or not, either spends his time trying to get his neck free, like a wild animal wrestling with a collar to which a log is fastened; or else he spends his days decorating his mill-stone, his log, with fantastic colours.

And a finely or fantastically decorated mill-stone is called a personality. Never trust for one moment any individual who has unmistakable *personality*. He is sure to be a life-traitor. His personality is only a sort of actor's mask. It is his self-conscious *ego,* his *ideal* self masquerading and prancing round, showing off. He may not be aware of it. But that makes no matter. He is a painted bug.

The *ideal* self: this is personality. The self that is begotten and born from the *idea,* this is the *ideal* self: a spurious, detestable product. This is man created from his own Logos. This is man born out of his own head. This is the self-conscious ego, the entity of fixed ideas and ideals, prancing and displaying itself like an actor. And this is personality. This is what makes the American authoress gush about babies. And this gush is her peculiar form of personality, which renders her attractive to the American men, who prefer so much to deal with personalities and *egos,* rather than with real beings: because personalities and *egos,* after all, are quite *reasonable,* which means, they are subject to the laws of cause-and-effect; they are safe and calculable: materialists, units of the material world of Force and Matter.

Your idealist alone is a perfect materialist. This is no paradox. What is the idea, or the ideal, after all? It is only a fixed, static entity, an abstraction, an extraction from the living body of life. Creative life is characterized by spontaneous mutability: it brings forth unknown issues, impossible to preconceive. But an ideal is just a machine which is in process of being built. A man gets the idea for some engine, and proceeds to work it out in steel and copper. In exactly the same way, man gets some ideal of man, and proceeds to work it out in flesh-and-blood, as a fixed, static entity: just as a machine is a static entity, so is the ideal Humanity.

If we want to find the real enemy today, here it is: idealism. If we want to find this enemy incarnate, here he is: a personality. If we want to know the steam which drives this mechanical little incarnation, here it is: love of humanity, the public good.

There have been other ideals than ours, other forms of personality, other sorts of steam. We quite fail to see what sort of personality Rameses II had, or what sort of steam built the pyramids: chiefly, I suppose, because they are a very great load on the face of the earth.

Is love of humanity the same as real, warm, individual love? Nonsense. It is the moonshine of our warm day, a hateful reflection. Is personality the same as individual being? We know it is a mere mask. Is idealism the same as creation? Rubbish! Idealism is no more than a plan of a marvellous Human Machine, drawn up by the great Draughtsmen-Minds of the past. Give God a pair of compasses, and let the designs be measured and formed. What insufferable nonsense! As if creation proceeded from a pair of compasses. Better say that man is a forked radish, as Carlyle did: it's nearer the mark than this Pair of Compasses business.

You can have life two ways. Either everything is created from the mind, downwards; or else everything preceeds from the creative quick, outwards into exfoliation and blossom. Either a great Mind floats in space: God, the Anima Mundi, the Oversoul, drawing with a pair of compasses and making everything to scale, even emotions and self-conscious effusions; or else creation proceeds from the for ever inscrutable quicks of living beings, men, women, animals, plants. The actual living quick itself is alone the creative reality. Once you abstract from this, once you generalize and postulate Universals, you have departed from the creative reality, and entered the realm of static fixity, mechanism, materialism.

Now let us put salt on the tail of that sly old bird of "attractive personality." It isn't a bird at all. It is a self-conscious, self-important, befeathered snail: and salt is good for snails. It is the snail which has eaten off our flowers till none are left. Now let us no longer be taken in by the feathers. Anyhow, put salt on his tail.

No personalities in our Democracy. No ideals either. When still more Personalities come round hawking their pretty ideals, we must be ready to upset their apple-cart. I say, a man's self is a law unto itself: not unto *himself,* mind you. Itself. When a man talks about *himself,* he is talking about his idea of himself; his own ideal self, that fancy little homunculus he has fathered in his brain. When a man is conscious of himself he is trading his own personality.

You can't make an *idea* of the living self: hence it can never become an ideal. Thank heaven for that. There it is, an inscrutable, unfindable, vivid quick, giving us off as a life-issue. It is not *spirit.* Spirit is merely our mental consciousness, a finished essence extracted from our life-being, just as alcohol, spirits of wine, is the material, finished essence extracted from the living grape. The living self is not spirit. You cannot postulate it. How can you postulate that which is *there?* The moon might as well try to hold forth in heaven, postulating the sun. Or a child hanging on to his mother's skirt might as well commence in a long diatribe to postulate his mother's existence, in order to prove his own existence. Which is exactly what man has been busily doing for two thousand years. What amazing nonsense!

The quick of the self is *there*. You needn't try to get behind it. As leave try to get behind the sun. You needn't try to idealize it, for by so doing you will only slime about with feathers in your tail, a gorgeous befeathered snail of an *ego* and a personality. You needn't try to show it off to your neighbour: he'll put salt on your tail if you do. And you needn't go on trying to save the living soul of your neighbour. It's hands off. Do you think you are such a God-Almighty bird of paradise that you can grow your neighbour's goose-quills for him on your own loving house-sparrow wings? Every bird must grow his own feathers; you are not the almighty dodo; you've got nobody's wings to feather but your own.

IV

INDIVIDUALISM

It is obvious that Whitman's Democracy is not merely a political system, or a system of government–or even a social system. It is an attempt to conceive a new way of life, to establish new values. It is a struggle to liberate human beings from the fixed, arbitrary control of ideals, into free spontaneity.

No, the ideal of Oneness, the unification of all mankind into the homogeneous whole, is done away with. The great *desire* is that each single individual shall be incommutably himself, spontaneous and single, that he shall not in any way be reduced to a term, a unit of any Whole.

We must discriminate between an ideal and a desire. A desire proceeds from within, from the unknown, spontaneous soul or self. But an ideal is superimposed from above, from the mind; it is a fixed, arbitrary thing, like a machine control. The great lesson is to learn to break all the fixed ideals, to allow the soul's own deep desires to come direct, spontaneous into consciousness. But it is a lesson which will take many æons to learn.

Our life, our being depends upon the incalculable issue from the central Mystery into indefinable *presence*. This sounds in itself an abstraction. But not so. It is rather the perfect absence of abstraction. The central Mystery is no generalized abstraction. It is each man's primal original soul or self, within him. And *presence* is nothing mystic or ghostly. On the contrary. It is the actual man present before us. The fact that an actual man present before us is an inscrutable and incarnate Mystery, untranslatable, this is the fact upon which any great scheme of social life must be based. It is the fact of *otherness*.

Each human self is single, incommutable, and unique. This is its *first* reality. Each self is unique, and therefore incomparable. It is a single well-head of creation, unquestionable: it cannot be compared with another self, another well-head, because, in its prime or creative reality, it can never be comprehended by any other self.

The living self has one purpose only: to come into its own fullness of being, as a tree comes into full blossom, or a bird into spring beauty, or a tiger into lustre.

But this coming into full, spontaneous being is the most difficult thing of all. Man's nature is balanced between spontaneous creativity and mechanical-material activity. Spontaneous being is subject to no law. But mechanical-material existence is subject to all the laws of the mechanical-physical world. Man has almost half his nature in the material world. His spontaneous nature *just* takes precedence.

The only thing man has to trust to in coming to himself is his desire and his impulse. But both desire and impulse tend to fall into mechanical automatism: to fall from spontaneous reality into dead or material reality. All our education should be a guarding against this fall.

The fall is possible in a two-fold manner. Desires tend to automatize into functional appetites, and impulses tend to automatize into fixed aspirations or ideals. These are the two great temptations of man. Falling into the first temptation, the whole human will pivots on some function, some material activity, which then works the whole being: like an *idée fixe* in the mental consciousness. This automatized, dominant appetite we call a lust: a lust for power, a lust for consuming, a lust for self-abnegation and merging. The second great temptation is the inclination to set up some fixed centre in the mind, and make the whole soul turn upon this centre. This we call idealism. Instead of the will fixing upon some sensational activity, it fixes upon some aspirational activity, and pivots this activity upon an idea or an ideal. The whole soul streams in the energy of aspiration and turns automatically, like a machine, upon the ideal.

These are the two great temptations of the fall of man, the fall from spontaneous, single, pure being, into what we call materialism or automatism or mechanism of the self. All education must tend against this fall; and all our efforts in all our life must be to preserve the soul free and spontaneous. The whole soul of man must *never* be subjected to one motion or emotion, the life-activity must never be degraded into a fixed activity, there must be *no fixed direction.*

There can be no ideal goal for human life. Any ideal goal means mechanization, materialism, and nullity. There is no pulling open the buds to see what the blossom will be. Leaves must unroll, buds swell and open, and *then* the blossom. And even after that, when the flower dies and the leaves fall, *still* we shall not know. There will be more leaves, more buds, more blossoms: and again, a blossom is an unfolding of the creative unknown. Impossible, utterly impossible to preconceive the unrevealed blossom. You cannot forestall it from the last blossom. We know the flower of today, but the flower of tomorrow is all beyond us. Only in the material-mechanical world can man foresee, foreknow, calculate, and establish laws.

So, we more or less grasp the first term of the new Democracy. We see something of what a man will be unto himself.

Next, what will a man be unto his neighbour?—Since every individual is, in his first reality, a single, incommutable soul, not to be calculated or defined in terms of any other soul, there can be no establishing of a mathematical ratio. We cannot say that all men are equal. We cannot say $A = B$. Nor can we say that men are unequal. We may not declare that $A = B + C$.

Where each thing is unique in itself, there can be no comparison made. One man is neither equal nor unequal to another man. When I stand in the presence of another man, and I am my own pure self, am I aware of the presence of an equal, or of an inferior, or of a superior? I am not. When I stand with another man, who is himself, and when I am truly myself, then I am only aware of a Presence, and of the strange reality of Otherness. There is me, and there is *another being*. That is the first part of the reality. There is no comparing or estimating. There is only this strange recognition of *present otherness*. I may be glad, angry, or sad, because of the presence of the other. But still no comparison enters in. Comparison enters only when one of us departs from his own integral being, and enters the material-mechanical world. Then equality and inequality starts at once.

So, we know the first great purpose of Democracy: that each man shall be spontaneously himself—each man himself, each woman herself, without any question of equality or inequality entering in at all; and that no man shall try to determine the being of any other man, or of any other woman.

But, because of the temptation which awaits every individual—the temptation to fall out of being, into automatism and mechanization, every individual must be ready at all times to defend his own being against the mechanization and materialism forced upon him by those people who have fallen or departed from being. It is the long unending fight, the fight for the soul's own freedom of spontaneous being, against the mechanism and materialism of the fallen.

All the foregoing deals really with the integral, whole nature of man. If man would but *keep* whole, integral, everything could be left at that. There would be no need for laws and governments: agreement would be spontaneous. Even the great concerted social activities would be essentially spontaneous.

But in his present state of unspeakable barbarism, man is unable to distinguish his own spontaneous integrity from his mechanical lusts and aspirations. Hence there must still be laws and governments. But laws and governments henceforth, we see it clearly and we must never forget it, relate only to the material world: to property, the possession of property and the means of life, and to the material-mechanical nature of man.

In the past, no doubt, there were great ideals to fulfil: ideals of brotherhood, oneness, and equality. Great sections of humanity tended to cohere into particular brotherhoods, expressing their oneness and their equality and their united purpose in a manner peculiar to themselves. For no matter how single an ideal may be, even such a mathematical ideal as equality and oneness, it will find the most diverse and even opposite expressions. So that brotherhood and oneness in Germany never meant the same as brotherhood and oneness in France. Yet each was brotherhood, and each was oneness. Souls, as they work out the same ideal, work it out differently: always differently, until they reach the point where the spontaneous integrity of being finally breaks. And then, when pure mechanization or materialism sets in, the soul is automatically pivoted, and the most diverse of creatures fall into a common mechanical unison.

This we see in America. It is not a homogeneous, spontaneous coherence so much as a disintegrated amorphousness which lends itself to perfect mechanical unison.

Men have reached the point where, in further fulfilling their ideals, they break down the living integrity of their being and fall into sheer mechanical materialism. They become automatic units, determined entirely by mechanical law.

This is horribly true of modern democracy–socialism, conservatism, bolshevism, liberalism, republicanism, communism: all alike. The one principle that governs all the *isms* is the same: the principle of the idealized unit, the possessor of property. Man has his highest fulfilment as a possessor of property: so they all say, really. One half says that the uneducated, being the majority, should possess the property; the other half says that the educated, being the enlightened, should possess the property. There is no more to it. No need to write books about it.

This is the last of the ideals. This is the last phase of the ideal of equality, brotherhood, and oneness. All ideals work down to the sheer materialism which is their intrinsic reality, at last.

It doesn't matter, now, who has the property. They have all lost their being over it. Even property, that most substantial of realities, evaporates once man loses his integral nature. It is curious that it is so, but it is undeniable. So that property is now fast evaporating.

Wherein lies the hope? For with it evaporates the last ideal. Sometime, somewhere, man will wake up and realize that property is only there to be used, not to be possessed. He will realize that possession is a kind of illness of the spirit, and a hopeless burden upon the spontaneous self. The little pronouns "my" and "our" will lose all their mystic spell.

The question of property will never be settled till people cease to care for property. Then it will settle itself. A man only needs so much as will help him to his own fulfilment. Surely the individual who wants a motor-car merely for the sake of having it and riding in it is as hopeless an automaton as the motor-car itself.

When men are no longer obsessed with the desire to possess property, or with the parallel desire to prevent another man's possessing it, then, and only then shall we be glad to turn it over to the State. Our way of State-ownership is merely a farcical exchange of words, not of ways. We only intend our States to be Unlimited Liability Companies instead of Limited Liability Companies.

The Prime Minister of the future will be no more than a sort of steward, the Minister for Commerce will be the great housekeeper, the Minister for Transport the head-coachman: all just chief servants, no more: servants.

When men become their own decent selves again, then we can so easily arrange the material world. The arrangement will come, as it must come, spontaneously, not by previous ordering. Until such time, what is the good of talking about it? All discussion and idealizing of the possession of property, whether individual or group or State possession, amounts now to no more than a fatal betrayal of the spontaneous self. All settlement of the property question must arise spontaneously out of the new impulse in man, to free himself from the extraneous load of possession, and walk naked and light. Every attempt at preordaining a new material world only adds another last straw to the load that already has broken so many backs. If we are to keep our backs unbroken, we must deposit all property on the ground, and learn to walk without it. We must stand aside. And when many men stand aside, they stand in a new world; a new world of man has come to pass. This is the Democracy, the new order.

THE PROPER STUDY

If no man lives for ever, neither does any precept. And if even the weariest river winds somewhere safe to sea, so also does the weariest wisdom. And there it is lost. Also incorporated.

> Know then thyself, presume not God to scan;
> The proper study of mankind is man.

It was Alexander Pope who absolutely struck the note of our particular epoch: not Shakespeare or Luther or Milton. A man of first magnitude never fits his age perfectly.

> Know then thyself, presume not God to scan;
> The proper study of mankind is Man—*with a capital M.*

This stream of wisdom is very weary now: weary to death. It started such a gay little trickle, and is such a spent muddy ebb by now. It will take a big sea to swallow all its alluvia.

"Know then thyself." All right! I'll do my best. Honestly I'll do my best, sincerely to know myself. Since it is the great commandment to consciousness of our long era, let us be men, and try to obey it. Jesus gave the emotional commandment, "Love thy neighbour." But the Greeks set the even more absolute motto, in its way, a more deeply religious motto: "Know thyself."

Very well! Being man, and the son of man, I find it only honourable to obey. To do my best. To do my best to know myself. And particularly that part, or those parts of myself that have not yet been admitted into consciousness. Man is nothing, less than a tick stuck in a sheep's back, unless he adventures. Either into the unknown of the world, of his environment. Or into the unknown of himself.

Allons! the road is before us. Know thyself! Which means, *really,* know thine own *unknown self.* It's no good knowing something you know already. The thing is to discover the tracts as yet unknown. And as the only unknown now lies deep in the passional soul, allons! the road is before us. We write a novel or two, we are called erotic or depraved or idiotic or boring. What does it matter, we go the road just the same. If you see the point of the great old commandment, *Know thyself,* then you see the point of all art.

But knowing oneself, like knowing anything else, is not a process that can continue to infinity, in the same direction. The fact that I myself *am* only myself makes me very specifically finite. True, I may argue that my Self is a mystery that impinges on the infinite. Admitted. But the moment my Self impinges on the infinite, it ceases to be just myself.

The same is true of all knowing. You start to find out the chemical composition of a drop of water, and before you know where you are, your river of knowledge is winding very unsatisfactorily into a very vague sea, called the ether. You start to study electricity, you track the wretch down till you get some mysterious and misbehaving atom of energy or unit of force that goes pop under your nose and leaves you with the dead body of a mere word.

You sail down your stream of knowledge, and you find yourself absolutely at sea. Which may be safety for the weary river, but is a sad look-out for you, who are a land animal.

Now all science starts gaily from the inland source of *I Don't Know*. Gaily it says: "I don't know, but I'm going to know." It's like a little river bubbling up cheerfully in the determination to dissolve the whole world in its waves. And science, like the little river, winds wonderingly out again into the final *I Don't Know* of the ocean.

All this is platitudinous as regards science. Science has learned an uncanny lot, *by the way*.

Apply the same to the Know Thyself motto. We have learned something by the way. But as far as I'm concerned, I see land receding, and the great ocean of the last *I Don't Know* enveloping me.

But the human consciousness is never allowed finally to say: "I Don't Know." It has got to know, even if it must metamorphose to do so.

> Know then thyself, presume not God to scan.

Now as soon as you come across a Thou Shalt Not commandment, you may be absolutely sure that sometime or other, you'll have to break this commandment. You needn't make a practice of breaking it. But the day will come when you'll have to break it. When you'll have to take the name of the Lord Your God in vain, and have other gods, and worship idols, and steal, and kill, and commit adultery, and all the rest. A day will come. Because, as Oscar Wilde says, what's a temptation for, except to be succumbed to!

There comes a time to every man when he has to break one or other of the Thou Shalt Not commandments. And then is the time to Know Yourself just a bit different from what you thought you were.

So that in the end, this Know Thyself commandment brings me

up against the Presume-Not-God-to-Scan fence. Trespassers will be prosecuted. Know then thyself, presume not God to scan.

It's a dilemma. Because this business of knowing myself has led me slap up against the forbidden enclosure where, presumably, this God mystery is kept in corral. It isn't my fault. I followed the road. And it leads over the edge of a precipice on which stands up a signboard: Danger! Don't go over the edge!

But I've *got* to go over the edge. The way lies that way.

Flop! Over we go, and into the endless sea. There drown.

No! Out of the drowning something else gurgles awake. And that's the best of the human consciousness. When you fall into the final sea of *I Don't Know,* then, if you can but gasp *Teach Me,* you turn into a fish, and twiddle your fins and twist your tail and grope in amazement, in a new element.

That's why they called Jesus: The Fish. Pisces. Because he fell, like the weariest river, into the great Ocean that is outside the shore, and there took on a new way of knowledge.

The Proper Study is Man, sure enough. But the proper study of man, like the proper study of anything else, will in the end leave you no option. You'll have to presume to study God. Even the most hard-boiled scientist, if he is a brave and honest man, is landed in this unscientific dilemma. Or rather, he is all at sea in it.

The river of human consciousness, like ancient Ocean, goes in a circle. It starts gaily, bubblingly, fiercely from an inland pool, where it surges up in obvious mystery and Godliness, the human consciousness. And here is the God of the Beginning, call him Jehovah or Ra or Ammon or Jupiter or what you like. One bubbles up in Greece, one in India, one in Jerusalem. From their various God-sources the streams of human consciousness rush variously down. Then begin to meander and to doubt. Then fall slow. Then start to silt up. Then pass into the great Ocean, which is the God of the End.

In the great ocean of the End, most men are lost. But Jesus turned into a fish, he had the other consciousness of the Ocean which is the divine End of us all. And then like a salmon he beat his way up stream again, to speak from the source.

And this is the greater history of man, as distinguished from the lesser history, in which figure Mr. Lloyd George and Monsieur Poincaré.

We are in the deep, muddy estuary of our era, and terrified of the emptiness of the sea beyond. Or we are at the end of the great road, that Jesus and Francis and Whitman walked. We are on the brink of a precipice, and terrified at the great void below.

No help for it. We are men, and for men there is no retreat. Over we go.

Over we must and shall go, so we may as well do it voluntarily, keeping our soul alive; and as we drown in our terrestrial nature, transmogrify into fishes. Pisces. That which knows the Oceanic Godliness of the End.

The proper study of mankind is man. Agreed entirely! But in the long run, it becomes again as it was before, man in his relation to the deity. The proper study of mankind is man in his relation to the deity.

And yet not as it was before. Not the specific deity of the inland source. The vast deity of the End. Oceanus whom you can only know by becoming a Fish. Let us become Fishes, and try.

They talk about the sixth sense. They talk as if it were an extension of the other senses. A mere *dimensional* sense. It's nothing of the sort. There is a sixth sense right enough. Jesus had it. The sense of the God that is the End and the Beginning. And the proper study of mankind is man in his relation to this Oceanic God.

We have come to the end, for the time being, of the study of man in his relation to man. Or man in his relation to himself. Or man in his relation to woman. There is nothing more of importance to be said, by us or for us, on this subject. Indeed, we have no more to say.

Of course, there is the literature of perversity. And there is the literature of little playboys and playgirls, not only of the western world. But the literature of perversity is a brief weed. And the playboy playgirl stuff, like the movies, though a very monstrous weed, won't live long.

As the weariest river winds by no means safely to sea, all the muddy little individuals begin to chirrup: "Let's play! Let's play at something! We're so god-like when we *play*."

But it won't do, my dears. The sea will swallow you up, and all your play and perversions and personalities.

You can't get any more literature out of man in his relation to man. Which, of course, should be writ large, to mean man in his relation to woman, to other men, and to the whole environment of men: or woman in her relation to man, or other women, or the whole environment of women. You can't get any more literature out of that. Because any new book must needs be a new stride. And the next stride lands you over the sandbar in the open ocean, where the first and greatest relation of every man and woman is to the Ocean itself, the great God of the End, who is the All-Father of all sources, as the sea is father of inland lakes and springs of water.

But get a glimpse of this new relation of men and women to the great God of the End, who is the Father, not the Son, of all our beginnings: and you get a glimpse of the new literature. Think of the true novel of St. Paul, for example. Not the sentimental looking-backward Christian novel, but the novel looking out to sea, to the great Source, and End, of all beginnings. Not the St. Paul with his human feelings repudiated, to give play to the new divine feelings. Not the St. Paul violent in reaction against worldliness and sensuality, and therefore a dogmatist with his sheaf of Shalt-Nots ready. But a St. Paul two thousand years older, having his own epoch behind him, and having again the great knowledge of the deity, the deity which Jesus knew, the vast Ocean God which is at the end of all our consciousness.

Because, after all, if chemistry winds wearily to sea in the ether, or some such universal, don't we also, not as chemists but as conscious men, also wind wearily to sea in a divine ether, which means nothing to us but space and words and emptiness? We wind wearily to sea in words and emptiness.

But man is a mutable animal. Turn into the Fish, the Pisces of man's final consciousness, and you'll start to swim again in the great life which is so frighteningly godly that you realize your previous presumption.

And then you realize the new relation of man. Men like fishes lifted on a great wave of the God of the End, swimming together, and apart, in a new medium. A new relation, in a new whole.

ON BEING RELIGIOUS

The problem is not, and never was, whether God exists or doesn't exist. Man is so made, that the word God has a special effect on him, even if only to afford a safety-valve for his feelings when he must swear or burst. And there ends the vexation of questioning the existence of God. Whatever the queer little word means, it means something we can none of us ever quite get away from, or at; something connected with our deepest explosions.

It isn't really quite a word. It's an ejaculation and a glyph. It never had a definition. "Give a definition of the word God," says somebody, and everybody smiles, with just a trifle of malice. There's going to be a bit of sport.

Of course, nobody can define it. And a word nobody can define isn't a word at all. It's just a noise and a shape, like pop! or Ra or Om.

When a man says: *There is a God,* or *There is no God,* or *I don't know whether there's a God or not,* he is merely using the little word like a toy pistol, to announce that he has taken an attitude. When he says: *There is no God,* he just means to say: *Nobody knows any better about life than myself, so nobody need try to chirp it over me.* Which is the democratic attitude. When he says: *There is a God,* he is either sentimental or sincere. If he is sincere, it means he refers himself back to some indefinable pulse of life in him, which gives him his direction and his substance. If he is sentimental, it means he is subtly winking to his audience to imply: *Let's make an arrangement favourable to ourselves.* That's the conservative attitude. Thirdly and lastly, when a man says: *I don't know whether there's a God or not,* he is merely making the crafty announcement: *I hold myself free to run with the hare and hunt with the hounds, whichever I feel like at the time.*–And that's the so-called artistic or pagan attitude.

In the end, one becomes bored by the man who believes that nobody, ultimately, can tell him anything. One becomes very bored by the men who wink a God into existence for their own convenience. And the man who holds himself free to run with the hare and hunt with the hounds doesn't hold interest any more. All these three classes of men bore us even to the death of boredom.

Remains the man who sincerely says: *I believe in God.* He may still be an interesting fellow.

I: *How* do you believe in God?
HE: I believe in goodness.

(*Basta!* Turn him down and try again.)

I: *How* do you believe in God?
HE: I believe in love.

(Exit. Call another.)

I: *How* do you believe in God?
HE: I don't know.
I: What difference does it make to you, whether you believe in God or not?
HE: It makes a difference, but I couldn't quite put it into words.
I: Are you sure it makes a difference? Does it make you kinder or fiercer?
HE: Oh!—I think it makes me more tolerant.

(*Retro me.*—Enter another believer.)

HE: Hullo!
I: Hullo!
HE: What's up?
I: Do you believe in God?
HE: What the hell is that to you?
I: Oh, I'm just asking.
HE: What about yourself?
I: Yes, I believe.
HE: D'you say your prayers at night?
I: No.
HE: When d'you say 'em, then?
I: I don't.
HE: Then what use is your God to you?
I: He merely isn't the sort you pray to.
HE: What do you do with him then?
I: It's what he does with me.
HE: And what does he do with you?
I: Oh, I don't know. He uses me as the thin end of the wedge.
HE: Thin enough! What about the thick end?
I: That's what we're waiting for.
HE: You're a funny customer.
I: Why not? Do you believe in God?
HE: Oh, I don't know. I might, if it looked like fun.
I: Right you are.

This is what I call a conversation between two true believers. Either believing in a real God looks like fun, or it's no go at all. The Great God has been treated to so many sighs, supplications, prayers, tears and yearnings that, for the time, He's had enough. There is, I believe, a great strike on in heaven. The Almighty has vacated the throne, abdicated, climbed down. It's no good your looking up into the sky. It's empty. Where the Most High used to sit listening to woes, supplications and repentances, there's nothing but a great gap in the empyrean. You can still go on praying to that gap, if you like. The Most High has gone out.

He has climbed down. He has just calmly stepped down the ladder of the angels, and is standing behind you. You can go on gazing and yearning up the shaft of hollow heaven if you like. The Most High just stands behind you, grinning to Himself.

Now this isn't a deliberate piece of blasphemy. It's just one way of stating an everlasting truth: or pair of truths. First, there is always the Great God. Second, as regards man, He shifts His position in the cosmos. The Great God departs from the heaven where man has located Him, and plumps His throne down somewhere else. Man, being an ass, keeps going to the same door to beg for his carrot, even when the Master has gone away to another house. The ass keeps on going to the same spring to drink, even when the spring has dried up, and there's nothing but clay and hoofmarks. It doesn't occur to him to look round, to see where the water has broken out afresh, somewhere else out of some live rock. Habit! God has become a human habit, and Man expects the Almighty habitually to lend Himself to it. Whereas the Almighty–it's one of His characteristics–won't. He makes a move, and laughs when Man goes on praying to the gap in the Cosmos.

"Oh, little hole in the wall! Oh, little gap, holy little gap!" as the Russian peasants are supposed to have prayed, making a deity of the hole in the wall.

Which makes me laugh. And nobody will persuade me that the Lord Almighty doesn't roar with laughter, seeing all the Christians still rolling their imploring eyes to the skies where the hole is, which the Great God left when He picked up his throne and walked.

I tell you, it isn't blasphemy. Ask any philosopher or theologian, and he'll tell you that the real problem for humanity isn't whether God exists or not. God always is, and we all know it. But the problem is, how to get at Him. That is the greatest problem ever set to our habit-making humanity. The theologians try to find out: How shall Man put himself into relation to God, into a living relation? Which is: How shall Man *find* God? That's the real problem.

Because God doesn't just sit still somewhere in the Cosmos. Why should He? He, too, wanders His own strange way down the avenues of time, across the intricacies of space. Just as the heavens shift. Just as the pole of heaven shifts. We know now that, in the strange widdershins movement of the heavens, called precession, the great stars and constellations and planets are all the time slowly, invisibly, but absolutely shifting their positions; even the pole-star is silently stealing away from the pole. Four thousand years ago, our pole-star wasn't a pole-star. The earth had another one. Even at the present moment, Polaris has side-stepped. He doesn't really stand at the axis of the heavens. Ask any astronomer. We shall soon have to have another pole-star.

So it is with the Great God. He slowly and silently and invisibly shifts His throne, inch by inch, across the Cosmos. Inch by inch, across the blue floor of heaven, till He comes to the stairs of the angels. Then step by step down the ladder.

Where is He now? Where is the Great God now? Where has He put His throne?

We have lost Him! We have lost the Great God! O God, O God, we have lost our Great God! Jesus, Jesus, Thou art the Way! Jesus, Jesus, Thou art the Way to the Father, to the Lord Everlasting.

But Jesus shakes His head. In the great wandering of the heavens, the foot of the Cross has shifted. The great and majestic movement of the heavens has slowly carried away even the Cross of Jesus from its place on Calvary. And Jesus, who was our Way to God, has stepped aside, over the horizon with the Father.

So it is. Man is only Man. And even the Gods and the Great God go their way; stepping slowly, invisibly, across the heavens of time and space, going somewhere, we know not where. They do not stand still. They go and go, till they pass below the horizon of Man.

Till Man has lost his Great God, and there remains only the gap, and images, and hollow words. The Way, even the Great Way of Salvation, leads only to the pit, the nothingness, the gap.

It is not our fault. It is nobody's fault. It is the mysterious and sublime fashion of the Almighty, who travels too. At least, as far as we are concerned, He travels. Apparently He is the same today, yesterday, and for ever. Like the pole-star. But now we know the pole-star slowly but inevitably side-steps. Polaris is no longer at the pole of the heavens.

Gradually, gradually God travels away from us, on His mysterious journey. And we, being creatures of obstinacy and will, we insist that He cannot move. God gave us a way to Himself. God gave us Jesus, and the way of repentance and love, the way to God. The salvation through Christ Jesus our Lord.

And hence, we assert that the Almighty cannot go back on it. He can never get away from us again. At the end of the way of repentance and love, there God *is,* and *must be.* Must be, because God Himself *said* that He would receive us at the end of the road of repentance and love.

And He *did* receive men at the end of this road. He received our fathers even, into peace and salvation.

Then He must receive us.

And He doesn't. The road no longer leads to the Throne.

We are let down.

Are we? Did Jesus ever say: *I am the way, and there is no other way?* At the moment there was no other way. For many centuries, there was no other way. But all the time, the heavens were mysteriously revolving and God was going His own unspeakable way. All the time, men had to be making the road afresh. Even the road called Jesus, the Way of the Christian to God, had to be subtly altered, century by century. At the Renaissance, in the eighteenth century, great curves in the Christian road to God, new strange directions.

As a matter of fact, never did God or Jesus say that there was one straight way of salvation, for ever and ever. On the contrary, Jesus plainly indicated the changing of the way. And what is more, He indicated the only means to the finding of the right way.

The Holy Ghost. The Holy Ghost is within you. And it is a Ghost, for ever a Ghost, never a Way or a Word. Jesus is a Way and a Word. God is the Goal. But the Holy Ghost is for ever Ghostly, unrealizable. And against this unsubstantial unreality, you may never sin, or woe betide you.

Only the Holy Ghost within you can scent the new tracks of the Great God across the Cosmos of Creation. The Holy Ghost is the dark hound of heaven whose baying we ought to listen to, as he runs ahead into the unknown, tracking the mysterious everlasting departing of the Lord God, who is for ever departing from us.

And now the Lord God has gone over our horizon. The foot of

the Cross is lifted from the Mound, and moved across the heavens. The pole-star no longer stands on guard at the true polaric centre. We are all disorientated, all is gone out of gear.

All right, the Lord God left us neither blind nor comfortless nor helpless. We've got the Holy Ghost. And we hear Him baying down strange darknesses, in other places.

The Almighty has shifted His throne, and we've got to find a new road. Therefore we've got to get off the old road. You can't stay on the old road, and find a new road. We've got to find our way to God. From time to time Man wakes up and realizes that the Lord Almighty has made a great removal, and passed over the known horizon. Then starts the frenzy, the howling, the despair. Much better listen to the dark hound of heaven, and start off into the dark of the unknown, in search.

From time to time, the Great God sends a new saviour. Christians will no longer have the pettiness to assert that Jesus is the only Saviour ever sent by the everlasting God. There have been other saviours, in other lands, at other times, with other messages. And all of them Sons of God. All of them sharing the Godhead with the Father. All of them showing the Way of Salvation and of Right. Different Saviours. Different Ways of Salvation. Different pole-stars, in the great wandering Cosmos of time. And the Infinite God, always changing, and always the same infinite God, at the end of the different Ways.

Now, if I ask you if you believe in God, I do not ask you if you know the Way to God. For the moment, we are lost. Let us admit it. None of us knows the way to God. The Lord of time and space has passed over our horizon, and here we sit in our mundane creation, rather flabbergasted. Let us admit it.

Jesus, the Saviour, is no longer our Way of Salvation. He *was* the Saviour, and is not. Once it was Mithras: and has not been Mithras for these many years. It never *was* Mithras for us. God sends different Saviours to different peoples at different times.

Now, for the moment, there is no Saviour. The Jews have waited for three thousand years. They preferred just to wait. We do not. Jesus taught us what to do, when He, Christ, could no longer save us.

We go in search of God, following the Holy Ghost, and depending on the Holy Ghost. There is no Way. There is no Word. There is no Light. The Holy Ghost is ghostly and invisible. The Holy Ghost is nothing, if you like. Yet we hear His strange calling, the strange calling like a hound on the scent, away in the unmapped wilderness. And it seems great fun to follow. Oh, great fun, God's own good fun.

Myself, I believe in God. But I'm off on a different road.

Adiós! and, if you like, *au revoir!*

BOOKS

Are books just toys? the toys of consciousness?

Then what is man? The everlasting brainy child?

Is man nothing but a brainy child, amusing himself for ever with the printed toys called books?

That also. Even the greatest men spend most of their time making marvellous fine toys. Like *Pickwick* or *Two on a Tower*.

But there is more to it.

Man is a thought-adventurer.

Man is a great venture in consciousness.

Where the venture started, and where it will end, nobody knows. Yet here we are—a long way gone already, and no glimpse of any end in sight. Here we are, miserable Israel of the human consciousness, having lost our way in the wilderness of the world's chaos, giggling and babbling and pitching camp. We needn't go any further.

All right, let us pitch camp, and see what happens. When the worst comes to the worst, there is sure to be a Moses to set up a serpent of brass. And then we can start off again.

Man is a thought-adventurer. He has thought his way down the far ages. He used to think in little images of wood or stone. Then in hieroglyphs on obelisks and clay rolls and papyrus. Now he thinks in books, between two covers.

The worst of a book is the way it shuts up between covers. When men had to write on rocks and obelisks, it was rather difficult to lie. The daylight was too strong. But soon he took his venture into caves and secret holes and temples, where he could create his own environment and tell lies to himself. And a book is an underground hole with two lids to it. A perfect place to tell lies in.

Which brings us to the real dilemma of man in his long adventure with consciousness. He is a liar. Man is a liar unto himself. And once he has told himself a lie, round and round he goes after that lie, as if it was a bit of phosphorus on his nose-end. The pillar of cloud and the pillar of fire wait for him to have done. They stand silently aside, waiting for him to rub the *ignis fatuus* off the end of his nose. But man, the longer he follows a lie, becomes all the surer he sees a light.

The life of man is an endless venture into consciousness. Ahead goes the pillar of cloud by day, the pillar of fire by night, through the wilderness of time. Till man tells himself a lie, another lie. Then the lie goes ahead of him, like the carrot before the ass.

There are, in the consciousness of man, two bodies of knowledge: the things he tells himself, and the things he finds out. The things he tells himself are nearly always pleasant, and they are lies. The things he finds out are usually rather bitter to begin with.

Man is a thought-adventurer. But by thought we mean, of course, discovery. We don't mean this telling himself stale facts and drawing false deductions, which usually passes as thought. Thought is an adventure, not a trick.

And of course it is an adventure of the whole man, not merely of his wits. That is why one cannot quite believe in Kant, or Spinoza. Kant thought with his head and his spirit, but he never thought with his blood. The blood also thinks, inside a man, darkly and ponderously. It thinks in desires and revulsions, and it makes strange conclusions. The conclusion of my head and my spirit is that it would be perfect, this world of men, if men all loved one another. The conclusion of my blood says nonsense, and finds the stunt a bit disgusting. My blood tells me there is no such thing as perfection. There is the long endless venture into consciousness down an ever-dangerous valley of days.

Man finds that his head and his spirit have led him wrong. We are at present terribly off the track, following our spirit, which says how nice it would be if everything was perfect, and listening to our head, which says we might have everything perfect if we would only eliminate the tiresome reality of our obstinate blood-being.

We are sadly off the track, and we're in a bad temper, like a man who has lost his way. And we say: I'm not going to bother. Fate must work it out.

Fate doesn't work things out. Man is a thought-adventurer, and only his adventuring in thought rediscovers a way.

Take our civilization. We are in a tantrum because we don't really like it now we've got it. There we've been building it for a thousand years, and built so big we can't shift it. And we hate it, after all.

Too bad! What's to be done?

Why, there's nothing to be done! Here we are, like sulky children, sulking because we don't like the game we're playing, feeling that we've been *made* to play it against our will. So play it we do: badly: in the sulks.

We play the game badly, so of course it goes from bad to worse. Things go from bad to worse.

All right, let 'em! Let 'em go from bad to worse. *Après moi le déluge.*

By all means! But a deluge presupposes a Noah and an Ark. The old adventurer on the old adventure.

When you come to think of it, Noah matters more than the deluge, and the ark is more than all the world washed out.

Now we've got the sulks, and are waiting for the flood to come and wash out our world and our civilization. All right, let it come. But somebody's got to be ready with Noah's Ark.

We imagine, for example, that if there came a terrible crash and terrible bloodshed over Europe, then out of the crash and bloodshed a remnant of regenerated souls would inevitably arise.

We are mistaken. If you look at the people who escaped the terrible times of Russia, you don't see many regenerated souls. They are more scared and senseless than ever. Instead of the great catastrophe having restored them to manhood, they are finally unmanned.

What's to be done? If a huge catastrophe is going only to unman us more than we are already unmanned, then there's no good in a huge catastrophe. Then there's no good in anything, for us poor souls who are trapped in the huge trap of our civilization.

Catastrophe alone never helped man. The only thing that ever avails is the living adventurous spark in the souls of men. If there is no living adventurous spark, then death and disaster are as meaningless as tomorrow's newspaper.

Take the fall of Rome. During the Dark Ages of the fifth, sixth, seventh centuries A.D., the catastrophes that befell the Roman Empire didn't alter the Romans a bit. They went on just the same, rather as we go on today, having a good time when they could get it, and not caring. Meanwhile Huns, Goths, Vandals, Visigoths, and all the rest wiped them out.

With what result? The flood of barbarism rose and covered Europe from end to end.

But, bless your life, there was Noah in his Ark with the animals. There was young Christianity. There were the lonely fortified monasteries, like little arks floating and keeping the adventure afloat. There is no break in the great adventure in consciousness. Throughout the howlingest deluge, some few brave souls are steering the ark under the rainbow.

The monks and bishops of the Early Church carried the soul and spirit of man unbroken, unabated, undiminished over the howling flood of the Dark Ages. Then this spirit of undying courage was fused into the barbarians, in Gaul, in Italy, and the new Europe began. But the germ had never been allowed to die.

Once all men in the world lost their courage and their newness, the world would come to an end. The old Jews said the same: unless in the world there was at least one Jew passionately praying, the race was lost.

So we begin to see where we are. It's no good leaving everything to fate. Man is an adventurer, and he must never give up the adventure. The venture is the venture: fate is the circumstance around the adventurer. The adventurer at the quick of the venture is the living germ inside the chaos of circumstance. But for the living germ of Noah in his Ark, chaos would have redescended on the world in the waters of the flood. But chaos *couldn't* redescend, because Noah was afloat with all the animals.

The same with the Christians when Rome fell. In their little fortified monasteries they defended themselves against howling invasions, being too poor to excite much covetousness. When wolves and bears prowled through the streets of Lyons, and a wild boar was grunting and turning up the pavement of Augustus's temple, the Christian bishops also roved intently and determinedly, like poor forerunners, along the ruined streets, seeking a congregation. It was the great adventure, and they did not give it up.

But Noah, of course, is always in an unpopular minority. So, of course, were the Christians, when Rome began to fall. The Christians now are in a hopelessly popular majority, so it is their turn to fall.

I know the greatness of Christianity: it is a past greatness. I know that, but for those early Christians, we should never have emerged from the chaos and hopeless disaster of the Dark Ages. If I had lived in the year 400, pray God, I should have been a true and passionate Christian. The adventurer.

But now I live in 1924, and the Christian venture is done. The adventure is gone out of Christianity. We must start on a new venture towards God.

THINKING ABOUT ONESELF

After all, we live most of our time alone, and the biggest part of our life is the silent yet busy stream of our private thoughts. We think about ourselves, and about the things that most nearly concern us, during the greater part of the day and night, all our life long. A comparatively small period is really spent in work or actual activity, where we say we "don't think." And a certain space is spent in sleep, where we don't know what we think, but where, in some sense, we keep on thinking. But the bulk of the time we think, or we muse, or we dully brood about ourselves and the things that most nearly concern us.

Perhaps it is a burden, this consciousness. Perhaps we don't want to think. That is why people devote themselves to hobbies, why men drink and play golf, and women jazz and flirt, and everybody goes to the brainless cinemas: all just to "get away from themselves," as they say. *Oh, forget it!* is the grand panacea. "You want to forget yourself," is the cry. The joy of all existence is supposed to be the "forgetting oneself."

Well, perhaps it is! and perhaps it isn't. While a boy is getting "gloriously drunk" in the evening, in the process of forgetting himself, he knows perfectly well all the time that he'll remember himself next morning quite painfully. The same with the girls who jazz through the gay night. The same even with the crowd that comes out of the cinema. They've been forgetting themselves. But if you look at them, it doesn't seem to have been doing them much good. They look rather like the cat that has swallowed the stuffed canary, and feels the cotton wool on its stomach.

You would think, to hear people talk, that the greatest bugbear you can possibly have is yourself. If you can't get away from yourself, if you can't forget yourself, you're doomed. The mill-stone is round your neck, so you might as well jump in and drown yourself.

It seems curious. Why should I myself be the greatest bugbear to myself? Why should I be so terrified of being in my own company only, as if some skeleton clutched me in its horrid arms, the moment I am alone with myself?

It's all nonsense. It's perfectly natural for every man and every woman to think about himself or herself most of the time. What is there to be afraid of? And yet people as a mass are afraid. You'd think everybody had a skeleton in the cupboard of their inside.

Which, of course, they have. I've got a skeleton, and so have you. But what's wrong with him? He's quite a good solid wholesome skeleton. And what should I do without him? No, no, I'm quite at home with my good and bony skeleton. So if he wants to have a chat with me, let him.

We all seem to be haunted by some spectre of ourselves that we daren't face. "By jove, that's me!" And we bolt. "Oh, heaven, there's an escaped tiger in Piccadilly! Let's rush up Bond Street!"—"Look out! There's a tiger! Make for Maddox Street!"—"My God, there's a tiger here too! Let's get in the underground."—And underground we go, forgetting that we have to emerge somewhere, and whether it's Holland Park or the Bank, there'll be a tiger.

The only thing to do is: "All right! If there's a tiger, let's have a look at him." As everybody knows, all you have to do is to look him firmly in the eye. So with this *alter ego,* this spectral me that haunts my thoughts.

"I'm a poor young man and nobody loves me," says the spectre, the tiger. Look him firmly in the eye and reply: "Really! That's curious. In what way are you poor? Are you nothing *but* poor? Do you *want* to be loved? *How* do you want to be loved, and by whom, for example? And why *should* you be loved?"—Answering these questions is really amusing, far greater fun than running away from yourself and listening-in and being inert.

If the tiger is a tigress, she mews woefully. "I'm such a nice person, and nobody appreciates me. I'm so unhappy!"—Then the really sporting girl looks her tigress in the eye and says: "Oh! What makes you so sure you're nice? *Where* are you nice? Are there no other ways of being nice but *your* way? Perhaps people are pining for a different sort of niceness from your sort. Better do something about it."

If it's a young married couple of tigers they wail: "We're so hard up, and there's no prospect."—Then the young he and she, if they've any spunk, fix their two tigers. "Prospect! What do you mean by prospect? Sufficient unto the day is the dinner thereof. What is a prospect? Why should we need one? What sort of a one do we need? What's it all about?"

And answering these questions is fun, fun for a life-time. It's the essential fun of life, answering the tiger back. Thinking, thinking about oneself and the things that really concern one is the greatest fun of all, especially when, now and then, you feel you've really spoken to your skeleton.

RESURRECTION

"Touch me not! I am not yet ascended unto the Father."

We have all this time been worshipping a dead Christ: or a dying. The Son of Man on the Cross.

Yet we know well enough, the Cross was only the first step into achievement. The second step was into the tomb. And the third step, whither? "I am not yet ascended unto the Father."

I have just read, for the first time, Tolstoy's *Resurrection*. Tolstoy writhed very hard, on the Cross. His Resurrection is the step into the tomb. And the stone was rolled upon him.

Now, as Christians, we have died. The War was the Calvary of all real Christian men. Since the War, it has been the tomb, with no rule at all. As the peasants in Italy used to say—after Christ was put in the tomb—on Good Friday eve: Now we can sin. There is no Lord on earth to see us.

Since the War, the world has been without a Lord. What is the Lord within us, has been walled up in the tomb. But three days have fully passed, and it is time to roll away the stone. It is time for the Lord in us to arise.

With the stigmata healed up, and the eyes full open.

Rise as the Lord. No longer the Man of Sorrows. The Crucified uncrucified. The Crown of Thorns removed, and the tongues of fire round the brows. The Risen Lord.

Man has done his worst, and crucified his God. Men will always crucify their god, given the opportunity. Christ proved that, by giving them the opportunity.

But Christ is not put twice on the Cross. Not a second time. And this is the great point that Tolstoy missed. It seemed to him, Christ would go on being crucified, everlastingly.

Bad doctrine. As man puts off his clothes when he dies, so the Cross is put off, like a garment. But the Son of Man will not be twice crucified. That, never again.

He is risen. And now beware! Touch me not.

Put away the Cross; it is obsolete. Stare no more after the stigmata. They are more than healed up. The Lord is risen, and ascended unto the Father. There is a new Body, and a new Law.

Christ and the Father are at one again. There is a new law. The Man has disappeared into the God again. The column of fire shoots up from the nadir to the zenith, and there is a new fierce light on our faces.

Men who can rise with the Son of Man, and ascend unto the Father, will see the new day. Many men will perish in the tomb, unable to roll the stone away. But the stone that is rolled away will roll on. It too has a course to run.

Christ has re-entered into the Father, and the pillar of flame shoots up, anew, from the nadir to the zenith. The world and the cosmos stagger to the new axis. There is a new light upon the hills, the valleys groan and are wrenched.

The tree shivers, and sheds its leaves. Never was the tree so vast in stature and so full of leaves. But the new fire spurts at its roots, the boughs writhe, the twigs crackle from within, and the old leaves fall thick and red to the ground. That is how a new day enters the Tree of Life.

The Cross has taken root again, and is putting forth buds. Its branches sprout out where the nails went in, there is a tuft of sprouts like tongues of flame at the top, where the inscription was. Even *consummatum est* is dissolved in a rising up.

When Christ rejoins the Father, the Cross is again a Tree, the wheel of fire flares up and spins in the opposite way. And little wheels of fire are seen round the brow of men who have ascended, reascended to the Father. There are kings in the cosmos once more, there are lords among men again.

It is the day of the Risen Lord. Touch me not! I am the Lord Arisen.

Men of the Risen Lord, rise up. The wheel of fire is starting to spin in the opposite way, to throw off the mud of the world. Deep mud is on the staggering wheel, mud of the multitudes. But Christ has rejoined the Father at the axis, the flame of the hub spurts up. The wheel is beginning to turn in the opposite way, and woe to the multitude.

Men of the Risen Lord, the many ways are one. Down the spokes of flame there are many paths which are one way still, to the core of the wheel. Turn round, turn round, away from the mud of the rim to the flame of the core, and walk down the spokes of fire to the Whole, where God is One.

For the multitudes shall be shaken off as a dog shakes off his fleas. And only the risen lords among men shall stand on the wheel and not fall, being fire as the wheel is Fire, facing in to the in-ordinate Flame.

The Lord is risen. Let us rise as well and be lords. The multitudes rolled the stone upon us. Let us roll it back.

Men in the tomb, rise up, the time is expired. The Lord is risen. Quick! let us follow Him.

The Lord is risen as Lord indeed; let us follow, as lords in deed. The Lord has rejoined the Father, in the flame at the hub of the wheel. Let us look that way, and cry "Behold!" down the spokes of fire. Let us turn our backs on the tomb, and the stone that is rolling upon the multitude. It is more than finished, it is begun again.

The lords are out of prison, with the Risen Lord. Let the multitudes tremble and fall down, as the black stone rolls towards them, back from the mouth of the tomb. Except you died with the Lord, you shall surely die. Except you rise with the Lord and roll the stone from the mouth of the tomb, the stone shall surely crush you. The greater the stone you rolled upon the mouth of the tomb, the greater the destruction overtakes you.

It is not given to you twice, oh multitudes, to put the Lord on the Cross. It was given you once, and once and for all, and now it is more than finished. If you have not died, you shall die. If you cannot rise, you shall fall. If you cannot note the coming day, if you're blind to the morning star, it is because the shadow of the stone is upon you, rolling down from the mouth of the tomb.

More blessed to give than to receive. So you gave the Judas kiss.

Now it rolls back on you, huge, an increasingly huge black stone, as big as the world, that kiss.

You thought *consummatum est* meant *all is over*. You were wrong. It means: *The step is taken*.

Rise, then, men of the Risen Lord, and push back the stone. Who rises with the Risen Lord rises himself as a lord. Come, stand on the spokes of fire, as the wheel begins to revolve. Face inward to the flame of Whole God, that plays upon the zenith. And be lords with the Lord, with bright, and brighter, and brightest, and most-bright faces.

CLIMBING DOWN PISGAH

Sometimes one pulls oneself up short, and asks: "What am I doing this for?" One writes novels, stories, essays: and then suddenly: "What on earth am I doing it for?"

What indeed?

For the sake of humanity?

Pfui! The very words *human, humanity, humanism* make one sick. For the sake of humanity as such, I wouldn't lift a little finger, much less write a story.

For the sake of the Spirit?

Tampoco!—But what do we mean by the Spirit? Let us be careful. Do we mean that One Universal Intelligence of which every man has his modicum? Or further, that one Cosmic Soul, or Spirit, of which every individual is a broken fragment, and towards which every individual strives back, to escape the raw edges of his own fragmentariness, and to experience once more the sense of wholeness?

The sense of wholeness! Does one write books in order to give one's fellow-men a sense of wholeness: first, a oneness with all men, then a oneness with all things, then a oneness with our cosmos, and finally a oneness with the vast invisible universe? Is that it? Is that our achievement and our peace?

Anyhow, it would be a great achievement. And this has been the aim of the great ones. It was the aim of Whitman, for example.

Now it is the aim of the little ones, since the big ones are all gone. Thomas Hardy, a last big one, rings the knell of our Oneness. Virtually, he says: Once you achieve the great identification with the One, whether it be the One Spirit, or the Oversoul, or God, or whatever name you like to give it, you find that this God, this One, this Cosmic Spirit isn't human at all, hasn't any human feelings, doesn't concern itself for a second with the individual, and is, all told, a gigantic cold monster. It is a machine. The moment you attain that sense of Oneness and Wholeness, you become cold, dehumanized, mechanical, and monstrous. The greatest of all illusions is the Infinite of the Spirit.

Whitman really rang the same knell. (I don't expect anyone to agree with me.)

The sense of wholeness is a most terrible let-down. The big ones have already decided it. But the little ones, sneakingly too selfish to care, go on sentimentally tinkling away at it.

This we may be sure of: all talk of brotherhood, universal love, sacrifice, and so on, is a sentimental pose for us. We reached the top of Pisgah, and looking down, saw the graveyard of humanity. Those meagre spirits who could never get to the top, and are careful never to try, because it costs too much sweat and a bleeding at the nose, they sit below and still snivellingly invent Pisgah-sights. But strictly, it is all over. The game is up.

The little ones, of course, are writing at so many cents a word —or a line—according to their success. They may say I do the same. Yes, I demand my cents, a Shylock. Nevertheless, if I wrote for cents I should write differently, and with far more "success."

What, then, does one write for? There must be some imperative.

Probably it is the sense of adventure, to start with. Life is no fun for a man, without an adventure.

The Pisgah-top of spiritual oneness looks down upon a hopeless squalor of industrialism, the huge cemetery of human hopes. This is our Promised Land. "There's a good time coming, boys, a good time coming." Well, we've rung the bell, and here it is.

Shall we climb hurriedly down from Pisgah, and keep the secret? Mum's the word!

This is what our pioneers are boldly doing. We used, as boys, to sing parodies of most of the Sunday-school hymns.

> They climbed the steep ascent of heaven
> Through peril, toil, and pain:
> O God, to us may grace be given
> To scramble down again.

This is the grand hymn of the little ones. But it's harder getting down a height, very often, than getting up. It's a predicament. Here we are, cowering on the brinks of precipices half-way up, or down, Pisgah. The Pisgah of Oneness, the Oneness of Mankind, the Oneness of Spirit.

Hie, boys, over we go! Pisgah's a fraud, and the Promised Land is Pittsburgh, the Chosen Few, there are billions of 'em, and Canaan smells of kerosene. Let's break our necks if we must, but let's get down, and look over the brink of some other horizon. We're like the girl who took the wrong turning: thought it was the right one.

It's an adventure. And there's only one left, the venture of consciousness. Curse these ancients, they have said everything for us. Curse these moderns, they have done everything for us. The aeroplane descends and lays her egg-shells of empty tin cans on the top of Everest, in the Ultimate Thule, and all over the North Pole; not to speak of tractors waddling across the inviolate Sahara and over the jags of Arabia Petræa, laying the same addled eggs of our civilization, tin cans, in every camp-nest.

Well then, they can have the round earth. They've got it anyhow. And they can have the firmament: they've got that too. The moon is a cold egg in the astronomical nest. *Heigho! for the world well lost!*

That's the known World, the world of the One Intelligence. That is the Human World! I'm getting out of it. *Homo sum. Omnis a me humanum alienum puto.*

Of the thing we call human, I've had enough. And enough is as good as a feast.

Inside of me, there's a little demon—maybe he's a big demon—that says *Basta! Basta!* to all my oneness. "Farewell, a long farewell to all my greatness." In short, come off the perch, Polly, and look what a mountain of droppings you've crouched upon.

Are you human, and do you want me to sympathize with you for that? Let me hand you a roll of toilet-paper.

After looking down from the Pisgah-top on to the oneness of all mankind safely settled these several years in Canaan, I admit myself dehumanized.

> Fair waved the golden corn
> In Canaan's pleasant land.

The factory smoke waves much higher. And in the sweet smoke of industry I don't care a button who loves whom, nor what babies are born. The sight of all of it *en masse* was a little too much for my human spirit, it dehumanized me. Here I am, without a human sympathy left. Looking down on Human Oneness was too much for my human stomach, so I vomited it away.

Remains a demon which says *Ha ha! So you've conquered the earth, have you, oh man? Now swallow the pill.*

For if the proof of the pudding is in the eating, the proof of a conquest is in digesting it. Humanity is an ostrich. But even the ostrich thinks twice before it bolts a rolled hedgehog. The earth is conquered as the hedgehog is conquered when he rolls himself up into a ball, and the dog spins him with his paw.

But that is not the point, at least for anyone except the Great Dog of Humanity. The point for us is, *What then?*

"Whither, oh splendid ship, thy white sails bending?" To have her white sails dismantled and a gasolene engine fitted into her guts. That is whither, oh Poet!

When you've got to the bottom of Pisgah once more, where are you? Sitting on a sore posterior, murmuring: *Oneness is all bunk. There is no Oneness, till you invented it and killed your goose to get it out of her belly. It takes millions of little people to lay the egg of the Universal Spirit, and then it's an addled omelet, and stinks in our nostrils. And all the millions of little people have over-reached themselves, trying to lay the mundane egg of oneness. They're all damaged inside, and they can't face the addled omelet they've laid. What a mess!*

What then?

Heigho! Whither, oh patched canoe, your kinked keel thrusting?

We've been over the rapids, and the creature that crawls out of the whirlpool feels that most things human are foreign to him. *Homo sum!* means a vastly different thing to him, from what it meant to his father.

Homo sum! a demon who knows nothing of oneness or of perfection. *Homo sum!* a demon who knows nothing of any First Creator who created the universe from his own perfection. *Homo sum!* a man who knows that all creation lives like some great demon inhabiting space, and pulsing with a dual desire, a desire to give himself forth into creation, and a desire to take himself back, in death.

Child of the great inscrutable demon, *Homo sum!* Adventurer from the first Adventurer, *Homo sum!* Son of the blazing-hearted father who wishes beauty and harmony and perfection, *Homo sum!* Child of the raging-hearted demon-father who fights that nothing shall surpass this crude and demonish rage, *Homo sum!*

Whirling in the midst of Chaos, the demon of the beginning who is for ever willing and unwilling to surpass the *Status Quo*. Like a bird he spreads wings to surpass himself. Then like a serpent he coils to strike at that which would surpass him. And the bird of the first desire must either soar quickly, or strike back with his talons at the snake, if there is to be any surpassing of the thing that was, the *Status Quo*.

It is the joy for ever, the agony for ever, and above all, the fight for ever. For all the universe is alive, and whirling in the same fight, the same joy and anguish. The vast demon of life has made himself habits which, except in the whitest heat of desire and rage, he will never break. And these habits are the laws of our scientific universe. But all the laws of physics, dynamics, kinetics, statics, all are but the settled habits of a vast living incomprehensibility, and they can all be broken, superseded, in a moment of great extremity.

Homo sum! child of the demon. *Homo sum!* willing and unwilling. *Homo sum!* giving and taking. *Homo sum!* hot and cold. *Homo sum!* loving and loveless. *Homo sum!* the Adventurer.

This we see, this we know as we crawl down the dark side of Pisgah, or slip down on a sore posterior. *Homo sum!* has changed its meaning for us.

That is, if we are young men. Old men and elderly will sit tight on heavy posteriors in some crevice upon Pisgah, babbling about "all for love, and the world well saved." Young men with hearts still for the life adventure will rise up with their trouser-seats scraped away, after the long slither from the heights down the well-nigh bottomless pit, having changed their minds. They will change their minds and change their pants. Wisdom is sometimes in a sore bottom, and the new pants will no longer be neutral.

Young men will change their minds and their pants, having done with Oneness and neutrality. Even the stork meditates on an orange leg, and the bold drake pushes the water behind him with a red foot. Young men are the adventurers.

Let us scramble out of this ash-hole at the foot of Pisgah. The universe isn't a machine after all. It's alive and kicking. And in spite of the fact that man with his cleverness has discovered some of the habits of our old earth, and so lured him into a trap; in spite of the fact that man has trapped the great forces, and they go round and round at his bidding like a donkey in a gin, the old demon isn't quite nabbed. We didn't quite catch him napping. He'll turn round on us with bare fangs, before long. He'll turn into a python, coiling, coiling, coiling till we're nicely mashed. Then he'll bolt us.

Let's get out of the vicious circle. Put on new bright pants to show that we're meditative fowl who have thought the thing out and decided to migrate. To assert that our legs are not grey machine-sections, but live and limber members who know what it is to have their rear well scraped and punished, in the slither down Pisgah, and are not going to be diddled any more into mechanical service of mountain-climbing up to the great summit of Wholeness and Bunk.

THE DUC DE LAUZUN

The Duc de Lauzun [Duc de Biron] belongs to the fag-end of the French brocade period. He was born in 1747, was a man of twenty-seven when Louis XV died, and Louis XVI came tinkering to the throne. Belonging to the high nobility, his life was naturally focused on the court, though one feels he was too good merely to follow the fashion.

He wrote his own memoirs, which rather scrappily cover the first thirty-six years of his life. The result on the reader is one of depression and impatience. You feel how idiotic that French court was: how fulsomely insipid. Thankful you feel, that they all had their heads off at last. They deserved it. Not for their sins. Their sins, on the whole, were no worse than anybody else's. I wouldn't grudge them their sins. But their dressed-up idiocy is beyond human endurance.

There is only one sin in life, and that is the sin against life, the sin of causing inner emptiness and boredom of the spirit. Whoever and whatever makes us inwardly bored and empty-feeling, is vile, the anathema.

And one feels that this was almost deliberately done to the Duc de Lauzun. When I read him, I feel sincerely that the little baby that came from his mother's womb, and killed her in the coming, was the germ of a real man. And this real man they killed in him, as far as they could, with cold and insect-like persistency, from the moment he was born and his mother, poor young thing of nineteen, died and escaped the scintillating idiocy of her destiny.

No man on earth could have come through such an upbringing as this boy had, without losing the best half of himself on the way, and emerging incalculably impoverished. Abandoned as a baby to the indifference of French servants in a palace, he was, as he says himself, "like all the other children of my age and condition; the finest clothes for going out, at home half naked and dying of hunger." And that this was so, we know from other cases. Even a dauphin was begrudged clean sheets for his bed, and slept in a tattered night-shirt, while he was a boy. It was no joke to be a child, in that smart period.

To educate the little duke—though when he was a child he was only a little count—his father chose one of the dead mother's lackeys. This lackey knew how to read and write, and this amount of knowledge he imparted to the young nobleman, who was extremely proud of himself because he could read aloud "more fluently and pleasantly than is ordinarily the case in France." Another writer of the period says: "There are, perhaps, not more than fifty persons in Paris capable of reading prose aloud." So that the boy became "almost necessary" to Madame de Pompadour, because he could read to her. And sometimes he read to the King, Louis XV. "Our journeys to Versailles became more frequent, and my education consequently more neglected. . . . At the age of twelve I was entered into the Guards regiment. . . ."

What sort of education it was, which was neglected, would be difficult to say. All one can gather from the Duc himself is that, in his bored forlornness, he had read innummerable novels: the false, reekingly sentimental falderal love-novels of his day. And these, alas, did him a fair amount of harm, judging from the amount of unreal sentiment he poured over his later love affairs.

That a self-critical people like the French should ever have wal lowed in such a white sauce of sentimentalism as did those wits of the eighteenth century, is incredible. A mid-Victorian English sentimentalist at his worst is sincere and naïve, compared to a French romanticist of the mid-eighteenth century. One works one's way through the sticky-sweet mess with repulsion.

So, the poor little nobleman, they began to initiate him into "love" when he was twelve, though he says he was fourteen. "Madame la Duchesse de Grammont showed a great friendship for me, and had the intention, I believe, of forming, gradually, for herself a little lover whom she would have all to herself, without any inconveniences." Her chambermaid and confidante, Julie, thought to forestall her mistress. She made advances to the boy. "One day she put my hand in her breast, and all my body was afire several hours afterwards; but I wasn't any further ahead." His tutor, however, discovered the affair, nipped it in the bud, and Mademoiselle Julie didn't have the honour of "putting him into the world," as he called it. He was keenly distressed.

When he was sixteen, his father began to arrange his marriage with Mademoiselle de Boufflers. The Duchesse de Grammont turned him entirely against the girl, before he set eyes on her. This was another part of his education.

At the age of seventeen, he had a little actress, aged fifteen, for his mistress, "and she was still more innocent than I was." Another little actress lent them her cupboard of a bedroom, but "an enormous spider came to trouble our rendezvous; we were both mortally afraid of it; neither of us had the courage to kill it. So we chose to separate, promising to meet again in a cleaner place, where there were no such horrid monsters."

One must say this for the Duc de Lauzun: there is nothing particularly displeasing about his love affairs, especially during his younger life. He never seems to have made love to a woman unless he really liked her, and truly wanted to touch her: and unless she really liked him, and wanted him to touch her. Which is the essence of morality, as far as love goes.

The Comtesse d'Espartes had thoroughly initiated him, or "put him into the world." She had him to read aloud to her as she lay in bed: though even then, he was still so backward that only at the second reading did he really come to the scratch. He was still seventeen. And then the Comtesse threw him over, and put him still more definitely into the world. He says of himself at this point, in a note written, of course, twenty years later: "All my childhood I had read many novels, and this reading had such an influence on my character, I feel it still. It has often been to my disadvantage; but if I have tended to exaggerate my own sentiments and my own sensations, at least I owe this to my romantic character, that I have avoided the treacherous and bad dealings with women from which many honest people are not exempt."

So that his novels did something for him, if they only saved him from the vulgar brutality of the non-romantic.

He was well in love with Madame de Stainville, when his father married him at last, at the age of nineteen, to Mademoiselle de Boufflers. The marriage was almost a worse failure than usual. Mademoiselle de Boufflers, apparently, liked Lauzun no better than he liked her. Madame de Stainville calls her a "disagreeable child." She did not care for men: seems to have been a model of quiet virtue: perhaps she was a sweet, gentle thing: more likely she was inwardly resentful from the day of her birth. One would gather that she showed even some contempt of Lauzun, and physical repugnance to the married state. They never really lived together.

And this is one of the disgusting sides to the France of that day. Under a reeking sentimentalism lay a brutal, worse than bestial callousness and insensitiveness. Brutality is wholesome, compared with refined callousness, that truly has no feelings at all, only refined selfishness.

The Prince de Ligne gives a sketch of the marriage of a young woman of the smart nobility of that day: "They teach a girl not to look a man in the face, not to reply to him, never to ask how she happened to be born. Then they bring along two men in black, accompanying a man in embroidered satin. After which they say to her: 'Go and spend the night with this gentleman.' This gentleman, all afire, brutally assumes his rights, asks nothing, but exacts a great deal; she rises in tears, at the very least, and he, at least, wet. If they have said a word, it was to quarrel. Both of them look sulky, and each is disposed to try elsewhere. So marriage begins, under happy auspices. All delicate modesty is gone: and would modesty prevent this pretty woman from yielding, to a man she loves, that which has been forced from her by a man she doesn't love? But behold the most sacred union of hearts, profaned by parents and a lawyer."

Did the Duc de Lauzun avoid this sort of beginning? He was really enamoured of Madame de Stainville, her accepted and devoted lover. He was violently disposed against his bride: "this disagreeable child." And perhaps, feeling himself compelled into the marriage-bed with the "disagreeable child," his bowels of compassion dried up. For he was naturally a compassionate man. Anyhow, the marriage was a drastic failure. And his wife managed somehow, in the first weeks, to sting him right on the quick. Perhaps on the quick of his vanity. He never quite got over it.

So he went on, a dandy, a wit in a moderate way, and above all, a "romantic," extravagant, rather absurd lover. Inside himself, he was not extravagant and absurd. But he had a good deal of feeling which he didn't know what on earth to do with, so he turned it into "chivalrous" extravagance.

This is the real pity. Let a man have as fine and kindly a nature as possible, he'll be able to do nothing with it unless it has some scope. What scope was there for a decent, manly man, in that France rotten with sentimentalism and dead with cruel callousness? What could he do? He wasn't great enough to rise clean above his times: no man is. There was nothing wholesome doing, in the whole of France. Sentimental romanticism, fag-end encyclopædic philosophy, false fiction, and emptiness. It was as if, under the expiring monarchy, the devil had thrown everybody into a conspiracy to make life false and to nip straight, brave feelings in the bud.

Everything then conspired to make a man little. This was the misery of men in those days: they were made to be littler than they really were, by the niggling corrosion of that "wit," that "esprit" which had no spirit in it, except the petty spirit of destruction. Envy, spite, finding their outlet, as they do today, in cheap humour and smart sayings.

The men had nothing to do with their lives. So they laid their lives at the feet of the women. Or pretended to. When it came to the point, they snatched their lives back again hastily enough. But even then they didn't know what to do with them. So they laid them at the feet of some other woman.

The Duc de Lauzun was one of the French anglophiles of the day: he really admired England, found something there. And perhaps his most interesting experience was his affair with Lady Sarah Bunbury, that famous beauty of George III's reign. She held him off for a long time: part of the game seemed to be

[Unfinished]

[THE GOOD MAN]

There is something depressing about French eighteenth-century literature, especially that of the latter half of the century. All those sprightly memoirs and risky stories and sentimental effusions constitute, perhaps, the dreariest body of literature we know, once we do know it. The French are essentially critics of life, rather than creators of life. And when the life itself runs rather thin, as it did in the eighteenth century, and the criticism rattles all the faster, it just leaves one feeling wretched.

England during the eighteenth century was far more alive. The sentimentalism of Sterne laughs at itself, is full of teasing self-mockery. But French sentimentalism of the same period is wholesale and like stale fish. It is difficult, even if one rises on one's hind-legs and feels "superior," like a high-brow in an East End music-hall, to be amused by Restif de la Bretonne. One just sits in amazement that these clever French can be such stale fish of sentimentalism and prurience.

The Duc de Lauzun belongs to what one might call the fag-end period. He was born in 1747, and was twenty-seven years old when Louis XV died. Belonging to the high nobility, and to a family prominent at court, he escapes the crass sentimentalism of the "humbler" writers, but he also escapes what bit of genuine new feeling they had. He is far more manly than a Jean Jacques, but he is still less of a man in himself.

French eighteenth-century literature is so puzzling to the *emotions,* that one has to try to locate some spot of firm feeling inside oneself, from which one can survey the morass. And since the essential problem of the eighteenth century was the problem of *morality,* since the new homunculus produced in that period was the *homme de bien,* the "good man," who, of course, included the "man of feeling," we have to go inside ourselves and discover what we really feel about the "goodness," or morality, of the eighteenth century.

Because there is no doubt about it, the "good man" of today was produced in the chemical retorts of the brain and emotional centres of people like Rousseau and Diderot. It took him, this "good man," a hundred years to grow to his full stature. Now, after a century and a half, we have him in his dotage, and find he was a robot.

And there is no doubt about it, it was the writhing of this new little "good man," the new *homme de bien,* in the human consciousness, which was the essential cause of the French revolution. The new little homunculus was soon ready to come out of the womb of consciousness on to the stage of life. Once on the stage, he soon grew up, and soon grew into a kind of Woodrow Wilson dotage. But be that as it may, it was the kicking of this new little monster, to get out of the womb of time, which caused the collapse of the old show.

The new little monster, the new "good man," was perfectly reasonable and perfectly irreligious. Religion knows the great passions. The *homme de bien,* the good man, performs the robot trick of isolating himself from the great passions. For the passion of life he substitutes the reasonable social virtues. You must be honest in your material dealings, you must be kind to the poor, and you must have "feelings" for your fellow-man and for nature. Nature with a capital. There is nothing to *worship.* Such a thing as worship is nonsense. But you may get a "feeling" out of anything.

In order to get nice "feelings" out of things, you must of course be quite "free," you mustn't be interfered with. And to be "free," you must incur the enmity of no man, you must be "good." And when everybody is "good" and "free," then we shall all have nice feelings about everything.

This is the gist of the idea of the "good man," chemically evolved by emotional alchemists such as Rousseau. Like every other homunculus, this little "good man" soon grows into a slight deformity, then into a monster, then into a grinning vast idiot. This monster produced our great industrial civilization, and the huge thing, gone idiot, is now grinning at us and showing its teeth.

We are all, really, pretty "good." We are all extraordinarily "free." What other freedom can we imagine, than what we've got? So then, we ought all to have amazingly nice feelings about everything.

The last phase of the bluff is to pretend that we *do* all have nice feelings about everything, if we are nice people. It is the last grin of the huge grinning sentimentalism which the Rousseau-ists invented. But really, it's getting harder and harder to keep up the grin.

As a matter of fact, far from having nice feelings about everything, we have nice feelings about practically nothing. We get less and less our share of nice feelings. More and more we get horrid feelings, which we have to suppress hard. Or, if we don't admit it, then we must admit that we get less and less feelings of any sort.

Our capacity for feeling anything is going numb, more and more numb, till we feel we shall soon reach zero, and pure insanity.

This is the horrid end of the "good man" homunculus.

Now the "good man" is all right as far as he goes. One must be honest in one's dealings, and one does feel kindly towards the poor man—unless he's one of the objectionable sort. If I turn myself into a swindler, and am a brute to every beggar, I shall only be a "not good man" instead of a "good man." It's just the same species, really. Immorality is no new ground. There's nothing original in it. Whoever invents morality invents, tacitly, immorality. And the immoral, unconventional people are only the frayed skirt-tails of the conventional people.

The trouble about the "good man" is that he's only one-hundredth part of a man. The eighteenth century, like a vile Shylock, carved a pound of flesh from the human psyche, conjured with it like a cunning alchemist, set it smirking, called it a "good man" —and lo! we all began to reduce ourselves to this little monstrosity. What's the matter with us, is that we are bound up like a China-girl's foot, that has got to cease developing and turn into a "lily." We are absolutely bound up tight in the bandages of a few ideas, and tight shoes are nothing to it.

When Oscar Wilde said that it was nonsense to assert that art imitates nature, because nature always imitates art, this was absolutely true of human nature. The thing called "spontaneous human nature" does not exist, and never did. Human nature is always made to some pattern or other. The wild Australian aborigines are absolutely bound up tight, tighter than a China-girl's foot, in their few savage conventions. They are bound up tighter than we are. But the length of the ideal bondage doesn't matter. Once you begin to feel it pressing, it'll press tighter and tighter, till either you burst it, or collapse inside it, or go deranged. And the conventional and ideal and emotional bandage presses as tight upon the free American girl as the equivalent bandage presses upon the Australian black girl in her tribe. An elephant bandaged up tight, so that he can only move his eyes, is no better off than a bandaged-up mouse. Perhaps worse off. The mouse has more chance to nibble a way out.

And this we must finally recognize. No man has "feelings of his own." The feelings of all men in the civilized world today are practically all alike. Men *can* only feel the feelings they know how to feel. The feelings they don't know how to feel, they don't feel. This is true of all men, and all women, and all children.

It is true, children do have lots of unrecognized feelings. But an unrecognized feeling, if it forces itself into any recognition, is only recognized as "nervousness" or "irritability." There are certain feelings we recognize, but as we grow up, every single disturbance in the psyche, or in the soul, is transmitted into one of the recognized feeling-patterns, or else left in that margin called "nervousness."

This is our true bondage. This is the agony of our human existence, that we can only feel things in conventional feeling-patterns. Because when these feeling-patterns become inadequate, when they will no longer body forth the workings of the yeasty soul, then we are in torture. It is like a deaf-mute trying to speak. Something is inadequate in the expression-apparatus, and we hear strange howlings. So are we now howling inarticulate, because what is yeastily working in us has no voice and no language. We are like deaf-mutes, or like the China-girl's foot.

Now the eighteenth century did let out a little extra length of bandage for the bound-up feet. But oh! it was a short length! We soon grew up to its capacity, and the pressure again became intolerable, horrible, unbearable: as it is today.

We compare England today with France of 1780. We sort of half expect revolutions of the same sort. But we have little grounds for the comparison and the expectation. It is true our feelings are going dead, we have to work hard to get any feeling out of ourselves: which is true of the Louis XV and more so of the Louis XVI people like the Duc de Lauzun. But at the same time, we know quite well that if all our heads were chopped off, and the working-classes were left to themselves, with a clear field, nothing would have happened, really. Bolshevist Russia, one feels, and feels with bitter regret, is nothing new on the face of the earth. It is only a sort of America. And no matter how many revolutions take place, all we can hope for is different sorts of America. And since America is *chose connue,* since America is known to us, in our imaginative souls, with dreary finality, what's the odds? America has no new feelings: less even than England: only disruption of old feelings. America is bandaged more tightly even than Europe in the bandages of old ideas and ideals. Her feelings are even more fixed to pattern: or merely devolutionary. Her art forms are even more lifeless.

So what's the point in a revolution? Where's the homunculus? Where is the new baby of a new conception of life? Who feels him kicking in the womb of time?

Nobody! Nobody! Not even the Socialists and Bolshevists themselves. Not the Buddhists, nor the Christian Scientists, nor the scientists, nor the Christians. Nobody! So far, there is no new baby. And therefore, there is no revolution. Because a revolution is really the birth of a new baby, a new idea, a new feeling, a new way of feeling, a new feeling-pattern. It is the birth of a new man. "For I will put a new song into your mouth."

There is no new song. There is no new man. There is no new baby.

And therefore, I repeat, there is no revolution.

You who want a revolution, beget and conceive the new baby in your bodies: and not a homunculus robot like Rousseau's.

But you who are afraid of a revolution, realize that there will be no revolution, just as there will be no pangs of parturition if there is no baby to be born.

Instead, however, you may get that which is not revolution. You may, and you will, get a *débâcle*. *Après moi le déluge* was premature. The French revolution was only a bit of a brief inundation. The real deluge lies just ahead of us.

There is no choice about it. You can't keep the *status quo*, because the homunculus robot, the "good man," is dead. We killed him rather hastily and with hideous brutality, in the great war that was to save democracy. He is dead, and you can't keep him from decaying. You can't keep him from decomposition. You cannot.

Neither can you expect a revolution, because there is no new baby in the womb of our society. Russia is a collapse, not a revolution.

All that remains, since it's Louis XV's Deluge which is louring, rather belated: all that remains is to be a Noah, and build an ark. An ark, an ark, my kingdom for an ark! An ark of the covenant, into which also the animals shall go in two by two, for there's one more river to cross!

THE NOVEL AND THE FEELINGS

We think we are so civilized, so highly educated and civilized. It is farcical. Because, of course, all our civilization consists in harping on one string. Or at most on two or three strings. Harp, harp, harp, twingle, twingle-twang! That's our civilization, always on one note.

The note itself is all right. It's the exclusiveness of it that is awful. Always the same note, always the same note! "Ah, how can you run after other women when your wife is so delightful, a lovely plump partridge?" Then the husband laid his hand on his waistcoat, and a frightened look came over his face. "Nothing but partridge?" he exclaimed.

Toujours perdrix! It was up to that wife to be a goose and a cow, an oyster and an inedible vixen, at intervals.

Wherein are we educated? Come now, in what are we educated? In politics, in geography, in history, in machinery, in soft drinks and in hard, in social economy and social extravagance: ugh! a frightful universality of knowings.

But it's all France without Paris, *Hamlet* without the Prince, and bricks without straw. For we know nothing, or next to nothing, about ourselves. After hundreds of thousands of years we have learned how to wash our faces and bob our hair, and that is about all we *have* learned, *individually*. Collectively, of course, as a species, we have combed the round earth with a tooth-comb, and pulled down the stars almost within grasp. And then what? Here sit I, a two-legged individual with a risky temper, knowing all about—take a pinch of salt—Tierra del Fuego and Relativity and the composition of celluloid, the appearance of the anthrax bacillus and solar eclipses, and the latest fashion in shoes; and it don't do me *no* good! as the charlady said of near beer. It doesn't leave me feeling no less lonesome inside! as the old Englishwoman said, long ago, of tea without rum.

Our knowledge, like the prohibition beer, is always near. But it never gets there. It leaves us feeling just as lonesome inside.

We are hopelessly uneducated in ourselves. We pretend that when we know a smattering of the Patagonian idiom we have in so far educated ourselves. What nonsense! The leather of my boots is just as effectual in turning me into a bull, or a young steer. Alas!

we wear our education just as externally as we wear our boots, and to far less profit. It is all external education, anyhow.

What am I, when I am at home? I'm supposed to be a sensible human being. Yet I carry a whole waste-paper basket of ideas at the top of my head, and in some other part of my anatomy, the dark continent of myself. I have a whole stormy chaos of "feelings." And with these self-same feelings I simply don't get a chance. Some of them roar like lions, some twist like snakes, some bleat like snow-white lambs, some warble like linnets, some are absolutely dumb, but swift as slippery fishes, some are oysters that open on occasion: and lo! here am I, adding another scrap of paper to the ideal accumulation in the waste-paper basket, hoping to settle the matter that way.

The lion springs on me! I wave an idea at him. The serpent casts a terrifying glance at me, and I hand him a Moody and Sankey hymn-book. Matters go from bad to worse.

The wild creatures are coming forth from the darkest Africa inside us. In the night you can hear them bellowing. If you are a big game-hunter, like Billy Sunday, you may shoulder your elephant gun. But since the forest is inside all of us, and in every forest there's a whole assortment of big game and dangerous creatures, it's one against a thousand. We've managed to keep clear of the darkest Africa inside us, for a long time. We've been so busy finding the North Pole and converting the Patagonians, loving our neighbour and devising new means of exterminating him, listening-in and shutting-out.

But now, my dear, dear reader, Nemesis is blowing his nose. And muffled roarings are heard out of darkest Africa, with stifled shrieks.

I say feelings, not emotions. Emotions are things we more or less recognize. We see love, like a woolly lamb, or like a decorative decadent panther in Paris clothes: according as it is sacred or profane. We see hate, like a dog chained to a kennel. We see fear, like a shivering monkey. We see anger, like a bull with a ring through his nose, and greed, like a pig. Our emotions are our domesticated animals, noble like the horse, timid like the rabbit, but all completely at our service. The rabbit goes into the pot, and the horse into the shafts. For we are creatures of circumstance, and must fill our bellies and our pockets.

Convenience! Convenience! There are convenient emotions and inconvenient ones. The inconvenient ones we chain up, or put a ring through their nose. The convenient ones are our pets. Love is our pet favourite.

And that's as far as our education goes, in the direction of feelings. We have no language for the feelings, because our feelings do not even exist for us.

Yet what is a man? Is he really just a little engine that you stoke with potatoes and beef-steak? Does all the strange flow of life in him come out of meat and potatoes, and turn into the so-called physical energy?

Educated! We are not even *born,* as far as our feelings are concerned.

You can eat till you're bloated, and "get ahead" till you're a byword, and still, inside you, will be the darkest Africa whence come roars and shrieks.

Man is not a little engine of cause and effect. We must put that out of our minds for ever. The *cause* in man is something we shall never fathom. But there it is, a strange dark continent that we do not explore, because we do not even allow that it exists. Yet all the time, it is within us: the *cause* of us, and of our days.

And our feelings are the first manifestations within the aboriginal jungle of us. Till now, in sheer terror of ourselves, we have turned our backs on the jungle, fenced it in with an enormous entanglement of barbed wire, and declared it did not exist.

But alas! we ourselves only exist because of the life that bounds and leaps into our limbs and our consciousness, from out of the original dark forest within us. We may wish to exclude this inbounding, inleaping life. We may wish to be as our domesticated animals are, tame. But let us remember that even our cats and dogs have, in each generation, to be tamed. They are not now a tame species. Take away the control, and they will cease to be tame. They will not tame *themselves.*

Man is the only creature who has deliberately tried to tame himself. He has succeeded. But alas! it is a process you cannot set a limit to. Tameness, like alcohol, destroys its own creator. Tameness is an effect of control. But the tamed thing loses the power of control, in itself. It must be controlled from without. Man has pretty well tamed himself, and he calls his tameness civilization. True civilization would be something very different. But man is now tame. Tameness means the loss of the peculiar power of command. The tame are always commanded by the untame. Man has tamed himself, and so has lost his power for command, the power to give himself direction. He has no choice in himself. He is tamed, like a tame horse waiting for the rein.

Supposing all horses were suddenly rendered masterless, what would they do? They would run wild. But supposing they were left still shut up in their fields, paddocks, corrals, stables, what would they do? They would go insane.

And that is precisely man's predicament. He is tamed. There are no untamed to give the commands and the direction. Yet he is shut up within all his barbed wire fences. He can only go insane, degenerate.

What is the alternative? It is nonsense to pretend we can untame ourselves in five minutes. That, too, is a slow and strange process, that has to be undertaken seriously. It is nonsense to pretend we can break the fences and dash out into the wilds. There are no wilds left, comparatively, and man is a dog that returns to his vomit.

Yet unless we proceed to connect ourselves up with our own primeval sources, we shall degenerate. And degenerating, we shall break up into a strange orgy of feelings. They will be decomposition feelings, like the colours of autumn. And they will precede whole storms of death, like leaves in a wind.

There is no help for it. Man cannot tame himself and then stay tame. The moment he tries to stay tame he begins to degenerate, and gets the second sort of wildness, the wildness of destruction, which may be autumnal-beautiful for a while, like yellow leaves. Yet yellow leaves can only fall and rot.

Man tames himself in order to learn to un-tame himself again. To be civilized, we must not deny and blank out our feelings. Tameness is not civilization. It is only burning down the brush and ploughing the land. Our civilization has hardly realized yet the necessity for ploughing the soul. Later, we sow wild seed. But so far, we've only been burning off and rooting out the old wild brush. Our civilization, as far as our own souls go, has been a destructive process, up to now. The landscape of our souls is a charred wilderness of burnt-off stumps, with a green bit of water here, and a tin shanty with a little iron stove.

Now we have to sow wild seed again. We have to cultivate our feelings. It is no good trying to be popular, to let a whole rank tangle of liberated, degenerate feelings spring up. It will give us no satisfaction.

And it is no use doing as the psychoanalysts have done. The psychoanalysts show the greatest fear of all, of the innermost primeval place in man, where God is, if He is anywhere. The old Jewish horror of the true Adam, the mysterious "natural man," rises to a shriek in psychoanalysis. Like the idiot who foams and bites his wrists till they bleed. So great is the Freudian hatred of the oldest, old Adam, from whom God is not yet separated off, that the psychoanalyst sees this Adam as nothing but a monster of perversity, a bunch of engendering adders, horribly clotted.

This vision is the perverted vision of the degenerate tame: tamed through thousands of shameful years. The old Adam is the for ever untamed: he who is of the tame hated, with a horror of fearful hate: but who is held in innermost respect by the fearless.

In the oldest of the old Adam, was God: behind the dark wall of his breast, under the seal of the navel. Then man had a revulsion against himself, and God was separated off, lodged in the outermost space.

Now we have to return. Now again the old Adam must lift up his face and his breast, and un-tame himself. Not in viciousness nor in wantonness, but having God within the walls of himself. In the very darkest continent of the body there is God. And from Him issue the first dark rays of our feeling, wordless, and utterly previous to words: the innermost rays, the first messengers, the primeval, honourable beasts of our being, whose voice echoes wordless and for ever wordless down the darkest avenues of the soul, but full of potent speech. Our own inner meaning.

Now we have to educate ourselves, not by laying down laws and inscribing tables of stone, but by listening. Not listening-in to noises from Chicago or Timbuktu. But listening-in to the voices of the honourable beasts that call in the dark paths of the veins of our body, from the God in the heart. Listening inwards, inwards, not for words nor for inspiration, but to the lowing of the innermost beasts, the feelings, that roam in the forest of the blood, from the feet of God within the red, dark heart.

And how? How? How shall we even begin to educate ourselves in the feelings?

Not by laying down laws, or commandments, or axioms and postulates. Not even by making assertions that such and such is blessed. Not by words at all.

If we can't hear the cries far down in our own forests of dark

[THE INDIVIDUAL CONSCIOUSNESS *V.* THE SOCIAL CONSCIOUSNESS]

The more one reads of modern novels, the more one realizes that, in this individualistic age, there are no individuals left. People, men, women, and children, are *not* thinking their own thoughts, they are *not* feeling their own feelings, they are *not* living their own lives.

The moment the human being becomes conscious of himself, he ceases to be himself. The reason is obvious. The moment any individual creature becomes aware of its own individual isolation, it becomes instantaneously aware of that which is outside itself, and forms its limitation. That is, the psyche splits in two, into subjective and objective reality. The moment this happens, the primal integral *I,* which is for the most part a living *continuum* of all the rest of living things, collapses, and we get the I which is staring out of the window at the reality which is not itself. And this is the condition of the modern consciousness, from early childhood.

In the past, children were supposed to be "innocent." Which means that they were like the animals, not split into subjective and objective consciousness. They were one living *continuum* with all the universe. This is the essential state of innocence, of naïveté, and it is the persistence of this state all through life, as the *basic* state of consciousness, which preserves the human being all his life fresh and alive, a true individual. Paradoxical as it may sound, the individual is only truly himself when he is unconscious of his own individuality, when he is unaware of his own isolation, when he is not split into subjective and objective, when there is no *me or you,* no *me or it* in his consciousness, but the *me and you,* the *me and it* is a living *continuum,* as if all were connected by a living membrane.

As soon as the conception *me or you, me or it* enters the human consciousness, then the individual consciousness is supplanted by the social consciousness. The social consciousness means the cleaving of the true individual consciousness into two halves, subjective and objective, "me" on the one hand, "you" or "it" on the other. The awareness of "you" or of "it" as something definitely limiting "me," this is the social consciousness. The awareness of "you" or of "it" is a *continuum* of "me"—different, but not separate: different as the eye is different from the nose—this is the primal or pristine or basic consciousness of the individual, the state of "innocence" or of naïveté."

This consciousness collapses, and the real individual lapses out, leaving only the social individual, a creature of subjective and objective consciousness, but of no innocent or genuinely individual consciousness. The innocent or radical individual consciousness alone is unanalysable and mysterious; it is the queer nuclear spark in the protoplasm, which is life itself, in its individual manifestation. The moment you split into subjective and objective consciousness, then the whole thing becomes analysable, and, in the last issue, dead.

Of course, it takes a long time to destroy the naïve individual, the old Adam, entirely, and to produce creatures which are completely social in consciousness, that is, always aware of the "you" set over against the "me," always conscious of the "it" which the "I" is up against. But it has happened now in even tiny children. A child nowadays can say: *Mummy!*—and his fatal consciousness of the cleft between him and Mummy is already obvious. The cleavage has happened to him. He is no longer one with things: worse, he is no longer *at one* with his mother even. He is a tiny, forlorn little social individual, a subjective-objective little Consciousness.

The subjective-objective consciousness is never truly individual. It is a product. The social individual, the me-or-you, me-or-it individual, is denied all naïve or innocent or really individual feelings. He is capable only of the feelings, which are really sensations, produced by the reaction between the "me" and the "you," the "I" and the "it." Innocent or individual feeling is only capable when there is a *continuum,* when the *me* and the *you* and the *it* are a *continuum.*

Man lapses from true innocence, from the at-oneness, in two ways. The first is the old way of greed or selfishness, when the "me" wants to swallow the "you" and put an end to the *continuum* that way. The other is the way of negation, when the "I" wants to lapse out into the "you" or the "it," and so end all responsibility of keeping up one's own bright nuclear cell alive in the tissue of the universe. In either way, there is a lapse from innocence and a fall into the state of vanity, ugly vanity. It is a vanity of positive tyranny, or a vanity of negative tyranny. The old villains-in-the-piece fell into the vanity of positive tyranny, the new villains-in-the-peace, who are still called saints and holy persons, or at worst, God's fools, are squirming in the vanity of negative tyranny. They won't leave the *continuum* alone. They insist on passing out into it. Which is as bad as if the eye should insist on merging itself into a oneness with the nose. For we are none of us more than a cell in the eye-tissue, or a cell in the nose-tissue or the heart-tissue of the macrocosm, the universe.

And, of course, the moment you cause a break-down in living tissue, you get inert Matter. So the moment you break the *continuum,* the naïveté, the innocence, the at-oneness, you get materialism and nothing but materialism.

Of course, inert Matter exists, as distinct from living tissue: dead protoplasm as distinct from living, nuclear protoplasm. But the living tissue is able to deal with the dead tissue. Whereas the reverse is not true. Dead tissue cannot do anything to living tissue, except try to corrupt it and make it dead too. Which is the main point concerning Materialism, whether it be the spiritual or the carnal Materialism.

The *continuum* which is alive can handle the dead tissue. That is, the individual who still retains his individuality, his basic at-oneness or innocence or naïveté, can deal with the material world successfully. He can be analytical and critical upon necessity. But at the core, he is always naïve or innocent or at one.

The contrary is not true. The social consciousness can only be analytical, critical, constructive but not creative, sensational but not passionate, emotional but without true feeling. It can know, but it cannot be. It is always made up of a duality, to which there is no clue. And the one half of the duality neutralizes, in the long run, the other half. So that, whether it is Nebuchadnezzar or Francis of Assisi, you arrive at the same thing, nothingness.

You can't make art out of nothingness. *Ex nihilo nihil fit!* But you can make art out of the collapse towards nothingness: the collapse of the true individual into the social individual.

Which brings us to John Galsworthy with a bump. Because, in all his books, I have not been able to discover one real individual —nothing but social individuals. *Ex nihilo nihil fit!* You can't make art, which is the revelation of the *continuum* itself, the very nuclear glimmer of the naïve individual, when there is no *continuum* and no naïve individual. As far as I have gone, I have found in Galsworthy nothing but social individuals.

Thinking you are naïve doesn't make you naïve, and thinking you are passionate doesn't make you passionate. Again, being stupid or limited is not a mark of naïveté, and being doggedly amorous is not a sign of passion. In each case, the very reverse. Again, a peasant is by no means necessarily more naïve, or innocent, or individual than a stockbroker, nor a sailor than an educationalist. The reverse may be the case. Peasants are often as greedy as cancer, and sailors as soft and corrupt as a rotten apple.

INTRODUCTION TO PICTURES

Man is anything from a forked radish to an immortal spirit. He is pretty well everything that ever was or will be, absolutely human and absolutely inhuman. If we did but know it, we have every imaginable and unimaginable feeling streaking somewhere through us. Even the most pot-headed American judge, who feels that his daughter will be lost for ever if she hears the word *cunt,* has all the feelings of a satyr careering somewhere inside him, very much suppressed and distorted. And the reason that Puritans are so frightened of life is that they happen, unfortunately, to be alive in spite of themselves.

The trouble with poor, pig-headed man is that he makes a selection out of the vast welter of his feelings, and says: I *only* feel these excellent selected feelings, and you, moreover, are allowed only to feel these excellent select feelings too. Which is all very well, till the pot boils over, or blows up.

When man fixes on a few select feelings and says that these feelings must be felt exclusively, the said feelings rapidly become repellent. Because we've *got* to love our wives, we make a point of loving somebody else. The moment the mind *fixes* a feeling, that feeling is repulsive. Take a greedy person, who falls right into his food. Why is he so distasteful? Is it because his stomach is asserting itself? Not at all! It is because his *mind,* having decided that food is good, or good for him, drives on his body to eat and eat and eat. The poor stomach is overloaded in spite of itself. The appetites are violated. The natural appetite says: I've had enough! But the fixed mind, fixed on feeding, forces the jaws, the gullet to go on working, the stomach to go on receiving. And this is greed. And no wonder it is repulsive.

The same is precisely true of drinking, smoking, drug-taking, or any of the vices. When did the *body* of a man ever like getting drunk? Never! Think how it reacts, how it vomits, how it tries to repudiate the excess of drink, how utterly wretched it feels when its sane balance is overthrown. But the mind or spirit of a man finds in intoxication some relief, some escape, some sense of licence, so the drunkenness is forced upon the unhappy stomach and bowels, which gradually get used to it. But which are slowly destroyed.

If only we would realize that, until perverted by the mind, the human body preserves itself continually in a delicate balance of sanity! That is what it is always striving to do, and always it is shoved over by the pernicious mental consciousness called the spirit. As soon as even a baby finds something good, it howls for more, till it is sick. That is the nauseating side of the human consciousness. But it is not the body. It is the mind, the self-aware-of-itself, which says: This is good. I will go on and on and on eating it! The human spirit is the self-aware-of-itself. This self-awareness may make us noble. More often it makes us worse than pigs. We need above all things a curb upon this spirit of ours, this self-aware-of-itself, which is our spirituality and our vice.

As a matter of fact, we need to be a little more *radically* aware of ourselves. When a man starts drinking, and his stomach simply doesn't want any more, it is time he put a check on his impudent spirit and obeyed his stomach. When a man's body has reached one of its periods of loneliness, and with a sure voice cries that it wants to be alone and intact, it is then, inevitably, that the accursed perversity of the spirit, the self-aware-of-itself, is bound to whip the unhappy senses into excitement and to force them into fornication. It is then, when a man's body cries to be left alone and intact, that man forces himself to be a Don Juan. The same with women. It is the price we have to pay for our precious spirit, our self-aware-of-itself, which we don't yet know how to handle.

And when a man has forced himself to be a Don Juan, you may bet his children will force themselves to be Puritans, with a nasty, *greedy* abstinence, as greedy as the previous gluttony. Oh bitter inheritance, the human spirit, the self-aware-of-itself! The self-aware-of-itself, that says: I like it, so I will have it all the time!—and then, in revulsion, says: I don't like it, I will have *none* of it, and no man shall have any of it. Either way, it is sordid, and makes one sick. Oh lofty human spirit, how sordid you have made us! What a viper Plato was, with his distinction between body and spirit, and the exaltation of the spirit, the self-aware-of-itself. The human spirit, the self-aware-of-itself, is only tolerable when controlled by the divine, or demonish sanity which is greater than itself.

It is difficult to know what name to give to that most central and vital clue to the human being, which clinches him into integrity. The best is to call it his vital sanity. We thus escape the rather nauseating emotional suggestions of words like soul and spirit and holy ghost.

We can escape from the trap of the human spirit, the self-aware-of-itself, in which we are entrapped, by going quite, quite still and letting our whole sanity assert itself inside us, and set us into rhythm.

But first of all we must know we are entrapped. We most certainly are. You may call it intellectualism, self-consciousness, the self aware of itself, or what you will: you can even call it just human consciousness, if you like: but there it is. Perhaps it is simpler to stick to a common word like self-consciousness. In modern civilization we are all self-conscious. All our emotions are mental, self-conscious. Our passions are self-conscious. We are an intensely elaborate and intricate clockwork of nerves and brain. Nerves and brain, but still a clockwork. A mechanism, and hence incapable of experience.

The nerves and brain are the apparatus by which we signal and *register* consciousness. Consciousness, however, does not take rise in the nerves and brain. It takes rise elsewhere: in the blood, in the corpuscles, somewhere very primitive and pre-nerve and pre-brain. Just as energy generates in the electron. Every speck of protoplasm, every living cell is *conscious*. All the cells of our body are conscious. And all the time, they give off a stream of consciousness which flows along the nerves and keeps us spontaneously alive. While the flow streams through us, from the blood to the heart, the bowls, the viscera, then along the sympathetic system of nerves into our spontaneous minds, making us breathe, and see, and move, and be aware, and *do* things spontaneously, while this flow streams as a flame streams ceaselessly, we are lit up, we glow, we live.

But there is another process. There is that strange switchboard of consciousness, the brain, with its power of transferring spontaneous energy into voluntary energy: or consciousness, as you please: the two are very closely connected. The brain can transfer spontaneous consciousness, which we are *unaware* of, into voluntary consciousness, which we *are* aware of, and which we call consciousness exclusively.

Now it is nonsense to say there cannot be a consciousness in us of which we are *always* unaware. We are never aware of sleep except when we awake. If we didn't sleep, we should never know we were awake. But we *are* very much aware of our "consciousness." We are aware that it is a state only. And we are aware that it displaces another state. The other state we may negatively call the unconscious. But it is a poor way of putting it. To say that a skylark sings unconsciously is feeble. The skylark of course sings consciously. But with the other, spontaneous or sympathetic consciousness, which flows up like a flame from the corpuscles of all the body to the gates of the body, through the muscles and nerves of the sympathetic system to the hands and eyes and all the organs of utterance. The skylark does *not* sing like the lady in the concert-hall, consciously, mentally, deliberately, with the voluntary consciousness.

Some very strange process takes place in the brain, the process of cognition. This process of cognition consists in the forming of ideas, which are units of transmuted consciousness. These ideas can then be stored in the memory, or wherever it is that the brain stores its ideas. And these ideas are alive: they are little batteries in which so much energy of consciousness is stored.

It is here that our secondary consciousness comes in, our mind, our mental consciousness, our cerebral consciousness. Our mind is made up of a vast number of live ideas, and a good number of dead ones. Ideas are like the little electric batteries of a flashlight, in which a certain amount of energy is stored, which expends itself and it not renewed. Then you throw the dead battery away.

But when the mind has a sufficient number of these little batteries of ideas in store, a new process of life starts in. The moment an idea forms in the mind, at that moment does the old integrity of the consciousness break. In the old myths, at that moment we lose our "innocence," we partake of the tree of knowledge, and we become "aware of our nakedness": in short, self-conscious. The self becomes aware of itself, and then the fun begins, and then the trouble starts.

The first thing the self-aware-of-itself realizes is that it is a derivative, not a primary entity. The second thing it realizes is that the spontaneous self with its sympathetic consciousness and non-ideal reaction is the original reality, the old Adam, over which the self-aware-of-itself has no originative power. That is, the self-aware-of-itself knows it can frustrate the consciousness of the old Adam, divert it, but it cannot stop it: it knows, moreover, that as the moon is a luminary because the sun shines, so it, the self-aware-of-itself, the mental consciousness, the spirit, is only a sort of reflection of the great primary consciousness of the old Adam.

Now the self-aware-of-itself has *always* the quality of egoism. The spirit is always egoistic. The greatest spiritual commands are *all* forms of egoism, usually inverted egoism, for deliberate humility, we are all well aware, is a rabid form of egoism. The Sermon on the Mount is a long string of utterances from the self-aware-of-itself, the spirit, and all of them are rabid aphorisms of egoism, back-handed egoism.

The moment the self-aware-of-itself comes into being, it begins egoistically to assert itself. It cuts immediately at the wholeness of the pristine consciousness, the old Adam, and wounds it. And it goes on with the battle. The greatest enemy man has or ever can have is his own spirit, his own self-aware-of-itself.

This self-aware ego *knows* it is a derivative, a satellite. So it must assert itself. It knows it has no power over the original body, the old Adam, save the secondary power of the idea. So it begins to store up ideas, those little batteries which *always* have a moral, or good-and-bad implication.

For four thousand years man has been accumulating these little batteries of ideas, and using them on himself against his pristine consciousness, his old Adam. The queen bee of all human ideas since 2000 B.C. has been the idea that the body, the pristine consciousness, the great sympathetic life-flow, the steady flame of the old Adam is bad, and must be conquered. Every religion taught the conquest: science took up the battle, tooth and nail: culture fights in the same cause: and only art sometimes—or always—exhibits an internecine conflict and betrays its own battle-cry.

I believe that there was a great age, a great epoch when man did not make war: previous to 2000 B.C. Then the self had not really become aware of itself, it had not separated itself off, the spirit was not yet born, so there was no internal conflict, and hence no permanent external conflict. The external conflict of war, or of industrial competition, is only a reflection of the war that goes on inside each human being, the war of the self-conscious ego against the spontaneous old Adam.

If the self-conscious ego once wins, you get immediate insanity, because our primary self is the old Adam, in which rests our sanity. And when man starts living from his self-conscious energy, women at once begin to go to pieces, all the "freedom" business sets in. Because women are only kept in equilibrium by the old Adam. Nothing else can avail.

But the means which the spirit, the self-conscious ego, the personality, the self-aware-of-itself takes to conquer the vital self or old Adam are curious. First it has an idea, a semi-truth in which some of the energy of the vital consciousness is transmuted and stored. This idea it projects down again onto the spontaneous affective body. The very first idea is the idea of shame. The spirit, the self-conscious ego looks at the body and says: You are shameful. The body, for some mysterious reason (really, because it is so vulnerable), immediately feels ashamed. A-ha! Now the spirit has got a hold. It discovers a second idea. The second idea is work. The spirit says: Base body! you need all the time to eat food. Who is going to give you food? You must sweat for it, sweat for it, or you will starve.

Now before the spirit emerged white and tyrannous in the human consciousness, man had not concerned himself deeply about starving. Occasionally, no doubt, he starved; but no oftener than the birds do, and they don't often starve. Anyhow, he cared no more about it than the birds do. But now he feared it, and fell to work.

And here we see the mysterious power of ideas, the power of rousing emotion, primitive emotions of shame, fear, anger, and sometimes joy; but usually the specious joy over another defeat of the pristine self.

So the spirit, the self-aware-of-itself organized a grand battery of dynamic ideas, the pivotal idea being almost always the idea of self-sacrifice and the triumph of the self-aware-of-itself, that pale Galilean *simulacrum* of a man.

But wait! Wait! There is a nemesis. It is great fun overcoming the Old Adam while the Old Adam is still lusty and kicking: like breaking in a bronco. But nemesis, strange nemesis. The old Adam isn't an animal that you can *permanently* domesticate. Domesticated, he goes deranged.

We are the sad results of a four-thousand-year effort to break the Old Adam, to domesticate him utterly. He is to a large extent broken and domesticated.

But then what? Then, as the flow of pristine or spontaneous consciousness gets weaker and weaker, the grand dynamic ideas go deader and deader. We have got a vast magazine of ideas, all of us. But they are practically all dead batteries, played out. They can't provoke any emotion or feeling or reaction in the spontaneous body, the old Adam. Love is a dead shell of an idea—we don't react—for love is only one of the great dynamic ideas, now played out. Self-sacrifice is another dead shell. Conquest is another. Success is another. Making good is another.

In fact, I don't know of one great idea or ideal—they are the same —which is still alive today. They are all dead. You can turn them on, but you get no kick. You turn on love, you fornicate till you are black in the face—you get no real thing out of it. The old Adam plays his last revenge on you, and refuses to respond *at all* to any of your ideal pokings. You have gone dead. You can't feel anything, and you may as well know it.

The mob, of course, will always deceive themselves that they are feeling things, even when they are not. To them, when they say *I love you!* there will be a huge imaginary feeling, and they will act up according to schedule. All the love on the film, the close-up kisses and the rest, and all the responses in buzzing emotion in the audience, is *all* acting up, all according to schedule. It is all just cerebral, and the body is just forced to go through the antics.

And this deranges the natural body-mind harmony on which our sanity rests. Our masses are rapidly going insane.

And in the horror of nullity–for the human being comes to have his own nullity in horror, he is terrified by his own incapacity to feel anything at all, he has a mad fear, at last, of his own self-consciousness–the modern man sets up the reverse process of katabolism, destructive sensation. He can no longer have any living productive feelings. Very well, he will have destructive sensations, produced by katabolism on his most intimate tissues.

Drink, drugs, jazz, speed, "petting," all modern forms of thrill, are just the production of sensation by the katabolism of the finest conscious cells of our living body. We explode our own cells and release a certain energy and accompanying sensation. It is, naturally, a process of suicide. And it is just the same process as ever: the self-conscious ego, the spirit, attacking the pristine body, the old Adam. But now the attack is direct. All the wildest Bohemians and profligates are only doing directly what their puritanical grandfathers did indirectly: killing the body of the old Adam. But now the lust is direct self-murder. It only needs a few more strides, and it is promiscuous murder, like the war.

But we see this activity rampant today: the process of the sensational katabolism of the conscious body. It is perhaps even more pernicious than the old conservative attack on the old Adam, certainly it is swifter. But it is the same thing. There is no *volte-face*. There is no new spirit. It may be a *Life of Christ* or it may be a book on Relativity or a slim volume of lyrics or a novel like the telephone directory: it is still the same old attack on the living body. The body is still made disgusting. Only the moderns drag in all the excrements and the horrors and put them under your nose and say: Enjoy that horror! Or they write about love as if it were a process of endless pissing–except that they write kissing instead of pissing–and they say: Isn't it lovely!

VII

Personalia and Fragments

THE MINER AT HOME

Like most colliers, Bower had his dinner before he washed himself. It did not surprise his wife that he said little. He seemed quite amiable, but evidently did not feel confidential. Gertie was busy with the three children, the youngest of whom lay kicking on the sofa, preparing to squeal; therefore she did not concern herself overmuch with her husband, once having ascertained by a few shrewd glances at his heavy brows and his blue eyes, which moved conspicuously in his black face, that he was only pondering.

He smoked a solemn pipe until six o'clock. Although he was really a good husband, he did not notice that Gertie was tired. She was getting irritable at the end of the long day.

"Don't you want to wash yourself?" she asked, grudgingly, at six o'clock. It was sickening to have a man sitting there in his pit-dirt, never saying a word, smoking like a Red Indian.

"I'm ready, when you are," he replied.

She lay the baby on the sofa, barricaded it with pillows, and brought from the scullery a great panchion, a bowl of heavy earthenware like brick, glazed inside to a dark mahogany color. Tall and thin and very pale, she stood before the fire holding the great bowl, her grey eyes flashing.

"Get up, our Jack, this minute, or I'll squash thee under the blessed panchion."

The fat boy of six, who was rolling on the rug in the firelight, said broadly:

"Squash me, then."

"Get up," she cried, giving him a push with her foot.

"Gi'e ower," he said, rolling jollily.

"I'll smack you," she said grimly, preparing to put down the panchion.

"Get up, theer," shouted the father.

Gertie ladled water from the boiler with a tin ladling can. Drops fell from her ladle hissing into the red fire, splashing on to the white hearth, blazing like drops of flame on the flat-topped fender. The father gazed at it all, unmoved.

"I've told you," he said, "to put cold water in the panchion first. If one o' th' children goes an' falls in . . ."

"You can see as 'e doesn't then," snapped she. She tempered the bowl with cold water, dropped in a flannel and a lump of soap, and spread the towel over the fender to warm.

Then, and only then, Bower rose. He wore no coat, and his arms were freckled black. He stripped to the waist, hitched his trousers into the strap, and kneeled on the rug to wash himself. There was a great splashing and sputtering. The red firelight shone on his cap of white soap, and on the muscles of his back, on the strange working of his red and white muscular arms, that flashed up and down like individual creatures.

Gertie sat with the baby clawing at her ears and hair and nose. Continually she drew back her face and head from the cruel little baby-clasp. Jack was hanging on to the kitchen door.

"Come away from that door," cried the mother.

Jack did not come away, but neither did he open the door and run the risk of incurring his father's wrath. The room was very hot, but the thought of a draught is abhorrent to a miner.

With the baby on one arm, Gertie washed her husband's back. She sponged it carefully with the flannel, and then, still with one hand, began to dry it on the rough towel.

"Canna ter put th' childt down an' use both hands?" said her husband.

"Yes; an' then if th' childt screets, there's a bigger to-do than iver. There's no suitin' some folk."

"The childt 'ud non screet."

Gertie plumped it down. The baby began to cry. The wife rubbed her husband's back till it grew pink, whilst Bower quivered with pleasure. As soon as she threw the towel down:

"Shut that childt up," he said.

He wrestled his way into his shirt. His head emerged, with black hair standing roughly on end. He was rather an ugly man, just above medium height, and stiffly built. He had a thin black moustache over a full mouth, and a very full chin that was marred by a blue seam, where a horse had kicked him when he was a lad in the pit. With both hands on the mantelpiece above his head, he stood looking in the fire, his whitish shirt hanging like a smock over his pit trousers.

Presently, still looking absently in the fire, he said: "Bill Andrews was standin' at th' pit top, an' give ivery man as 'e come up one o' these."

He handed to his wife a small whity-blue paper, on which was printed simply:

February 14, 1912.

To the Manager–

I hereby give notice to leave your employment fourteen days from above date.

Signed ––

Gertie read the paper, blindly dodging her head from the baby's grasp.

"An' what d'you reckon that's for?" she asked.

"I suppose it means as we come out."

"I'm sure!" she cried in indignation. "Well, *tha'rt* not goin' to sign it."

"It'll ma'e no diff'rence whether I do or dunna–t'others will."

"Then let 'em!" She made a small clicking sound in her mouth. "This 'ill ma'e th' third strike as we've had sin' we've been married; an' a fat lot th' better for it you are, arena you?"

He squirmed uneasily.

"No, but we mean to be," he said.

"I'll tell you what, colliers is a discontented lot, as doesn't know what they *do* want. That's what they are."

"Tha'd better not let some o' th' colliers as there is hear thee say so."

"I don't care who hears me. An' there isn't a man in Eastwood but what'll say as th' last two strikes has ruined the place. There's that much bad blood now atween th' mesters an' th' men as there isn't a thing but what's askew. An' what *will* it be, I should like to know!"

"It's not on'y here; it's all ower th' country alike," he gloated.

"Yes; it's them blessed Yorkshire an' Welsh colliers as does it. They're that bug nowadays, what wi' talkin' an' spoutin', they hardly know which side their back-side hangs. Here, take this childt!"

She thrust the baby into his arms, carried out the heavy bowlful of black suds, mended the fire, cleared round, and returned for the child.

"Ben Haseldine said, an' he's a union man–he told me when he come for th' union money yesterday, as th' men doesn't want to come out–not our men. It's th' union."

"Tha knows nowt about it, woman. It's a' woman's jabber, from beginnin' to end."

"You don't intend us to know. Who wants th' Minimum Wage? Butties doesn't. There th' butties'll be, havin' to pay seven shillin' a day to men as 'appen isn't worth a penny more than five."

"But the butties is goin' to have eight shillin' accordin' to scale."

"An' then th' men as can't work tip-top, an' is worth, 'appen, five shillin' a day, they get th' sack: an' th' old men, an' so on."

"Nowt o' th' sort, woman, nowt o' th' sort. Tha's got it off 'am-pat. There's goin' to be inspectors for all that, an' th' men'll get what they're worth, accordin' to age, an' so on."

"An' accordin' to idleness an'–what somebody says about 'em. I'll back! There'll be a lot o' fairness!"

"Tha talks like a woman as knows nowt. What does thee know about it?"

"I know what you did at th' last strike. And I know this much, when Shipley men had *their* strike tickets, not one in three signed 'em–so there. An' *tha'rt* not goin' to!"

"We want a livin' wage," he declared.

"Hanna you got one?" she cried.

"Han we?" he shouted. "Han we? Who does more chaunterin' than thee when it's a short wik, an' tha gets 'appen a scroddy twenty-two shillin'? Tha goes at me 'ard enough."

"Yi; but what better shall you be? What better *are* you for th' last two strikes–tell me that?"

"I'll tell thee this much, th' mesters doesna' mean us to ha'e owt. They promise, but they dunna keep it, not they. Up comes Friday night, an' nowt to draw, an' a woman fit to ha'e yer guts out for it."

"It's nowt but th' day-men as wants the blessed Minimum Wage –it's not butties."

"It's time as th' butties *did* ha'e ter let their men make a fair day's wage. Four an' sixpence a day is about as 'e's allowed to addle, whoiver he may be."

"I wonder what you'll say next. You say owt as is put in your mouth, that's a fac'. What are thee, dost reckon?–are ter a butty, or day-man, or ostler, or are ter a mester?–for tha might be, ter hear thee talk."

"I nedna neither. It ought to be fair a' round."

"It ought, hang my rags, it ought! Tha'rt very fair to me, for instance."

"An' arena I?"

"Tha thinks 'cause tha gi'es me a lousy thirty shillin' reg'lar tha'rt th' best man i' th' Almighty world. Tha mun be waited on han' an' foot, an' sided wi' whativer tha says. But I'm *not!* No, an' I'm not, not when it comes to strikes. I've seen enough on 'em."

"Then niver open thy mouth again if it's a short wik, an' we're pinched."

"We're niver pinched that much. An' a short wik isn't no shorter than a strike wik; put that i' thy pipe an' smoke it. It's th' idle men as wants th' strikes."

"Shut thy mouth, woman. If every man worked as hard as I do . . ."

"He wouldn't ha'e as much to do as me; an' 'e wouldna. But *I've* nowt to do, as tha'rt flig ter tell me. No, it's th' idle men as wants th' strike. It's a union strike, this is, not a men's strike. You're sharpenin' th' knife for your own throats."

"Am I not sick of a woman as listens to every tale as is poured into her ears? No, I'm not takin' th' kid. I'm goin' out."

He put on his boots determinedly.

She rocked herself with vexation and weariness.

THE FLYING FISH

I. DEPARTURE FROM MEXICO

"Come home else no Day in Daybrook." This cablegram was the first thing Gethin Day read of the pile of mail which he found at the hotel in the lost town of South Mexico, when he returned from his trip to the coast. Though the message was not signed, he knew whom it came from and what it meant.

He lay in his bed in the hot October evening, still sick with malaria. In the flush of fever he saw yet the parched, stark mountains of the south, the villages of reed huts lurking among trees, the black-eyed natives with the lethargy, the ennui, the pathos, the beauty of an exhausted race; and above all he saw the weird, uncanny flowers, which he had hunted from the high plateaux, through the valleys, and down to the steaming crocodile heat of the *tierra caliente,* towards the sandy, burning, intolerable shores. For he was fascinated by the mysterious green blood that runs in the veins of plants, and the purple and yellow and red blood that colours the faces of flowers. Especially the unknown flora of South Mexico attracted him, and above all he wanted to trace to the living plant the mysterious essences and toxins known with such strange elaboration to the Mayas, the Zapotecas, and the Aztecs.

His head was humming like a mosquito, his legs were paralysed for the moment by the heavy quinine injection the doctor had injected into them, and his soul was as good as dead with the malaria; so he threw all his letters unopened on the floor, hoping never to see them again. He lay with the pale yellow cablegram in his hand: "Come home else no Day in Daybrook." Through the open doors from the patio of the hotel came the heavy scent of that invisible green night-flower the natives call *Buena de Noche.* The little Mexican servant-girl strode in barefoot with a cup of tea, her flounced cotton skirt swinging, her long black hair down her back. She asked him in her birdlike Spanish if he wanted nothing more. "*Nada más,*" he said. "Nothing more; leave me and shut the door."

He wanted to shut out the scent of that powerful green inconspicuous night-flower he knew so well.

No Day in Daybrook;
For the Vale a bad outlook.

No Day in Daybrook! There had been Days in Daybrook since time began: at least, so he imagined.

Daybrook was a sixteenth-century stone house, among the hills in the middle of England. It stood where Crichdale bends to the south and where Ashleydale joins in. "Daybrook standeth at the junction of the ways and at the centre of the trefoil. Even it rides within the Vale as an ark between three seas; being indeed the ark of these vales, if not of all England." So had written Sir Gilbert Day, he who built the present Daybrook in the sixteenth century. Sir Gilbert's *Book of Days,* so beautifully written out on vellum and illuminated by his own hand, was one of the treasures of the family.

Sir Gilbert had sailed the Spanish seas in his day, and had come home rich enough to rebuild the old house of Daybrook according to his own fancy. He had made it a beautiful pointed house, rather small, standing upon a knoll above the river Ashe, where the valley narrowed and the woods rose steep behind. "Nay," wrote this quaint Elizabethan, "though I say that Daybrook is the ark of the Vale, I mean not the house itself, but He that Day, that lives in the house in his day. While Day there be in Daybrook, the floods shall not cover the Vale nor shall they ride over England completely."

Gethin Day was nearing forty, and he had not spent much of his time in Daybrook. He had been a soldier and had wandered in many countries. At home his sister Lydia, twenty years older than himself, had been the Day in Daybrook. Now from her cablegram he knew she was either ill or already dead.

She had been rather hard and grey like the rock of Crichdale, but faithful and a pillar of strength. She had let him go his own way, but always when he came home, she would look into his blue eyes with her searching uncanny grey look and ask: "Well, have you come, or are you still wandering?" "Still wandering, I think," he said. "Mind you don't wander into a cage one of these days," she replied; "you would find far more room for yourself in Daybrook than in these foreign parts, if you knew how to come into your own."

This had always been the burden of her song to him: *if you knew how to come into your own.* And it had always exasperated him with a sense of futility; though whether his own futility or Lydia's, he had never made out.

Lydia was wrapt up in old Sir Gilbert's *Book of Days;* she had written out for her brother a fair copy, neatly bound in green leather, and had given it him without a word when he came of age, merely looking at him with that uncanny look of her grey eyes, expecting something of him, which always made him start away from her.

The *Book of Days* was a sort of secret family bible at Daybrook. It was never shown to strangers, nor ever mentioned outside the immediate family. Indeed in the family it was never openly alluded to. Only on solemn occasions, or on rare evenings, at twilight, when the evening star shone, had the father, now dead, occasionally read aloud to the two children from the nameless work.

In the copy she had written out for Gethin, Lydia had used different coloured inks in different places. Gethin imagined that her favourite passages were those in the royal-blue ink, where the page was almost as blue as the cornflowers that grew tall beside the walks in the garden at Daybrook.

"Beauteous is the day of the yellow sun which is the common day of men; but even as the winds roll unceasing above the trees of the world, so doth that Greater Day, which is the Uncommon Day, roll over the unclipt bushes of our little daytime. Even also as the morning sun shakes his yellow wings on the horizon and rises up, so the great bird beyond him spreads out his dark blue feathers, and beats his wings in the tremor of the Greater Day."

Gethin knew a great deal of his *Book of Days* by heart. In a dilettante fashion, he had always liked rather highflown poetry, but in the last years, something in the hard, fierce, finite sun of Mexico, in the dry terrible land, and in the black staring eyes of the suspicious natives, had made the ordinary day lose its reality to him. It had cracked like some great bubble, and to his uneasiness and terror, he had seemed to see through the fissures the deeper blue of that other Greater Day where moved the other sun shaking its dark blue wings. Perhaps it was the malaria; perhaps it was his own inevitable development; perhaps it was the presence of those handsome, dangerous, wide-eyed men left over from the ages before the flood in Mexico, which caused his old connexions and his accustomed world to break for him. He was ill, and he felt as if at the very middle of him, beneath his navel, some membrane were torn, some membrane which had connected him with the world and its day. The natives who attended him, quiet, soft, heavy, and rather helpless, seemed, he realized, to be gazing from their wide black eyes always into that greater day whence they had come and where they wished to return. Men of a dying race, to whom the busy sphere of the common day is a cracked and leaking shell.

He wanted to go home. He didn't care now whether England was tight and little and over-crowded and far too full of furniture. He no longer minded the curious quiet atmosphere of Daybrook in which he had felt he would stifle as a young man. He no longer resented the weight of family tradition, nor the peculiar sense of authority which the house seemed to have over him. Now he was sick from the soul outwards, and the common day had cracked for him, and the uncommon day was showing him its immensity, he felt that home was the place. It did not matter that England was small and tight and over-furnished, if the Greater Day were round about. He wanted to go home, away from these big wild countries where men were dying back into the Greater Day, home where he dare face the sun behind the sun, and come into his own in the Greater Day.

But he was as yet too ill to go. He lay in the nausea of the tropics, and let the days pass over him. The door of his room stood open on to the patio where green banana trees and high strange-sapped flowering shrubs rose from the water-sprinkled earth towards that strange rage of blue which was the sky over the shadow-heavy, perfume-soggy air of the closed-in courtyard. Dark-blue shadows moved from the side of the patio, disappeared, then appeared on the other side. Evening had come, and the barefoot natives in white calico flitted with silent rapidity across, and across, for ever going, yet mysteriously going nowhere, threading the timelessness with their transit, like swallows of darkness.

The window of the room, opposite the door, opened on to the tropical parched street. It was a big window, came nearly down to the floor, and was heavily barred with upright and horizontal bars. Past the window went the natives, with the soft, light rustle of their sandals. Big straw hats balanced, dark cheeks, calico shoulders brushed with the silent swiftness of the Indian past the barred window-space. Sometimes children clutched the bars and gazed in, with great shining eyes and straight blue-black hair, to see the Americano lying in the majesty of a white bed. Sometimes a beggar stood there, sticking a skinny hand through the iron grille and whimpering the strange, endless, pullulating whimper of the beggar—"*por amor de Dios!*"—on and on and on, as it seemed for an eternity. But the sick man on the bed endured it with the same endless endurance in resistance, endurance in resistance which he had learned in the Indian countries. Aztec or Mixtec, Zapotec or Maya, always the same power of serpent-like torpor of resistance.

The doctor came—an educated Indian: though he could do nothing but inject quinine and give a dose of calomel. But he was lost between the two days, the fatal greater day of the Indians, the fussy, busy lesser day of the white people.

"How is it going to finish?" he said to the sick man, seeking a word. "How is it going to finish with the Indians, with the Mexicans? Now the soldiers are all taking *marihuana*—hashish!"

"They are all going to die. They are all going to kill themselves—all—all," said the Englishman, in the faint permanent delirium of his malaria. "After all, beautiful it is to be dead, and quite departed."

The doctor looked at him in silence, understanding only too well. "Beautiful it is to be dead!" It is the refrain which hums at the centre of every Indian heart, where the greater day is hemmed in by the lesser. The despair that comes when the lesser day hems in the greater. Yet the doctor looked at the gaunt white man in malice:—"What, would you have us quite gone, you Americans?"

At last, Gethin Day crawled out into the plaza. The square was like a great low fountain of green and of dark shade, now it was autumn and the rains were over. Scarlet craters rose the canna flowers, licking great red tongues, and tropical yellow. Scarlet, yellow, green, blue-green, sunshine intense and invisible, deep indigo shade! and small, white-clad natives pass, passing, across the square, through the green lawns, under the indigo shade, and across the hollow sunshine of the road into the arched arcades of the low Spanish buildings, where the shops were. The low, baroque Spanish buildings stood back with a heavy, sick look, as if they too felt the endless malaria in their bowels, the greater day of the stony Indian crushing the more jaunty, lean European day which they represented. The yellow cathedral leaned its squat, earthquake-shaken towers, the bells sounded hollow. Earth-coloured tiny soldiers lay and stood around the entrance to the municipal palace, which was so baroque and Spanish, but which now belonged to the natives. Heavy as a strange bell of shadow-coloured glass, the shadow of the greater day hung over this coloured plaza which the Europeans had created, like an oasis, in the lost depths of Mexico. Gethin Day sat half lying on one of the broken benches, while tropical birds flew and twittered in the great trees, and natives twittered or flitted in silence, and he knew that here, the European day was annulled again. His body was sick with the poison that lurks in all tropical air, his soul was sick with that other day, that rather awful greater day which permeates the little days of the old races. He wanted to get out, to get out of this ghastly tropical void into which he had fallen.

Yet it was the end of November before he could go. Little revolutions had again broken the thread of railway at the end of which the southern town hung revolving like a spider. It was a narrow-gauge railway, one single narrow little track which ran over the plateau, then slipped down, down the long *barranca,* descending five thousand feet down to the valley which was a cleft in the plateau, then up again seven thousand feet, to the higher plateau to the north. How easy to break the thread! One of the innumerable little wooden bridges destroyed, and it was done. The three hundred miles to the north were impassable wilderness, like the hundred and fifty miles through the low-lying jungle to the south.

At last however he could crawl away. The train came again. He had cabled to England, and had received the answer that his sister was dead. It seemed so natural, there under the powerful November sun of southern Mexico, in the drugging powerful odours of the night-flowers, that Lydia should be dead. She seemed so much more *real,* shall we say actually vital, in death. Dead, he could think of her as quite near and comforting and real, whereas while she was alive, she was so utterly alien, remote and fussy, ghost-like in her petty Derbyshire day.

"For the little day is like a house with the family round the hearth, and the door shut. Yet outside whispers the Greater Day, wall-less, and hearthless. And the time will come at last when the walls of the little day shall fall, and what is left of the family of men shall find themselves outdoors in the Greater Day, houseless and abroad, even here between the knees of the Vales, even in Crichdale. It is a doom that will come upon tall men. And then they will breathe deep, and be breathless in the great air, and salt sweat will stand on their brow, thick as buds on sloe-bushes when the sun comes back. And little men will shudder and die out, like clouds of grasshoppers falling in the sea. Then tall men will remain alone in the land, moving deeper in the Greater Day, and moving deeper. Even as the flying fish, when he leaves the air and recovereth his element in the depth, plunges and invisibly rejoices. So will tall men rejoice, after their flight of fear, through the thin air, pursued by death. For it is on wings of fear, sped from the mouth of death, that the flying fish riseth twinkling in the air, and rustles in astonishment silvery through the thin small day. But he dives again into the great peace of the deeper day, and under the belly of death, and passes into his own."

Gethin read again his *Book of Days,* in the twilight of his last evening. Personally, he resented the symbolism and mysticism of his Elizabethan ancestor. But it was in his veins. And he was going home, back, back to the house with the flying fish on the roof. He felt an immense doom over everything, still the same next morning, when, an hour after dawn, the little train ran out from the doomed little town, on to the plateau, where the cactus thrust up its fluted tubes, and where the mountains stood back, blue, cornflower-blue, so dark and pure in form, in the land of the Greater Day, the day of demons. The little train, with two coaches, one full of natives, the other with four or five "white" Mexicans, ran fussily on, in the little day of toys and men's machines. On the roof sat tiny, earthy-looking soldiers, faces burnt black, with cartridge-belts and rifles. They clung on tight, not to be shaken off. And away went this weird toy, this crazy little caravan, over the great lost land of cacti and mountains standing back, on to the shut-in defile where the long descent began.

At half-past ten, at a station some distance down the *barranca,* a station connected with old silver mines, the train stood, and all descended to eat: the eternal turkey with black sauce, potatoes, salad, and apple pie—the American apple pie, which is a sandwich of cooked apple between two layers of pie-crust. And also beer, from Puebla. Two Chinamen administered the dinner, in all the decency, cleanness and well-cookedness of the little day of the white men, which they reproduce so well. There it was, the little day of our civilization. Outside, the little train waited. The little black-faced soldiers sharpened their knives. The vast, varying declivity of the *barranca* stood in sun and shadow as on the day of doom, untouched.

On again, winding, descending the huge and savage gully or crack in the plateau-edge, where no men lived. Bushes trailed with elegant pink creeper, such as is seen in hothouses, enormous blue convolvuluses opened out, and in the unseemly tangle of growth, bulbous orchids jutted out from trees, and let hang a trail of white or yellow flower. The strange, entangled squalor of the jungle.

Gethin Day looked down the ravine, where water was running.

He saw four small deer lifting their heads from drinking, to look at the train. *"Los venados! los venados!"* he heard the soldiers softly calling. As if knowing they were safe, the deer stood and wondered, away there in the Greater Day, in the manless space, while the train curled round a sharp jutting rock.

They came at last to the bottom, where it was very hot, and a few wild men hung round with the sword-like knives of the sugar-cane. The train seemed to tremble with fear all the time, as if its thread might be cut. So frail, so thin the thread of the lesser day, threading with its business the great reckless heat of the savage land. So frail a thread, so easily snapped!

But the train crept on, northwards, upwards. And as the stupor of heat began to pass, in the later afternoon, the sick man saw among mango trees, beyond the bright green stretches of sugar-cane, white clusters of a village, with the coloured dome of a church all yellow and blue with shiny majolica tiles. Spain putting the bubbles of her little day among the blackish trees of the unconquerable.

He came at nightfall to a small square town, more in touch with civilization, where the train ended its frightened run. He slept there. And next day he took another scrap of a train across to the edge of the main plateau. The country was wild, but more populous. An occasional big *hacienda* with sugar-mills stood back among the hills. But it was silent. Spain had spent the energy of her little day here, now the silence, the terror of the Greater Day, mysterious with death, was filling in again.

On the train a native, a big, handsome man, wandered back and forth among the uneasy Mexican travellers with a tray of glasses of ice-cream. He was no doubt of the Tlascala tribe. Gethin Day looked at him and met his glistening dark eyes. *"Quiere helados, Señor?"* said the Indian, reaching a glass with his dark, subtle-skinned, workless hand. And in the soft, secret tones of his voice, Gethin Day heard the sound of the Greater Day. *"Gracias!"*

"Padrón! Padrón!" moaned a woman at the station. *"Por amor de Dios, Padrón!"* and she held out her hand for a few centavos. And in the moaning croon of her Indian voice the Englishman heard again the fathomless crooning appeal of the Indian women, moaning stranger, more terrible than the ring-dove, with a sadness that had no horizon, and a rocking, moaning appeal that drew out the very marrow of the soul of a man. Over the door of her womb was written not only: *"Lasciate ogni speranza, voi ch'entrate,"* but: *"Perdite ogni pianto, voi ch'uscite."* For the men who had known

these women were beyond weeping and beyond even despair, mute in the timeless compulsion of the Greater Day. Big, proud men could sell glasses of ice-cream at twenty-five centavos, and not really know they were doing it. They were elsewhere, beyond despair. Only sometimes the last passion of the death-lust would sweep them, shut up as they were in the white man's lesser day, belonging as they did to the greater day.

The little train ran on to the main plateau, and to the junction with the main-line railway called the Queen's Own, a railway that still belongs to the English, and that joins Mexico City with the Gulf of Mexico. Here, in the big but forlorn railway restaurant the Englishman ordered the regular meal, that came with American mechanical take-it-or-leave-it flatness. He ate what he could, and went out again. There the vast plains were level and bare, under the blue winter sky, so pure, and not too hot, and in the distance the white cone of the volcano of Orizaba stood perfect in the middle air.

"There is no help, O man. Fear gives thee wings like a bird, death comes after thee open-mouthed, and thou soarest on the wind like a fly. But thy flight is not far, and thy flying is not long. Thou art a fish of the timeless Ocean, and must needs fall back. Take heed lest thou break thyself in the fall! For death is not in dying, but in the fear. Cease then the struggle of thy flight, and fall back into the deep element where death is and is not, and life is not a fleeing away. It is a beauteous thing to live and to be alive. Live then in the Greater Day, and let the waters carry thee, and the flood bear thee along, and live, only live, no more of this hurrying away."

"No more of this hurrying away." Even the Elizabethans had known it, the restlessness, the "hurrying away." Gethin Day knew he had been hurrying away. He had hurried perhaps a little too far, just over the edge. Now, try as he might, he was aware of a gap in his time-space *continuum;* he was, in the words of his ancestor, aware of the Greater Day showing through the cracks in the ordinary day. And it was useless trying to fill up the cracks. The little day was destined to crumble away, as far as he was concerned, and he would *have* to inhabit the greater day. The very sight of the volcano cone in mid-air made him know it. His little self was used up, worn out. He felt sick and frail, facing this change of life.

"Be still, then, be still! Wrap thyself in patience, shroud thyself in peace, as the tall volcano clothes himself in snow. Yet he looks down in him, and sees wet sun in him molten and of great force, stirring with the scald sperm of life. Be still, above the sperm of life, which spills alone in its hour. Be still, as an apple on its core, as a nightingale in winter, as a long-waiting mountain upon its fire. Be still, upon thine own sun.

"For thou hast a sun in thee. Thou hast a sun in thee, and it is not timed. Therefore wait. Wait, and be at peace with thine own sun, which is thy sperm of life. Be at peace with thy sun in thee, as the volcano is, and the dark holly-bush before berry-time, and the long hours of night. Abide by thy sun in thee, even the onion doth so, though you see it not. Yet peel her, and her sun in thine eyes maketh tears. Each thing hath its little sun, even in the wicked house-fly something twinkleth."

Standing there on the platform of the station open to the great plains of the plateau, Gethin Day said to himself: My old ancestor is more real to me than the restaurant, and the dinner I have eaten, after all. The train still did not come. He turned to another page of cornflower-blue writing, hoping to find something amusing.

"When earth inert lieth too heavy, then Vesuvius spitteth out fire. And if a nightingale would not sing, his song unsung in him would slay him. For to the nightingale his song is Nemesis, and unsung songs are the Erinyes, the impure Furies of vengeance. And thy sun in thee is thy all in all, so be patient, and take no care. Take no care, for what thou knowest is ever less than what thou art. The full fire even of thine own sun in thine own body, thou canst never know. So how shouldst thou load care upon thy sun? Take heed, take thought, take pleasure, take pain, take all things as thy sun stirs. Only fasten not thyself in care about anything, for care is impiety, it spits upon the sun."

It was the white and still volcano, visionary across the swept plain, that looked back at him as he glanced up from his *Book of Days*. But there the train came, thundering, with all the mock majesty of great equipage, and the Englishman entered the Pullman car, and sat with his book in his pocket.

The train, almost with the splendour of the Greater Day, yet rickety and foolish at last, raced on the level, entered the defile, and crept, cautiously twining round and round, down the cliff-face of the plateau, with the low lands lying thousands of feet below, specked with a village or two like fine specks. Yet the low lands drew up, and the pine trees were gone far above, and at last the thick trees crowded the line, and dark-faced natives ran beside the train selling gardenias, gardenia perfume heavy in all the air. But the train nearly empty.

Veracruz at night-fall was a modern stone port, but disheartened and tropical, mostly shut up, abandoned, as if life had quietly left it. Great customs buildings, unworking, acres of pianofortes in packing-cases, all the endless jetsam of the little day of commerce flung up here and waiting, acres of goods unattended to, waiting till the labour of Veracruz should cease to be on strike. A town, a port struck numb, the inner sun striking vengefully at the little life of commerce. The day's sun set, there was a heavy orange light over the waters, something sinister, a gloom, a deep resentment in nature, even in the washing of the warm sea. In these salt waters natives were still baptized to Christianity, and the socialists, in mockery perhaps, baptized themselves into the mystery of frustration and revenge. The port was in the hands of strikers and wild out-of-workers, and was blank. Officials had almost disappeared. Even here, a woman, a "lady" examined the passports.

But the ship rode at the end of the jetty: the one lonely passenger ship. There was one other steamer–from Sweden, a cargo boat. For the rest, the port was deserted. It was a point where the wild primeval day of this continent met the busy white man's day, and the two annulled one another. The result was a port of nullity, nihilism concrete and actual, calling itself the city of the True Cross.

2. THE GULF

In the morning they sailed off, away from the hot shores, from the high land hanging up inwards. And world gives place to world. In an hour, it was only ship and ocean, the world of land and affairs was gone.

There were few people on board. In the second-class saloon only seventeen souls. Gethin Day was travelling second. It was a German boat, he knew it would be clean and comfortable. The second-class fare was already forty-five pounds. And a man who is not rich, and who would live his life under as little compulsion as possible, must calculate keenly with money and its power. For the lesser day of money and the mealy-mouthed Mammon is always ready for a victim, and a man who has glimpsed the Greater Day, and the inward sun, will not fall into the clutches of Mammon's mean day, if he can help it. Gethin Day had a moderate income, and he looked on this as his bulwark against Mammon's despicable authority. The thought of earning a living was repulsive and humiliating to him.

In the first-class saloon were only four persons: two Danish merchants, stout and wealthy, who had been part of a bunch of Danish business men invited by the Mexican government to look at the business resources of the land. They had been fêted and feasted, and shown what they were meant to see, so now, fuller of business than ever, they were going back to Copenhagen to hatch the eggs they had conceived. But they had also eaten oysters in Veracruz, and the oysters also were inside them. They fell sick of poison, and lay deathly ill all the voyage, leaving the only other first-class passengers, an English knight and his son, alone in their glory. Gethin Day was sincerely glad he had escaped the first class, for the voyage was twenty days.

The seventeen souls of the second class were four of them English, two Danish, five Spaniards, five Germans, and a Cuban. They all sat at one long table in the dining-saloon, the Cuban at one end of the table, flanked by four English on his left, facing the five Spaniards across the table. Then came the two Danes, facing one another, and being buffer-state between the rest and the five Germans, who occupied the far end of the table. It was a German boat, so the Germans were very noisy, and the stewards served them first. The Spaniards and the Cuban were mum, the English were stiff, the Danes were uneasy, the Germans were boisterous, and so the first luncheon passed. It was the lesser day of the ship, and small enough. The menu being in correct German and doubtful Spanish, the Englishwoman on Gethin Day's right put up a lorgnette and stared at it. She was unable to stare it out of countenance, so she put it down and ate uninformed as to what she was eating. The Spaniard opposite Gethin Day had come to table without collar or tie, doing the bluff, go-to-hell colonial touch, almost in his shirt-sleeves. He was a man of about thirty-two. He brayed at the steward in strange, harsh Galician Spanish, the steward grinned somewhat sneeringly and answered in German, having failed to understand, and not prepared to exert himself to try. Down the table a blonde horse of a woman was shouting at the top of her voice, in harsh North-German, to a Herr Doktor with turned-up moustaches who presided at the German head of the table. The Spaniards bent forward in a row to look with a sort of silent horror at the yelling woman, then they looked at one another with a faint grimace of mocking repulsion. The Galician banged the table with the empty wine-decanter: wine was "included." The steward, with a sneering little grin at such table-manners, brought a decanter half full. Wine was not *ad lib.*, but *à discrétion.* The Spaniards, having realized this, henceforth snatched it quickly and pretty well emptied the decanter before the English got a shot at it. Which somewhat amused the table-stewards, who wanted to see the two foreign lots fight it out. But Gethin Day solved this problem by holding out his hand to the fat, clean-shaven Basque, as soon as the decanter reached that gentleman, and saying: "May I serve the lady?" Whereupon the Basque handed over the decanter, and Gethin helped the two ladies and himself, before handing back the decanter to the Spaniards.—Man wants but little here below, but he's damn well got to see he gets it.—All this is part of the little day, which has to be seen to. Whether it is interesting or not depends on one's state of soul.

Bristling with all the bristles of offence and defence which a man has to put up the first days in such a company, Gethin Day would go off down the narrow gangway of the bottom deck, down into the steerage, where the few passengers lay about in shirt and trousers, on to the very front tip of the boat.

She was a long, narrow, old ship, long like a cigar, and not much space in her. Yet she was pleasant, and had a certain grace of her own, was a real ship, not merely a "liner." She seemed to travel swift and clean, piercing away into the Gulf.

Gethin Day would sit for hours at the very tip of the ship, on the bowsprit, looking out into the whitish sunshine of the hot Gulf of Mexico. Here he was alone, and the world was all strange white sunshine, candid, and water, warm, bright water, perfectly pure beneath him, of an exquisite frail green. It lifted vivid wings from the running tip of the ship, and threw white pinion-spray from its green edges. And always, always, always it was in the two-winged fountain, as the ship came like life between, and always the spray fell swishing, pattering from the green arch of the water-wings. And below, as yet untouched, a moment ahead, always a moment ahead, and perfectly untouched, was the lovely green depth of the water, depth, deep, shallow-pale emerald above an under sapphire-green, dark and pale, blue and shimmer-green, two waters, many waters, one water, perfect in unison, one moment ahead of the ship's bows, so serene, fathomless and pure and free of time. It was very lovely, and on the softly-lifting bowsprit of the long, swift ship the body was cradled in the sway of timeless life, the soul lay in the jewel-coloured moment, the jewel-pure eternity of this gulf of nowhere.

And always, always, like a dream, the flocks of flying fish swept into the air, from nowhere, and went brilliantly twinkling in their flight of silvery watery wings rapidly fluttering, away, low as swallows over the smooth curved surface of the sea, then gone again, vanished, without splash or evidence, gone. One alone like a little silver twinkle. Gone! The sea was still and silky-surfaced, blue and softly heaving, empty, purity itself, sea, sea, sea.

Then suddenly the faint whispering crackle, and a cloud of silver on webs of pure, fluttering water was soaring low over the surface of the sea, at an angle from the ship, as if jetted away from the cut-water, soaring in a low arc, fluttering with the wild emphasis of grasshoppers or locusts suddenly burst out of the grass, in a wild rush to make away, make away, and making it, away, away, then suddenly gone, like a lot of lights blown out in one breath. And still the ship did not pause, any more than the moon pauses, neither to look nor catch breath. But the soul pauses and holds its breath, for wonder, wonder, which is the very breath of the soul.

All the long morning he would be there curled in the wonder of this gulf of creation, where the flying fishes on translucent wings swept in their ecstatic clouds out of the water, in a terror that was brilliant as joy, in a joy brilliant with terror, with wings made of pure water flapping with great speed, and long-shafted bodies of translucent silver like squirts of living water, there in air, brilliant in air, before suddenly they had disappeared, and the blue sea was trembling with a delicate frail surface of green, the still sea lay one moment ahead, untouched, untouched since time began, in its watery loveliness.

Sometimes a ship's officer would come and peer over the edge, and look at him lying there. But nothing was said. People didn't like looking over the edge. It was too beautiful, too pure and lovely, the Greater Day. They shoved their snouts a moment over the rail, then withdrew, faintly abashed, faintly sneering, faintly humiliated. After all, they showed snouts, nothing but snouts, to the unbegotten morning, so they might well be humiliated.

Sometimes an island, two islands, three, would show up, dismal and small, with the peculiar American gloom. No land! The soul wanted to see the land. Only the uninterrupted water was purely lovely, pristine.

And the third morning there was a school of porpoises leading the ship. They stayed below surface all the time, so there was no hullabaloo of human staring. Only Gethin Day saw them. And what joy! what joy of life! what marvellous pure joy of being a porpoise within the great sea, of being many porpoises heading and mocking in translucent onrush the menacing, yet futile onrush of a vast ship!

It was a spectacle of the purest and most perfected joy in life that Gethin Day ever saw. The porpoises were ten or a dozen, round-bodied torpedo fish, and they stayed there as if they were not moving, always there, with no motion apparent, under the purely pellucid water, yet speeding on at just the speed of the ship, without the faintest show of movement, yet speeding on in the most miraculous precision of speed. It seemed as if the tail-flukes of the last fish exactly touched the ship's bows, under-water, with the frailest, yet precise and permanent touch. It seemed as if nothing moved, yet fish and ship swept on through the tropical ocean. And the fish moved, they changed places all the time. They moved in a little cloud, and with the most wonderful sport they were above, they were below, they were to the fore, yet all the time the same one speed, the same one speed, and the last fish just touching with his tail-flukes the iron cut-water of the ship. Some would be down in the blue, shadowy, but horizontally motionless in the same speed. Then with a strange revolution, these would be up in pale green water, and others would be down. Even the toucher, who touched the ship, would in a twinkling be changed. And ever, ever the same pure horizontal speed, sometimes a dark back skimming the water's surface light, from beneath, but never the surface broken. And ever the last fish touching the ship, and ever the others speeding in motionless, effortless speed, and intertwining with strange silkiness as they sped, intertwining among one another, fading down to the dark blue shadow, and strangely emerging again among the silent, swift others, in pale green water. All the time, so swift, they seemed to be laughing.

Gethin Day watched spell-bound, minute after minute, an hour, two hours, and still it was the same, the ship speeding, cutting the water, and the strong-bodied fish heading in perfect balance of speed underneath, mingling among themselves in some strange single laughter of multiple consciousness, giving off the joy of life, sheer joy of life, togetherness in pure complete motion, many lusty-bodied fish enjoying one laugh of life, sheer togetherness, perfect as passion. They gave off into the water their marvellous joy of life, such as the man had never met before. And it left him wonderstruck.

"But they know joy, they know pure joy!" he said to himself in amazement. "This is the most laughing joy I have ever seen, pure and unmixed. I always thought flowers had brought themselves to the most beautiful perfection in nature. But these fish, these fleshy, warm-bodied fish achieve more than flowers, heading along. This is the purest achievement of joy I have seen in all life: these strong, careless fish. Men have not got in them that secret to be alive together and make one like a single laugh, yet each fish going his own gait. This is sheer joy—and men have lost it, or never accomplished is. The cleverest sportsmen in the world are owls beside these fish. And the togetherness of love is nothing to the spinning unison of dolphins playing under-sea. It would be wonderful to know joy as these fish know it. The life of the deep waters is ahead of us, it contains sheer togetherness and sheer joy. We have never got there."

There as he leaned over the bowsprit he was mesmerized by one thing only, by joy, by joy of life, fish speeding in water with playful joy. No wonder Ocean was still mysterious, when such red hearts beat in it! No wonder man, with his tragedy, was a pale and sickly thing in comparison! What civilization will bring us to such a pitch of swift laughing togetherness, as these fish have reached?

3. THE ATLANTIC

The ship came in the night to Cuba, to Havana. When she became still, Gethin Day looked out of his port-hole and saw little lights on upreared darkness. Havana!

They went on shore next morning, through the narrow dock-streets near the wharf, to the great boulevard. It was a lovely warm morning, already early December, and the town was in the streets, going to mass, or coming out of the big, unpleasant old churches. The Englishman wandered with the two Danes for an hour or so, in the not very exciting city. Many Americans were wandering around, and nearly all wore badges of some sort. The city seemed, on the surface at least, very American. And underneath, it did not seem to have any very deep character of its own left.

The three men hired a car to drive out and about. The elder of the Danes, a man of about forty-five, spoke fluent colloquial Spanish, learned on the oil-fields of Tampico. "Tell me," he said to the chauffeur, "why do all these *americanos,* these Yankees, wear badges on themselves?"

He spoke, as foreigners nearly always do speak of the Yankees, in a tone of half-spiteful jeering.

"Ah, Señor," said the driver, with a Cuban grin. "You know they all come here to drink. They drink so much that they all get lost at night, so they all wear a badge: name, name of hotel, place where it is. Then our policemen find them in the night, turn them over as they lie on the pavement, read name, name of hotel, and place, and so they are put on a cart and carted to home. Ah, the season is only just beginning. Wait a week or two, and they will lie in the streets at night like a battle, and the police doing Red Cross work, carting them to their hotels. Ah, *los americanos!* They are so good. You know they own us now. Yes, they own us. They own Havana. We are a Republic owned by the Americans. *Muy bien,* we give them drink, they give us money. Bah!"

And he grinned with a kind of acrid indifference. He sneered at the whole show, but he wasn't going to do anything about it.

The car drove out to the famous beer-gardens, where all drank beer—then to the inevitable cemetery, which almost rivalled that of New Orleans. "Every person buried in this cemetery guarantees to put up a tomb-monument costing not less than fifty-thousand dollars." Then they drove past the new suburb of villas, springing up neat and tidy, spick-and-span, same all the world over. Then they drove out into the country, past the old sugar *haciendas* and to the hills.

And to Gethin Day it was all merely depressing and void of real interest. The Yankees owned it all. It had not much character of its own. And what character it had was the peculiar, dreary character of all America wherever it is a little abandoned. The peculiar gloom of Connecticut or New Jersey, Louisiana or Georgia, a sort of dreariness in the very bones of the land, that shows through immediately the human effort sinks. How quickly the gloom and the inner dreariness of Cuba must have affected the spirit of the Conquistadores, even Columbus!

They drove back to town and ate a really good meal, and watched a stout American couple, apparently man and wife, lunching with a bottle of champagne, a bottle of hock, and a bottle of Burgundy for the two of them, and apparently drinking them all at once. It made one's head reel.

The bright, sunny afternoon they spent on the esplanade by the sea. There the great hotels were still shut. But they had, so to speak, half an eye open: a tea-room going, for example.

And Day thought again, how tedious the little day can be! How difficult to spend even one Sunday looking at a city like Havana, even if one has spent the morning driving into the country. The infinite tedium of looking at things! the infinite boredom of things anyhow. Only the rippling, bright, pale-blue sea, and the old fort, gave one the feeling of life. The rest, the great esplanade, the great boulevard, the great hotels, all seemed what they were, dead, dried concrete, concrete, dried deadness.

Everybody was thankful to be back on the ship for dinner, in the dark loneliness of the wharves. See Naples and die. Go seeing any place, and you'll be half dead of exhaustion and tedium by dinner time.

So! good-bye, Havana! The engines were going before breakfast time. It was a bright blue morning. Wharves and harbour slid past, the high bows moved backwards. Then the ship deliberately turned her back on Cuba and the sombre shore, and began to move north, through the blue day, which passed like a sleep. They were moving now into wide space.

The next morning they woke to greyness, grey low sky, and hideous low grey water, and a still air. Sandwiched between two greynesses, the long, wicked old ship sped on, as unto death.

"What has happened?" Day asked of one of the officers.

"We have come north, to get into the current running east. We come north about the latitude of New York, then we run due east with the stream."

"What a wicked shame!"

And indeed it was. The sun was gone, the blueness was gone, life was gone. The Atlantic was like a cemetery, an endless, infinite cemetery of greyness, where the bright, lost world of Atlantis is buried. It was December, grey, dark December on a waste of ugly, dead-grey water, under a dead-grey sky.

And so they ran into a swell, a long swell whose oily, sickly waves seemed hundreds of miles long, and travelling in the same direction as the ship's course. The narrow cigar of a ship heaved up the upslope with a nauseating heave, up, up, up, till she righted for a second sickeningly on the top, then tilted, and her screw raced like a dentist's burr in a hollow tooth. Then down she slid, down the long, shivering downslope, leaving all her guts behind her, and the guts of all the passengers too. In an hour, everybody was deathly white, and sicklily grinning, thinking it a sort of joke that would soon be over. Then everybody disappeared, and the game went on: up, up, up, heavingly up, till a pause, ah!—then burr-rr-rr! as the screw came out of water and shattered every nerve. Then whoo-oosh! the long and awful downrush, leaving the entrails behind.

She was like a plague-ship, everybody disappeared, stewards and everybody. Gethin Day felt as if he had taken poison: and he slept—slept, slept, slept, and yet was all the time aware of the ghastly motion—up, up, up, heavingly up, then ah! one moment, followed by the shattering burr-rr-rr! and the unspeakable ghastliness of the downhill slither, where death seemed inside the entrails, and water chattered like the after-death. He was aware of the hour-long moaning, moaning of the Spanish doctor's fat, pale Mexican wife, two cabins away. It went on for ever. Everything went on for ever. Everything was like this for ever, for ever. And he slept, slept, slept, for thirty hours, yet knowing it all, registering just the endless repetition of the motion, the ship's loud squeaking and chirruping, and the ceaseless moaning of the woman.

Suddenly at tea-time the second day he felt better. He got up. The ship was empty. A ghastly steward gave him a ghastly cup of tea, then disappeared. He dozed again, but came to dinner.

They were three people at the long table, in the horribly travelling grey silence: himself, a young Dane, and the elderly, dried Englishwoman. She talked, talked. The three looked in terror at *Sauerkraut* and smoked loin of pork. But they ate a little. Then they looked out on the utterly repulsive, grey, oily, windless night. Then they went to bed again.

The third evening it began to rain, and the motion was subsiding. They were running out of the swell. But it was an experience to remember.

ACCUMULATED MAIL

If there is one thing I don't look forward to it's my mail.

Look out! Look out! Look out!
Look out! The postman comes!
His double knocking makes us start,
It rouses echoes in the heart,
It wakens expectation, and hope and agitation, etc., etc.

So we used to sing, in school.

Now, the postman is no knocker. He pitches the mail-bag into a box on a tree, and kicks his horse forward.

And when one has been away, and a heap of letters and printed stuff slithers out under one's eyes, there is neither hope nor expectation in the heart, but only repulsion, as if it were something nauseous one had to eat.

Business letters—all rather dreary. Bank letters, with the nasty green used-up checks, and a dwindling small balance. Family letters: *We are so disappointed you are not coming to England. We wanted you to see the baby, he is so bonny: the new house, it is awfully nice: the show of the daffodils and crocuses down the garden.* Friends' letters: *The winter has been very trying.* And then the unknown correspondents. They are the worst. . . . *If you saw my little blue-eyed darling, you could not refuse her anything—not even an autograph.* . . . The high-school students somewhere in Massachusetts or in Maryland are in the habit of choosing by name some unknown man, whom they accept as a sort of guide. A group has chosen me—will I send them a letter of encouragement or of help in the battle of life? Well, I would willingly, but what on earth am I to say to them? *My dear young people: I daren't advise you to do as I do, for it's no fun, writing unpopular books. And I won't advise you, for your own sakes, to do as I say. For in details I'm sure I'm wrong. My dear young people, perhaps I need your encouragement more than you need mine.* . . . Well, that's no message!

Then there's the letter signed "A Mother"—from Lenton, Nottingham: telling me she has been reading *Sons and Lovers,* and is there not misery enough in Nottingham (my home town) without my indicating where vice can be found, and (to cut short) how it can be practised? She saw a young woman reading *Sons and Lovers,* but was successful in preventing her from finishing the book. And the book was so well written, it was a pity the author could not have kept it clean. "As it is, although so interesting, it cannot be mentioned in polite society." Signed "A Mother." (Let us hope the young woman who was saved from finishing *Sons and Lovers* may also be saved from becoming, in her turn, A Mother!)

Then the letter from some gentleman in New York beginning: *I am afraid you may consider this letter an impertinence.* If he was afraid, then what colossal impertinence to carry on to two sheets, and then post his impudence to me. The substance was: *I should like to know, in the controversy between you and Norman Douglas* (I didn't know myself that there was a controversy), *how it was the Magnus manuscript came into your hands, and you came to publish it, when clearly it was left to Douglas? In this case, why should you be making a lot of money out of another man's work?—Of course, I know it is your* Introduction *which sells the book. Magnus's manuscript is trash, and not worth reading. Still, for the satisfaction of myself and many of my readers, I wish you could make it clear how you come to be profiting by a work that is not your own.*

Apparently this gentleman's sense of his own impertinence only drove him deeper in. He has obviously read neither Magnus's work nor my *Introduction*—else he would plainly have seen that this MS. was detained by Magnus's creditors, at his death, and handed by them to me, in the poor hope of recovering some of the money lost with that little adventurer. Moreover, if I wrote the only part of the book that is worth reading (*I* don't say so)—the only part for which people buy the book (they're not *my* words)—then it is my work they buy! This out of my genteel correspondent's own mouth—because *I* do *not* consider Magnus's work trash. Finally, if I get half proceeds for a book of which practically half was written by me and the other half sells on my account, who in heaven's name is going to be impertinent to me? Nobody, without a kick in the pants. As for Douglas, if he could have paid the dead man's debts, he might have "executed" the dead man's literary works to his heart's content. Why doesn't he do something with the rest of the remains? Was this poor Foreign Legion MS. the only egg in the nest? Anyhow, let us hope that those particular debts for which this MS. was detained, will now be paid. And R.I.P. Anyhow, I shan't be a rich man on the half profits.

But this is not all my precious mail. . . . From a London editor and a friend (*soi-disant*): *Perhaps you would understand other people better if you did not think that you were always right.* How one learns things about oneself! Or is it really about the other person? I always find that my critics pretending to criticize me, are analysing themselves. My own private opinion is that I have been, as far as people go, almost every time wrong! Anyhow, my desire to "understand other people better" is turning to dread of finding out any more about them. This "friend" goes on to say, will I ask my literary agent to let him have some articles of mine at a considerably cheaper figure than the agent puts on them?

It is not done yet. There is Mr. Muir's article about me in the *Nation*. Never did I feel so baffled, confronting myself in my worst moments, as I feel when I read this "elucidation" of myself. I hope it isn't my fault that Mr. Muir plays such havoc between two stools. I think I read that he is a young man, and younger critic. It seems a pity he hasn't "A Mother" to take the books from him before he can do himself any more harm. Truly, I don't want him to read them. "There remain his gifts, splendid in their imperfection,"—this is Mr. Muir about me—"thrown recklessly into a dozen books, fulfilling themselves in none. His chief title to greatness is that he has brought a new mode of seeing into literature, a new beauty which is also one of the oldest things in the world. It is the beauty of the ancient instinctive life which civilized man has almost forgotten. Mr. Lawrence has picked up a thread of life left behind by mankind; and at some time it will be woven in with the others, making human life more complete, as all art tends to. . . . Life has come to him fresh from the minting at a time when it seemed to everyone soiled and banal. He has many faults, and many of these are wilful. He has not fulfilled the promise shown in *Sons and Lovers* and *The Rainbow*. He has not submitted himself to any discipline. The will (in Mr. Lawrence's characters) is not merely weak and inarticulate, it is in abeyance; it does not come into action. To this tremendous extent the tragedy in Mr. Lawrence's novels fails in significance. We remember the scenes in his novels; we forget the names of his men and women. We should not know any of them if we met them in the street, as we should know Anna Karenina, or Crevel, or Soames Forsyte. . . ." (Who is Crevel?)

Now listen, you, Mr. Muir, and my dear readers. You read me for your own sakes, not for mine. You do me no favour by reading me. I am not indebted to you in the least if you spend two dollars on a book. You do it entirely for your own delectation. Spend the dollars on chewing-gum, it keeps the mouth busy and doesn't fly to the brain. I shall live just as blithly, unbought and unsold. When you buy chewing-gum, do you feel you acquire divine rights over the mind and soul of Mr. Wrigley? If you do, it's like your impudence. Therefore get it out of your heads that you are throned aloft like the gods, called upon to utter divine judgment. Your lofty seats, after all, are more like tall baby-chairs than thrones of the gods of judgment. . . . But here goes, for an answer.

1. I have lunched with Mr. Banality, and I'm sure I should know him if I met him in the street. . . . Is that my fault, or his?—Alas, that I should recognize people in the street, by their noses, bonnets, or beauty. I don't care about their noses, bonnets, or beauty. Does nothing exist beyond that which is recognizable in the street?—How does my cat recognize me in the dark?—Ugh, thank God there are more and other sorts of vision than the kodak sort which Mr. Muir esteems above all others.
2. "The will is not merely weak and inarticulate, it is in abeyance."—Ah, my dear Mr. Muir, the will of the modern young gentleman may not be in your opinion weak and inarticulate, but certainly it is as mechanical as a Ford car engine. To this extent is the tragedy of modern young men insignificant. Oh, you little gods in the machine, stop the engine for a bit, do!
3. "He has not submitted himself to any discipline."—Try, Mr. Muir *et al.,* putting your little iron will into abeyance for one hour daily, and see if it doesn't need a harder discipline than this doing of your "daily dozen" and all your other mechanical repetitions. Believe me, today, the little god in a Ford machine cannot get at the thing worth having, not even with the most praiseworthy little engine of a will.
4. "He has not fulfilled the promise of *Sons and Lovers* and *The Rainbow.*"—Just after *The Rainbow* was published, the most eminent figure in English letters told me to my nose that this work was a failure. Now, after ten years, Mr. Muir finds it "promising." Go ahead, O Youth. But whatever promise you read into *The Rainbow,* remember it's like the little boy who "promised" his mother to be good if she'd "promise" to take him to the pantomime. I promise nothing, inside or out of *The Rainbow.*
5. "Life has come to him fresh from the minting at a time when it seemed to everyone stale and banal."—Come! Come! Mr. Muir! With all that "spirit" of yours, and all that "intellect,"

and with all that "will," and all that "discipline," do you dare to confess that (I suppose you lump yourself in among everyone) life seemed to you stale and banal?—If so, something must be badly wrong with you and your psychic equipment, and Mr. Lawrence wouldn't be in your shoes for all the money and the "cleverness" in the world.

6. "Mr. Lawrence has picked up a thread of life left behind by mankind."—Darn your socks with it, Mr. Muir?
7. "It is the beauty of the ancient instinctive life which civilized man has almost forgotten."—He may have forgotten it, but he can put a label on it and price it at a figure and let it go cheap, in one and a half minutes. Ah, my dear Mr. Muir, when do you consider ancient life ended, and "civilized" life began? And which is stale and banal? Wherein does staleness lie, Mr. Muir? As for "ancient life," it may be ancient to you, but it is still alive and kicking in some people. And "ancient life" is far more deeply conscious than you can even imagine. And its discipline goes into regions where you have no existence.
8. "His chief title to greatness is that he has brought a new mode of seeing into literature, a new beauty," etc., etc.—Easy, of course, as re-trimming an old hat. Michael Arlen does it better! Looks more modish, the old hat.—But shouldn't it be a new mode of "feeling" or "knowing" rather than of "seeing"? Since none of my characters would be recognizable in the street?
9. "There remain his gifts, splendid in their imperfection."—Ugh, Mr. Muir, think how horrible for us all, if I were perfect! or even if I had "perfect" gifts!—Isn't splendour enough for you, Mr. Muir? Or do you find the peacock more "perfect" when he is moulting and has lost his tail, and therefore isn't so exaggerated, but is more "down to normal"?—For "perfection" is only one of the attributes of "the normal" and "the average" in modern thought.

Well, I don't want to be just or to be kind. There is a further justice and a greater kindness than this niggling tolerance business, and suffering fools gladly. Fools bore me—but I don't mean Mr. Muir. He is a phœnix, compared to most. I wonder what it is that the rainbow—I mean the natural phenomenon—stands for in my own consciousness! I don't know all it means to me.—Is this lack of intellectual capacity on my part? Or is it because the rainbow is somehow not quite "normal," and therefore not quite fit for intellectual appreciation? Of course white light passing through prisms of falling raindrops makes a rainbow. Let us therefore sell it by the yard.

For me, give me a little splendour, and I'll leave perfection to the small fry.

But oh, my other anonymous little critic, what shall I say to thee? *Mr. Lawrence's horses are all mares or stallions.*

Honi soit qui mal y pense, my dear, though I'm sure the critic is a gentleman (I daren't say a *man*) and not a lady.

Little critics' horses (*sic*) *are all geldings.*

Another little critic: "Mr. Lawrence's introspective intelligence is too feeble to balance this melodramatic fancy in activities which cater for a free play of mind."

Retort simple: Mr. Lawrence's intelligence would prevent his writing such a sentence down, and sending it to print.—What can those activities be which "cater for a free play of mind" (whatever that may mean) and at the same time have "introspective intelligence" (what quite is this?) balancing "melodramatic fancy" (what is this either?) within them?

Same critic, finishing the same sentence: ". . . and so, since criticism begins at home, his (Mr. Lawrence's) latter-day garment of philosopher and preacher is shot through with the vulgarity of aggressive self-ignorance."

Retort simple: If criticism begins at home, then the professional, and still more so the amateur critic (I suspect this gentleman to be the latter), is never by any chance at home. He is always out sponging on some author. As for a "latter-day garment of philosopher and preacher" (I never before knew a philosopher and a preacher transmogrified into a garment) being "shot through with the vulgarity of aggressive self-ignorance," was it grapeshot, or duck-shot, or just shot-silk effect?

Alas, this young critic is "shot through" with ignorance even more extensive than that of self. Or perhaps it is only his garment of critic and smart little fellow which is so shot through, *percé* or *miroité,* according to fancy—"melodramatic fancy" balanced by "introspective intelligence," "in activities which cater for a free play of mind."

"We cater to the Radical Trade," says Jimmie Higgins's advertisement.

Another friend and critic: "Lawrence is an artist, but his intellect is not up to his art."

You might as well say: Mr. Lawrence rides a horse but he doesn't wear his stirrups round his neck. And the accusation is just. Because he hopes to heaven he is riding a horse that is alive of itself, not a wooden hobbyhorse suitable for the nursery.–And he does his best to keep his feet in the stirrups, and to leave his intellect under his hat, when he is riding his naughty steed. No, my dears! I guess, as an instrument, my intellect is as good as yours. But instead of sitting in my own wheelbarrow (the intellect is a sort of wheelbarrow about the place) and whipping it ecstatically over the head, I just wheel out what dump I've got, and forget the old barrow again, till next time.

And now, thank God, I can throw all my mail, letters, used checks, pamphlets, periodicals, clippings from the "press," Ave Marias, paternosters, and bunk, into the fire.–When I get a particularly smelly bit of sentiment, I always burn it slowly, invoking the Lord thus: "Lord! *Herrgott! nimm du diesen Opferrauch!* Take Thou this smoke of sacrifice.–The sacrifice of blood is no longer acceptable, for blood has turned to water: all is vapour! Therefore, O Lord, this choice titbit of the spirit, this kidney-fat of sentiment, accept it, O Lord, from Thy servant. . . . This firstling of the sentimental herd, this young ram without spot or blemish, from the æsthetic flock, this adamantine young he-goat, from the troops of human "stunts"–see, Lord, I cut their throats and burn the cardboard fat of them. Lord of the Spirit, Lord of the Universal Mind, Lord of the cosmic will, snuff up the smoke of this burnt-paper offering, for it makes my eyes smart–"

I wish they'd make His eyes smart as well! this Lord of sentimentalism, æstheticism, and stunts. One day I'll make a sacrifice of Him too: to my own Lord, who broods at the centre of all the worlds, over His own fathomless Desire.

THE LATE MR. MAURICE MAGNUS: A LETTER

To the Editor of The New Statesman:

Sir,—Referring to the review published in your last issue of Mr. Norman Douglas's *Experiments,* will you give me a little space in which to shake off Mr. Douglas's insinuations—to put it mildly—regarding my introduction to Maurice Magnus's *Memoirs of the Foreign Legion?* When Mr. Douglas's "pamphlet" first appeared I was in New Mexico, and it seemed too far off to trouble. But now that the essay is enshrined in Mr. Douglas's new book, *Experiments,* it is time that I said a word. One becomes weary of being slandered.

The whole circumstances of my acquaintance with Maurice Magnus, and the facts of his death, are told in my introduction as truthfully as a man can tell a thing. After the suicide of Magnus, I had continual letters from the two Maltese, whom I had met through Magnus, asking for redress. I knew them personally—which Douglas did not. Myself, I had not the money to repay Magnus's borrowings. All the literary remains were left to Douglas, in the terms of Magnus's will. But then, after his death, all Magnus's effects were confiscated, owing to his debts. There was really nothing to confiscate, since the very furniture of the house had been lent by the young Maltese, B——. There were the MSS.—the bulk of them worthless. Only those *Memoirs of the Foreign Legion,* which I had gone over previously with Magnus, might be sold.

I wrote to B—— that Norman Douglas would no doubt get the *Memoirs* published. The reply came from Malta, B—— would never put anything into the hands of Douglas. I then wrote to Douglas—and, remembering the care with which he files all his letters, I kept his reply. Parts of this reply I quote here:

> Florence,
> 26*th December,* 1921.
>
> Dear Lawrence,
>
> So many thanks for yours of the 20*th.*
>
> Damn the Foreign Legion. . . . I have done my best, and if B—— had sent it to me the book would be published by this time, and B—— £30 or £50 the richer. Some folks are hard to please. By all means do what you like with the MS. As to M. himself, I may do some kind of memoir of him later on—independent of Foreign Legions. Put me into your introduction, if you like. . . .

Pocket all the cash yourself. B—— seems to be such a fool that he doesn't deserve any.

I'm out of it and, *for once in my life,* with a clean conscience. . . .

Yours always,

NORMAN DOUGLAS.

The italics in this letter are Douglas's own. As for his accusation of my "unkindness" to Magnus, that too is funny. Certainly Magnus was generous with his money when he had any; who knew that better than Douglas? But did I make it appear otherwise? And when Magnus wanted *actual* help—not postmortem sentiment—where did he look for it? To the young Maltese who would have no dealings whatsoever with Norman Douglas, after the suicide.

Then I am accused of making money out of Magnus's effects. I should never have dreamed of writing a word about Magnus, save for the continual painful letters from the Maltese. Then I did it solely and simply to discharge a certain obligation. For curiously enough, both B—— and S—— seemed to regard me as in some way responsible for their troubles with Magnus. I had been actually there with them and Magnus, and had driven in their motor-car. To discharge an obligation I do not admit, I wrote the Introduction. And when it was written, in the year 1922, it started the round of the publishers, as introducing the *Memoirs of the Foreign Legion,* and everywhere it was refused. More than one publisher said: "We will publish the Introduction alone, without the Magnus Memoirs." To which I said: "That's no good. The Introduction only exists for the Memoirs."

So, for two years, nothing happened. It is probable that I could have sold the Introduction to one of the large popular American magazines, as a "personal" article. And that would have meant at least a thousand dollars for me. Whereas I shall never see a thousand dollars, by a long chalk, from this *Memoirs* book. Nevertheless, by this time B—— will have received in full the money he lent to Magnus. I shall have received as much—as much, perhaps, as I would get in America for a popular short story.

As for Mr. Douglas, he must gather himself haloes where he may.

Yours, etc.,

D. H. LAWRENCE.

THE UNDYING MAN

Long ago in Spain there were two very learned men, so clever and knowing so much that they were famous all over the world. One was called Rabbi Moses Maimonides, a Jew—blessed be his memory!—and the other was called Aristotle, a Christian who belonged to the Greeks.

These two were great friends, because they had always studied together and found out many things together. At last after many years, they found out a thing they had been specially trying for. They discovered that if you took a tiny little vein out of a man's body, and put it in a glass jar with certain leaves and plants, it would gradually begin to grow, and would grow and grow until it became a man. When it had grown as big as a boy, you could take it out of the jar, and then it would live and keep on growing till it became a man, a fine man who would never die. He would be undying. Because he had never been born, he would never die, but live for ever and ever. Because the wisest men on earth had made him, and he didn't have to be born.

When they were quite sure it was so, then the Rabbi Moses Maimonides and the Christian Aristotle decided they would really make a man. Up till then, they had only experimented. But now they would make the real undying man.

The question was, from whom should they take the little vein? Because the man they took it from would die. So at first they decided to take it from a slave. But then they thought, a slave wasn't good enough to make the beginnings of the undying man. So they decided to ask one of their devoted students to sacrifice himself. But that did not seem right either, because they might get a man they didn't really like, and whom they wouldn't want to be the beginning of the man who would never die. So at last, they decided to leave it to fate; they gathered together their best and most learned disciples, and they all agreed to draw lots. The lot fell to Aristotle, to have the little vein cut from his body.

So Aristotle had to agree. But before he would have the little vein cut out of his body, Aristotle asked Maimonides to take him by the hand and swear by their clasped hands that he would never interfere with the growth of the little vein, never at any time or in any way. Maimonides took him by the hand and swore. And then

Aristotle had the little vein cut out of his body by Maimonides himself.

So now Maimonides alone took the little vein and placed it among the leaves and herbs, as they had discovered, in the great glass jar, and he sealed the jar. Then he set the jar on a shelf in his own room where nobody entered but himself, and he waited. The days passed by, and he recited his prayers, pacing back and forth in his room among his books, and praying loudly as he paced, as the Jews do. Then he returned to his books and his chemistry. But every day he looked at the jar, to see if the little vein had changed. For a long time it did not change. So he thought it was in vain.

Then at last it seemed to change, to have grown a little. Rabbi Moses Maimonides gazed at the jar transfixed, and forgot everything else in all the wide world; lost to all and everything, he gazed into the jar. And at last he saw the tiniest, tiniest tremor in the little vein, and he knew it was a tremor of growth. He sank on the floor and lay unconscious, because he had seen the first tremor of growth of the undying man.

When he came to himself, the room was dusk, it was almost night. And Rabbi Moses Maimonides was afraid. He did not know what he was afraid of. He rose to his feet, and glanced towards the jar. And it seemed to him, in the darkness on the shelf there was a tiny red glow, like the smallest ember of fire. But it did not go out, as the last ember of fire goes out while you watch. It stayed on, and glowed a tiny dying glow that did not die. Then he knew he saw the glow of the life of the undying man, and he was afraid.

He locked his room, where no one ever entered but himself, and went out into the town. People greeted him with bows and reverences, for he was the most learned of all rabbis. But tonight they all seemed very far from him. They looked small and they grimaced like monkeys in his eyes. And he thought to himself: They will all die! They grimace in this fashion, like monkeys, because they will all die. Only I shall not die!

But as he thought this, his heart stood still, because he knew that he too would die. He stood still in the street, though rain was falling, and people crept past him humbly, thinking he was praying some great prayer. But he was only locked in this one thought: I shall die and pass away, but that little red spark which came from Aristotle the Christian, it will never die. It will live for ever and ever, like God. God alone lives for ever and ever. But this man in the jar will also live for ever and ever, even that red spark. He will be a man, and live for ever and ever, as good as God. Nay, better than God! For surely, to be as good as God, and to be also a man and alive, that would be better even than being God!

Rabbi Moses Maimonides started at this thought as if he had been stung. And immediately he began to walk down the street towards home, to see if the red glow were really glowing. When he got to his door, he stood still, afraid to open. He could not open.

So suddenly he cried a great fierce cry to God, to help him and His people. A great fierce cry for help. For they were God's people, God's chosen people. Though they grimaced in the sight of Rabbi Moses Maimonides like monkeys, they were beautiful in the sight of God, and the best Jews among them would sit in high, high places in the eternal glory of God, in the after-life.

This thought so emboldened Maimonides that he opened his door and entered his room. But he stood again as if pierced through the body by that strange red light, like no light of God, which glowed so tiny and yet was so fierce and strong. "Fierce and strong! fierce and strong!" he kept muttering to himself as he paced back and forth in his room. "Fierce and strong!" His servant thought he was praying, and she dared not bring his food to the door. "Fierce and strong!"—he paced back and forth. And he himself thought he was praying. He was so used to praying the ritual prayers as he paced in his room, that now he thought he was praying to the one and only God. But in fact, all he was saying was "Fierce and strong! Fierce and strong!"

At last he sank down in exhaustion, and then his woman tapped at his door and set down the tray. But he told her to take the tray away, he would not eat in his room, but would come downstairs. For he could not eat in the presence of that little red glow.

So he made his ablutions and went downstairs and ate. And he slept in the guest-room, for he could not sleep in the presence of the little red glow. Indeed he could not sleep at all, but lay and groaned in spirit, thinking of that little red light which alone of all light was not the light of God. And he knew it would grow and grow, and be a man, most splendid, a man who would never die. And all the people would think: What is the most wonderful of all things, seen or unseen?—And there would come the

[Unfinished]

NOAH'S FLOOD

NOAH
SHEM (the Utterer) and KANAH (the Echoer)
I am, it is. it was, it shall be.
HAM (Heat) and SHELAH (Flux)
JAPHET (encompassing, spreading, Father of All: also Destroyer) and
COSBY (female-male. Kulturträger)

1st Man. What ails the sun, that his mornings are so sickly?

2nd Man. You heard what the Old One said: the sun is dark with the anger of the skies.

1st Man. The Old One is sly. Himself is angry, so he says the anger breathes from the hollows of the sky. We are not fools altogether. What think you? Are the sons of men more stupid than the sons of God?

3rd Man. I don't think! The Old One and his demi-god sons, what are they? They are taller than the sons of men, but they are slower. They are stronger, but it seems to me they are duller. Ask women what they think of the sons of Noah, the demi-gods! Ah, the sons of God! They follow at the heels of the daughters of men, and the daughters of men laugh beneath the black beards, as they laugh when the bull snorts, and they are on the safe side of the wall. Big is the bull by the river, but a boy leads him by the nose. So, if you ask me, do we lead these big ones, these demigods, old Noah and his sons, Shem and Ham and Japhet.

1st Man. If we had the secret of the red flutterer.

3rd Man. Ha! I have the name of that Bird. Ham told a woman that the name is Fire.

1st Man. Fire! It is a poor name. What is its father, and who its mother?

3rd Man. Nay, that Ham did not tell. It is a secret of these demigods. But I tell you. It comes out of an egg. And the Old One knows where the eggs of that bird called Fire are laid. So he gathers them up, for his house.

2nd Man. He shall tell us.

3rd Man. No, he will never tell us. But his sons may. Because if we knew the secret of the red bird they call Fire, and could find the eggs and have the young ones flutter in our houses, then we should be greater than Noah and his sons. The sons of men already are wittier than the sons of God. If we had the scarlet chicken they call Fire, between our hands, we could do away with the sons of God, and have the world for our own.

1st Man. So it should be. The sons of men are numberless, but these sons of God are few and slow. The sons of men know the secret of all things, save that of the red flutterer. The sons of men are the makers of everything. The sons of God command and chide, but what can they make, with their slow hands? Why are they lords, save that they guard the red bird which should now be ours. What name do they give it, again?

3rd Man. Fire.

1st Man. Fire! Fire! And that is all their secret and their power: merely Fire! Already we know their secret.

3rd Man. Ham told it to a woman, and even as she lay with him she laughed beneath his beard, and mocked him.

1st Man. Yet this red bird hatches the pale dough into bread, into good dark bread. Let us swear to catch the red bird, and take it to our houses. And when it has laid its eggs, we will kill the demi-gods, and have the earth to ourselves. For the sons of men must be free.

2nd Man. Yes, indeed! Free! Free! Is it not a greater word than Fire? We will kill the demi-gods and be free. But first we must catch the red bird, take him alive, in a snare.

1st Man. Ah, if we could! For Ham has told us that the feathers shine like feathers of the sun, with warmth, even hotter than the sun at noon.

2nd Man. Then it were very good if we had him, seeing the sun in heaven has lost his best feathers, and limps dustily across the heavens like a moulting hen. Ah men, have you learnt what it is to shiver?

3rd Man. Have we not! Even in the day-time shivers seize us, since the sun has moulted his rays. And shivering in the day-time is like dying before one's hour. The death-shiver is on us. We must capture the red bird, so that he flutters his wings in our houses and brightens our flesh, as the moulting sun used to do, till he fell poor and mean.

2nd Man. You know what Shem says? He says there are three birds: the little red bird in the houses of the demi-gods–

3rd Man. The one Ham calls Fire. We must lay hold of that one.

2nd Man. Then the bigger bird of the sun, that beats his yellow wings and makes us warm, and makes the ferns unroll, and the fern-seed fall brown, for bread.

3rd Man. Ay, the bird of the sun! But he is moulting, and has lost his ray-feathers and limps through grey dust across the sky. He is not to be depended on. Let us once get hold of the red chick Ham calls Fire, and we will forget the sick sun of heaven. We need our sun in our grasp. A bird in the hand is worth two in the bush.

2nd Man. Yet you know what Shem says. Far, far away beyond the yellow sun that flies across the sky every day, taking the red berries to his nest, there lives the Great White Bird, that no man has ever seen.

3rd Man. Nor no demi-god either.

2nd Man. In the middle of the tree of darkness is a nest, and in the nest sits the Great White Bird. And when he rises on his nest and beats his wings, a glow of strength goes through the world. And the stars are the small white birds that have their nests among the outer leaves. And our yellow sun is a young one that does but fly across from the eastern bough to the western, near us, each day, and in his flight stirs with his feathers the blue dust of space, so we see him in the blue of heaven, flashing his sun-pinions. But beyond the blue fume of the sky, all the time, beyond our seeing, the Great White Bird roosts at the centre of the tree.

3rd Man. Hast thou seen thy Great White Bird, fool?

2nd Man. I? No!

3rd Man. When dost thou expect to see him?

2nd Man. I? Never!

3rd Man. Then why dost thou talk of him?

2nd Man. Because Shem told me.

3rd Man. Shem! He is fooling thee. Did he tell thee the secret of the little red bird?

2nd Man. That, no!

3rd Man. That, no! Rather will he tell thee of a Great White Duck that no man ever did see or ever will see. Art thou not a fool?

2nd Man. Nay, for listen! Shem says that even the yellow sun cannot fly across from the eastern bough to the western, save on the wind of the wings of the Great White Bird. On the dead air he cannot make heading. Likewise, Shem says, the air men breathe is dead air, dead in the breast, save it is stirred fresh from the wings of the Great White Bird.

3rd Man. The air in my breast is not dead.

2nd Man. And so it is, the sun struggles in grey dust across the heavy sky, because the wings of the Great White Bird send us no stir, there is no freshness for us. And so we shiver, and feel our death upon us beforehand, because the Great White Bird has sunk down, and will no more wave his wings gladly towards us.

1st Man. And pray, why should *he* be moping?

2nd Man. Because the sons of men never breathe his name in answer. Even as the ferns breathe fern-seed, which is the fume of their answer to the sun, and the little green flowers that are invisible make a perfume like the sky speaking with a voice, answering deep into heaven, so the hearts of men beat the warmth and wildness of an answer to the Great White Bird, who sips it in and is rejoiced, lifting his wings. But now the hearts of men are answerless, like slack drums gone toneless. They say: We ourselves are the Great White Birds of the Universe. It is we who keep the wheel going!–So they cry in impertinence, and the Great White Bird lifts his wings no more, to send the wind of newness and morning into us. So we are stale, and inclining towards deadness. We capture the yellow metal and the white, and we think we have captured the answerer. For the yellow gold and the white silver are pure voices of answer calling still from under the oldest dawn, to the Great White Bird, as the cock crows at sunrise. So we capture the first bright answerers, and say: Lo! we are lords of the answer.–But the answer is not to us, though we hold the gold in our fist. And the wings of the Bird are slack.

1st Man. What is all this talk? Is the humming-bird less blue, less brilliant?

2nd Man. It is Shem's word, not mine. But he says, the Great White Bird will waft his wings even to the beast, for the beast is an answerer. But he will withhold his draught of freshness from the new beast called man, for man is impertinent and answerless. And the small white birds, the stars, are happy still in the outer boughs, hopping among the furthest leaves of the tree, and twittering their bright answer. But men are answerless, and dust settles on them; they shiver, and are woe-begone in spite of their laughter.

1st Man. Nay, thou art a mighty talker! But thy Great White Bird is only a decoy-duck to drag thee into obedience to these demigods, who cannot stoop to sweep the fern-seed for themselves, but must bid the children of men.–And thou art a fool duck decoyed into their net. Did Japhet ever talk of a Great White Bird? And Japhet is shrewd. Japhet says: Ah, you sons of men, your life is a predicament. You live between warm and cold; take care. If you fall into great heat, you are lost, if you slip down the crevices of cold, you are gone for ever. If the waters forsake you, you are vanished, and if the waters come down on you, you are swept away. You cannot ride on the heat nor live beneath the waters. The place you walk on is narrow as a plank across a torrent. You must live on the banks of the stream, for if the stream dries up, you die, but if the stream flows over its banks, likewise you die. Yet of the stream you ask not whence it cometh nor whither it goeth. It travels for ever past you, it is always going, so you say. The stream is there! I tell you, watch lest it be not there. Watch lest the banks be gone beneath the flood. For the waters run past you like wolves which are on the scent. And waters come down on you like flocks of grasshoppers from the sky, alighting from the invisible. But what are the wolves running for, and what hatched the flying waters in mid-heaven? You know not. You ask not. Yet your life is a travelling thread of water for ever passing. Ask then, and it shall be answered you. Know the whither and the whence, and not a wolf shall slip silently by in the night, without your consent. Ask and it shall be answered unto you. Ask! Ask! and all things shall be answered unto you, as the cock answers the sun. Oh, wonderful race of Askers, there shall be no answer ye shall not wing out of the depths. And who answers, serves.–So says Japhet, and says well. And if we had the red flutterer, it should answer to us, and all things after should answer to us for their existence. And we should be the invincible, the Askers, those that set the questions.

3rd Man. It is so. If we had the red bird in our hand, we could force the sun to give himself up in answer; yea, even the Great White Bird would answer in obedience. So we could unleash the waters from the ice, and shake the drops from the sky, in answer to our demand. The demi-gods are dumb askers, they get half-answers from us all. What we want is the red bird.

1st Man. It is true. That is all we need.

2nd Man. Then let us take it. Let us steal it from their house, and be free.

3rd Man. It is the great word: let us be free. Let us yield our answer no more, neither to gods nor demi-gods, sun nor inner sun.

1st Man. Men, masters of fire, and free on the face of the earth. Free from the need to answer, masters of the question. Lo, when we are lords of the question, how humbly the rest shall answer. Even the stars shall bow humbly, and yield us their reply, and the sun shall no more have a will of his own.

2nd Man. Can we do it?

1st Man. Can we not! We are the sons of men, heirs and successors of the sons of God. Japhet said to me: The sons of men cannot capture the gift of fire: for it is a gift. Till it is given to them, by the sons of God, they cannot have it.—I said to him: Give us the gift.—He said: Nay! for ye know not how to ask. When ye know how to ask, it shall be given you.

3rd Man. So! What they will not give, we will take.

2nd Man. Yes, we will take it, in spite of them. We are heirs of the gods and the sons of God. We are heirs of all. Let us take the flutterer and be free. We have the right to everything; so let us take.

1st Man. Japhet said: it is a gift!

(Enter Noah)

[Unfinished]

[AUTOBIOGRAPHICAL FRAGMENT]

Nothing depresses me more than to come home to the place where I was born, and where I lived my first twenty years, here, at Newthorpe, this coal-mining village on the Nottingham-Derby border. The place has grown, but not very much, the pits are poor. Only it has changed. There is a tram-line from Nottingham through the one street, and buses to Nottingham and Derby. The shops are bigger, more plate-glassy: there are two picture-palaces, and one Palais de Danse.

But nothing can save the place from the poor, grimy, mean effect of the Midlands, the little grimy brick houses with slate roofs, the general effect of paltriness, smallness, meanness, fathomless ugliness, combined with a sort of chapel-going respectability. It is the same as when I was a boy, only more so.

Now, it is all tame. It was bad enough, thirty years ago, when it was still on the upward grade, economically. But then the old race of miners were not immensely respectable. They filled the pubs with smoke and bad language, and they went with dogs at their heels. There was a sense of latent wildness and unbrokenness, a weird sense of thrill and adventure in the pitch-dark Midland nights, and roaring footballing Saturday afternoons. The country in between the colliery regions had a lonely sort of fierceness and beauty, half-abandoned, and threaded with poaching colliers and whippet dogs. Only thirty years ago!

Now it seems so different. The colliers of today are the men of my generation, lads I went to school with. I find it hard to believe. They were rough, wild lads. They are not rough, wild men. The board-school, the Sunday-school, the Band of Hope, and, above all, their mothers got them under. Got them under, made them tame. Made them sober, conscientious, and decent. Made them good husbands. When I was a boy, a collier who was a good husband was an exception to the rule, and while the women with bad husbands pointed him out as a shining example, they also despised him a little, as a petticoat man.

But nearly all the men of my generation are good husbands. There they stand, at the street corners, pale, shrunken, well-dressed, decent, and *under*. The drunken colliers of my father's generation were not got under. The decent colliers of my generation are got under entirely. They are so patient, so forbearing, so willing to listen to reason, so ready to put themselves aside. And there they stand, at the street corners and the entry-ends, the rough lads I went to school with, men now, with smart daughters and bossy wives and cigarette-smoking lads of their own. There they stand, then, and white as cheap wax candles, spectral, as if they had no selves any more: decent, patient, self-effacing sort of men, who have seen the war and the high-water-mark wages, and now are down again, under, completely under, with not a tuppence to rattle in their pockets. There they are, poor as their fathers before them, but poor with a hopeless outlook and a new and expensive world around them.

When I was a boy, the men still used to sing: "There's a good time coming, boys, there's a good time coming!" Well, it has come, and gone. If anybody sang now, they'd sing: "It's a bad time now, and a worse time coming." But the men of my generation are dumb: they have been got under and made good.

As for the next generation, that is something different. As soon as mothers become self-conscious, sons become what their mothers make them. My mother's generation was the first generation of working-class mothers to become really self-conscious. Our grandmothers were still too much under our grandfathers' thumb, and there was still too much masculine kick against petticoat rule. But with the next generation, the woman freed herself at least mentally and spiritually from the husband's domination, and then she became that great institution, that character-forming power, the mother of my generation. I am sure the character of nine-tenths of the men of my generation was formed by the mother: the character of the daughters too.

And what sort of characters? Well, the woman of my mother's generation was in reaction against the ordinary high-handed, obstinate husband who went off to the pub to enjoy himself and to waste the bit of money that was so precious to the family. The woman felt herself the higher moral being: and justly, as far as economic morality goes. She therefore assumed the major responsibility for the family, and the husband let her. So she proceeded to mould a generation.

Mould it to the shape of her own unfulfilled desire, of course. What had she wanted, all her life?—a "good" husband, gentle and understanding and moral, one who did not go to pubs and drink and waste the bit of wages, but who lived for his wife and his children.

Millions of mothers in Great Britain, in the latter half of Victoria's reign, unconsciously proceeded to produce sons to pattern. And they produced them, by the million: good sons, who would make good, steady husbands who would live for their wives and families. And there they are! we've got 'em now! the men of my generation, men between forty and fifty, men who almost all had Mothers with a big *m*.

And then the daughters! Because the mothers who produced so many "good sons" and future "good husbands" were at the same time producing daughters, perhaps without taking so much thought or exercising so much will-power over it, but producing them just as inevitably.

What sort of daughters came from these morally responsible mothers? As we should expect, daughters morally confident. The mothers had known some little hesitancy in their moral supremacy. But the daughters were quite assured. The daughters were always right. They were born with a sense of self-rightness that sometimes was hoity-toity, and sometimes was seemingly wistful: but there it was, the inevitable sense that I-am-right. This the women of my generation drew in with their mothers' milk, this feeling that they were "right" and must be "right" and nobody must gainsay them. It is like being born with one eye; you can't help it.

We are such stuff as our grandmothers' dreams are made on. This terrible truth should never be forgotten. Our grandmothers dreamed of wonderful "free" womanhood in a "pure" world, surrounded by "adoring, humble, high-minded" men. Our mothers started to put the dream into practice. And we are the fulfilment. We are such stuff as our grandmothers' dreams were made on.

For I think it cannot be denied that ours is the generation of "free" womanhood, and a helplessly "pure" world, and of pathetic "adoring, humble, high-minded" men.

We are, more or less, such stuff as our grandmothers' dreams are made on. But the dream changes with every new generation of grandmothers. Already my mother, while having a definite ideal for her sons, of "humble, adoring, high-minded" men, began to have secret dreams of her own: dreams of some Don Juan sort of person whose influence would make the vine of Dionysus grow and coil over the pulpit of our Congregational Chapel. I myself, her son, could see the dream peeping out, thrusting little tendrils through her paved intention of having "good sons." It was my turn to be the "good son." It would be my son's turn to fulfil the other dream, or dreams: the secret ones.

Thank God I have no son to undertake the onerous burden. Oh, if only every father could say to his boy: Look here, my son! These are your grandmother's dreams of a man. Now you look out!—My dear old grandmother, my mother's mother, I'm sure she dreamed me almost to a *t,* except for a few details.

But the daughter starts, husbandly speaking, where the mother leaves off. The daughters of my mother, and of the mothers of my generation, start, as a rule, with "good husbands," husbands who never fundamentally contradict them, whose lifelong attitude is: All right, dear! I know I'm wrong, as usual. This is the attitude of the husband of my generation.

It alters the position of the wife entirely. It is a fight for the woman to get the reins into her own hands, but once she's got them, there she is! the reins have got her. She's got to drive somewhere, to steer the matrimonial cart in some direction. "All right, dear! I'll let you decide it, since you know better than I do!" says the husband, in every family matter. So she must keep on deciding. Or, if the husband balks her occasionally, she must keep up the pressure till he gives in.

Now driving the matrimonial cart is quite an adventure for a time, while the children are little, and all that. But later, the woman begins to think to herself: "Oh, damn the cart! Where do *I* come in?" She begins to feel she's getting nothing out of it. It's not good enough. Whether you're the horse or whether you're the driver doesn't make any odds. So long as you're both harnessed to the cart.

Then the woman of my generation begins to have ideas about her sons. They'd better not be so all-forsaken "good" as their father has been. They'd better be more sporting, and give a woman a bit more "life." After all, what's a family? It swallows a woman up until she's fifty, and then puts the remains of her aside. Not good enough! No! My sons must be more manly, make plenty of money for a woman and give her a "life," and not be such a muff about "goodness" and being "right." What is being "right," after all? Better enjoy yourself while you've got the chance.

So the sons of the younger generation emerge into the world—my sons, if I'd got any—with the intrinsic maternal charge ringing in their ears: "Make some money and give yourself a good time—and all of us. Enjoy yourself!"

The young men of the younger generation begin to fulfil the hidden dreams of my mother. They are jazzy—but not coarse. They are a bit Don-Juanish, but, let us hope, entirely without brutality or vulgarity. They are more elegant, and not much more moral. But they are still humble before a woman, especially *the* woman!

It is the secret dream of my mother, coming true.

And if you want to know what the next generation will be like, you must fathom the secret dreams of your wife: the woman of forty or so. There you will find the clue. And if you want to be more precise, then find out what is the young woman of twenty's ideal of a man.

The poor young woman of twenty, she is rather stumped for an ideal of a man. So perhaps the next generation but one won't be anything at all.

We are such stuff as our grandmothers' dreams are made on. Even colliers are such stuff as their grandmothers' dreams are made on. And if Queen Victoria's dream was King George, then Queen Alexandra's was the Prince of Wales, and Queen Mary's will be—what?

But all this doesn't take away from the fact that my home place is more depressing to me than death, and I wish my grandmother and all her generation had been better dreamers. "Those maids, thank God, are 'neath the sod," but their dreams we still have with us. It is a terrible thing to dream dreams that shall become flesh.

And when I see the young colliers dressed up like the Prince of Wales, dropping in to the Miners' Welfare for another drink, or into the "Pally" for a dance—in evening suit to beat the band—or scooting down the black roads on a motor-bike, a leggy damsel behind—then I wish the mothers of my own generation, my own mother included, had been a little less *frivolous* as a dreamer. In life, so deadly earnest! And oh, what frivolous dreams our mothers must have had, as they sat in the pews of the Congregational Chapel with faces like saints! They must unconsciously have been dreaming jazz and short skirts, the Palais de Danse, the Film, and the motor-bike. It is enough to embitter one's most sacred memories. "Lead Kindly Light"—unto the "Pally."—The eleventh commandment: "Enjoy yourselves!"

Well, well! Even grandmothers' dreams don't always come true, that is, they aren't allowed to. They'd come true right enough otherwise. But sometimes fate, and that long dragon the concatenation of circumstance, intervene. I am sure my mother never dreamed a dream that wasn't well-off. My poor old grandmother might still dream noble poverty—myself, to wit! But my mother? Impossible! In her secret dreams, the sleeve-links were solid gold, and the socks were silk.

And now fate, the monster, frustrates. The pits don't work. There's reduced wages and short pay. The young colliers will have a hard time buying another pair of silk socks for the "Pally" when these are worn out. They'll have to go in wool. As for the young lady's fur coat—well, well! let's hope it is seal, or some other hard-wearing skin, and not that evanescent chinchilla or squirrel that moults in a season.

For the young lady won't get another fur coat in a hurry, if she has to wait for her collier father to buy it. Not that he would refuse it her. What is a man for, except to provide for his wife and daughters? But you can't get blood out of a stone, nor cash out of a collier, not any more.

It is a soft, hazy October day, with the dark green Midlands fields looking somewhat sunken, and the oak trees brownish, the mean houses shabby and scaly, and the whole countryside somewhat dead, expunged, faintly blackened under the haze. It is a queer thing that countries die along with their inhabitants. This countryside is dead: or so inert, it is as good as dead. The old sheep-bridge where I used to swing as a boy is now an iron affair. The brook where we caught minnows now runs on a concrete bed. The old sheep-dip, the dipping-hole, as we called it, where we bathed, has somehow disappeared, so has the mill-dam and the little water-fall. It's all a concrete arrangement now, like a sewer. And the people's lives are the same, all running in concrete channels like a vast cloaca.

At Engine Lane Crossing, where I used to sit as a tiny child and watch the trucks shunting with a huge grey horse and a man with a pole, there are now no trucks. It is October, and there should be hundreds. But there are no orders. The pits are turning half-time. Today they are not turning at all. The men are all at home: no orders, no work.

And the pit is fuming silently, there is no rattle of screens, and the head-stock wheels are still. That was always an ominous sign, except on Sundays: even when I was a small child. The head-stock wheels twinkling against the sky, that meant work and life, men "earning a living," if living can be earned.

But the pit is foreign to me anyhow, so many new big buildings round it, electric plant and all the rest. It's a wonder even the shafts are the same. But they must be: the shafts where we used to watch the cage-loads of colliers coming up suddenly, with a start: then the men streaming out to turn in their lamps, then trailing off, all grey, along the lane home; while the screens still rattled, and the pony on the sky-line still pulled along the tub of "dirt," to tip over the edge of the pit-bank.

It is different now: all is much more impersonal and mechanical and abstract. I don't suppose the children of today drop "nuts" of coal down the shaft, on Sunday afternoons, to hear them hit, hit with an awful resonance against the sides far down, before there comes the last final plump into the endlessly far-off sump. My father was always so angry if he knew we dropped coals down the shaft: If there was a man at t'bottom, it'd kill 'im straight off. How should you like that?—We didn't quite know how we should have liked it.

But anyhow Moorgreen is no more what it was: or it is too much more. Even the rose-bay willow-herb, which seems to love collieries, no longer showed its hairy autumn thickets and its last few spikes of rose around the pit-pond and on the banks. Only the yellow snapdragon, toad-flax, still was there.

Up from Moorgreen goes a footpath past the quarry and up the fields, out to Renshaw's farm. This was always a favourite walk of mine. Beside the path lies the old quarry, part of it very old and deep and filled in with oak trees and guelder-rose and tangle of briars, the other part open, with square wall neatly built up with dry-stone on the side under the plough-fields, and the bed still fairly level and open. This open part of the quarry was blue with dog-violets in spring, and, on the smallish brambles, the first handsome blackberries came in autumn. Thank heaven, it is late October, and too late for blackberries, or there would still be here some wretched men with baskets, ignominiously combing the brambles for the last berry. When I was a boy, how a man, a full-grown miner, would have been despised for going with a little basket lousing the hedges for a blackberry or two. But the men of my generation put their pride in their pocket, and now their pockets are empty.

The quarry was a haunt of mine, as a boy. I loved it because, in the open part, it seemed so sunny and dry and warm, the pale stone, the pale, slightly sandy bed, the dog-violets and the early daisies. And then the old part, the deep part, was such a fearsome place. It was always dark—you had to crawl under bushes. And you came upon honeysuckle and nightshade, that no one ever looked upon. And at the dark sides were little, awful rocky caves, in which I imagined the adders lived.

There was a legend that these little caves or niches in the rocks were "everlasting wells," like the everlasting wells at Matlock. At Matlock the water drips in caves, and if you put an apple in there, or a bunch of grapes, or even if you cut your hand off and put it in, it won't decay, it will turn everlasting. Even if you put a bunch of violets in, they won't die, they'll turn everlasting.

Later, when I grew up and went to Matlock—only sixteen miles away—and saw the infamous everlasting wells, that the water only made a hoary nasty crust of stone on everything, and the stone hand was only a glove stuffed with sand, being "petrified," I was disgusted. But still, when I see the stone fruits that people have in bowls for decoration, purple, semi-translucent stone grapes, and lemons, I think: *these* are the real fruits from the everlasting wells.

In the soft, still afternoon I found the quarry not very much changed. The red berries shone quietly on the briars. And in this still, warm, secret place of the earth I felt my old childish longing to pass through a gate, into a deeper, sunnier, more silent world.

The sun shone in, but the shadows already were deep. Yet I had to creep away into the darkness of bushes, into the lower hollow of the tree-filled quarry. I felt, as I had always felt, there was something there. And as I wound my way, stooping, through the unpleasant tangle, I started, hearing a sudden rush and clatter of falling earth. Some part of the quarry must be giving way.

I found the place, away at the depth under the trees and bushes, a new place where yellow earth and whitish earth and pale rock had slid down new in a heap. And at the top of the heap was a crack, a little slantingly upright slit or orifice in the rock.

I looked at the new place curiously, the pallid new earth and rock among the jungle of vegetation, the little opening above, into the earth. A touch of sunlight came through the oak-leaves and fell on the new place and the aperture, and the place flashed and twinkled. I had to climb up to look at it.

It was a little crystalline cavity in the rock, all crystal, a little pocket or womb of quartz, among the common stone. It was pale and colourless, the stuff we call spar, from which they make little bowls and mementoes, in Matlock. But through the flat-edged, colourless crystal of the spar ran a broad vein of purplish crystal, wavering inwards as if it were arterial. And that was a vein of the Blue John spar that is rather precious.

The place fascinated me, especially the vein of purple, and I had to clamber into the tiny cave, which would just hold me. It seemed warm in there, as if the shiny rock were warm and alive, and it seemed to me there was a strange perfume, of rock, of living rock like hard, bright flesh, faintly perfumed with phlox. It was a subtle yet most fascinating secret perfume, an inward perfume. I crept right into the little cavity, into the narrow inner end where the vein of purple ran, and I curled up there, like an animal in its hole. "Now," I thought, "for a little while I am safe and sound, and the vulgar world doesn't exist for me." I curled together with soft, curious voluptuousness. The scent of inwardness and of life, a queer scent like phlox, with a faint narcotic inner quality like opium or like truffles, became very vivid to me, then faded. I suppose I must have gone to sleep.

Later, I don't know how much later, it may have been a minute, or an eternity, I was wakened by feeling something lifting me, lifting me with a queer, half-sickening motion, curiously exciting, in a slow little rhythmic heave that was at once soft and powerful, gentle and violent, grateful and violating. I could do nothing, not even wake up: yet I was not really terrified, only utterly wonder-struck.

Then the lifting and heaving ceased, and I was cold. Something harsh passed over me: I realized it was my face: I realized I had a face. Then immediately a sharpness and bitingness flew into me, flew right into me, through what must have been my nostrils, into my body, what must have been my breast. Roused by a terrific shock of amazement, suddenly a new thing rushed into me, right into me, with a sweep that swept me away, and at the same time I felt that first thing moving somewhere in me, there was a movement that came aloud.

There were some dizzy moments when my I, my consciousness, wheeled and swooped like an eagle that is going to wheel away into the sky and be gone. Yet I felt her, my I, my life, wheeling closer, closer, my consciousness. And suddenly she closed with me, and I knew, I came awake.

I knew. I knew I was alive. I even heard a voice say: "He's alive!" Those were the first words I heard.

And I opened my eyes again and blinked with terror, knowing the light of day. I shut them again, and felt sensations out in space, somewhere, and yet upon *me*. Again my eyes were opened, and I even saw objects, great things that were here and were there and then were not there. And the sensations out in space drew nearer, as it were, to me, the middle me.

So consciousness swooped and swerved, returning in great swoops. I realized that I was I, and that this I was also a body that ended abruptly in feet and hands. Feet! yes, feet! I remembered even the word. Feet!

I roused a little, and saw a greyish pale nearness that I recognized was my body, and something terrible moving upon it and making sensations in it. Why was it grey, my own nearness? Then I felt that other sensation, that I call aloudness, and I knew it. It was "Dust of ages!" That was the aloudness: "Dust of ages!"

In another instant I knew that violent movingness that was making sensations away out upon me. It was somebody. In terror and wonder the realization came to me: it was somebody, another one, a man. A man, making sensations on me! A man, who made the aloudness: "Dust of ages." A man! Still I could not grasp it. The conception would not return whole to me.

Yet once it had lodged within me, my consciousness established itself. I moved. I even moved my legs, my far-off feet. Yes! And an aloudness came out of me, even of me. I knew. I even knew now that I had a throat. And in another moment I should know something else.

It came all of a sudden. I saw the man's face. I saw it, a ruddy sort of face with a nose and a trimmed beard. I even knew more. I said: "Why–?"

And the face quickly looked at me, with blue eyes into my eyes, and I struggled as if to get up.

"Art awake?" it said.

And somewhere, I knew there was the word Yes! But it had not yet come to me.

But I knew, I knew! Dimly I came to know that I was lying in sun on new earth that was spilled before my little, opened cave. I remembered my cave. But why I should be lying grey and stark-naked on earth in the sun outside I did not know; nor what the face was, nor whose.

Then there was more aloudness, and there was another one. I realized there could be more than one other one. More than one! More than one! I felt a new sudden something that made all of me move at once, in many directions, it seemed, and I became once more aware of the extent of me, and an aloudness came from my throat. And I remembered even that new something that was upon me. Many sensations galloping in all directions! But it was one dominant, drowning. It was water. Water! I even remembered water, or I knew I knew it. They were washing me. I even looked down and saw the whiteness: me, myself, white, a body.

And I remembered, that when all of me had moved to the touch of water, and I had made an aloudness in my throat, the men had laughed. Laughed! I remembered laughter.

So as they washed me, I came to myself. I even sat up. And I saw earth and rock, and a sky that I knew was afternoon. And I was stark-naked, and there were two men washing me, and they too were stark-naked. But I was white, pure white, and thin, and they were ruddy, and not thin.

They lifted me, and I leaned on one, standing, while the other washed me. The one I leaned on was warm, and his life softly warmed me. The other one rubbed me gently. I was alive. I saw my white feet like two curious flowers, and I lifted them one after another, remembering walking.

The one held me, and the other put a woollen shirt or smock over me. It was pale grey and red. Then they fastened shoes on my feet. Then the free one went to the cave, peering, and he came back with things in his hands: buttons, some discoloured yet unwasted coins, a dull but not rusted pocket-knife, a waistcoat buckle, and a discoloured watch, whose very face was dark. Yet I knew these things were mine.

"Where are my clothes?" I said.

I felt eyes looking at me, two blue eyes, two brown eyes, full of strange life.

"My clothes!" I said.

They looked at one another, and made strange speech. Then the blue-eyed one said to me:

"Gone! Dust of ages!"

They were strange men to me, with their formal, peaceful faces and trimmed beards, like old Egyptians. The one on whom I was unconsciously leaning stood quite still, and he was warmer than the afternoon sunshine. He seemed to give off life to me, I felt a warmth suffusing into me, an inflooding of strength. My heart began to lift with strange, exultant strength. I turned to look at the man I was resting on, and met the blue, quiet shimmer of his eyes. He said something to me, in the quiet, full voice, and I nearly understood, because it was like the dialect. He said it again, softly and calmly, speaking to the inside of me, so that I understood as a dog understands, from the voice, not from the words.

"Can ta goo, o shollt be carried?"

It sounded to me like that, like the dialect.

"I think I can walk," said I, in a voice that sounded harsh after the soft, deep modulation of the other.

He went slowly down the heap of loose earth and stones, which I remembered had fallen. But it was different. There were no trees in an old quarry hollow. This place was bare, like a new working. And when we came out, it was another place altogether. Below was a hollow of trees, and a bare, grassy hillside swept away, with clumps of trees, like park-land. There was no colliery, no railway, no hedges, no square, shut-in fields. And yet the land looked tended.

We stood on a little path of paved stone, only about a yard wide. Then the other man came up from the quarry, carrying tools and wearing a grey shirt or smock with a red cord. He spoke with that curious soft inwardness, and we turned down the path, myself still leaning on the shoulder of the first man. I felt myself quivering with a new strength, and yet ghostlike. I had a curious sensation of lightness, not touching the ground as I walked, as if my hand that rested on the man's shoulder buoyed me up. I wanted to know whether I was really buoyant, as in a dream.

I took my hand suddenly from the man's shoulder, and stood still. He turned and looked at me.

"I can walk alone," I said, and as in a dream I took a few paces forward. It was true. I was filled with a curious rushing strength that made me almost buoyant, scarcely needing to touch the ground. I was curiously, quiveringly strong, and at the same time buoyant.

"I can go alone!" I said to the man.

They seemed to understand, and to smile, the blue-eyed one showing his teeth when he smiled. I had a sudden idea: How beautiful they are, like plants in flower! But still, it was something I felt, rather than saw.

The blue-eyed one went in front, and I walked on the narrow path with my rushing buoyancy, terribly elated and proud, forgetting everything, the other man following silently behind. Then I was aware that the path had turned and ran beside a road in a hollow where a stream was, and a cart was clanking slowly ahead, drawn by two oxen and led by a man who was entirely naked.

I stood still, on the raised, paved path, trying to think, trying, as it were, to come awake. I was aware that the sun was sinking behind me, golden in the October afternoon. I was aware that the man in front of me also had no clothes on whatsoever, and he would soon be cold.

Then I made an effort, and looked round. On the slopes to the left were big, rectangular patches of dark plough-land. And men were ploughing still. On the right were hollow meadows, beyond the stream, with tufts of trees and many speckled cattle being slowly driven forwards. And in front the road swerved on, past a mill-pond and a mill, and a few little houses, and then swerved up a rather steep hill. And at the top of the hill was a town, all yellow in the late afternoon light, with yellow, curved walls rising massive from the yellow-leaved orchards, and above, buildings swerving in a long, oval curve, and round, faintly conical towers rearing up. It had something at once soft and majestical about it, with its soft yet powerful curves, and no sharp angles or edges, the whole substance seeming soft and golden like the golden flesh of a city.

And I knew, even while I looked at it, that it was the place where I was born, the ugly colliery townlet of dirty red brick. Even as a child, coming home from Moorgreen, I had looked up and seen the squares of miners' dwellings, built by the Company, rising from the hill-top in the afternoon light like the walls of Jerusalem, and I had wished it were a golden city, as in the hymns we sang in the Congregational Chapel.

Now it had come true. But the very realization, and the very intensity of my *looking,* had made me lose my strength and my buoyancy. I turned forlorn to the men who were with me. The blue-eyed one came and took my arm, and laid it across his shoulder, laying his left hand round my waist, on my hip.

And almost immediately the soft, warm rhythm of his life pervaded me again, and the memory in me which was my old self went to sleep. I was like a wound, and the touch of these men healed me at once. We went on again, along the raised pavement.

Three horsemen came cantering up, from behind. All the world was turning home towards the town, at sunset. The horsemen slackened pace as they came abreast. They were men in soft, yellow sleeveless tunics, with the same still, formal Egyptian faces and trimmed beards as my companions. Their arms and legs were bare, and they rode without stirrups. But they had curious hats of beech-leaves on their heads. They glanced at us sharply and my companions saluted respectfully. Then the riders cantered ahead again, the golden tunics softly fluttering. No one spoke at all. There was a great stillness in all the world, and yet a magic of close-interwoven life.

The road now began to be full of people, slowly passing up the hill towards the town. Most were bare-headed, wearing the sleeveless woollen shirt of grey and red, with a red girdle, but some were clean-shaven, and dressed in grey shirts, and some carried tools, some fodder. There were women too, in blue or lilac smocks, and some men in scarlet smocks. But among the rest, here and there were men like my guide, quite naked, and some young women, laughing together as they went, had their blue smocks folded to a pad on their heads, as they carried their bundles, and their slender, rosy-tanned bodies were quite naked, save for a little girdle of white and green and purple cord fringe that hung round their hips and swung as they walked. Only they had soft shoes on their feet.

They all glanced at me, and some spoke a word of salute to my companions, but no one asked questions. The naked girls went very stately, with bundles on their heads, yet they laughed more than the men. And they were comely as berries on a bush. That was what they reminded me of: rose-berries on a bush. That was the quality of all the people: an inner stillness and ease, like plants that come to flower and fruit. The individual was like a whole fruit, body and mind and spirit, without split. It made me feel a curious, sad sort of envy, because I was not so whole, and at the same time, I was wildly elated, my rushing sort of energy seemed to come upon me again. I felt as if I were just going to plunge into the deeps of life, for the first time: belated, and yet a pioneer of pioneers.

I saw ahead the great rampart walls of the town–then the road suddenly curved to gateway, all the people flowing in, in two slow streams, through the narrow side entrances.

It was a big gateway of yellow stone, and inside was a clear space, paved mostly with whitish stones, and around it stood buildings in the yellow stone, golden-looking, with pavement arcades supported on yellow pillars. My guides turned into a chamber where men in green stood on guard, and several peasants were waiting. They made way, and I was taken before a man who reclined on a dark-yellow couch, himself wearing a yellow tunic. He was blond, with the trimmed beard and hair worn long, cut round like the hair of a Florentine page. Though he was not handsome, he had a curious quality of beauty, that came from within. But this time, it was the beauty of a flower rather than of a berry.

My guides saluted him and explained briefly and quietly, in words I could only catch a drift of. Then the man looked at me, quietly, gently, yet I should have been afraid, if I had been his enemy. He spoke to me, and I thought he asked if I wanted to stay in their town.

"Did you ask me if I want to stay here?" I replied. "You see, I don't even know where I am."

"You are in this town of Nethrupp," he said, in slow English, like a foreigner. "Will you stay some time with us?"

"Why, thank you, if I may," I said, too helplessly bewildered to know what I was saying.

We were dismissed, with one of the guards in green. The people were all streaming down the side street, between the yellow-coloured houses, some going under the pillared porticoes, some in the open road. Somewhere ahead a wild music began to ring out, like three bagpipes squealing and droning. The people pressed forward, and we came to a great oval space on the ramparts, facing due west. The sun, a red ball, was near the horizon.

We turned into a wide entrance and went up a flight of stairs. The man in green opened a door and ushered me in.

"All is thine!" he said.

My naked guide followed me into the room, which opened onto the oval and the west. He took a linen shirt and a woollen tunic from a small cupboard, and smilingly offered them to me. I realized he wanted his own shirt back, and quickly gave it him, and his shoes. He put my hand quickly between his two hands, then slipped into his shirt and shoes, and was gone.

I dressed myself in the clothes he had laid out, a blue-and-white striped tunic, and white stockings, and blue cloth shoes, and went to the window. The red sun was almost touching the tips of the tree-covered hills away in the west, Sherwood Forest grown dense again. It was the landscape I knew best on earth, and still I knew it, from the shapes.

There was a curious stillness in the square. I stepped out of my window on to the terrace, and looked down. The crowd had gathered in order, a cluster of men on the left, in grey, grey-and-scarlet, and pure scarlet, and a cluster of women on the right, in tunics of all shades of blue and crocus lilac. In the vaulted porticoes were more people. And the red sun shone on all, till the square glowed again.

When the ball of fire touched the tree-tops, there was a queer squeal of bagpipes, and the square suddenly started into life. The men were stamping softly, like bulls, the women were softly swaying, and softly clapping their hands, with a strange noise, like leaves. And from under the vaulted porticoes, at opposite ends of the egg-shaped oval, came the soft booming and trilling of women and men singing against one another in the strangest pattern of sound.

It was all kept very soft, soft-breathing. Yet the dance swept into swifter and swifter rhythm, with the most extraordinary incalculable unison. I do not believe there was any outside control of the dance. The thing happened by instinct, like the wheeling and flashing of a shoal of fish or of a flock of birds dipping and spreading in the sky. Suddenly, in one amazing wing-movement, the arms of all the men would flash up into the air, naked and glowing, and with the soft, rushing sound of pigeons alighting the men ebbed in a spiral, grey and sparkled with scarlet, bright arms slowly leaning, upon the women, who rustled all crocus-blue, rustled like an aspen, then in one movement scattered like sparks, in every direction, from under the enclosing, sinking arms of the men, and suddenly formed slender rays of lilac branching out from red and grey knot of the men.

All the time the sun was slowly sinking, shadow was falling, and the dance was moving slower, the women wheeling blue around the obliterated sun. They were dancing the sun down, and dancing as birds wheel and dance, and fishes in shoals, controlled by some strange unanimous instinct. It was at once terrifying and magnificent, I wanted to die, so as not to see it, and I wanted to rush down, to be one of them. To be a drop in that wave of life.

The sun had gone, the dance unfolded and faced inwards to the town, the men softly stamping, the women rustling and softly clapping, the voices of the singers drifting on like a twining wind. And slowly, in one slow wing-movement, the arms of the men rose up unanimous, in a sort of salute, and as the arms of the men were sinking, the arms of the women softly rose. It gave the most marvellous impression of soft, slow flight of two many-pinioned wings, lifting and sinking like the slow drift of an owl. Then suddenly everything ceased. The people scattered silently.

And two men came into the oval, the one with glowing lamps

hung on a pole he carried across his shoulder, while the other quickly hung up the lamps within the porticoes, to light the town. It was night.

Someone brought us a lighted lamp, and was gone. It was evening, and I was alone in a smallish room with a small bed, a lamp on the floor, and an unlighted fire of wood on the small hearth. It was very simple and natural. There was a small outfit of clothing in the cupboard, with a thick blue cloak. And there were a few plates and dishes. But in the room there were no chairs, but a long, folded piece of dark felt, on which one could recline. The light shone upwards from below, lighting the walls of creamy smoothness, like a chalk enamel. And I was alone, utterly alone, within a couple of hundred yards of the very spot where I was born.

I was afraid: afraid for myself. These people, it seemed to me, were not people, not human beings in my sense of the word. They had the stillness and the completeness of plants. And see how they could melt into one amazing instinctive thing, a human flock of motion.

I sat on the ground on the dark-blue felt, wrapped in the blue mantle, because I was cold and had no means of lighting the fire. Someone tapped at the door, and a man of the green guard entered. He had the same quiet, fruit-like glow of the men who had found me, a quality of beauty that came from inside, in some queer physical way. It was a quality I loved, yet it made me angry. It made me feel like a green apple, as if they had had all the real sun.

He took me out, and showed me lavatories and baths, with two lusty men standing under the douches. Then he took me down to a big circular room with a raised hearth in the centre, and a blazing wood fire whose flame and smoke rose to a beautiful funnel-shaped canopy or chimney of stone. The hearth spread out beyond the canopy, and here some men reclined on the folded felts, with little white cloths before them, eating an evening meal of stiff porridge and milk, with liquid butter, fresh lettuce, and apples. They had taken off their clothes, and lay with the firelight flickering on their healthy, fruit-like bodies, the skin glistening faintly with oil. Around the circular wall ran a broad dais where other men reclined, either eating or resting. And from time to time a man came in with his food, or departed with his dishes.

My guide took me out, to peep in a steaming room where each man washed his plate and spoon and hung them in his own little rack. Then my guide gave me a cloth and tray and dishes, and we went to a simple kitchen, where the porridge stood in great bowls over a slow fire, the melted butter was in a deep silver pan, the milk and the lettuce and fruit stood near the door. Three cooks guarded the kitchen, but the men from outside came quietly and took what they needed or what they wanted, helping themselves, then returning to the great round room, or going away to their own little rooms. There was an instinctive cleanliness and decency everywhere, in every movement, in every act. It was as if the deepest instinct had been cultivated in the people, to be comely. The soft, quiet comeliness was like a dream, a dream of life at last come true.

I took a little porridge, though I had little desire to eat. I felt a curious surge of force in me: yet I was like a ghost, among these people. My guide asked me, would I eat in the round hall, or go up to my room? I understood, and chose the round hall. So I hung my cloak in the curving lobby, and entered the men's hall. There I lay on a felt against the wall, and watched the men, and listened.

They seemed to slip out of their clothing as soon as they were warm, as if clothes were a burden or a slight humiliation. And they lay and talked softly, intermittently, with low laughter, and some played games with draughtsmen and chessmen, but mostly they were still.

The room was lit by hanging lamps, and it had no furniture at all. I was alone, and I was ashamed to take off my white sleeveless shirt. I felt, somehow, these men had no right to be so unashamed and self-possessed.

The green guard came again, and asked me, would I go to see somebody whose name I did not make out. So I took my mantle, and we went into the softly-lighted street, under the porticoes. People were passing, some in cloaks, some only in tunics, and women were tripping along.

We climbed up towards the top of the town, and I felt I must be passing the very place where I was born, near where the Wesleyan Chapel stood. But now it was all softly lighted, golden-coloured porticoes, with people passing in green or blue or grey-and-scarlet cloaks.

We came out on top into a circular space, it must have been where our Congregational Chapel stood, and in the centre of the circle rose a tower shaped tapering rather like a lighthouse, and rosy-coloured in the lamplight. Away in the sky, at the club-shaped tip of the tower, glowed one big ball of light.

We crossed, and mounted the steps of another building, through the great hall where people were passing, on to a door at the end of a corridor, where a green guard was seated. The guard rose and entered to announce us, then I followed through an antechamber to an inner room with a central hearth and a fire of clear-burning wood.

A man came forward to meet me, wearing a thin, carmine-coloured tunic. He had brown hair and a stiff, reddish-brown beard, and an extraordinary glimmering kind of beauty. Instead of the Egyptian calmness and fruit-like impassivity of the ordinary people, or the steady, flower-like radiance of the chieftain in yellow, at the city gates, this man had a quavering glimmer like light coming through water. He took my cloak from me; and I felt at once he understood.

"It is perhaps cruel to awaken," he said, in slow, conscious English, "even at a good moment."

"Tell me where I am!" I said.

"We call it Nethrupp—but was it not Newthorpe?—Tell me, when did you go to sleep?"

"This afternoon, it seems,—in October, 1927."

"October, nineteen-twenty-seven!" He repeated the words curiously, smiling.

"Did I really sleep? Am I really awake?"

"Are you not awake?" he said smiling. "Will you recline upon the cushions? Or would you rather sit? See!"—He showed me a solid oak armchair, of the modern furniture-revival sort, standing alone in the room. But it was black with age, and shrunken-seeming. I shivered.

"How old is that chair?" I said.

"It is just about a thousand years! a case of special preservation," he said.

I could not help it. I just sat on the rugs and burst into tears, weeping my soul away.

The man sat perfectly still for a long time. Then he came and put my hand between his two.

"Don't cry!" he said. "Don't cry! Man was a perfect child so long. Now we try to be men, not fretful children. Don't cry! Is not this better?"

"When is it? What year is this?" I asked.

"What year? We call it the year of the acorn. But you mean its arithmetic? You would call it the year two thousand nine hundred and twenty-seven."

"It cannot be," I said.

"Yet still it is."

"Then I am a thousand and forty-two years old!"

"And why not?"

"But how can I be?"

"How? You went to sleep, like a chrysalis: in one of the earth's little chrysalis wombs: and your clothes turned to dust, yet they left the buttons: and you woke up like a butterfly. But why not? Why are you afraid to be a butterfly that wakes up out of the dark for a little while, beautiful? Be beautiful, then, like a white butterfly. Take off your clothes and let the firelight fall on you. What is given, accept then–"

"How long shall I live now, do you think?" I asked him.

"Why will you always measure? Life is not a clock."

It is true. I am like a butterfly, and I shall only live a little while. That is why I don't want to eat.

[Unfinished]

Appendix

APPENDIX

The information given below will enable interested readers to tell: first, which of the selections in this volume are now newly published; second, when and where selections reprinted here first appeared in print. The listing in this appendix follows that of the table of contents.

I. Nature and Poetical Pieces

"Whistling of Birds." *Athenæum,* April 11, 1919.
"Adolf." *Dial,* September 1920. Also *New Keepsake: 1921,* Chelsea Book Club, London.
"Rex." *Dial,* February 1921.
"Pan in America." Previously unpublished.
"Man Is a Hunter." Previously unpublished.
"Mercury." *Atlantic Monthly,* February 1927. Also *Nation and Athenæum,* February 5, 1927.
"The Nightingale." *Forum,* September 1927. Also *Spectator,* September 10, 1927.
"Flowery Tuscany." *New Criterion,* October, November, December, 1927. Also *Travel,* April 1929.
"The Elephants of Dionysus." Previously unpublished.
"David." Previously unpublished.
"Notes for *Birds, Beasts and Flowers.*" Cresset Press edition of *Birds, Beasts and Flowers,* London, 1930.

II. Peoples, Countries, Races

"German Impressions: I. French Sons of Germany." *Westminster Gazette,* August 3, 1912.
"German Impressions: II. Hail in the Rhineland." *Westminster Gazette,* August 9, 1912.
"Christs in the Tirol." *Westminster Gazette,* March 22, 1913. In revised form, *Atlantic Monthly,* August 1933.
"America, Listen to Your Own." *New Republic,* December 15, 1920.
"Indians and an Englishman." *Dial,* February 1923. Also *Adelphi,* November 1923.
"Taos." *Dial,* March 1923.
"Au Revoir, U. S. A." *Laughing Horse,* No. 8, 1923.
"A Letter from Germany." *New Statesman and Nation,* October 13, 1934. This letter may almost certainly be dated February 19, 1924, the day before the Lawrences left Baden for Paris. See Lawrence's letter to J. M. Murry, February 13, 1924, in *Letters of D. H. Lawrence.*
"See Mexico After, by Luis Q." Previously unpublished.
"Europe *v.* America." *Laughing Horse,* April 1926.
"Paris Letter." *Laughing Horse,* April 1926.
"Fireworks in Florence." *Nation and Athenæum,* April 16, 1926. Also *Forum,* May 1927.
["Germans and Latins."] No record of previous publication.
"Nottingham and the Mining Countryside." *Adelphi,* June–August 1930. Also *Architectural Review,* August 1930, under the title, "Disaster Looms Ahead."
"New Mexico." *Survey Graphic,* May 1931.

III. Love, Sex, Men, and Women

"Love." *English Review,* January 1918.
"All There." No record of previous publication.

"Making Love to Music." Previously unpublished.
"Women Are So Cocksure." Previously unpublished.
"Pornography and Obscenity." *This Quarter,* July–September 1929. Also separate pamphlet, Faber and Faber, Ltd., London, 1929; Knopf, N. Y., 1930.
"We Need One Another." *Scribner's Magazine,* May 1930. Also separate book, Equinox, N. Y., 1933.
"The Real Thing." *Scribner's Magazine,* June 1930.
"Nobody Loves Me." *Virginia Quarterly,* July 1930. Also *Life and Letters,* July 1930.

IV. Literature and Art

Prefaces and Introductions to Books:

1. *All Things Are Possible,* by Leo Shestov; trans. by S. S. Koteliansky. Secker, London, 1920.
2. *New Poems,* by D. H. Lawrence. Huebsch, N. Y., 1920.
3. [*Mastro-don Gesualdo,* by Giovanni Verga.] No record of previous publication; possibly written for Lawrence's translation of this novel and then for some reason rejected in favour of a much briefer prefatory notice.
4. *A Bibliography of D. H. Lawrence,* by Edward D. McDonald. Centaur Book Shop, Philadelphia, 1925.
5. *Max Havelaar,* by E. D. Dekker (Multatuli, pseud.); trans. by W. Siebenhaar. Knopf, N. Y., 1927.
6. *Cavalleria Rusticana,* by Giovanni Verga; trans. by D. H. Lawrence. Cape, London, 1928.
7. *The Collected Poems of D. H. Lawrence.* Never heretofore published, this long and personal introductory essay was evidently designed for Lawrence's *Collected Poems* and then rejected.
8. *Chariot of the Sun,* by Harry Crosby. Black Sun Press, Paris, 1931. Also in *Exchanges,* with text in English and French, under the title, "Chaos in Poetry," December 1929. In point of fact this essay was written some time before its publication anywhere.
9. *The Mother,* by Grazia Deledda; trans. by M. G. Steegmann. Travellers' Library, Cape, London, 1928.
10. *Bottom Dogs,* by Edward Dahlberg. Putnam, London, 1929. Also Simon & Schuster, N. Y., 1930.
11. *The Story of Doctor Manente,* by A. F. Grazzini; trans. by D. H. Lawrence. G. Orioli, Florence, 1929.
12. *Pansies,* by D. H. Lawrence. From the edition of *Pansies* privately printed for subscribers by P. R. Stephensen, London, 1929.
13. *The Grand Inquisitor,* by F. M. Dostoievsky; trans. by S. S. Koteliansky. Elkin Mathews and Marrot, London, 1930.
14. "Introduction." *London Mercury,* July 1930. Connected in some way not altogether understood with Mr. Frederick Carter's MS entitled *The Dragon of the Apocalypse.* See introduction to present volume.

Reviews of Books:

1. *Georgian Poetry: 1911–1912. Rhythm,* March 1913.
2. "German Books: Thomas Mann." *Blue Review,* July 1913.
3. *Americans,* by Stuart P. Sherman. *Dial,* May 1923.
4. *A Second Contemporary Verse Anthology.* New York *Evening Post Literary Review,* September 29, 1923.
5. *Hadrian the Seventh,* by Baron Corvo. *Adelphi,* December 1925.
6. *The Origins of Prohibition,* by J. A. Krout. New York *Herald-Tribune Books,* January 31, 1926.
7. *In the American Grain,* by William Carlos Williams. *Nation,* April 14, 1926.
8. *Heat,* by Isa Glenn. No record of previous publication.
9. *Gifts of Fortune,* by H. M. Tomlinson. No record of previous publication.
10. *The World of William Clissold,* by H. G. Wells. *Calendar of Modern Letters,* October 1926.
11. *Saïd the Fisherman,* by Marmaduke Pickthall. *Adelphi,* January 1927.

12. *Pedro de Valdivia,* by R. B. Cunninghame Graham. *Calendar of Modern Letters,* April 1927.
13. *Nigger Heaven,* by Carl Van Vechten; *Flight,* by Walter White; *Manhattan Transfer,* by John Dos Passos; *In Our Time,* by Ernest Hemingway. *Calendar of Modern Letters,* April 1927.
14. *Solitaria,* by V. V. Rozanov. *Calendar of Modern Letters,* July 1927.
15. *The Peep Show,* by Walter Wilkinson. *Calendar of Modern Letters,* July 1927.
16. *The Social Basis of Consciousness,* by Trigant Burrow. *Bookman* (American), November 1927.
17. *The Station: Athos, Treasures and Men,* by Robert Byron; *England and the Octopus,* by Clough Williams-Ellis; *Comfortless Memory,* by Maurice Baring; *Ashenden,* by W. Somerset Maugham. *Vogue* (English), July 20, 1928.
18. *Fallen Leaves,* by V. V. Rozanov. *Everyman,* January 23, 1930.
19. *Art Nonsense and Other Essays,* by Eric Gill. *Book Collector's Quarterly,* October–December 1933.

"Study of Thomas Hardy." Only the third chapter of this treatise has been published heretofore: in *Book Collector's Quarterly,* January–March 1932; also in *John o' London's Weekly,* March 12 and 19, 1932.
"Surgery for the Novel—or a Bomb." *International Book Review,* April 1923.
"Art and Morality." *Calendar of Modern Letters,* November 1925.
"Morality and the Novel." *Calendar of Modern Letters,* December 1925.
"Why the Novel Matters." No record of previous publication.
"John Galsworthy." *Scrutinies,* by Various Writers, Wishart, London, 1928.
"Introduction to These Paintings." *The Paintings of D. H. Lawrence,* Mandrake Press, London, 1929.

V. Education

"Education of the People." Heretofore unpublished.

VI. Ethics, Psychology, Philosophy

"The Reality of Peace." *English Review,* June, July, August, 1917.
"Life." *English Review,* February 1918.
"Democracy." No record of publication.
"The Proper Study." *Adelphi,* December 1923. Also *Vanity Fair,* January 1924.
"On Being Religious." *Adelphi,* February 1924.
"Books," "Thinking about Oneself," "Resurrection," "Climbing down Pisgah," "The Duc de Lauzun," ["The Good Man"], "The Novel and the Feelings," ["The Individual Consciousness *v.* the Social Consciousness"], and "Introduction to Pictures" are, so far as is known, all published here for the first time.

VII. Personalia and Fragments

"The Miner at Home." London *Nation,* March 16, 1912.
"The Flying Fish." Unpublished heretofore.
"Accumulated Mail." *The Borzoi: 1925,* Knopf, N. Y., 1925.
"The Late Mr. Maurice Magnus: A Letter." *New Statesman,* February 20, 1926.
"The Undying Man," "Noah's Flood," and ["Autobiographical Fragment"] are now published for the first time.

Index

INDEX